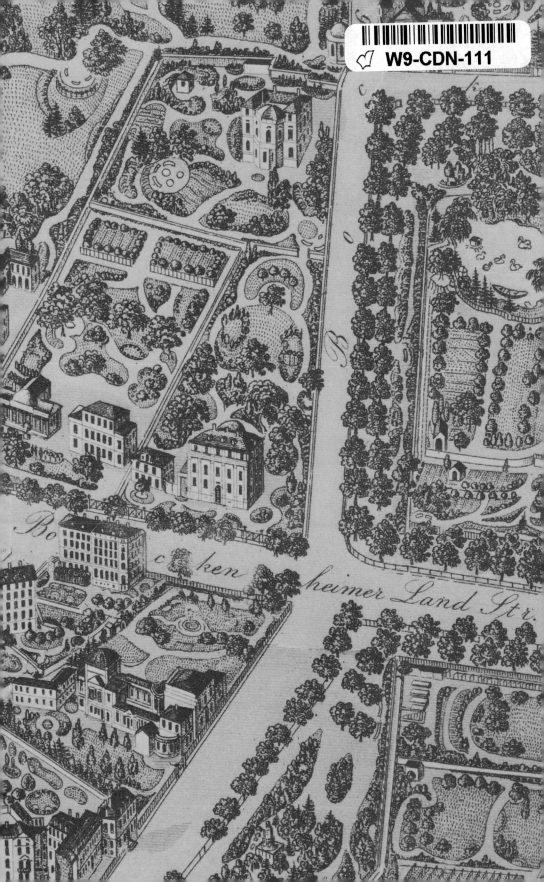

YESTERDAY'S
STREETS

SILVIA TENNENBAUM

YESTERDAY'S STREETS

RANDOM HOUSE
NEW YORK

*Grateful acknowledgment is made to the following for permis-
sion to reprint previously published material:* Houghton Mifflin
Company: Excerpt from *The Duino Elegies & Sonnets to Or-
pheus* by Rainer Maria Rilke, translated by A. Poulin, Jr.
Copyright © 1975, 1976, 1977 by A. Poulin, Jr.
Reprinted by permission of the publisher,
Houghton Mifflin Company.

Library of Congress Cataloging in Publication Data
Tennenbaum, Silvia.
Yesterday's streets.
I. Title.
PS3570.E646Y4   813'.54   81-1119
ISBN 0-394-51478-5   AACR2

Manufactured in the United States of America
2 4 6 8 9 7 5 3
First Edition

Dedicated to the memory of my mother,

LOTTI STEINBERG, *née* STERN,

whose presence is everywhere

in my life and work

Es bleibt uns vielleicht
irgend ein Baum an dem Abhang, dass wir ihn täglich
wiedersähen; es bleibt uns die Strasse von gestern
und das verzogene Treusein einer Gewohnheit,
der es bei uns gefiel, und so blieb sie und ging nicht.

Maybe what's left
for us is some tree on a hillside we can look at
day after day, one of yesterday's streets,
and the perverse affection of a habit
that liked us so much it never let go.

From the first *Duino Elegy*, by Rainer Maria Rilke,
translated by A. Poulin, Jr.

The Wertheim Family

MORITZ m. **HANNCHEN**
(1836–1912) | (LEVI)
(1848–1933)

Eduard **Jacob** **Gottfried** **Siegmund** **NATHAN** m.
(1883–) (1878– (Gerald F. (1874–) (1873–1933)
1944) Worth) m. Pauline
m. Lore (1875–1930)
m. Blanche

3 children

Jenny **Julia** **Willy**
(1901–) (1902–) (1904–)

EMMA **ERNST & ANDREAS**
(1900–) (1902–) (1902–?)

m. **m. Miriam**
Otto Radowitz

The Süsskind Family

BENEDICT m. TÄUBCHEN
(1832–1918)   (HERZ)
                (1842–1890)

CAROLINE
(1880–1942)

Jonah
(1881–1938)
m.
Hildegard

4 children

Eva
(1882–)

Elias
(1883–)
m. Bettina

Benno
(1910–)

HELENE
(1903–)

m. (1st) Thomas — m. (2nd) Manfred Solomon
von Brenda-Badolet   (1898–)
(1900–)

Clara
(1928–)

Peter
(1938–)

YESTERDAY'S
STREETS

1

1903

EDUARD WERTHEIM thought all babies ugly and never failed to pass this information on to their mothers. When he entered his sister-in-law's sitting room on a ravishing spring day to have his first look at Helene, nestled in Caroline Wertheim's arms, he cried, "My God! She looks like an angry aborigine!"

Hedwig, the nurse, gave a snort of disgust, and the tentative smile faded from Caroline's face. She was seated on an elegant Empire chaise, wearing a soft white challis robe over her voluminous, old-fashioned muslin nightgown, but she was in some pain; her breasts had been tightly bound to dry the flow of milk. Dr. Schlesinger, the family doctor, paid no attention when she complained about the discomfort, and continued to prescribe rest and a light diet. "No goose fat," he said cheerfully.

Despite the pain, Caroline tried to be friendly to all her visitors, especially Edu, who frequently rubbed her the wrong way. "*I* think she's beautiful," she said. "You simply do not like babies!"

"She *will* be beautiful, once she begins to resemble her mother,"

Edu answered gallantly. A cloud of cigar smoke drifted out of his nostrils as he waited for Caroline to forgive him.

Hedwig, muttering "You'll choke the child to death," abruptly took Lene from her mother and swept out of the room with her.

Caroline, who had not been mollified, wondered what there was to say to Edu, who, although he was only twenty, gave himself the airs of a man of the world. He had just returned from a two-year sojourn in America and held decided opinions on every subject. But he, too, was momentarily at a loss for words. He had not yet developed ease in his discourse with women or the assurance to skip lightly over conversational pauses. He was quick-witted, but he needed a masculine foil to be at his best; with women his wit too readily turned to insult.

"Now that I've admired the little monster, I can take my leave," he said, and Caroline smiled at him in sweet relief. She cared for neither the smoke of his cigars nor his humor, and his vanity seemed an insult to her.

"I thank you for coming," she said, accepting the peck of his dutiful kiss. "We all wondered if you would stay in America."

"America is not for me," he announced pompously. "The men haven't a cultivated bone in their bodies; they might as well be running around in war paint like the Indians. And the women! Harridans all! And feminists," he added. He had risen to go but stood for a minute—a slim, handsome man dressed in the best that English tailoring could provide—glancing around the room. He noticed how the light, playing over the mahogany furniture, turned the old carpet into a rich and colorful Oriental garden. It was good to be back home in Germany, but especially in Frankfurt, among his own.

Edu put out his cigar in the clean marble ashtray that stood exactly in the center of the brocade cloth covering the little table next to the door. "Be well," he said to Caroline, who had closed her eyes against the encroaching sun, "and say hello to my brother Nathan for me."

"I'll see you Saturday," she murmured.

He made certain to shut the door quietly. There was no one in the downstairs hall to let him out, so he took his bowler from the hatrack himself and did not leave a tip for the inattentive parlormaid. Strolling down the broad steps of his brother's house, he noticed the lilacs cascading over the garden wall in fragrant profusion and the stately chestnut tree crowned by a batch of lamblike clouds hovering in the endless blue May sky. But he also noticed that the curving balustrade needed polishing and that the metal gate wanted a coat of paint.

Edu was pleased with himself and therefore pleased with the world as well. He decided to take a detour through the Palmengarten back to his parents' house. As he walked he reflected on the time he had spent in New York, working for the banking house of Kuhn, Loeb & Co.; to him, it was an exile. He attended to his work scrupulously, even zealously, but he was unable to conquer his loneliness. The boisterous Americans, full of optimism and innocence, made him feel unaccountably shy. He made no friends. He was not, as he had hoped, received with open arms by the best American families, although his father, Moritz Wertheim, had bragged of his connection to Jacob Schiff.

"My grandfather lived directly across the street from the Schiffs in the Judengasse," Moritz always said, thinking back to the days in the Jewish quarter, "and the families were exceedingly close. You know, everyone talks about the Rothschilds, but they're not the only family of consequence to come out of the Frankfurt ghetto. They're the richest, to be sure, but some of the rest of us didn't do too badly either." At this point he invariably leaned forward. The little speech was one he gave, almost by rote, to each of his children, and grandchildren as soon as they were old enough to understand him. "There's something else you mustn't forget," he would say. "It's prestige of another sort—the old Jews used to call it *yichus*—and our family possessed plenty of that, even when we didn't have the money."

"I know," Edu would answer his father, but the little lecture seemed to drift about his head like the vapors his mother used to cure chest colds, smelling odd, like a whiff from the past, unconnected to what he knew to be the present.

"It has to do with righteousness and goodness, with charitableness and a reverence for those who possess riches of the mind: learning

and scholarship. Just go and read if you can—but of course you can't
—the words on those tombstones in the old cemetery and see what
your forebears thought was important for the world to see and God
to remember."

Moritz would lean back in his chair, and Edu would look serious,
for he knew it was expected of him. But now he wondered why he
had seen so little of Jacob Schiff during his months of apprenticeship
if the family connection was as close as his father had claimed. Once
—only once—had he been asked to Friday-night dinner. He was,
as he told his family, not impressed. The piety appalled him. "Imagine, they made the men wear skullcaps! In this day and age!" Fur-
thermore (and this was not, he admitted, the fault of Jacob Schiff),
New York was filling up with a million or more poor immigrants,
many if not most of them Jews from Eastern Europe. "Just wait and
see what sort of anti-Semitism that will cause in their precious
democracy," he said, and his mother, Hannchen, nodded her head.
She always agreed with Edu; he was the youngest of her five sons
and her favorite.

Edu strolled happily through the Palmengarten, whose varieties
of familiar and exotic plants he adored. He had been exploring its
paths and greenhouses for as long as he could remember, observing
in every detail the flowers and cacti, the tropical palms and orchids,
even learning their Latin names. The gardeners had come to know
him and doffed their caps to him. Now and again, though they were
a taciturn lot, they even explained the care of a particularly precious
plant to him. It seemed to Eduard Wertheim that to raise flowers
was a splendid and rewarding occupation, which repaid hard work
with beauty or sweet perfume and never required maudlin displays
of affection.

THE WHOLE Wertheim family gathered at Nathan and Caroline's
house in the Guiollettstrasse on the Saturday afternoon following
Edu's visit to the baby. Saturdays, if there was nothing else on the
social calendar, they usually dropped in for tea at Nathan's. Sunday
belonged, irrevocably to the parents, Hannchen and Moritz, and
included dinner promptly at one o'clock. Nathan, an attorney-at-

law, was the eldest son and the most "settled." He was punctilious and melancholy and somewhat reclusive. His small Vandyke beard was closely trimmed, and the ends of his mustache twirled ever so slightly. At thirty he was nearly bald and so sensitive about it that he would not allow himself to be photographed without a hat.

The next son, Siegmund, twenty-nine, worked in his father's wholesale woolen business and was considered the most dapper of the group. He was also the most carefree and played the cello—badly. He was frequently heard to say that he should have been born to the landed gentry and thus spared the need to go to work each day. At the office he flirted with the secretaries and charmed traveling salesmen. He never worked a minute longer than necessary. His father-in-law was very rich. Pauline, his wife, having grown up in luxurious surroundings, had developed an eye for clothes and a taste for lavish parties at an early age.

Gottfried, twenty-eight and unmarried, had been complimented on his good looks since he was three, and it was expected that he would grow up vain. But no one thought that self-indulgence would play so large a part in his life and put so great a limit on his capacity for friendship. Gottfried, too, worked in his father's business and pressed Moritz to take greater risks than the old man thought prudent. Their relationship was not a happy one.

Twenty-five-year-old Jacob, laconic and intelligent, had never been told that he was handsome. Indeed, he was considered the ugly duckling, but he had discovered, when he was only a child, that his father prized his intellectual gifts and would indulge him because of them. He had spent, as his mother said, "more years than were good for him" at the university, and he played second violin in his brother Siegmund's amateur quartet.

All the brothers but Gottfried arrived at Nathan's on time that Saturday afternoon. It was another glorious May day, and Edu held forth on his favorite topic, dissecting the American character and describing the miserable conditions of life on New York's Lower East Side. Nathan, who had just returned from a brief visit to Berlin, remarked that the influx of Jews from Poland was becoming a threat there too.

"Thank God we live in Frankfurt, then," said Jacob, an edge of sarcasm to his voice.

"They will come here as well," said Siegmund.

"I used to lie in my bed at night in New York," said Edu, "and imagine myself back here, wandering in the Palmengarten, or taking the trolley out to Bockenheim. I would put myself to sleep listing the stops."

"Was there *nothing* about New York you liked?"

"I learned to survive among savages. I liked the idea of becoming master of my fate."

The men were sitting together in the salon while the women chatted in the sunroom facing the garden, which, in the fullness of spring, showed an amazing variety of greens, from the glistening dark of the magnolias to the feathery yellowish leaves of the lindens. Above them all towered two red beeches and an ancient chestnut tree. Older than the house, older than anyone now living, they had stood on this piece of land before the walls of the city had been torn down, before the Jews had been allowed out of the narrow confines of the ghetto. Perhaps they had been there—striplings, to be sure—when Goethe said adieu to his native city.

The windows of the sunroom had been thrown open, and the women talked in animated voices while the children—Caroline's twins, Ernst and Andreas; her eldest, Emma; and Pauline Wertheim's two girls, Jenny and Julia—played on the gravel walks under the watchful eye of Fräulein Gründlich, the governess. Lene was asleep in her pram, shaded from the wind and the sun, her little hands, despite the mild spring weather, encased in mittens of pink wool, her unruly shock of black hair contained by a matching pink bonnet.

It was not unusual for the men and women to congregate separately. When the family was together—"*entre nous,*" as they said— the men liked to unburden themselves of business vexations, while the women preferred to discuss the servants and the latest scandals in Frankfurt's fashionable West End. Although they were, all of them, emancipated and cultivated, they recognized that the life of a well-to-do bourgeois family was governed by established rules and regulations which recognized several spheres: women had their do-

main and men theirs; children inhabited a sort of nether world
("seen but not heard"); and servants belonged to the great unwashed
masses. Hannchen Wertheim herself inspected the fingernails of her
maids every morning and discreetly sniffed at all her servants'
clothes. Only Jacob, who was bored by the men's endless business
talk, and Caroline's sister Eva Süsskind ever questioned the immuta-
bility of the social order. Eva, who was nineteen, wanted to study
or to work; she did not want to marry. She had "advanced" ideas,
and it was thought that her mother's early death and her own gruff
character had contributed equally to her unorthodox opinions.
Hannchen believed that she would have been less outspoken had she
been prettier, but Caroline knew that it was her sister's heart, not
her face, that was responsible for her independent ways. She sometimes wished in a vague, desultory fashion that she had Eva's
strength of purpose.

The Süsskinds were of more humble origin than the Wertheims.
(In Moritz's eyes this meant that they had not breathed the sophisticated air of Frankfurt for as long.) Caroline's father was a druggist.
He was, to be sure, successful, but his shop and apartment were on
the Grünestrasse, near the Zoo, in the horribly unfashionable East
End. He had come from a small village near Mainz as a young man.
His people were simple and pious *Dorfjuden*, village Jews, who
walked around in muddy boots and slept in a single room, no doubt
with the chickens! It was true—Moritz Wertheim had to admit it
—that Süsskind was ambitious and had worked his way up. He was
going to send his elder son, Jonah, to medical school, and Elias, the
younger, to study art history at the University of Freiburg. Elias and
Edu had been school friends, and it was to Elias that the homesick
young apprentice had sent most of his plaintive letters from America.

Hannchen Wertheim presided over the group gathered in the
sunroom that Saturday with her usual charm and wit. The fact that
it was her son's house rather than her own did not concern her in
the least. She dominated the conversation everywhere, even among
the men, and had reduced many a salesperson to tears and instilled
terror in the hearts of countless tradesmen. She was proud, proud
to be married to a good and successful man, proud to be the mother

of five sons, proud to be a citizen of Frankfurt am Main. She pronounced judgment on everything, even her sons, and never disguised who was her favorite or who displeased her. That her marriage to Moritz was a happy one was evident; she never disguised that, either. Moritz adored her and credited her with all the good that happened within the family. If something went wrong, it was because Hannchen had not had a hand in it. She was a stout woman, good-looking but not beautiful, who stood a head taller than her husband and walked with an ebony cane which she did not need. She had been born in Bockenheim, the hamlet west of Frankfurt, where her family owned a small furniture factory. Her father had sloughed off his pious observances when he was a young man, but Hannchen never failed to attend synagogue on the High Holy Days or to send it a contribution on the anniversary of her parents' death.

Moritz was a native of Frankfurt. His family had resided in the Judengasse of the Old City since the early seventeenth century, and he knew the histories of its inhabitants and the topography of its ancient dwellings as well as he knew the textile business. He told all who would listen, often and with great delight, that more Jews than Christians could trace their roots back to the Frankfurt of 1500. Now that he was near retirement and ailing a little, he had become something of a bore on the subject, and many of his acquaintances, especially those who were Gentile, had begun to avoid him. Although he was a short man, his large head with its snowy white hair and old-fashioned mustache and side whiskers made him an impressive figure still. He was obstinate in his dislike of the Prussians, who had marched into Frankfurt as conquerors in 1866, and just with his sons. Jacob was the one closest to his heart, the one most likely to revive the cherished tradition of learning and scholarship which had been lost in the tenacious struggle to rise from the ghetto into a position of prominence in Frankfurt's mercantile community. That world was powerful indeed, for Frankfurt had a long history of commerce, which Goethe himself had looked down upon with all the contempt his genius could muster.

Moritz had established a trust fund for Jacob, in case he should one day find himself unable to earn a proper living. The chances of his receiving a university appointment were slim indeed; one still had to convert to be found eligible, and given Jacob's stubborn pride, it was highly unlikely that he would take such a step. His brothers were not overtly hostile to the arrangement; nevertheless, they reserved their sharpest criticisms for him. Edu particularly was quick to call him down for the sloppy way he dressed and his unregulated life. But he could never remain angry for long, since Jacob was generous and good-humored and amused them all with his gift for mimicry.

"Having a worthless intellectual for a son lends the family a certain cachet," Moritz was saying this afternoon, under a cloud of blue smoke in the salon. And then, lowering his voice and raising his right index finger, he added, "It's a whole lot better than having a black sheep, a homosexual or a thief whom one must send to the tropics. As you may recall, even the Haggadah mentions the 'bad' son. He appears in numerous good Jewish families."

At that moment, as if on cue, the door opened to admit Gottfried. He wore a flower in his buttonhole and gave off a strong scent of hair lotion.

"Phew!" Edu made a face.

"We were just talking about you," said Jacob, avoiding his father's stern eye.

"I'm sure it wasn't kind," said Gottfried. "Forgive me for being late," he said to Nathan, "but the barber kept me waiting. He said the fault was not his, he had had to shave the French cultural attaché. Have I missed many of Edu's American tales?"

"He's complaining about New York's lower depths," said Siegmund, "and thinks the natives will grow restless."

"I'd sooner hear about the better class of people," Gottfried said, turning toward Edu. "Didn't you meet a single Kuhn or Loeb?"

Edu blushed angrily.

"Leave the poor boy alone," said Moritz, "and go say hello to your mother."

Gottfried found the women talking about Hannchen's parlormaid. "She got herself pregnant *again*?" Pauline was asking incredulously.

"I couldn't believe it either," said Hannchen. "The third time, my dear! Thank God the first two died."

"Didn't she try to abort it?" Caroline asked warily. She had lived a sheltered life, both before and since her marriage, and the word "abort" made her shudder. It conjured up a host of dreadful images of the poor in sunless rooms, fetid with the odors of cabbage and disinfectant. Dirty old women with knitting needles went about their awful tasks there. It was a wonder not more of their victims died.

"She *did* abort the first one," said Hannchen, "and didn't come in to work for days. When she finally arrived, pale as a ghost, she was still bleeding and I had to call Dr. Schlesinger in to look at her. Bless his soul, he came right away. The second baby was born prematurely and lived only a few hours. She cried about it for months, without ever telling me the true details of what happened."

"I can't get mine to talk about her private life either," said Pauline, to whom it had never before occurred that maids had a private life.

"They think we're prying," said Caroline.

"When we're only trying to help," Gottfried, who had been standing in the doorway, chimed in.

"Don't make fun of us," said Hannchen.

"Rest assured," Gottfried told her, "the so-called Christians treat their domestics a lot worse than we do."

Hannchen's sister Berthe, so small and fat that she was nicknamed Queen Victoria, tapped her mouth delicately with a linen napkin, one she herself had hemmed and edged for Caroline's wedding, and said, "It seems to me that we do nothing but talk about servants." She was a spinster and employed only a part-time cleaning woman.

It had grown darker in the sunroom, the day was slowly drawing toward dusk, the green garden fading to violet; the children had long since been taken to the nursery.

"I think it's time we joined the men," said Pauline, and they all rose and moved toward the salon.

Gottfried looked at his pocket watch. "I must go," he said. He shook his father's hand and dutifully kissed his mother on the forehead.

"Can't wait to be done with us?" Moritz asked, as he invariably did when Gottfried rushed off.

"I'm late for an engagement" came the equally invariable answer.

"I don't know why he bothers to show up at all," Edu remarked after the door slammed behind his brother.

"I was at the bookseller's today," Pauline told the company at large, "and saw that a German translation of *The Picture of Dorian Gray* has been published . . ."

"I'm surprised they allowed it," said Berthe.

"Of course I read it in English," Pauline continued, "but I glanced at the translation and found it adequate. I recommend the book highly. It's very original."

"The man was put in jail," said Berthe.

"Whatever are you talking about?" asked Hannchen with some annoyance. She did not like control of the conversation to fall into her sister's hands.

"He's a moral degenerate," said Berthe haughtily.

"What other cultural news have you brought us?" Moritz Wertheim asked Pauline.

"I hear the Städel Museum is looking for funds to buy a large Rembrandt from a Viennese collection."

"There's your chance!" said Jacob. "Giving money to the Städel will guarantee your ascension to the heaven of *Kultur* as well as your acceptance in the best circles."

"Did the Schiffs have good paintings?" Hannchen asked Edu.

"It was so dark the night I was there, I couldn't really see what they had on the walls," he replied. "The furniture was massive; I guess the pictures were, too."

"Surely they don't have a taste for good works of art in America?" said Jacob, ironic as always.

"Big big big," his father snorted, "Edu says they care only about size over there."

The walls of Moritz and Hannchen's large and stately house on the Neue Mainzer Strasse were hung with copies of the masters, mostly those they could see in the original right across the river Main in the galleries of the Städel.

"I advise you to subscribe to the fund to buy the 'Samson and Delilah,'" said Edu.

"How did you know its name?" Pauline asked him, miffed that he was privy to information that had been withheld from her.

"I have my sources," he said, smiling benignly.

"They tell me that the new work being shown by the artists of the Berlin 'Secession' is absolutely stunning," Pauline said quickly and was pleased to find that she had the last word in the matter. Edu made a mental note to ask Elias about the pictures in question.

At that moment a last golden ray of sunlight, bursting from the dark clouds on the horizon, flooded the room. It seemed to glide across the glass doors of the breakfront, causing the silver objects within to brighten for a moment. And then, before it was extinguished by the high wall and its overreaching lilacs, it cast a fiery glow on the bouquet of tearoses that stood atop the grand piano in a slender crystal vase.

Caroline, sitting alone on the corner sofa, perceived the moment as "magical." She allowed herself to be consumed by such small colorful details. They made her feel like an artist.

"The days are growing longer," said Hannchen, and then, apropos of nothing at all, continued, "I'm reading *Buddenbrooks*, by Thomas Mann." She sighed. "It's very long, as novels go."

"Not longer than *War and Peace*," said Jacob, "nor quite as good."

"He tells all the family secrets," said Berthe, proud to have read it when it had first appeared, two years before. "It has the whole city of Lübeck in an uproar."

"I met him in Munich once," said Pauline with satisfaction, "at a fancy-dress ball."

The old Biedermeier clock struck six, and Moritz took out his watch to make sure the two timepieces agreed. Siegmund and Jacob yawned, more or less in unison. There was plenty of time yet before supper, and for a few minutes all of them were still, occupied with private thoughts.

Hannchen remembered the quiet Sabbath afternoons of perfect peace in her parents' house. She had never again found their like. Now there were worries and distractions, undercurrents of bitterness. Her thoughts never strayed far from the subject of Gottfried —he was certain to come to grief. She recalled the first time her suspicions about his character had been confirmed. It was when he stole the gold coin from the nursemaid's purse. Moritz had punished him, of course, whipped him soundly, sent him to return the coin and apologize. Gottfried did it sullenly, knowing that he would not be forgiven. Children from good families simply did not steal from servants.

It had grown quite dark all of a sudden; Hannchen could not see into the corners of the room. Perhaps she was wrong and things would turn out all right. She preferred to banish unpleasant thoughts. It was better to think of cheerful things. Where, for instance, ought they to spend their summer vacation? There were so many lovely places, the world was growing more accessible each day.

"Someone make some light, for heaven's sake!" said Moritz, and then they all slowly prepared to leave.

GOTTFRIED was glad he had made his escape early. The evening was pleasant, the air mild—if only his own feelings could match the season! He was angry, and yet he could not put the blame on any one thing. The city's placid prospect irked him. It was stifling, self-satisfied, a city of bourgeois virtue—and vice. No wonder his family adored it! All afternoon he had had to listen to their praises, harmonizing perfectly with Edu's slighting remarks about New York. How absurdly pleased his brother was to be "home." Why hadn't they sent him instead? He would have taken the place by storm, beaten it at its own game. Edu hadn't the character it took to succeed in that land of boundless opportunity. You needed to be a gambler—Gottfried was certain of that—to tame New York. Only an ass would think the future was *here*.

He walked rapidly through the gathering darkness. He did not look where he was going, he knew the way by heart. He never noticed the two men approaching him on the sidewalk, but all at once they were directly in front of him. He walked into the shorter of the two before he realized they were there. "Excuse me," Gottfried said, but they blocked his way, and he had to look into their faces. Of course they were drunk. They were near a streetlight which had just gone on. "*Saujude!*" said the taller one, "Jewish swine," and the other echoed, "*Saujude!*"

"What?" Gottfried drawled, unprepared for the confrontation. They raised their fists—two solid burghers, in derby hats and well-cut suits, their eyes glazed with drink. "You heard us," said the shorter, and it was then that Gottfried bolted. He simply took off and ran the rest of the way home—like a little boy shitting in his pants with fear, he thought when he reached the safety of his building's foyer. He was ashamed. Nothing had taken place, really, he had just been called a nasty word, it happened all the time. It had never happened to him before, but he knew that had been mere chance. Why did he feel so ashamed? There was sweat on his neck and between his legs, and his knees shook. As soon as he was inside his apartment, he drew a bath. He poured himself a cognac and sat in the hot tub for a long time, making his mind a blank.

THE CARRIAGE came for Moritz and Hannchen promptly at six-thirty. "Come along," Hannchen said to Berthe, "*vite, vite!*" Quick, quick! She was anxious to get home, and vented her impatience on the short fat woman, whose only response was to make her farewells all the more lengthy and elaborate. Sitting in the carriage at last, they made their small noises, each of them, of acceptance, comfort and fatigue.

"We really *must* get an automobile," said Hannchen, putting her stubby gloved hand on Moritz's knee as the horse clip-clopped smartly past the opera house, past the equestrian statue of Wilhelm I and the weeping beeches in the Anlagen, the gracious, English-style park that formed a green belt around the Old City.

"Don't forget *me!*" said Berthe, who lived just to the north and could never understand why she was not dropped off first.

"Bruno knows all about it," said Moritz, nodding toward the coachman. "He'll take you after he's brought us home. Are you in a special hurry?"

"No, no," said Berthe, who was dependent on the favors of others.

"Mathilde Rothschild has one," Hannchen said.

"One what?" Moritz asked.

"An automobile. You said yourself that the time will come when no one will use a horse and carriage any longer."

"What I say and what I mean aren't always the same thing."

"It would make a grand birthday present," Hannchen whispered, not wanting Bruno to hear.

The Wertheim house on the Neue Mainzer Strasse dated from the 1830s. Its simple, almost severe classical style was considered old-fashioned now that a more eclectic and ostentatious architecture had come into favor, but it suited Hannchen and Moritz. It was a very large house which, when they bought it in 1878, represented the ultimate in refinement and a stateliness that Moritz's grandfather, selling notions in the Judengasse, could not have imagined for one of his descendants.

They had raised their five sons here, and Edu still lived in a tastefully "modern" apartment on the third floor. (The rest of the interior had been refurbished in the prevailing dark, overcrowded Victorian style.) The large garden behind the house had a great green smooth-as-velvet lawn, on which croquet was sometimes played. The lawn could not match the Rothschilds' in size, though its texture, the gardener swore, was of comparable quality.

Moritz thought it foolish to compete with the Rothschilds, but he allowed Hannchen the pleasure—within bounds. He just might buy her the automobile, he thought, if Bruno could be taught to drive it.

EDU HAD NOT accompanied his parents; he wanted to have a private conversation with Nathan about a delicate and unpleasant family matter. "Let's have a cognac in your study," he said.

Siegmund and Pauline, having sent the children home with the English governess long before dark, were getting ready to leave. "Pauline needs plenty of rest," said Siegmund. "You know, she is *enceinte* again."

"For the third time," said Jacob.

"After two girls, perhaps it will be a boy," said Siegmund.

"I meant to say that you have told us the good news for the third time today," said Jacob.

"Good news bears repeating," said Caroline, who was always made uncomfortable by the verbal jousting her brothers-in-law indulged in. A great reserve had marked the atmosphere in her own family, no doubt a reaction to the death of her mother. When his wife died at forty-eight of cancer of the breast, Benedict Süsskind had made a determined effort to maintain his family without the aid of a full-time housekeeper or—God forbid—a second wife. They became a close-knit family, but it required forbearance on everyone's part. Benedict constantly cautioned the children to behave kindly to one another and to swallow nasty words and angry retorts.

The Wertheim clan had no need for such restraints. They were in lively competition from the start, and it was only in front of outsiders that they felt the need to maintain a properly dignified and united façade. The boys were reminded not to talk with their hands in the manner of *Ostjuden,* East European Jews, and a conscious effort was made to teach them to enunciate their German with as little as possible of the vulgar Frankfurt dialect. Here, however, Moritz was a pernicious influence, since all his favorite jokes and stories had to be told with the local inflection.

As soon as Siegmund and Pauline had left, Caroline hurried upstairs to check on the baby and the twins, Ernst and Andreas. Jacob followed close behind her, because three-year-old Emma had asked to say good night to him. She was a dark-eyed little girl with a beautiful round face framed by cascading corkscrew curls. She had inherited her father's melancholy expression, which lent her a gravity that, so it seemed to Jacob, was too great for such a small girl.

"How does my little niece fare?" he asked her.

"I knew you would come," she whispered.

Jacob kissed her.

"Kiss my baby doll too," she said, and he did.

"What's a 'niecefare'?" she asked.

"A what?"

"You said 'how's my little niecefare' to me."

Jacob laughed. "It's a special name uncles give their favorite girls."

"Is baby Lene your 'niecefare' too?"

"Absolutely not!" Jacob assured her. "Promise me you'll get up smiling tomorrow morning?"

"If you read me a story."

"Now?"

She nodded.

"It's late."

"Then I won't smile!"

Jacob turned up the light and took *Struwwelpeter* down from the shelf. "Which story shall I read?" he asked. "The one about Paulinchen, who played with matches and got all burned up?"

By the time he got to the place where the two cats are weeping over the little girl's ashes, Emma was sound asleep.

Caroline, looking into the nursery, saw Hedwig giving the baby her bottle. Lene's small pink hands waved contentedly in the air as she sucked the formula with all her might. "I hope she's not cold," said Caroline, gently touching a bare little foot. She got a withering glance from the nurse. Caroline's breasts still ached, and she wondered, for the hundredth time, why it was considered—by doctors as well as by other women of her class—wrong to nurse one's child. She sensed that she was as much a prisoner of her place in life as those who were less fortunate than she.

Hedwig put the baby on her shoulder to burp her and gently patted her back.

"She *does* look like an aborigine," said Caroline, watching the red, squooshed-up face with its halo of unruly hair droop sleepily on the nurse's shoulder.

"I beg your pardon?" said Hedwig.

"She's a sweet fat baby," said Caroline.

The boys slept soundly in their own room, Ernst clutching a bear, Andreas sucking a corner of his blanket.

When Caroline came downstairs again, she found Jacob waiting in the hall. "I wanted to say good-bye," he said. "Your daughter and I had a very nice little tête-à-tête."

"She's always so pale," said Caroline, "and even though her face is round—she has that from my side of the family—she's delicate. I worry about her."

Caroline found Jacob the most sympathetic of her brothers-in-law. He was the only one willing to display a gentle side. But he was also, in some way, the most distant; after a point, he would disappear like a genie.

"I must go," he said. "Give Nathan and Edu my best. Tell them I know they're discussing secrets."

"Where are they?"

"In the study."

He kissed Caroline lightly and went out the door, though he was back in a minute, having forgotten his hat.

Caroline went back upstairs to her sitting room to rest. She was tired and did not wish to think about Emma. Fräulein Gründlich took excellent care of the children, there was really no need to worry, even if Emma was a poor eater. Dr. Schlesinger said she was one of those children who would grow up slender and tough. Caroline took off her dress and stretched out on the chaise longue. It was dark and pleasant in the room, the window was open, and she could smell the lilacs.

She was suddenly overcome by a lassitude far greater than mere tiredness. It occurred to her that she had no real love for her children, that she was, in her heart of hearts, a cold and unfeeling person. Those "magic" moments that had the power to move her were rarely an expression of love—except the kind of love Narcissus found when he looked into the pool. They were a precious congruence of inanimate objects, of color, of light, divorced from human passion. Had she been a true artist, she might have been forgiven for responding only to them, but she was not. She had a small talent, her sketchbook was filled with charming little watercolors, but—so what? She would work a little harder, she thought, as drowsiness began to muddle her thoughts. She had forgotten that a moment earlier she had felt a sense of emptiness.

EDU AND NATHAN sat opposite each other in the comfortably appointed study that served as Nathan's office. Hannchen had chosen the furnishings. They included a truly imposing desk, whose top was inlaid with a great expanse of morocco leather and whose drawers—complete with secret compartments—were decorated with brass fittings. Nathan, whose law practice did not match his princely surroundings, sat at the desk, playing with a letter opener.

"You seem nervous," said Edu, looking older than his twenty years. His face, save for the neatly trimmed mustache, was clean-shaven, his faintly wavy hair carefully combed. He resembled Nathan, and indeed all of his brothers, in the straight, firm line of his mouth, the slightly drooping eyelids, and the manner in which his eyebrows petered out all at once. The hooded look, which the drooping lids gave him, made him seem withdrawn and often led people to think that he was not paying attention, when in fact he picked up every detail. Nathan, on the other hand, appeared to look out from under the same lids as from a great and unfathomable depth. He caught not details, but the logic behind them; he would remain silent for long periods and then, all at once, make some startling connection. He did not have Edu's elegance, or Siegmund's charm, or Gottfried's willfulness, or Jacob's intelligence. People found it difficult to characterize him. Perhaps it was simply that he was the first-born, the one his parents had watched over more than the others.

"I'm not nervous," Nathan said. "What are we going to talk about?"

"You know I'm to start work on Monday at Wertheim and Sons —officially, that is." Edu sounded a touch pompous. "Unofficially I've been going in to acquaint myself with the way things work there. I did learn a few things in New York."

"You want to apply those things?" Nathan caught his brother by surprise. Edu had meant to proceed more slowly.

"Yes, of course."

"Why are you talking to me? Speak to Papa."

"I think there are problems . . ." Nathan said nothing, so he went on, "Quite frankly, they involve Gottfried."

"He's careless and inconsiderate. That's nothing new."

"He gets his share of the profits, he must pull his weight."

"What do you propose to do?"

"We must reorganize—slowly, carefully, but from the bottom up and totally."

"I'm still puzzled that you've come to me. Do you mean to go to the courts? Do you want to take legal action?"

"I doubt that that will be necessary—just yet."

"But you've thought about it?"

"I've thought about *everything.*" Edu's face became animated and intense. "I have a lot of ideas, and I want you to be on my side if I run into trouble. Papa is getting older, he pays less attention, he no longer thinks ahead. It is necessary not only to keep up but to be prepared for the future."

Nathan did not look at his brother, but he listened to his words. They had the ring of steel.

"I want to succeed," he was saying, "and I have the knowledge, the tools for it. I'm not a gambler like Gottfried, I haven't got that vein of wildness . . . but, I'll make the business prosper as never before."

Nathan was impressed with Edu's ambition. "And Siegmund?" he asked.

"Siegmund is honest and decent, but his mind wanders. He's interested in other things. Pauline's money will always provide a measure of safety for him. He does his work—and does it well—but no more. It is *I* who'll succeed Papa. I think he knows that, even though he's never talked about it. He wants to be 'fair,' but why did he send *me* to America? Because he understands that, ten years from now, I'll have built Wertheim and Sons into the biggest business of its kind in Frankfurt—perhaps in Germany."

"And Gottfried is in your way?"

Edu stood up and came to the desk. "Gottfried must resign," he said calmly and evenly. "It will be cheaper for everyone in the long run if Papa buys his way into another business."

GOTTFRIED could not put the unpleasant street encounter out of his mind. Stepping from the tub, he poured himself another cognac and stretched out on the bed. He had a ticket for that evening's performance of *Die Meistersinger* and an engagement for a late supper with Nellie, a young woman in the chorus. Her picture, showing her dressed for a bit part in some opera whose name he could never remember, stood in his bedroom on a small table. He had not permitted his mother to furnish his flat; she had been to see it only once and had objected to its somewhat Byzantine flavor. He could see Nellie's picture now, and it helped him direct his thoughts to the evening ahead.

Gottfried had first noticed her on a snowy day, walking on the footbridge over the Main from Frankfurt to Sachsenhausen. She was dressed like a little girl, her hands in a white rabbit-fur muff, a

matching hat on her blond curls. There were literally hundreds like
her in the city, but Gottfried remembered her face when he saw her
a second time, a week later, at the Christmas market on the square
by City Hall. He smiled at her, and she looked quickly away. The
third time he saw her was on the Opernplatz, on a cold and windy
day. This time he followed her and saw her enter the stage entrance
at the opera. By now he was determined to meet her. It was not
difficult. A well-to-do young man from a good family could arrange
such things without trouble. Nellie was not interested; Gottfried
assumed it was feigned. He could not imagine someone in her
position unwilling to have an affair with someone in his. She met
him once for coffee and explained that there was no room in her life
for a liaison—with him or with anyone else. She said (and Gottfried
thought she was lying) that she was the sole support of a widowed
mother (one could only laugh at such a cliché) and worked hard at
her "career." Gottfried continued to send flowers and candy. Her
intransigence appealed to him. And Nellie continued to allow him
to buy her coffee or a glass of wine. Once or twice she went walking
with him on a Sunday morning.

But then, one day, what he knew would eventually happen happened. He met her on a Saturday afternoon at the Zoo. When she
said she was tired he took her to the restaurant, which had a pretty
view and was a favorite spot for tourists and young couples in love.
Here Nellie burst into tears and sobbed out her tale of woe. Of
course, it involved a confidence man who sold false insurance poli-
cies and did old widows out of their meager pensions. Gottfried did
not bother to listen very carefully, he merely said, "How much do
you need?" When Nellie protested that he misunderstood her, that
she wanted only a small loan, he kissed her hand, told her she was
charming and put 100 marks into her purse, begging her to say no
more.

That had been three weeks ago, and Gottfried looked forward to
reaping the benefits of the transaction—perhaps even tonight. He
had no wish to be crass and had not pressed her, but he had taken
her to dinner in some of Frankfurt's best restaurants and to the
theater. Every time she ate an oyster or sipped champagne she knew
she must repay him; every rose and every strawberry dipped in

cream was an acknowledgment of her debt; and every time her tongue darted from between her lips to lick a dollop of Italian ice from her spoon, Gottfried's desire for her grew stronger.

Stretched out on his bed, Gottfried looked down on his naked body. He planned—with great care—what he would wear. He had forgotten the two men; he thought only of Nellie and the night before him.

SIEGMUND and Pauline had been invited to a party at the Seligmans'. They both enjoyed the preparations for an evening in splendid company and allowed themselves enough time to get ready so that they would be relaxed and in their best form when at last they left their modest house for the short carriage ride to yet another sumptuous West End villa. The Seligmans owned one of the grandest of these. Built in 1870, it had three floors and a fully finished basement with bar and servants' quarters. Each of the rooms on the ground floor was done up in a different style, from the Louis Quinze music room to the Florentine High Renaissance dining room; there was even a flower room with Pompeiian frescoes—all in all, a "palace," as Pauline often said. The *pièce de résistance* (and a constant source of amusement for the irreverent Wertheim sons) was a cupola over the great stairwell, on which was painted, in glorious colors, the figure of Liberty. "She watches their investments," Siegmund had remarked dryly on first seeing the lady.

But much as she might snicker at such pretension, Pauline longed to have a "palace" of her own and to entertain in the grand style. She could not understand Caroline's reluctance to enter the social whirl, could not comprehend the moment of agonizing trepidation that gripped her sister-in-law whenever she stepped from her carriage beneath the porte-cochere of a dazzling, brightly lit villa.

Pauline had been thinking about Caroline ever since they left Nathan's house, and now, as her maid was brushing her hair—a hundred strokes in the morning and a hundred strokes at night—she found herself repeating a litany of charges, beginning with how complaisant Caroline had been in allowing her mother-in-law to oversee the purchase of furniture for her house. The old lady had simply taken the girl to the firm of A. Bembé (granted it was the best) and ordered eight rooms of furniture just like that. She seemed to buy her clothes all at once too and was always a little behind the current fashion, as if she had to make certain how a style looked on all the other women in town before daring to try it herself. And then, if she liked something, she wore it much too long.

Siegmund came into the bedroom just as the maid was done with the last stroke of the brush. He stood behind his wife and tied his white tie in the mirror that reflected her animated countenance. The maid stepped back and watched the couple with her dull, protruding eyes.

"Will they have music tonight?" Pauline asked.

"Don't they always?" Siegmund answered. "I just hope it's not some child prodigy."

"I hope they've had the piano tuned," Pauline said. "Remember how out of tune it was last time?"

Siegmund lifted her hair and kissed her on the nape of her neck. She felt a shiver of lust flutter through her body.

She had always thought him the handsomest of the Wertheim boys. She remembered seeing him pass her house on his way to school as a youngster of thirteen. She had set her cap for him then, and he knew it. From the beginning their love had had a strong sensual aspect to it, and they had married young, despite Moritz's grumblings.

"Be ready in fifteen minutes," she said. How she looked forward to the evening's entertainments!

JACOB LIVED in a large and disorderly flat on the Fahrgasse in a building which dated from the early eighteenth century. Like many of the houses in the Old City, it was no longer in the best shape, nor was it occupied by the best people. Hannchen did not go there, but Moritz, who liked sniffing out traces of his past, stopped by now and then, breathing hard after having climbed the three flights of stairs to chat with his son.

Jacob employed a housekeeper named Gerda, who was also his mistress, this being perhaps the main reason Hannchen would not set foot in his apartment. The relationship was not exactly scandalous, but it raised eyebrows here and there however discreetly Jacob behaved—and he was by nature discreet. He never brought Gerda to public functions and he had never introduced her to any member of his family. In some ways, he often thought guiltily, it was as if she were no more than a stick of furniture.

Gerda was not yet twenty. She had a speech defect, which caused her much distress and made her exceedingly shy and virtually mute. She spoke to almost no one but Jacob, who was kind and gentle to her. She had been thought to be simple-minded, but it was only her inarticulateness, her desperate searchings for the shape of a word, that had made the people in the small Hessian village she came from regard her as an idiot. Jacob had taught her to read and write, and she took delight in setting down her droll, sometimes garbled impressions of Frankfurt's street life.

She had come from the country to find work, but because of her trouble with words, the employment agency refused to recommend her. She ended up working from dawn to dusk as a laundress in a steam-filled basement on a cold stone floor. One day when she had returned some shirts to one of Jacob's neighbors who was noted for her stinginess and been refused payment on some pretext or other, he found her weeping on his doorstep. With great patience, he managed to get the story out of her and then, in a fit of anger, went to the woman and demanded that she give him the laundress' money. Gerda was grateful and offered to take in his wash, but Jacob somewhat sheepishly confessed that he took it home to his mother's house. But he asked her if she would come and clean for him. In a rush of pity he offered her much too much money, and she accepted immediately.

Jacob had no idea that the relationship would grow in intimacy. It was his nature to make light of things, and he never admitted, even to himself, how much he loved her. When she came into his life he had just finished six years of studying history and philosophy at Göttingen; now he was writing a thesis on Immanuel Kant, learning Hebrew privately with a rheumy old rabbi and reading Greek with a retired classics professor. Despite these pursuits, his friends considered him a clown because he could impersonate almost anything, from a flea to the Kaiser. His face, unhandsome by the standards of his family, was expressive, but he, too, thought of himself as fit only for comedy.

Looking back on it, Jacob realized that the relationship was probably decided (as all such things are) the moment he stopped to help
the girl. Having once been asked into his life, she fitted herself to
his routine with rare tact.

They did not become intimate for a long time. Both of them were
shy and fearful of being rebuffed. When Jacob finally took her to
bed, it was unpremeditated. He had been at his desk, working on
his dissertation, while Gerda sat in an armchair, doing some mending. Looking up from his work to speak to her, Jacob noticed
that she had dozed off. He got up to send her to bed, and when
he bent over her she put her arm around his neck like a small
child. Only when she opened her eyes did she see who it was.
But the gesture had been made, and both of them responded to
it.

JACOB SEEMED thoughtful and a little out of sorts when he came
home that Saturday evening. Gerda had noticed that he was often
tense when he had been to visit his relatives, but she said nothing
to him about it. His family was a closed book to her; she had formed
no impression of them save what she had gleaned from the pictures
that stood on Jacob's cluttered desk, and these might as well have
been the stone faces of kings on the portals of Chartres or the painted
profiles of pharaohs from an Egyptian tomb for all that she could
imagine of their persons or lives. Moritz, who was careful to "drop
in" only when she was out shopping, was scarcely more real to her
than the photographs. If they happened to meet on the stairs, she
averted her face, and he looked straight ahead.

Gerda had never known a Jew until she met Jacob. She was not
even aware that he *was* Jewish until a neighbor's maid told her. The
idea frightened her for a while, and she sometimes looked at him
suddenly as if to catch him in his Jewishness, but she never did—
much to her relief.

At the dinner table Jacob muttered indistinctly as he waited to be
served. Gerda, thinking he was speaking to her, said, "What?"

"There'll be trouble," he said. "Edu and Gottfried will have a go
at each other sooner or later, probably sooner."

She brought him a bowl of hot cabbage soup. She did not know
—for he had never told her—that he was used to different fare.

"Edu thinks, because he's been to America, that he knows it all. Not that he can tell you anything interesting about the place, except to repeat the familiar criticisms. Ask him to describe the social context, and he fails utterly. 'You should have read Tocqueville,' I said to him. 'Who's that?' was all he answered. Not that he wanted to *know.*"

Jacob spoke to Gerda as though he were talking to himself. He had done it for so long that he no longer even noticed that Gerda understood only about half of what he was saying.

"That was delicious," he said when he had finished the last of his soup. He knew how to compliment Gerda only on the quality of her cooking. The other things he loved about her he did not put into words.

Gerda took away the empty bowl and set a plate of veal sausage and fried onions before him. She poured him a glass of beer and sat down, arms folded on the table, to watch him eat. She always ate later, by herself, and Jacob never tried to change her ways, although when they went out to a tavern in Sachsenhausen or to the Taunus Mountains for apple wine and ribs, she ate and drank heartily in his company.

After dinner he smoked a cigar, and while Gerda ate and washed up, he took his usual walk, down to the Main and along its quai to the Friedberger Anlage, then back past the old tollgate, along the abandoned Jewish cemetery and home again. He noticed that the air had grown damp, and there was a mist rising from the river. "We'll have rain," he told Gerda. He stayed up late that night, reading Greek, while Gerda darned his socks.

EDU HAD MADE a reservation for himself and Elias for dinner at eight at a restaurant said to be excellent. He planned to put business out of his mind and concentrate on pleasant company and good food. He was learning his way around. He went to the opera now and then, and to the theater, or to concerts with Siegmund and Pauline —he enjoyed not only the music but the liveliness of an evening out with his brother and sister-in-law. Here, too, he was watchful so that he might learn a thing or two. Understanding was the key to every-thing. If one had it, one could interpret any situation as though it were a plan for battle, and one could take control of it. That way one moved alone, forever rid of the herd. That way one was free.

Edu lived frugally. He ate at home whenever possible, never gambled or spent large amounts of money on women. His wardrobe was small, but the suits he owned were of the best material and expertly tailored.

This evening's dinner, planned several weeks in advance, was to celebrate his return to Frankfurt. He wanted to share it with his friend Elias because he liked him but also—more obscurely—because he wanted to show himself off to him. Elias was his foil. Like Edu he stood at the beginning of his career, but unlike him, he cared only for his work. He denied that he was ambitious, but Edu knew otherwise. It was one of the reasons they were friends. Besides, Edu loved to hear him tell about his courses in art history. He might go to the theater and the concert hall out of a sense of duty, but he went to the Städel out of a sense of wonder and something close to love. Paintings never failed to move him, and he envied Elias the many hours he spent looking at works of art.

Edu arrived at the restaurant a little early. The head waiter did not know him but seemed to respond with polite recognition when he gave his name. Edu was not kept waiting, and the table at which he was seated was good. Elias breezed in a few minutes late, looking disorganized and harried, trailing a scarf behind him.

"Am I late?" he asked, breathing extra hard to emphasize the effort he had made to get there on time.

"Not at all," said Edu grandly, forgiving him.

Elias was short and delicate-looking, but his head was large and his tousled hair as dark as his jet-black eyes. He resembled his sister Caroline only in the shape of his face and mouth. Despite the fact that he was clean-shaven, there was something of the anarchist about his appearance; now and then he was watched surreptitiously by agents of the police, particularly when he showed up in elegant establishments.

But Elias never noticed such things. Unlike Edu, he paid not the slightest attention to what went on around him. He was generally in a state of high excitement over some intellectual discovery.

"Guess what!" he said as soon as he was seated.

"Let's look at the menu first," said Edu, "and choose the wines, then we'll talk." He had made up his mind never to be embarrassed by the behavior of his friends or relations but to make every effort to guide their erratic deportment into more acceptable channels.

"I saw some new Cézannes on my trip to Paris," said Elias. "He's becoming more and more austere—"

"Would you like the lamb," Edu asked, "or the breast of veal?"

"Lamb sounds good. You knew I'd been to Paris, didn't you?"

"Indeed. Do you know anything about wines?" he whispered.

"Not a damn thing. Why don't you ask the wine steward, he's supposed to be the expert."

"He'll recommend the most expensive if he thinks I don't know anything."

"That way you'll learn. If you believe it's so important, the right wine and such, then you just have to sit down and learn all about it."

That settled it for Elias and he returned to his favorite subject, telling Edu of the Monets he had seen, all shimmering color, and the Munchs and Van Goghs in Berlin, where he had also been and admired nearly everything at the Secession Annual.

"You must tell me about that," said Edu, remembering his sister-in-law's casual reference. He spread the napkin on his lap and ordered the dinner as well as the wines. The maître d' was respectful, and Edu felt that he had made a good impression. He could relax now and listen to everything Elias had to tell him. His friend could hardly stop talking.

"It's great to have you back," he said as a bite of the delicate quenelles disappeared in his mouth. "You know," he went on, "it seems to me that the art of today is moving in several directions at once . . ." He wiped his mouth with his napkin. Edu noticed that there were crumbs and spots of sauce on the cloth around Elias' plate.

"The white wine is dry, I like it," Edu said.

"Styles did not used to come and go so quickly," Elias continued. "Nor did inventiveness play so large a role."

"Taste the lamb," Edu told him.

"Mmm! Pink and lovely," Elias said. He washed it down with a large drink of red wine.

"The white was better," Edu said.

"Do you know Meier-Graefe?" Elias asked suddenly.

Edu shook his head.

"He's a very perceptive critic. I don't always agree with him, but he's one of the few voices speaking out intelligently on the new art. Meier-Graefe says, for instance, that Cézanne has come to over-throw Impressionism, a bourgeois art, superficial and philistine."

He paused a minute to let his words sink in. "Like social democracy, something for everyone. But Cézanne does away with that. He arrives like Rembrandt, uncompromising. An aristocrat who disdains palaces."

Edu wasn't entirely certain he understood. He found theoretical and critical studies useless to his need to develop a quick and perceptive eye and an understanding of what was good and why, what was of value and what not. He was a practical man and not ashamed of it.

"I'm more interested in connoisseurship than in criticism," he said.

"You cannot have one without the other," Elias cried, tilting back dangerously in his chair. "Especially when it comes to contemporary painting, which breaks so radically with the past and does not yield its secrets readily."

"I thought your field of study was the early medieval manuscript," said Edu.

"It is, it is," said Elias, "but you can't escape the moderns. They are everywhere around us. We're living in wonderful times, just look at what's happening in Paris, Berlin, Munich, Vienna . . ."

"You haven't explained Secession to me yet," said Edu. They had finished their *fraises du bois* and were sipping an after-dinner brandy.

"I will, I will"—Elias' words always tumbled out in staccato repetitions—"but before I forget—have you made any other plans for tonight?"

Edu shook his head. All his energy had gone into arranging the dinner.

"The reason I ask you is that I've met a young painter here in Frankfurt—hard as that may be for you to believe, since there hasn't been a painter of note working here since Courbet. We had a long talk, and he asked me if I would like to see his work. I have no idea what it's like, but we had a splendid conversation, and I said I might stop by later tonight. Would you like to come with me?"

Edu, who needed time to think about anything he planned to do, was taken aback by the abruptness of the invitation. "I don't know any painters at all," he said. "The only one I ever met was that man who did Papa's portrait, and he seemed like a proper businessman."

"You won't find Franz Bleicher a proper businessman, I can assure you. He's a Bohemian through and through. But he really knows a lot about painting."

"I'm not sure . . ."

"Don't be so cautious," Elias cried. "Come and see how the other half lives."

"Is he quite poor?" Edu asked.

"What does it matter?"

"It makes things awkward."

"Nonsense! You have to realize, Edu, that not everyone looks on your privileged position with envy. Franz is quite happy with his life. A poor artist doesn't want to be a wealthy merchant. He dreams of being a successful artist. When he meets someone with a little bit of money he sees only a potential patron."

Edu wondered why he had not seen the visit in this light himself. To buy a work of art directly from the artist—what a wonderful idea! Not only would it be cheaper than going through a dealer, but he might have the good fortune to discover someone! He remembered the countless stories he had heard of painters—now famous, whose works were selling for thousands of francs—who gave away masterpieces for the price of a piece of bread and a bottle of wine.

Edu asked for the bill, studied it carefully and paid it, adding a generous tip. The waiter bowed low, and the maître d' said "Good night, Herr Wertheim" as they left. Edu felt certain he would be remembered the next time he came. Elias in his usual unconcerned way made no offer to pay his share. Edu was both pleased to be playing the gracious host and slightly irked at Elias' unthinking acceptance.

"Shall we take a cab?" Edu asked.

"They'll make a fuss about finding their way through the Altstadt," said Elias. "Let's walk."

"Where in God's name does he live?" asked Edu, growing cautious and doubt-ridden again.

"Near the old Judengasse, where they're tearing down a lot of old buildings—including, I hear, some historic ones—to extend the Braubachstrasse."

"Why does he live there? Most of those houses have been condemned."

"Exactly," said Elias. "He probably pays no rent, or else just a pittance."

They walked awhile in silence through the shrouded night. The roofs of the old buildings seemed at times to close over their heads; there was no sky visible, only a pale glow whenever they crossed one of the many small squares.

"Thank you for dinner," Elias suddenly said.

"You're welcome," Edu answered him.

FRANZ BLEICHER lived on the top floor of a building that was already half abandoned. Windows had been knocked out on almost every floor; the damp air stirred torn wallpaper in some apartments where doors hung loose on their hinges. Edu shuddered in the cool night air. Elias ran up the stairs two at a time and knocked peremptorily on the painter's door.

Bleicher opened it without first asking who was there, an act that seemed to Edu foolishly trusting, given the nature and condition of the building. Stepping into the cavernous, candle-lit studio, he very nearly tripped on a rotten floorboard. The glass in the immense skylight rattled at every gust of wind from the river, every footfall. The painter himself was heavyset, with a protruding stomach and pudgy, dirty hands. He wore a corduroy suit and a heavy sweater and smelled of paint, sweat and wine. There was a gap in his mouth where two teeth were missing, but the slur in his speech seemed rather to come from the wine.

Elias and Bleicher began almost immediately to talk animatedly and with excited gestures about a painter whose name Edu did not catch. It was a conversation of which he made no sense whatever, since he could not conjure up an image to go with the works in question. He sat on the hard-backed chair to which he had been directed as though he were waiting for something unpleasant, a reprimand in school or a painful procedure at the dentist's. Once or twice he tried to see if there were paintings on the walls or on an easel anywhere, but the darkness of the garret was all-pervading.

"So you like painting, eh?" Franz Bleicher asked him abruptly.

"Why, yes," said Edu, "as a friend of Elias' I have no choice but to like art." The statement seemed to him to come out of his mouth garbled. It was not what he would have said if he had spoken more thoughtfully. But he was angry with Elias for bringing him here, and he was letting the words tumble out any which way. It was something he had learned to do in America, where there was a lot of prattle going on all the time.

"Have you ever bought anything by a living artist, or don't you have the courage?"

"No," Edu said, "and I won't until I've sharpened my under-standing a little more."

"Don't you trust your friend? He brought you here."

"He didn't say that he had seen your work, only that you talked well."

"We'll remedy that," the painter shouted, jumping up from the crate on which he had been sitting and going to rummage about in a distant corner where there appeared to be a number of large canvases stacked against the wall.

"He's drunk," Elias whispered, by way of apology.

Edu kept his eye on the painter, who was moving with the exag-gerated motions of a jester, although he handled the large canvases with delicacy and care. Edu saw that the part of the studio where Bleicher apparently worked was neat, in contrast to the littered place in which he entertained—and drank and ate and cooked as well. Paint brushes stood in simple, graceful jars, the large palette was wiped clean and the tubes of paint were lined up on an old oak table like tin soldiers on parade. Edu felt himself an alien. Rain began pelting the roof. A small puddle formed at his feet.

He did not like the paintings. He had wanted to like them, but the work, like its creator, was disturbing and rude. There were many dancing figures, still lifes with bloody fruit, horsemen of the apocalypse. The paint was thick, the colors intense.

"You don't like them!" Bleicher crowed triumphantly.

"No, I don't," Edu said equally bluntly, even though he had been searching for words that would convey his meaning diplomatically.

"Perhaps you should look at a few more," Elias suggested, "before you leap to a judgment."

"It was he who put the words in my mouth," said Edu.

"I read the expression on your face," said the painter. "I can always tell. Even in the dark. I shan't ask you what *you* think," he said to Elias, and turned all the pictures back to the wall.

Elias tried to engage Bleicher in conversation again, to draw him out with technical questions about his work. But the painter refused to respond. He sat on his crate looking at his stubby hands, picking at the black fingernails. There was nothing to do but leave.

The two young men walked down the stairs without speaking. The street was full of dirty puddles. It was clear they would never find a cab; Edu's suit would be spattered with mud; they would catch cold.

"Don't say anything," Elias said.

"I can't believe—"

"Please shut up. I don't want to hear your opinions."

"It stank in there, the man was a drunk, his pictures were horrid, and he despised and insulted me, but you don't want to hear my opinions! Do you expect me to apologize because I wash and have manners?"

They walked rapidly through the rain, and neither said another word. At the Goetheplatz, where they usually parted, they stood for a minute, and neither knew what to say. They were more embarrassed than angry now, and had their feet not been so wet, they might have embraced and smiled at each other.

"*Tschüss,* so long," Elias said as he turned to sprint away from the evening's disaster. "Next time I'll invite *you.*"

"When will that be?" Edu shouted, but there was no answer, only the sound of splashing footsteps hurrying across the glistening cobbled pavement.

GOTTFRIED had sent the landlady's son to fetch a cab and the coachman to pick out a dozen roses for Nellie. The cognac had made him gloomy, and the damp air intensified the city's mingled smells of soot and horse manure. The performance had already begun by the time he reached the opera house, so he dropped off the flowers at the stage door, paid the driver and went into the brightly lit foyer. He felt the void of anxious desire within him, which the music of Richard Wagner—he could hear it faintly in the carpeted halls of the handsomely decorated building—did nothing to fill. He sat on a plush bench cracking his knuckles, unwilling to enter his box in the middle of an act.

At intermission he told everyone he met that he thought the performance dull, lifeless. Since Nellie did not permit him backstage until after the final curtain call, he had to wander through the crowds by himself, smiling and bowing to his family's acquaintances, knowing full well that everyone he greeted went off to whisper about him.

Rain had begun to fall by the time the opera was finally over. Gottfried waited for Nellie inside the stage door. He was not the only one; a mob of well-dressed men bearing flowers surrounded him. Not wanting to catch anyone's eye, he kept looking at the clock above the watchman's cage and set his mouth in a contemptuous smile. Nellie was a slow dresser and always the last of the dancers to appear.

"Did you get the flowers?" Gottfried asked her when she finally came out of the dressing room empty-handed.

"Oh yes, thank you. I gave them to a friend whose sister is in the hospital. I hope you don't mind."

Gottfried's face betrayed his chagrin.

"They were *old* and withered," she said. "Didn't you notice?" Gottfried silently damned the driver.

A table had been reserved for them at the same restaurant where Edu and Elias had dined a few hours earlier. Gottfried and Nellie ate sumptuously and drank a considerable quantity of wine. They did not talk a great deal, but what they said was laced with malice. Nellie criticized the chorus master; Gottfried said he had found the singers uninspired.

It was very late by the time they reached Nellie's house. Gottfried dismissed the cabbie. "Don't do that," Nellie said as the horse trotted away. "Call him back!" she said, with great urgency in her voice.

"Why, in heaven's name?"

"I don't want you to stay here," she said, and her teeth chattered. "I'm terribly tired."

The cab had turned the corner, and the rainy street was still.

"Let me stay," said Gottfried. "Please! I've waited so long."

"Not tonight," said Nellie.

But Gottfried, consumed by the afternoon's insults, the evening's tedium, felt he was owed some pleasure. "I must have you," he said and held her so tightly in his arms that she grew more frightened than ever. He pushed her against the wall and kissed her, not in love but in anger. He took her by the shoulders and shook her. She was almost lifeless with terror, and this exacerbated his rage. He shook her harder and harder, until she began to resist him, trying to tear herself away. She almost succeeded, but he lunged after her, slipped on the wet stones and, falling, brought her down with him. The fall hurt him, and he heard Nellie's cry of pain at his throat. She lay beneath him now, and he thought she was about to give in to him when she cried again, and he saw her teeth for a moment, as if ready to bite him. He put his mouth over hers, to shut it, and he tasted blood just before he came to orgasm.

The shock of his eruption left him sweating and dizzy. All at once he smelled the pavement, dirty with slops and refuse. Nellie lay very still. A light went on somewhere; he heard a window being opened. He bolted. He limped home, staying close to the walls of the houses. When he got to his apartment, not long before dawn, he fell exhausted on his bed. He slept only in fits and starts, alternately racked by the cold chills and damp sweats of a fever. His head ached with a pain like drumbeats. In lucid moments he thought he must call his mother during the course of the morning and excuse himself from the next day's dinner. He did not think about Nellie at all.

SUNDAY DINNER with all her family in attendance gave Hannchen more pleasure than any other event of the week. At her table she was empress. She could guide the conversation, spoil her sons by feeding them their favorite delicacies, scrutinize her daughters-in-law's faces for signs of failing health or flagging courage.

Hannchen planned the dinners carefully, as though each one

were her first (or last, if one wanted to look at it that way), and only
the meals at Christmas, New Year's and Easter, the Seder and dinner
on Rosh Hashanah were prepared on a grander scale.

She kept careful track of her Sundays. In a leather-covered diary
she noted what she served, what everyone wore, what the most
discussed subject was. She even reported on the weather. Moritz
pretended to be amused by it all, but he would have been affronted,
not to say heartbroken, had some calamitous event prevented even
one of the gatherings from taking place. They were suspended only
in the two summer months and during winter vacation, these dates
being as rigidly kept as October 16, the day on which the landlords
of Frankfurt turned on the heat and women and children decked
themselves out in their new winter coats and hats.

GOTTFRIED called at ten-thirty in the morning and announced, in a
voice that sounded, as Hannchen later said, "as if it came from the
grave," that he was ill and would not be able to come to dinner.
Hannchen asked if he needed Dr. Schlesinger or whether she should
send him a tureen of broth; she was certain that Bruno could deliver
it while it was still hot. Gottfried declined both doctor and soup and
said he merely needed bed rest and a day's fast.

At about the same time, Nathan received a call from the police.
The officer, whom he knew slightly, told him—neither as briefly
nor as directly as Nathan might have wished—that a young woman
(and he stopped to read her name very carefully, though, of course,
it meant nothing at all to Nathan) who had been found unconscious
and bruised in the courtyard of her apartment building and brought
to the hospital by the police, had claimed that it was Gottfried
Wertheim who had attacked her and beat her when she refused his
advances. Here the policeman sighed heavily. He was calling, he
said, at the behest of his superior to warn Nathan that charges might
be preferred.

Nathan thanked him and hung up.

Hannchen had not yet been told the news of Gottfried's latest
peccadillo, but she clearly suspected, even before the family sat
down to dinner, that there was something "rotten in the state of
Denmark," as she herself later expressed it. A somber sense of preoc-
cupation gripped everyone.

Jacob tried to be amusing, but all his jokes fell flat, and he, too, at a withering look from his father, sank into glum silence. Only Pauline seemed insensible to the atmosphere and chatted merrily away, describing the previous evening's party at the Seligmans'.

It was a relief to everyone when dessert had at last been served and dutifully eaten.

"The coffee mousse is delicious," Caroline ventured to say.

"Too bad we can't enjoy it," said Hannchen.

At that, the men rose, as if by command, and excused themselves to go into the smoking room.

"Now, then," said Moritz, "tell us the bad news. *All* of it."

Nathan told the story, more or less as it had been conveyed to him by the policeman.

"Have you done anything?" Moritz asked at the end.

"No," said Nathan. Edu wondered why Nathan still seemed to cower before his father.

"Why not?" he interjected. Moritz glanced at him with annoyance.

"I didn't want to do anything before consulting with all of you."

"*You*'re the one who has the legal training," said Siegmund.

"It isn't a question of legal training. It's a matter of coming to some general decision about Gottfried and the mess he seems to be making of things."

"In business as well," Edu put in boldly.

"Did you speak to Gottfried?" Jacob asked.

"He was incoherent. That's what Mama said."

"What are we going to do?" Siegmund asked.

"Pay her off," said Moritz.

"She has *some* rights," Jacob mumbled.

"What rights?" Moritz demanded.

"She may have rights," said Nathan, "but as long as she doesn't know about them . . . The police are on our side."

"What if she loses her job?"

"I know the assistant director," said Siegmund.

Nathan, it was decided, would visit the young woman in the hospital and talk to her. A sum of money with which he was to start negotiations was agreed upon. A further sum was chosen as the maximum he could offer her.

"And Gottfried?" Jacob asked.

"I do not wish to see him again," said Moritz.

"Ever?" said Edu.

"Ever!" said Moritz.

His four sons stiffened. It was as if a cold wind had swept through the room. The old man's voice had a terrible, hoarse sound to it.

"But what will he do?" asked Siegmund.

"He'll go to America," said Jacob, "like everyone else."

"*Enough!*" cried Moritz.

"We'll discuss it another time," said Nathan.

Nellie, it turned out, did not require more than a few days' rest and recuperation. She received Nathan with dignity and a certain touching pride and was happy to accept an amount of money not much above what he first offered her. She was back singing in the chorus within two weeks.

Edu's careful perusal of the books at Wertheim and Sons showed some irregularities, but by the time Nathan had checked them out and they had been shown to Moritz, it was too late to ask Gottfried about them. He was on his way to New Orleans with a sum of money and a letter of recommendation to a Frankfurt gentleman on the cotton exchange. He had not seen his father again, but Jacob and Siegmund had gone to say good-bye to him. He had told them— a touch defiantly, Jacob thought—that he was as glad to be going as the family was to see him go.

11

1913

MORITZ WERTHEIM died peacefully in his sleep one night in February of 1913. He was properly eulogized and buried, his sons put mourning bands on their sleeves, and his widow wore voluminous black. She would later say that it was just as well that Moritz hadn't lived to see the Great War, but she missed him bitterly those first few months. She had loved him well.

By Christmas of that year, with the period of mourning almost over, the thoughts of most of the family, most especially the children, turned to the impending holiday. All of Frankfurt was astir, bustling with commerce, glittering with gifts, redolent with the buttery scent of cakes and cookies.

On the square in front of the Römer the annual Christmas bazaar was in full swing. The Römer, as every child learned in school, had been not only Frankfurt's City Hall since 1405, but also the place where the German emperors held their coronation festivities in the years between 1564 and 1794.

Fragrant pine trees were stacked in lush green rows waiting for buyers, wooden booths were crammed with good things to eat, with *Lebkuchen* and *Kwetschemännche* and other seasonal delicacies, with colorful candles and brightly shimmering Christmas ornaments, with carved, hand-painted figures for the crêche, with whistles and tin drums, with entire regiments of toy soldiers, their cannons and their adversaries in colorful costumes from every corner of the earth: India and Turkey, Russia and Africa. At several of the booths the visitor could stop for a drink of hot punch or cider or *Glühwein* to wash down the roasted chestnuts that the Italian vendors sold from atop their portable ovens. The chestnuts were charred on the outside, soft and yellow and sweet inside. The Italians who sold them wore fedoras and had large black mustaches and eyes as dark as coal. They cried *"Marroni, marroni!"* in their melodious southern voices, which mingled (and would always be remembered like that) with the tinny sounds of Christmas carols from a dozen different calliopes.

There had been a dusting of snow the week before Christmas which clung to the sloping roofs in the Altstadt and gave it properly picturesque aspect. This delighted the adults no end, and they kept pointing it out to the children, who didn't care anything at all about such things, for their eyes were on the toys in the shop windows and the booths of the Römer.

Hannchen and Moritz Wertheim had celebrated Christmas ever since the year Edu was born. *Everyone*, they reasoned, celebrated Christmas, why shouldn't they? It was a good German holiday, and they were good German citizens. Oddly enough, this year, with Moritz dead and buried in the Jewish cemetery on the Rat-Beil Strasse, Hannchen felt some trepidation about the forthcoming festivities. What if Moritz, up there in heaven (where he belonged, she was certain of *that*) was talking to the Jewish God, and He asked him, "Moshe, Moshe, tell me please, why did you celebrate Christmas all those years? Didn't you know it's supposed to celebrate the birthday of my *son*? *I have no son!* Or, better to say: I have a hundred million sons—you are all my sons, the children of men everywhere are my sons . . ." What would Moritz answer him? He would probably say, "Everybody does it back home," and God would say (and He would be perfectly right), "What kind of an answer is *that*?" She hadn't thought about the religious significance of Christmas in years and years, even as her eyes grew damp when she gazed at the sweet baby lying on its bed of straw in a manger surrounded by donkeys and cows and sheperds, or when she lifted her voice, along with the others, to sing "Silent Night, Holy Night."

Of course, she couldn't take Christmas away from her grandchildren. Perhaps they would, she thought, grow up in a world where all these differences would be forgotten, though *who* would do the forgetting was a problem no one had yet been able to solve. But she would no more think of doing that than she would of forbidding them to look at the religious paintings in the Städel—there'd be precious little to look at if she did *that*—especially since her own very favorite one was the van Eyck Madonna, which she had looked at so many times that she could close her eyes now and see it in every detail, from the red cloak hemmed in pearls and precious stones to the apples on the windowsill and the four lions made of brass (like the bowl full of water in the niche on the right wall) which graced the arms and back of her throne . . .

Hannchen had decided that Nathan and Caroline should have the family celebration at their house on Christmas Eve. She offered her own servants to help Caroline's and promised to provide all the Christmas cookies and *Stollen*. At night, in her large canopied bed, she tried to think about every decision she had made during the day. And while she used to talk everything over with Moritz after dinner when they sat alone together in the salon, drinking coffee and listening to the distant sounds of servants and the clip-clop of traffic outside, she now talked to—she wasn't quite certain, maybe to God? Or was it simply Moritz in celestial garments, who listened, as he always had, with serious mien to her chatter, interrupting only when it seemed to him that she was being unreasonable?

Hannchen was relieved when her solution to the problem of Christmas found favor with her family and occasioned no complaints from on high.

HELENE WERTHEIM had celebrated her tenth birthday this year. From having been considered an "angry aborigine" by her Uncle Edu, she had progressed to being called his "dumpling." A plump little girl with a head of untamed curls, she was clearly his favorite. True, she had a temper, but she was of a far healthier disposition than Emma, skinny at thirteen, who still had a puny appetite and nerves that were easily strained. Nevertheless, she was a loving older sister, who took Lene and the twins in hand so often that the family called her "little mother."

Ernst and Andreas, eleven this year, formed a separate brotherhood, not only because they were boys and therefore expected to follow their own, different pursuits, but because, as twins they were natural companions, self-sufficient and tuned to each other's personalities like finely matched instruments. They were fraternal, not identical twins, which was a blessing, for it prevented them from being forever confused and allowed them, even though they were dressed alike, some measure of separateness. Caroline thought that Andreas rather resembled Emma, and that Ernst and Lene were more alike. All of the relatives agreed that the boys were winsomely coupled, and that the sisters, who, much to Emma's chagrin, were also dressed alike, made an appealing pair.

The family members never tired of discussing the children. Pauline and Siegmund had presented Julia and Jennie with a little brother, Wilhelm, called Willy, now a stripling of nine with ears that extended far from his head; a scared sort of child, who was the butt of his sisters' silly laughter. At Hannchen's Sunday dinners everyone chatted happily about the progress being made by the youngsters or censured one of the lot for having failed, in some nominal way, to come up to expectations. All too often it was forgotten that the children were at the table too—albeit at the far end, under the protection and care of Nanny and Fräulein Gründlich—and Nathan had to pass on the stern reminder "Not before the children," which he delivered in English.

Fräulein Gründlich had been with Caroline and Nathan Wertheim ever since the twins were born. As infants, the children were cared for by a nurse; the governess took over only after they were safely out of the nursery. Fräulein Gründlich was from the north of Germany, a stout woman of peasant stock who had done her best to overcome the narrow chauvinism of her Schleswig-Holstein upbringing. She looked older than her twenty-eight years, wearing her hair flattened back tightly against her head before it was caught up in a small round bun.

She had left home to look for a job when she was sixteen, much against the wishes of her dour and superstitious mother. She had not liked the monotonous farm work, the flat moors oppressed her, she hated the sea. Domestic service seemed to promise escape from all this. Before coming to the Wertheims, she had held a job in Hamburg for a year and never regretted the course she had chosen. Children, she found, were no trouble at all; they liked to be left alone. She never had to cook, only to eat, and no dustcloth ever soiled her fingers. At table she listened to conversations which opened horizons far greater than any she had imagined back home. She began to read, first the children's books and then those she found on the shelves of her employers' library. Since she was expected to speak only when spoken to, she did not have to expose her ignorance; she built up her knowledge slowly, behind a wall of silence. And the children loved her, right from the start. They recognized, before the adults did, that she was kind and good-natured. She was there to supervise the children, to walk them to school (the boys, before they were allowed to go alone, had learned to walk several paces ahead of her, so that it was not clear to those who might be watching whether they were with her or not), to see to it that they did their homework, dressed properly and displayed good manners. When a chaperone was needed, she was there, at dancing school, at parties and on shopping trips. When the family went on vacation, she had her own room at the hotel and saw to it, as she did at home, that the children all went on their daily walk.

And so it happened that most of the small crises of the children's lives took place in the presence of Fräulein Gründlich. It was given to her to wipe their tears, to adjudicate their quarrels and to sing them to sleep. Mama and Papa drifted through their young lives like visiting royalty. None of them ever saw Caroline quarrel with Nathan or weep tears of pain or grief or rage. They had all posed for a portrait the autumn just past, looking casual and elegantly affectionate. The finished picture suggested an ease of companionship that was a complete invention. The painter would have done better to show the parents alone—setting out for the theater, perhaps, or sitting together at the piano. There *were* such moments in their lives. As for the children, they might have been posed holding their attributes—a sailboat, a teddy bear—two on each side of Frieda Gründlich, sitting up straight as a preacher's wife, her hands folded in her lap. But, of course, the painter was hired to represent the approximation of a bourgeois ideal.

THE CHRISTMAS season was replete with parties that year. There was hardly a day when there was not some entertainment, either for the children or the adults. In retrospect it seemed the entire populace had been gripped by an unspoken premonition that, before the next Advent, the world would plunge into a war from which it would emerge forever changed.

Costume balls were especially popular, particularly for young people who went about Frankfurt dressed as chimney sweeps and clowns, dairymaids and shepherdesses. Lene enjoyed these parties more than the other children did. She loved dressing up in costumes of faraway times and places. The twins felt foolish going out in velvet suits or disguised as Neapolitan peasants, and Emma had got it into her head that she was homely. She looked out at the world with large dark eyes that reflected her fear of its dangers rather than her anticipation of its pleasures. She had once overheard her nose discussed. Hannchen said it was the least attractive aspect of her face, to which Caroline had replied that it was a "Wertheim nose," and Siegmund, with a wicked laugh, had added, "a Jewish nose." Now she looked in the mirror rather frequently to see if, like Pinocchio's nose, it might have shrunk. She had not noticed it before, and now it was all she saw.

Lene, on the other hand, seemed not to hear when the grownups talked with some exasperation of her chubbiness. "We're going to exhibit you as the 'fat child' at the fair," Hannchen admonished her, but Lene happily ate another piece of cake.

On the twenty-first of December, the von Brenda-Badolets had their annual party, which was held in celebration of young Thomas' birthday. Fräulein Gründlich spent a long time with the girls, planning their costumes, and accompanied them into town to make the necessary purchases. Lene was to go as the young Mozart, whose picture hung near the piano in an oval frame. "He is making sure you don't play false notes or the wrong tempi," Herr Sauerwein, the piano teacher, said. Emma had rather more reluctantly chosen the costume of a shepherdess, after a painting by Watteau. She was fitted out in yards and yards of flowered chintz and even carried a real crook. Her own dark curls were hidden beneath a blond wig, on which perched a small cap. She looked, except for her very dark eyes, like a Dresden figurine.

The diminutive, round-faced Mozart also wore a wig—a powdered one with a pigtail, exactly as in the picture. It proved difficult to get the girls' winter coats over their costumes, and there was a lot of moaning and groaning, but Fräulein Gründlich did her best to bundle them up without putting them awry.

Tom von Brenda-Badolet was a classmate of the twins at the Goethe *Gymnasium*, where they had just begun studying Greek and Latin. (The girls went to a private school run by two maiden-lady sisters which provided a decent enough education for those who were up to it but also served as finishing school for those who were not.) The students at the Goethe *Gymnasium* were divided less by their religious affiliation than by their social standing: it was not so much whether you were Jew or Gentile, Catholic or Protestant as whether you lived in the West End. The von Brenda-Badolets were an old Frankfurt family whose antecedents came of Italian as well as French-Huguenot stock. Both of these groups had been an integral part of Frankfurt's merchant community since the sixteenth and seventeenth centuries. Never forced to live in a ghetto like the Jews, they had nevertheless suffered some discrimination in the early years but were, by now, among the most respected "old" families in Frankfurt and had in many cases been knighted.

Tom was a child of his parents' old age. His brothers and sisters were adults, married, out in the busy world or studying at the university. Tom was the recipient of the sort of uncomprehending, indulgent love parents usually reserve for their children's children. He grew up dandled on many knees, dressed too long in lace, wearing curls down to his shoulders until the age of three. He was a solitary child, separated from his contemporaries by the

memory of all that lace, those curls and the grandeur of his surroundings. His parents' house was one of the oldest and most
beautiful mansions in the West End. But he was alone in it so
much that he felt friendless and estranged; his closest companions
were most often Jews. He was thought to be delicate, but this was
to some extent an illusion. He was scarcely ever ill with anything
but the normal childhood diseases. Like many solitary children,
Thomas read a good many books and was wise about the world
from what he had learned in them. He often sat reading for hours
and hours, lost in some adventure which he relived—with himself
as hero—that night in bed. His mother often forgot to come kiss
him good night, and his old nurse was close to senility, so he
enjoyed very little attention and practically no interference in his
choice of reading material. His imagination was not looked upon
as an asset by his family. His mother was a cold woman and his
father a businessman of the old school, with a seat on the stock
exchange and frugal habits.

Tom was dressed as Pierrot for his party. The costume had been
made for one of his elder brothers and had seen much use over the
years, but its multicolored patches were of fine silk, and all the work
had been done by hand. Tom wore a cocked hat and a mask over
his blue eyes; he felt well-protected and managed to play the role
of host with a patrician grace he did not always feel.

Most of the children were awed by the von Brenda-Badolets'
great house, which had been built as a summer villa in the days when
the West End was still country, and was set back a long way from
the street with its own orangerie and carriage house. The awe
translated itself into a lot of giggling and whispering and wide-eyed
glances into the distant corners of the neoclassic rooms.

The little pierrot stood at the foot of a grand staircase greeting his
guests. Directly above him hung a chandelier of truly magnificent
proportions, shedding its soft lights over a thousand crystal pieces,
so that the space above the boy's head seemed as alive with stars as
the Milky Way. Tom recognized almost everyone who came in,
even those who wore masks. He knew the Fräuleins and the nannies
and the mademoiselles who brought his guests. He was used to
playing host. His parents preferred him to entertain his friends at

home rather than go to their houses, and Tom accepted this as a fact of life.

A magician had been engaged to provide entertainment for the party. He not only did magic tricks but organized the party games. The dancing master to whose school all those present were sent once a week was on hand to lead the dances. A beautifully decorated table had been set up at one end of the ballroom, and the children studied it with care, but almost everything was still in the kitchen, kept in readiness for the moment when it would finally be time to eat.

Fräulein Gründlich left the children alone, once they had shaken hands with Thomas, and withdrew to the large, plainly furnished sitting room in a wing off the kitchen which the house provided for the help. There the assorted governesses had their own chaste party and gossiped about their employers. They formed a group almost as exclusive as that of the families for whom they worked. Those whose *Herrschaften* were Christian felt slightly superior to those who were employed by Jews.

Lene walked into the crowd of children with resolute, quick steps. She loved wearing knickers like the boys; it gave her the freedom to take big strides, to spread her legs and climb a tree if she wished, as dresses never did. She pirouetted about, all by herself, half boy, half girl, and almost knocked over a chair. She had lost Emma; the boys (a pirate and a hussar) had lost her. She wanted to dance, but it wasn't time yet; she wanted to eat, but it wasn't time yet for that either. The magician was just calling them all to order; a violin and a piano made thin music somewhere. Emma in her many skirts had trouble moving around and sat, primly and shyly, on a chair near the entrance. School friends often came over and whispered in her ear. She listened for a while and then broke in with a word or two to make them laugh. She caught the looks passed between friends, and sometimes she was too rash in her comments. Then the girls covered their mouths and turned away, saying, "Did you hear what Emma said? Really now!"

When the magic show was over, it was time for the dance. A young chimney sweep came over to Lene and asked her to dance. Tom did not join the waltz but walked among his guests, as his parents had taught him, making certain that everything was in order. He tried his twelve-year-old best to be gallant. He was sensible to the feelings of his companions to an extraordinary degree; in his solitary journeys through untold literary countries he had entered the lives of so many characters that he understood in a way far beyond his years the varieties of anguish that lurked behind the human face.

Tom had noticed the little Mozart as soon as she came in. After a moment of confusion—was it boy or girl?—he saw by the delicate mouth and the studied posture and walk that it was indeed a girl. Shaking hands with her, he noticed her merry eyes. After that, he watched for her as much as he could.

He saw that her next partner was a bullfighter with a large embroidered cape that seemed to get in his way a lot. What he couldn't see were the boy's sweaty hand in Lene's and his labored breath as he tried his best not to step on her toes. Lene was glad when the dance was over and she could slip away. She started to look for Emma just as the servants began to bring in the food. At the sight of so many delectable tidbits her stomach suddenly contracted with hunger, as though she hadn't eaten for days.

"Where have you been?" asked Emma, coming upon her in a corner near the pantry. "I'm supposed to keep my eye on you."

"Who said?" Lene often approached her sister with great good feelings and the wish to share some secret, only to find Emma acting annoyed and critical.

"I'm your older sister, and as such I'm responsible for you."

"That boy stepped all over my feet. I think I'll get myself something to eat. I'm starved."

"You're not supposed to eat yet," Emma said. "They'll tell us when it's ready."

But Lene was already on her way. She surveyed the table with the eyes of an expert as she thought hard about what it would be best to try first. The cinnamon stars or the tiny sandwiches with anchovy butter? The meringues or the mocha petits fours? The deviled eggs or the *madeleines*?

Lene could not resist. Thinking that no one was looking, she quickly took two of the butter cookies and had just put one into her mouth when she felt a bony hand on her shoulder. In her guilty fright she gave a small cry and turned around, expecting Herr von Brenda-Badolet had come to turn her out of his house. But it was only the dancing master. "Time for another dance," he said, "and I've got a partner for you, child."

His face was oddly animated. Lene turned away from him and stuffed the second cookie into the pocket of her kneepants. Her hand was greasy now and her lips studded with buttery crumbs. "Dance, children, dance," the old man cried and pushed Lene into the arms of a knight as the violin and piano started to play a fox trot.

The knight's name was Günter. He was taller than Lene and much older. "I didn't want to dance with you," he whispered in her ear. "The dancing master made me. You're fat, like a pig."

Lene stared at the boy's throat where his striped tunic ended and his pulse beat a steady rhythm. Tears started into her eyes and she wondered where Emma was. Günter held her to him with a cruel boyish strength. But once the music stopped, she pushed him away angrily, so that he tripped backwards, looking surprised, and bumped awkwardly into another couple before he caught himself. Lene ran out of the room and into the hall, thinking of nothing but escape. She wanted to find a spot where she could cry, all alone, but the house was so immense, there seemed to be no small spaces in it, no hiding place for a little girl.

At last she found the back stairs and hurried up, into a hall with many doors, most of them closed. But one was open, and she entered a study much like her father's, only larger. On one wall hung a beautiful tapestry, done in deep reds and blues, full of animals of every kind—rabbits and birds and mice, weasels and pheasants and cats with the round faces of babies. There were flowers, too, of every description. Lene forgot that she was going to cry. She stood transfixed, looking at the tapestry. There was a white beast, a unicorn, with a wound bleeding red blood in its white neck, and it was hemmed in by dogs. Lene saw how its eye was turned upward to heaven, full of suffering and the agony of death.

She forgot Günter and his insult. The tears on her cheeks dried; she could taste the salt they'd left when she put out her tongue as far as it would go. She did not hear Tom step into the room behind her. He had seen the incident with Günter and instantly recognized her hurt. He knew Günter to be a bully, stupid and thick-skulled and vain. Because he was in his own house, he felt both protective and bold. He followed her. When he sensed that she was aware of his presence—that he wouldn't frighten her—he said, "That's a copy of a famous tapestry from Paris. My grandfather had it made." Lene did not turn around right away. When she did look at him, he could not help noticing the last tear, still clinging to her cheek, right beside her nose.

"Don't cry," he said, but Lene was already smiling again.

A few of her dark locks stuck out from under the white wig. Tom kissed her on the cheek, and she didn't move. She simply stood there and looked up at him as if she had always known that one day Thomas von Brenda-Badolet would kiss her in his father's study. He took her hand and said, "Come back downstairs. The food is ready, you'll want something to eat. I'll protect you," he added grandly.

But Lene could not yet tear herself away from the tapestry. "Do you know the story?" she asked.

Tom nodded. "I've seen the rest of the tapestries, this is only one of them," he told her, and his way of explaining what he knew was, Lene thought, not at all stuck-up.

"That poor unicorn," she said.

"It comes back to life," said Tom.

They walked down the main staircase, back to the crowded ballroom.

"Can you tell that I cried?" Lene asked, and Tom studied her by the light of the great chandelier. He took out his handkerchief and wiped the last trace of tears away.

"I'm really hungry now," said Lene, but she remembered what Günter had said and decided she would eat only a little.

Emma had once again been looking for her sister, and when she saw her on the stairs with Thomas, she felt the anger that relief brings and a stab of jealousy at the natural way the two stood beside each other. Her voice sounded a little too shrill when she called, "Lene! Where have you been? What have you done? I was so worried, I couldn't find you!"

Lene would not answer, for Emma's voice had made heads turn to look at her more than the crooked wig or even tear-stained cheeks could have done.

The party seemed to be ending; some of the governesses had already come with coats and muffs in their hands to collect their charges. Lene headed for the food with determination, but she found almost everything had been eaten. Only broken pieces of cookies and melted ices were left, and there was a layer of dark, wrinkled skin on the hot chocolate.

"Remember to say good-bye nicely," Fräulein Gründlich said. "And to tell the host what a good time you had."

"But I didn't," Lene said. "The food's all gone, and Günter called me a pig." She almost began to cry again.

"That's not young von Brenda-Badolet's fault. Good guests don't complain," the governess admonished.

Lene went over to Thomas, who stood perfectly composed under the chandelier accepting the compliments of his departing guests.

"Thank you," she said, with a little curtsy, "I had a nice time."

His smile had the twinkle of conspiracy in it. "Bye, little Lene," he said. "I'll see you again."

They all walked home together, the boys skipping and running ahead. They arrived with cold cheeks and red noses, and no sooner had they entered the front door than they heard the voices of adults coming from the salon.

"Uncle Edu is here!" Emma cried and ran into the warm, comfortably lit room where the family sat on winter evenings. She hadn't even bothered to take off her coat. Lene, being smaller, fatter and slower, stayed behind and let herself be unbundled. The twins had run upstairs.

Uncle Edu kissed Emma on her cold cheek.

"Let me see you in your beautiful dress!" he said and watched as she dropped her coat to the floor and slowly turned around and around for him, hardly taking her eyes off his face. He was smiling, and she was pleased, and then she saw his smile grow fuller and brighter until it transformed his entire face. He was looking past her to the door where Lene had just appeared with her wig slightly askew and her vest unbuttoned.

Der kleine Mozart!" said Edu. "What a wonderful idea. Who thought of it?"

He looked around the room. Nathan and Caroline were there, and Jacob and Hannchen.

"Nathan thought of it," Hannchen said.

"I'm certain it was Caroline," said Jacob. "My brother is too practical for such charming conceits. He even *plays* Mozart as if Mozart had never been young and carefree. Forgive me for being critical," he added, with a nod toward Nathan.

"*Your* Mozart is nothing but fun and games, which is surely as much of a distortion," Nathan said, "but you're right, it *was* Caroline's idea."

Edu kissed the little prodigy and took her on his lap. "How was the party?" he asked.

"I didn't get to taste very much," Lene replied with a pout, "and some boy named Günter called me a name."

"She tried to eat before it was time," said Emma. "She's always trying to stuff herself."

"We'll exhibit her at the fair," said Jacob.

"Let the child alone," said Hannchen. "Eating is healthy. I wish Emma didn't pick at her food like a bird."

"What would you like more than anything else for Christmas?" Edu asked her.

"I am not allowed to tell you," she said, "or the *Christkind* won't bring it. I left a message on my window sill two weeks ago, and it came to fetch it that night, but Fräulein Gründlich says I musn't talk about it."

"Even to your Uncle Edu?"

"That's what she said."

"You're a baby still to believe that," said Emma. "You want to know what *I* want, Uncle Edu?"

He looked at her and she was pleased to see that his eyes took in hers with love too. She drew close to him so that she could whisper in his ear, "A doll in a carriage, as big as a real baby."

"But you already have a million dolls," said Edu. "How can you take care of yet another one?"

"Oh, I *can,*" said Emma. "You'll see, when I grow up I'll have lots and lots of children, and then I'll know just what to do."

"Aren't you getting too big to play with dolls?" Nathan asked.

"Fräulein Gründlich is showing me how to sew for them now,

and I can crochet and knit too. Mama says it's all very useful. Isn't it, Mama?"

Emma looked to her mother for confirmation, but Caroline was sitting, as usual, with her needlepoint, totally absorbed in what she was doing.

"What did you say?" she asked vaguely. And then, by way of apology, added, "I was fussing with a difficult spot here. Come take a look."

"I was telling Papa that I wasn't too old to play with dolls," said Emma.

"Of course you're not, dear."

"And I've learned to sew very well, haven't I?"

"Indeed you have." Caroline was all attention now. "Perhaps your father will let you have drawing lessons soon."

Caroline had been thinking about drawing lessons for quite a long time now. They were something she had always wanted and been refused by her father, so she had transferred her wish to Emma, to whom she felt closest.

"If I take drawing lessons," Emma asked excitedly, "will I be able to stop piano lessons?"

"You haven't learned enough yet to stop," said Nathan.

"But I don't really like the piano," said Emma, "and you yourself said I wasn't talented."

"We'll see," said Nathan.

During the course of this conversation, Ernst and Andreas had come into the room and sat down quietly to play dominoes. They accepted all the attention their sisters got—it was natural, Fräulein Gründlich said, with all those uncles around—and were perfectly happy with each other. They kept away from Uncle Edu, who clearly preferred the girls, and were closer to Uncle Jacob, who was, they thought, much more amusing. He told them jokes and played games with them; he was never ashamed to play hide-and-go-seek and get the knees of his pants dirty. He never teased them, as Uncle Edu did, and there was no malice to his practical jokes.

Andreas, who was the smaller of the two, was particularly sensitive. When he looked in the mirror, he found that his face always looked sad and a little worried. Unlike Ernst, he was afraid to climb trees and scale walls. His Uncle Jacob had told him the story of Jacob and Esau many times. "Though I don't recall your coming out clutching your brother's heel," he said, "nevertheless, the moral of the story is clear and unequivocal: cleverness wins out over brute strength. The Jews continue to draw important lessons from that."

"Don't fill his head with such nonsense," Edu had said more than once. "This is the twentieth century. The Jews are like everyone else, and if they're not, they ought to be."

Nathan felt the need to act as peacemaker. "We cannot ignore history," he said, "but there's no reason to be its slaves. Things *do* change. Let's hope the worst is over for the Jews."

"*Plus ça change, plus c'est la même chose,*" said Jacob. "The more things change, the more they stay the same."

Hannchen had been trying hard to read her book, but she was not in the mood for it. Sometimes at night she still missed Moritz, but it was no longer the fierce hurt it had been. She sighed, thinking about it, and looked at the scene around her with pleasure. Her clear gray eyes fell on Jacob, who was watching the twins at their game. He had, just before his father's death, asked for and been given part of his inheritance to buy a bookstore near the Römer. It had made him respectable in his dying father's eyes and had lessened the resentment his brothers had always felt toward his indolent existence.

"You look more disreputable every time I see you," Hannchen said. "What in the world do people coming into your bookstore think when they see you looking like that?"

"They come for my books, not my looks," Jacob said. He was not easily admonished. Ernst and Andreas both laughed, and he winked at them.

"You're a terrible influence on the children," his mother said, but the tone of her voice was not forbidding.

"Suppose I tell you that I'm contemplating marriage?" he asked. The question had an electrifying effect on all those present. No one moved.

Hannchen was the first to speak. "You've found someone suitable?"

"*I* think she's suitable."

"Not your Gerda?"

Jacob nodded. He felt as if he had the situation in control, and a touch of giddiness assailed him.

"Have you found out something that you didn't know before?" Nathan asked. "Is she the illegitimate daughter of the crown prince of Austria?"

"I think it's far better to be the legitimate child of working-class parents than a bastard of royalty," Jacob said with some heat.

"*Pas devant les enfants!*" Hannchen muttered and turned to the children. "Go see where Fräulein Gründlich is; it must be nearly time for your supper."

It took the girls a long time to walk the few steps to the door. The boys began to put away their dominoes one at a time and dropped a few for good measure.

"*Vite, vite!*" said Hannchen. "You may come back later."

"We want to stay with Uncle Jacob," Andreas pouted.

"I'll be here Christmas Eve," said Jacob and ran his hand over Ernst's close-cropped hair. "Tell them to let your hair grow a little," he added. His own was disheveled, which was one of the bones of contention within the family. "If you're good," Jacob went on, "maybe they'll let you come down to visit me at the store tomorrow."

"Will you buy us hot sausages for lunch?" Ernst asked.

"Absolutely! I'll close up shop and hang a sign in the window: 'Out for *heisse Würstchen.*'"

Once the children were safely out of the room, the conversation returned to the question at hand.

"Are you serious?" Nathan asked.

"I would not joke about anything of such importance to me." Jacob's voice had a cutting edge.

"You know how we feel about Gerda . . ." said Edu.

"I'm sure you've done wonders with her . . ." said Nathan.

"To come from such humble beginnings into a home such as yours, I know she is grateful to you and devoted," said Hannchen, "but Jacob . . . marriage!"

"I love her, Mama."

This admission, spoken in a very low voice but with an intensity all the stronger for its gravity, was greeted by profound silence.

"Does my love strike terror in your hearts?" Jacob asked.

"Only puzzlement . . ." Edu ventured.

"You don't understand love, then."

"That's one of your typically arrogant statements. Just because I don't parade my affairs around town . . ."

"You have affairs?"

"Come now," said Nathan, "we're getting off the subject."

"You cannot marry Gerda," said Hannchen with what struck them all as chilling finality. "It is out of the question. I also speak for your father of blessed memory. He would not have made a penny of your money available to you if he had thought that it would end up in the hands of this woman. If you do not conduct yourself respectably, there is no need to have you set up in a respectable business.

"You find it respectable that I *live* with a woman who is not my wife?"

"She is your housekeeper."

"But you know, Mama . . . that's, that's"—Jacob hesitated—"an illusion."

"We live by such illusions," his mother replied. "That's how society preserves itself. If you were to marry her, you would have to bring her into the *beau monde,* into our company, you would have to bring her *here.* And I will not have it."

"Would the world really come to an end?"

"No. But our small piece of it would be changed irrevocably."

"Before long, it will be changed irrevocably, anyway. War will come, perhaps even revolution. Do you think that *we,* this little group here, will escape unscathed?"

"Enough!" said Hannchen with great agitation. "I don't want to hear about it."

FRÄULEIN GRÜNDLICH always took the children for walks. It was as much a part of each day as the carefully planned meals or the obligatory eight hours of sleep. Sometimes all four of them accompanied the governess, sometimes only the girls went, but always their path took them to one of Frankfurt's parks. On special occasions they took the trolley across the river and out to the city woods, the Stadtwald, and took long leisurely walks on its sun-dappled paths, between the stately beeches and the firs.

Ernst and Andreas had received permission from their father to visit Uncle Jacob, and so, on this day, their *Spaziergang* proceeded in a less leisurely fashion, with fewer interruptions. The boys were anxious to get to the bookstore. To be with Uncle Jacob was to taste some of the joys of manhood.

Jacob's particular affection for the twins, he had to admit to himself, had been taken away from Emma, his first love. Once upon a time she had been lovely, shy and dark. But she was no longer a little girl, and her shyness now had something morbid about it. And she had withdrawn from him, he felt certain of that. She seemed to take the side of those who were against him in his relationship with Gerda, and she was drawn to Edu more and more, almost as though she knew instinctively that the power in the family would hence-forth lie with him. The boys, Jacob thought, were simpler and less devious. This was a delusion, but Jacob felt slightly oppressed by women these days.

The street on which Jacob's bookstore was located had not changed very much since Goethe's time. People liked to wander there on days when they had nothing much to do. Around Christ-mas the neighborhood seemed never to go to sleep. It was a perfect place for a bookstore.

Jacob knew every book on his shelves and could find anything anyone asked to see—Jules Verne or H. G. Wells, Heine, Schiller, Shakespeare, Mark Twain or James Fenimore Cooper. It was a magic place, and neither Ernst nor Andreas ever tired of visiting it. A red-headed Austrian named Alois who clerked for Jacob added to the magical quality of the place; he looked like a genii, always rubbing his hands as if to summon exotic Oriental gifts from some dusty corner. Jacob had found a very pretty old bottle when he bought the store and had placed it in the window among the maps and fine old volumes put there to catch the passing eye. The twins liked to imagine that Alois disappeared into it each evening.

Alois had surprising odds and ends of knowledge in his head. He was expert at recognizing and classifying eighteenth-century book illustrations, and he knew medieval armor as well as a tailor knows men's fashions. He loved the Russian writers and even knew a little of their language. He stayed in the small back office, answering mail and filling orders, unless Jacob summoned him out front.

Fräulein Gründlich, Andreas had noticed, liked to chat with Alois. She would come into the store and stand there as if she were lost, waiting for him to come out so that she could ask him some carefully worded question in her quaint north German accent.

The boys burst into the shop that morning with happy cries, startling a slightly deaf old gentleman who was giving Jacob a long and complicated order. Fräulein Gründlich peeked into the dark interior looking for Alois.

"Excuse me," Jacob finally said to the old gentleman, "my nephews are here, and I want to greet them; Alois will take the rest of your order."

"Eh?" said the man.

"My nephews . . ."

"Who?"

"The princes of Hohenlohe-Schillingsfürst!"

The gentleman turned to the twins with a beaming face and bowed from the waist as best he could, "*Enchanté . . .*" he said.

The boys, giggling, bowed in return. Jacob took them into the "children's corner," putting an arm around each.

"Pick out a book, my princes," he said, "one for each of you, a present from your uncle."

They sat down on a pair of footstools near the front door. A small bell tinkled whenever someone came in or went out, and its sound was one of the pleasures the children associated with the bookstore. It sounded almost like the bell that called them into the festive living room on Christmas Eve. It rang almost continuously that day, for there were many customers in the last hectic hours before the holiday, and Alois was kept too busy to talk to Fräulein Gründlich.

"Come back to pick the boys up around four o'clock," Jacob said to her.

"Be very good," she told them before she went out into the street.

It was long after the bells in the cathedral had struck the noon hour that Jacob found a minute to ask the boys if they were hungry.

Indeed they were, and Ernst's stomach growled in confirmation. The sun had moved behind the gabled buildings across the street, the window was in shadow, and a milky curtain of clouds advanced slowly across the pale blue sky.

"It looks like snow," said Jacob. "Are you bundled up?" They wore matching blue coats and gray scarves and hats with flaps to cover their ears.

It was only a short walk to the *Schirn*, where the hot sausages were sold. Jacob bought them each a fat *Gelbwurst*, made of veal, bursting its seams as it was handed them, dripping from the cauldron, with a dollop of sharp mustard and a crisp round Kaiser roll still warm inside its hard, flour-dusted crust. There surely was nothing better in the world than to walk through the wintry Altstadt, taking first a bite of the sausage and then a bite of the roll, washing it all down with a large glass of fresh cider. Uncle Jacob enjoyed it as much as the boys did, but he drank apple wine instead of cider, which made him, as he said, *"très gai."*

When they had finished eating and drinking they walked, one boy on each side of Jacob, and looked into shopwindows and down courtyards and up to see the varied roofs and wall decorations. They never tired of the variety of the Altstadt, especially in the company of Uncle Jacob, who knew every fountain and every monument and the stories that went with each.

"Let's buy something for Alois for Christmas," he said, and before they knew it he'd picked out a piggy bank in the shape of Goethe's house with the poet's likeness painted on the back in vivid colors.

"He can contemplate the likeness of Germany's greatest poet while he's saving money for his wedding," said Jacob.

"Who'll be his wife?" Andreas asked.

"I think he's sweet on Fräulein Gründlich," said Ernst.

They were back at the shop by two o'clock.

"Don't get in the way now," said Jacob, "I'm sending Alois out to lunch." He was anxious to return to his orders and his customers. Much as he loved his nephews, it never occurred to Jacob that they might be getting a little bored with the store by now.

"Let's go outside," said Ernst, "we can wait for Gründlich there."

The boys left the store without a word to anyone. The little bell jingled, but Jacob paid no attention. They stood on the sidewalk for a few minutes, aware that there was even less to do out here than in the shop. The narrow street was crowded. It had grown colder, and a dampness from the river seemed to drift over the cobblestones. In some of the store windows, the first lights of evening had been lit.

"Do you have any money?" Andreas asked.

"Just a little," said Ernst. "Why?"

"We passed a tiny little store, coming back from the Römerplatz, that had the most beautiful tin soldiers. I want to go back and take another look and buy one maybe, if it doesn't cost too much. It was a wonderful mounted hussar. It would go perfectly with the others they bring out for Christmas. I'll pay you back."

"Do you want to go back there *now*?"

"If we have time before Gründlich comes. Uncle Jacob won't miss us; it isn't far away."

They both wanted very much to go, but neither was entirely sure that he wasn't breaking some rule. By now they were already at the next corner, out of sight of the store, and that gave them courage. No one had called after them or come running to fetch them. They sauntered on.

"Do you really think Gründlich will marry Alois?" Andreas asked.

"She might," said Ernst. "Women marry all the time, even servants. But I hope she doesn't."

"She'd have to leave us, wouldn't she?"

"Yes—and go live in a little house with Alois in Offenbach or Rödelsheim, filled with little banks in the shape of the Goethehaus . . ."

"And somebody else would come to work for us."

"Who probably wouldn't be as nice as Gründlich."

"*Nobody* is as nice as she is."

"She never gets angry . . ."

"And she doesn't play favorites."

"And leaves you alone when you want to be alone."

"We'd better hurry," said Ernst, "it'll be dark soon."

They went on more quickly now, excited by the unaccustomed

freedom. They rarely went anywhere alone except to school, though they knew the whole of Frankfurt from their many walks and had learned the destinations of the streetcars too.

"Are you sure you can find it?" Ernst asked after they had gone about a dozen blocks and seemed still to be just around the corner from where they had started.

"It's only a little farther," said Andreas, but he was not at all certain, and the note of bravado in his voice was, as Ernst immediately recognized, a cover for doubt. They turned another corner, hoping to see the Cathedral of St. Bartholomew, the Dom, at the end of the little street, but they saw the river instead.

"Oh damn," said Andreas, "it's not this way at all."

"Do you want to ask directions?" Ernst asked gently, so as not to make Andreas even more unsure of his way. He was feeling chilly, and his teeth chattered a little, as much with apprehension as with the cold. Andreas, because it had all been his idea and he felt to blame, pretended unconcern.

"I'll find it, don't worry," he said. "If we go down as far as the Main, we can get our bearings. We'll see the Dom and head straight back for it."

They walked to the end of the little street and found themselves on the bank of the river. Everything was still; the sky, gray with late afternoon winter clouds, pressed on the city's familiar skyline. The trees on the island in the middle of the river were spidery black; the Sachsenhausen shore seemed far away and snow-enclosed. A group of neatly up-ended boats on the island looked like a row of teeth. The water lapped gently against the stone abutments of the bridge. There were already ice floes drifting downstream.

The familiar view gave the boys confidence and dissipated some of their uneasiness.

"You shouldn't have gone out like that unless you knew where you were going," said Ernst.

"I still want to find the shop with the soldiers," said Andreas stubbornly, "so I can go back there another time. I really want that hussar."

"They're probably too expensive. I bet they come from some foreign country and cost a fortune."

It was beginning to snow. The fine white flakes fluttered down slowly from the wan gray sky. At first they melted when they landed and turned into tiny drops of water, but soon they gained strength and remained whole and white in the deepening cold, and it was as if the sky, too, grew white with them.

"Shouldn't we go back?" Ernst asked.

"Maybe we should go home instead," said Andreas. "What if it's four o'clock already and they miss us and there's a ruckus. We can always say we were on our way back to the Guiollettstrasse."

They were walking westward, along the quai, where it was deserted and lonely at that time of day. All at once a figure emerged out of the snow and stood before them, blocking their way. At first it seemed that it was a vendor or delivery boy or perhaps a slightly tipsy apprentice on his way home. The man was small and thin and hunched over in the crooked way people sometimes have when they have carried too heavy loads too long. He seemed uncertain whether to step out of their way or wait for them to go around him. He was too well-dressed, Ernst noticed, to be a workingman. His coat was well-cut, and he wore a tie, a rather florid one, Andreas thought. When it became clear that the man was about to address them, the boys instinctively drew close, until their arms touched, as though joined by a common membrane.

"You two children must be lost," the man said with a voice full of friendly concern and not a trace of Frankfurt accent. Ernst saw, with a shock of relief not unmixed with apprehension, that it was the dancing master.

"No, we're not lost," said Andreas.

"What are you doing down here all alone then?"

Now Andreas had recognized him too. "We're looking for a shop with toy soldiers," he said, meaning to address the dancing master by his title but finding it impossible. Though the sharp eyes looked directly into his, the little man showed not the slightest sign of recognition.

"Down at the river's edge?" he asked in feigned incredulity. He seemed to sniff at them with his sharp nose.

"We came down here to see the Main," Ernst said. "We're going right back, before they close."

"What street is the shop on?" The dancing master wore no gloves and kept blowing into his hands.

"I don't exactly remember the name of the street," said Andreas.

"But we can find it," Ernst chimed in.

"I think I know the shop you mean," said the man. "And I can help you find it." He put a bony hand on Andreas' shoulder. "You shouldn't be running around alone down here. Is this your brother?"

Andreas nodded, pleased that they had not been taken for twins but puzzled that they had not been recognized.

"Don't you know us?" he asked. The bent figure said nothing.

They started to cross the street, heading for one of the alleys leading into the Altstadt. Ernst hung back a little, feeling as though his brother had been pulled away from him. The dancing master walked with his hand on Andreas' shoulder until they had crossed the quai and then dropped it suddenly, though he continued to direct his attention toward him. Andreas looked at Ernst, with an embarrassed shrug.

They walked briskly now and were soon on more familiar streets. Nothing much was said, and both boys looked with pleasure and relief at the landmarks all around them. They *had* been lost. Andreas expected to see the window filled with its hundreds of colorful figures any minute now.

Then, quite without warning, the dancing master stopped in front of a building in which there was a small tavern on one side and a junk shop, billed as "Fine Antiques," on the other. "This is where I live," he said. "Let's stop here for a minute. I may, I just remembered, have a little soldier like the one you described, in my collection."

Andreas and Ernst both hesitated. The dancing master had opened an ornate wooden door that led into a dark passage between shop and tavern. He stood there exactly as he did in dancing class, a little irritable, expecting more than his pupils could give.

"Come, come now," he said, and there was no disobeying him. He led them through the passage and up a flight of stairs into an apartment that seemed to have many rooms leading in different directions. Ernst was glad to see that it faced the street—which represented escape to him—and that the noise of the tavern was a distinct, lively presence.

A very fat, bushy-tailed cat jumped off a chair as they entered, and startled both boys. It was hot in the apartment, which was filled with furniture, a little threadbare but of good quality; the boys recognized it as the sort with which they were familiar. There were innumerable music boxes, as befitted the home of one who made his living from the dance. What startled them was the figure of a young man stretched out on a low armchair reading a book. He scarcely moved when they came in but lifted his pale and handsome face to smile at the dancing master and greet him with a casual nod.

The two men conversed for a few moments in French, speaking so low and so rapidly that neither boy understood what was being said. Then the younger man got up from his seat and went into another room. Andreas saw that the dancing master's face had grown more calm as he gazed after his friend.

"He's gone to look for the soldiers," he said. "He'll be only a minute. Take off your coats. My assistant," he added.

"We can't stay," said Ernst, fearful of the reprimands they would receive when they returned. Andreas threw him an exasperated look, he seemed to find the adventure delightful. And indeed, at the sight of the assistant, the last residue of his fear had left him; the young man had an angelic look about him as if nothing that happened in his presence could possibly be touched with ugliness or evil. His face, pale and smooth, framed by soft, rather long brown hair, had the perfection some painters seek, and to the young boy, who knew far more about art than about life, the assistant was like Verrocchio's striding angel.

Ernst saw exactly the same figure as his brother, and he, too, noticed the young man's grace and beauty, but its perfection did not conjure up for him figures of angels and works of art; it reminded him, more insistently than ever, that they had strayed from their uncle's shop and were even now causing all sorts of trouble—for Jacob, for Fräulein Gründlich, even for Alois perhaps. It seemed to grow darker with every second they were away—his father would certainly be angry; his mother would look at them with her sad eyes, resigned and pained and helpless; they would be punished, and she would withdraw still farther from them.

The assistant brought back a large box and set it on the floor. Andreas kneeled down to look, and his face shone with pleasure at what he saw. The dancing master clapped his hands, as he did when he sought their attention to begin a Virginia reel.

"What did I tell you?" he exclaimed. "It's just as I promised."

Andreas set up the toy soldiers, one by one. He had forgotten the hussar he was searching for in his admiration for the dozens of colorful figures before him.

"We have to go," said Ernst, and he felt dull as a clod. "It's dark outside. If you don't come with me, I'll go by myself."

The heat in the room was stifling, but Ernst would not take off his coat. He did not want to go without Andreas, but with every passing second he felt himself drawn further and further away. Something had come between them, for the first time.

"Good-bye," he said.

No one seemed to be listening, and he had to repeat himself. "Good-bye, I'm leaving," he said and headed toward the door.

"I'll be right along," said Andreas and made as if to get up. But something else, some other figure, caught his eye, and he bent back over the soldiers again. Ernst opened the door, and the cold draft from the hall made them all shudder. The lights flickered and the cat raised her head from the dancing master's lap, where she had settled. Ernst hurried downstairs and out into the street.

He felt the cold bitterly after the overheated apartment, and it struck him like a pang of loneliness. He stood undecided for a second, then walked very slowly, counting his steps, through the falling snow to the corner. He recognized the little square with its fountain, and all of a sudden he knew exactly where he was. From here it would take only ten minutes, if they ran, to get home.

The streets seemed brighter now in their snow shroud, and Ernst stood still again, keeping his eyes on the door of the dancing master's house, waiting for Andreas. He hadn't sold his birthright for a mess of pottage, as Esau had, but he felt hungry and hairy now, the awkward, dull-witted brother, done out of his blessing. He stamped his feet, both in anger and against the cold. Then he saw Andreas coming out of the door next to the tavern, saw him look around, heard him call his name in a clear, high voice just this side of trembling.

"Here I am!" he called, even though he had intended to remain silent and watch Andreas grow panicky, to teach him a lesson. Andreas ran toward him.

"Let's hurry," Ernst said, "it's late."

In the window of a clockmaker's shop they saw the time—five minutes to five. Without another word they took off, Ernst in the lead, and raced the whole way home. At the monument to Wilhelm I, opposite the opera house, they finally halted to catch their breath and walked the short block from there, in order not to arrive in a sweat.

They found a delegation of distraught adults waiting for them. Fräulein Gründlich was in tears. "Where did you go?" she said to them. "Where have you been? Why did you do this?"

Caroline stood at the foot of the stairs, leaning against the balustrade, looking distracted. Lene and Emma in their robes, fresh from their baths, stood beside her with wide-open eyes—Lene's showing excitement and Emma's concern. They smelled of soap and fresh towels and talcum powder. Andreas became aware of them almost as soon as he saw the crying Fräulein, and their sweet-smelling cleanliness made him feel dirty.

Nathan came striding out of his office. He had been on the telephone with Jacob when the boys appeared, discussing the advisability of calling the police. "It isn't necessary now," he had said, "they've apparently come home on their own." He wanted to call his brother to account, but his angry words evaporated in relief.

Ernst and Andreas were punished by being sent to bed without supper. They received a stern lecture from Nathan, but it was Fräulein Gründlich's sobs and tear-stained face that caused them the greatest chagrin.

When the lights were out and they were in bed, Ernst tentatively brought the conversation back to their adventure.

"Do you really think he didn't recognize us?" he asked.

"We're all the same to him," Andreas answered, already beginning to drowse off.

"Did anything happen after I left you?"

"What should have happened?"

"I don't know. I didn't like them."

"That's too bad," Andreas mumbled. "I thought they were rather nice. Imagine, our dancing master at home with an angel."

"What?" said Ernst. Again he felt heavy, weighed down. He and Andreas were no longer one flesh and soul.

"Go to sleep," Andreas said, turned to the wall and was himself asleep in an instant. But Ernst thought about their adventure for a long time, and when he finally slept, it invaded his dreams. He was running through snowy streets pursued by a man with flapping wings. The man did not catch him, but neither did Ernst reach safety.

THE CHILDREN's Advent calendar had reached its final day: the little paper door with the date on it could now be opened to reveal the last tableau in the snowy Christmas landscape. Everyone knew what it would show, but that made its discovery no less exciting. Lene was allowed to lift the flap. And there it was—the baby in the manger on a bed of straw, its head surrounded by a bright yellow halo. It was December 24, the hallowed evening was at hand.

The day had dawned clear and cold. A pale-blue sky suffused with light stretched over the snow-covered city. Helene and Emma awoke early, and when they pulled the curtains back and glimpsed the wintry scene beyond, they both caught their breath at once. The sunlight was intense behind the frosty glass and it seemed to the girls that they were looking out from within a glittering glacier.

Fräulein Gründlich was already up and busy, the boys were still asleep, not a sound came from anywhere on the second floor. The girls put on their long wool robes and went carefully over their store of hand-made gifts one more time. They had been hard at work for months, crocheting and knitting, drawing and pasting, stringing and cutting, to make presents for everyone, from Mama and Papa right down to Anna in the kitchen and Liese the maid, not to speak of cousins, aunts, uncles and friends. They had wrapped the gifts carefully the day before, tied them with ribbon and tagged them, and were checking them now to make certain no one had been left out. Sometime during the day Mama or Fräulein Gründlich would carry them downstairs to the curtained living room, where the Christmas preparations went on mysteriously, behind locked doors, out of sight, but clearly not out of the children's mind. Stealing about the house on tiptoe, they sometimes heard the tinkling of small bells or smelled the fresh scent of the pine tree (brought in late at night, when they were fast asleep) or became aware of scurrying steps and the rustle of tissue paper.

Delicious aromas began wafting through the house early in the day. The kitchen, where they liked to go when not shooed away by a perspiring Anna, was a wonderland of steaming puddings, baking tarts, kettles of red cabbage simmering with clove-spiked apples, chestnuts roasting in gleaming pans, unfolding to be peeled and stuffed in the goose. The goose, it was said, was Frankfurt's eagle, and the fatter the better. Anna had already rendered a crock of its fat with onions, and it was cooling now (Lene's mouth watered, thinking about it) so as to be ready to be spread on chunks of black bread, lightly sprinkled with salt. And then there were the *Grieben*, the cracklings left after the rendering, which sat on a piece of absorbent paper, draining their fat, and which Lene tasted, whenever no one was looking, just as she'd steal a broken piece of cookie or lick off the whipped cream that clung to the wire beaters.

"Don't spoil your appetite!" Anna would admonish, but gently, and Sophie, who had been hired for the day to help in the kitchen, would smile benignly and slip the little girl another bit of crackling. "Eat hearty," she'd whisper. Sophie had been the elder Wertheims' cook before she retired a dozen years ago. She was an immense woman, unrivaled in the preparation of fowl, who could stuff the largest goose ever bred and make the fluffiest dumplings in the world. She was partial to Lene because Lene loved to eat, and when Anna was about to throw the child out of the kitchen, Sophie always pleaded with her to let her stay "just a little longer."

The day passed with excruciating slowness and was apt to get the children quarreling, although they had been warned of the dire consequences of not being good right up to the last minute before the doors to the living room were opened.

In the early afternoon Fräulein Gründlich suddenly decided that it was time for them all to take a walk. The children immediately suspected that some gift was on its way that could not be got into the house without being noticed, and all four obediently put on their coats and accompanied the governess to the Palmengarten. That tropical paradise, hot and steamy as the Christmas kitchen but suffused with a host of other, different smells, was a favorite destination. There were a number of greenhouses adjacent to the main one, which housed the palms, and each one simulated another kind of foreign climate, from arid desert to sweltering jungle. But it was the main house with its huge palms that held the greatest attraction for the children. Its floor was covered with a carpet of green grass and stone walks meandered over it. A waterfall splashed in the forest, forming several pools alive with goldfish. Birds flew in and out among the trees, twittering and singing in rapture over this perpetual summer.

But Christmas Eve, they all agreed, was not the proper time for a tropical paradise, and so they tramped through the park itself where the paths had been cleared and the landscape was truly northern. Children were ice-skating on the pond, and the great pines wore gossamer mantles of snow. Everything sparkled in the sunshine, and the icicles that hung from the roof of the delapidated little garden restaurant dripped water onto the stacked metal chairs of summer.

When they returned home again, it was time to begin preparations for the festive hours ahead. Fräulein Gründlich sent the boys to bathe first. They often sat together in the tub, washing each other's backs and splashing a little, usually under her supervision. ("No fooling around," she always said, very sternly, and they were never quite certain what she meant.)

The girls took their baths separately. They had had their hair washed the day before; it was wrapped in towels and piled high atop their heads for the bath. Emma washed herself methodically, even between the toes, but Lene liked to play in the tub, and there was usually water all over the floor by the time she was finished. "Hurry, hurry," Fräulein Gründlich urged. "It's almost time for the Christ Child." But Helene Wertheim hurried for no one.

When, at last, they were all properly dressed and combed and powdered and had brushed their teeth, it was still not quite time to go downstairs, after all. So they all sat, stiff and polished, in the upstairs sitting room, waiting for the great moment to arrive. Fräulein Gründlich, dressed in her Sunday best with her hair curled, perspired a little, for she was at least as excited as the children.

And then they heard it! What an unmistakable sound it made— silvery and pure, it seemed to ring not only in this house, but in every other house in Frankfurt. The girls grasped each other's hand, and then they all walked downstairs together, to find the hallway crowded with family and all the servants lined up in a row, in their cleanest, best uniforms. Sophie had tears in her eyes. She had seen Nathan and his brothers grow up, and here they were—all except Gottfried—men of substance, two of them fathers of beautiful children. Sophie involuntarily started to curtsey before she stopped herself: it wasn't done anymore, but the children coming down the stairs had an almost haughty look. Caroline looked regal this evening too. Sophie took the corner of her apron and wiped the tears away.

Everything in the large living room had been set up beautifully. The Christmas tree, ablaze with candles, stood at the very end of the room, between the tall windows that led to the garden. The lamps had not yet been turned on, so that the tree gave off the only light. The candles flickered slightly, and whenever they did, the golden globes on the tree shimmered more brightly and the wooden angels bobbed from the delicate tips of the branches. Some blew trumpets, others held cymbals, and between them all wound garlands of silver threads, while the cinnamon stars added their spicy fragrance to the forest smell of the pine.

The crèche was at the foot of the tree, on an old white sheet arranged to resemble a snowy hillside. The shepherds were there, and the three kings; inside an alpine hut, Joseph and Mary knelt at the cradle with its haloed infant surrounded by the obligatory sheep and donkeys and cows. And all around the room itself stood the tables piled high with gifts, each with a white card on which Caroline had written the recipient's name. The children made a dash for their presents, only to be brought up short by Fräulein Gründlich calling out in her brittle north German voice, "Wait! Wait! We haven't sung 'Silent Night' yet!" She knew, in her good Protestant heart, that Christmas was incomplete without carols, and she always chose this one, the most German of them all. She began, in her uncertain, unmusical voice, to sing the opening words, her hand held up for silence first, then moving in time to the music as, slowly, the others chimed in. Nathan went quickly to the piano and began to accompany the singers as they went through all the stanzas, one by one.

The gifts that year were of an almost Oriental splendor. It seemed as if everyone had tried his best to make this the most memorable Christmas ever. Emma got the largest and prettiest dollhouse imaginable, and the boys got a train that was realistic in every detail, and several companies of soldiers, including a couple of mounted hussars. Lene received a tea service of Meissen china for her teddy bears, and a beautiful edition of Andersen's *Fairy Tales,* but best of all and totally unexpectedly, she got what she had wanted as long as she could remember—a live puppy! It was the puppy that had been brought to the house while they were all on their walk in the Palmengarten. Lene had eyes for nothing else and almost overlooked the little figurine of Mozart that Fräulein Gründlich had bought for her. Had Emma not brought it up to her room late that evening and set it on her night table where the governess could see it when she came to say good night, Lene would surely have forgotten it and neglected to thank her for it.

All four children had pooled their resources to buy *one* gift for Fräulein Gründlich: a beautiful piece of genuine leather luggage. Mama had taken their jar full of change and added the necessary monies to it so that she could buy a suitcase nearly as stylish as her own.

"This is from all of us," Emma had written on a small card in her fine handwriting. "A new suitcase for Fräulein Gründlich, who says she is ashamed, when we travel, to see her old suitcase in among ours." Quite naturally and expectedly, the governess was brought close to tears.

Edu's gifts to the children were, as always, the most carefully thought out. He went out to buy presents for his nieces and nephews with the same clearheadedness with which he approached all things that involved decisions about money or matters of taste. The boys invariably received books. Not ordinary ones, but first editions that would form the nucleus of a library when they were grown.

Little as they might appreciate these gifts now, they were awed and impressed by them. The girls were always given something precious —not for the mind but for the body. Edu loved to adorn them with pretty baubles, but these presents were meant for now, and he never made the mistake of giving them something too grown-up, too womanly, for them. This Christmas, Emma received a single black pearl suspended within a silver teardrop studded with tiny slivers of diamonds. It came in a small leather box with a velvet lining from the jeweler Koch. Emma was delighted with it and immediately asked Caroline to put it around her neck.

Lene hadn't yet acquired any sort of taste for jewelry, so she simply glanced at Uncle Edu's delicate gold necklace of tiny pearls, emeralds and turquoises and went from it to a small chest with many drawers, a gift from Uncle Jacob, which pleased her much more.

"Don't you like the necklace?" Edu asked her. Lene realized guiltily that he had seen her almost pass it by.

"Oh yes I do," she said quickly, "it's beautiful!" And she went to hug him, still holding the puppy.

"If you set the dog down, I'll put the necklace on you so we can see how it looks," he said, affecting a jovial tone, for he wanted it understood that he was impervious to what the children thought of his presents. Lene sat down on the couch next to him and gently set the puppy at her feet. She lifted up her hair with both her hands and felt Edu's cool fingers and the prickly necklace touch her skin at the same time. She shuddered a little, just for a moment, and then Edu's mustache tickled the nape of her neck, and she felt his dry kiss. She giggled. "You can let your hair down now," he said, and she did and turned to plant a kiss on his cheek.

Caroline's relatives arrived fifteen minutes before dinner, just in time to see Jacob, who did not want to leave Gerda alone this evening, make his farewells.

Benedict Süsskind and his three other children were not regularly invited to the Wertheim get-togethers. The families were cordial but preferred to keep a certain distance. Benedict did not have social ambitions; he wanted his children to do useful and productive work and assumed that happiness would come from that. He was convinced that it would not come with money and felt just slightly superior to the Wertheims, who so clearly believed that it would.

The Wertheims, on their part, found the Süsskinds very nice and generally good company, but they were also quite certain that in some unalterable way, the Süsskinds would never "fit in." There was, for one thing, the business of their religion. Benedict was not a practicing Jew, which is to say that he was not by any standards Orthodox, but he was opposed to taking up the practices of the *goyim* wholesale. He did not believe one should celebrate their festivals with such enthusiasm as he saw here this night. He could not refuse his daughter's invitation to Christmas dinner, but the tree with its crèche—never mind that it was an antique one which Edu had found on a trip to the Tyrol—annoyed him, and he made it a point to bring his grandchildren gifts that would remind them of the faith of their fathers. This year, he brought them all a lovely eighteenth-century menorah, from Prague. It was made of silver and had nine tiny lamps at its base in which to burn oil for the eight days of the festival—the ninth lamp was called the *shammash*, the beadle —with an embossed scene on it showing in bloody detail and eighteenth-century dress the victory of Judas Maccabeus over the Romans. All around this were other scenes celebrating a variety of Jewish triumphs over oppression, and some silver bells attached to its crown jingled with a light and airy tone.

The menorah brought outcries of pleasure from the children and was immediately given a place of honor by them, on the mantel behind the piano, under the portrait of Mozart.

Hannchen studied the gift through her pince-nez and turned her most supercilious smile upon the giver. Clearly, it was a valuable piece, but Benedict had made a gaffe, she thought, in bringing it for Christmas. Caroline kept her eyes cast down and prayed that Nathan would not make an unkind remark or Siegmund a bad joke or Edu a sarcastic comment. The brothers took their cues from Hannchen and acted out their own roles for her, as if to give extra emphasis to all her opinions. Fräulein Gründlich was intrigued and fascinated by the menorah. She was the only one who knew her Bible well enough to decipher the Old Testament scenes without a hitch.

Of Benedict's three other children, Eva, the eldest, had made the most strenuous objection to coming this evening. She did not like these large jolly parties at her sister's house. By dint of iron-willed determination and endless hours of hard work she had succeeded in becoming a chemist and had obtained a position in Dr. Paul Ehrlich's laboratory. Her experience had not made her exactly bitter but had convinced her that nothing in life came easily, and she distrusted the comfort and perfectly appointed elegance of her sister's house. She liked to think that she had no illusions, but her illusions were simply of a different order from those of her sister or even her brothers. At twenty-nine, determined and opinionated, she was her father's favorite.

Of the three siblings, Elias felt the most comfortable among the Wertheims. His friendship with Edu, his interest in Frankfurt's cultural life and his sense of himself as a purveyor of scholarly connoisseurship to the city's *haute bourgeoisie* (he had, for several years now, had a position at the Städel and was making a name for himself there) put him at ease with these people.

He had also married a woman of spirit and talent named Bettina, who was a Frankfurt native but not Jewish. Her father, a well-to-do patrician lawyer with a well-nigh prophetic instinct for modern painting, had been on the board of directors of the Städel, and it was said that Elias married her in order to secure his position. Nothing could have been further from the truth. They had met in her parents' drawing room, and Bettina, who was shy and rather homely, possessed of that peculiar combination of solitariness and volubility that is the mark of the talented woman, had set her cap for Elias at once. He proved able to understand her better than anyone she had ever met. Elias, in turn, was charmed by her sometimes wayward thoughts—and powerfully attracted to her sexually. He could not name that attraction, for it lay far outside his fields of expertise, and he persisted in thinking it had something to do with her striking resemblance to one of Hans Baldung Grien's "Weather Witches," a painting that had hung in the museum since 1878. They had a small son, Benno, alternately adored and ignored by his mother, and the only reason Bettina had not come with Elias to the Wertheims' this evening was that she was loving Benno intensely just then, and he was in bed with a high fever.

Jonah, Caroline's other brother, was a physician. Still unmarried, he pursued his work in a hospital in Höchst, Frankfurt's industrial satellite, well-known for its chemical plants, with the single-mindedness of one who does not wish to face more than a small and clearly marked out plot of land in the midst of the confusing variety of the world's landscape. He was putting in his years of service at this awful place in the hope that one day soon he would find his way to a small but lucrative practice in some town filled with ailing rich widows.

It was the Wertheims' hope that a festive meal would integrate the Süsskinds into their company. Caroline clearly shared the view that only by stuffing everyone to the gills—much as the goose had been stuffed with chestnuts—could one avoid disagreement or the propensity to argue.

The Christmas tree was visible through the door that led from the living room to the dining room, where the table had been extended to its full length in order to seat the eighteen persons present. Caroline, observing them all, felt that it would be a happy occasion; there was a feeling about the white-clothed table that seemed most auspicious, as if everyone was pleased with himself, content to enjoy the food and to beam upon the happy children. Hannchen at the head of the table looked down from her perch with regal certitude.

"You look exactly like a benevolent despot," said Siegmund. Hannchen took it as a compliment, whether because of "benevolent" or "despot" no one could tell. She had apparently forgiven Benedict the menorah and turned to him now and said, with a twinkle in her eye, to be sure, "Do we say grace?"

"Not usually" was Edu's acerbic aside.

"Well, tonight we shall ask Benedict to make a blessing."

Benedict, who was seated at Hannchen's right, looked quizzically about. The servants had paused in the doorway pantry and bowed their heads, Fräulein Gründlich had folded her hands. He began, *"Baruch atah adonai . . . eloheinu melech ho'olom . . . ,"* looked triumphantly about him and then continued in idiomatic Frankfurt dialect to thank God for bread from the earth and fruit from the vine and to express the assembled persons' gratitude for having been brought to this happy season in good health. When he stopped they all said "Amen," and dinner was served. It had seemed, to most of them, an odd interlude, but since it established a bond between Hannchen and Benedict, they let it pass.

The first course was a clear soup, "to give us the strength—in case

God fails us—to eat the rest of the meal," said Siegfried. The children beamed at him. The cousins saw one another frequently and were sometimes taken for siblings in school. They had an easy way among themselves, the four girls especially. Willy was liked by the twins, but he shied away from camaraderie, as though his protruding ears made him hear voices behind or underneath those heard by the rest of the world.

"Did Edu tell you the news?" Pauline asked when they had finished the soup.

"What's that?" asked Aunt Berthe, who was convinced that she was always the last to know anything.

"Edu is buying a house," said Hannchen.

"Leaving you all alone?" said Berthe, but her sister ignored her.

"Where?" Caroline and Eva asked simultaneously. Elias, because he was Edu's friend, had already been told. No one knew where Pauline had heard it.

"I've been thinking about it for a long time," said Edu, ignoring the question. "When Papa died I dropped the idea for a while, but now there's a house come on the market that I cannot resist." He wiped his mouth carefully on the damask napkin, happy to be the center of attention. "Real estate is a good investment," he continued, "especially in this part of town. After I took over the firm"—he paused—"after Siegmund and I took over the firm," but he was already too late, a frown had crossed Siegmund's face. "After that," he continued quickly, "I thought it might be a good idea—for any number of reasons, which I won't go into here—to move into my own house. Mama has said often enough that we must be independent."

The soup plates had all been taken away, and it was time for the second course, which was a specialty of Anna's, though the children found it difficult to eat, for it involved eels in a white sauce sharp with allspice.

"There'll always be an apartment in my house for her," said Edu, "but she says at the moment she wants to stay where she is."

"It's a large house then?" Nathan asked.

"What do *you* think?" said Siegmund.

"The city is soon going to stop expanding," Edu went on, "it will be harder and harder to find good houses within its boundaries, especially in the West End."

"Where the stench of the factories doesn't waft into your windows," Eva Süsskind said suddenly.

"What factories?" Elias asked her.

"The prevailing winds are westerly," she explained, with, Edu noticed, a mouthful of eel. "That's true all over Europe, and the reason why the west ends of cities are always where the 'better class' of people live."

"Please tell us where the house is?" said Pauline.

"On the Bockenheimer Landstrasse," said Edu.

Several of the guests said "Aah!" Edu smiled. There was a look of pride on his face. His mother, who saw it, had one of those flashes of insight: That is a look that will never leave him, she thought.

"Which house is it?" Siegmund asked as all the houses on the street passed in review before his eyes.

"Number Thirty-two," said Edu, "four houses down from the Rothschild Palace."

Siegmund whistled. "I know it. It's a beauty." And then everyone began to talk at once.

"And how much did it cost, Uncle Edu?" Willy asked from behind his thick glasses.

"That's none of your business," said his father.

"Not before the servants," Hannchen said, in English, although none of the servants was at that moment visible, except Fräulein Gründlich, whose position was ambiguous.

"Well, *mazel tov*, in any case!" said Benedict Süsskind and raised his glass of very good white wine. Everyone chimed in and drank to Edu's purchase. ("A hundred thousand at least," Siegmund whispered to Nathan, across Caroline's pale, bare shoulder.)

Just then the goose was brought in, and the conversation went directly from Edu's house to the bird.

"I do hope she's fat," said Elias.

"We've got three crocks of fat from her already," Caroline said. "You may take one home with you."

"Will there be enough left for us?" Lene asked, to everyone's amusement.

The red cabbage was brought in and the mashed potatoes and the goose-liver pâté in its crust, and a bowl of cucumber salad, sharp with vinegar and caraway seed, to help cut the richness and fat of the other foods.

"This is the best goose we've ever had," said Edu.

"I recall one or two at *my* table, which were at least as good," said Hannchen. "Not that we're in competition here. Caroline is a superb housekeeper, I always said so." And she smiled at Benedict, who found himself, much against his wishes, becoming entangled in some sort of conspiracy with her. "You know," she announced to all who would listen, "matters are not totally in the hands of the *Hausfrau*, or even the cook. It's the butcher you have to trust, ultimately, and it's getting harder and harder to find a trustworthy butcher. When old Fritz Hanauer was alive, he always gave me the fattest, most succulent birds. 'For you, Frau Wertheim, anything,' he used to say to me. The new man is something else again. All business. He gives the best not to those who appreciate it, but to those who order the most from him. When I tell him he's not half the butcher Fritz was, he says, 'Times change, Frau Wertheim, times change.' "

"Indeed they do," Berthe said emphatically, taking a piece of the wing, on which she had been sucking, out of her mouth with great delicacy.

"This time next year there'll likely be war," said Benedict.

"Don't spoil our dinner," Berthe said.

"You're an old pessimist," Hannchen told him.

"Haven't you been following the news?" he asked. "It gets worse all the time."

"I can't be bothered," said Hannchen. "There have been so many crises in the past several years, you can't keep worrying about each new one."

"Two years ago we had that trouble in Morocco . . ."

". . . you know how the French are!"

". . . still smarting over 1871 . . ."

". . . and our cousins the English take up the French cause all the time . . ."

"The English think they can tell the whole world what to do," said Pauline.

"Of course they rule the seas . . ."

"Germany must protect itself from encirclement . . ."

"They say if we support the Austrians in a war against Russia, we must be prepared to fight France at the same time."

"Those damned Austrians! Rotten through and through . . ."

"That Empire has been patched up again and again, usually at someone else's expense . . ."

"We'll pay dearly, you'll see."

"Germany must challenge England on the sea . . ."

"Nonsense! A strong army has always been our trump."

"If the Kaiser would show more confidence in Bethmann-Hollweg and listen less to his generals . . ."

"If, if, if," said Hannchen. "Do let's talk of more cheerful things."

The main course had been cleared away, and a chorus of sighs could be heard from around the table. The children's eyes were slightly glassy and Fräulein Gründlich's glistened.

"I suggest we skip dessert," said Siegmund. There was a thunderous *"No!"* from the children. Plates filled with *Weihnachtgebäck*, the Christmas cookies, were brought to the table along with the *pièce de résistance*, a long chocolate-covered, almond-studded yule log of the lightest, fluffiest sponge cake rolled in a blanket of sweet thick whipped cream.

It was greeted with the same enthusiasm that had, earlier in the evening, greeted Edu's plan to buy the house on the Bockenheimer Landstrasse. Everyone had room for a slice and no one refused a cookie, or even two.

"We must assume that trouble will come from the Balkans," said Edu, who had not, he felt, been sufficiently heard, "and in that case the Russians will surely step in."

"Trouble always comes from the Balkans," said Berthe.

"The navy will do you no good against Russia," said Elias.

"It will all depend on what steps the Austrians take," said Siegmund. "And God only knows how much control old Franz Josef has, or if he still knows what he's doing. He might be dead a week or two and nobody would notice. On the throne since '48! Do you know how long that is? Sixty-five years!"

"If we *do* go to war," said Nathan, "you can put the fault for it straight on the doorstep of our Prussian rulers."

"Germany is under the control of the militarists," said Eva, irritated at those around her for expressing such reactionary, chauvinist views and angry that her opinions counted for so little here. I'm not silly like Pauline or muddled like my sister, she thought bitterly, but they treat me like a damn fool woman just the same.

"If there's a war," said Elias, "and we lose it, you know who they'll blame?"

"The Jews, of course," said his father morosely.

"We always seem to come back to the Jews," said Edu.

"If there *is* a war," said Caroline hesitantly, "then you'll all be called upon to fight it."

"God preserve us," cried Hannchen, "you mustn't mention such a thing!"

"A war, especially one that goes badly, might hasten the Revolution," said Eva.

The company at table fell silent. One did not speak of revolution at the dinner table. And in front of the servants!

"Not in Germany," said Pauline finally, as if she had it from some higher authority.

"Have you seen the conditions under which some of your fellow citizens live and work?" Eva asked bristling.

"No, and I don't want to," said Pauline, "thank you."

"If they'd get off their butts and do an honest day's work," said Jonah, "instead of waiting for the revolution . . ."

"There is no work for many of them," said Eva.

"All right, children," Hannchen said, sternly determined to bring the conversation out of this particular thicket, "we will stop the discussion now. To talk of politics at the dinner table is to bring on stomach disorders. That's what my grandmother always said, and she was right, in this as in so many other things." She paused a minute, as if making sure that the image of her grandmother was securely fixed in her mind. "You cannot imagine what a sleepy little village Bockenheim was in her day, and so far from Frankfurt! She'd be overwhelmed if she could see us here now in this beautiful house, at Christmas dinner, having just eaten the biggest and best goose imaginable . . . She'd probably think it was a dream."

"Didn't they have geese in those days?" asked Lene, to the sound of relieved laughter. They were safely out of the woods now, and Hannchen lost her concerned look. She allowed her grandchildren to persuade her to talk about the old days in Bockenheim, and the whole family, Eva included, leaned back to listen to her.

At last the children's eyelids began to droop. Lene had already nodded off to sleep several times but awoke with a start when she heard her name called. "Time to go to bed, Lenchen," her father said, but she objected, pouting, that she wanted another cookie, wanted to see the gifts once more, wanted to play with the puppy.

"*He's* gone to sleep," said Caroline.

The candles on the Christmas tree had long since burned out, and the smell of hot wax and charred wicks mingled with the rich odor of pine. It was almost midnight, and the adults were nearly as tired as the children.

Downstairs, in the kitchen, the servants were finishing their own holiday meal and talking about what they had heard in the dining room. They knew which house it was Edu was buying, and they guessed how much it must cost. The parlormaid had a friend she thought might be interested in a job with Herr Wertheim. "I told her that Jews were good to work for, not to listen to what the others said."

"What others?" asked August, the big Hessian coachman. He was kind-hearted and could never imagine ill of anyone.

"Don't you listen to them downtown? Haven't you seen that newspaper they read? You should hear what Hans-Friedrich, who works for the von Varrentrapps, has to say!"

"It doesn't concern us," said August.

"Oh, you're so old-fashioned," exclaimed Anna's sister, who had helped with the serving.

August took another piece of cake and shrugged his shoulders.

"I'm happy the way I am," he said. "I don't want to change the world."

"It's people like you they make fun of," said the parlormaid. "You'd better learn a new tune. Times are changing."

"And what are they changing to?" August asked.

"There'll be a revolution—they even said so upstairs," she answered.

"It makes the old lady uncomfortable," said Anna's sister.

"Whatever happens," August concluded, "there'll always be some who are on top and some who are on the bottom. That's human nature." He finished what was left of a bottle of red wine in one large draft. "Merry Christmas!" he said.

IT SNOWED again before New Year's, and the talk about war continued. Edu contracted to buy the house on the Bockenheimer Landstrasse for 150,000 reichsmarks and planned to move in by Easter. On the last day of the year he called Jacob and told him that he thought they ought to have a "little chat."

"Come by my house about noon," said Jacob, "and we can take a walk."

Frankfurt was wrapped in white, sleigh-bells sounded everywhere, and the air was crisply cold. There was a harshness in the cold now, a drain of color from the landscape, which seemed always to come after Christmas, but it was particularly cruel this year, and on the quai by the Main the poor followed the coal trucks to watch for the small lumps that fell into the street. Sometimes they fought over them. Most of the good burghers of Frankfurt averted their eyes from the scene, though some increased their charitable contributions. Jacob often walked down here, lost in his own turbulent thoughts. He felt a sadness growing within what seemed to him— who liked to be happy—to be an oppressive weight, driving him further into himself. He was not at all certain that he really wanted to marry Gerda, but his conscience demanded it. It was his sadness that linked them now more than his love. If he could marry her, perform that decent and unselfish act, he might yet come to terms with his life's limitations.

Edu appeared at his door promptly at twelve.

"Is it too early to wish you a happy New Year?" Jacob asked, ready to embrace his brother. He noticed, just in time, that Edu, who was wearing his finest pale-gray suit, moved slightly to the side to avoid contact.

"It is too early, but you may wish it, anyway," said Edu. He did not enter the apartment. "If you're ready," he added, "we can go."

Jacob wound his long wool muffler around his neck and pulled his soft felt fedora down over his too long hair.

"You'll need a coat," said Edu, who had his chesterfield on his arm and carried a malacca cane. Jacob took down his oldest, shabbiest coat and put it on. Edu looked at him in exasperation but said nothing until they reached the street.

"What a Bohemian you've turned into," he said.

Jacob, who had decided to be impervious to criticism, merely shrugged his shoulders. "We're very different," he said, "you and I. But there's no need to make moral judgments about it all the time."

They walked in silence up the Fahrgasse. Edu grew increasingly nervous. "I'm here for a reason," he said finally. "I must talk to you about Gerda. You're not really going to marry her?"

Jacob had expected the question, but he had been unable, even in the privacy of his own mind, to find an answer to it. He said, "I'm older than you are, why are you pressing me?" He would have liked nothing better than to talk to Edu openly and honestly about his feeling, but it was obviously impossible.

"You may be older," said Edu, "but I'm more responsible."

"Responsibility should extend no further than the self," responded Jacob.

"In a family such as ours, that isn't far enough. We have a widowed mother to think about, children—even if they aren't ours—a business"—he hesitated a moment—"which, even if you take no part in it, you look to for sustenance. *Someone* has to assume responsibility for all of that. You don't agree?"

"You're very quick," said Jacob. "Maybe that's the reason I find it hard to talk to you. Everything is worked out in your mind, logically and clearly. You admit no doubts. I don't believe that I could convince you of anything—even if it concerned my own life."

"Some things *are* very clear, aren't they? Duty, honor, truth . . ."

"Precisely the things I would have chosen to prove to *you* how difficult it is to believe in anything wholeheartedly. There are subtleties in all those concepts . . ."

"We always think differently, you and I . . ."

"Only about the really great issues of our time. Tell me, Edu, do you think there'll be a war?"

"I think we have to be prepared for one."

"Anything *you* prepare for is more than a possibility—it's likely to become a certainty. So I assume we shall have a war, and if we do, we shall have to fight in it."

"We ought to be proud to."

"You have such old-fashioned ideas for one so young," said Jacob. He was much happier talking about these things than about his private life. "Wars are not what they used to be. They never will be again. You know, I've been rereading *War and Peace,* and one of the things that struck me—apart from the realization that it truly is one of the greatest novels ever written—is the simplicity of waging war in those times. I don't mean that there weren't men killed, and that death then was better than death anytime, anywhere. But they were governed by rules, it was like a dance or a game. However random men's actions are, they seem more so when they're not under close scrutiny and control. It's like a fire, burning down whole cities, forests . . . With the technology we have at our disposal today we can, and we will, slaughter millions, create a conflagration that will engulf the whole world."

"What a pessimist you are! And where do you get the information on which you've built your gloomy outlook?"

"I read."

"Novels?"

"Of course. What better place is there to get one's *Weltanschauung*?"

"I thought you read the newspapers."

"The *newspapers*? The *Frankfurter Zeitung* is a good newspaper, but I wouldn't count on it to give me information by which I could conduct my life. The stock-market reports, yes, those you can read and believe. For the rest, they print all the nonsense that someone —usually a politician or high official—makes up as he goes along, or reads from a piece of paper that somebody else made up. Then, once it's down in black and white, the next day someone comes and denies it all. It isn't that the newspapers are culpable, it's only that they have to appear every day, and there's so much useless information around that they can't be expected to be anything more than superficial."

"How did we get on this subject?" said Edu.

"Books. I like to read books."

"No."

"Yes. We were talking about war. You said there'd be one."

"Did I?"

"You believe in progress. I believe the industrialists need to get richer. As if they weren't rich enough already."

"The French want to avenge 1871."

"That's what the Prussians say."

"Let's get off this depressing subject."

"And get on a *more* depressing one?" asked Jacob.

It was a bitterly cold day, and Jacob, who had forgotten to bring gloves, put his hands deeper into his pockets and bent his head so that the scarf covered his chin. He noticed that Edu wore gray kid gloves.

"Would you be interested in moving back to the Neue Mainzer Strasse with Mama?" Edu asked.

"What an idea!" It was such an unexpected proposition that Jacob could scarcely grasp it.

"She would not have to be alone, then. The apartment I have is —how shall I put it?—finer than yours. I'm sure you agree. There's a staff, a beautiful garden, no rent to pay. The idea came to me just a day or so ago. Of course I've said nothing to Mama."

"And Gerda?"

"I was coming to that. If you're really committed to the relationship, why don't you set her up in a small flat, give her a little business —millinery perhaps—and spend as much time with her as you like. Other men do it."

"She's not good enough at sewing, she hasn't got the taste to create hats—there are probably a hundred women in Frankfurt who are better than she could ever be, and *they're* hard put to it to make ends meet."

"If she's frugal, she wouldn't need much to live on. Maybe she could learn to make something else—artificial flowers perhaps? And she might meet someone she could marry."

Jacob gazed at his brother. Look how straight and confidently he walks, he thought. He knows exactly what he wants, he has a solution to every problem; he can tell you whether or not the horse has to be shot and what's the right flower to put in your buttonhole.

Edu, aware of his brother's dark glance, continued to look straight ahead. He felt no pleasure in what he saw himself called upon to do. It was simply his duty. If he was the strongest, then he must show it and take charge. Even Nathan had begun to defer to his judgment.

"Listen to me, Edu," Jacob said, his voice, partly muffled by his wool scarf, sounded strained, but only because he was trying very hard to say exactly what he meant. "I love Gerda, and I expect you to respect that. I want to marry her. I may not, but I want to. Call it honor, if you will. *I* think it is something else, something perhaps more modern. One ought not, in the year of our Lord 1913, take advantage of women, of *poor* women like Gerda."

"Take advantage?" said Edu. "Whatever do you mean? She has a good life, better than anything she could have dreamt about when she came to Frankfurt. You've given her a great deal."

"But I haven't given her respectability."

"Do you really think she values respectability more than a comfortable life? *You* may have an idea of what she's missing, but does she? Will she appreciate being brought into your mother's house? You may wish to bring her, but have you ever thought that, for her, it would be torture? Not because any of us would behave badly, we would not, but because she knows, and will always know, that she does not belong there."

"It won't always be like that," said Jacob. "Our world is going to be turned into dust. Don't you feel it? Can't you sense it? Warnings are being sent out, but no one's listening. You know how animals go a little mad just before an earthquake strikes? That's how I feel. You see it rationally. 'War is inevitable,' you say, and you approach it as you would the harvest, betting on it as though you

were trading in commodities. No doubt the generals see it like that
too. But to me it is a promise of terrible upheaval. I see it in human
terms. It will be the end of our world . . ." He spread his arms out
wide, as if to take in the entire placid city on the Main, and Sachsenhausen too.

"And you want to greet the millennium as Gerda's husband?"
Edu asked him. "You are doing something on the strength of an
abstract conviction. You want to do what is right and proper and
'modern.' Your passion, it seems to me, is not for Gerda but for
justice."

"I won't leave Gerda," Jacob said, but it sounded to Edu as
though there was more spite than conviction in his voice. "I may
marry her still." He sounded distant, as if he was talking to himself.
"We made it out of the Judengasse," he said, "when no one wanted
us or believed we could be like the others, like *them*. It ill behooves
us to forget that and keep another group 'in their place.' "

Edu would not argue with him. He felt he had won his case. They
had walked across the Opernplatz and down Bockenheimer Landstrasse and stood in front of the house that Edu had bought.

"It's beautiful, isn't it?" he said, and Jacob was touched by that
foolish pride, which was so like a child's that it could not be despised. "You can't see the garden at this time of year, but the garden
is what I always admired," said Edu. "I often walk by here on my
way to the Palmengarten, and I feel I know the house. You'll see,
in the spring, how splendid the garden is."

They parted after that. Edu went to see his mother, while Jacob,
disturbed and tense but feeling so free and open to the world that
he noticed everything that crossed his path as though it was of great
significance and portent, wandered for a long time through the
ice-bound city.

EDU PLANNED to spend New Year's Eve at home alone with Hannchen. She had refused all invitations to go out; her mind was on
Moritz and it agitated her. She was glad Edu was there. They took
a sherry together, and he told her what had appeared to him to be
the outcome of his conversation with Jacob. "He made no promises," Edu said, "but I sensed him to be, himself, curiously relieved."

"Promise me, Edu, that you'll always take charge of the family problems," she said. She felt old just then and would not have wished to look in the mirror.

Edu nodded. "I spoke with Papa about all that, not long before he died."

"He knew you could best be entrusted with the care of the family."

"I promised him that, as long as I ran the business, I would see to it that nobody in the family lacked anything, that a portion of our profits would go to each and every one—Gottfried excepted, of course. Which reminds me, he sends me a letter every Christmas, bragging of his successes. Did I tell you he changed his name?"

"To what, pray tell?"

"Let me look, I have the letter right here." He took a folded paper from his wallet. "Gerald F. Worth," he read from the envelope.

"Sounds peculiar," said Hannchen.

"He took the *heim* off Wertheim and changed the *e* to an *o*. 'Worth' means 'Wert' in English. He's moved to New York and claims to have become a valued member of society in his adopted land."

"Perhaps he's come to his senses," said Hannchen and took another glass of sherry. "I shall go to bed early and forget everything," she announced. She had gained weight and resembled her sister Berthe to an astonishing degree that evening.

Edu had not finished all he wanted to say. "I also promised Papa that, should anything—God forbid, of course—happen to Siegmund or Nathan, I would see to it that the children were provided for, regardless of what their fathers' financial situation might be."

"Especially the girls," said Hannchen.

"Especially the girls."

Somewhat later they sat down to dumplings stuffed with apricots and served in melted butter with bread crumbs. Sophie had come by especially to make them. The church bells had begun to toll.

"I meant to go to bed early," said Hannchen over brandy. "Oh, but I miss your father! And you'll be in your new house soon."

"You may come to live with me anytime."

"No, no, no. But I want to give you a nice house gift. What would you like?"

"A painting."

"Your tastes are so different from mine . . ." It was almost an accusation.

"I'll choose it myself," said Edu, "and show it to you so you can approve."

AT NATHAN and Caroline's, the children were still playing with their Christmas toys. Lene faithfully fed her dog and was trying her best to train him. The boys lay on their stomachs all day, playing with their trains and toy soldiers. On New Year's Eve, Andreas brought in some small rocks he had dug out of the snow and dropped them on the tracks. The train derailed.

"What's that?" Ernst shouted.

"War," Andreas answered.

The church bells tolled and tolled, but the children were all asleep when 1914 rolled in.

III

1918

BY THE SUMMER of 1918, the war was a bitter component of every civilian's life, in Frankfurt as well as elsewhere in the German Reich. The poor, of course, suffered more than the rich. The previous winter had been very cold. People had too little coal, too little food, and they stood in lines for hours, waiting in the biting wind to buy a head of cabbage. They cursed the rich, and they cursed the government. Hungry children went into the nearby countryside to beg and to forage for potatoes, which—if they were not caught by a police patrol—they smuggled home to dingy workers' flats. Except for the police there were few able-bodied men in the city; on the streets, in the factories, in the shops, one saw only women.

The coming of summer did not change the course of the war or alter the political realities, but it lessened some of the hardships. People went walking in the Stadtwald and swimming in the Main, they tended their small garden plots out past the city limits and hoped that they would see peace before another winter set in.

Lene Wertheim had helped Fräulein Gründlich plant a small

vegetable garden in among the beds of roses and peonies. Cucumbers trailed along the ground, and tomatoes climbed their stakes along with peas and beans. A few homely potato plants bordered the white gravel paths. Even Edu's one remaining gardener, a bent old man, had put in vegetables that year. Edu was an officer in the German army, a member of the Duke of Hesse's Dragoons, stationed on the Eastern Front. Nathan was too old for active service, and Siegmund, who volunteered during the first months of the war, had been released after two years to run the family business, which was supplying necessary wool material to clothe the army. Jacob had also volunteered, not so much in a spirit of patriotism as in a desperate, ultimately vain attempt to change his life and his character. He had been wounded at the Somme and was recovering slowly in a hospital at Mainz. Gerda went down each week to visit him, hard as it was to find transportation, and sat mute at his bedside, staring at his drawn face.

Because there had been several air raids on Frankfurt in the past year, many of those parents who could afford it sent their children to the country in the summer of 1918. Fräulein Gründlich accompanied Lene and the twins to Königstein in the Taunus Mountains, where they stayed in a modest *Pension*. Emma, who was eighteen, had asked to be allowed to join a group of her contemporaries at a country estate near Kronberg where young women of good family had gone to aid the war effort by helping to farm and bring in the harvest.

She wrote enthusiastic letters home and sent a photograph of herself among the group, all of them wearing dirndls and kerchiefs about their heads like Russian peasants, holding hay rakes and looking tanned and healthy. As it happened, Emma was off to the side in the small snapshot and only half of her profile was visible, but she appeared to have a smile on her face. "Anyway, the *others* look healthy," said Nathan.

Caroline was struck by her daughter's dark beauty there among the pigtailed gentry looking haughty even in their rustic dresses and casual poses. If Nathan noticed it, he said nothing. His children puzzled him, he did not know why. They were attentive and polite, they chatted about their lives and ventured opinions on a host of issues, but no one, neither his sons nor his daughters, ever allowed him a glimpse into their hearts. Emma reported on her activities, from stove cleaning to chicken feeding, with the same determined good cheer with which, at home, she had regaled them with her stories about teachers and maids and salesgirls. No pain or doubt ever entered these letters; if, by accident, something troublesome reared its head, it was dismissed in the next sentence.

Caroline was quite right—Emma had grown into a beautiful young woman. Her black eyes seemed to have grown deeper still, her skin whiter; it would never have the healthy glow that shone in Lene's face when the summer sun touched it, but her bones were finer, the curve of her jaw more delicate. The anxiety, the almost trembling uncertainty before life, had never left Emma, and she kept people at a distance, afraid it might be uncovered. She did not like to be touched and was so quick and nervous in her movements that it was, indeed, hard to approach her. And yet she had a need for friendship, a desperate longing for intimacy which she dared not articulate and could not consummate. She wanted a bosom friend to kiss and pet and share secrets with, but when she found someone, she could neither hug her nor whisper, even at night under cover of darkness, the thoughts and fears that tortured her. The comradeship of the group was, the family said, "good for her." She was now one of a gaggle of girls working, chattering, living responsibly and well, enjoying fresh air, fresh food and a full night's sleep. Emma conspired with them to pass this story on as fact.

Caroline had been hesitant to give Emma permission to go to the country. She instinctively distrusted experiences that radically altered one's way of life. She herself had become utterly dependent upon her husband, her house, her servants. When Nathan was rejected for army duty, she became positively light-headed with relief. The idea that she would have to manage the house by herself had weighed on her like an incubus. Eva, appalled at her sister's dependence, urged her again and again to take charge of her own life, but Caroline could not be brought out of her castle refuge. Frustrated there, Eva turned to Emma to encourage her to take some small steps of her own. When Emma announced that she intended to work on a farm, her aunt was delighted.

Eva did not, of course, have an accurate picture of the conditions under which Emma would be working. She imagined a kind of collective where sturdy peasant children mixed with the daughters of the bourgeoisie and everyone shared equally in the routines of daily life. She would have been shocked to see the estate and observe the style in which these girls of privilege lived. Drawn ever more to the left, Eva had joined a small and secret group of Spartacists, who met for weekly discussions and talked about the Revolution. Eva, unlike some of her comrades, approached that subject with a good heart and an innocent mind. A peace treaty had been concluded with the new Bolshevik regime the year before, and the German Left looked eastward with anxious hope.

Had Edu, serving at an outpost in eastern Galicia in the far reaches of a crumbling Austro-Hungarian Empire, known what Eva Süsskind's sympathies, let alone affiliations, were, he would surely have made every effort to have her arrested. He clung, as if for life itself, to the beliefs of his class. Yet his experiences in the imperial army had been anything but pleasant. He had received his commission in the exclusive Dragoons only because a Gentile friend and associate, a man of high rank, had vouched for his wealth and his abilities. It had been virtually impossible, up to this time, for a Jew to become an officer. Those who had received commissions because of the war found the anti-Semitism of their fellow officers a burden to which each had to adjust in his own way. Edu, as was his wont, responded by calling upon his considerable reserves of self-sufficiency, serving wordlessly and punctiliously at a polite and discreet distance from his fellow officers. He made only one friend, a fellow Jew and doctor from Darmstadt named Max Demant. But Demant was transferred to a hospital in Lithuania, where he died of typhus shortly before the treaty of Brest-Litovsk was signed. He had cared for the wounded and ill without respite for three weeks on end. The two friends had often confessed to each other that they found the army grim and life in it intolerable. When he heard of his friend's death, Edu vowed never to talk about his years in the army. He put them out of his mind with the same resolve with which he later burned his uniforms and buried his decorations in the attic in a box which he never looked at again.

Most of the officers in Edu's regiment detested the part of the world in which they found themselves. They had seen some action, most of them wanted to see more. It was clear to them that the important, the "real" war was being fought in France, and now that Russia was out of it, they saw no reason why they should have to stay where they were. But a million and a half German troops remained in place between the Ukraine and the Baltic. In part they were kept there because the government felt that the political situation was too volatile to remove them, but in part, too, they stayed at their posts because General Ludendorff had a dream that Germany would create and administer a large Russian satellite state to stretch from the Crimea to the Caucasus. Neither the men in the field nor their officers had any idea of this plan, even though it was simply an extension of an idea shared by many, including the officers with whom Edu served. He made it a point to avoid all political discussions. Had anyone asked his opinion—and no one did—he would have said he knew nothing whatever about the situation.

He had been assigned a Jewish orderly, but the vast social gulf between them discouraged intimacy. Still, there was a feeling of mutual affection and good will, and in a number of veiled, secret ways they made common cause against the other officers, against "them," against, though the word was never mentioned, the *goyim*. With his usual ironic detachment, Edu noticed that there was far greater comradeship between his "boy" Solly and the other soldiers of the regiment than there was between himself and his confreres.

They were quartered in one Galician village after another, and to the men they all looked alike. Coming as they did from gently rolling, fertile lands, from neat villages and respectable towns where the houses were whitewashed regularly and the streets swept, this poor, flat countryside dotted with broken-down huddled houses at crossroads that were a sea of mud in the rain and dusty as the desert in heat seemed a truly barbarian land. Many of the peasants in these border regions spoke no German, and even when they did, it was hard for the German soldiers to look upon them as anything but aliens. And there were Jews everywhere. Most of the army had never seen so many Jews all at once and in such wretched poverty. Because of the fighting in and around the provinces, many of the inhabitants had had to flee their homes again and again, living from hand to mouth, facing starvation. Edu, riding Pegasus, his chestnut gelding, at the head of his troop, often passed these miserable people on the dirt roads. They would scurry to the ditches, laden down with bedding and copper pots and baby carriages full of their pitiful possessions. He never stopped, he barely looked at them, but they haunted his dreams night after night. "Did you see them?" he asked Solly one evening.

The orderly was polishing his boots to a mirrorlike shine. "See who, sir?"

"Those poor Jews we passed on the road today."

"They're there all the time, sir."

"But they've got no land, no crops, no jobs."

"They're used to it. That's the way it is here. They survive."

"Why don't they go to America?" Edu asked, and he remembered New York.

"I don't know, sir. I never bother my head with history or politics. I just want to get home to my family in one piece. The war won't last much longer. That's what they all say. We're lucky, you know—we might have been in the trenches in France. Nobody hardly gets out of them alive.

"I really don't know about the Jews," he went on, "but I wouldn't worry about them. This is their home, they know every rock and every brick, they're used to hard work. They'll crawl back and start over to make children. It's something I ought to be doing, instead of presenting arms and parading in the town square. I'm sure you feel the same way."

"Have you ever talked with the Jews here?" Edu asked.

"Yes, sir."

"And what do they speak, what language?"

"Yiddish. And a little bit of Polish and some German. A few even know Russian. The innkeeper—you know, the red-bearded man— he said if I was here on Rosh Hashanah . . ." He looked at Edu shrewdly for a second to see if he knew what he was talking about. When he was satisfied that Edu was not so big an apostate that the festivals had to be explained to him, he went on, "He said to come and have dinner with him and his family. I said thank you, but we'd better not still be here come Rosh Hashanah. Have you ever been to his inn?"

Edu shook his head. He sometimes went riding by himself or walked through the town on market day, but he had never entered any building, not even a store.

"You ought to visit the inn," said Solly. "He has good vodka, ninety-proof, and it keeps you from being so lonely and so bored."

One of the few things Edu found it possible to do in the midst of the restricted, aimless round of his life was to write letters home to his family. He wrote to his mother, and he wrote to his brothers, and he wrote to his nieces and nephews. He even wrote to Aunt Berthe, and of course he wrote to Elias, who had managed to find himself a safe job at headquarters. When Edu heard that Jacob had been wounded and was in a hospital, he wrote to him more often than to the others, and he allowed some of his chagrin and homesickness to show, though he felt it unseemly to express any bitterness toward the other officers.

Dear Jacob:

My orderly says the war cannot go on much longer. He expects to be home for the Jewish holidays (you may know when they are this year, I don't and am not going to display my ignorance before Solly, who thinks of me as a *goy* in any case). The town where we are stationed is one of those dreary Galician towns that hasn't changed in hundreds of years. It looks exactly like the old photos you see, for it seems not to contain any color, just black and white and gray. The sky is overcast most of the time, the streets are unpaved, there's a church with two steeples (the church is white) and a brick house or two, for the rest it's all stucco and tin roofs, except where the Jews live, there it's wooden shacks with leaking roofs and a thousand filthy children. The poverty is indescribable, especially now since the armies of Austria, Russia and Germany have been fighting on this pitiful bit of earth. The Austrians have been particularly harsh with the local populations, since they suspect many of the ethnic minorities of being against them, and therefore accuse them of spying. I myself have seen any number of these poor dumb peasants executed by firing squads, after being convicted by a kangaroo court in a matter of minutes. They string the dead bodies up on the nearest tree or hang them on a lamppost, as a warning to others. (It is true, I hear, that some of the Austrian army have deserted to the Russians, and that many of those who were taken prisoner by them are now released through the Bolsheviks and come back convinced revolutionaries. Where will it all lead?) The hanging bodies are something I cannot get used to, even after nearly four years of war. The others merely laugh at them, but I keep remembering Goethe's horror at the three heads which they had up on stakes on the old bridge across the Main as a warning to a rebellious population.

I keep in shape, ride daily, look after myself, my men, my horse. I have little contact with the regular officers; they live in a world all their own. News does not reach us very quickly here, but the rumors seem to indicate that—now that the Americans have joined the fray—things will be over before another winter comes. My imagination sometimes leads me to the macabre picture of Gottfried—or Gerald, as he now calls himself—riding in a charge against us, his own brothers. Another reason to be happy that you're done with fighting and I'm stuck way out here.

Of course, we keep right on drilling and exercising, as if we were going to charge into battle tomorrow. Sometimes it strikes me as totally absurd, but the other officers take it very seriously. They do not seem to understand that we are preparing for another kind of war, a war that is no longer being fought. If I remember correctly, you and I had a discussion about that once, years ago, walking through the snowy streets of Frankfurt. I wish I were there now—you cannot imagine how I long for the familiar streets, the sounds of voices speaking the homely patois. Sometimes I hear one of my Hessians talking *frankfurterisch*, and I want to go up to him and embrace him.

Mama writes me that you are on the mend, which I am glad to hear. She also says that Siegmund is managing the business faithfully, which I don't doubt, but she doesn't say how *well* he's managing it. Nathan looks in on him regularly. We certainly seem to have had exceptionally good earnings, but considering that it's wartime and we're supplying the government, I can't see how we'd fail to turn a profit. I only hope that the end of the war doesn't bring total collapse.

I look forward to a reunion soon.

Your loving brother
Edu

Jacob read Edu's letter several times. There was little to do in the hospital *but* read, and Jacob found himself reading everything over and over again. He was still in considerable pain. He slept very little because of it and the battlefield memories that overwhelmed him in the dark of the night. He could make it through the day, but when the lights were turned out, the smallest noise would become the rattle of machine-gun fire and the bump of a wagon somewhere the start of another round of bombardment. The muffled groan of another soldier, turning in his sleep nearby, would re-create the endless carnage, screams of pain, torn bodies trailing their entrails after them, trenches running with blood and muddy water. Everywhere he looked, when his eyes were closed, there was this huge slaughterhouse. He was afraid to dream.

Edu's description of the corpses dangling from the trees seemed like nothing more than a curtain raiser for the terrible drama that unfolded in his mind every evening. Jacob found his brother's letters surprisingly gentle and revealing. He suspected that Edu was unhappy, but when he wrote back, he pretended not to be aware of anything below the surface of the letters. He had his own troubles.

It was Sunday, the day on which Hannchen usually steamed into the hospital for her biweekly visit. She always brought something good to eat with her and a cheerful face. Both set Jacob's nerves on edge, the food because he found it difficult to eat—a hole had been blown in his gut by a mortar-shell fragment as he led a charge against some Senegalese troops dug in at the Somme—and the cheerful face because it seemed an affront to his own misery. He had gotten it into his head that his mother didn't like him, and this perception further blackened his already black mood.

Hannchen was not a reflective person, certainly not about her own feelings, which she took to be the expression of some elemental force within her. She accepted Jacob's scowl as an extension of his injury and his battlefield experiences. She certainly did not believe she loved him less than she loved her other sons, though she was aware that she loved Edu more. Jacob had been decorated with the Iron Cross, first class, and Hannchen—though she would not admit it—was proud of this. She told everyone about it, but her Gentile friends had to listen to the story more than once.

"How is my brave son feeling today?" Hannchen appeared, as if on cue, just as Jacob, having read Edu's letter a third time, began thinking about how he would deal with her.

"Not very good." Jacob's response was always the same.

"I brought you some goose-liver pâté. Just a very little bit, which I was able to hunt up, don't ask me how. It cost a fortune and is very light and can't possibly hurt your stomach. And guess what? To wash it down, a small bottle of exceptionally good wine."

Hannchen put everything on Jacob's night table and settled into the chair beside his bed. Someone had drawn the curtain that hung between Jacob and the other man in the ward, who had been blinded at Verdun and said very little, though he seemed to be listening all the time.

"Thank you, Mama," said Jacob. "I appreciate your concern, but it isn't necessary, really. The doctors allow me almost no solid food."

"Doctors!" she snorted. "If they'd let me, I'd be here nursing you. Anyway, you can drink the wine, that's liquid."

"I had a letter from Edu," Jacob said. "He seems to be well. Says the war will be over before long."

"How does he know that, over there in Galicia?"

"His orderly hears rumors."

"We've heard those rumors in Frankfurt for two whole years. What else does he say?" Hannchen was always a little jealous when someone else heard from Edu. She liked to think that she was if not his only, then his favorite correspondent.

"He writes about corpses hanging from trees . . ."

"Come on, be serious, Jacob!"

Jacob looked at her with such ferocity that she could not return his gaze. He had grown a beard, and its thick black growth exaggerated whatever expression came across his face. It is almost as if he hates me, thought Hannchen, but the thought was so awful she couldn't bear it and dismissed it immediately.

"I'm sorry," she said, "I'm a foolish woman who knows nothing about war. Can I read the letter or does it contain secrets?"

Jacob handed her the letter wordlessly. He knew he ought not to show the raw edges of his nerves or make a virtue of his contempt, especially to his mother, who understood nothing about the more complicated strains of his character, who probably didn't even understand her own. As soon as she glanced at it, Hannchen gave him the letter back. Edu's handwriting was small and neat, and appeared to hasten, in a straight line toward the right edge of the paper. He still partially wrote the old German script, but one could see that he was slowly freeing himself from its Gothic flourishes.

"It must be awful," she said, but it was hard to tell what she thought was awful. Jacob asked her how everyone was, going most carefully down the line and leaving no one out.

"I think that Gründlich is bringing the children down to see you soon," she said. "They're out in Königstein for the summer. Frankfurt is no place for them this year. Did I tell you they poisoned Lene's dog?"

"Whatever for?"

"No one seems to know. Either out of mischief or because they wanted to break into the house. That's what the police think; they stole vegetables out of the garden and tried to open the cellar door but couldn't."

"Poor Lene! I have such a sweet photo of her on the lawn, shaking hands with the dog and wearing someone's uniform . . . maybe even mine. She looks adorable."

"When you talk about the children, you sound more like a human being."

"Hmmm," Jacob murmured in acknowledgment. He closed his eyes for a minute.

"Do you have pain?" his mother asked.

"Just a little."

"Shall I call the doctor?"

"No, no."

"Or the nurse for medicine?"

"It's not necessary, Mama."

"A little wine?"

"That's a good idea."

The corkscrew had been wrapped in a napkin and put in the wicker basket along with the pâté and some biscuits, two pears and a piece of yeasty yellow *Gugelhupf*.

"Sophie packed it for you," said Hannchen. "You know, she's come back to work since Marie went off to the munitions plant. They'll find it hard, those girls, to go back to domestic service once the war is over. And we'll have to suffer their tempers and their arrogance."

It was rather touching, Jacob thought, those delicacies from a world of peace and luxury, even if they had nothing to do with his life. He was groggy and didn't want to have to be on his best behavior. Hannchen was fussing with the cork, which Jacob had not offered to extract. Oh damn, he thought, let me sleep. He dropped off right after those words crossed his mind, but shortly—it could not have been more than a few minutes later—he was awakened by the sense that someone else had come in the room. My neighbor's wife, he thought, hearing a rustle of skirts. The cork popped out of the bottle, Jacob opened his eyes, and there was Gerda. She had pulled the curtain back just a little—to surprise him—and seen Hannchen. The look on her face was one of panic. She opened her mouth as if to scream, but then, seeing Jacob's open eyes, she froze, exactly as if she'd been painted there, playing a role in some neoclassical tableau.

"Come back later," Jacob said to her, as though she were the nurse. Hannchen sat in the stiff-backed chair, as still as Gerda. They stared at each other for a few long seconds, then Hannchen turned back to Jacob, poured him a glass of the wine, took another glass herself and said *"Prosit!"*

"Go away!" Jacob shouted, loud enough for the whole ward to hear. "Go, go, *go!*" Gerda left. Jacob and Hannchen listened to her hurried steps, fleeing down the length of the corridor.

Jacob drank his wine in a single swallow. His mother poured him another and yet another until he sank back on his pillows, his mind edged with fuzz.

"That was good," he said, his speech slurred.

"There's a little more," said Hannchen. "You'll save it for later. I have to go now. Bruno is waiting downstairs."

"Did you drive here?" Jacob asked. "In the war?"

"He came with me on the train. 'You shouldn't ought to go alone, Frau Wertheim,' he said to me."

Those were the last of his mother's words he heard. When he woke again, an hour or more had passed, and Gerda sat beside him on the straight-backed chair in Hannchen's place. The wine had given him a headache. Gerda looked thin and drawn, her skin had an unhealthy yellow-gray cast, and her hair was dull and greasy. Jacob felt a revulsion for her. He compared her to one of the sad, puny whores he used to see along the way of the army's march where they were often the only live things left. They and the mangy, howling dogs.

"You don't look well," he said. "Haven't you been eating properly?"

Gerda's eyes were red from crying.

"You have enough money?"

"It's hard to get f-f-food," she said. "There are always l-l-lines, and the w-w-women fight with you."

"You must take care of yourself," Jacob said desperately. "For me —do it for me, so that I'll have a pretty Gerda to look at when I come home." He let the words spill out as one might in talking tender nonsense to a baby. But he felt no tenderness whatever. She put her hand on his. It was a suppliant gesture. The veins along the back of her hand ran like thick blue strings into her bony wrist.

"I'll send you more money," Jacob said.

She shook her head.

"I'll marry you, then," Jacob shouted, and everyone in the ward heard him, and no one listened. "I'll marry you, I swear it!" His voice was filled with hatred and despair. "Don't just sit there," he screamed, "I told you I'd marry you!"

Tears ran down her cheeks. She covered her face with both her hands and shivered violently. Jacob whispered, "I'm sorry, I'm sorry, Gerda," innumerable times and stroked her knee; he could not reach her head or even her shoulder. They remained like that, chained in dumb misery, until dark, when Gerda got up, saying only, "The last train . . ."

"Take the basket of food with you," Jacob said.

"It's y-yours."

"Please take it."

Again she shook her head in the dumb stubbornness that so infuriated him.

"I told you to take it!"

She made a move as though to obey him, but the specter of Hannchen stood in her way, and she dropped her hands and left quickly without it.

THREE DAYS later Fräulein Gründlich brought the twins and Lene for a visit. The children stood around the hospital bed with serious, questioning faces. Fräulein had done her best to prepare them for what they would find, so that they all expected the worst and were slightly disappointed. Surreptitiously they looked around them for the horrors they'd been promised. Lene sniffed and wrinkled her nose. The smell of ether made her feel slightly nauseous, but it was the only unpleasant sensation she felt.

"How can you stand the smell, Uncle Jacob?" she asked.

"I've had to get used to it," he said, "like a lot of other things."

The children admired his black beard.

"You look like a revolutionary," said Ernst.

"I think you look like a prophet," said Andreas.

"And what do you think?" Jacob asked Lene.

"You look like one of those Jewish secondhand dealers in the Altstadt," she said. Fräulein Gründlich's eyes grew severe with disapproval. But Lene was, however dimly, aware of her charm. She smiled at Jacob conspiratorily.

"How's your summer been?" he asked.

"Boring! We're in this dreary *Pension* with nothing to do but walk in the fresh air, drink fresh milk and eat fresh bread."

"I thought you liked to eat?"

"But not the same thing all the time. Besides, didn't you notice, Uncle Jacob, I lost weight!"

Lene had indeed grown thinner, had shed the baby-fat that had kept her a child. Jacob noticed that she was more aware of herself as a woman and the world as a stage.

"Don't forget your uncle's gifts," Fräulein Gründlich prompted. Lene put the bouquet she had been clutching on the bedcover, just about where Jacob's chest was.

"I'm not yet dead," he joked and sniffed the wild flowers, which had no particular odor. Lene had picked them that morning, but they had already begun to wilt a little. It was all so like Lene! Fräulein Gründlich suddenly noticed with horror that she had apparently stolen two dahlias from the pension garden and put them with the daisies and cornflowers and poppies.

"Fräulein Gründlich can find a glass and some water, I'm sure," said Jacob, handing the bouquet to the governess, who gave Lene another stern look and a shake of the head.

The twins were physically at the most awkward age. Sixteen and gangly, they looked as if they were about to break apart. Ernst had pimples and a faint, downy mustache on his upper lip. Andreas' skin was transparent, hairless still; his eyes were in restless pursuit of—

What? thought Jacob. What's he looking for?

Ernst, working with an old carpenter who puttered about the pension, had made Uncle Jacob a box with several compartments.

"It's beautiful," said Jacob. "What is it for?"

"It's good for anything and everything," said Ernst. "It will hold pencils or studs or erasers or paper clips or nibs for your pen or cuff links . . ."

"You've thought a lot about it." Jacob smiled.

"And you can put Andreas' gift in it!" Ernst concluded.

Andreas pulled something out of his pocket. It had been wrapped, not very neatly, in a small piece of tissue paper and tied with string.

"I'm not as good at making things as Ernst," he said, "so I bought you this. I found it in a little shop in Königstein one day when we were out for a walk."

Jacob unwrapped the package and found a flat bronze paperweight, finely sculpted on both sides in low relief. On one side there was a portrait of Heinrich Heine writing with a quill; on the other, a floating female figure carrying a laurel wreath. Below her, in sinuous Art Nouveau lettering, were the words: *"Aus meinen grossen Schmerzen mach' ich die kleinen Lieder"*— "Out of my large sorrows I make small songs."

Jacob turned it over and over in his hand. It was such a lovely gift; he was profoundly touched, and because the usual joking words would not rise to his lips, speechless. Something close to tears lurked in his throat. "What a lucky man I am to have such a bunch of generous and well-brought-up nieces and nephews," he mumbled.

"Have Jenny and Julia and Willy been to see you yet?" Lene asked.

"They're at the seashore," Fräulein Gründlich reminded her.

"They send me charming letters," said Jacob, "and so does your sister Emma."

Fräulein Gründlich, whose task it was to notice everything, saw that Jacob had grown very still. "It's time we left," she told the children.

"I thank you for coming," said Jacob in his most formal manner, "and I thank you for your beautiful gifts. You are a credit to Fräulein Gründlich's upbringing."

The governess looked pleased. She was rarely thanked or complimented, though the children depended on her for great things and small ones. Even Emma, at eighteen, was not yet free of her strict though benign influence. Fräulein Gründlich would be with them all the days of their lives. There was but one secret place she could not enter, the realm of their sexual initiation. Try as she might, she would never be able to interpose herself between them and the temptations of the flesh, which she saw quite literally in the guise of the serpent whispering into the ear of the woman, Eve.

Fräulein Gründlich was proud that she knew the difference between good and evil. As for the limitations of her life, she understood these too and conducted herself accordingly. Everyone had a place in this world and was expected to stake it out with virtue. The sisters in the wards, sweeping up, dispensing codeine, dressing wounds, all in their striped blue-and-white cotton dresses and white aprons and caps knew their work as well as she did and surely slept soundly in that knowledge every night.

Jacob, dozing in his bed, let his thoughts wander. The visit had provoked a sentimental response in him; he found himself mulling over the nature of Fräulein Gründlich's relationship to his nieces and nephews. What did the homilies and good habits she struggled to teach them have to do with survival in this time of war and suffering? It seemed to Jacob that everyone was acting as if nothing would ever change. But then, he thought, what else is there to do? Habits, once set in motion, go on and on and on, even as a nation crumbles and revolution threatens. The comfort of the well-worn path, the dinner served just so, the mail opened each day at the exact moment the clock strikes noon . . . these are what give men comfort and allow them to face down despair.

The children kissed their Uncle Jacob one by one. He tried his best to smile. They reached the railroad station in plenty of time to catch the train back to Königstein. After the dusty heat of the city and the stench of the hospital, it was pleasant to smell the fresh country air as the train chugged on its way. The windows of the carriages were open (there was no distinction made between first and second class, the governess noted, because of the war, no doubt), and the children leaned out, smelling the new-mown hay and the leafy aroma of the forests. Fräulein Gründlich nodded a little, sitting primly upright even in sleep. Lene kept herself apart from her brothers; she was miffed with them for having managed to upstage her in their gifts to Uncle Jacob. It wasn't the first time it had happened, for she tended to think too little about the quality of her presents, assuming always that at the last minute her full and generous heart would transform the dingiest object into a shining star. She had spent a long time that morning picking the wild flowers, thinking tenderly of Uncle Jacob all the time. She had had to be brave to steal the striped dahlias out of the pension garden. But she had hardly got to her uncle's bedside when she noticed how limp they were. The boys' gifts, on the other hand, were solid and permanent and would remind Uncle Jacob of their visit forever.

EMMA LIKED working in the barn with the animals best. It was away from the broiling sun and smelled of cow's milk, manure and bedding straw. Each morning, soon after dawn, the herd was brought in from the far meadow by the tenant farmer's two sons and those of the girls who were on "milking detail" that week. At first Emma had been afraid of the cows' hoofs and swinging, swishing tails, but she overcame her fear once the farmer had shown her exactly what to do, and she came to know each of the cows and could milk expertly, with the pail in place and herself comfortable on the little stool. She hadn't liked getting up so early, either, but then she got used to it, all except that first awful, sharp ring of the alarm clock. She would jump quickly out of bed and wash her face in the cold water from the farmyard pump. With a kerchief tied around her head and a sweater over her dirndl she would run the whole way to the barn just as the sun climbed above the low purple mountains to the east and the mists began to fade from the valleys.

The dozen girls lived in one wing of a stately manor house belonging to the Countess of Albers-Eschenbach, an elderly widow who spent much of her time on good works and socially uplifting activities. She was a lean woman, intense and somewhat masculine, an avid card player and reader of trashy novels. Much of the land in that part of Hesse belonged to her, but she was a woman of principle, and the peasants and villagers respected and liked her. She knew them all by their first names and inquired after their children and wives when she met them on her drives around the countryside. They would stand before her, hats in their hands, heads bowed, listening to her lectures and giving her estimates on the harvest that were always much too low. They squirreled things away for themselves, and she knew that they did, but she closed her eyes to it up to a point. During wartime the government demanded a certain portion of the produce for itself, and the countess was strict in collecting it. She had been glad to provide living quarters for the young women "from good homes" who were spending their summer helping the war effort and learning good housekeeping, for they were being instructed in every aspect of house management by two home economics teachers and took their turns cooking and baking, darning and mending, canning and preserving. They gathered eggs and fed the chickens in addition to milking the cows, raking hay and tending the large vegetable garden.

There was also a gym teacher, named Ilse Stauffer, who lectured on hygiene and saw to it that everyone got some exercise and washed her hair once a week. "Die Stauffer," as she was invariably called, did a prescribed number of push-ups and other exercises each morning, bathed in ice-cold water and said lengthy prayers at night, kneeling beside her bed. Most of the girls adored her. Emma in fact had a schoolgirl crush on her; a good part of every one of her letters, as Caroline remarked, was a testament to Ilse Stauffer's sterling qualities.

She was a fair-haired young woman of Teutonic build and visage. In the aristocratic confines of the Albers-Eschenbach estate she was admired but expected to know her place. She was also an innocent, one of those people who because they are insulated from others by lack of knowledge and understanding are capable of doing irreparable harm. They know neither friend nor foe, every day is a blank to them, they lack both memory and imagination.

Die Stauffer found Emma a puzzle. She appeared to be weak and yielding, the sort of girl who would complain of headaches and menstrual problems. But she was not like that at all. She was tough and resilient, and she never complained about anything. Emma, of course, had her own reasons for playing the good sport. Although she was not frail in body, her feelings were tender, and she was vulnerable precisely because no one—least of all the gym teacher—could see the qualities and fears and strains beneath the silky skin.

Early one morning as they stood next to each other brushing their teeth—Die Stauffer made it a point to live exactly like the girls in her charge—she turned to Emma and said, "You're a Jew, aren't you?"

The sun had not yet broken through the mist, and it was at that pale hour when subtle details remain invisible. Emma felt herself flush deeply, but she knew that Ilse Stauffer could not see her. She made some gargling sound of assent but nothing that could be understood for words.

"Do you know I never met a Jew before?" Die Stauffer went on. "You're the very first one. In the school where I teach, they don't allow them, and in the town where I grew up, there weren't any as far as I know, except an old man who used to come around selling pots and pans. We were all frightened of him."

"I don't resemble him at all," said Emma, "do I?"

Her irony was lost on Ilse Stauffer. "Well, of course not," she protested, "but you have to admit that you're different from us."

Emma looked up from the washbasin and into the mirror that hung there. It was still not light enough to see clearly, but she made out her dark hair and eyes and the Pinocchio nose that grew and grew and grew while she was looking at it. Her face seemed ugly and alien even to herself. "I'll soon be baptized," she told her companion.

"And then you won't be Jewish anymore! Oh, Emma, let's talk about it soon again. I'll teach you all about our dear Lord, and I'll pray with you."

She impulsively flung her arms about Emma's neck and kissed her on the cheek, but near enough to her mouth to give Emma an unpleasant shock.

"It's time to fetch in the cows," said Emma and left the room quickly.

Emma ran out of the house without waiting for the other girls on her "detail" that morning. The grass was still wet with dew, and her knee socks were soon sopping. But the sky was filled with the early-morning gold of the sun, the trilling swallows swooping high above the barnyard and a few tiny, distant clouds. Everything was touched by the gold of the sun: the yellow wheat rippled like a placid sea, and the cornflowers and poppies opened their brilliant blue and scarlet petals to its light until the peace and beauty of the scene momentarily banished the curious encounter with Ilse Stauffer from Emma's mind and transformed her from a pale, apprehensive Jewish girl from the city into a rosy-cheeked country maid at home with nature and in any company.

The farmer's boys had gone out first and were already driving the cows to the barn. The animals' udders were heavy with milk and wobbled as they trudged along the worn, familiar paths. They were creatures of habit, easily controlled. The lead cow walked almost daintily, Emma noticed, her bell clanging with every step. Emma closed the barnyard gate and helped to put the cows into their accustomed stalls. She fetched her pail and stool and began milking. She had learned the skill quickly. Her thin strong fingers pulled expertly on the pink teats and the milk squirted out in a long warm white stream, sounding a rhythmic tattoo against the sides of the pail. Emma liked this job; she felt strong in her competence. She carefully "stripped" the last drop of milk from each teat until the udder hung empty, like an old handbag, between the cow's legs.

When the pail was almost full she carried it to the milk house, where it was poured through a strainer into the large cans the estate manager picked up in his horse-drawn cart twice a day. The milk house was cool and dark and kept scrupulously clean. After each milking it was hosed down and all the implements were washed and scrubbed. Gregor, a crippled old man whose strength had once been great but now remained only in his arms, was in charge of the barn and the milking and did the dirty work of shoveling the manure out to the heap where it sat steaming and decomposing until it was ready to be carried back to the fields to nourish them for the next year. Gregor saluted Emma as he did every morning and praised her speed and cleanliness.

Emma returned to the milking. It was quiet work, no one talked. A few flies buzzed about, the rays of the sun started to come through the dusty windows, it was growing hotter. Why had Ilse Stauffer said *that* to her? Why? Why? Why? She felt as though she had been branded. As though the other girls would now look at her strangely, even if nothing had been said publicly. She had not ever thought of herself as different—not in that way, surely. And now, having been articulated, it could never be taken back. It was there, like her nose; it wouldn't go away.

Gregor and the tenant farmer's sons always behaved deferentially and politely to the "young ladies." There was an understanding that very heavy or very dirty work would be done by the men and boys. Even the gatekeeper's very small children understood this. They turned up on everyone's snapshots, for they were cute and picturesque, a little grimy, of course, barefoot, dressed in cotton smocks, with tangled hair. When parents came to visit, carrying cameras and picnic baskets, the children stood around looking photogenic, begging for pennies and candy. The teachers said it should not be encouraged, but it was hard to resist them.

Gregor and the two boys stayed away on those visiting days, as if to emphasize the gulf that separated them from the gentlefolk. Gregor drank his beer, and the boys skipped rocks across the pond, tied the cats' tails together, and stole peaches from the orchard. Christoph, the older of the boys, was well-meaning and friendly toward the girls. He always offered to help them and truly expected nothing in return. He was not yet seventeen but large for his age, and his face was disfigured by a livid red scar that ran from the end of his eyebrow to the corner of his mouth and pulled the whole side of his face out of shape. Emma was afraid of him. She dreaded looking at him, and because he was ungainly, she had come to the conclusion that he was a lout. Emma often made cruel snap judgments. If she had understood that he was good-hearted and quite as shy of people as she was, she might have been kinder to him.

She did the milking quickly that morning in order to rush back to the house and write her father a letter. If she hurried, she could do it in the time allotted for breakfast and bed-making. Her mind, circling about Ilse Stauffer's remarks, had fastened on the reply she herself had made. She would tell Papa that she was sick and tired of being Jewish and wanted to be baptized! That was a perfect solution, simplicity itself. Many of her contemporaries—including, she believed, her three cousins—had been baptized at birth. No one said much about it, they simply took the baby to Pastor So-and-so down at the Evangelical Congregation, and he sprinkled some water on it and gave the parents a baptismal certificate, which was put in the locked desk drawer with other papers, passports and army discharges, never to be looked at again. It was there as proof, if one needed it; and had no effect whatever in one's private or family life, but perhaps in another three generations one might really no longer be Jewish.

The idea appealed to Emma more and more. Her last pail full of milk was quite heavy, and a little of it spilled as she went to lift it. She suddenly got a strong whiff of the rich sweet milk and was repelled by it. She had no taste for fresh, still-warm milk, thick with yellow cream. Only after it had been cooled and the cream skimmed off could she drink it. She had a horror of growing fat, blowing up like a balloon if she ate too much, being made fun of like tubby little Lene.

As Emma carried the last heavy pail into the milking shed, she noticed Christoph waiting next to the outside door. He stood directly in front of the slanting morning rays of the sun and she could not see his face at all, which was a blessing.

"How are you this morning?" he asked. "I see you working faster and faster these days. You'll soon be a real farm girl." He used the familiar *Du*, which did not please Emma. She smiled at him mechanically, stiffly, the sort of smile one uses to keep beggars away or mental defectives from hanging on to one's sleeve.

"You never say a nice word to me," the boy went on. "Is it my scar that bothers you?"

Emma shook her head and did not shut off her smile.

"I'm going away tomorrow," Christoph said. "I got me a job in a factory. They're short-handed, you know, on account of the war. They don't care how I look. A lot of them coming back from the war look worse. And when I've gone from here, I'll not return."

"Where is the factory?" Emma asked. She felt he would not let her go unless she responded.

"In Höchst."

"That's not far from Frankfurt," Emma said. "It's an ugly factory town."

"That's all the same to me."

Emma knew suddenly that Lene would have been kinder to this boy. It made her impatient. "I have to go back to the house," she said. "Breakfast is on the table, and I've got letters to write before we go out to the fields."

"It's going to rain, I can feel it." He touched his crimson scar. "We'll have to work hard to bring in the hay before the weather changes."

Emma walked past him, out the door into the bright sun. She made certain not to come close to him, but her skirt brushed his knee. The sky was clear and a deep summer blue. There was no hint of a rain cloud anywhere. In the barnyard the chickens scratched in the dirt, the ducks quacked their waddling way to the small pond, the geese craned their necks as though they were spectators at a parade.

Emma did not turn around, but she knew Christoph was following her. She did not want to hurry on his account, so she walked with a slow measured step. The path she followed led through the apple orchard and past the raspberry patch to the wide gravel drive that curved round the fountain in front of the baroque manor house. In the middle of the orchard, in the dappled shade of one of the apple trees, Christoph caught up with Emma. He smelled of manure and milk, and his heavy rubber boots were caked with mud. Emma smelled him and saw his washed-out shirt and corduroy pants flecked with bits of straw. She did not look at his face.

"You're a beautiful girl," Christoph said, "I want a kiss from you. A good-bye kiss to remember you by in Höchst."

Emma shook her head resolutely, but the boy put his rough hand on her chin and tilted her face up to his. Emma closed her eyes. She was trembling and her stomach drew together in a painful cramp.

"Don't be afraid," Christoph said. "I don't want anything from you but a kiss." He pressed his lips against hers, and they were rough too, like his hands. She felt his teeth and his tongue trying to pry into her mouth, and his stableboy smell seemed to envelop her. She gagged. Christoph held her tightly now, and his smell made her faint. She tried to step back but tripped over a rock in the high grass and felt herself falling. Christoph fell on top of her, and his hand was on her breast.

"I'm sorry," he whispered, "forgive me, I didn't mean it, I'm sorry."

He had pulled back immediately and was squatting on his heels now, a terrified look on his face. Emma felt the sickness rise so quickly she had time only to turn her face to the side and vomit a small stream of bitter water over her shoulder into the grass. When she opened her eyes, Christoph was gone, and only the disarray of her clothes and his smell, stronger than her sour vomit, proved he had been there.

Emma washed herself off thoroughly in the washbasin, rinsed her mouth and combed her hair. Back in the bedroom, which she shared with a girl named Gertrude, she took off her dress and hid it in her laundry bag. She crawled into bed feeling as if she had a high fever. It no longer occurred to her to write to her father. Every time a whiff of Christoph's barnyard smell reached her nostrils, she felt nauseated again.

When Gertrude came up after breakfast, she found Emma shivering under the down comforter. "Are you sick?" she asked. "We're all supposed to help with the haying."

"I'll be along," said Emma, but when Ilse Stauffer came to check on her half an hour later, she was sleeping soundly. The teacher detected a faint odor of vomit and thought that Emma had probably eaten too many of the sweets her parents sent—in fact, Emma always gave them away—and would be well by dinner time. She was the only one who did not help bring in the hay.

Christoph left early the next day, and Emma did not see him again. She thought she was better, but when she went out to the barn to do the milking and smelled the manure and the milk, she felt nauseated once more. She tried by force of will to do her job, but she was gripped by such revulsion, such an inexplicable fear, that she begged to be excused. Old Gregor finished the chore for her. Ilse Stauffer was puzzled and alarmed when Emma asked to be excused from any further work in the barn. She pressed her for a reason, but Emma would give her none.

"I never heard of such a thing!" Die Stauffer said. "You cannot simply stop. It is your duty to go on." But Emma would not promise to go back. The gym teacher took her refusal as both moral lapse and personal affront. She turned away from Emma, who watched in anguish, and did not speak to her again.

They put Emma on the kitchen and canning detail and had her weed the garden and boil the laundry. It rained heavily for several days. The summer was half over. The Countess Albers-Eschenbach invited her charges to dinner on her Saint's Day, the first Sunday in August.

SUMMER LAY thick and heavy over Frankfurt. It was feared there would be illness. Cholera had broken out in a number of German regiments in distant places. The war dragged on, even though it was clear to many that it was lost. Everywhere in the land voices were raised against continuing the fighting. Revolution seemed possible, the way a storm does on a sultry afternoon when there are gray clouds heaped high on the horizon and distant thunder is heard.

A new director had been hired to take charge of both opera and theater in Frankfurt. He promised to bring contemporary plays to the city and caused a sensation with several Expressionist works that kept theatergoers in a turmoil of argument even in the dog days of summer. Max Beckmann had settled in Frankfurt. He took up his position at the Städel, and his savage paintings and etchings of the world as a madhouse were received with shock and horror by a society that refused to recognize itself.

"What awful things!" Pauline Wertheim said. "How can you call them art?" she asked Elias Süsskind.

"Have you ever looked closely at some of the fifteenth-century martyrdoms in the Städel?" he asked her back.

"But that's in the *museum*," she protested. "Of course that's art. Besides, it was done five hundred years ago. They saw cruelty, death and disfigurement every day of their lives. They got used to it."

Alone in her house, Caroline devoted herself to her painting. She had made her upstairs sitting room into a studio and spent many hours a day sketching still lifes and the view from her window. She continued copying romantic eighteenth-century landscapes and aristocratic portraits. Nathan found her boring but could not imagine anyone else in her place. They loved each other under a mantle of sadness.

Pauline and Siegmund had sent the children and their nanny to a resort on the Baltic. They themselves continued to be fixtures at charity balls and to attend the opera and the theater enthusiastically, no matter what was being presented. Neither one ever seemed to feel the need for privacy. It was always lively at their house.

When the children, in their letters home, complained that because of the war the resort hotel was positively desolate, Pauline called her sister-in-law. "Why not send your children up there too?"

"They're perfectly happy in the Taunus," said Caroline.

"I think the air is better on the Baltic," Pauline told her and then called Fräulein Gründlich to ask if the boys wouldn't like to be at the seashore for a while. "Willy hasn't a soul for company," she said, "and the girls would adore having Lene around. She's become such a young lady."

"What does Mrs. Wertheim think?" Fräulein Gründlich asked. She was used to Pauline's ways.

"She hasn't made up her mind yet, *you* know how she is. But don't tell her I called you."

Pauline herself rang up Caroline to tell her she had spoken to the governess. "It's practically arranged," she said. "They'd love to come. You have only to say yes. I'll get Siegmund to make the reservations and I'll send the chauffeur for the train tickets."

"Is the hotel dreadfully expensive?" Caroline asked. "Nathan says we must save money."

"Nathan is becoming a miser," said Pauline. "You had better talk to him. Your daughters won't be able to make a decent marriage if he watches his pennies all the time. Going about like paupers, they'll never meet any of the right people, and even if they *should*, none will have them, lovely as they are, if there's no dowry."

"Nathan tries to teach them that money isn't everything. He

wants them to understand the value of it and not think it grows on trees or that they're entitled to it no matter what."

"His law practice would be better if he were more aggressive."

"You can't change him."

"But tell him from me, please, not to try to tell rich children that they're poor when they're *not*. It will only confuse them and send them to one of those new head doctors."

The train to Travemünde took longer than usual. Fräulein Gründlich kept a close watch over the children. "Be very careful!" she said to them more than once. The train was crowded with haggard women, crippled soldiers and children with great dark circles under their eyes. "They'll rob you if they get half a chance," said Fräulein Gründlich. "This country is on the verge of revolution."

"So much the better," said Lene, "we'll have peace."

"You don't know what you're talking about, or have you been listening to your Aunt Eva? If there's a revolution, blood will run in the streets of Frankfurt, and people like your parents will be stood up against the wall and shot."

"And you?" asked Ernst.

"I'll go back home, back to the country," Fräulein Gründlich said. "And take you all with me. You'll be safe with me back home. In bad times it's always better to be in the country where you can hide, because you know every nook and cranny and the enemy doesn't. There's always food, and eventually the stranger moves on and leaves you in peace again. Or, if he stays, you swallow him up, he becomes part of the land, and his loyalty is to the land, not to the conqueror. The revolution doesn't concern us, it comes from the cities and is meant for the cities."

The children had never heard Fräulein Gründlich talk like that before; they were astounded and looked at one another in silence. All the same, they were comforted by her expressed intention of taking them with her to safety.

THEY ARRIVED at the beach resort late in the evening and took a horse-drawn cab from the station to the hotel. The nag and driver both were nothing but skin and bones. The children were so tired that they remembered nothing of their night journey but the pleasure with which they sank into clean sheets, surrounded by the salty fragrance and cool winds of the nearby sea.

When they awoke the next morning, the first thing they heard was the pounding of the surf, and the first thing they saw was the brilliant sun flooding an immense sky. Lying in their beds, slowly growing used to their surroundings, they listened to the sea gulls' cries and breathed deeply, observing the bleached colors of the things in their rooms, even the wood.

"Wouldn't it be nice if Emma were here?" Lene said at breakfast. She felt lonely. The rolls were crisp and fresh, the hot chocolate dark and sweet, but her two cousins, sitting at the next table with Nanny, paid her no attention whatever. Andreas and Ernst had marched off with Willy down to the sea, and Julia and Jenny seemed interested only in young men, even though there was clearly a dearth of them. The hotel was oversupplied with young women and little boys.

"All they can talk about is 'love,' " said Lene disgustedly, putting another dab of apricot jam on her roll.

"Don't eat too much of the sweet stuff," said Fräulein Gründlich. "Soon you'll find it interesting to talk about love too."

"The boys and Willy don't act like that. They get along splendidly, and I bet they never even think about girls."

"That will come too," said Fräulein Gründlich, and removed the jam to her side of the table. "The word is 'patience,' my child. 'Everything comes to him who waits.' "

When the boys got to the end of the boardwalk, they all took off their shoes and walked barefoot in the sand. Far off on the horizon they could see boats.

"Those are warships," said Willy, who was very short-sighted and wore thick glasses. He could barely see the boats, but he had been there awhile and was an old hand. Some other boys had told him about the warships on his first day. When they returned to the hotel, they found the town photographer in the lobby taking pictures. Lene was pleading with Fräulein Gründlich to let her pose for one.

"I'm not sure your parents would approve. It costs money."

"Please!" said Andreas.

As the governess searched her mind for an answer, Ernst said, "We'll pay for it out of our allowances . . ."

"If necessary," said Lene.

They were posed, all three of them, in front of a painted backdrop showing the ocean and sailboats, little white clouds in the sky and beach chairs and flags on a terrace.

Hanno Altenburg, the novelist, who was staying at the hotel, watched the children take their poses for the old photographer, who was adjusting his camera and kept disappearing under his black cloth, calling out instructions. The children were at once serious and full of laughter; the two emotions kept following hard upon each other, and as soon as one child had succeeded in looking grave, one of the others would begin to grin and smiles would ripple across all three faces again.

Hanno had taken a seat in one of the white wicker chairs in the hotel's sunroom, where it was easy to observe what went on in the lobby as well as in the main salon. He had very sharp eyes and was, even more than most novelists, a voyeur. He traveled a great deal, always with a satchel full of lined notebooks, which he wrote in wherever he alighted. Many prizes and honors had come to him in the fifty-seven years of his life. He was a good rather than a great novelist, but he was popular, his books were well received and his reputation reached beyond the borders of his native land.

Hanno took careful note of the photographing session and smiled at the children's antics. He was particularly taken with the two boys. He had a weakness for adolescents; it was one of the reasons for his restless travels. Men of his own age interested him only as friends; he never sought lovers among them. His work took up the greater part of his life, so since he had no energy left for grand passions, he had decided early on to stand a little to the side, remain a spectator and never become *engagé.* He considered himself a bourgeois in the best sense of the word.

As Hanno watched the three, he became aware that his attention was more and more drawn to one of them. The more delicate of the boys kept intruding into his consciousness; he recognized the birth of desire. Before long he was watching only Andreas. The notebook lay untouched in his lap, the open fountain pen caught between its pages, while Hanno Altenburg fell slowly and deliciously in love with Andreas Wertheim.

When the children had disappeared, Hanno approached the concierge and asked, "Who is the family that arrived last night?"

"The children with their governess?"

"Yes."

"Their name is Wertheim, from Frankfurt, sir. Frankfurt on the Main. Shall I spell the family name for you?"

"Not necessary, thank you."

Andreas had noticed the writer even before the writer noticed him. The boy's eye was quick. He took in the whole of a scene at a glance. Every room was to him a stage on which a drama might unfold at any minute, and he had to know his place in it. More often than not, nothing actually happened, but Andreas had committed all the necessary details to memory so that he would henceforth never become lost. That morning at breakfast, while Ernst and Willy traded stories on a variety of schoolboy subjects and Lene tried to get the attention of her cousins, Andreas had seen the gentleman with the mane of graying hair enter the dining room and go directly to the best-placed table from which he could observe without being observed.

Andreas saw that the man was vain—he seemed slightly over-dressed—and anxious to keep his youth. He did not think all this out word for word, but he understood it, as one instinctively understands the elements of a drama one has come to see. Here is the villain, there the heroine, this one's not to be trusted. Andreas could not get the man out of his mind even while he frolicked with his brother and cousin in the sand. "Who was that man," he asked Willy casually, "the one with all the hair?"

"A famous writer," Willy said, "except I don't know his name, I never heard of him."

Andreas was convinced that this time it would be his fate to have a part in the play.

Fräulein Gründlich sent them all to bed after lunch. "The sea air, like the air of the mountains is fatiguing," she said. "We have to be careful not to overdo things the first day." She closed the shutters in their rooms and turned down their beds. Ernst fell asleep almost instantly, having run hard that morning over the dunes and through the soft sand trying to elude the waves, chasing them when they swept back out to sea, sprinting before them when they poured across the sand. His mind was untroubled, his dreams uncomplicated. Andreas looked at him, asleep, spread wide across the bed, his face already burned by the sun. He often envied him, but not this day. He felt keyed up, happy, poised on the edge of adventure; he could not sleep.

Next door in her own room, Lene slept too. She snored a little, and her brown curls were salty from the spray of the sea. Fräulein Gründlich, who meant only to take a brief rest, found she could not keep her eyes open and slept soundly for two hours.

By the following day clouds had swept across the sea and were sending large drops of rain splattering against the windows. The children spent a long time over breakfast and then went off to explore the hotel. Andreas pointed out the game room to them, but it smelled of stale cigars. Jenny and Julia had relented enough to allow Lene to accompany them to the music room, where they took turns playing the piano. Ernst tried to read one of the books he had brought with him, but something always caught his attention; he was bored and distracted at the same time. Only Andreas did not feel the malaise of the rainy weather upon him. At breakfast he had again watched Hanno Altenburg enter the room and had, as soon as he noticed the older man's eyes straying over the assembled guests, smiled at him. He hoped the smile was right, neither too brazen nor too shy. Hanno Altenburg smiled back and inclined his head in greeting. Andreas felt pure pleasure spread over his face.

The actual meeting between them took place that evening at about dusk. The rain had gradually subsided, and the sky had suddenly been lighted by the brilliant red of the setting sun. The guests assembled on the terrace to look at the sunset, and Andreas found himself standing next to the novelist.

"How beautiful it is," Andreas, as if to himself.

"It means we'll have a nice day tomorrow," Hanno Altenburg answered.

They had not yet actually looked at each other.

"My name is Andreas Wertheim," the boy said. "I understand you are a famous writer. I saw you watching the guests yesterday."

Hanno laughed, and there was a hint of embarrassment in that quick, distinctive bark.

"You're one of the clever ones," he said. "I should have known it. Are you going to be a writer too?"

"Not so far as I know," said Andreas. "I hope I didn't catch you at something you want to keep a secret. But don't be afraid—I won't tell anyone."

Hanno thought he detected amusement in the boy's eyes. How refreshing it was!

"Allow me," he said with mock seriousness, clicking his heels together. "Hanno Altenburg, from Berlin."

They shook hands and watched the sunset in silence. Lene, who had been standing nearby, edged over. She had a thin sweater draped across her shoulders and was shivering in the evening air. "You ought to go inside," said Andreas. "You look as though you're freezing."

"Let me borrow your jacket. I want to stay and watch some more. I love sunsets when you can see the whole sky."

"If I give you my jacket, I'll be cold."

"We can both get under it," Lene said, and snuggled up to her brother, who reluctantly threw part of his loden jacket over her shoulder. Hanno moved some distance away and kept his eyes on the setting sun. Andreas had not introduced his sister to him.

"Who is that man?" she whispered.

"A famous novelist," he whispered back.

Lene studied Hanno in the fading light. "He's handsome," she said, "but not the sort of man I like at all. He's supercilious. And stuck-up."

"Shh! He'll hear you. Go on inside now, it's getting dark."

It had, indeed, suddenly grown darker. Only a faint yellow glow remained in the western sky. The dunes had turned black, and the lights in the hotel were turned on. The guests all went inside, except for a young wounded soldier and his fiancée, who kissed under the cover of darkness.

The next morning was clear and nearly windless. Fräulein

Gründlich took her charges to the beach at midmorning. The boys had decided to build a really large sand castle, and the girls went searching for shells with which to decorate it. Julia and Jenny did less searching than talking. They speculated on the course of the wounded soldier's love and wondered what the latest fashions in Frankfurt were. Travemünde was *such* a backwater, they had not seen a decent illustrated magazine in all the time they'd been there. Lene listened to them, saying very little so that she would make no foolish mistakes, but she felt that they tolerated her a touch more each day. Julia, especially, who was only a year older, made an effort not to exclude her. Jenny was two years older and like her mother a great chatterer.

"Did you meet Hanno Altenburg?" Julia asked Lene as they walked along the beach.

"No, but Andreas did, on the terrace last night," said Lene.

"What can he find to say to him?" Julia asked. "I'd be afraid to go up to such a famous man and speak to him. And you know"— her tone was conspiratorial—"I have decided I want to become a writer."

"I'd like to be a doctor," Lene said. It was a wish that had developed since she had gone to visit Jacob in the hospital.

"A doctor? Why not a nurse?"

"People like us don't become nurses!"

"Girls don't become doctors much either."

"Nowadays they do. But anyway, I've got plenty of time to think about it." That was a sentence that seemed to have come straight out of Fräulein Gründlich's mouth.

"What are you two having such a serious conversation about?" Jenny asked them.

"We're talking about what we plan to do with our lives," Julia said with a deep sigh.

FRÄULEIN GRÜNDLICH and Nanny Ida were sitting over their busywork in the shade of two large wicker beach chairs, deep in conversation.

"Here comes Herr Altenburg, the famous novelist," Fräulein Gründlich whispered. "I wonder what he wants."

Hanno Altenburg had come to have a look at the sand castle.

"Magnificent!" he said. "Which one of you is the architect of this edifice?"

"We all three built it," said Willy, pushing the heavy glasses up his nose with sandy hands.

"The girls are bringing shells for decoration," said Ernst.

Only Andreas was silent.

"After you have all had lunch and taken your rest, would you like me to show you an old wreck, up along the shore? It's best seen at low tide, which comes about four o'clock today." Hanno was pleased with his ploy, even if it meant taking all three boys for a walk.

"We have to tell our governesses," said Ernst.

"I'm surprised that children interest him," said Nanny Ida, after the children had spoken to them.

"He's probably got a grandchild somewhere," said Fräulein Gründlich.

"He doesn't look to *me* as though he's ever been married," said Nanny.

While they were at lunch, there was a telephone call from Frankfurt. Fräulein Gründlich blanched when the waiter came to call her to the desk.

"Not to worry," the concierge said, seeing her face. "Madame tells me that the news is good, everyone is in the best of health."

When the governess returned to the table, she was smiling. "Guess who'll be here tomorrow!"

"Emma!" Lene guessed. She had not had a letter from her sister in a week and had been thinking about her.

"Yes, Emma," said Fräulein Gründlich. "She has had enough of that farm work, I think. Your mother didn't say so, but I believe it. Emma isn't cut out for the barn and the stable."

"Is Mama still on the phone?" Lene asked.

"Good heavens, no. It's much too expensive to talk on the phone such a long time over so great a distance. But she sends all of you her love."

The walk to the shipwreck and back took nearly an hour. Ernst and Willy were disappointed, for the wreck was just a few heavy wooden ribs sticking out of the sand, barnacled and blackened by water and age. Hanno walked a few steps behind the boys and watched Andreas, who did everything possible to demonstrate his youth and joyfulness. He jumped from the dunes and chased the waves, once he even turned a cartwheel. The sea was almost as calm as a mountain lake. Andreas and Hanno exchanged hardly a word. It seemed enough for the moment to admire and be admired.

EMMA ARRIVED the next afternoon and was met at the station by all the children. Fräulein Gründlich looked at her searchingly for signs of malaise but found none. Emma was tanned, she had lost no weight, and her arms and hands, which she proudly showed them when the boys offered to carry her luggage, were as strong and brown as any milkmaid's. In fact, Fräulein Gründlich did not entirely approve of such arms "on a young lady."

"What happened?" Lene asked as soon as they had a minute alone together.

"Oh, nothing, really," said Emma in a light-hearted tone that seemed to Lene not to ring true. "I thought I'd spent enough time just working, I wanted to spend some part of my vacation with you. Especially after I heard you were here at the beach."

"Were you *homesick?*" The idea of homesickness was one that Lene could grasp in all its horror. Sometimes, even on a vacation like this, surrounded by siblings and under the familiar protection of Fräulein Gründlich, there were moments when she longed for her own bed, the beloved view from her window, and the comforting sense that everything in the house had been there as long as she could remember and would always enfold her.

"A little," Emma admitted.

"Well, *that* explains it," said Lene and did not ask her sister for further explanations. She observed, however, that Emma was more than usually quiet; even the giggling banter she engaged in with her cousin Jenny seemed a little forced.

HANNO ALTENBURG, though he had exchanged no more than a few words with Andreas, knew that he had to arrange a meeting soon, if only to know how far he could go—what pleasures to expect. Andreas was not some wise, mean street Arab whom one could order to one's room with a wink and the show of a coin. Besides, this was a family hotel. It was, to be sure, sparsely populated because of the war, but there were dozens of snotty children, one more curious than the next, and the Wertheims hung around one another like a litter of puppies, especially now that the eldest sister had come. And the governess! What a fierce demon *she* was! Hanno did not wish to tangle with her. All these considerations, of course, gave the affair a piquancy no assignation with a Neapolitan ragamuffin could ever have and increased his desire hundredfold.

The hotel had a pleasure pavilion, a sort of large Victorian gazebo, where in better times band concerts had taken place. It was closed now, the chairs within stacked up, the stage dusty, the piano covered with a sheet, the parquet floor spotted with mouse droppings, and the windowpanes grimy with alternating layers of dust and rain. It was not kept locked, and on occasion its porch was used as a refuge from a sudden storm. It was to this place that Hanno hoped to bring Andreas for a long conversation and whatever else they might agree on.

Hanno had come upon the building and discovered its piano on one of his tours the first week he was at the hotel. He went there to play it once in a while, being much too self-conscious to use the instrument in the music room, where he could imagine all the guests whispering, "Listen to how badly Hanno Altenburg plays the piano." He was very much aware of his public persona and assumed that everyone was always looking at him, talking about him and waiting to entrap him in stupid conversations. If ever he suspected that this was *not* what they were doing, he became sullen. He also did not allow his self-consciousness to stop him from sitting, notebook in hand, behind the potted palms, as though he wore a cloak of invisibility.

Andreas was nervous. His appetite suffered, and he slept badly. He could not keep the writer's face out of his waking dreams, he was constantly aware of his presence. When Hanno's cool gray eyes strayed toward him and fastened themselves on him, he imagined they were caresses. He was a virgin, and like many virgins of his age, yearned not to be. The fact that his seducer was a man did not trouble him. It seemed, actually, rather natural. Andreas knew his own body and understood it. He often played naked in front of the mirror in his room at home now that he and Ernst had been given separate bedrooms. He missed the closeness that had once existed between them, but their subtle differences in tastes and desires had grown from a thin breath to a thick pane of glass. Real understanding seemed impossible. The trouble was that he wanted, more than anything, to talk and confide in Ernst, wanted Ernst to understand, to receive his confessions and forgive him.

Toward the end of the week a strong offshore wind began blowing. Since there was also a full moon, the tides ran very high, and the guests at the hotel spent many hours watching the rough sea. The waves broke a long way from the shore, often from a great height, and thundered in with a booming sound that never ceased. The cabanas had been secured and the beach chairs brought to safety. The water was an ugly grayish brown and carried much debris with it. The sky, too, was dirty, and the air felt as if there were snow in it.

Andreas, wearing a sweater under his oilskin jacket, stood at the start of the pier, which was slick and dangerous to walk on. It shook with the pounding of the surf, and when the high waves broke, a cascade of salt spray burst over its railings. Andreas could not tear himself away from the spectacle even after his trousers had become soaked. Hanno saw him standing there, braced against the wind, like a lonely figure in a snowstorm, his mouth open in a shout half glee, half fear. The writer dressed himself warmly and went out on the beach. No one paid any attention to him, the spectacle that day was the sea. At the bottom of the pier he looked up at Andreas but did not trust himself to join him. He was not as agile and sure-footed as the boy.

"Hello there!" he shouted, not at all certain that he could be heard. "I've been watching you watching the ocean. It's magnificent, isn't it?"

Andreas understood only a few of the words, but he nodded blissfully. Hanno took his courage in his hands and climbed the steps of the pier, holding the banister tightly. For a few minutes he stood there, next to the boy, letting his heartbeat slow, leaning on the railing.

"Do you think we might have a talk, you and I?" Hanno asked. "Too many women and children in this hotel," he added by way of explanation. Andreas nodded, and Hanno noticed a smile on his face—the kind that comes from within, full of happiness not unmixed with self-satisfaction. When he grew serious again, he looked directly into the older man's face and said, "I'm afraid I haven't read your books." Although his honesty was charming, a tremor of annoyance fluttered in the writer's head.

"There are other things we can talk about," he said mildly. "It's good to relax once in a while from the immense concentration that's required in my line of work. When I let it go for a while—of course I can never forget it completely—I come back to it refreshed."

"Would you like to take a walk down the beach?" Andreas asked. "I think I can persuade my brother and my cousin that the shipwreck isn't worth seeing again."

"That's splendid for the nice weather," said Hanno, "but God knows when we'll have another good day. No, no, no . . . we've wasted enough time already." He could not help himself, the words skipped out even as he meant to be more judicious. He started to put his hand on the boy's head but withdrew it quickly, afraid of being seen.

"Whatever you say." Andreas with his sensitivity to geography of both place and mind had caught a hint of Hanno Altenburg's egotism, and it served as a warning. He recognized that he must take care and protect himself, that this person would cosset him with sweet words and then disappear like the froth on a wave as soon as something else was required. But the wind and the sea and his own physical desire made him daring, and he let himself go.

"Look, look!" cried Hanno. "That huge wave out there, just about to break! Tremendous!" As Andreas turned his head out to sea, the wind blew his hair, which had not been cut since they left Frankfurt, into a tangle, and the writer, pointing with his left hand, his head bent toward Andreas', felt it on his cheek. He put his mouth close to the delectable shell of the boy's ear and whispered "I love you" just as the wave crashed down a short distance from the end of the pier and sent water spraying high into the air, so that a thin wall of rain fell on them. Andreas did not find the declaration startling, but he kept his eyes on the water and said "Thank you," which was the only answer that came to his mind.

"We can meet at the pavilion," said Hanno. "Do you know where it is? The door on the side, next to the bar, is open. I go there regularly and play the old piano. It is dusty in there but romantic, you'll see. We shan't be found out. When can you come?"

"Tomorrow morning, after breakfast?"

"No sooner?"

"When?"

"In an hour. We have all afternoon, supper isn't served till seven-thirty."

"I'll be missed."

"Tell them you're going to the village."

Andreas' heart was beating as hard as if he had just completed some great physical feat. He had made a conquest, his first! His heart expanded with joy. He had never experienced anything quite like this before. What power it gave him! He felt that were he to throw himself into the churning sea, he would survive its fury, he would come out alive.

Hanno parted from the boy at the edge of the terrace. He shook his hand quite formally, as if they were saying good-bye at the end of a casual meeting. Hanno, too, was excited, as he always was on these occasions, but his own feelings were dampened by age and experience. He knew that the burst of passion that occurs between two lovers at their first tryst is the most fragile of emotions, even though it may seem the most beautiful. He looked beyond the meeting in the gazebo and sighed a long sigh for the inevitable loss that awaited them both.

Most of the guests at the hotel spent the late afternoon either in their rooms or in one of the peaceful retreats of the hotel. Andreas knew he would be missed if he absented himself too obviously at that hour. It was now already three o'clock, he had to find a good excuse to be gone for a while. Fräulein Gründlich thought the boys were given quite enough freedom; it was her job, after all, to see to it that they remained safe, and the only way to make certain that they were safe was to know at all times where they were.

Ernst was in the armchair by the window reading an adventure novel by Karl May. His knobby knees were covered with scratches and scabs. Ernst was always cutting himself, banging his fingers with hammers and tearing his pants on barbed wire. He needed to prove his physical courage, he was determined to be strong and brave. Like all of Caroline's children, he suffered from shyness, and like all of Nathan's, he lacked the competitive spirit. Although the two boys had grown apart, each still had a profound and subtle sensitivity to the other's inner clockwork.

Ernst looked up when Andreas came into the room. "You're prowling," he said.

"What do you mean?"

"There's a certain nervousness about you, the way you came into the room. I can always tell when you're simply strolling and at ease or crouched like a panther—"

"—waiting to pounce?"

"No. Just waiting for something to happen."

"Ernst?"

"Yes?"

"I want to ask you a favor."

Ernst sat very still in his chair, aware that the occasion was somehow momentous. But Andreas was doing his best not to allow the excitement he felt to escape through his words or to flame in his eyes.

"It isn't much. I want to go into the village. I want to buy something to bring home with me"—he grew a little apprehensive at the lie—"for my friend Wolfgang. But you know how Gründlich is, she'd probably say no if I asked her. Now, I don't want her to worry. So if she should come looking for me while I'm gone, would you tell her that I've gone for a walk down to the shipwreck with a group of those boy scouts from the other hotel. Don't say anything, though, unless she asks. It's better not to lie if you don't have to." He blushed when he said this and was absolutely certain that Ernst didn't believe a word he was telling him.

But Ernst was very casual. "You'll be back in time for dinner?" he asked.

"Of course. I shan't be *that* long."

Ernst did not ask any further questions. His mind had gone

back to the adventures of Winnetou. He did not give Andreas' nervous request any thought until much later, when it had become part of a pattern. At the moment he was ready to believe his brother and happy to accommodate him. He said, "Have a good time."

"Why do you say that?"

"You're going into town, aren't you? That's an adventure here. Just be careful you're not run down by a wild horse."

Andreas walked down the long corridors of the hotel as quietly as possible, thinking that he *was* a panther, allowing his excitement to take hold of him now that he was on his way. He met no one. He crossed the empty dining room, which was already set for supper. A waiter dozed in the corner of the big lounge, no one had yet arrived for tea. Andreas walked unhurriedly across the lawn and through a small pine wood. He heard Hanno's piano playing before he reached the gazebo. It struck him, quite irrelevantly, that Hanno did not play very well. Andreas was musical, and it seemed natural to him to make these judgments. What he did not recognize was the affectation of the gesture: Hanno Altenburg setting the stage for his seduction.

Andreas stopped for a moment before the door, which stood slightly ajar. A moment of panic, followed immediately by a rush of desire, gripped him. He slipped through the door and caught sight of the writer—who knew he was there because the door creaked on its hinges—bent over the keyboard. It was theatrical, but no matter; Andreas felt that it had to be. The boy closed the door, and the room sank into dingy twilight. Hanno finished a badly played run with a flourish and rose from the piano stool to greet his young lover. He spread his arms wide, and Andreas flung himself into them.

THE HOTEL was awake again when Andreas sauntered back from the gazebo. Mothers chatted quietly in the sunroom, children played sedate games, young ladies read magazines or stood in little groups listening to the harpist, who played the same trippingly sentimental music each afternoon from five to seven. Andreas felt a little drunk

and full of the false sense of strength alcohol may induce. He wanted
to jump and shout, but he walked very casually through the public
rooms of the hotel, waved to his sisters and his cousins who were
playing cards, and then went out again across the terrace and down
to the water's edge. He took off his shoes and walked barefoot. The
sea was still raging, but within bounds; the danger of its spilling over
and charging across the land seemed to have passed. The sun, beginning to set, promised nothing. Andreas put his hands into the cold
water and brought them to his hot face. He smelled the writer's
cologne on him and felt his hands and lips on his tender skin, which
bloomed from the love made to it. But all that had to be washed
away. Andreas rubbed the salty sandy water into his cheeks, his neck
and along his arms. Then he ran down the beach in a spurt of
panther energy until he felt a ringing in his ears and sweat on his
back.

Hanno Altenburg, who had taken his usual seat on the terrace and
ordered an aperitif, watched him from afar. He felt contentment as
well as satisfaction in his own generosity. He had given the boy
more than he would ever know, he had made him a man and
brought him as close as he was likely to come to genius. Hanno
thought of himself as a sentimental fool, an old loser, a man destined
never to meet his equal. He loved Andreas dearly—for his youth and
his beauty and the way he had swooned before him; but he envied
him too, for the many years that stretched in front of him.

They met nearly every day in the few short weeks that remained
before Andreas returned to school. Since Fräulein Gründlich had
not missed him, Andreas felt secure and prepared no more lies for
Ernst. He simply said, "I'm going for my walk," each day at the
appointed hour. Ernst paid his brother no mind. He was too deeply
involved in his books, which were forbidden reading at home.
Karl May was a prolific author, and the holiday was drawing to its
close.

Andreas hoped there'd be no long farewells. He had felt the
stirring winds of love and desire and derived pleasure from an illicit
affair, but with the cool shrewdness of his youth, he saw Hanno
more clearly than Hanno saw him. He was growing impatient with
the writer for his romantic posturing, his narcissim and his elderly

habits. Andreas was anxious to return to his uncomplicated daily routine.

"Can you meet me tonight to wish me farewell?" Hanno Altenburg asked on the afternoon before the day of their departure for Frankfurt. "Maybe we can take a walk on the beach, it's so mild and lovely out and the Milky Way is grand at this time of the year. I have a gift for you," he added. They were sitting on the terrace playing chess. It was one of the little ruses Hanno had thought up to facilitate conversations between them. "I shall teach this young man a game to sharpen his intellect," he had told Fräulein Gründlich, who was happy to see such a famous man take an interest in Andreas.

"Will you come out—after the others are asleep?" Hanno asked again, more importunately this time.

"Yes, of course," Andreas reassured him. It would be an adventure, nothing much could happen now, and he'd gotten very good at dissembling.

At ten-thirty the writer said good night to a boring old lady, kissing her hand gallantly, sighing his regrets. "I need my constitutional, dear friend," he said.

He waited, slightly chilled, beside some overturned buoys at the end of the boardwalk. A few swift clouds raced by the waning moon. He won't come, Hanno thought, but he waited nevertheless. He had the gift—a privately printed edition of some of his erotic poetry—in his coat pocket. A cryptic inscription was on the flyleaf in Hanno's own hand. "He cannot be that thoughtless, he must come," the man said to himself as he looked toward the darkened hotel with furious, sad regret.

But Andreas, waiting in his bed, only half undressed, until Ernst was asleep, had dozed off, oblivious of the tolling bell on the buoy out at sea, and Hanno gave up his vigil.

It was already gray dawn when Andreas awoke with a start and the guilty realization that he had failed his lover. He raced to the window and drew back the curtains, but the light of morning hung in the thick white fog and the steps from the terrace led nowhere. Andreas went back to bed and did not wake up until Fräulein Gründlich came to tell them it was nearly time to go.

The book of poems came in the mail some weeks later with a

bittersweet note which, as Andreas recognized, contained more literary flourishes than emotional depth.

EDU'S REGIMENT was recalled to Germany in the early fall of 1918. In January of that year, a metalworkers' strike in Berlin, put down with typical harshness by the government, had spread to other cities. Those workers whose punishment it had been to be sent from the factory into the army fomented discontent among the soldiers in the field. The working population was totally disenchanted with the war, but neither the Kaiser nor the generals were ready for peace, and there were still those in the right-wing parties who dreamt of expansion and empire as fervently as ever.

The troops sent to Berlin were kept in reserve to quell the expected revolution. Edu was desperate; much as he supported law and order, he had no stomach for police work, no wish to shoot civilians. All he wanted was to go home to his house and his garden. He dreamt constantly of walking down the Bockenheimer Landstrasse in spring when the chestnuts were in bloom and turning into the Palmengarten, where he lost himself in the green of its tropical jungle. But every morning he woke up in the miserable room near the railroad station where he was billeted.

Berlin in those autumn days was a city balanced between desperate gaiety and looming threat. Tatters of flags hung from the windows, the women wore dresses made from the rags of old ball gowns. The streets were filled with whores and the wounded. The grotesque became the norm, daily life was viciously distorted. The bitter, biting drawings by George Grosz were not exaggerations but unvarnished truth. Everyone in the cafés seemed to know the artist who had very nearly been executed by a military tribunal for treason. Only the intervention of Harry, Count Kessler, had saved him.

Edu, wandering through the shabby capital, was repelled by what he saw. It seemed to him that he walked through hell, not the hell of the trenches, but the hell of a society in disintegration, which for a man of Edu's sensibilities was almost more horrifying than war. At every step, his soul kept crying out, "Is this what we fought for?" Like many others, he believed that the despair and disorder he saw on the streets of Berlin threatened everything he held sacred.

One evening, walking on the Kurfürstendamm, he was spat on by a haggard man sitting at the curb in a little four-wheeled cart. The stumps of his legs were covered by the fragment of an army blanket, the stumps of his bare arms waved in the air in jerky, fretful rhythm. "Pig!" the man shouted after Edu. "See what you've done to me!" His chest was covered with medals, a tin cup was squeezed between his thighs.

Edu felt the eyes of the other pedestrians on him. His uniform made him as conspicuous as if he'd been wearing prisoner's stripes. An air of hostility and rage filled the cool night air around him. He saw people snicker at him, saw scowls on the faces of others. Edu had never before been the butt of so much public contempt. He thought: If just one of those men raises a fist, all the others will beat me unconscious! The spittle had lodged on his polished cavalry-man's boot. Edu was both afraid and ashamed. His officer's uniform, the shiny boots, his clean-shaven face were the stigmata of the conqueror. The wretch in the cart had doubtlessly had very little before the war, now he had nothing, not even a body. Compared to him, Edu was blessed. He wanted to defend himself, but what was there to say? In the minutes it took him to walk away from the crowd, he tried to articulate an answer. But there was no answer. All he could do was escape.

He turned the nearest corner and walked for almost an hour through the bourgeois part of the city where large apartment houses decorated in the stucco curlicues of Art Nouveau stood silent and dark and uninviting. He knew no one here, the city itself was strange to him, the only person who spoke to him was a whore who did not think the solitary handsome officer would refuse her. But Edu shook his head. The whore cursed him roundly; he heard her voice for a long time echoing down the empty street.

It was not until his feet grew tired and his mind groggy that he began to forget the insults he had just suffered. It was time to go home, but he was somewhat uncertain as to where he was. He passed several art galleries and looked into their barred windows, but what he saw did not especially interest him until he came to a very dimly lit window in which a single shining painting was hung against a background of black velvet. Edu stood still and stared at it. It had been so long since he saw an object of beauty that he did not realize until now how barren his life had been these past few years. He could not quite read the signature in the picture's bottom right-hand corner, but he knew he would never "lose" the painting, his mind would preserve it forever, even if he failed to find it in this particular window again. The subject, as far as he could make out, was an orgiastic dance. But subject matter was not what struck him —it was the raw color and the passionate movement. His Impressionists paled beside its purples, blues and reds, its fiery yellows and oranges. Edu stood for a long time leaning against the iron bars, gazing at the work, before he wrote the address of the gallery in the little notebook he carried with him.

He did not have the opportunity to return to the gallery for more than a week. When he finally had some free time, he went there directly, afraid that the whole thing had been a mirage, that he would reach the address only to find an empty lot or a blank wall. But the gallery was there, the painting was still in the window, and this time the door was unlocked and opened, like Jacob's, with the tinkle of a bell. The gallery was a single room with an office to the rear, behind an arched opening curtained off by strings of beads that moved slightly when he entered with a sound like teacups being set on their saucers. All around the walls hung more of the brilliant pictures. Edu looked at them with the kind of attention that made him oblivious to anything else. He was startled when he heard someone say, "May I help you?" An owlish, corpulent man had appeared from behind the beads. He stared at Edu with a Berliner's morose and mocking stare.

"Whose work is this?" Edu asked.

"Emil Nolde's," the man said. "And is it he who brought you here? It isn't every day I'm visited by an officer of the Kaiser's army. What are you, a cossack? No, they don't have cossacks in our army . . ."

Edu made sure he didn't click his heels together, but he bowed slightly and said, "I'm Eduard Wertheim from Frankfurt am Main. I'm interested in pictures . . ." He hesitated a moment and then decided to go on, "I collect them."

The man held out his hand. "If you don't know Nolde in Frank-

furt," he said, "you're way behind Berlin. I'm Levy." They shook
hands. Levy looked at Edu shrewdly. "Are you going to buy something?"

"Yes," Edu replied, trying not to sound surprised at the frankness
of the question.

"Very good. I hope you have money?"

"I've been getting paid, and there's nothing to spend it on."

"Very good. You send nothing home to your wife or your Frau
Mama?"

"That's none of your business!"

"It's not, you're quite right. *Chutzpa*, wouldn't you say? Or don't
you understand such expressions?"

Edu decided the best thing to do was to ignore the rude questions.
"How much is the painting I liked, the one in the window?"

" 'The Dance around the Golden Calf'? A biblical subject. You
say you have cash?"

He quoted a price which seemed not unreasonable. Edu, uncertain whether one bargained here, was silent for a moment and
looked at the other pictures. None struck him with the same force
as the Golden Calf, though there was a beautiful seascape to which
he almost lost his heart.

"We don't bargain here," said Levy. Edu noticed that his sweater
was unraveling. "On the other hand, if you're going to buy more
than one picture—if you're going to buy two or three—we might
be able to quote another price: *en gros*, as they say in business. I take
it you're in business when you're not in the army?"

Edu nodded. Much as he had begun to detest this man, he could
not tear himself away. "Let me see what else you have," he said, and
Levy led him into a room behind his office where there were racks
filled with paintings. Levy systematically took certain pictures from
them; he seemed to have analyzed Edu's preferences with a magician's finesse. There wasn't a single one he brought out that was not,
to a greater or lesser degree, to Edu's taste. At the end of three hours
Edu had chosen four paintings and spent all the money he carried
in his money belt.

"I will get someone to help you bring them home," Levy said.

Half the day had passed and Edu was hungry, but he felt happier than he had in years. No other feeling could compare to the rush of exultation that acquisitions brought. And he would have the pictures to look at every day until he was discharged.

The boy who appeared to help Edu carry the paintings back to his room was about sixteen, Edu guessed. He wore a long black coat over his knickers, a collarless white shirt buttoned to the neck and a delivery boy's cap on his shaved head. Edu did not immediately notice that he also had earlocks pushed behind his ears. He said very little, but those words he uttered in reply to Edu's polite questions revealed him to be better in Yiddish than in German. When they reached Edu's room, which was twenty minutes' walk away, Edu gave him a small gold piece for a tip. The boy was pleased; he had apparently not expected so generous a reward. He stood there trying to formulate something. *"Er is a yid?"* he finally asked. Edu did not understand him immediately. Yiddish was a language he simply refused to hear. When the question, repeated twice, did penetrate his mind, his first impulse was to deny that he was a *yid,* but a look at the boy's knowing black eyes showed him that the question was really a statement of fact; the boy had been watching him, had seen into his heart and mind (or, Edu ruefully decided, into his pants) and recognized a brother.

"Whatever you should need or want," the boy said, having carefully wrapped the coin in a corner of his handkerchief and knotted it, "I can get it for you." Edu nodded absently; he wanted to close the door and look at his purchases. "I can get almost anything. Even a girl." There was no bravado in the way the boy said it. Instead he seemed to breathe out desire with the remark, as though it were less an offer made to the gentleman officer than an expression of his own heart's wish.

Edu was so struck with what was almost a plea that he hesitated a minute before he answered stiffly, "No, no, absolutely not."

"My cousin," the boy persisted, "a Jewish girl. She is very pretty. I would not deceive you."

I've never had a Jewish girl, thought Edu.

"I'll bring her tonight," the boy said.

"No," said Edu. "Not tonight."

"Tomorrow?" The boy would not let go.

Edu shrugged his shoulders with what, he realized in horror, was a most Jewish gesture. He felt trapped. The boy started to offer him his hand but changed his mind and saluted him instead in a touchingly childish gesture. Then he ran down the winding stairs, two steps at a time. "Wait!" Edu called after him, but the clatter of his feet on the stone stairs kept the word from reaching his ears.

The paintings, once he had unwrapped them and leaned them against the wall so that the light from his two lamps might strike them to best advantage, looked even more beautiful than in the gallery. Had his pleasure in owning them really deepened their colors? In addition to the two Noldes, he had bought a small abstract Franz Marc and a portrait of a woman by Kirchner. When he had finished looking at them, he wrapped them up again. There was no place to hang them, his landlady would not permit it, anyway, and besides, he wanted no one else here to see them.

Edu wished to maintain as much distance from his surroundings as he possibly could. He did not want anything from this time to lodge in his memory. Punctually at ten each night, just before he went to bed, he put a line through the day in the leather-bound pocket calendar his mother gave him for Christmas every year. When it was necessary to speak to other officers, he maintained an aloofness as chilling as theirs. There was no need now to be courteous or smiling; peace negotiations, as everyone knew, were going forward, and Edu was certain to be mustered out the minute an armistice was declared.

He sat in his stuffy room the evening after his visit to Levy and wondered if the boy would return with a young woman. The hot day had left the room stuffy and close, and he opened both windows to let in the cool night air. It had an unpleasant city smell, and the noises from the courtyard floated on it—screechings and yowlings from cats and dogs and the bawling of angry humans. It was a habitation as alien to Edu as a tribal village on the African veldt.

The knock on his door startled him, although he had been thinking about the promised assignation. He almost did not answer, but at the second knock he found his courage and let the ear-locked boy and his "cousin" in. The boy was dressed exactly as before. The young woman with him could not have been more than nineteen with a delicate oval face. She was not beautiful, but the loveliness of youth was still on her features. She wore her dark hair loosely wound around her head, so that it covered her ears; her mouth was full and her dark eyes expressed absolute, dumb terror.

"This is Friedl," the boy said. "She's very quiet." The young woman tried to smile but seemed to find it impossible. It occurred to Edu that she might be a deaf-mute.

"Can she speak?" he asked. "Does she know German?"

"A little. She's from out there . . ." The boy made a gesture toward what he assumed was the east. "She had a hard time with the Russians. But she's all right. She's clean. You can pay me."

Friedl sat down on the edge of the red plush armchair, her hands pressed together between her stiffly held knees, making a deep valley in her lap. Her shoulders were narrow, a child's shoulders, and her dress was thin and just covered her knees. The pose reminded Edu of a girl in a painting by Edvard Munch, but her face was that of his niece Emma, only a little more common. It was an unsettled face. Besides the terror, there was sensuality and an abjectness that touched Edu and aroused him. He took out some paper money.

"She's worth more than an ordinary whore," the boy said, but his voice was unsteady. "And her brothers and sisters are hungry. Her mother is dead and her father sick and can't work . . ."

"That's enough," said Edu. Friedl had not changed expression during this litany. He peeled off some bills, hardly counting them, thinking of his house and his family and his paintings, growing suddenly furious to find himself in a situation from which there was now no escape, no honorable withdrawal. With a gesture that looked as if he was about to strike the boy, he shoved the money at him and told him to get out.

"This is where she lives," the boy said and gave Edu a piece of paper with an address written on it. He put the money, which he had counted with his eyes while Edu peeled it off his roll, in his back pocket and once again ran down the stone stairs two at a time.

Edu closed the door and sat on the day bed, facing Friedl.

"Well," he said, "what shall we do?" He was unwilling to approach Friedl as he would a real whore. She looked down at the floor

and shrugged her shoulders in that infuriating way of the Jews. He
almost grabbed her to shake her free of her multitude of bad habits,
but he recognized at once he must not.

"Shall I undress?" Friedl asked in a German that sounded like
pure Yiddish to Edu's ears.

"No," he answered, "not just yet. We have plenty of time."

Friedl looked at him and seemed to summon up all her courage.
"I'm hungry," she said. It was the first time her eyes met his.

"I'll take you out to dinner," Edu said and got up immediately
to fetch his hat and coat, glad to have something to do. Out in the
street the chill of night met them with a suddenness that sent a shiver
through Edu and set Friedl's teeth to chattering.

"You don't have a jacket?" he asked her, and she shook her head.
He took off his coat and put it around her. "I shall buy you one,"
he said. If he had found a store open, he would have gone into it
then and there and made the purchase.

They went to a nearby restaurant where Edu often ate, and he
ordered a meal for Friedl and a bottle of wine for himself. She looked
at him for a second when the plate was brought to her and then
began to eat ravenously. She looked like a small, delicate animal, a
Siamese cat perhaps, that had just had a dish of something delectable
set before it. Edu, drinking the awful wine slowly, watched her, and
an odd assortment of thoughts followed one another through his
mind. Foremost among them was the puzzlement he felt at being
there. He was suddenly reminded of the long-ago time when he
went to see that dreadful painter. For someone like Edu, who felt
safe only in a world he knew and controlled, moments like this were
rare, and he could explain his presence in the restaurant with Friedl
only by thinking himself in the grip of some fever, as though he'd
been put under a spell. Even alone in America, he had never allowed
himself to become involved in such a bizarre affair. He had always
been certain that the things he needed to learn—his education, in
other words—would never come to him on the street or in a
woman's arms. He doubted that it was even necessary to have
experienced love to be the kind of man he wanted to be. He had
never until now felt a longing for romance or fear for his sanity.
Now he was floating on the cheap wine toward both.

"Oh, good," said Friedl, finishing the last bit of bread with the last dab of gravy on her plate.

"What would you like to do now?" Edu asked.

Friedl lowered her eyes. She seemed even younger than Emma; she ought to have been rolling a hoop down the Berlin streets.

"How old are you?" Edu asked.

"Twenty-two," she said, and he wondered if he should believe her.

"Do you dance?" he asked, and again she shrugged her Jewish shrug. "I like to watch dancing," she said.

When they walked back to Edu's room he saw that she was no longer shivering so hard, but he gave her his coat, anyway. No one looked at the two walking down the street; there were too many other couples like them. But they did not touch, they walked side by side, only their breaths mingled.

Edu poured brandy into the two silver tumblers that had come with his leather traveling set. The brandy was good. He had bought it from someone on the black market. Friedl did not touch hers. There was nothing to say. The questions Edu might have asked seemed pointless: Friedl wanted to reveal nothing, know nothing.

"Would you like to see my pictures?" he asked, and Friedl to his surprise said yes. Edu unwrapped them all and arranged them to their best advantage. "The light is terrible," he said. "You can see them much better in the daytime."

Edu felt the excitement that always possessed him when he looked at pictures—his pictures. He squatted before them and began to tell Friedl what he saw there. He talked about the colors and the composition, and some of what he said he knew was pure nonsense, but he didn't care particularly, the words were words of love. He chattered on and did not look up at Friedl until, in the middle of a sentence, he needed some confirmation. It was then that he saw her, sitting stark naked on the day bed. Her hands were squeezed between her thighs again, the hollow between her shoulders was in shadow, but Edu could see her two small white breasts, the breasts of a young girl. She looked almost in a trance.

Edu carefully put away the pictures, undressed, turned off the light and made love to the silent girl. Friedl's body was pliant and cool, and she held it very still for him. She made no demands, and she did not reach orgasm, nor did she try to pretend that she had. When Edu had come and lay beside her, she licked his ear and began to hum a tune that sounded like a Slavic lullaby. "Don't," he said, and she was still again, stiller than death.

When Edu woke up, an hour or so later, it had gotten cold in the room and Friedl was asleep, curled into herself, at the foot of the bed. "I must take you home," Edu said, and she awoke as silently as she did everything else. She dressed as though in a dream and sat waiting for him on the red-plush armchair. Edu gave her one of his sweaters. "You may keep it," he said. It reached below her hips and the sleeves were too long, the shoulders too wide.

"How soft it is," she said and pushed up the sleeves and took the belt from her dress to tie it over the sweater.

She looked almost chic, and Edu saw that if she had a mind to, she could make herself over, the instinct for style was there.

"It's cashmere," he said, but the word meant nothing to Friedl. She rubbed her hand over the wool and put her nose to her shoulder. "It smells of you," she said.

Edu could not find a cab, so they walked hurriedly through the streets. Friedl knew her way, Edu did not need to refer to the piece of paper with her address on it. In front of an old six-story apartment building in the Jewish quarter, Friedl stopped. "I live here," she said.

"Will you come to see me again?" Edu asked.

Friedl shrugged. He took some money from his wallet and went to press it into her hand, but she dropped it at his feet and shook her head. Edu picked up the bills. "Please take them," he said, "for the jacket I promised you."

"You already paid me," she said. *"Gut' Nacht."* Edu heard her measured steps retreating up the stairs.

A week or so later Edu saw her again—or thought he did—in an artists' café. Friedl, if it was she, sat between two slovenly Bohemians who were talking with great intensity and many gestures. The café was impossibly crowded and Edu could not get in; he saw the scene only as a dumbshow. "Don't block the door," the bouncer said, "wait your turn."

Edu looked into the smoke-filled room through the window and saw Friedl sit as still and untouchable between the two as she had sat in his room. The steamy breath from his mouth clouded the glass after a few minutes, and he could see no more. It began to rain, and Edu went home. The two Bohemians reminded him again of the painter in that Frankfurt garret—Franz Bleicher, that was his name! Edu had never heard it again, and neither, as far as he knew, had anyone else.

He passed by the café several more times in the following week but did not see Friedl. He waited for the boy, but he did not come either. Then he went to the gallery, intending to ask Levy to send him the boy to help him move some furniture. But Levy was sick and Edu could not bring himself to make inquiries of the woman who was there in his place. Finally he took the piece of paper he had saved and found the street of miserable tenements where he had left Friedl. But no one would give him any information. The old men pretended not to understand German, the young ones said "not here" or "wrong place." They must have thought Edu was with the police, but that was something he could not possibly have understood. He retreated before their bearded, contemptuous faces, knowing that they despised him but powerless to do anything about it.

A few days later, news of the mutiny at Kiel reached Berlin. Throughout the land, a population grown tired of the war rebelliously shouted for the abdication of the Kaiser. City after city fell to an advance guard of mutinous sailors, industrial workers and soldiers who would no longer fight.

Even Frankfurt was taken over by the Reds for a brief time. Mercifully, no blood was shed. The bourgeoisie looked on apprehensively, even though the speeches that rang out from the throats of the revolutionaries were filled with familiar, time-worn rhetoric. "We believe in truth, we do not fear it," they said. Alas, they had neither the support of the populace nor control over its institutions. They did not carry the day. In Berlin, where everything was finally decided, events moved swiftly to their conclusion. The Kaiser was forced into abdication and flight. An unwilling Social-Democratic government took over and turned to the generals to help it quell "the threat from the Bolsheviks." The Armistice was signed. The war was over.

Edu was mustered out soon thereafter. Along with thousands of others he headed home. Although he had to stand most of the way or lie on the floor of the baggage car and the journey took four days, he finally stood in the wintry garden of his house once more, ready to take up where he had left off four years before. The lights were on, the butler greeted him with a warm handshake, the maid curtsied, there was a fire in the grate. He could hang his pictures on the walls of his house and sleep without doubt or fear or romantic delusions.

ERNST and Andreas Wertheim walked home from school almost every day with Thomas von Brenda-Badolet when they were let out shortly after one o'clock. After dinner they were expected to do their homework, but they sometimes spent part of the afternoon together in the Palmengarten or walking through the Anlagen.

It was not a good winter. Peace had brought an end to hostilities but not to hunger and privation. The ranks of the needy were swelled by hundreds of thousands of returning soldiers, most of them jobless. The Wertheim offspring, like other wealthy children, were only dimly aware of events and lived much as they always had. Tables were set a little less sumptuously, and there were fewer servants for a while. The teachers warned them to avoid certain squares and places where the proletariat gathered, for there was still danger of violence, but if they stayed in the West End, safely on *their* side of the Taunus Anlage and the Bockenheimer Anlage, they could walk unmolested, their eyes on the beautiful villas.

When the boys stopped in front of the Wertheim house on the Guiollettstrasse, Ernst or Andreas would often try to invite Tom to come in with them. He always refused. This embarrassed them, and they therefore never talked about it. One particular day was very cold and they had walked fast. At the steps to their house, Andreas said, "It's early today, do you want to come in?"

Tom hesitated for once. "Maybe for just a few minutes," he said. "My parents are away for the day."

"If you want to call home to your governess and ask if you can stay for dinner . . ." Andreas began, but Tom shook his head. "I couldn't do that," he said.

Emma and Lene, who had a shorter walk from the *Höhere Töchter-*

schule, a private academy for girls, were already home and had changed their clothes when the three boys appeared. They met in the front hall, and Andreas noticed that Lene's face brightened with pleasure and a blush when she saw Tom. He greeted her, and his eyes never strayed from hers. Emma frowned, and Andreas, too, felt excluded.

"What are *you* doing here?" Lene asked.

"Your brothers invited me in."

"I'm going to show him my room," said Andreas, "he doesn't have much time."

"All right," said Lene with an elaborate display of nonchalance, "don't share your friends!"

Fräulein Gründlich came to the head of the stairs at that moment and saw the guest immediately. "How very nice to see you, Tom," she said, and if one were not well tuned to subtleties of voice and manner, one might have believed she was the children's mother. "Perhaps you'll join us for our midday meal," she added. Fräulein Gründlich had always realized that Thomas von Brenda-Badolet was a person of importance.

"Oh, no, thank you, I couldn't. I'm not allowed. That is to say, I must be home for all my meals." Tom's gracious tone made the governess smile at him as though he had just paid her a compliment. Ernst thought it no wonder that mothers and maids adored him.

All three boys hurried upstairs, and when he passed Fräulein Gründlich, Tom gave her another of his handsome smiles.

"Don't play too long," she called after them, "dinner will be ready in twenty minutes."

"We're too *old* to play," said Ernst with outraged dignity.

They went directly to Andreas' room, where most of the treasures were kept in almost military order and neatness. Tom studied everything he was shown with polite attention. He was surprised and a little appalled at the opulence of his friends' possessions and was afraid that his feelings would show. His father believed that children should be raised in Spartan simplicity—even when they lived in a world where riches were taken for granted—and Tom never received but a single, useful gift for Christmas.

Andreas had just started up the electric train when Lene entered the room without knocking.

"Don't you know better than to come bursting in like that?" Andreas yelled, irritated because he had just begun to set out his collection of tin soldiers.

"I brought Tom a cookie," said Lene. She was munching on one herself.

"Only for me?" Tom asked. "How about your brothers?"

"They can fend for themselves," she said. "They know where we keep them."

"Have you gotten taller since last spring," Tom asked, "or merely thinner?" He was paying no attention to either the train or the soldiers.

"I lost a little weight," said Lene.

"You'll put it back with all those cookies," said Ernst.

"Did you hear that my dog died?" Lene asked Tom. "He was killed by a burglar, we think, who put poison in some meat. Isn't that awful? I'm only glad I wasn't here to see him. Mama offered me a new puppy for Christmas, but I don't want to have such a terrible thing happen again. Papa had them put big new locks on all the doors."

"Tom doesn't want to hear about a dead dog," said Andreas.

He sat cross-legged among his possessions while Ernst on the window seat watched Tom and Lene. He had wanted to take Tom to see his hidden cache of Karl May novels, but he knew that he hadn't a chance now. Lene was urging Tom to look at her collection of stuffed animals.

"It isn't proper to go into a girl's room," said Andreas, putting his soldiers back into their boxes.

"Gründlich is watching," said Lene. "Her door is open," she whispered, "she can hear every word we're saying."

Tom dutifully allowed himself to be introduced to every one of the Steiff animals, which Lene did with mock seriousness. "They have very distinct personalities," she said. Because it was winter they all wore sweaters, which Lene had crocheted "when I was much younger," she added, "years and years ago."

All too soon Fräulein Gründlich appeared at the door to call her to dinner. Tom quickly made his adieux.

"I'll see you in school tomorrow," he said to Ernst and Andreas.

Lene had trailed after him to the front door. "Can you visit me again?" she asked.

"I'll take you for a walk in the Palmengarten," he said and raced home, afraid of what the governess would tell his parents.

THAT EVENING there was a very large gathering at Hannchen's house to welcome Edu home from the army. The children went, even though it promised to be a late night. They stayed for a while with the grownups, then withdrew with their cousins to the library and had their own party.

The adults had opened the last of the good prewar bottles of champagne. All who had been invited came, even Jacob, who was not yet fully mended. Elias and Bettina had brought eight-year-old Benno with them, to everyone's strong disapproval. He was left in the care of the maid, who put him to sleep in Moritz's old bedroom and went back to reading her paper.

It was chilly in the big house, and Bruno had to keep putting more coal in the grate.

"Here we all are," said Hannchen, "it is like old times, thank God."

No one contradicted her. She had grown heavier still, and her hair had turned snow white, but her face was as rosily cheerful as ever. "I love *all* my sons," she said, lifting her glass of champagne, "but I must tell you that I missed Edu very, very much." Something like a sob entered her voice, but she swallowed it bravely. "Welcome home!" she said, and they all drank a toast to Edu.

Hannchen patted Jacob on his knee and told him he looked well. She inquired after Siegmund's quartet and asked Nathan to tell her how the children had enjoyed their summer. "They've been home for three months," said Nathan. "They seem none the worse for wear."

"You always say that," Hannchen scolded. "You pay no attention at all to what they're doing and how they're growing up. It's a disgrace!"

"Why not ask them yourself?" Siegmund said. "They're all here tonight."

"*You* know they don't talk to an old lady like me," Hannchen said. "And even when they have something to say, it's not very illuminating. I look to their parents to tell me how they are faring and whether they are developing satisfactorily. Emma is old enough to be married, after all. I hope you are keeping an eye on her," she said to Caroline.

"Have you seen the beautiful paintings Edu bought in Berlin?" Caroline asked her.

"But of course," she answered, "I was the first person he showed them to."

The old lady continued to lead the conversation. It was a merry and congenial evening, but Hannchen wondered now and then why neither her sons nor her daughters-in-law ever knew any more about their children than the state of their health and obedience and how well they did in school.

THOMAS VON BRENDA-BADOLET, true to his word, stopped by the house again two weeks later. It was a Sunday afternoon, and he asked to see Caroline Wertheim because he wanted to take Lene to the opera the following Saturday. "They are playing *The Magic Flute*," he said. "I thought Lene would enjoy Mozart." He did not mention that he had never forgotten her appearance as the young composer five years before at his party.

Caroline told him that she felt certain Lene would adore *The Magic Flute*, and she had no objection whatever but would ask her husband to be absolutely sure that there were no other family plans. She disappeared into Nathan's study while Tom sat on the chintz-covered couch in the living room and studied the large paintings which were so dark with varnish that it was hard to make out their subject matter.

"Why should I have any objection?" Nathan asked Caroline. He hadn't expected to be bothered for such a trifle. "The Brenda-Badolets are one of the first families of Frankfurt."

"But Lene is only fifteen," Caroline said.

"*The Magic Flute* won't corrupt her."

"And Thomas?"

"Thomas *certainly* won't. Don't you know that boys at that age are innocence personified? Just look at your own two. Better worry about Thomas' virtue! Lene knows what she wants."

And so permission was given. Lene was happy all week.

"Will you ask me for the carriage?" Tom's father wanted to know. They had an automobile, but old von Brenda-Badolet, as he was known around town, kept it in the garage and tried to use it only when absolutely necessary. He had become more and more crotchety with age. Two of his sons had been killed in the war. Tom had told Andreas that his father reminded him of old Prince Bolkonsky, Prince Andrew's father in *War and Peace*. Tom was forever finding people in real life who were like characters in novels. Andreas decided he ought to read Tolstoi. Hanno Altenburg had recommended him too.

"I don't want the carriage," said Tom. "We're only going up to the Opera House."

"Don't be surprised if that little Jewish girl is disappointed in you," the old man muttered.

"She's not like that at all, Papa," said Tom.

"Nonsense! They're *all* like that. Women are either gold diggers or pious fools." (His wife had developed the unpleasant habit of constantly doing church work. Missions to the heathen and the poor were her favorite charities. "She's just like the old Consul Buddenbrook's wife in the second generation," said Tom. But Andreas was too busy with Tolstoi to take up Thomas Mann.)

Tom stood respectfully in front of his father. He never tried to convince him of the justice of any of his opinions. Most of the time he met both of his parents' idiosyncrasies with silence. They had tried in vain to enlist him in their causes. At seventeen Thomas was already fully independent in thought and spirit, but he never made an issue of it. Courtly in his relationships with everyone, he was unfit for any role save that of an enlightened eighteenth-century man of the world, a character, as he was the first to recognize, out of *Elective Affinities*. Of course, one always returned to Goethe.

Lene wore her favorite party dress. It was lined, belted loosely at the hips and reached just above her ankles. Caroline let her wear the single strand of pearls she kept in a safe place for her. Her new coat, made by the seamstress from one of Caroline's which had gone out of style, and the matching hat suited her perfectly. Her face was already aglow with pleasure when Tom called for her, and she seemed to him beautiful indeed. He was proud to have her on his arm and certain that every head turned to look at them. Walking to the Opera House through the Anlagen, they held hands. They knew they were in love though they were as yet too inexperienced to articulate it and perhaps too frightened of the idea to try.

Tom had been given his parents' seats in a box, and they felt very grown-up indeed. "It's as if we were royalty," Lene whispered as they sat down in the soft plush seats beneath a host of garlands and gilded putty. She did not actually think that princes and princesses lived an enviable life. They had, she knew, no freedom at all, and freedom was what she currently craved more than anything. Still, the eyes of the whole world were upon them, and they lived in castles and were taken everywhere in coaches. She had never forgotten the tapestry in Tom's father's study, and when she found a book in Uncle Jacob's store in which there were illustrations for the whole unicorn cycle, she pestered him to let her have it and forever after preserved that vision of the royal life. And Tom was the perfect prince, no doubt about that. He was so very handsome, with his wide-set deep-blue eyes, his shock of blond hair—not straw-colored but honey—unruly above his high forehead. He wore a signet ring with the family crest on it, and Lene saw it glint now and then on his slender hand. Fräulein Gründlich always said one could tell character and class from a person's hands.

"Have you ever heard *The Magic Flute*?" Tom asked. Lene shook her head. "Me neither," he said.

"Mama told me the story before I came today. She got the whole libretto out for me to read, but that was too much!"

"The same thing happened at my house," Tom said, and in his delight he took her hand.

The houselights dimmed, the conductor entered the pit, the audience clapped and then, very quickly, the overture rang out. Soon the curtains opened, and Lene allowed a surprised rapturous "Oooh . . ." to escape her. The sets were old and dusty—no new production of any kind had been mounted during the war—but they seemed magical nonetheless. And the music turned out to contain one familiar tune after another. Lene had not realized before how surrounded by music she had been all her life. The house was forever filled with it—Papa made chamber music with Uncle Siegmund and Uncle Jacob, the boys practiced daily, and she—she absolutely *must* go back to the piano; maybe Papa would allow her to resume lessons if she promised to practice very hard.

The action on the stage drew the two children forward in their seats. Even knowing that it would end happily, they could not help fearing for the lovers, hating the evil Queen of Night. They laughed over Papageno in his bird feathers, blowing on his pipe. Only Sarastro with his deep voice and priestly garments puzzled them a little. Intermission seemed to come in no time at all, and when they walked down to the lobby, they both felt themselves deep in the magic land of the magic flute.

"Would you like some orangeade?" Tom asked.

"Of course," said Lene, "isn't that part of going to the opera?"

It tasted terrible and not even the color was orange.

"It wasn't good before the war, either," said Tom, and they poured their drinks into a potted palm.

A group of people standing near the bar noticed them.

"Isn't that old von Brenda-Bandolet's boy?"

"Indeed, and with a Jewish girl."

"Do you know her?"

"One of the Wertheim clan, I believe."

"Money there."

"Isn't there always?"

"Lucky von Bre-Ba!"

"Would *you* encourage such a liaison?"

"I have certain principles, but I might bend them for financial considerations."

There was some laughter, none of it pleasant.

"They're only children, for heaven's sake," said one member of the group, a woman who was in the box next to Tom and Lene and had been charmed by their innocence.

"Such things often begin in the cradle."

"Especially when there's ambition involved."

"Or money."

"Aren't they the same?"

"Push push push."

"I've yet to find a good argument for Emancipation."

"It hardly matters, we're stuck with it."

"Your conversation is revolting," the same woman said and turned on her heel to walk away. Her husband looked after her. "Don't pay any attention to the whore," he said. "She gives herself airs. Her father was Rothschild's barber."

Tom and Lene, who thought all eyes were upon them because they were in love and beautiful, did not hear this conversation. They did not, that day, hear any conversation but their own. They watched the opera and listened intently, and during intermissions they told each other about their vacations. Tom had been in a distant part of East Prussia to visit relatives of his mother.

"It's so very desolate out there," he said to Lene, "it seems you can see the whole world spread to the horizon. Even the colors aren't like those in our countryside. It's as if earth and sky squeeze something out of the landscape in between."

He was a little embarrassed at having given voice to these perceptions, which he had thought about a great deal, and a slight stutter entered his speech, but Lene was obviously happy to hear him out. So he finished smoothly and even added a spontaneous coda.

"Living in such a place, you become absorbed by the immensity of nature, but it also forces you back on your own thoughts, and if they desert you or seem intolerably vain and artificial, life can be terribly lonely. The people there are caught in the rhythm of the seasons and the farm work that follows them; you have to be in tune with that. But I'm not, I guess. You know, I realize I'd hate to give up living in Frankfurt, going to the opera like this or taking the tram just anywhere . . . But I understand better about Tolstoi now," he said in conclusion.

Just then the bell rang, and the two returned to their seats.

Dusk and a cold mist had settled over the city when they left the Opera House to walk home. Frankfurt had a grim aspect in this light. There were police barricades everywhere and debris in the streets. In the bareness of winter, the city's unkempt look was exaggerated and had a sinister dimension. Lene shuddered. The contrast with the warm, bright Opera House and its enchanted land of make-believe was too strong. Tom put his arm around her, and they walked in step close together toward home.

The Wertheim family was at tea when they got back. Hannchen was there, and the children felt the curious eyes of the grownups upon them. Tom's conversation was smooth and polite. He answered all the questions put to him—who sang which part and was the performance well attended; how did the old sets look and did the Queen of Night reach those high notes? Everyone had a contribution to make, and Nathan at one point got up and played Papageno's aria "Ein Mädchen oder Weibchen" for them on the piano. Lene was a little embarrassed; she remembered the chill formality of Tom's house, but he seemed not to mind the lively attention and sat down next to Hannchen to have a cup of tea.

"Who was in the box with you?" Caroline asked her daughter.

"I didn't know them," said Lene, "but Tom told me his father called them *parvenus* who got rich in the war."

When Tom at last decided he could not stay another minute, he took his farewell as politely as he had made his salutations, and Lene walked him to the front door.

"I like your family," Tom said. "They're articulate and warm. I especially like your Uncle Jacob."

Lene groaned, but she was flattered all the same. They shook hands.

"Remember when I kissed you in front of my father's tapestry?" Tom said.

"Of course I do! I'll never forget it."

"Well—I'll kiss you again—next time!" And Tom bounded down the steps laughing like an impish child and turned to wave once more before he disappeared around the corner of the garden wall.

That evening Lene sat for a long time in front of the mirror brushing her hair. Fräulein Gründlich looked in on her every few minutes, wondering when she would finish.

"So you had a good time with Thomas at the opera?" she asked. It wasn't the first time she had posed the question. "You're becoming vain, I notice, brushing your hair like that. I remember when you used to jump into bed without giving it a single stroke."

Fräulein Gründlich experienced life through her charges. She had not had the opportunity to fall in love herself, her flirtation with Alois notwithstanding, so she painted pictures of love from the models she saw around her. She collected information from books and newspapers, gossip and old wives' tales, and poured it into those outlines she knew best. She experienced the children's joy as well as their pain. She wanted to comfort and advise them but realized only too well that they probably knew more about these things than she ever would.

Lene, still dreaming about the afternoon, was in no mood for Fräulein Gründlich tonight. Love had carried her into another world, removed her temporarily from her governess' mundane concerns and pithy maxims. Those of her thoughts that were clear enough to divulge she wanted to share with Emma.

Saying good night to Fräulein Gründlich rather abruptly, Lene turned off the light and got into bed. But sleep would not come, and when the house was utterly still except for the snoring sounds issuing from Fräulein Gründlich's room, Lene tiptoed into the hall to see if there was still a light under Emma's door. There was. Lene knocked softly.

"Come in," said Emma, who had been expecting her. She was lying down with a book resting on the quilt in front of her. Lene sat cross-legged on the foot of the bed. Emma thought her very beautiful just then with her hair wild about her face and her cheeks pink.

"You came to talk to me about *The Magic Flute*?" Emma asked in a jocular, sisterly fashion.

"Oh, Emma," said Lene, "Tom is like no one I ever met. He's all the things you dream about and think are only romantic nonsense. I want to talk about him."

And the words poured out as she recapitulated her afternoon with Tom. She did not mention the opera, the singers or the crowd, except as they were reflected in the mirror of her feelings.

"Do you think I could *marry* him one day?" she asked finally and blushed at having said such a thing.

"He comes from an old and prominent family," said Emma.

"Does that matter?" Lene's indignation rang false, she knew, for the same thought had crossed her mind.

"Of course it matters, dummy. If the world were a better place than it is, it wouldn't matter, but in the scheme of things, birth and privilege count. I hope you won't try to tell me I'm wrong."

"Not only is he from a distinguished family, he's handsome too." Lene was trying to be sarcastic, but her tone must have been wrong, for Emma didn't appear to catch the sarcasm.

"So much the better. Blond and blue-eyed, a veritable Teutonic god. Not one of your Jewish misfits."

Lene heard anger in Emma's voice. Her sister did not look at her but sat primly among her pillows, her quilt drawn up to her throat, looking vexed. Her thin face, which Lene had often envied her, was Jewish in every nuance of color, every finely etched line from brow to chin.

"I like Jewish misfits," Lene said defiantly.

"I suppose that's how come you're in love with Thomas von Brenda-Badolet?"

Lene had no ready answer to that.

"Jews cut such an absurd figure in the world," Emma went on heatedly. "They should all disappear."

"What an awful thing to say! Do you want *us* to disappear?"

"I want us to be like everybody else. Not to be different all the time, sticking out like weeds in the garden."

"I don't think we stick out. We *are* like everyone else. At least here in Frankfurt we are. We don't go around, you know, dressed in a crazy costume, talking with our hands."

"We don't, I know, but the Christians see us like that."

"Only the dumb ones."

"No, Lene, no. We deserve their contempt, we're so stiff-necked —the chosen people! Oh, how I wish I were Christian!"

"But you are what you are, you can't change that. It would be like cutting off your hair and wearing trousers and saying you're a man."

Emma turned her head toward Lene and saw her own face in the mirror of the dressing table that stood behind her sister.

"Damn my face," she said with heartrending bitterness, "damn my Jewish nose and my kinky Jewish hair . . ."

"You're perfectly lovely!" cried Lene, absolute honesty ringing in her voice. "You've always been prettier than I am. I've envied you all my life!"

"But it's you who's caught Tom . . ."

"I didn't plan it that way, Emma. You don't mean to tell me that you're jealous? It isn't that *you* want him, is it?"

"No, no! Of course not. He's much too young, he's still only a boy, and he's soft too, almost Jewishly soft . . . I would just like to climb out of my skin and into theirs. Don't you understand that?"

Lene shook her head. She did not understand it at all. "Have you ever told Mama or Papa about this?"

"No. How could I, Lene? I've never said anything except to you, and you musn't tell anyone either."

Lene was flattered by her sister's confidence. As much as she longed to talk about Tom, she knew that what Emma carried in her heart was of greater urgency, if only because Emma's unhappiness was so clear and specific—what was it Thomas had quoted to her from Tolstoi?—and her own happiness filled the world and would, she felt in her innocence, always be there.

"Shall I tell you what happened this summer? Why I left the farm early? It wasn't homesickness."

Emma's voice shifted ever so slightly into a tone more appropriate for confession than casual conversation. She had thought about the humiliations of the summer continuously without being able to bring herself to talk about them. Now she was suddenly ready to tell Lene the whole awful story.

She began by talking about Ilse Stauffer, whom she evoked in minute and loving detail. Her memory reached back over the events of the summer and fastened on her first impression.

"She was so full of vigor, so wholesome a person, I never met anyone like her before. Even Fräulein Gründlich has been corrupted by city life . . . by us. And she was pious in so simple and natural a way. I liked her so much," Emma sighed, "and she liked me too. Until that day when I said I couldn't go back into the barn."

"Why couldn't you?" Lene immediately understood that there were yet greater secrets hidden away in the depths of Emma's heart.

"I . . . I had a bad experience, but never mind."

Lene saw that it was useless to press her sister.

"Not long after that," Emma said, "during the week it rained, we were invited up to the countess' apartments in the manor house. I was looking forward to it, we all were. It was supposed to be the highlight of the summer, and our one opportunity to meet this remarkable woman. Don't laugh. I know you think me foolish to respect aristocratic women of her sort, but she isn't as you'd imagine at all. The peasants adore her."

"Tell Aunt Eva that!"

"Never mind her, she's impossible. So let me continue. The countess was charming and polite. She said she wanted us to feel at home. She spoke to everyone in the kindliest way. Only . . ." Emma's voice was close to breaking, but she caught herself and rushed on, "She didn't say a word to me."

"And you still think she's wonderful?"

"It was a misunderstanding. They play by their own strict rules."

"Go on, tell me the rest."

"We sat down to eat, and I was placed at the end of the table by myself. It was clear by then that I was to be considered a leper." A sob escaped Emma. "The girls all noticed it; how could they not? One by one they stopped talking to me. They all went over to her side, even the ones I thought were my friends. When it came time to say good-bye, we lined up to shake hands and curtsy, but as soon as I approached her, she placed her hands behind her back—not wanting to touch me—and said, 'I understand you let your companions down.' I stammered something. 'Fräulein Stauffer tells me that you refuse to do your appointed chores. She says you shirk your duty. We have no use here for girls like you.' I tried to tell her that I had felt ill, that the odor didn't agree with me, but she cut me off. 'There can be no excuses,' she said. 'God and country demand that we serve without regard for our private desires. But perhaps, being Jewish, you don't understand that.' Everyone was listening, I could only shake my head by then. No, no! my mind cried silently. But she wouldn't have listened, even if I'd fallen on my knees before her. 'I suppose your father made his money in the war,' she said, 'from the blood of our *German* youth.' 'My father is a lawyer,' I told her, 'and my uncle was wounded at Verdun.' 'Lawyers and pawnbrokers,' she sneered. Her last words to me were 'Learn what duty and honor are!'

"I went to Ilse Stauffer and asked her why she had told the countess such a story about me, but she acted as if she didn't know what I was talking about. 'The countess knows what she's doing; unlike me, she's had plenty of experience with Jews. A little discipline never hurt anybody. Be glad she didn't kick you out.'

"Of course I couldn't stay. The girls turned against me, I became their scapegoat. Slips of paper kept showing up among my belongings with little messages on them, like *'Do your duty, Jew.'* The first chance I got I went to the village to find a telephone and called Mama to let me come home."

Emma put her face in her hands and allowed herself the relief of tears at last. She cried bitterly, silently. Lene, who couldn't bear to see anyone cry, sat helplessly at the foot of the bed saying, "Don't, Emma, please don't . . ."

But, to herself, she admitted some doubts, questions that would not go away. Had Emma asked for it? Had she wanted to be humiliated, cast out? Why wasn't she angry? Did she agree with them? Lene thought of what she would have done, what she would like to do this very minute. And all her feelings centered on revenge.

"Don't cry," she said, "they're terrible people and not worth your tears. Fräulein Gründlich would tell you 'Sticks and stones may break your bones,' and so forth and so on. You must forget it, Emma. Stop thinking about them."

"But I wanted so much to have them like me," Emma sobbed.

Not until the clock in the hall struck midnight did Lene leave her sister's room and go to bed. Emma was calm by then and could muster a smile. They kissed each other good night, and there were dark circles of tiredness under their eyes. Their black hair fell in tousled curls down to their white gowns; they resembled each other very much—two princesses from the Orient cast up on a snowy northern shore.

IT PROVED to be a very bad winter, blowing in on the heels of a war that had sapped the country's strength and a peace that left a legacy of resentments. Pestilence struck not only Germany but the whole world. It was like the havoc sent by an avenging God to chastise an obstreperous people. Millions died as the winter howled on; every family counted its dead. Aunt Berthe, who was old and senile, was the first to go. Jacob lay in bed delirious for two weeks, and no one believed he would live. Gerda nursed him with her usual silent sufficiency, only to be stricken herself as soon as Jacob had passed the crisis. She was ill no more than three days, and then one morning early she died. She had said nothing during her illness, she left the world as silently as she had dwelt in it. Jacob sat at her bedside scarcely strong enough to move from his chair, but it was not his physical weakness that kept him there. He sat dry-eyed and unbelieving, reciting a litany of his love and dereliction. He sat through the dank daylight hours and into the evening when it began to snow. He did not answer the phone or call a doctor, and it was Siegmund who finally came and found him, toward ten in the evening.

Jacob arranged for the funeral and went to it alone. He forbade his brothers to come because he was afraid they would not, and this way the decision had been his. On her stone he put her name and his behind it. The only other word he had inscribed on it was BELOVED. He secretly bought a plot next to hers, though the cemetery was not the Jewish one, and wrote a letter which he filed with his papers noting his wish to be buried beside her.

Weeks and months followed when he sat in his rooms and wished he would die. But he could never find the way, and after a while the thoughts of death left him and he began to remember Gerda without anguish or guilt.

IV

1923

THE SEVERAL years after the end of the First World War were years of tumult. Events followed one another in panic succession, and inflation was rampant. Rosa Luxemburg and Karl Liebknecht were murdered in 1919, the French occupied the Ruhr in 1920, and on April 6 of that year their troops marched into Frankfurt. The year 1920 also saw the birth of the National Socialist Party. But the single most awful and doom-shrouded act of those years was the death of Walther Rathenau, the Jewish Foreign Minister, who was murdered on June 24, 1922, by a group of nationalists who believed they were serving their country's interests.

Nathan Wertheim grew increasingly melancholy in those years, but it was not, as with others of his class, for mourning the past. He simply could not remember a time when he had been happy, when Caroline had not been fearful, when there had been no crises or tragedies.

Edu threw himself into the business, trying to hold on to gains large and small, to reach a market that promised to grow beyond all expectation. The children enjoyed themselves on the whole, although sometimes Frankfurt struck them as dangerous and decayed. Yet that decay had helped to loosen the bonds of convention that, twenty years earlier, would have kept them safe, the boys in the counting house, the girls in the garden, walking with parasols to shield them from the sun. Codes of conduct were no longer so rigid, even as clothes had become looser, simpler, more casual.

Siegmund Wertheim maintained his happy-go-lucky way of life; he was incapable of serious reflection and did not know how to mourn. Jacob had had his fill of grief in the months after Gerda died.

Eva Süsskind certainly did not mourn the past. She returned to Frankfurt from a pilgrimage to the Soviet Union convinced, like Lincoln Steffens, that she had seen the future and it worked. All her dreams and hopes were for the moment concentrated on the vision she had brought back with her. She visited Caroline and sat on the sofa, which had recently been re-covered in gold velvet, smoking her Russian cigarettes and telling her sister about collective farms and hydroelectric plants. She wore the same baggy blouse and blue serge skirt she always wore, but she had added a colorful Russian peasant scarf, which she tied around her neck and exhibited with a mixture of challenging pride and vanity.

Her mind had responded immediately, almost instinctively, to the stimulus of Soviet technology, to socialist equality for women, to facts and figures on production and modernization and the heady proclamations of a classless society. Eva had never had any patience with the convolutions and intricacies of human relationships; she made "the best friend of my life" every other day and could wax enthusiastic over someone with whom she had spent an hour discussing the wheat harvest in the Ukraine. She had never stolen a kiss or had one stolen from her. She was brave and true and kind, and her intelligence was sharp—"too sharp for a woman" she was told again and again—but it did not help her overcome her naïve trust in the goodness of all who embraced her and called her "Comrade."

One late morning, on a hot summer's day, she was there, at the Guiollettstrasse, and the doors to the garden were open. Caroline gazed out, only half listening to her sister. The view calmed her, not only because it was gracious and lovely but, even more important, because it was familiar. Caroline clung to the familiar with what Eva thought amounted to terror. The sisters were tense in each other's company. Caroline found Eva's cigarette smoke annoying and waved her hand in front of her face. She also suspected that Eva did not wash as often as she should, she had the aura, the mottled look, of someone too preoccupied with larger matters to care about personal habits or tastes.

"What you're telling me about the Russians," Caroline said suddenly with greater vehemence than she had meant to betray, "means nothing to me, nothing at all. They seem to me to be an Asiatic, strange and savage people, brutes who are no different now than they were under the Czar—whom they murdered so brutally with his wife and small children. You cannot change people overnight. Hydroelectric plants won't make the Russians into civilized Westerners."

"They were so oppressed under the czars, naturally they became brutalized," Eva said, determined not to lose her composure, "but they are at heart a good and generous people, and under the Soviet rule, under Socialism, their better nature is given free reign. I *do* think you can change people when you change the conditions under which they live." Her voice rose passionately. Her cigarette ash fell on the couch and lay in a small gray pile on the new velvet upholstery. Caroline meant to ignore it, but she could not take her eyes from the spot until Eva, aware of her sister's pained gaze, hastily brushed it off. It rose in a small cloud and scattered onto the Bokhara carpet.

"The French Revolution changed the course of world history, and so will the Russian. No one will be able to halt it, no one can ignore its message: 'Arise ye prisoners of starvation, arise ye wretched of the earth . . .' That's what we sing, and that's what the peasants and the workers of the world hear. It cannot be held up— it is inevitable. And it is *right* that it should be so."

"I really don't want to argue with you," said Caroline. "I know too little about history. That may be a failing, but you remember I could never remember all the emperors of Germany crowned down in the Cathedral next to the Römer . . ."

"Learning the names of emperors by rote isn't history!"

"I do know something about other things, and I'm interested in what Russia has to offer culturally. They say that the Hermitage is filled with great treasures, and that Moscow and St. Petersburg—"

"They call it Petrograd now . . ." Eva interrupted.

"—are beautiful cities."

"What is a beautiful city if the people are wretched who live there? Beautiful cities testify to the tastes of the ruling cliques, the courts and princes. The glory that was Greece is the glory of a civilization that practiced slavery."

"Didn't the czars free the serfs?"

"Not until 1861. Which is exactly what I meant when I said the long history of oppression under the czars."

"You saw nothing beautiful then?"

"I saw people struggling to build a new world. *That* was beautiful!"

"Eva, for heaven's sake stop speaking in slogans! You sound like a propaganda machine."

"I tell you no more than the truth. Everywhere I went I was welcomed with open arms, with hugs and kisses. And if the people had one loaf of bread, they shared it with me; and if they had only half a loaf, they'd share it with me too. Do you know something that happened to me, that I witnessed there, riding one day in Moscow on a crowded tram? A man made an anti-Semitic remark, which is to say he called another passenger a dirty Jew. And the conductor —who, incidentally, was a woman—hauled him off the bus and handed him over to a policeman, all the while giving him a lecture on the moral as well as the legal wrong of what he had done. My Russian isn't good enough to understand it all, but a comrade who was with me translated most of what I missed."

"That's very nice," said Caroline. "All that and hydroelectric plants too."

"They began six years ago a hundred years behind the West. The magnitude of their achievement is both technical and human."

"I still say you cannot change human nature, and neither can you change a culture overnight."

Eva put out her cigarette with great energy. "There's no reason for us to be arguing," she said. "You have your views, and I have mine. But I never cease hoping that I'll be able to bring a breath of something new and fresh into your life. You are like a prisoner in this house, removed from the world, but I'm not certain that you even know it. And if they ever come and set you free, it'll probably seem like the end of life to you."

"Don't attack me," said Caroline, her voice mournful. A sudden rush of pity for her sister swept over Eva. At the same time she wanted to shake her, march her out into the "real" world, where one was jostled by crowds and had to make one's way alone. Caroline in turn felt the panic she always felt when threatened by the forces of passion; her breath caught in her chest, as though a hand had been put to her throat. She looked about the room, which was filled with sunlight. Everything was where it was supposed to be. Caroline breathed more easily. She would take some valerian drops as soon as Eva had gone. She would lie down and rest, a thin handkerchief over her eyes. And then, when she was quite relaxed, she would arrange some flowers for the dinner table and go back to her miniatures if it had got a little cooler.

Eva noticed Caroline's distracted expression, but she lit another cigarette and prepared to launch into a new barrage of stories. She had spent twelve weeks in the Soviet Union, and those weeks had been filled with incidents, every one capable of being transformed into a moral tale like the one she had told Caroline about the anti-Semite on the bus. It was Lene who finally put an end to the tête-à-tête by appearing unannounced at the garden door. Tom was directly behind her. They were out of breath and moved with impetuous haste.

"Calm yourselves and sit down," said Caroline. "You see Aunt Eva is here."

"We've been bicycling," Lene said. "I'd give you a kiss, Aunt Eva, but I'm all perspired. You know Tom by now. Traffic in the city is brutal. We got out as fast as we could and headed for the Stadtwald and drank some beer at the Oberschweinstiege, where it was jammed . . . with 'proletarians,' as Tom said in his arrogant way. Please excuse us, Aunt Eva. It's horribly hot."

Lene wore her hair short, brushed back from her forehead and held by a long thin cotton scarf tied around her head Indian fashion.

Her face, tanned from the sun, was covered with freckles. She was wearing a sleeveless cotton blouse and knickers. At twenty, there was something of the gamin about Lene. Her mind flitted between animation and reflection. She could be a whirlwind of talk and laughter, or she could fall into utter stillness. Tom sometimes thought she resembled a Renaissance portrait, a young contessa looking over her shoulder, aware of her beauty and her station in life, neither mannered nor hard, and not quite certain that all was right with the world.

Tom wore knickers too, and a shirt open at the collar, but there was nothing about either his clothes or his bearing that suggested he had just been on a hot, dusty bicycle ride. He shook hands with Eva and Caroline and carried the latter's hand to his lips. Caroline felt his breath for a single moment before he let her hand sink again.

"You've been to Russia, I hear," he said to Eva. "Was it all you expected?"

"Yes, and much more," she said.

It was hard for her not to like Tom, who was always charming and seemed to have almost no prejudices. He had grown tall—he stood a head higher than Lene—and his face always seemed ready to break into a cordial smile. Actually, he kept his true feelings much more to himself than Lene did, and relied on his poise and good looks to see him through his social obligations.

Lene sat down on the couch next to Eva and hugged her. Caroline motioned to Tom to sit beside her in one of the comfortable armchairs.

"You may talk to me," she said, "while Eva gives Lene a brief—or not so brief—rundown of her journey." She raised her eyes and said in a voice just above a whisper, "God save me from the mention of tractors or other heavy machinery. You, I hope, will talk of something else."

"I give you my promise," said Tom. He had gotten into the habit of telling Caroline amusing stories about people she knew and about the actors and singers at the Frankfurt theaters. He made no demands whatever on her, having realized long ago that this was the surest way to her heart.

Lene tried to settle down to listen to Eva's report on the Soviet Union, but her aunt's enthusiasm sat no better with her than with her mother. Lene was, however, very fond of her Aunt Eva, so she hid her impatience.

"Guess what I've decided to do," she interrupted at last. "I think that you'll be very proud of me. I've decided to become a kindergarten teacher. They've accepted me at the Pedagogical Institute, I begin classes in less than a month. We work with poor children in a nursery school while taking courses, and at the end of our studies we take the state exam to become certified."

"How very good," said Eva. "I *am* proud of you, and if I've played even a small role in your decision to take up some worthwhile work, I'll be even prouder. You know, I always feel sure that my convictions are enough to crush empires, but the idea that a single person has changed her ways on account of *me* is utterly baffling . . ."

"She hasn't exactly changed her life *yet*," said Tom. "Wait until she's spent a day among snot-nosed children."

"I hope Lene realizes that there's hard work ahead," said Caroline, who understood the side of her daughter's personality that was closest to her own—her tendency to give up, to sink into the soft pillow of lethargy at the first sign of difficulty. Eva, on the other hand, in keeping with her own view of the world, felt that the enthusiasm shining from her niece's face was the genuine expression of a deeply felt commitment.

Lene quickly tried to encourage her aunt's view and disparage her mother's. "I've been taking some courses in sociology at the university, and you'd be surprised how much I've learned. Not that I'll ever be a scholar, but I'm convinced that we have to prepare ourselves for great changes, and I want to do some good in this world. Tom makes fun of me"—she threw a look of affectionate disdain toward him—"but that doesn't bother me a bit. We've all lived rather frivolous lives—all except you, Aunt Eva—and I'm going to change all that. Whatever Tom may say, he admitted one day when he saw me playing with some children in the playground of the Palmengarten that I looked as natural there among them as if I'd been born to play with children . . ."

"They were clean and neat," said Tom, "and about as wild as a bunch of newborn chicks."

"I'm convinced that Lene will do well," said Eva. "We'll have a long talk about it one day, you and I." She patted Lene's knickered knee. "You have a lot to learn, and I will tell you about the mistakes you must avoid. It's so easy to misperceive those who aren't like you, especially when your life is lived in so different a world."

"Soon there'll be fewer and fewer differences," said Lene.

"God save us from such equality," Caroline said fervently.

"Speaking of the Palmengarten," Tom interjected, though no one else remembered that it had been spoken of, "we have tickets for the concert tonight."

"When does it begin?" Lene asked.

"Seven o'clock, I think."

"I'll have to eat very early, then. Shall I tell Anna?"

"Thinking of food, as usual," said Caroline. "You know, you look so much better since you lost weight."

"I suggest you don't eat supper," Tom said, "and we'll go out after the concert."

"When had you planned to have dinner today?" Lene asked her mother.

"The same time as always," said Caroline. "Your father would have a fit if we ever changed the dinner hour."

"Who's coming?"

"No one special . . . Eva will stay, of course, and Emma after her ride in the Stadtwald."

"I forgot today is Emma's riding day!" cried Lene. "We should have looked for her galloping through the forest while we pedaled our bikes."

"The Stadtwald is large," said Caroline. "Andreas isn't coming, he said he was busy. But perhaps Tom will stay?"

"I promised my parents to be home," said Tom.

"How *is* your father?" Caroline asked.

"Growing worse every week. But he clings to life with the strength of a young wrestler."

"No one wants to die," said Eva.

"That's not true," said her sister, "there are many who give up and let themselves slip away . . ."

"Or commit suicide," said Lene, shuddering slightly.

"My father isn't one of those," Tom muttered. "You know, he's eighty and suffers from hardening of the arteries. Sometimes he's lucid as the day, other times so senile he doesn't remember the war or his dead children. Nothing more recent than the year 1901 seems to exist for him—but he always remembers to chide me for my 'irresponsible' ways."

"You must understand and forgive him," said Caroline, who dealt with unpleasant subjects by pronouncing formulas over them like benedictions. She gave very little thought to what she said, but she wanted it known that her ideas were as correct as the décor of her house, even though they were no more profound than Frieda Gründlich's.

"Where is Fräulein Gründlich?" Tom was anxious to change the subject. His parents, especially his father, depressed him, and he did not like to be depressed. But for all that, he loved his father, largely because his early memories of him were tender.

"What made you think of her, all of a sudden?" Lene asked. "You must have read my thoughts. She's on vacation, the old dear. Back home on the farm, with her family. Probably drinking raw milk and munching fresh vegetables to her heart's content, shuddering to think of the garbage we have to eat here."

"Anna cooks as best she can," Caroline said mildly.

"If you think it's hard for *you* in this inflation, imagine what the poor have to contend with," said Eva.

"Do you think they'll *ever* do away with ration cards?"

"Here comes Emma," said Tom, rising to greet her, "just in time to rescue us from our dispiriting conversation."

"We looked and looked for you," said Lene, believing this to have been true, "but you were nowhere to be seen."

Emma wore her riding habit, gloves and a hat, and only a slight flush on her cheeks hinted at the heat of the day. Her hair, which she wore long, was tied wth a large red ribbon. She still held the riding crop in her hand. "Guess what happened to me today," she said.

"What?" Lene asked without much enthusiasm. Her sister usually found her pleasure in observing such things as a mare foaling.

"I met a handsome cavalry officer, and he rode with me through the most beautiful, distant part of the woods for an hour. It was just lovely."

"No wonder we didn't see you," said Lene.

"Who is he? What's his name?" Caroline asked.

"Wait, wait," said Emma, "I'll get to that part. Let me tell you the story."

"I've never seen you so excited," said Eva, and there was a clear vein of derision in her tone. "It's amazing how the sight of a handsome man can turn the head of the most sensible girl!"

Emma very rarely took the center of the stage for herself. It was clear that she had, indeed, had an unusual adventure. She took as much pleasure in the telling of it now as she had had in the experience itself.

"I was riding the chestnut gelding," she said, "the one I like, with the white splash down his right foreleg. They call him Onufri."

"A funny name," said Lene.

"Yes. Well, I had been going around the ring with him, as I usually do before I go out on the trail, as a kind of exercise, when I noticed a commotion near the stable. One of the grooms was having a terrible time with Black Savage, a vicious horse, which only the most foolhardy ever ride. They won't let women near him. He was rearing and kicking, behaving like some horse you might see at a Wild West show. The groom apparently could do nothing to control him and finally took a stick to him and whacked him across the flank with it. That was the end of it for the horse, it kicked with both rear legs and hit the boy. I saw him fall, bleeding from his head. It was awful, but I must say, anyone who hits a horse like that deserves what he gets—the poor beast!"

"How can you say such a thing?" cried Eva.

"Say what?" Emma was startled.

"That the boy 'deserved' to be kicked. Was he badly hurt?"

"How should I know? I didn't go over to stare, that was all that was needed at that point," Emma said sarcastically. "And they took him away very quickly, once Otto had caught the horse. *He* probably saved the poor wretch's life."

"A stupid beast remains just that, especially if it's a *mean* stupid beast. But a man . . . a boy!" Eva couldn't bear people who made a fuss over animals.

"Is Otto your officer?" Lene asked.

"Yes. Otto Radowitz. He caught Black Savage before he could inflict any more damage on the groom. Calmed him down and rode him about for a bit until he was gentle as a lamb. I spoke to him, to compliment him, not many people know how to treat animals like that. He's a colonel."

"How many workers did he shoot?" Eva asked.

"I will ignore that question, Aunt Eva!"

"The whole story sounds like something out of the illustrated newspapers. One of those serials by ladies with long invented triple names," said Tom. "I didn't know girls in real life still fell in love with dashing hussars."

"I'm not in love," said Emma.

"Did he wear a uniform?" Lene wanted to know.

"Of course! How else would I have known he was an officer?"

"He might have worn a sign around his neck: 'Handle with care —I am an officer!' " Lene said.

"You're all making fun of me."

Caroline felt it was time to intervene. "You two promised to go visit Uncle Jacob this afternoon!"

"But we're invited to Uncle Edu's for tea."

"You can go right after dinner, he takes a long break these days and probably won't go back to the store until three-thirty. Anna baked a chicken for him, which you're to bring. He can have it cold for his supper. You know he'd never eat a thing if left to his own devices."

"I'll pick you up at six-thirty," said Tom to Lene, getting ready to leave. "Wear something enchanting for me."

"I'll walk you out," said Lene, putting her arm through his. At the gate to the garden, where he had left his bicycle, Lene stood on her toes and kissed him on the cheek.

"Do you think Emma has finally found a beau?" she said.

"A German army officer? Good Lord, I hope not!"

"She's *starved* for sex, haven't you noticed?"

"For *love.*"

"*I* think for sex."

"What does she tell you?"

"Nothing, not a thing."

"You're being catty—and unkind."

"I think, too, that she doesn't approve of us."

"Dare I ask you why?"

"At first it was jealousy, now it is that she doesn't believe you're serious."

"I thought we got along splendidly, she and I."

"Oh, you do. But Emma is very critical."

Tom got on his bicycle and gave Lene a kiss on her freckled forehead. "I'll see you tonight. Go take a bath now."

EMMA LEFT the door to her room open while she undressed for her bath. She was almost twenty-three, still as thin as a rail. Her black hair reached to her waist. Most of the time she wore it parted in the middle and gathered into a heavy bun at the nape of her neck, held up with large hairpins of tortoise shell. The effect was that of a black cap, which showed no more than the soft lobe of her ear and sank in a graceful line from forehead to neck.

Emma was at the moment in her life when her beauty was at its peak. Men stopped to stare at her everywhere, at the theater, the museum, in the shops and on the street. She did not know why they did, assuming only that it was part of their animal nature to do so. She held herself erect and stared straight ahead, exuding a chill rigidity that turned men away as soon as they had drawn near. She was like an angel, they said, brilliantly inhuman, or like a marble bust by Laurana, exquisitely hewn in cold stone. She had become an excellent horsewoman and rode sidesaddle regally, ramrod-straight in her formal habit, exerting a fine control with hands alone. And still—something like fire smoldered beneath it all, and one could not tell whether it would bring warmth or destruction.

Seeing the open door, Lene walked into her sister's room, stretched herself out on the chintz-covered chair and said, "Tell me more about your admirer." She liked the way the smell of horses clung to Emma's clothes, even though Emma did not and therefore always hung them outside to air. Her boots were carried right down to the basement, where August cleaned and polished them to a high gloss.

"He's slender and his eyes are grayish blue. There is a tremendous power in him, even though he isn't tall. You feel that he's muscular through and through, perfectly balanced, hard."

"You like that?"

"I don't like soft men." She thought back to the action she had witnessed, remembered the way Otto had tamed the angry wild horse, whose eyes had been like blind white orbs, whose body was sleek with sweat, except where the groom had drawn blood.

"I hope he's nice and not only handsome."

"He was very gallant. He bowed before he introduced himself and kissed my hand after we were done riding together."

"Tom is right, it does sound exactly like a story out of the illustrated papers."

"Tom makes fun of everything in that superior way of his. It's despicable. I wish you wouldn't take it up."

"Have you lost all sense of humor, Emma?"

"I don't like to be laughed at."

"No one is laughing, we're only trying to fathom this bizarre meeting. Where's your beau from?"

"East Prussia."

"Good heavens—a Junker. Do you think Eva is right, did he shoot workers during the Revolution?"

"Eva is a blind fool. Wait until her beloved proletariat turns on her and tears her to pieces."

"She has a heart of gold."

"Like many fools."

"When are you two going to meet again?"

"I don't know. But he asked me on what days I ride and I told him."

"Will we meet him? Maybe the four of us can go to the theater together—or on a picnic if he doesn't like theater."

"Why shouldn't he like the theater? He seems like a cultivated man, 'a gentleman of the old school' Gründlich would say."

Emma sat on her bed, naked except for the silk robe she had put on. Lene could still faintly smell the horses.

"However," Emma said resolutely, "we haven't got that far. I don't want to think about what might be. And I don't want to talk about it any longer. I'm going to bathe and get rid of this stable odor."

THE DINING ROOM, facing north, was the coolest room in the house. Nathan arrived home punctually at one o'clock and dinner was served at one-thirty, which gave him time to read the mail and glance at the day's newspaper. He always looked into the dining room as he walked to his study, to see how many places had been set so that he might have an idea whom to expect. Today there were five places, which might mean that Andreas was coming. But the voices that reached him from the living room were the voices of women, and he remembered that his sister-in-law was back from Russia. Eva and Caroline and his two daughters made four, so he would—alas!—be alone among the women again.

It was always a pleasant interlude for him when Andreas came. They talked about music. Andreas was studying at the university, with an eye to becoming a musicologist. Several of his reviews of concerts had been accepted by the *Frankfurter Zeitung*. He knew contemporary music better than most of the local critics, and his style was excellent. But he was unambitious, his life seemed to hang in painful balance between lassitude and restlessness. He could lie about for days making plans he was unable to carry out; then again, he might prowl the streets looking for an encounter, some goad to his feelings, a dangerous elation in which to lose himself. He wished he could find that elation in his work. Once or twice he had done so, and it had been intoxicating. He understood what it was to be an artist. But these moments were so rare that he was driven again and again into the streets and the tiny dismal bars of the Altstadt. His family refused to acknowledge his homosexuality. It would have comforted him to know that they did not think of it as a secret they must keep for fear of the world and what it might say. Even Ernst, who had fled to the University of Berlin and sat there growling his dissatisfaction at them all, grew fearful and blank whenever Andreas tried to bring up the subject.

Lene had once mentioned it to Emma—Lene considered herself

enlightened, a child of her time—saying that she did not think that Andreas liked *women,* and Emma had agreed in a vague way, which was unusual for her. She clearly did not wish to dwell on the subject.

"He sleeps with *men,*" Lene said. "I try to imagine it, but find it hard to do."

"I don't imagine it at all," said Emma. "My mind stops at the threshold of that door. I will not open it."

Nathan greeted the four women with a wan smile and a mumbled welcome for his sister-in-law. He shook her hand but did not kiss her. "I hope dinner is better today than it was yesterday," he said. It had become his daily, dry comment.

"It won't be until more food becomes available," said Caroline. "With the way inflation is going, we're lucky to get anything at all. You have to have a baby carriage full of money to buy six eggs, and by the time you get to the store, you find you've only got enough for four."

"You can't blame the farmers for not wanting to take worthless money," said Eva.

"Have you tried the black market?" Nathan asked with apparent innocence.

"Let Pauline fool around with that," said Caroline. "You won't catch me dealing with criminals."

"They've been dealing very harshly with black marketeers in Berlin," said Eva, "as well they should."

"Can we talk of more pleasant things?" asked Lene.

Nathan sniffed at the croquettes Liese was handing around. Anna had done her best to dress them up, chopping a lot of chives from the garden into them and surrounding them with mounds of parsley. There were also fresh tomatoes from the garden, which did not always escape thieves, and a green salad. But the rolls were dark and rubbery. Caroline broke off some pieces and rubbed them into doughy balls, quite unaware of what she was doing.

"I think I'm going to have to fire Eisenstein," said Nathan, picking at the croquette on his plate, trying to mix it up with some tasteless rice.

"Why, in these hard times?" Caroline asked.

"Times are hard for all of us," Nathan said in his customary dejected voice. "I don't think I can keep him, the way things are going. It seems that no matter how well and scrupulously I conduct my practice, it grows smaller instead of larger. Eisenstein is getting old."

"He's not much older than you are, Papa," said Lene. "Poor Eisenstein, what will he do?"

"Take out an unemployment card," Eva said quietly.

"I'll try to find him another position," Nathan said. "Perhaps Edu can take him on."

"What would we do without Edu?" murmured Emma. Everyone pretended not to have heard, but everyone had had the exact same thought.

"Since Edu has become a partner in the Goldschmidt bank, he ought to be able to find something, somewhere," said Caroline. "Your brother's ventures prosper, no matter what. War, revolution, inflation . . . nothing seems to be able to stop him."

"Be thankful," said Nathan, "it keeps food—bad as it is—on all our tables."

Silence fell. The heat from outside seemed to press in on everyone. Caroline ate next to nothing and continued playing with her bread. Her hands were very white; except for the blue veins traveling up their backs, they might have been made of ivory. Eva was overcome with pity for her sister but at the same time felt a great urge to be done with her. She wanted to relegate her to the past she thought she had left behind her forever during her weeks of travel in the Soviet Union. *That* was the future, damn these relics of the old order, so full of melancholy decadence and nervous disease. Eva withdrew into her cozy, private recollections of wandering with the comrades of the Workers' Youth out in the Taunus, singing folksongs and dancing around a campfire. She had been told, by a high party official, that the Politburo hoped for a German Revolution on November 7, the anniversary of the Russian Revolution. Though she did not quite believe it—her instincts told her the hope was a delusion—she fixed her mind on it.

"Eisenstein is a good man," Nathan said, breaking the silence, "trustworthy and decent. I'll do what I can for him. Edu must surely have an opening for such a man. His wife is ailing and his two sons are worthless." He sighed.

Dessert was a yellow-colored pudding, specked with bits of candied fruit. It seemed to be made of powders, chemicals and synthetic grit.

"Any messages for Uncle Jacob?" Emma asked. She had pushed aside her pudding and was anxious to leave the table.

"Tell him he is to take our tickets for the recital next Wednesday. We're expected at the Schlesingers'."

"How boring," said Nathan, "you didn't tell me. Can't you refuse invitations on the nights we have concert tickets?"

"I'd forgotten. It's summer, and there's no rhyme or reason to when they give performances. When I realized we had a conflict, it was too late to cancel."

"I'd sooner hear the recital. I'm told it's a new and very talented pianist, a local boy, though he was born in Poland, by the name of Manfred Solomon. Tell those pompous Schlesingers we cannot come."

"I'll do nothing of the sort," said Caroline.

"You may have to go alone, then, or in the company of your son or one of your daughters. I do not want to miss the concert."

Caroline drummed her fingers on the table. Eva forced herself—in a daydream—to dwell on a trip to the Vogelsberg, the highest mountain in the Taunus, with "The Friends of Nature" to see the sun rise.

"May we be excused?" Emma asked. "We've got a lot yet to do today, especially if we have to stop at Uncle Jacob's."

"I'll get the chicken from Anna," Lene said. She had eaten most of the dessert and noticed that Aunt Eva, too, was finishing hers.

"What chicken?" Nathan asked.

"Oh, God," said Caroline, "another scene. Go, girls . . . and don't be late at Edu's."

"Are you sending my worthless brother Jacob a chicken?" Nathan stormed. He had roused himself into a fury, he hardly knew why. If only Andreas had been there, to keep the accusations and the whine of these women from him. He blamed Eva for it all but dared not attack her. "After you serve me this garbage, you turn around and ask the cook to prepare a chicken for Jacob, who doesn't care if he eats sawdust as long as he has a bottle of wine to wash it down with?"

"We're also having chicken," Caroline said wearily, "tomorrow. Your mother and Edu are coming for dinner, and Andreas as well. I thought—I hope you'll forgive me, Eva—that I would save the birds until then. Anna was able, don't ask me how, to extract three pullets from the butcher. One was rather smaller than the others, and I thought that Jacob . . ." Caroline's tone of voice was pleading now. The girls had folded their napkins and put them into their silver rings and slipped out of the room. "Since Jacob cannot or will not come to dinner, I thought he could use the smaller pullet. He has no one to do the shopping for him, he's nothing but skin and bones. He's never recovered from Gerda's death, I think, or from the fact that he didn't marry her—all because of the family—before she died. He's become stranger and queerer since her death . . ."

"Gerda's death does not, after all these years, I think, deserve a chicken."

Eva, unable to avoid the quarrel, got up from the table as well. She kissed her sister, who took no notice of her, and grasped her hand to whisper "Good-bye" into her ear, wanting to show her solidarity even as she got ready to flee.

Emma and Lene had gone down to the kitchen. They missed Fräulein Gründlich, whose presence inhibited quarreling.

"Papa is angry about the chicken," Lene said.

"I would think so," said Anna, "especially after the croquettes, which he doesn't like. How was the pudding? I notice that almost no one touched it."

"Well"—Lene hesitated—"it was sweet."

"Soon they'll begin harvesting apples and then we'll do better," said Anna. "Don't you envy Fräulein Gründlich, up there in the country, wherever it is?"

"Schleswig-Holstein," said Emma.

"You know, I never thought the country was such a good place, but after all I've seen, and it's not getting better, I don't know anymore." Anna had wrapped the chicken in an old clean dishtowel and then in a checked napkin, put it in a basket and added a couple of tomatoes for good measure. "Tell him to bring the basket back sometime," she said, "and go now, like Little Red Riding Hood and beware of the wolf!"

Lene and Emma took their time walking down to the Fahrgasse and Uncle Jacob's house. Passing the store, they waved to Alois, who sat near the open door reading a book.

"You know, I was sure he'd marry Gründlich," Lene said after they had turned the corner. "I wonder what went wrong there."

"She told me about it once," Emma said.

"Why you and not me?" Lene said, offended.

"She probably thought that, being the older, I'd have more under-standing."

"And you never told me!"

"I didn't feel it was right. And then I forgot."

"I bet he was unfaithful!"

"No, it was something quite different. Gründlich became fright-ened. They had seen each other a lot, and he proposed marriage one day on a trip down the Main on the little excursion steamer. At first, she said, she was thrilled and happy. But the more she thought about it—living with him in some little flat in Sachsenhausen, or worse yet, she said, in Niederrad or Rödelsheim—the more the idea began to seem foolish to her. They looked at furniture, and Alois talked about her place in his life, and in his kitchen, and she thought about it and thought about it till, she said, she got panicky, already feeling trapped at the mere thought of an apartment in the suburbs, taking up the sort of life her mother led, seeing the walls close in. So she broke the engagement. She told him she wanted to stay with her job. Isn't that amazing?"

"Did she tell you what his reaction was?"

"He was stunned and furious, of course. To think she preferred bondage to the *Herrschaft* to bondage to him! I think he probably made her feel terrible. He pursued her for a while and then found someone else, I guess. That's all there is to the story."

"Good old Gründlich! She'll be there for my children and my children's children—like an old Russian nurse!"

"She lives in *our* world, you see. I really ought to tell Aunt Eva the whole story, to see what she'd say."

"She would see the sadness of it."

They had reached Jacob's house and rang his bell. Frau Koeppening, who came in twice a week to clean and do the laundry, opened the door for them. Both Emma and Lene had a strong dislike for the heavyset woman, who seemed to spend most of her time deep in conversation with Frau Strüpler, the super's wife. Jacob was unaware that his apartment was a shambles. It had deteriorated gradually, and he in his solitude noticed neither her sloppiness nor her occasional thefts. Frau Koeppening knew that Jacob was blind to her, that he did not see her slovenly bulk and was unaware of the work required of her, so she did the barest minimum.

"I do as little as I can and still live with myself, taking his money," she said to Frau Strüpler regularly. She had come to him, she was convinced, full of good will and a true German delight in hard work and cleanliness. But his blind and damning unwillingness to take her into account, to care, even to notice whether she lived or died, had wounded her so deeply that she had become his enemy. Frau Koeppening knew that his two nieces, always so well-dressed, so pretty, so *superior*, saw through her and hated her, but it didn't matter, it was nothing to her; they could not reach their uncle either.

Jacob had not expected them. He sat at his desk taking notes for an article he was writing in refutation of something that had been published in a learned philological journal.

"We brought the chicken for your supper," Lene said. He remembered now that Caroline had promised him a chicken yesterday when she called to invite him and he had refused. How young and pretty his nieces looked. Why did he never take them anywhere? He sniffed at the chicken. "Delicious," he said, and he took one of the tomatoes and bit into it. The juice spurted out and left a bloody pulp on top of the learned journal.

"I suppose my brother, your papa, was furious about the chicken?"

The sisters looked at each other.

"I was right! Nathan is growing stingier each day. But it's nice to see you two—I really ought to see you more often. When your brothers were small, I used to take them out for lunch at the Schirn. We'd buy hot sausages straight from the boiling pot and eat them, walking through the Altstadt. I must take you both to dinner soon. This inflation can't possibly go on forever. I'm sorry your papa was angry about the chicken. It looks good enough to eat." He leaned forward across the desk. Emma saw that there was still some tomato juice and a seed or two stuck to his chin. "I shall hide the chicken from Frau Koeppening. She *steals.*"

"Papa gets furious about a lot of things these days," said Lene soothingly. "He says he has to fire Eisenstein."

"That poor devil. What will he do? Where will he go? He must be in his fifties . . ."

"And his wife is sick," said Lene.

"And his sons are no good" Emma added, "but Papa said he would talk to Uncle Edu and see if he can find some work for him."

"What other good news have you brought me?"

"Emma has found a beau!"

"Don't tell me."

"It's nothing at all," said Emma, "don't listen to Lene, she's exaggerating as always."

"A Prussian army officer!" said Lene. "Don't let her deny it."

"I was riding this morning," Emma began, determined to tell it in her own words, "and he caught a horse that had gone wild after the groom beat it. We went riding together. That's really all there is to the story."

Jacob had settled down in his old office chair, put his feet on the desk, right on top of his notes for a rebuttal, and watched his nieces closely. The curtains were drawn and there was a smell, which bothered Emma. She could not make it out, except that it was of stale air and unclean clothes and mildew.

Jacob noticed her sniffing, noticed her trying to pretend that she wasn't doing it. He folded his hands over his stomach and trans-ferred his attention to Lene, whose eyes roamed uncritically around the room. She had the dreamy expression on her face that protected her. Emma had no such protection. Jacob should have liked her better, and he was irked that he did not. Both girls, he thought, were a little silly, and it was really time to get back to the shop. He wound the silk scarf he always wore another couple of turns around his neck. It had tomato stains on it, too, now, and Emma had probably noticed it. He smelled the fresh scent of the ripe fruit. Frau Koeppening was lurking about the kitchen.

"Time to go home, Frau Koeppening!" he called out, but she was still as a mouse, gulping down her second lunch and what was left of a bottle of wine.

"She shan't have my chicken," Jacob said. "I'll wait her out. Did I thank you for it? And your mother and the good and trusty Anna?" He spoke rather loudly but suddenly lowered his voice again. "Frau Koeppening is a witch, one has to be very careful around her. She's in league with the enemy."

"Why don't you fire her?" Emma said. She was growing uncomfortable as she always did when disorder seemed to come creeping through the cracks in the floorboards. It struck her all at once that what seemed to her most compelling about Otto Radowitz was the neat and orderly way he was put together, the precise articulation of his speech, all of it hinting at a seamless existence, the calm of routine, the blessing of certainty.

"I know her too well," said Jacob. "I know every one of her faults, and I know she has no redeeming features. She will never surprise me with a kindness. Such consistency is not only rare but admirable."

"We must go," said Emma.

"Uncle Edu expects us for tea," Lene explained.

Jacob got up. Frau Koeppening stood in the doorway wearing her hat and coat, probing her teeth with her tongue for the poppy seeds stuck between them. "I'm leaving," she said.

"How are your brothers?" Jacob asked his nieces. He never said "Good-bye" or "Good morning" to the housekeeper. She closed the door loudly behind her, but Jacob suspected she stood listening on the other side.

"Ernst writes gloomy letters," said Emma.

"He's thinking of going to Palestine," Lene added. "He says there's no hope whatever for the Jews in Germany."

"Berlin always makes me think so too."

They left as soon as Frau Koeppening's heavy tread had receded down the stairwell. Jacob went with them as far as his store. He remembered much later that he had left the chicken sitting on his desk, among the learned journals and the dictionary and the tomato-stained papers.

Even the hot summer air was a welcome relief, Emma thought, from the stuffiness of the apartment.

"Thank God *that's* over," she said as soon as they had parted from Jacob. "You must admit that he gets more peculiar every time we see him."

"He's unhappy and lonely, poor thing."

"That's no excuse," said Emma.

They looked at their watches and decided to take a leisurely stroll through the main shopping street and up the Goethestrasse. The trees were in full leaf, the colors of the women's summer dresses were gay, there was a pleasant feeling of small-town life in the air. Uncle Edu had asked them to come at four-thirty. They watched the time carefully; it was well known that Edu did not like it any better if one came too early than if one came late.

The broad leaves of the chestnut trees on the Bockenheimer Landstrasse allowed only a little sunlight to filter down to the sidewalks and increased the walker's sense of being on hallowed ground. The great houses, each behind its ornate iron fence and mighty shut gate, appeared to have spread themselves in tranquil poses among their green gardens, looking more substantial and immutable than ever. Few cars disturbed the peace of the hour, even the trolley seemed to glide along its tracks more quietly. The loudest noise was the occasional tramp of a horse, pulling a deliveryman's cart, bringing back memories of the years before the war. If one stood very still one could hear the bees humming at their work in the gardens. To walk this way at this hour was to feel the magic of worldly riches, to understand how they protect fragile life and create for it a paradise on earth.

Uncle Edu's villa was replete with mansard roof and a Renaissance frieze of garlands and flowers, which appeared much too ornate to the sophisticated eye of the 1920s, schooled as it was in the new esthetic of the Bauhaus. Tom had pointed out all of its hideous incongruities to Lene, praised the Landhaus Rothschild down the street and the Villa Leonhardsbrunn behind the Palmengarten for their classic façades, but to no avail: Lene had a deep and abiding affection for her uncle's house, sinful though it was, as sinful as her love of chocolate éclairs bursting with whipped cream. An ornately wrought iron gate, made by the same blacksmith who had fashioned the intricate grills that topped the mansard roof, allowed cars and carriages to enter; pedestrians like Lene and Emma came through a smaller gate beside it, which was an exact replica. A bell pull attached to the stone pillar into which the gates were fastened had to be rung before one could enter, after having been observed by Humboldt, the butler, through a small window next to the front door. Humboldt was very selective. If no company was expected, he might not push the buzzer that unlocked the gate even once in a day.

The shutters of the house were all let down at the hot time of day in this season, to keep the paintings and gobelins safe from the bleaching rays of the sun. Emma looked at her watch as they reached the gate. It was four twenty-five. They had time for a quick turn around the garden. Humboldt let them in—he had been looking for them—and noting the time as well on his large pocket watch, decided that they would be walking in the garden for five minutes.

Once they had stepped through the gate, the two sisters again felt the excitement and awe they had felt the very first time Fräulein Gründlich brought them here, ten years before. The garden, Edu's pride and joy, was a richly colored paradise of sweetly scented summer flowers, luxuriant as one of Monet's Giverny canvases. Walking along the graveled paths, Lene and Emma were drawn, as always, into another world. Here was a stunning profusion and variety of flowering shapes and colors, yet everything was planned with exquisite care as precisely as a military parade drill. It was this latter aspect that pleased Emma—everything in its place and labeled, though the effect was one of casual, almost accidental beauty—while Lene responded to the voluptuous prodigality of it all.

At four-thirty precisely, they stepped through the front door and returned Humboldt's greetings with friendly exclamations. They had both involuntarily caught their breath as they entered the dark of the front hall from the sunshine of the garden. The interior of the house had been as ornately eclectic as the exterior when Edu bought it, but he had made alterations, following the advice of Elias, who wanted nothing to distract from the paintings and *objets d'art* that Edu was accumulating. Elias was now first assistant to the director of the Städel.

Humboldt led them into the drawing room. He wore a proper uniform and white gloves and had that year joined the fledgling, apparently innocuous NSDAP, the National Socialist German Workers' Party, with whom he occasionally fought in street brawls against the Communists.

As always, Uncle Edu kept his young visitors waiting a few minutes before appearing, dapper and distinguished-looking in his English-cut suit and his polka-dot silk tie.

"Good afternoon, my dear nieces," he said, coming quietly over the cushioned carpet from his study across the hall. His mustache was neatly trimmed (a barber came every morning to shave him) and a faintly tantalizing scent of cologne accompanied him into the room. Edu rose at dawn every morning that it wasn't raining to ride in the Stadtwald. The only other people up and about then were a few poor street workers, and the dew was still fresh on the meadows at the edge of the forest. It was an hour in which Edu savored his solitude and collected his thoughts. The exercise invigorated him, and when he arrived at his office at eight, a full hour before Siegmund did, he was in full command of his wits and ready to slay all manner of commercial dragons.

He allowed both Lene and Emma to kiss him on the cheek before he sat down opposite them on a Louis Quinze chair and took their measure. He felt very strongly that a neat and tasteful choice of dress reflected a well-regulated mode of life, and he never hesitated to criticize his nieces if he felt that some aspect of their clothing exhibited signs of bohemianism, old-maidenhood or the pernicious influence of some Oriental or Near Eastern cult, of which there were many in those years.

"You both look lovely today," he said, and the girls smiled at each other. They wore simple dresses which extended several inches past the knee, were pleated below the belt and had a scooped-out neckline, above which they both wore a single strand of natural pearls, which Edu had given them. Their silk stockings were white, complementing their dresses, and their pumps were flat-heeled with a buttoned strap across the instep.

Edu noted their exchange of smiles and saw how each face was illuminated differently by it. Lene's smile gave her a look of bemused irony, as if she saw behind all this. Emma's smile drove a fragment of the tension from her watchful face and laid bare her innocence and her desire to please. Edu was well satisfied with all his nieces' progress, which he had overseen as carefully as his brothers and sisters-in-law allowed. He was certain that neither Siegmund nor Nathan was fully aware of the ravishing creatures they had begot. Both of them had left the girls' education to the charge of their wives, and they, in turn, had left it in the hands of governesses. Edu had no illusions about Caroline or Pauline, which is to say that he saw their bad sides sooner than their good ones. He thought them selfish and blamed any narrowness of vision he detected in his brothers to the influence of their wives. He was glad that Jacob had had no children. What Gottfried had produced in America was anyone's guess.

"What have you two been doing?" Edu asked.

"I went riding this morning . . ." Emma began.

". . . and she met a beau," Lene said. She always felt some anxiety under Uncle Edu's gaze, never quite sure whether everything was up to his exacting standards. She was the one most likely to have a run in her stocking or a torn hem on her dress. She wished tea would be served quickly, but she knew that the amount of elapsed time between their arrival and the entrance of Marie, the maid, with the tea tray, was also counted out exactly.

"No doubt he's a dashing officer," said Edu. News traveled fast in the Wertheim circle.

"How did you guess?" Emma asked, quite startled.

Edu's smile was sly. "I can always tell what's in your heart, be it a Christmas wish or a romantic throb. But I warn you: beware of dashing officers. Many a young maiden has lost her heart to one and suffered bitterly for it."

"You're joking, Uncle Edu. Those days are gone forever. The army is a pretty dull place nowadays. Otto said so."

"I'm joking," said Edu, "but I'm also completely serious. The army is full of men of cruelty and limited intelligence." Seeing Emma's stricken face, he added, "But I don't doubt that your Otto isn't like that at all."

Marie appeared at five minutes to four, first with a white cloth, which she spread over the table, and then with the tray, which held the silver tea service and three platters filled with a multitude of open sandwiches: smoked salmon, anchovy paste, black caviar, cucumbers, watercress and deviled egg. There were sweets, too, petits fours and tiny éclairs, rich butter cookies and delicate napoleons. The dishes were Nymphenburg china, pink-flowered with a gold border, and the small napkins were delicately edged in lace, freshly laundered and stiff with starch. It was clearly worth a visit, thought Lene.

"How did you manage to get such delicacies?" she asked, trying to choose between the pale-pink salmon and the shiny dark globules of caviar and finally taking one of each.

"Are the poor children being starved at home?" Edu asked her, his sarcasm untouched by concern.

"We certainly haven't sat down to anything like this in quite a while," Lene exclaimed. "Caviar!"

"Mama manages very well, all things considered," Emma said loyally. She had no taste for rich foods, and *her* plate held neither caviar nor smoked salmon nor a cream-topped raspberry tart, as Lene's did, but two cucumber sandwiches and one with watercress.

"How thin you are," Otto Radowitz had said as they rode next to each other that morning, "like a dark and slender pine." Emma remembered the words the moment she sipped the hot, unsweetened tea. A lemon slice floating on top gave up the pungent odor of cloves stuck in its rind, and Emma saw herself again riding at a canter along the leafy bridle path. The horses had moved in unison, their riders holding the reins loosely and feeling the animals' speed and strength become their own. Emma hoped that Otto hadn't noticed how large her nose was, or how unnerved she felt in his presence. She rode well, however; he had tried to compliment her on it in his stiff and gallant manner. He confessed that he read poetry and made it sound like some fatal, dooming flaw.

"I can't eat another thing." Lene sat back comfortably in the cushions of the sofa. "It was delicious."

"I'm glad I was able to help bring you back from the brink of starvation," Edu said. "You've got some crumbs on your lap."

Lene brushed them off.

"That's fine, now they're on my Chinese rug!"

"Thank God you've got such a large and able staff, Uncle Edu." Lene gave him an unintimidated smile. Edu liked her for standing up to him. He knew she would never become impudent, she was too well brought up for that; the only thing he feared was that she would descend into Bohemia. The horror he had of that went back to his encounter with Franz Bleicher so many years before. These days Bohemia was everywhere. One couldn't walk down the street without encountering groups of young people looking as if they were vagrants or Italian peasants or Russian anarchists. No costume was too crazy, no style too outlandish. Edu often worried that Lene would marry Tom. The boy was nice enough, and his background was impeccable, but Edu distrusted his languid gaze, his bookish turn of mind. He was the sort who would never amount to anything and believe until his dying day that he was meant to be a poet, even though he hadn't written more than half a dozen mediocre rhymes.

"I've got a surprise for you," said Edu. "Actually it's two surprises, one for me and one for you. The one for me is a new painting I bought, which I want to show you. I think you'll like it. The other, *your* surprise, is something I thought up just the other day that I know will please you. I want to invite the two of you to spend a week in Venice with me early in October." The girls squealed their delight. "You'll be my guests, and so will Julia and Jenny, who will be told tomorrow, when *they* come to tea. I can see you *are* pleased."

They clapped their hands together and would have hugged, had they not felt that it was too childish a thing to do.

"Venice!" said Lene. "We've never been there."

"I know you haven't," said Edu. "It's a city no one should miss, especially when they're young and romantic. Someday I plan to take you on a tour of all Italy, a Grand Tour, to see the most beautiful places: Florence, Naples, Pisa, Rome, Sicily—the list is endless. It would make me most happy to think that I was the one who showed

you the treasures of that land where, as Goethe said, the lemon trees
bloom. But it will have to wait another year, better times."

"Thank you, Uncle Edu!" Emma was the one who never forgot
to express her gratitude.

"Will better times come soon?" Lene asked.

"Things can't get much worse," said Edu. "The government will
have to stabilize the currency one of these days; this inflation is
hurting the middle class fiercely. It takes away people's savings and
makes their pensions worthless . . . But come, let's talk about more
pleasant things—why should you two bother your beautiful heads
with business, anyway? You'll be taken care of, come what may. I'll
see to that." The last words were spoken quietly, almost inaudibly.
The girls did not quite catch them but were comforted by the tone
of assurance in which they were uttered.

"Papa told us today that he has to fire Eisenstein," Lene blurted
out, ignoring her sister's look, which clearly said, "Don't talk about
it."

"Why, for heaven's sake? Eisenstein's been with him as long as
I can remember!"

"He says his practice is shrinking, he gets fewer and fewer clients."

"He seems depressed," said Emma. "We shouldn't talk about it."

"Society goes elsewhere these days," said Edu. "They like things
modern, fast and jazzy. I'll have to speak to him. I'm sure we can
hunt up some clients. But come now, you two, and let's look at the
picture." They rose, and as they were about to leave the room Edu
turned smilingly to Lene and asked, "You're sure, now, that you've
had enough to eat?"

"Quite enough, thank you."

The new painting hung in the dining room over the buffet. It was
a most extraordinary blue.

"Do you know—can you tell—who painted it?"

Both nieces shook their heads.

"It's by a modern painter," said Emma.

"It's very blue," said Lene.

"You're both right," said Edu. "You should, however, begin to
recognize contemporary masterpieces, not only old masters, all of

whom I'm sure you *do* know. This picture was painted by Henri Matisse."

"I should have known," said Emma.

"Next time you will," Edu assured her.

"What's it supposed to be?" Lene asked. "I recognize the pot and the flowers, but there's more to it."

"All paintings, all great paintings, are more than merely flowers or landscapes or Nativities," said Uncle Edu. "This painting is no exception . . ."

The sisters heard him in silence. Edu became a different man when he spoke about his paintings. He would never have talked about a woman in just this way, yet it seemed as if he were singing the praises of his beloved.

"Look," he said, "look how incredibly varied the blue is, how deep, how subtle the shifts in the brush strokes. That touch of lavender there is the heart of the picture. And Matisse, you'll notice, used the same lavender as underpainting for the blue vase. Do you see it?"

"It's beautiful," said Lene, who hadn't thought so at first, "once you get used to it."

Somewhere in the house a bell sounded, and Edu looked at his watch. "I must send you home; it's after five o'clock." He escorted them from the dining room, through the front hall to the door, his arm around their waists. As they passed by the salon Lene noticed a woman sitting on the couch. Her face was turned to the side and Lene glimpsed no more than her profile under a large summer hat. And then, abruptly, Humboldt appeared and quietly shut the salon door. They kissed Uncle Edu, thanked him, and strolled out through the garden. The sun was still above the chestnut trees; the dahlias hung heavy on their stalks, saturated with vivid color.

"I'm not sure I liked the picture," Emma said to Lene. "There was something unnatural about it, something *willed.* But then, blue is not my favorite color."

"Did you see the woman who came in?"

"What woman?"

"On the couch just now, in the salon. You were on the wrong side of Uncle Edu to see her. She must have been early, for Edu is usually careful about his time arrangements. Humboldt shut the door in a hurry when he saw me peek."

"I wonder who she is?" They both asked the question at the same time and in the same tone of voice. It made them giggle, and they walked home arm in arm, speculating on the lady on Edu's sofa.

Lene barely had time to rest and change her clothes before it was six-thirty and Tom was at the door. She had put on a long satin dress she particularly loved. Its smooth line made her appear taller, besides hiding her legs, which were too thick at the ankles. This was a family failing; even skinny Emma had thick legs. The dress was gold-colored, like clear sherry. A thin belt circled her hips, she wore her strand of pearls and very little lipstick. Her hair was brushed back from her forehead to expose her widow's peak.

"Do you remember the first time I took you to the opera?" Tom asked.

"Yes, I do. We heard *The Magic Flute.* Remember our first hike in the Taunus?"

"We went to the Saalburg, and you got so excited when you saw it was an old Roman fort you decided you were going to study Roman history and brush up on your Latin."

"I never got very far with it."

"It takes a special taste to appreciate Caesar's campaigns." Tom laughed. "We're collecting memories like an old married couple."

They walked arm in arm through the summer evening. Tom wore a tuxedo and patent-leather shoes. A silk scarf trailed over his shoulder. They were a handsome couple, and they knew it. Their gait was assured, and part of the love they felt for each other was this—they were enchanted with their appearance, the tall blond young man with the blue eyes and the brown-eyed, dark young woman, her face like a heart.

"Afterwards we'll go to the Café Rumpelmayer and have a bite to eat," said Tom. "You know, we rarely go out in company, we spend most of our time alone together or sitting in your garden, visiting with your family. We hike, we bike, we take daytrips down the Main, but never with anyone else."

"I like that, don't you?"

"I like it, Lene, but it's not the only way to spend one's time. It's good to be with others now and then, hearing different voices and exchanging ideas about life and art. We're social creatures, after all."

"Some of us more than others."

"You mustn't be so shy."

"I don't choose what I am."

"Well, then, try to overcome it . . ."

"Look who's talking about 'overcoming'! You're more set in your ways than a member of the Versailles court!"

"All right. We won't talk about it. I promise you this evening will be great fun. There'll be a lot of theater people and reporters from the *Frankfurter Zeitung*, writers, artists . . . you'll see."

Lene tightened her hold on his arm, and he pressed her hand against the black sleeve of his tuxedo.

It was not yet dusk, and the Palmengarten was bathed in the dusty blue light that precedes evening in the city. Row upon row of Japanese lanterns had been strung between the trees all over the park. As yet their light could not compete with the light of the fading day, but their reflections danced merrily on the waters of the lake and the duck pond. The members of the orchestra straggled in to tune their instruments. Waiters poured champagne for the elegant crowd sitting and standing about the small tables on the open veranda of the clubhouse. The champagne was German and second-rate, but the magic of the evening was not dampened by that. It was the last party of the summer.

"Look, look!" Lene cried suddenly and pointed to the sky above the trees, now almost purple, where the moon hung full and white and round.

"It isn't real, Lene," said Tom, "they brought it over from the theater, just for this concert." Lene almost believed him. Fireflies flew about the perimeter of the small meadow in front of the band shell, and the lanterns shone brightly now. People took their seats, the waiters stopped serving champagne.

"It's the very same person!" Lene cried suddenly.

"What's that?" Tom asked, startled.

Lene whispered in his ear, "Don't look right this second, but

when you can, take a peek over there, in the first row—naturally—
where Uncle Edu is sitting, and see . . . he's with a strange lady and
I saw her this afternoon, at his house!"

"Why are you so excited?"

"A strange married lady with Uncle Edu!"

"How do you know she's married?"

"Oh, Tom! I can tell. She looks married. Women of that age and
station are bound to be married. She surely doesn't look like an old
maid."

"Did he introduce you?"

"No. I only saw her for a second, in the salon."

"You saw a *lot* in that second."

"I'm very observant."

"When it comes to your Uncle Edu."

Everyone clapped at that moment, for the conductor had arrived
on the podium. He was a man with a great reputation and very
much in demand that year. He had just come from Bayreuth.

"They say he's better than Hermann Scherchen," said Tom in a
low voice.

"Nonsense!" Lene hissed back at him. All the young women of
Frankfurt adored Hermann Scherchen.

Lene kept craning her neck to see the woman who was with
Uncle Edu. The orchestra was ready, the conductor raised his baton
and the familiar sounds of "Eine kleine Nachtmusik" filled the
evening air. Much as she loved the piece and the Schubert Spring
Symphony that followed it, Lene found it difficult to pay attention,
she was so curious about Edu's companion. She was determined to
see the couple during intermission, and as soon as the conductor had
bowed to the applauding audience for the last time, she got up to
make her way there. Tom followed her. They came upon Edu in
the midst of a crowd of Frankfurt's leading citizens, which included
the *Bürgermeister* and the composer Paul Hindemith, whose new
piece was to conclude the evening's program. Determined as Lene
was to break through the crowd, she found it hard going. Society
gives way only before the most persistent onslaught. At this moment
—and she would remember it forever after—Lene discovered the
difference between those who are recognized and those who are not.

It had, in this case, nothing to do with the usual trappings of power —this was the Weimar Republic, after all—but everywhere in that circle courtiers fawned and sycophants grinned and she was ignored. Pretty as she was, well-dressed and in the company of a handsome escort, no one paid her the slightest attention.

But she caught her uncle's eye at last, and he came to her and kissed her and told her how enchanting she looked. He shook hands with Tom coolly; Edu often did not seem to notice the young men who accompanied his nieces in public. He had, however, seen with what curious looks Lene devoured his companion, so he took her gently by the hand and introduced her. "This is Lady Samuel," he said, "an acquaintance from England who is visiting here in Frankfurt."

Lene shook hands with the Englishwoman, and Edu saw immediately how carefully the two appraised each other. Lene was capable at such moments of rising to self-contained womanhood. She found Lady Samuel stunningly handsome in the grand manner; there was a touch of divine serenity about her as she smiled benignly at Lene. She obviously spoke next to no German but wanted it known that she would have said something pleasant if only she had the words. Lene was quite taken with her. It was one of those immediate sympathies that young women develop with those they suspect of being the beloved of one of their elders. Lady Samuel seemed to recognize the touch of *Schwärmerei* in Lene and said something that sounded like "Hope to meet you again" before she turned back to Edu to suggest, in English, that they return to their seats. Tom and Lene then ran into Elias and Bettina Süsskind. Bettina was, as usual, distracted or playing at being distracted. She composed funny, mordant rhymes in her head, mostly at public functions, and some of them had found their way into the *Frankfurter Zeitung* under a pseudonym. She was a woman of sharp wit, but hardly the sort on whom a young woman like Lene could develop a crush.

The Hindemith piece which ended the concert was greeted with polite applause. Lene unfortunately had so much on her mind after intermission that she barely heard it.

She and Tom took the trolley to the Café Rumpelmayer; "slumming" had become a favorite pastime of the rich. Lene stayed close

behind Tom when they entered the crowded, noisy café. She felt
tired, and it was clear to her that not a single scintillating sentence
would rise from her throat.

Tom found a table, at which there was just barely room for them.
He seemed to know several of those present and made the introduc-
tions, which fluttered in and out of Lene's head as quickly as the
Hindemith had done. The only person to catch her attention was
a small-boned, homely man who scribbled continuously in a blue
notebook and hardly bothered to look up when he was introduced.
He had thinning hair, his homely features were finely drawn, almost
delicate, and he had the saddest eyes Lene had ever seen. In front
of him was an ashtray filled with cigarette butts, beside it a glass
from which he drank constantly an evil-looking liquid that turned
out to be brandy. The phrase Emma had once flung at her suddenly
came to her mind: "one of your Jewish misfits." Lene had not
known quite what her sister meant until this moment. Here he was,
the Jewish misfit; his name was Paul Leopold.

There was also a lion-maned painter, who had spots of paint on
him as if to advertise his profession; a poet with a mannish haircut
who referred to herself in the third person as Lulu; two actors from
the chamber theater; and a man who said he was a playwright. Paul
Leopold was a reporter for the *Frankfurter Zeitung*.

Tom ordered a bottle of wine and "something light" to eat without asking Lene what she wanted. There was so much noise around
the table that it was impossible to hear what anyone except the
nearest person was saying. Lene sat between the artist with the hair
and Paul Leopold. No sooner had the waiter left than a bearded
figure in shorts approached. He carried a green flag on his shoulder
and tried to sell them a hand-printed magazine called *Love*. He was
dismissed with heckled comments by most of the people at the table,
but Paul Leopold took some change from his pocket and bought a
copy of the magazine before returning to his compulsive scribbling.
"He's a harmless fool," he muttered, "but you're all a bunch of
villainous dilettantes."

"Who is that?" Lene asked.

"Karlchen Wassmann," said the journalist, as if that explained it
all.

"And who is Karlchen Wassmann?" persisted Lene.

"A good man, following his own dream, doing no evil to anyone, eating vegetables, preaching love. I shall have to write a piece about him one day. What was your name?"

"Lene Wertheim."

"Are you here alone?"

"I came with Thomas there . . ." Lene pointed to Tom, who was deep in conversation with Lulu.

"You're both dressed for better things," Paul Leopold said.

"We've been to a concert at the Palmengarten," Lene explained, but he was already back in his notebook.

"He's writing the most important philosophical work of our time," the painter told her.

"Nonsense," said Paul Leopold.

"What *are* you writing?" Lene asked.

"The most important novel of our time."

"Your friend Tom over there looks like one of those black-and-white birds from the South Pole," said the painter. "What do you call 'em?"

"Penguins," said Lene.

"Playboys," said Paul Leopold, and the painter cackled. Lene sipped her glass of wine, trying to think of an interesting subject with which to initiate a conversation. The painter leered at her with tipsy insolence. Paul Leopold turned the page, his pen scratched out a word and then flew on. A waiter brought Lene a portion of runny and tasteless chicken à la king. Lene tried to keep busy with the food, for no one would talk to her. The painter had turned away and was having an animated discussion with the playwright. Now and then a key word drifted toward Lene—"agitprop," "stylization," "*Sachlichkeit*"—but she lost the thread in the noise and the numbness that attacked her head after the second glass of wine. Someone, she did not know who, kept refilling her glass. Tom looked over at her, and she saw his lips move in what she took to be expressions of loving concern, but she felt more and more isolated. Paul Leopold had started another glass of brandy.

"May I have a cigarette?" Lene asked him, and he handed her one without looking up. She knew she ought not to smoke in her tipsy condition, but the smoke was so thick at the table that she thought it would counteract it, the way rangers sometimes set other fires to halt a runaway forest fire. As she inhaled the first puff, an attack of nauseous dizziness assailed her.

Just then Paul Leopold shut his notebook and announced in a ringing voice that he had finished for the night. He called the waiter over, ordered black coffee and another brandy "to wash it down" and immediately took charge of the conversation. His transformation astounded Lene. He was a mesmerizing storyteller, taking some small, observed event—like a drunk's insult hurled at a *grande dame* walking her dog—and turning it into a wonderful tale, full of invention and a resonance that took in not merely Frankfurt but the entire country, even the world, even, sometimes, God in heaven.

His Jewish-misfit's face and body were suddenly exchanged for those of sage, prophet and court jester. Paul Leopold disappeared in the suspense of his fables. He had put his hand on Lene's arm, and she saw with amazement that it was broad and flat with slender fingers—an artisan's hand, not a Talmudist's. She had continued sipping her wine, and while she was caught up in the journalist's story her head seemed clear, but as soon as he had finished she felt worse than ever. She was gratified to hear him say to her, "You've had too much to drink, my dear, and you'll think ill of us for it tomorrow morning—if not tonight. I want you to think well of this little band and would hope you'll return another night, when you've learned to hold your wine. Then perhaps our stimulating conversation won't put a glaze over your pretty eyes. Take the young lady home!" he shouted across the table at the startled Tom, who recognized the truth of what had been said and immediately rose, staring guiltily at Lene, who was trying to hold herself very straight.

"Leave us some money," Paul Leopold said.

"Come back later!" Lulu said. "We'll be here till dawn. Paul can't go to sleep before the sun rises."

Lene got up from her seat and nodded to everyone. The fixed smile was still on her face. She had seen heads turn at her entrance, had felt it might be possible with one or two seemingly simple gestures, like brushing the hair back from her face, to remain fixed in everyone's memory. Now she still felt the eyes resting on her, but she was humiliated. Her exit was not nearly as splendid as her entrance had been.

She dared not speak on the way home. Tom had gotten a horse cab nearby, and they rode in silence through the summer night. Lene fought desperately to keep the sour wine and the vile food from rising in her throat. It seemed an eternity before they reached the Guiollettstrasse. She closed her eyes and did not open them until she heard Tom say, "Here we are."

He tried to kiss her at the door, but she turned away. The carriage was waiting for him.

"Are you going back to the café?" she asked.

"I think so," he said, sounding a little embarrassed.

"Lulu will eat you." Lene's voice was slurred.

"I'll sit in her stomach like Jonah in the whale until she spits me up again."

"Don't say 'spit up'!" Lene said.

"I love you," Tom said, "no one else matters."

"Next time I will be like a tiger. I will glide silently through the café with glowing eyes and make them all stiffen with fright . . ."

"Go to sleep, Lene."

"Or maybe I'll just be a striped orange cat . . ."

"Good night, Lene, sleep well."

Lene closed the door behind her as silently as she could; it was heavy and full of creaks and sighs and the rattle of locks. She tiptoed upstairs and saw that the door to her mother's room was shut; the sound of voices came from behind it dimly, like the light slipping out from under it. The commotion at such a late hour was odd. Lene's curiosity almost got the better of her nausea, and she stood still for a minute on the top step of the staircase, trying to make out the intense voices behind the closed door. Then the waves of illness rose up again, and she realized she had just enough energy to reach her room and fall through the darkness onto her bed. The maid had turned back the covers and laid out her nightgown, but Lene dropped, fully clothed, across the white sheets into a sleeplike stupor. An hour later the upheaval in her stomach woke her. She made it to the washstand just in time.

ANDREAS HAD taken a small flat not far from the university the previous year, at the beginning of the fall term. He wanted to put some distance between the family and himself, to have privacy to

pursue his life without explanations or excuses. He had soon realized
that he would have to go much farther than the few blocks from the
Guiollettstrasse to the Sophienstrasse to escape the closeness of
those ties. The Wertheims' oppressive interest in one another did
not stop at the doorstep of their houses. No doubt it would pursue
him even if he moved to another city. Mama was on the telephone
several hours each day. She talked to Eva—only to complain about
her later to whoever would listen—and to Pauline. She daily called
her mother-in-law, who had sold her house just before the inflation
struck with full force and was living in a light and airy apartment
in Edu's house. She had conversations once a week with her brother
Jonah in Wiesbaden, who had married a Gentile and retired from
hospital work to a lucrative private practice. She talked to Elias or
Bettina every other day at least. And she could not help talking to
Edu, who always wanted to know what the "children" were doing.
Andreas found it unbearable and stifling, but it was not so easy to
escape.

He had unfortunately taken up with a young laborer who worked
for the coal company. Andreas found his lust and his innocence and
the pride with which he offered his body irresistible. Heiner did not
care where the love that enfolded and caressed and petted him came
from. He had a string of girl friends too. Andreas had no idea how
he had found his way into the underground world of the homosexual. Heiner had told him many different stories, none of which
sounded true. He had a flair for making up the most outlandish lies,
which he defended to the bitter end, withdrawing in an angry pout
if he was challenged with proof that he had been blatantly untruth-
ful. It had taken Andreas a while to get used to the lies. At first he
was exasperated, then he realized that Heiner's innocence extended
to his fictions. He lied because the truth was so ordinary, so dull,
like the workers' suburb where he had grown up. Heiner was one
of nine children, a cipher, a nobody. He lied to make himself the
equal of the "gentlemen" who picked him up and bought him good
food and drink and gave him trinkets.

"Oh, man," he said the first time he saw Andreas naked, "will you
look at that li'l Jew-tail." He didn't mean it to be an insult, he simply
took note of it in his inimitable Frankfurt accent and went on to talk
of something else. He was the same age as Andreas, which made him

seem less like a whore but provoked the struggle for dominance between them. Andreas, growing up in sheltered West End rooms and gardens, had never known a boy from the working class until he fell in love with one.

While he continued to devote himself to the study of music, he found that the affair was occupying more and more of his time. When he was alone, he would have to tear his mind back forcibly from dreams of Heiner or monologues directed at his absent lover. If something had been wrong between them at their last meeting, Andreas would return again and again to accusations of cruelty or thoughtlessness. While he dissected his lover's dishonesty, analyzed his unfaithfulness, afternoon would turn into night, or night into morning, and Andreas' book would still lie open at the same page.

He never broached these subjects when he was with Heiner. He wanted desperately to be as free and unconcerned as Heiner was. To live from day to day. To swim in the river in summer and take a sled down the steep and dangerous hill in the winter and never be asked "Where have you been?" But he himself continuously asked "Where have you been?" and was furious when Heiner lied or told him to mind his own business.

Heiner knew that he made Andreas unhappy, that he tormented him and deceived him. He knew that Andreas had every right to be angry. But he could not stand his friend's childish sulks and girlish sighs. They embarrassed him in front of his friends, and Heiner cared about his friends. He was a sociable person. He couldn't stand it when Andreas wanted him alone to himself, and he grew furious when he was reproached, ever so mildly, with accusations that had given Andreas not a moment's peace for days. Heiner's parent had never in all of his twenty-one years managed to make him feel guilty. Why should Andreas succeed where they had failed?

This night they had been drinking at a bar where many of Frankfurt's sleazier Bohemians hung out. There were a number of homosexuals, but it was not an exclusively *Schwule* bar. Andreas, who had given up a ticket to the Palmengarten concert and was behind in his summer-course work, was edgy and dissatisfied. The bar was quiet —it was a weekday night—and the prices for beer had just gone up another several thousand marks.

"I ought to be home working," Andreas muttered, not for the first time.

"Then go home," Heiner said. "Shut up and leave."

He took his beer over to another table where a girl with slavic features was sitting with an empty glass, leafing through a movie magazine. For a while Andreas sat alone while Heiner talked to the girl about Charlie Chaplin and Anny Ondra and ordered another drink for her, which he told the bartender to put on Andreas' tab. The girl was not very talkative and kept looking at Andreas nervously with her cold flat eyes. She allowed Heiner to put his arm around her but never took her eyes off Andreas, who had gotten up and was rummaging through his pockets for enough bills to pay the check.

"Go back to him," she said to Heiner, loud enough that Andreas heard her. "Go to your friend before he cries."

"He can cry forever for all I care," said Heiner. "He can float away on his tears down the Main and into the Rhine and out to sea. I'm tired of his moods."

Andreas didn't want to go alone, but he didn't want to stay either. He wanted to take Heiner to his room and be alone with him. Not merely to touch him and undress him and make love to him, but to bring him under his influence, talk to him so Heiner could stop being the braggart. Alone together, they were more nearly equals, and Heiner's stories lost some of their shrillness and began moving toward the truth.

Heading for the door, his mind on Heiner and the girl, Andreas didn't look where he was going—or else the man's foot was there intentionally—and tripped over the leg of a customer sprawled in a chair near the door. He fell to the floor, his glasses went skidding under a table, and the money he held in his hand flew in all directions. It was so unexpected that Andreas had no time to protect himself; he fell heavily, awkwardly and painfully. The people in the bar laughed. The loudest laughter of all came from Heiner in the corner with his arm around the girl.

Andreas groped under the tables for his glasses and his money while the laughter rose around him. Suddenly he was enraged. As soon as he had found the glasses, he got up and charged at Heiner.

He toppled him from his chair, and they both went rolling to the floor locked together in combat, hitting out at whatever they could reach, clawing, biting, boxing. But Andreas was no match for the young laborer. If the barkeeper had not separated them and thrown them both out the door, it would have ended badly for Andreas.

"That's it," said Heiner, once they had recovered their breath. "You can lick my ass from now on. I've had enough. Go find yourself another playmate."

Andreas knew better than to ask his pardon, although he desperately wanted to do just that. He didn't want to see him go. At that moment he wanted more than ever to be with him, naked, playing Indian, wrestling and making believe they were engaged in great feats of endurance. But Heiner straightened his jacket, threw back his shoulders, set the visored cap firmly on his head and sauntered away. He turned once, to make an obscene gesture, which Andreas interpreted as an enticement, and then headed for the railroad underpass and home.

"Meet me tomorrow after work," Andreas called after him. "I'll have something for you."

"What?"

"Whatever you like, I'll bring it."

"I thought you already had something in mind." Heiner, who had stopped under a street lamp, his chest thrust out so that Andreas could see the shirt pulled tightly across it, made as if to move on again. Andreas' mind raced through all his possessions.

"My ring!" he shouted. "I'll give you my ring!"

"What kind of ring?"

"A gold ring with a precious stone in it."

"A diamond?"

"No, not a diamond. I don't know what kind. But it's green."

"Who does it belong to?"

"I told you it's mine."

"You'll say I stole it."

"No I won't."

"Then write me a letter to say you're giving it to me."

"I will. Meet me at the Bockenheimer Watchtower at five o'-clock."

"Maybe."

Heiner disappeared in the murk of the underpass. Andreas heard his friend's steps for a little while. Then there was silence.

Andreas headed straight home to fetch the ring. The large bruise on his cheek stung and his rib cage ached. Limping along the moonlit streets, away from the scene of his unhappy encounter, he suddenly felt some vague but persistent discomfort—it could hardly be called a pain—and the certainty, more palpable than the discomfort, that he had been touched by the cold hand of death. His knees grew weak with fear. He sat down on the nearest stoop, but started up again when he heard footsteps approaching and went loping off toward his parents' house, amazed that his legs were able to carry him. When he reached his house, he rested for a while beside the garden gate that led to the kitchen entrance. He was certain that his parents were either asleep or out. But their quarrel about the dinner invitation had ended with the decision to stay home and nurse their wounded feelings. Caroline, having given in and made her excuses to Frau Doktor, locked herself in her rooms, saying she had palpitations. She took several drops of valerian to calm herself but still found it impossible to sleep.

Nathan chose to respond to his wife's agitation by withdrawing to his study to read *The Decline and Fall of the Roman Empire*. He had taken it up in opposition to the current vogue for Oswald Spengler and his *Decline of the West*, which he considered the work of a charlatan. Nathan never ceased to be amused at Gibbons' bias in favor of the Romans and against the upstart Christians. He often mused in his melancholy way on the hopes implicit in the Age of Enlightenment and wished that it had been given to him to be one of its children—even if it had meant living in the Judengasse. Who knew, he might have been a friend of Börne's. The only things that still gave him pleasure these days were activities like reading and music in which he could lose himself sufficiently to forget the painful present. The law had once offered him such a haven, but he had grown weary of it; it had been too much abused. He felt that it could, in the hands of unscrupulous practitioners or a totalitarian state, become the instrument of monstrous perversions of justice, divorced from all moral ends. He had begun writing an essay on this subject, but he wrote slowly and laboriously, and with his usual pessimism he doubted it would ever get done.

It had been Andreas' intention to slip quietly into the house, pick up the ring, a gift from his grandfather Wertheim, wash his face and hands, put on a clean shirt and leave again without being detected. He knew that Fräulein Gründlich was on vacation; he had no great fear of meeting Emma, whom he trusted and with whom he saw himself allied; and Lene was out with Thomas von Brenda-Badolet.

As soon as he let himself in, Andreas realized that his parents were home. A minute later he heard his mother's anxious voice, calling from upstairs. "Who's there?" Her voice was full of fear. "Who just came in?"

"It's only me, Mama," Andreas said. He was halfway up the stairs and saw that the door to her room was partly open. "I've come to get something."

"At this hour of the night?" she said. "Come in and talk to me, tell me what's happened."

Andreas could see her through the door, lying on her chaise longue dressed for bed. She could not see him.

"I'll be right there, Mama," he said. "Let me go quickly to the bathroom first."

He meant to wash his bruised face with cold water and comb his hair and see if the rest of him could pass muster.

"What are *you* doing here?" Emma's voice so startled Andreas that he let out an involuntary cry. "You must have done something wrong," Emma said, "to be so frightened of me." She looked closely at him. "You've been in a brawl!" she said. "Oh, Andreas!"

"It wasn't a brawl."

"Who attacked you?"

"Nobody. I had a fall, in a bar."

Emma made a face. She did not believe him.

"I must go and see Mama," he said, "and first make myself presentable. Let's meet for supper soon and talk."

"When? I have much to tell you."

"Soon."

"Next week?"

"I have a paper due. The week after. I promise."

Andreas kissed her quickly, and in a fever of activity saw to his face, his clothes, and went like a whirlwind through his chiffonier searching for the ring. He found it in its small green leather box and stuffed it deep into his pocket. He was sweating, so he wiped his neck with some cologne and put the comb through his hair once more. Then he went to see his mother, closing the door behind him. The first thing she noticed was the bruise on his face.

"My God!" she exclaimed. "What's that?"

"I tripped and fell."

"That doesn't look as though it came from a fall. You were in a fight!"

"Only a small one—with a friend."

"If that's what a friend does, I would hate to see an enemy's work."

Andreas felt like a small boy. He was never prepared for his mother's maternal insight. Aloof though she was, her powers of observation were acute; now and then she penetrated directly to the heart of a secret her children wanted to keep hidden from her.

"Sit down a minute," she said to him. "You're not going out again?"

"I have a paper due. I must get back to work. Next weekend I'll come to dinner, I swear it. But don't press me, Mama, I don't want to be pressed."

"You don't look like a young man who's been working on a paper. If you have fistfights with your friends, you can't be getting much studying done. Will you pass the examinations in January?"

"What if I don't?"

"You know the answer as well as I do. You won't receive your degree. You'll have to stay here. Your father will doubtless withdraw his support. Uncle Edu—"

"I'll pass the examinations, Mama."

Caroline looked at him slouched in the chair, thin, pale, handsome, easily bruised. His hair was slicked down unnaturally. His right hand was in the pocket of his pants. He smelled of the street.

"These are not good times," Caroline began. The whiff of the gutter hung about her son. She feared for them all. "Tell me, Andreas," she said, her hands folded demurely in her lap, "is it true what . . . what they say about you?"

"What is it that they say about me, Mama?"

"That you are . . . that you prefer men."

"Yes, it's true, Mama."

Caroline looked into his eyes for a swift moment, to see if she could find something new there, something she hadn't seen before. Andreas returned her gaze steadily, without the familiar veil, without mockery. Tears shimmered on his lids. She saw now that his mouth had puffed up, his cheeks were scratched and the bruise was turning purple.

"So that's how you got those injuries," Caroline said in a low, husky voice. She cleared her throat. "They sent your Uncle Gottfried to America for far less cause."

" 'They' can send *me* to America too! I don't give a damn—the farther away the better!"

"Be careful, Andreas, *please* be careful."

Caroline had gotten up and turned toward the window. She wanted to hide from Andreas and shut herself off from any more revelations. But he followed her and they embraced. Caroline realized as she held him tightly that she had not—for how long?—held anyone in her arms. Not her children, not her husband, not her sister or her brothers. Tears streamed down her face. She suddenly longed for little children again. For grandchildren.

"If you need anything," she whispered in his ear, "please ask me for it. Whatever it is, I'll get it for you. Don't allow yourself to be . . . blackmailed."

Andreas kissed her hand. The ring weighed in his pocket like a stone. He went back to his room and flung the empty green leather box back into the drawer. Walking to his apartment he was uncertain whether it was relief he felt or merely the emptiness that remains when the hand of death is briefly removed.

NATHAN's telephone rang very late that evening. He had dozed off, the Gibbon in his lap, his hand like a bookmark on the page. Edu's voice was cool and crisp over the receiver. "I'm sorry if I woke you, but I wanted to reach you at home and alone. I just got in from the concert and a party, and it seemed like a good time to call."

"I was sitting here reading," said Nathan.

"It's come to my attention that you plan to fire Eisenstein."

"He doesn't have enough to do, Edu. My practice . . . well, you know . . . I thought you might be able to use him."

"I'm not the Home Relief, Nathan, nor is the firm a retirement home for pensioned imbeciles. Keep Eisenstein on. Your monthly dividends from the firm are being increased by fifty percent. We have been having some good luck—for those who can borrow, as we can, inflation is not such a terrible thing. You borrow good marks and pay back bad ones. We've done well. Business with America is picking up, and now that I'm a partner in the bank . . . well, never mind."

"Thank you, Edu, thank you very much." Nathan was half under the impression that he was dreaming.

"Don't thank me. It was father's wish that all his sons share in the profits of Wertheim and Sons."

"I will keep Eisenstein on until he's old enough to receive his pension. I think that's seven more years . . ."

"Nathan! Listen to me, I don't give a damn about Eisenstein, but it's important that your children are provided for. Do you understand me? Politically, if not necessarily financially, things are going to get worse and worse for us. I'm afraid the murder of Rathenau was only the beginning . . ."

"I've been writing a treatise on law and morality which I'll be glad to let you read when it's done."

"Lots of luck," said Edu dryly. "Good night." And he hung up.

HANNCHEN WAS not prepared for the letter she received, on a Monday in mid-August, from Gerald F. Worth, in New York. At first, looking at the envelope with its engraved name and an address on Park Avenue, she wondered idly, with just a touch of apprehension, whether it was a plea for money from a stranger or bad news from some other quarter. Not until she saw the salutation did she remember who Gerald F. Worth was. As she began to read she thought that the handwriting had grown elusively cursive and the language stiff.

Dear Mother:

Twenty years have passed since I left Frankfurt for America. The letters I wrote to Edu have remained unanswered, but I can no longer allow his intransigence to stand in my way—I must write to you. It's not as though

I have done poorly in life, quite the contrary, I am what one calls here in America an "unqualified success." I have a seat on the stock exchange and on the boards of several private banks, and I own a half-interest in a company that manufactures cosmetics. All in all, not a bad record.

I am married to a lovely woman and have three children, who are our pride and joy. Blanche, my wife, comes from a distinguished Jewish family in New Orleans, where we met and were married. Her father gave me my start in this country and has always treated me like a son. They do not judge a person's small trespasses so harshly here. But let me not speak of the past. "Let by-gones be by-gones" as they say here.

We have lived in New York since just before the war. I served in the American army (being a proud citizen of this great land) but was not sent overseas, so that I did not fight against Germany and my brothers, though I would have done my duty in any case.

Life has been good to me, but I think of you now and then, Mama, and wonder how you are. Have the years treated you well? Are you happy? Do you enjoy the opera and the theater still? I would like very much to hear from you. I know that you live in my brother's house, but I ask you please not to show him this letter. I do not know why he has never forgiven me, I never did anything to him. But I would like to see you again before death separates us forever. I would like to feel free to visit you, should fate bring me to Frankfurt . . .

Gerald,

your son

Hannchen read the letter carefully. As soon as she was finished, before she allowed her mind to dwell on its contents, she began to worry about what she should do about it. Should she show it to Edu? Could she? Her youngest son and her favorite had become her keeper. She always said that she was "but a guest" in his house, yet she felt, at moments such as these, that she was more nearly a prisoner. Edu had to know everything about her: what she ate for dinner and how she spent her afternoons, what she purchased and what she saw in her dreams. He would ask her what mail she had received and she would have to answer, "A letter from Gottfried." Or would she? What if she said, "Only some bills and circulars?" Would he know? Did Humboldt, who brought her mail twice a day, keep track of what she got? A stab of annoyance with Gottfried for disturbing the peace of this pleasant day cut through her thoughts. He had always been difficult. He fought harder and cried less than the others. He had a fearful temper. Hannchen saw the child he was, looking the other way in the family photograph. Unsmiling.

In the end she compromised. She did not show Edu the letter, but she told him that it had come in the morning mail. Edu seemed uninterested. Hannchen was annoyed. "Gottfried's done well," she said, "he has a seat on the stock exchange, directorships in many banks and owns a powder factory."

"He seems to be a braggart now, too," Edu murmured. "Do you mean to stay in touch with him?"

Hannchen looked away. "I hadn't thought about it," she lied.

"Just don't become involved," he warned her. "He's the same blackguard as ever. Once a thief, always a thief."

After a week of much soul-searching, Hannchen wrote Gottfried a letter. She wrote effusively and asked for pictures of his children. But: "Don't think about coming to visit," she added, "I'm an old lady, good for nothing but sitting in the sun in my beautiful room in Edu's house, rocking and dreaming." She made herself appear fragile. She put the blame on Edu. Still, she had not remained silent, no one could fault her.

EMMA'S LIFE changed overnight. Lene had been right, she had a beau; she was in love. Otto loomed larger in her life than anything, anyone, ever had before. She continued to go riding three times a week, but those three days were the ones around which all the others turned. Otto, mounted on his dappled gray gelding, waited for her, and when she rode up to him, he rose in his stirrups and lifted his cap. The weather was glorious that year, summer seemed to hold on and on deep into September. The two of them galloped along the still paths in sunlight and shade until the horses were glistening with sweat. Then they would slow to a walk and find a pleasant spot under some large tree where they dismounted and sat for a while talking. They had much to tell each other, for they were truly strangers.

"When are we to meet this paragon of German manhood," Nathan asked at dinner one day, "your dashing young Siegfried?"

"He isn't *young*," said Emma.

"He's not?" There was something in the even tone of Caroline's voice and the level stare that accompanied it that made Emma uneasy.

"Oh, he isn't *old*," she said.

"How old would you say he was?"

"In his late thirties . . ."

"Has he told you?"

"No—I never asked." It was a lie. Otto had told her. He had turned forty-four in July.

"Is there some problem?" Nathan asked. "If so, let's hear about it. I simply asked if we were ever going to make the man's acquaintance. I don't see what his age has got to do with it."

"Soon, Papa," said Emma.

She brought Otto to tea one rainy afternoon. Anna had baked an elaborate Sachertorte especially for the occasion, under the misapprehension that the officer was Austrian. Emma was so nervous that she could not get a bit of it down her throat. The visit did not go well. The conversation was stilted, without warmth. Emma threw herself valiantly into the breach and chattered with the heedless intensity of someone in the grip of delirium. Nathan said almost nothing; Caroline questioned the officer about home and family and discovered that he had an old mother to whom he was quite attached. He had served his country "with honor" in the war, didn't care about politics but was against all things "radical" or "extreme."

"I believe in the *middle*," he said, "the middle of everything."

"You must meet my sister Eva," said Caroline.

"I would be glad to," Otto replied, though he was aware that the remark, etched in sarcasm, did not mean what it said. Emma's heart cried out angrily against her family, and Otto caught the indignant look she threw at her mother. He recognized something she saw only dimly—that her parents understood the willful element in her love. Emma wanted desperately to be seared by a white-hot flame, to be purified and to emerge reborn. What her parents found odd, and therefore unbelievable, was that all this should have found an echo in Otto Radowitz. They wrote him off as a fortune hunter.

Caroline found him handsome enough, but he was not acceptable. He was, as Nathan later said, "the enemy."

"It's not as though I insist that my children marry within the faith," he proclaimed before Hannchen. "It might even be a blessing to lose some of the Jewish *Angst* with which we're all cursed. The way things are going, the next generation might even thank us for breaking their connection with 'the chosen people.' However"—he paused to give his words added weight—"a Thomas von Brenda-Badolet is one thing, an Otto Radowitz quite another."

"I've never seen Emma so radiant," said Hannchen.

It was hoped that the trip to Venice would put a brake on the affair.

"A week is hardly time enough to wean her away," said Caroline to Edu on the telephone one Sunday morning.

"I'm sorry that I didn't know the trip was to serve the additional purpose of separating my niece from her beloved, or I might have taken the girls on a trip around the world," he replied.

"Perhaps *you* can talk her out of it," said Caroline. "I suspect him of being after her money."

"It's easy enough to find out what his financial position is," Edu replied, and the very next morning gave the order to check Otto Radowitz's credit rating. The report came back a week later. There was nothing in the man's financial history to lead one to suspect him of fortune hunting. The family was not rich, but its estate was profitable, and Otto, an only child, had a decent income besides his army pay. He was not known to be a gambler. Edu gave Caroline the information. "And what about his private life?" she asked. "Has he ever been married?"

"We didn't inquire into that," said Edu. "We're not a detective agency, my dear."

The following Saturday, Edu and his four nieces boarded the night express to Venice. Edu had taken two double rooms and a single at the Hotel Danieli. "Facing the water, on one of the upper floors, please," he had written, and his request had been granted.

"It is best to do very little the first day," he said as they were being shown to their rooms. "Acclimatize yourselves, the way you do in the mountains."

"We've got so little time!" said Lene.

"I'm certain you'll return," said Edu. "You don't have to see *every* painting in Venice this trip."

"We'll just take a turn around the Piazza San Marco," Julia said.

"With frequent rests," Jenny chimed in.

The young women set off, guidebooks in hand. They had made a concerted effort to learn some Italian before leaving home, but the only one with any aptitude for the language was Emma, so they put her in charge of asking directions. "*Dove* . . ." she would begin, in her German accent, articulating the words very clearly.

At supper that night the girls brought their impressions to Edu, and he bathed in the light of their volatile enthusiasm. In the middle of dessert he was called to the telephone. The girls continued to eat their zuppa inglese.

Lene said, "I wonder who *that* could be?"

"Who *should* it be?" Jenny wanted to know.

"Lene is convinced that Uncle Edu is involved in a secret affair with a married woman," Emma explained.

"Of the highest rank!" Lene added.

"Do tell us," said Julia, lighting a cigarette now that Edu was gone. Julia was bright and intense, and her gift for stylistic mimicry made her small literary talent appear greater than it was. She had sworn she would never marry and had already sold some short essays and features to provincial newspapers.

Lene told her story. Since there was not much to it—a glimpse through the door and a brief meeting at intermission between Schubert and Hindemith—she had to embellish it with conjectures and opinions. The cousins were delighted. A faint smile played about Jenny's mouth, and Julia giggled with delight. "If she *is* here in Venice, we'll have to be on the lookout for her every minute," she said. "That'll be so exciting! My God, I might even make it into a little story . . ."

"Shhh . . ." whispered Emma. "Here he comes." Julia put out her cigarette, but Edu, who had no patience with women who smoked, sniffed at the traces of smoke in the air and said that he thought cigarettes spoiled the taste buds.

"I'm finished eating," Julia said by way of apology.

"It's rude to those who are *not*," he said sternly.

Julia colored and said, "I'm sorry, Uncle Edu," with proper humility. Like the rest of them, she hadn't the courage to oppose him, but unlike them she yielded not with love but with a calculation she did her best to hide. She saw her dependence on him more clearly than the others.

The week in Venice was unforgettable. From the first stroll in the Piazza to the final ride down the Grand Canal the girls thought every moment touched with magic. The weather was mild and sometimes just a little misty, putting the city into a melancholy perspective.

The day after their arrival, they took a *vaporetto* over to San Giorgio. Uncle Edu stayed inside, protected from wind and water, but the girls rode outside, squealing a little when the waves slapped the sides and sent the spray into their faces. Emma read the descriptions from Baedeker to them while they admired the Tintorettos as best they could in the darkness of the choir. Then they took the elevator to the top of the campanile to look at all Venice spread out before them.

Uncle Edu did not accompany them up into the bell tower. There was an exhibition of sixteenth-century Venetian drawings at the library adjacent to the church which he very much wanted to see, having just bought a drawing attributed to a follower of Titian. While there, he met Lady Samuel and her party, who had also come to view the drawings. Edu proved to be an eloquent guide. Elias would have been proud of his friend and pupil. Lady Samuel smiled her divine smile and confided to her friends that Mr. Wertheim was a noted collector. She asked him whether he planned to take his nieces to the island of Torcello. "I've left that for the last day," he said. Lady Samuel opined that the twelfth-century mosaics were "simply grand." She had been to see them on her last trip and remembered their splendor most vividly. "I know them well," said Edu.

By the time the girls found their way to the exhibition, Lady Samuel had gone in her private water taxi to visit the Church of the Redeemer. "I'm doing Palladio today," she had told Edu before sweeping out the door into the grassy enclosed courtyard, where she stopped to open her parasol against the sun. She knew Edu was watching.

The days flew by, until but one was left. Lene had not even sent postcards to all the people on her list. Julia's notes filled scarcely half her diary. Only Emma looked forward to their return. She had written long letters to Otto every evening in the room overlooking the Grand Canal. "I'll no doubt see you before you receive this," she wrote on the next-to-last evening. "Tomorrow we're taking the *vaporetto* to Torcello, where there is a Romanesque church and mosaic. We're taking a picnic lunch."

The day set aside for Torcello dawned unseasonably warm and foggy. As they set out from the quai the mist still covered the horizon, and it seemed as if they were heading into the shrouded vapors that hide a lost continent. They passed the island of San Michele and heard the wailing of the ships and tugs that ply the lagoon. All that was visible of the cemetery island were a few dark cypresses, looking like spectral galleons sailing out of Venetia's past. It was not until after they had left Burrano that the sun burned off the last traces of fog, and the morning blazed up in the fullness of golden autumn.

They were the only ones to get off at Torcello, and once the boat had left again, they were the only ones in the still, flat landscape. They followed the path that ran alongside the canal, speaking very little. Uncle Edu walked ahead, more anxious than the girls to get to their destination. Now and then he would stop and point with his walking stick at the peaceful landscape. "Look there, how lovely it is," he said, although he preferred works of art to landscapes. He would sooner gaze at Turners than at Alpine gorges or storm-tossed seas.

They reached the small square at the end of the canal in about fifteen minutes. The church stood off to the side, beyond a grassy lot ringed with the rubble of statues and bits of fluted columns. It looked older than antiquity; there was something triumphantly desolate about it. Edu and his nieces stepped inside, to be met by a breath-takingly cold darkness. It took them several minutes to grow accustomed to it and make out the mosaics emerging from the walls. Twelve white-robed apostles circled the apse below an elongated figure of the Virgin dressed in black. On an opposite wall a monstrous vision of hell and damnation seemed to quiver in the dusty sunlight that fell from the narrow windows. Edu read to them in a calm, dispassionate voice, but mesmerized by the torments of the damned, the girls listened without comprehension.

"Shall we have our lunch now?" Uncle Edu asked, and his voice was a reminder that they lived in a civilized present, which had pushed demons out of sight and dispensed with mysteries and found holiness in the trappings of the state.

"When we get back to Venice today, we musn't forget to have our pictures taken in the Piazza San Marco," he said as they were looking for a place to spread their picnic. The concierge at the Danieli had packed a delectable lunch and they sat down in the shade of a fig tree at a table of rough-hewn wood, in sight of the ancient church. Emma and Jenny unpacked the cheeses, the prosciutto, the bottle of wine and the crusty loaves of bread. There were fresh sweet tomatoes and pickled olives, and for dessert purple grapes and fresh green figs.

"It looks wonderful!" Lene exclaimed.

"Eating well, even when you're eating simply, is one of life's great joys," said Uncle Edu. "A person who appreciates good food is well on the way to being civilized."

He liked dispensing such homilies to his nieces, for he knew that they would, like mirrors, come to reflect the substance of his ruminations. He sought to go no further. To have listened to their beating hearts would have made him privy to secrets he did not wish to hear.

They drank the wine from small silver mugs and spread the sharp cheese over the fresh bread. The prosciutto was sliced thin as tissue paper.

They were packing up the remains of the picnic when another party appeared on the road from the docks to look at the cathedral mosaics. Lene and Edu recognized Lady Samuel at the same instant.

"Ah," said Edu, "I must go over to say hello to my old friend."

"You see," Lene whispered, when he was out of earshot, "I was right, I'm always right. She's *here*!"

By the time Edu returned, the last crumb had been cleared away and the leftovers carefully returned to the basket. The girls were ready to start back. If Edu noticed the self-satisfied smile on Lene's face, he did not acknowledge it.

"Lady Samuel has asked me to join her at the Lido tonight," he said. "I hope you'll forgive me if I take the evening off. You'll be safe at the hotel. I trust you're all old enough to eat supper without me."

Walking leisurely to the dock to catch the *vaporetto* for the ride back to Venice, Edu fell in step with Emma. "You others go ahead," he said. "I want to have a little private conversation with my oldest niece."

He took her by the arm, and instantly her sense of the landscape vanished; she was aware only of Edu and the details of his suit, the pale buttons, the thin red stripe on his tie, the curve of the brim of his derby. She looked at his face, but it was more difficult to take in than his clothing. He seemed to resemble her father today, and Hannchen. His nose had grown quite pointed and sharp.

"Your mother tells me you're serious about the man you've just met."

So that was it. She ought to have known. Edu pronounced the word "man" with particular emphasis and, Emma thought, distaste.

"I don't want to interfere in your life," he continued, "but your mother's concern for you is genuine, and I want you to know that I, too, care very much about you. Your future is something we have to think about seriously. Do you love this man?"

"I do. Very much," Emma said. It was hard for her to remain calm. She felt dread seeping through her limbs.

"You sound very certain. How long have you known . . . ?"

"Otto. We met in August."

"That's two months."

"Almost three."

"Still not very long. How old is he?"

"Forty-four." Emma knew that it was pointless to lie.

"I'm forty this year."

"Then you should understand him well."

"Your mother thinks you want to marry . . . Otto."

"We haven't talked about it. But I *do.*" Emma thought that it showed courage and determination not to equivocate.

"Have you thought about the consequences?"

"What consequences?" She felt chilled, her hands were like ice.

"All our acts provoke consequences, my dear." Edu fell into his lecturing style. Then he stopped himself. He knew that he had to prevent this ridiculous union. Compared to a Prussian army officer, von Bre-Ba was a prize!

"If you had fallen in love with a street-sweeper," he went on, holding her arm more tightly, "we could convince you how unsuitable a match that would be. We could forbid it, send you away, pay the man off."

Was he threatening her with all of this? "I'm twenty-three," Emma said in a small voice.

"You've led a sheltered life, you don't know how dangerous the world can be. A Prussian army officer"—he searched for appropriate words—"a colonel in the German army is not a groom with horse manure under his fingernails. But he is not someone I would wish you to marry . . ."

"You don't know him at all! He's a fine, a wonderful man!"

"Hear me out, Emma."

"You're being unfair, it isn't right . . ." If only Otto knew what she was going through!

"It *is* right," Uncle Edu insisted. "Parents and relatives have a responsibility to their children. I don't want to argue with you, nor do I want to tell you what you must do. I simply want to forewarn you. To tell you to make certain that you know what awaits you in a marriage such as this—between people of such different backgrounds, habits, ages. I know something more than you do about Prussian officers. I served with them for four years. They are a breed apart."

"Not Otto!"

"They're cruel, cold and unfeeling. They're anti-Semitic. For generations they've known nothing but war . . . 'Blood and iron,' as Bismarck put it. Oh no, my dear! You cannot understand them."

Edu spoke with terrible hatred. Emma wanted to cover her ears, close her eyes. The autumn landscape, the whole beautiful island, the canal, the flowers, the calm lagoon had all been destroyed, desolated, laid waste.

"We're almost at the dock," Edu went on in his normal voice. "I want to drop the subject now."

"You've said enough," Emma replied coldly.

"Here comes the *vaporetto*. We're just in time."

The three other girls crowded around. Edu tried to act gay and unconcerned as he herded them aboard and made some foolish jokes. They were the only foreigners, the object of everyone's attention.

Emma went to the stern to be alone, but her sister and cousins followed like a band of protective angels. She looked down at the boat's wake. The water was inviting. How easy it would be to slip beneath its gray-green surface. Emma considered the advantages of death, the temptations of oblivion. But the moment passed; she felt Lene's arm around her waist, heard Jenny's giggle. Suicide was a matter for poets, after all, and untidy.

When they got back to Venice, they went directly to the Piazza, and Uncle Edu chose a photographer to take their picture, all together, as a memento of their trip. The pigeons swarmed around them, and Emma, who detested birds, had to clench her teeth to keep from screaming out in terror. She could think of nothing but their claws and beaks pecking at her face. Uncle Edu conferred with the photographer, paid him, gave him their address and a tip, took his name, and they were done. The photos arrived weeks later, imprinted upon postcards that said *Cartolina Postale Italiana,* and showed all five of them in a hail of pigeons, Emma holding herself as stiffly as if the waters of the lagoon were closing over her.

They left the next morning. The young women did not know when Uncle Edu had returned from the Lido. He was ready and packed to catch the train at the appointed time. He did, however, sleep soundly all the way through Italy and awoke only briefly when they crossed the border into Switzerland. In Lucerne he drank black coffee, and in Basel he joined his nieces for a meal in the dining car. By the time they reached Frankfurt it was night.

Caroline and Nathan were waiting up for their daughters.

"How was it?" Nathan asked, after embracing them.

"I hope you thanked Uncle Edu," said Caroline.

"I'm certain we did," said Lene. "We'll send him a beautiful letter in any case."

"It's good to be home," Emma said. And then, pretending it was an afterthought, she asked, "Any messages for me?"

"Your friend Otto called," said Caroline, "wanting to know whether we expected you home tonight."

"Oh!" said Emma, relieved and happy. It suddenly seemed to her that she had experienced the entire beautiful trip through a miasma of longing and emptiness. She had missed Otto every minute of every day. Edu's "little talk" which had so upset her was now no more than a spur to her to go her own way. The familiar surroundings of home gave her courage. "I must call him back," she said.

"Can't that wait?" Nathan asked her. "You've only just walked in the door. We want to hear about the trip. Was it wonderful?"

"Lovely, lovely," said Emma. "The country is beautiful, and Uncle Edu was marvelous, and the food was grand. Ask Lene." She could not, at that moment, make the effort to remember particulars.

"I've never been any place where you eat *so* well *all* the time," said Lene.

"I hope you haven't gained weight." Seeing the look of annoyance on Lene's face, Caroline added, "It doesn't look as if you did."

"We did so much walking, Mama," said Emma.

"I saw Tom at Jacob's bookstore today, and he said to me, 'Lene promised to send me daily postcards and I haven't got *one.*' So I told him that the Italian postal service is an abomination and he'd be lucky if they arrived in time for Christmas. I hope you posted them yourself? It's my belief that if you give them to the concierge, he pockets your stamp money and throws the cards into the wastebasket."

Emma excused herself and went into her father's study to call Otto. Her heart was beating wildly. She had never called him before, even though he had given her his telephone number. She had always assumed that it was *forward* of a woman to call a man. She realized as soon as he answered the phone that he had been asleep.

"Who's this?" he asked.

"Emma."

He seemed to be struggling hard to wake up. She heard him drop the telephone, mutter, pick it up again, curse.

"Emma," he said and lost half the name in a yawn.

"You do remember me?" she said with a little laugh.

"Ah, Emma," he said. "Are you calling from abroad?"

"I'm home," she said, "we just arrived. I had to call you. I'm sorry I woke you up. I shan't talk any longer."

"How long were you gone?"

"Ten days. It seems like forever. I missed you." She had meant to say it, but at that moment it seemed not right. "When will I see you?" That, too, was wrong, but it was part of the script. She had thought about it the entire trip, rehearsed it—but without him, of course.

"When do you ride?"

"Tomorrow. I can ride tomorrow. The usual time."

"Yes, of course, Emma," he said. "Glad you're back."

They hung up, both of them at once. Emma felt ashamed. She should not have called. He must think her pushy now, she had disturbed the delicate balance of things. He was such a punctilious man, so careful in all he did. He was used to making arrangements himself—he had told her that he even did women's work. In the army you didn't always have a boy to help you. He had learned from his mother, an excellent housekeeper. Sometimes he would flick a piece of straw from her skirt or brush some dust from her sleeve. Once he had even taken a loose strand of hair and pushed it back in place. Oh, how precise he was! If he said that a march to the front had been twenty-four kilometers, she knew it was so. Not twenty-six or twenty-three, but twenty-four. Why had she called him?

She awoke early the next morning. Lene was at breakfast, still muddled by sleep. "I have to go to the Pedagogical Institute," she said. "They weren't pleased with me at all when I requested time off to go to Italy so soon after the start of the term. They're asking me to come in early to help out with the children in the day-care program." She let out a plaintive sigh. "I hadn't expected to work with the children so soon."

"I'm certain it will go all right," Emma assured her.

She arrived at the stables fully an hour before her time. Otto, as always, came at two minutes before ten. He kissed her hand.

"I must take you hunting with me, very soon," he said, following some train of thought of his own. He had never thought much of Italy or the Italians.

"Hunting?" Emma asked.

"Autumn always makes me eager for it. If I were home, I wouldn't be riding in tame woods like these. Did I ever tell you we still hunt boar?"

"I sent you letters every day," said Emma.

"I haven't received any."

"My mother says the Italian postal service is bad."

"You should have saved all the letters and mailed them once you got back across the border."

"Are you angry with me?"

"Of course not, why do you ask me that?"

"I feel a constraint. It must be *my* fault." When Emma quarreled with someone she loved she always blamed herself for the dissension.

They dismounted at their usual spot, a small clearing where a weathered oak cast its shadow over a velvet pallet of moss. The sun, too warm for mid-October, released the odor of sweet grass and wild flowers. Emma and Otto sat down in the dappled shade of the oak while their horses grazed nearby.

"I'm sorry my letters didn't arrive," Emma said to her preoccupied lover, who, once again, mentioned his desire to hunt. The idea of riding out early in the morning to shoot animals and bring their bloody bodies home at night appalled her. She wanted to talk about Venice, having stored up innumerable facts about the origin and growth of the city, the height of the campanile, the number of churches and bridges, the size of the Piazza. Though Otto might not care to know who Tintoretto was, surely he would appreciate the many facts and figures she had memorized for him. But he paid so little attention to her report that all her enthusiasm left her, and she sat beside him close to tears, biting her lip.

"I have some news for you," Otto said. "It came while you were away, and I have been trying to find a way to tell you, but your own experiences are uppermost in your mind. It is hard to find a bridge to you today."

Otto had spent the previous night with a whore. When Emma called she was lying curled against his side with her head on his chest.

"What news?" Emma asked, fearing the worst but not knowing what the worst might be.

"I'm being transferred next month. The orders came in three days ago; my regiment is being sent to Weimar."

"Oh no!" she cried. "Don't tell me that! Say that you've made it up! We've only just got to know each other. I'll be so alone—what will I do? Please, Otto—please! Don't go!"

He was dumfounded by the intensity of her response. She spoke in an urgent, desperate tone. She seemed to want to clutch at him, but she kept her hands in her lap, twisting and turning them. Otto was fascinated. She is wringing her hands, he thought, and nothing entered his mind but that irrelevant phrase. He could not take his eyes off her white knuckles. The sight touched and repelled him at the same time.

"I've come to love you," Emma said before she could stop herself. Once the words were out, her hands flew to her mouth as though to shut it forcibly.

Otto was stunned. The fear he had had of her terrible self-control evaporated. Her declaration seemed to set him free and at the same time to make her softer, bring her closer to the point where she would submit to him. He grew bold with anticipation and kissed her full on the mouth that had just declared her love. Taken by surprise, Emma responded with fervor and they sank back onto the mossy ground. Otto, however, wanted more than a kiss. He thought that he had received permission to bed her here and now, in a forest clearing, under a pale-blue autumn sky. But as soon as Emma felt Otto's hand plucking at her skirt, tearing at her underclothes, she grew rigid again. She smelled the earth and remembered Christoph. Otto's fingers reached her skin. Emma began a terrible struggle to free herself. "Don't do that, don't," she said, escaping his mouth. "*No!*" she screamed, rocking from side to side to try to escape.

"I thought you loved me," he said, forcing himself into a calmness

cold as frost. He stood up. It had cost him every bit of his strength
not to take her then. He did not believe that there was such a thing
as rape, but he was afraid that Emma would accuse him of it. He
was pale with his effort at self-control and turned in anger away
from the young woman on the ground. Taking up a large branch,
he broke it in two and then in two again and threw the pieces as
far as he could, into the woods. The horses shied, startled by the
sounds.

Emma had sat up and folded her arms about her knees. She was
covered with bits of moss and grass, her hair had broken loose from
its ribbon. She, too, had fought to control her desire, had pulled back
from the abyss. Her sexuality frightened her, it opened up the
possibility of something dark and dreadful within her, which must
not be let out. Was that an aspect of her Jewishness? Were those
monsters of temptation some racial nightmare that would pursue her
forever?

"You are so very beautiful," Otto said to her, "and so very hard.
I have never known anyone so hard."

She knew that he cursed her, but she also knew that her refusal
was the only trump she possessed. If once he saw those demons, if
once he penetrated her dark secrets, he would surely leave her. It
was only in marriage that she was safe. He could not leave her then.
She would let him tame her and be forever free of her inheritance.

Emma saw that he had regained his self-control. She saw, too, that
he was determined to have her, and that he would do anything
toward that end. He reached out his hand to her. "Get up," he said.
His voice revealed nothing. His face was blank. Emma allowed him
to pull her to her feet and brush her off. She felt exhausted.

They rode back to the stables side by side. Neither of them spoke.
Otto knew that he was faced with a decision. In a few weeks' time
he would have to leave Frankfurt and go through all the motions of
acclimatizing himself to a new town. He would have to put his
things in order in a new set of rooms, find a tailor and a shoemaker,
restaurants, taverns, women. And when everything was settled, he
would fall back into his familiar trains of thought, read the usual
newspapers. Was there another life? Did he have a choice? Could
he enjoy bourgeois comforts, a home presided over by a beautiful
Jewish wife? He stole a glance at Emma. Her profile was ravishing;

she would keep her beauty into old age. And there would be a dowry. Perhaps a large one. He could indulge himself now and then, he would not have to be so cautious. And he had caught a glimpse of her repressed fires. God only knew what she might give him when aroused. He imagined her in a dozen different positions, picture after lurid picture flashing through his mind. He rode his horse hard, galloping ahead of Emma, until he reached the end of the meadow, beside the ring, where he waited for her.

"Will you be my wife?" he asked, and when she turned her face toward him, radiant with devotion, he felt a pang of regret.

"Oh, I hope you mean that!" she said.

"I'm not in the habit of making frivolous declarations of love," he replied, knowing full well that he had not declared his love at all.

"Of course I'll be your wife," she said. "You're the first man I've ever loved."

The following Saturday, Otto came to see Nathan, to ask for Emma's hand. There was much consternation in the family, but Emma did not tell her betrothed. He suspected nothing, for it was unimaginable to him that anyone in his right mind would object to having him for a son-in-law. There had been a terrible scene when Emma announced to her parents that she intended to marry the officer. It was after dinner, on the day he proposed. Caroline begged her to give it a year's time, Nathan said it would be her life's ruin. Emma sat opposite them, pale and composed, and told them that she would run away if she didn't have their permission. She said that she planned to marry Otto even if she was disinherited and had to live with him in a single room in a dull gray garrison town near the Polish border—this being the most awful thing any of them could imagine. She said that Edu had talked to her and that she had felt betrayed and outraged by his interference and had considered suicide. Her parents were mute. They could not refuse their consent.

Edu was consulted the next day. "What can I do?" Nathan asked.

"Tell her you'll not give her a penny."

"She'll run away with him, she already told me so." Nathan sighed. "She is like a madwoman. Possessed."

Edu had to give in as well. Emma was triumphant.

Saturday was a cloudy, cool day. Nathan received Otto in his study, Caroline sat in the salon, Emma remained upstairs in her room. The two men said very little to each other. Nathan kept imagining himself in the role of a nineteenth-century *pater familias* standing beside his desk, pointing his finger at the door and shouting *"Out!"* while the bent, cur-like figure of the colonel slunk into the rainy night. But he sat still and dryly discussed Emma's income, her dowry, plans for the wedding. Otto marked everything down on a small pad and gave the exact figures of his own financial worth, the acreage in East Prussia, his plans and hopes for advancement, his current army pay. If he had been able, he might have tried to charm the dour attorney, but he had neither grace nor a talent for flattery. Without his uniform, no one would have noticed him.

He was honest, thrifty and patriotic, and truly not interested in money. He could have looked straight into Nathan's eye and said this, but he didn't bother to. Let the Jew think it mattered. He put a look of distaste on his face. He wished it were all over, the wedding too, so he could begin his married life, regulated like the army, but with better food, more comfortable living quarters and the promise of orgiastic encounters each night.

"Good luck," said Nathan, but he could not bring himself to reach out his hand to Otto. "Take care of my daughter," he said in his melancholy, throaty voice.

THE WEDDING was to take place in the week between Christmas and New Year's. Emma and Caroline began the preparations immediately. They chose the announcements at the printer's and went to see the caterer about the dinner. They made a date with the seamstress, and Emma picked out the material for her wedding dress. They discussed the flowers with the florist and engaged the photographer. Otto had promised to look for an apartment in Weimar which Emma would furnish at her leisure once they returned from their honeymoon. Fräulein Gründlich promised she would come to help Emma as soon as she was needed, for as long as she was wanted. Gründlich did not like Otto Radowitz any better than the *Herrschaft* did, but she did not allow herself the luxury of saying so. She felt that her love for the children required a certain loyalty. Should Emma ever want to pour out her heart to her, how could she possibly do so if she knew that she, Frieda Gründlich, had been one of those who had inveighed against him? When Lene made a face to her at the mention of the officer, Fräulein Gründlich chastised her gently. "You haven't any idea what they mean to each other," she said. "Nobody can understand lovers. All we can do is hope they understand each other."

Emma went to have tea with Uncle Edu. He did not refer to their conversation at Torcello but showed her a newly purchased Byzantine ivory and told her that he had given the blue Matisse to the Städel, in honor of Elias, now associate director and curator of the modern collection. When they had finished the last drop of tea and Emma had refused the butter cookies a third time, Edu took an envelope from his pocket and gave it to her. His stationery was always the best, made in England, with his name engraved on the flap of the envelope in small black letters.

"That's my wedding gift to you," he said. "It is a check, for a not inconsiderable amount of money. However, it is in American dollars and drawn on an American bank. I advise you to keep it in a safe place, until our own currency is stabilized, which I expect to happen within the month. I wish you luck. I hope you will be happy."

Emma nodded her head. The gesture was automatic. She always agreed with Edu.

"Just remember one thing, my dear," he continued. "You can always turn to me for help. You must not be ashamed. It is my pleasure, the reason I am here."

Emma said "Thank you," but it was clear from her expression that she did not believe she would ever need help.

"Only one thing you must never ask me. Don't ask me for money for your husband. Ever! If he gets into trouble, gambling or whatever, bad business deals, I don't care. He must know that he cannot come to me. If he thinks there's a marvelous opportunity to 'make a bundle,' and all he needs is a few thousand in seed money, tell him I'm not interested."

He knew that he sounded harsh. But it was something Emma had always understood. She felt only a touch of annoyance to think that Edu should for a minute doubt that she knew exactly what his rules in such matters were.

The day set for the wedding arrived. It was one of those winter days when the wind shifts and brings with it warm air from the south, which even the Alps do not succeed in cooling down to winter temperatures. It was raining softly when Emma awoke, and as mild as a day in September.

"'Happy Wedding Day!" said Lene, when they met at breakfast. The Christmas tree was still standing in the living room in front of the French windows, and its piney smell wafted through the house mixed with the spicy scent of Christmas cookies. The sisters kissed. They had not confided in each other for some time. Their lives had little in common just then, yet they both understood that a time would come when they would grow close again.

Lene said nothing about Otto. Her silence was an indictment Emma could not help but notice. She had not been stinting in her criticism of Tom, but her criticism, even when it stung, was never as inflexible as Lene's silence.

The wedding feast was planned for the evening. Late that morning Otto came to take Emma to City Hall for the wedding ceremony, at which only a handful of witnesses was present. Emma wore her new gray traveling suit, part of her trousseau, which had been chosen with Pauline's help and advice. After the ceremony they stopped at Edu's house for champagne and caviar and then went to their respective rooms for a rest. Otto's old mother, tiny and fragile and already afflicted with senility, which showed itself in sudden flashes of confused childishness, had traveled to Frankfurt with a dour retainer, a deposed gentlewoman of Polish descent. Otto had put them up at the Frankfurter Hof, where he had also taken a suite for his wedding night.

Two fellow officers, resplendent in their parade uniforms, like strutting peacocks next to the darkly clad Wertheim and Süsskind clans, were Otto's only guests besides his mother and her companion. Nathan and Caroline had limited their list to relatives, with one exception: Tom, who was by now considered a member of the family. He spent more of his free time at the Wertheims than he did at home.

It had not grown perceptively cooler by night, and everyone felt oppressed. Otto stayed close to his mother, and the two officers never left each other's side. Lene was with Tom, and the cousins with one another. The crowd seemed to Emma to be divided into antagonistic circles, like drops of oils floating on a deep and troubled sea. She tried desperately to go from one group to the other, chatting gaily, but she was everywhere met with polite smiles which barely covered the aura of discomfort and dread.

Emma began to blame her family for the sense of oppression, which neither good wine nor delectable hors d'oeuvres could dispel. They looked to her troubled eyes like evil caricatures of hook-nosed Jews, moving their hands in time to the singsong Yiddish they spoke. Not knowing that Emma saw them like that, they talked innocently about ordinary things, gossiped, helped themselves to canapés and washed them down with wine. When the time came to be seated, they spread their napkins in their laps and made toasts and praised the good food, helping themselves to goose-liver pâté and crisp duck in orange sauce and fresh trout amandine and beef Wellington and green salad and tiny peas and sweet yellow carrots —all provided by one of Frankfurt's finest caterers.

"*Judenfrass!*"—Jew-swill—the old woman cackled all at once, loud enough to be audible to most of her dinner companions. She had several times in the course of the evening laughed to herself like a blackbird settling in a tree and clutched at the air as if she were pushing brambles from her face. Most of the people in her vicinity tried to ignore the remark; within seconds several were already convinced that they had misheard her. But Andreas, who sat on her right, knew exactly what she had said. He turned to her now.

"Apologize for that remark," he said coldly.

"Eh?" the old lady crowed. "What say?"

"Mother!" Otto cautioned from across the table. His voice contained not only a warning but fear as well.

"Jews!" the old woman cried, and the entire company grew still. "Ruining our country, starving our people, filling up their bellies like pigs." She had been eating heedlessly, the way old people often do, cramming the food into the hole of her mouth like a sly, hungry child. "Look," she cried, "look look look . . ." and then subsided, forgetting what it was she wanted seen. Gravy clung to her chin. The officers smiled.

"My mother doesn't know what she's saying"—Otto had risen from his seat—"please forgive her."

"Take her out of this house," said Edu, flinging his napkin on the table. His fury was like an icy wind. "I will not allow such talk at our table, I don't care whose mouth it comes from. Send her away." He looked at the officers. "These gentlemen can take her back to the hotel."

"What happened?" asked the old lady, who was still eating. "What have I done?" She looked around, her eyes flickering with malice.

"You must go home," Otto said to her quietly. "You have been bad. And it's getting late for you." He put her black shawl over her shoulders and helped her to her feet. His two friends got up and bowed stiffly to the assembled company. The Polish retainer, who had said nothing all evening, bared a set of yellow teeth and smiled at her employer. "Don't mind," she whispered to her, "you speak the truth. They'll learn."

"Go!" Otto shouted at them and turned back to the table and to Emma, whose eyes spilled streams of tears down her cheeks, although she made no sound. Her wedding suit was wet with tears.

"She doesn't know what she is saying," said Otto. "She's a senile old woman."

But Emma sat still as a rock while the tears continued to fall on her suit.

"Emma!" he pleaded and got on his knees beside her, "Emma, please forgive us." Everyone at the table watched him. "It means nothing. I love you." He buried his head in her lap. The Jews sat in their seats, implacably staring at him; how well he knew their judgment now!

A few minutes later the party broke up. Emma was surrounded by her well-wishers; no one spoke to Otto. They embraced her and whispered words of love in her ear. It was raining outside. Police sirens wailed—there had been another altercation in the suburb of Bockenheim, Brown Shirts against the Reds. There were cracked heads, bloody noses, broken glass. Somewhere a band of fleeing youths were singing: *"Verreckt ist Walther Rathenau, die gottver-dammte Judensau"* ("Wasted is Walther Rathenau, the goddamn Jewish sow").

With her gray suit Emma wore her pearls and a matching gray hat. A pale-pink silk scarf was wrapped around her neck. Fräulein

Gründlich said, "Don't forget your raincoat." She hugged Emma tightly. "God bless you," she said. "I'll follow you to Weimar in a little while."

"I'm frightened," said Emma.

"Every girl is, on her wedding night," Fräulein Gründlich told her. "You're not the first, you won't be the last."

The suitcases were brand-new in matching gray leather with her initials on them: E.R-W. Emma Radowitz-Wertheim. Fräulein Gründlich kissed Emma and embraced her once again. She did not seem to want to let her go.

At the Frankfurter Hof the bridal suite awaited them, filled with flowers. There was more champagne. The bed was large and canopied and its white sheets were drawn back invitingly. Emma did not remove her hat. She kept the raincoat wrapped around her. She had taken a seat on the edge of an armchair and was listening to her beating heart.

Otto opened a bottle of champagne so that the cork flew up to the ceiling and the wine bubbled out onto the napkin he had carefully wrapped around the neck of the bottle. He filled both glasses.

"Not for me, thank you," said Emma.

"But for me," said Otto. "Lots and lots of champagne for me." He drank down several glasses rapidly. "I've waited a long time," he said. "As you know, that makes the pleasure that much sweeter." He went over to Emma, a little tipsy now, with the ease and sense of perfect rightness one feels at such moments.

"Take off your coat," he said, "take off your shoes, take off all your many pretty new clothes."

Emma's teeth chattered. "I must have a fever," she said.

"Undress!" said Otto, pulling off his own clothes.

"I'm not feeling well." Emma allowed him to hear the uncontrolled chatter of her teeth. Her arms were wrapped around her body. "I'm cold cold cold," she said. She felt an ache of desire while at the same time she shook with the terrible fear of being trampled, crushed, forever violated. Otto, naked before her, with his narrow shoulders and cylindrical body, pranced a little.

"Come on, come on," he said, "let's play." He found the sight of the frightened girl before him more tempting than that of the most worldly woman. He knew she would be unable to resist him, she would rush to him finally, as all the others had, crying with pleasure, even in the midst of pain. He was a good lover.

"I'm awfully good," he said to her now, by way of encouragement. "I know all the tricks. I may not be able to talk about paintings in Venice or architecture in Rome, but I'm a master at making love. I can satisfy any woman and turn her inside out with delight." He knelt on the floor and started to take off Emma's shoes, then her stockings. He had to reach all the way to her girdle. She shuddered.

"Be gentle," she begged. Her tears flowed again.

"Crybaby," he said. "I'll nip you and lick you and bite you and bathe you with my kisses and suck the sex out of you with my lips."

His penis had grown huge. Such small hands and feet . . . Emma thought and screamed. His fingers, like a pail full of eels, had reached her pubic hair and plucked at it.

"Shut up now," he said. "Shut up!"

For the next several hours Otto Radowitz tried every trick he knew on the body of the sobbing Emma. Again and again he rode her in triumph, groaning and sweating to try to arouse her, to make her respond. He poured champagne on her lovely thin white body —like a birch tree, he said—and then on his own and made her lick him until she gagged. He did nothing he had not done a hundred times before, but he did not know what he was doing. He wanted to give pleasure as well as take it, but his tricks all failed him with this inexperienced, frightened virgin of a girl. Had he but listened to Emma and been gentle, he might have enticed a response from her, might have brought all the love and the locked-up sensuality to fruition, to climax. But the more he felt her resist, the more she wept and pleaded with him to stop, the more he drove himself to show her his mastery and his strength and cunning.

When he lay asleep at last, sprawled among the sheets, drained and sweat-soaked and besotted with champagne, Emma got up and washed herself. Had she had the strength or some instrument of death in her possession, she might well have killed him. She put on her new shoes and stockings and her gray suit and hat and raincoat and stole out of the hotel room. She ached as though she had been beaten with chains. In order not to be seen, she went down the servants' stairs and past several sleepy bakers and pastry chefs, out the back door of the hotel where the garbage rotted. It was nearly dawn, and the rain had stopped. There was a pink glow in the eastern sky. Emma walked home. Anna was the only one up. She sat in the kitchen with a cup of hot coffee; it was the time of day she loved. She got the fire going first and then she planned her work. She was puzzled when the doorbell rang, but she wasn't afraid, so she went to answer it, and there was Emma.

Later she told the story again and again. "Poor child," she would say, "looking like death. She fell into my arms, weeping and wailing. I had to hold her there and pet her till I could get Gründlich up, and then we put her to bed, the two of us."

Toward midmorning Dr. Schlesinger came and gave her a sedative. She was not hurt physically, and since she refused to talk about what happened, there was nothing to be done. Edu arranged for an annulment. Otto disappeared, the wedding gifts were sent back, vague explanations given. Emma stayed in her room, in bed, most of the rest of that winter. Fräulein Gründlich brought her meals, the family came to visit, but it was spring before she was able to put the experience out of her mind. The only image that remained, for some reason, was of Otto kneeling to take off her shoes. Everything else had been sealed away in a most secret place.

Uncle Edu made her a gift of a Cézanne watercolor. The dollars went back into the American account. The German inflation had been checked. Hitler was in jail. November seventh had long come and gone and the Revolution the Communists promised had not materialized. There were some who said that the worst was over.

V

1928

IT WAS EARLY March, and there was a chill in the air. Only the day before it had seemed like spring; now a cold wind whipped out of the northwest. Lene sat by the window of her third-floor bedroom, gazing down at her parents' garden. She was eight months pregnant, and her marriage to Tom was going badly. They had been married for three years and had lived the entire time in the house on the Guiollettstrasse. Nathan and Caroline had rebuilt the top floor to make a charming apartment out of unused storage rooms and servants' quarters. Anna was the only servant who still lived "in," and Fräulein Gründlich had her old room on the second floor, enlarged by the addition of Lene's former bedroom.

Fräulein Gründlich looked hardly a day older than she had when she came to work for the Wertheims. The skin on her round, open peasant face was stretched smooth and tight, the wrinkles around her eyes were fine, and her hair, though it had become a little sparser, was still the same brown color it had always been. She was looking forward to the birth of Lene's baby. So many years in the bosom of a Jewish family with no religious faith had not shaken her simple Christian belief but had expanded and enriched it with good taste and urban broad-mindedness. She often thought that a stroke of good fortune, initiated by the Almighty, had kept her from marrying Alois, who still worked for Jacob and had a tiny, careworn slip of a wife and many children.

Lene's third-floor apartment was completely "modern," well-designed, clean and simple in line and proportion, bare of ornamentation. Lene often wondered why none of this functionalism worked its magic upon the complicated, messy interior part of their lives. There, baroque confusion and anxiety prevailed.

Tom worked in a small but prestigious publishing house which had made its reputation by printing beautiful books in limited editions. He had muddled through a number of ventures before landing in his present occupation. His father, who was still alive, did not approve. But then, he had never approved of Tom. He had tried and tried to make a businessman out of him and had given up only because his strength began to fail him. When it became clear that Tom was going to marry "the little Wertheim girl," the old man had called him to a conference.

"I have no objection to your marrying a Jewess," he said. "Her family is respectable and *rich*. They've been in Frankfurt longer than we have. But that's beside the point. Eduard Wertheim is a man of great abilities and considerable wealth. He can do all kinds of things. I want him to do some of them for you. No matter where I have sent you, to work or to study, you have returned home muttering that the place or the subject doesn't suit you. I got you a position in a bank; six months later you walked out. I don't think you even learned what a mortgage is. If you are going to marry that pretty little girl, I want you to draw some benefit from it. Ask Eduard Wertheim for a job."

Tom was terrified. He lacked the ambition that gives one courage to take a bold step.

"Go!" said his father. "Don't be shy. Your name alone should give you strength. Tell him—don't ask—to put you into his business. If you don't like banking, where he has some power, then try the woolen business. I cannot imagine that a son of mine is so without business acumen that he cannot hold the simplest of jobs in a commercial enterprise! All you have to do is be punctual and honest and work hard—you aren't stupid, I know that—and before long you'll be vice president. Our civil service and our corporations are filled with men who do just that and live long and productive lives. There's no shame attached to it."

Tom spoke to Lene, and that was as far as he got. Lene dropped some hints to her father, who mumbled of it to Edu in the course of a lunch they were having. Edu invited Lene for tea and explained to her that he was neither the Salvation Army nor the unemployment office. He was not harsh with her, as he had been with Emma, but he was firm. "Let him find his own job," he said. "If ever he proves himself capable at something, we can talk about it again. Marry him if you wish; you will receive a dowry and have an income, but I'll promise no more."

Lene reported back the gist of this conversation, stressing its positive rather than its negative tone, and by the time the information filtered back to old Bre-ba, it sounded as if his son had been promised something in the future, something almost certain, a year or two after the marriage.

Lene, her belly large, her body unwieldy under the tent of her wool dress, watched the bare branches of the chestnut tree bend stiffly in the wind. She was thinking about the state of her marriage. That seemed to be the only thing she ever thought about these days, especially when she was alone. The child kicked in her belly. She loved to feel it, it meant it was alive. Lifting her dress, she could see her stomach change shape, grow lopsided or pointed with the child's twisting. She liked being pregnant. There were times when she thought that being pregnant was better than being married. It was something she had completely to herself. Even if she hadn't created it alone, she was nurturing it alone. She had only to eat and drink and get enough sleep. She had something living within her, she was going to be a mother. Nothing she had ever done could compare to that.

As a matter of fact, she had done precious little. She had spent less than a year at the Pedagogical Institute before she was asked to leave. The humiliation had been awful and was probably one of the reasons she had married. She had encountered difficulties at work from the very beginning, and when she returned from Italy, she felt like an outcast. No one wanted to help her or share with her, and she had trouble getting the class notes for the sessions she had missed. She was plunged directly into working with the children, which turned out to be more troublesome than she had imagined. The children were dirty, they were hellions, they had no respect. At least, they had no respect for her; they refused to obey her, they ran wild under her care. She simply could not cope with them.

Lene told no one at home about it but went to see Aunt Eva, who had moved into one of the apartments in Ernst May's workers' estates, designed exclusively for professional women. Eva listened closely and did her best to explain the social conditions under which these children had grown up. Lene nodded her head. She understood all that and she didn't lack sympathy, still . . .

"Has it ever occurred to you that you may simply lack the gift to be a teacher?" Eva asked.

Not too many months later, after failing an examination and being kicked in the shins by a seven-year-old, Lene was called into the director's office and told, gently but firmly, that the faculty felt it was best if she withdrew and let her place be taken by someone "more likely to derive maximum benefit from the curriculum offered at the Pedagogical Institute, and to leave its precincts capable of giving German youth the discipline, the respect for order and the sense of duty to which it aspires."

Every member of the family rallied to her support, but even their kindest remarks and most refined rationalizations could not ease the bitterness of her hurt. Of all the people who loved her, the one whose aid and comfort was the most practical was Uncle Jacob. He suggested that she take a job in his bookstore, three days a week.

"You'll earn money, you'll do something worthwhile," he said, "and who knows, you may even learn the business." His offer was gratefully accepted. Lene enjoyed the work and stayed with it until she became pregnant, but it could not quite drive the haunting memory of her failure from her mind.

While she was working part-time at Jacob's store, she had signed up to take cooking lessons. She wanted to be as busy as possible, and cooking was something at which she knew she would not fail. One day when she had prepared a particularly delectable ragout at home with very little help from Anna, her father said, "Are you and Tom ever going to get married?"

Lene shrugged her shoulders. Her mind had been wholly on the ragout.

"He would get himself a superb cook," said Nathan.

The following night Tom and Lene were sitting in their usual seats in the highest reaches of the opera house—the Brenda-Badolets no longer had their box—listening to *La Forza del Destino* and feeding bits of chocolate to the resident mice, when Lene said, "My father thinks we ought to get married."

"He doesn't approve of our present arrangement?"

"I don't think he considers it an arrangement."

"Oh," said Tom. One of the mice had almost learned to eat out of his hand.

"What do you think?" said Lene.

"I have no objections."

Someone behind them shushed them with a loud long hissing sound. Not too many months after that they were married.

Still anxious as a result of the terrible events surrounding Emma's wedding, the Wertheim family looked forward with relief to Lene's. It turned out to be simple and gay, more like a children's party than a wedding. The young people danced, and Tom was amusing and gracious as he had been so long ago at his costume party. Lene was charmingly shy and looked happy. The party lasted long into the night. No one seemed to want to leave the protection of the gracious house.

Tom's parents did not attend; they never ventured out of the house where they lived alone with their servants. The once beautiful mansion no longer served as a stage for festive gatherings. The great ballroom lay in an eternal gloom of dusk, its curtains drawn, its floors dusty, the furniture covered with white sheets. The old couple had buried all of their children except Thomas. They did not always remember who he was.

And so Tom and Lene moved upstairs into the third-floor apartment on the Guiollettstrasse, and there were many hours on many days when Lene did not feel married at all. Though they had a little kitchen, they took most of their meals downstairs. Lene had forgotten the recipe for the ragout. The cleaning woman was paid a little extra by Caroline to "go over" the apartment thoroughly once a week. And there was Fräulein Gründlich, and Lene got it into her head that she wanted a child.

Tom, vague and noncommittal as ever, could not imagine himself a father. Not yet, at any rate. Perhaps one day—when everything was in order.

"What do you mean?" Lene asked.

"The world's in disarray. It's full of disharmony, people are hysterical, constantly in contention. I'm fearful of putting a child—a delicate small bit of life—into that world."

"Babies are tough," said Lene, "and times have been bad before."

"Not like this."

"It's always bad for those caught up in the whirlwind. Imagine living during the Thirty Years' War."

"I probably wouldn't have wanted to become a father then, either."

"But you wouldn't have known how to prevent it!"

Lene had decided that Tom was made out of vapor. He offered almost no resistance, he was here today, gone tomorrow, a wisp of smoke gently curling from a farmhouse chimney on a cool summer morning. When she had to ask him about the accounts or tell him about her worries and fears, he was gone. When something displeased him, he disappeared. He might remain next to her in body, but his spirit had flown. Still, one day she held him tight, and four months later her belly began to swell and life began to stir within it.

Their social life centered more and more around the café. They had their *Stammtisch* now, their regular table, and a circle of friends who cruised about it. They were at the fringes of Frankfurt's intellectual and artistic elite, familiar faces, recognized but never quite known. Lene was Edu Wertheim's niece, but the painter May Beckmann could never remember her last name. Her husband was handsome and charming, but what exactly did he do? Lene was bored. Tom started to write a novel. At the café, while Tom discussed plot and character with Lulu, Lene talked to Paul Leopold.

Lene looked at her watch. Not yet time for lunch. She loved her apartment. Everything was in its place, the tubular steel of her Breuer chairs gleamed whenever the sun emerged from behind the clouds, the hand-woven tablecloth looked warmer and richer to her than her mother's damask. The baby was quiet just then. Tomorrow was Ash Wednesday.

That meant today was *Karneval.* The artists' annual masked ball this evening promised to be an unusually brilliant affair. A jazz band said to be made up of *real* American Negroes playing the latest music from Harlem had been hired. Lene and Tom planned to meet their friends at the café and go to the ball in a group from there.

Lene, who could not hide her condition, had elected to come as the Virgin Mary looking for a room at the inn. Tom thought it a fine idea, but balked at the prospect of going as Joseph. After much agitation and the perusal of many books, he decided to go as a sultan. This costume demanded a turban and a scimitar, a false beard, yards of cloth for baggy pants, wide sash, a flowing cape, and the help of Fräulein Gründlich. Lulu said she would be Scheherezade. Paul declared that the whole thing was utter nonsense, and he would come as himself.

Tom thought Lene ought to appear on a donkey so that everyone would understand immediately who she was, but that proved impractical, so Lene decided to bring a stuffed Steiff donkey with her. She based her costume—a voluminous blue cloak over a white chemise and a warm red wool jumper—on the Rogier van der Weyden "Medici Madonna" at the Städel. She actually liked the van Eyck Madonna much better, but *her* cloak was red, and there was no red material in the house, whereas Fräulein Gründlich had found a blue velvet curtain and turned it into a handsome cloak. Lene cut a halo out of gold paper, pasted it on a stiff piece of cardboard and attached it to a white ribbon, which she wound about her head.

Frankfurt was full of revelers that day. They marched and danced

through the streets of the Altstadt, pierrots and clowns and mino-
taurs. The Brown Shirts who joined them here and there were
hardly visible in the shouting, singing crowd.

Tom and Lene took a taxi as far as possible. The driver let them
off several blocks from the café; the crowd was too thick to allow
him to proceed any farther. He shook his head at the costumed
couple. "Better watch your pregnant lady," he said to Tom.

"She's a virgin," Tom told him.

Confetti swirled about the revelers, paper streamers wound down
from the windows and curled around the paper hats and grotesque
masks of the throng. Those who didn't wear masks had painted their
faces in vivid colors. Lene saw the demons all around her; the Last
Judgment at Torcello had come alive. The horrible masks gave their
wearers an intoxicating anonymity. Lene wished her face were not
so bare.

Never before had Lene seen the café so filled with smoke, so
crowded, so noisy. Paul Leopold in his usual shabby dark suit,
creased white shirt and jaunty bow tie was sitting in the corner
writing in his notebook, the glass of brandy and the cup of coffee
on the table before him. His fingers were black with ink, and he
appeared as gnomelike as ever.

Lene sat down next to him. She had come to depend on his
presence; he was the center of the ever-shifting crowd. When he was
absent, quarrels broke out and were not stilled, boredom made
everyone cranky. Paul looked up from his notebook for a minute,
acknowledging her presence. Lene felt in thrall to him. Tom had
been caught in a crush of admirers. He stood tall and straight, his
blue eyes contrasting oddly with his black shoe-polish mustache.
The laughter of the women swelled about him, their hands fluttered
over his costume. Lulu's voice was louder than the rest.

"Evening, Lene," said Paul. He stopped writing briefly and
cocked his head as though he were listening to sounds from another
world. He often did that.

"What do you hear?" she asked him.

"Leonore Overture Number Three," he said. "Hear the offstage
trumpet?" He sang the notes in perfect tune, though his voice was
full of whiskey cracks.

"Ah, Beethoven!" he said, and when he looked directly at Lene, she saw how bloodshot his eyes were. "Do you realize," he whispered, "that Nazis are on the march in the land of Goethe and Schiller? And do you know what they're singing? They're singing a charming ditty, and it goes like this . . ."—he didn't raise his voice very much—" 'Let Jewish blood squirt from your knife and see how good it feels!' Charming, isn't it?"

His melodious Austrian inflection contrasted queerly with the ominous lines. Paul Leopold insisted he came from Vienna, but in the course of a tipsy monologue one night, he had confided to Lene that he was born in a Jewish hamlet in Galicia. No sooner was the confession out of his mouth than he growled, "I never told you that, and if you bring it up, I'll deny it."

Now he said, "And what do you think the good German bourgeois says to that? He says, 'Shut the door, Sieglinde, and turn up the phonograph. How about some of the Ninth Symphony? *Alle Menschen werden Brüder,* all men will be brothers, etc. etc. *That's* the real Germany, our Fatherland. The other will pass.' And Sieglinde says, 'I wouldn't want to live under the Bolsheviks.' And they drink another glass of beer. They might even be Jewish, our good German burghers."

"Don't talk about such things," said Lene.

"You believe it will go away too?" he asked her.

"There's always been anti-Semitism."

"And pogroms."

"But—"

"Not in Germany, you'll tell me. Mother of God," he said, "your Jewish beauty is extraordinary. Maybe that child you're carrying will *be* our Savior."

"I hope it's a girl," said Lene.

"That's the punch line of a famous Yiddish joke. Shall I tell it to you?"

"If it's funny."

"A newspaper reporter comes to interview Mary. 'How does it feel to be the mother of the Lord Jesus Christ?' he asks. 'Actually,' she says, 'we were hoping for a girl.' "

"It's only medium funny," Lene said, but she was smiling. Paul returned to his notebook and began writing again. He moved quickly from the café table into the mysterious and mythic world of his novel.

"Why aren't you in costume?" Lene asked.

"Don't you think I look grotesque enough the way I am, without benefit of masquerade?"

"You don't look grotesque at all," Lene said. She wanted to touch his hands, but he had folded his arms and they were safely tucked away.

"When is your baby coming?" Paul asked.

"Any day now."

"Why do you want to bring a child into this world?"

"That's a question only a man would ask."

"Am I going to get a feminist lecture?"

"Not from me. But your question was so abstract I couldn't let it pass. To feel a baby kicking in your belly is beautiful—it makes all these considerations meaningless. I keep thinking: If I do nothing else in my life but this, it will have been enough. And I think I want a girl because only a girl will ever understand the things I know to pass on to my children. Besides, boys always get sent off to war. You know, Paul, here I am, hardly able to bend down, short of breath, and yet I've never felt better or healthier in my whole life. And I feel invulnerable too. I feel nothing can hurt me or hurt my baby. I'm fat as a cow and strong as an ox!"

Paul unfolded his hands to light a new cigarette. Lene's halo had slid down to the nape of her neck. Tom and Lulu sat, deep in conversation, at the adjacent table.

Shuffling the papers piled beneath and around his notebook, Paul, inhaling deeply, suddenly said, "You know I have a wife?" He was looking at his ink and nicotine-stained hands.

"No," said Lene. "You never told me. Where do you keep her?"

"She's in a sanatorium in Davos. She has tuberculosis."

"I shouldn't have been flip. I'm sorry."

"I'm sorry too. It helps neither of us. If she were well, we'd probably be divorced. But I can't leave her as long as she's ill. I'm trapped."

"Why did you tell me this, just now?"

Paul still kept his eyes averted. "Because I know without your ever having said anything that you're not happy in your marriage. My writer's sense gives me insight, and my lover's heart confirms it."

"You're very perceptive."

"I'd like very much to bring some . . . humor? good times? into your life, Lene. But I thought I'd better tell you about having a wife."

Paul cocked his head to one side and finally met her eyes, and Lene saw the embarrassed affection he did his best to hide behind a screen of smoke.

Around eleven o'clock there was a general exodus from the café. Everyone was already a little high. There was a shrill edge to the laughter and a clownish looseness to the movements of the figures. Lulu clung to Tom's arm. He looked uncomfortable, pretending to lack the strength to extricate himself. Lene had come to despise Lulu, who flirted with every man she met and sought to exchange intimacies with every woman. She talked about her friends behind their backs and sulked when they retaliated by snubbing her. But what angered Lene most was her false innocence, her childlike naiveté. She complained of being used but was always among the first to meet a new patron, to politick for a prize or to offer to give a public reading. She told Tom that Lene had insulted her the first time they met. When he asked her how, she looked into the distance and said, "I don't want to make it worse by talking about it."

They trooped from the café in a gay mood. There was a chill in the air, the kind that comes in late winter as a reminder that it is too early still to look for spring. Tom had come around to put his arm through Lene's, though Lulu still held his other hand. Lene carried her stuffed donkey, which made braying sounds whenever it was squeezed, and tried to walk with as much dignity as possible. She was angry with Tom, but her mind, dwelling on Paul Leopold, could not sustain her anger for long.

The streets were still filled with revelers, but the stinging wind had diminished their celebrations. Trampled hats, broken horns, and a thousand curled ringlets of colored streamers clogged the gutters. Paul walked behind the group, carrying his papers and notebook. The masked ball was being held in a cavernous hall, recently a restaurant, decorated with three-dimensional historical scenes. Most of these had been removed, but enough of Napoleon's shade and Hannibal's ghost were left to give the place an air of the surreal. The black jazz band played the latest American tunes, and the costumed couples danced the latest American steps. Tom danced with Lulu, and Lene sat with Paul Leopold.

"You'd better not dance," Lulu had told Lene. "In your condition it might turn out badly." She was, among other things, the perennial prophetess of doom.

"Paul will watch out for you," Tom said. When he was tipsy, he moved out of reach more magically than ever and his smile masked his face completely.

"Your husband is a weakling and a fool." The words startled Lene. Paul had spoken them harshly.

"What?" she said, confused. Then the anger surfaced. "Don't say that," she said.

Paul knew he had made a mistake. He did not like to appear unkind. Changing the subject quickly, he pointed to a corner table. "Do you recognize that creature over there?" he asked Lene. "The one dressed as a stork? It's Gareis, the tenor."

"I wouldn't know my own mother if she showed up here as a stork." Lene looked in wonderment at the gathering of two-legged beasts and other dissemblers.

"That's because you believe in illusion," said Paul. "I do not. I can see through every disguise. It's a great help to me, it makes me a good reporter. I watch the poses, the tricks, the gestures of my friends as well as my enemies. They can't fool me with a mask. But you, my dearest, in addition to believing in goodness and truth, take the world as it presents itself, you allow your judgment to be formed —at least in the beginning—by what you *see*. Take me, for instance. Didn't you look at me and say, 'A ghastly Jewish gnome, that Leopold.' Don't deny it! I won't hold it against you, for you changed your mind soon enough, I know that. It is one of the touching things about you, fair Helene. You are without the pride that keeps people clinging to first impressions. It takes you a while —like the tortoise—but you reach the correct, that is, the same conclusions I do. Which is why we are meant for each other."

Lene felt herself blushing, though she didn't want to seem to be the sort of woman who blushed. For Paul she wanted to be *une femme du monde*—even if she didn't have a clear idea of how to achieve that state. Just then she felt a hand on her shoulder and, looking up, saw the figure of a pierrot all in white with great black pompons on the front of his baggy suit. His face was beautifully made up, white as chalk. It was Andreas.

Lene introduced him to Paul Leopold, who shook hands and gazed shrewdly into his face. Another figure, this one black, in the costume of a chimney sweep, hovered behind Andreas but was not introduced.

"Isn't it a beautiful ball?" Lene said.

"Where's Tom?" Andreas asked.

"Dancing with Lulu."

"I heard there'd be trouble here." Andreas appeared more tense than usual. "Get Tom to take you home soon."

"What kind of trouble?" Lene was more excited than scared.

"Nazi trouble."

"Aha!" Paul exclaimed and repeated the grisly refrain he had sung to her earlier.

"There aren't only Jews here," she said with a kind of perverse reasoning.

"In their eyes we're all the same." Paul flung out his arms to include the mob of costumed artists and their friends.

"Please go home, Lene," Andreas urged. But he spoke too late. At that moment there was a commotion at the door. At first it appeared as if it was just another group of masked arrivals. Then a woman screamed, and the dancers began slowly to give way before the ten or so brown-shirted men, each one wearing a red armband with a black swastika in a round white field. The armbands were visible against even the most colorful costume on the floor.

One of the Brown Shirts jumped up on a table and shouted for the band to stop. Slowly and raggedly the musicians complied, one by one. "Don't stop!" a voice in the crowd cried, and the trumpeter blew a few wailing tones into the smoke-filled air. The man on the table began to harangue the crowd. "Germans awake!" he screamed. "Turn from your wicked ways." Andreas put his hands over Lene's ears, but she removed them gently.

All at once, while the man continued to shout his imprecations, there was a movement in the crowd. Perhaps they had grown bold behind their masks, perhaps they felt the strength of numbers and their own anonymity. Like a wave they pressed forward. The ones in front linked arms and pressed close to the Nazis. Another group surrounded the musicians—"those jungle niggers drumming their bastard music," the Nazi leader had called them—and the band began to play again, not tentatively but with all its strength. It was protected by several strong men in fantastic costumes armed with chairs.

Slowly the rest of the revelers came closer and closer, and the Nazis shrank back. One of them raised a hand with a blackjack in it, and it came down on the head of a young waiter who was in the front line. He fell back. No one heard him cry out, but many saw him sag, and they fell on the Brown Shirts while the band played more and more stridently, blues and marching tunes, an American medley with countless variations.

The Nazis were routed. One by one, disheveled and bruised, they escaped into the street.

"We'll be back!" their leader cried. "We'll be back in the name of our Führer. *Heil Hitler!*" Then he was gone, his cap trampled on the floor among the shards of glass and the spilled wine.

Order was soon restored on the dance floor, but a pall of exhaustion and fear lay over the crowd. They had all been touched by a profound fear, shaken in the depths of their hearts. They danced on slowly, as in a dream, to the last tunes of the night. Lene and Tom and Andreas and Paul Leopold and Lulu and Andreas' nameless friend the chimney sweep sat at their table, and no one spoke a word. Paul had been writing on a piece of paper, rapidly and continuously, since the uproar began.

"What are you doing?" Lene asked.

"The only thing I know how to do. I am a writer; my instinctive reaction to anything I see or hear is to take up my pencil and scribble. Later on I'll analyze it, and later still, cut the text in half."

Tom put his hand on Lene's arm. Tentative as the gesture was, it served to re-establish the link between them. Lulu had nodded off. Andreas sat close to the chimney sweep, and Lene noticed that their knees touched.

"How do you feel?" Tom asked her.

"Fine," Lene said. "I'm not even tired."

It took them a long time to find a taxi. Dawn was breaking. The cathedral's silhouette rose black against the pale-gray sky. It was Ash Wednesday. Here and there women were hurrying to church to receive the spot of ash on their foreheads. They passed the last of the costumed revelers heading home. In the early light they looked like the stragglers of an army in retreat. As the city around them came to life, stirred by the ringing of church bells, the last masked ghosts vanished. The street sweepers moved in, and it looked for a brief moment as if even the brown-shirted swastika-wearers had disappeared with the other spooks of the night.

Once she had closed the bedroom curtains against the morning light, Lene fell into a deep sleep. She was wrapped in the quilt and so perfectly comfortable that she did not want to wake up, even when she felt the stabbing pain in her lower abdomen. The pain was not dreadful but it was unusual, new. She had never, even during her periods, experienced anything like it. She was terribly tired and wanted only to sleep, but the silly pain came and went, came and went. I hope the baby's all right, she thought, remembering Lulu's evil eye. She sat up and opened her own eyes wide. "Tom!" she cried, shaking him, but he only dug himself deeper into the covers. "The baby's coming," she said and thought he heard her. "I'll be right there," he mumbled. She dressed herself quickly, only to discover when she was ready that he was fast asleep again.

Downstairs in her parents' apartment, the day had already begun. Caroline was having breakfast in her room, Fräulein Gründlich had just ironed six handkerchiefs and a blouse. Emma was watering the plants. "I'm ready!" Lene called out. Within five minutes she was on her way to the hospital in a taxi with Emma. Tom, dressed in a good suit, his hair neatly combed, his shoes polished, his teeth brushed, appeared in due time. "Where's Lene?" he asked Fräulein Gründlich. "I hope she hasn't left without me?"

The baby girl was born four hours later. It was an easy birth, even though she weighed a hefty eight pounds. She cried loudly and turned red when she did. Her round wrinkled face was crowned by a shock of light-brown hair. "She looks like an angry aborigine!"

said Edu when he saw her. Lene laughed at him and kissed the soft spot on top of the baby's head.

They named her Clara.

LENE NURSED the baby for three months. It was a time of contentment and bliss for her. Sitting on the new Thonet rocker in the sunny living room of their apartment, only meters away from her parents and Emma and Fräulein Gründlich, she watched the baby suck happily on her suddenly voluptuous breasts. She had been afraid that she might not have enough milk—the governess had warned her more than once that she was too flat-chested—but the fear proved groundless.

"Clara looks exactly like Lene when *she* was a baby," Hannchen said every Sunday when she came to visit. "Except for her blond hair and blue eyes," Emma would note. Caroline was easily persuaded to fetch the photo album, and they would all study it. Indeed, the fat, placid little girl was the image of baby Lene. "Her father deserves little credit," Edu remarked dryly.

Caroline insisted that a nurse be hired to help Lene out. "I'll pay," she said. That was the end of it, and Schwester Adele appeared one day with the highest recommendations. There was trouble right from the start. She had not expected to find a nursing mother, and she did her best to sabotage the undertaking. But Lene, with her usual stubbornness, would not be intimidated. Schwester Adele criticized the baby's diet, weighed her constantly and claimed she wasn't gaining weight properly. She accused Fräulein Gründlich of interfering, and even had words with good-natured Anna in the kitchen, over the preparation of her meals.

One day, when Fräulein Gründlich had retired to her room in tears, Caroline in a rare display of determination told the nurse to be out of the house by five o'clock that afternoon. Schwester Adele took her wages—Caroline had generously paid her through the end of the week—and left in an unrepenting rage. After she had gone, they discovered that her small room was filthy and littered with Nazi tracts, including a pamphlet on the genetic basis for Jewish inferiority.

Lene brooded over this for some time. Nevertheless, when elections were held on May 20, they provided a small basis for cautious optimism. Although the Democratic coalition suffered some losses, the Socialists won a total of 153 seats in the Reichstag and the Nazis took only 12. Unfortunately, their voting ranks were swelled by the Nationalists, who got 73 seats. The often unpredictable Communists won 54. For the moment—it being delightful, balmy spring weather—most liberals heaved a sigh of relief and concentrated on other things. But Lene found herself dreaming obsessively of Brown Shirts chasing her through the city. Once she woke up in the middle of the night with a loud cry.

"The Nazis are coming," she wept. Tom tried to comfort her. "They're after me," she said.

"Nonsense," Tom told her, "who'd want to hurt you?"

The next day at dinner, he said, "My friends at the office think that as long as the economy stays healthy, there's hope that the parties of the right can be contained. The Nazis will fight the Communists, the two will knock each other senseless, and the rest of us will benefit—safe behind our garden walls."

"Have you ever thought how precarious everything is?" Lene asked. "If one thing crumbles, the whole comes tumbling down. I look at Uncle Jacob's super, or his cleaning woman—they're so angry. They think the world is wicked because women wear short skirts and smoke cigarettes. Anything can set them off. And the Nazis have given them the Jews for a scapegoat. Don't you understand, Tom?"

"They just want to salvage their pride. They never got over losing the war. They're servile, and they like someone to tell them what to do, what to think. I hate them as much as you do, maybe more. They're out to destroy *our* world, not yours alone."

"What will we do?"

Tom shrugged his shoulders helplessly.

"We'll leave!" cried Lene.

"I couldn't do that," Tom said.

Lene talked to Nathan. They were sitting in the garden drinking tea. Clara slept in her carriage in the shade of the chestnut tree. A clean white cloth covered the wrought-iron table. Caroline had just bought new pillows for the chairs. "What's going to happen, Papa?" Lene asked.

"I wish I knew," said Nathan, who seemed to Lene to grow

wearier and older every day. "If you ask me whether I think there's a dictatorship coming, I will tell you yes, I think so. Look at Mussolini! Mass movements will shape the future. Fascists in the West, the Communists in the East. We will have to learn to live with it."

"But they say they'll kill the Jews!"

"We've been through pogroms before. Nations rise and fall, but the Jews seem to go on forever. We are the conscience of the world, and no one can do away with us."

Just then Caroline came into the garden and sat down beside Lene. She had brought her watercolors. The peonies were in full bloom, and she wanted to sketch them massed against the pale new green of the shrubs.

"I refuse to waste my precious time thinking about political problems," she announced, and the air of finality in her voice made it abundantly clear that she was serious.

"Anti-Semitism has poisoned the German psyche for decades," said Nathan. "There's probably no Western country where Jews have played such an important role in the life of the nation and at the same time been so despised."

"Ernst is still talking about going to Palestine," Lene said. "He apparently thinks it's the only hope."

"We've lived here since early in the sixteenth century," said Nathan. "We're *Germans*. What does Palestine mean to us?"

"Your brother Ernst is a romantic," said Caroline.

It was impossible to talk to Emma about the problem at all. "The filth of the earth!" she cried. "Scum, nothing but scum. I know Aunt Eva loves the proletariat, but they'll turn into Nazis as quickly as they'll turn into Communists. They're not to be trusted. They blame the rich for everything, but wouldn't they just love to be rich themselves? But you know," she added, "the Jews aren't faultless by any means. They're pushy. Too many of them are visible in the government, in the theater, in the newspapers. Everywhere you look there are Jews. They think they're smarter than anyone else, which may well be true, except they needn't rub people's noses in it."

Lene couldn't tell who made Emma more livid, the Brown Shirts or the Jews. She decided it was best not to discuss politics with her sister at all.

Aunt Eva had her own interpretation and her own answer to these questions. "You have to understand that it all reduces to class war," she told Lene one Sunday afternoon when she came to visit. Eva never changed. Her clothes were always the same, her hair— a little grayer now—was always worn short with bangs, her shoes were sensible and sturdy. Lene was touched by Eva's earnest goodness and defended her against her detractors. She thought that Eva's only major fault was her tenacious belief that man was perfectible and Utopia attainable.

"The Nazis' appeal is to the petite bourgeoisie, to the militarists and to the robber barons. The CP is trying to mobilize the workers so that the revolution can be effected from the left, not from the right." Eva sighed. "I used to believe it would be easy. I used to think that all you had to do was show the working class the logic of their position in capitalist society, and *piff!*, they'd rise up and slay the dragon. But it isn't so easy. And the fascists are clever—by using the Jews as scapegoats, they direct the attention of the people away from the *real* issues. The workers, who are in very great need—I hope you know that, Lene—shout, 'Give us bread!,' and the Nazis shout back, 'The Jews have bread, take it from them!' "

"But what's to be done?" Lene asked. She had just finished nursing Clara and was holding her against her shoulder. The baby was half asleep, and Eva looked at her with such affection and longing that Lene thought her heart would break with pity for this barren spinster so filled with tender compassion that she had to love the whole world because she never found a single soul to respond to her need.

"If everyone will support the parties of the left instead of trying to prove how much of a German patriot he is, perhaps we can present a united front. It will be the only way to defeat them." For just a moment Eva's face reflected hopelessness. But hopelessness was not a condition of which she approved. "Whatever happens," she said, "we cannot give up."

Clara gave a loud and gurgling belch.

"May I hold her?" Eva asked. When Lene put the little girl into her arms, she cradled her and kissed the round face, and again Lene was touched by her aunt's awkward love.

JACOB MADE a long face when asked about the state of the world. Lene had stopped at the bookstore on her way to the theater to pick up tickets to a play by Ernst Toller. Jacob made fun of the new playwrights. He called them "parlor pinks" and accused them of substituting slogans for ideas, and politics for talent.

"Artists won't change the world with their work," he said. "You can give your friends that message from me. The people who change the world are soldiers and inventors. Artists are commissioned to build monuments after the fact. They're individualists who guess wrong as often as not. When the dictatorship—of whatever stripe—sneaks up on us, they'll be among the first in jail."

"Will it be the Nazis who'll come to power?"

"Maybe not the Nazis, but it'll be the right," said Jacob. "The left will never hold their gains. As soon as things get bad again, as soon as enough people are out of work, the gospel the Nazis are preaching will be like the Christianity preached to the slaves of Rome. A place in heaven and a religion to call their own. They'll gladly be martyrs for that. And in Hitler they've got a messiah as well."

"Is he serious about the Jews?"

"I'm certain he is. People are always serious when it comes to hating Jews."

"And—what's to become of us?"

"We'll be put back into the ghetto. It will be more of a move for you than for me."

"Not if they make the West End the ghetto."

"It'll be crowded in any case," he said.

"Uncle Jacob thinks we'll all be put in a ghetto," Lene reported to Edu. They had met for a stroll through the Städel early on a sunny Sunday morning.

"My brother always makes those grim little jokes."

"Is he wrong?"

"Probably not—though I would think that enforced emigration might be the more likely fate. The best thing is to be ready for anything. A takeover from the left would be no picnic either. I have friends among the White Russians who fled after the Bolshevik Revolution; their stories don't make for pleasant listening, whatever your Aunt Eva may think."

"But it's not the same thing to have your money taken away for the sake of the poor as it is to be deprived of everything—perhaps even life—because you're Jewish."

"To be dead is to be dead, my child."

Elias joined them. He had important news for Edu and did not wish to have its impact diluted by gloomy reveries.

"Enough of all this nonsense," he said, "we have to think about better times, the legacies we leave our children. You've heard that some more works from the Hohenzollern-Sigmaringen collection are up for sale?" He had put his arm through Lene's as if to keep her from straying, but his attention was on Edu. "The director will try to get some for us—for the Städel—but that will take lots of money. We're tapping all the sources and then some."

"Am I 'all the sources' or 'then some'?" asked Edu.

"Probably both. We're sure to come around twice."

"Is there a chance I might get in there to do some bidding myself?"

"Why not? We shan't be able to get *everything*. But we'll have to make certain you're not bidding against us. You know, those works of art should *all* be in museums, really they should."

"What a thing to tell a collector!"

"Perhaps, my friend, your collection will turn up in a museum one day—for all the world to see."

"Do you truly believe 'all the world' appreciates this art?" Edu waved his hand gracefully about the room. "Shopkeepers and clerks and bored children?" They were in the room with Rembrandt's "Triumph of Delilah."

"I think they love it," said Lene.

A small boy holding tightly to his mother's hand looked in open-mouthed wonder at the great dramatic scene before him.

"It's a truly Baroque composition," Elias said rather absent-mindedly.

"A perfect picture for bloodthirsty children," Edu remarked.

"I love it too," said Lene.

"But of course," said Edu; "it is a Rembrandt."

JONAH SÜSSKIND, living in Wiesbaden with his wife, Hildegard, and their four children, had withdrawn almost completely from the family circle. The blame for this was usually put squarely on his wife. But although she held provincial views and was excessively concerned with her place in Wiesbaden society, this alone could not explain the change—one might almost call it a conversion—that had taken place in Jonah's life. In addition to being a successful general practitioner, treating the rich and the corpulent, the self-indulgent and the dyspeptic who flocked to Wiesbaden for the "cure," he was also something of a fanatic in matters of health and personal hygiene. He and Hildegard believed that virility came through joy and that joy came from a regimen of cold baths, long hikes, swims in mountain lakes, setting-up exercises and contests of strength consummated under a broiling sun. They wanted to be ready for anything. They thought a time might come when they would need to demonstrate both their vigor and their discipline.

Elias' wife, Bettina, whose opinions were often ignored because she was thought to be merely amusing, was not content to blame Hildegard. "He's a free man," she said. "He chose his life."

"He always wanted to marry a rich woman and take his place in good society," Eva added.

"I still think it's all *her* fault," said Caroline. "She pulled him down to her level."

"He couldn't have been easy to live with," said Emma. "He has no respect for women."

"Let's drop the subject," Nathan suggested. "As long as he's happy, a prosperous doctor in Wiesbaden, esteemed by patients and colleagues alike . . ."

"I don't think he's happy," Caroline insisted. Emma wondered why she had to have the last word.

AS SPRING turned into summer and Clara grew happier and fatter with each passing day, the gulf between Lene and Tom grew wider and wider. It was not something to put one's finger on, they never quarreled, but it happened as surely and steadily as the baby's increase in weight. He was absent from the house for longer and longer periods of time. When he did appear, he was as considerate as ever; he spoke to his in-laws and kissed the baby and smiled at Lene. Sometimes he even held Clara. But he always seemed to be stepping out of the way, and before anyone knew it he had gone out the door again. Lene could not hold him at all. He said he was working on an anthology of contemporary German poetry and had to travel across the length and breadth of the country to meet poets and talk to them about their work. Often he called from the office to say he was working late. Lene, still living within the bosom of her family, became used to Tom's absences. She decided that it was rather pleasant to be alone, since she was never truly alone.

Clara smiled a lot and grew a dimple on either side of her mouth and was adored by everyone. Lene often went with Emma to a concert or an exhibition and regularly saw her cousins Jenny and Julia. One weekend they all went on a trip to Salzburg, and when Clara was weaned, Emma and Lene spent a week in St. Moritz. They met Elias and Bettina there with Benno, who was now eighteen and overweight but terribly smart. They took long hikes, and Lene rarely thought about Tom.

When they returned to Frankfurt, where Fräulein Gründlich had taken charge of Clara, a chore she didn't intend to give up, Lene discovered that Tom had packed most of his clothes into his matched leather suitcases and gone off to spend the summer in Weimar, where his publisher had just opened a small branch office.

Neither Caroline nor Nathan discussed Tom's disappearance—if such it was—with Lene. They did not even allude to it in their private conversations. Only Fräulein Gründlich mentioned it one day as she and Emma were walking in the Palmengarten with Clara in the pram.

"I don't like to see them separated. It's sure to turn out badly."

Emma disagreed. "Lene doesn't have to have a man," she said with some vehemence. "She's perfectly happy the way things are. So what if Tom leaves for good? As long as Lene has the baby, her family and the apartment, she needn't worry."

Fräulein Gründlich was sorry she had spoken. She realized that

Emma saw everything through the distorting glass of her own unhappy experience. One had to be careful not to open the old wound. Fräulein Gründlich thought that Emma suffered from tender nerves. She occupied herself increasingly with good works and spent the better part of her time aiding and comforting the sick and the blind, counseling working-class women who had been abandoned by their husbands or beaten senseless by their lovers. Every charitable association in Frankfurt knew that it could call on Emma for a generous donation.

Lene had not been to the café in months when she decided, early one mild summer evening, to stop in for a glass of wine. She had not seen Paul Leopold since the artists' ball. The night was sweet, nothing remained of the raw air of winter or the sullen face of violence. Lene walked along the streets of the Altstadt unafraid. Women gossiped at the side of the fountains while their little girls played hopscotch in chalked squares, their husbands worked on motorbikes or drank beer at the corner tavern. Lene did not feel out of place; she patted the children's heads, smiled at the women, nodded at the men. No hint of the terror gleamed in their eyes.

At the café the same serenity prevailed. The doors and windows were open, and the street intruded gently, bringing with it the scent of geraniums and the laughter of little girls. Paul sat at his accustomed place. It was still early, and he was alone. Lene went directly to him, the smile on her face so radiant that he could not help but smile back at her. He reached for her hand to kiss it, but she drew it away, slid into the chair beside him and kissed him on the cheek.

"Enough of your Viennese tricks," she said. "You know how I detest 'Küss' die Hand, Madame.' "

"It's a charming custom from another, more generous age."

"Nonsense," said Lene, "you romanticize it. You, of all people, with your cynical view of the world should know better what rotten apples moldered at the bottom of that barrel. Lehár and Strauss and the Hapsburg court—did you never hear of Dr. Freud?"

"I never thought I'd hear that name come tripping from *your* tongue, my child."

"Oh—it's not that I believe in all that stuff and nonsense about curing people by psychoanalysis, but I do think those skeletons he dug out of the closet are very real."

"I'm certain the good doctor is grateful that Lene Wertheim of Frankfurt am Main recognizes the validity of his theories. However, I'm certain he would agree that gallantry is never out of place, never out of date. I'm certain *he* kisses the hand of every pretty young woman who walks into his office."

"How is your work going? What are you doing?"

"First let's hear about *you,* your life, your baby. You look more beautiful than ever!"

"The baby is fat and adorable."

"And your life?"

"My life is the same, or very nearly so."

"Fat and adorable?"

"Uneventful, boring."

"And Tom?"

"I see very little of him." Lene tried to sound airy and cool, but she could not hold back the faint tremor in her voice. She could not look at Paul; she knew his eyes were on her. "He's been traveling."

"With Lulu?"

"Why do you say that?"

Paul's sharp ears heard the surprise, verging on shock, in Lene's voice, and he realized that he had said too much. He tried to withdraw. "It was a silly question."

"You never ask silly questions," Lene said. "You make lightning connections, and they're rarely wrong. Now that you've said it, there's no way you can take it back."

"I'm sorry. I thought you knew."

"My suspicions are not easily aroused."

"Perhaps you aren't jealous?"

"That could well be."

"Perhaps you do not love Tom enough."

"That too may be true."

"Will you keep on as you are?"

"As long as nothing happens."

"That might be forever."

"Don't let's discuss it," Lene said. "I'd rather know what you've been doing."

"I'm rich as Croesus! My book is going well, I may be sent to the Balkans, I may go to Paris—and I will take you with me if I do!" He flung a handful of silver on the table. "Order the best wine. Leopold is king!"

"I'd love to go to Paris with you."

"You don't know me, Lene. I'm a person of unstable character."

"You're a person of talent and wit."

"Is that enough for you?"

Lene did not answer. It had grown dark outside. The café had become more crowded and noisier; people began to stop at Paul's table. It was no longer possible to talk quietly with him. He was a public person, the writer-at-the-café. Lene noticed slyly curious looks directed at her, she felt a guarded friendliness. It was clear that they were uncertain how to approach her. The past few months had altered their perception of Lene—would they be altered again? Lulu ranked higher in their estimation than Lene did. Lulu was a poet, not a bourgeoise from a good house. But then, Paul ranked higher than Tom, perhaps even higher than Tom and Lulu combined, and if Lene had taken up with Paul, it meant she had been admitted, as it were, to the peerage.

At the café, affairs of the heart were discussed as minutely as the novels of Proust or the music of Alban Berg. Lene realized that she had missed the banter and the shop talk. She enjoyed her new position and took it to mean that she was clever. She saw, as she had not seen before, that Paul was central to the "theater" of the group. He was the puppet master who ran the show, his anecdotes set the tone and regulated the laughter. It was he who changed the subject or turned the conversation around. When he stopped talking to return to his notebooks, a kind of depression settled over them all; the talk became quieter and more distracted.

It was after midnight when Lene looked at her watch for the first time. "It's late," she said, without conviction. "I should be going home." She did not believe that Paul would offer to accompany her but saw no harm in testing him.

"How do you propose to get home?" he asked.

"There are cabs nearby."

"I'm glad you're independent," said Paul. "I don't like clinging women."

Lene got up. "You're snotty," she said.

"Forgive me. It is my heritage again. The Viennese are supposed to be gallant—but a little fresh."

"Your freshness outstrips your gallantry by as much as the distance between Galicia and Vienna."

"*Touché,*" said Paul. "If you wait half an hour, I'll walk you home."

"I think I want to leave now."

Paul caught up with her just outside the door. He had stuffed all his papers in a new leather briefcase. "The very best," he said, patting it. "Excellence deserves excellence. Do you know where I got it?"

"Your concern with 'the very best' should never be advertised," Lene told him testily, "that makes it vulgar." She remembered Emma's reference to Jewish misfits and suddenly felt bereft.

"*I* need good clothes more than my work does," Paul said, walking beside her. He was not quite as tall as she was. "I'm ugly, my work is not. My work is probably the most handsome in Germany and Austria. It needs no fancy wrapping. But those who meet me on the street don't know that. So I carry an expensive briefcase too."

"What if it appeals to some thief?"

"I never let it out of my sight. And coming as I do from the land of thieves, I am not easily conned."

The night was crowned by a full moon. It hung directly above the Dom and cast its soft light over the city. It stole into garret and garden, and flitted between the leaves of the chestnut trees to tremble in dainty powdery spots on the empty sidewalks. Paul and Lene walked along the Main quai as far as the Anlagen and then turned north to walk beneath the trees. Everything seemed safe this night. Even the streetwalkers strolled softly, as though on bare feet. Paul and Lene did not touch but walked close together, so close that Lene could smell the cigarettes and brandy and the clean-laundry smell of his white shirt. At the corner where the Guiollettstrasse turned off, they stopped and kissed. All the stiffness in Lene's body, put there by the control she maintained over it, loosened, melted, opened up. An aching wish she had never known could be so strong flooded her limbs. She put her arms around Paul and pressed against him, thinking she must be moon-struck, for she had never realized that she knew the images of sexual pleasure that suddenly flooded into her mind.

"We can go to my house," Paul whispered. "It isn't too far from here. And I have some good wine. Are you expected at home?"

"No."

"Are you certain?"

"Didn't I ever tell you I was grown-up?"

They continued, arm in arm, to Paul's rented room. The boardinghouse was a plain, solid building behind a freshly painted iron fence. Nothing in the room belonged to Paul except his clothes, a typewriter and an alarm clock. He did not turn on the lights. Lene saw nothing but the moon beyond the window. They undressed each other by its cream-colored dusty glow and made love.

EDU WERTHEIM's fortune had grown enormously. He had traded wisely, eschewed speculation and diversified his holdings. The value of his collection, too, had increased, but he bought only things he truly cherished and scoffed at suggestions that he was interested in bargains. Within the family he maintained his benign, ironic rule, and no one challenged his decisions. It was easier to do as he said, to lose oneself in the calm order of his plans. Only his nephews— Ernst in Berlin and Siegmund's Willy studying mathematics at Göttingen—moved outside his influence. They recognized his cool punctiliousness toward them for what it was: disappointment, unrequited expectation. Had he dreamed that one or the other might become a son and partner to him? If so, he never mentioned it, but the hint of disparagement that entered his voice when he spoke of his "two beloved trolls" always sounded to Lene like sour grapes. Andreas escaped his strictures, perhaps because he had made a small reputation as music critic in Frankfurt, perhaps because he regularly came to tea impeccably dressed, exuding an odor of lemon soap.

Edu traveled a great deal. He went to the opera in Paris and to his tailor and the theater and Lady Samuel in London, but like so many Germans, he loved Italy best of all. While Nathan and Caroline vegetated in a stodgy hotel in the Swiss mountains, and Siegmund and Pauline motored to Monte Carlo and the races at Longchamps, he visited Naples and Sicily, clambering over the ruins of temples and jouncing about in donkey carts. He never lost his aplomb and never tore a thread in his fine English suits or scuffed his polished shoes.

In August of 1928 he invited Emma to go to Florence with him. Ever since her "disastrous experience," as it was called, he had shown a special concern for her. Edu had asked Julia as well, but she was involved in a complicated affair with a second-rate writer, and Edu was afraid that the complication would pursue her to Florence, so he put his invitation in the form of an ultimatum.

"Resolve your difficulties and you can join us," he said to her. "You know you're always welcome, but I don't approve of affairs with married men, especially when the woman is young and unmarried. It is bad form and will only make you unhappy."

Julia repeated the conversation word for word to Lene. "He's such a hypocrite," she said. "We all know that he's had this affair with Lady What's-her-name for years now."

"She's not young and unmarried."

"And how do *you* manage?"

"I've learned to be secretive."

Hannchen was the only one who spoke to Edu about his private life. The old lady was seventy-five and still vigorous, though she rarely left her apartment in Edu's house.

"Marry her—don't marry her, you'll be sorry either way," she said. Edu made no reply but merely smiled, patting her hand.

Elias, Bettina and Benno joined the expedition to Florence, where they all stayed at the Hotel Minerva at Edu's expense. From there they made daily forays to see the local splendors. They made excursions into the countryside, Baedeker in hand, and once, to please Bettina, they motored as far as Pisa, eighty kilometers away. She had always found the Campo Santo there overwhelmingly beautiful and had published a droll poem in the *Frankfurter Zeitung* on the varieties of objects made in the shape of the leaning tower for sale in the booths that lined its grassy green periphery. She drew pictures of the German tourists in their leather shorts, clutching the replicas.

Benno, who had grown from a pudgy boy to an obese young man, kept up with the others, though he huffed and puffed a great deal. He climbed the many steps up the inclining bell tower, and when he got to the top, felt such a weakness in his knees that he had to sit down. He closed his eyes and rested against the worn old stones, fanning himself with his hat.

"You'll get your fine linen suit dirty!" Emma cried. "Let me spread a handkerchief under you."

"There's not one made that's large enough," he said, smiling sheepishly. "Help me back down." Emma guided him the length of the spiraling staircase. He was one of the few men she knew whom she did not in any way fear, and she hung on his arm as much as he leaned on her. They reached the bottom giggling with relief. "Never again," said Emma.

Benno, following in the steps of his father, had studied art history and puttered about now in the Kaiser Friedrich Museum in Berlin, taking periodic measurements of the Pergamon altar, on which he was preparing a monograph. He had crossed out more words than he had left in and was on his fifth draft. Benno had the courtly manner and encyclopedic mind of his father, together with his mother's abstracted and amused air. Only his body was his own. Its great weight seemed less to weigh him down than to preserve him.

Later in the week, at an elegant party, they met Bernard Berenson, the expatriate American connoisseur of Italian painting. He was sixty-three years old and tiny. The minute he laid eyes on Emma, he asked to be introduced to her. She was flattered to have been singled out by the famous man, and they conversed for a while in English, which Emma had learned—"long ago," she said—in school.

"Your idiomatic use of the tongue is astounding," B.B. said gallantly. He invited her to come visit him. But by then Emma had caught the satyr's look in his delicate, bearded face and declined the invitation. B.B. was convinced, however, that her refusal was only temporary.

He spoke to Elias Süsskind about her. "That young woman's beauty is quite extraordinary. I understand she's Eduard Wertheim's niece?"

"She's my niece as well," said Elias. "My sister's eldest daughter."

"Exquisite, absolutely exquisite!"

"Are you buying or selling?" Elias did not like B.B.

The old man's face betrayed only a trace of the anger that welled up in him. The assistant director of the Städel had, he remembered, disputed his attributions on several occasions and been correct. He hoped the man would not get in the way of his pursuit of Eduard Wertheim and his niece. He suggested a joint trip to Siena. They would make a day of it, hire two motorcars, enjoy lunch on the Piazza del Campo and see all the sights, including some, B.B. hinted, not usually seen by tourists.

"My nephew is arriving tomorrow and bringing a friend," Edu told him. He had received a telegram from Andreas that morning. He hoped the old gentleman would not be overwhelmed by them all.

"*Ich bin Kummer gewöhnt,*"—I'm used to trouble—B.B. said slyly, indicating that he was familiar with the pitfalls of family outings.

The day proved glorious in typically Italian fashion. There was a good deal of discussion as to how the party was to be divided between two cars. B.B. cleverly jockeyed himself into a place beside Emma, who had chosen to ride with Andreas and his friend Kurt, who was said to be a composer, although Emma had never heard of him. Her fears that Andreas would bring an impossible person with him had blessedly not been realized. Kurt was quiet and respectable and about the same age as Andreas. In gratitude for this show of good taste, Emma felt called upon to treat the pair graciously. As a result, she spent the entire journey—which took a little more than an hour—talking with them, and B.B. was left to sulk in the corner.

They were let off in front of the Duomo, and the two drivers promised to be back by six-thirty. After inspecting the building inside and out, they descended to the Piazza del Campo along the winding streets. Now and then they were able to catch a glimpse of the piazza through the spaces between the brick houses, in the shell of its sloping pavement. When they reached it, they were pleasantly struck by the heat of the morning sun and sat down briefly at the café to drink espresso. B.B. began to expound his views on the place of Siena in the galaxy of central Italian cities, while Elias interjected occasional acerbic comments.

Emma sat nervously over her coffee, hoping that conflicts between them would be kept to a minimum. Edu was amused by the group; he thought it great fun to see all these people in one place contending for attention, observing, judging, jousting, all of it against the centuries-old backdrop of this rosy-stoned city. Bettina took notes in her large, illegible hand. She understood the subtle ways in which Edu orchestrated the relationships around him and knew that much as he respected Elias, he felt that his money gave him an edge, a superiority. It took the three of them, herself, Benno and Elias, to stand up to him.

Andreas, who was in love, could not have been happier. He experienced the beauties of Siena with a rare intensity, seeing them reflected in the eyes of his lover. He wanted to touch Kurt but was afraid that an explosion would occur and wipe them all off the face of the earth. He drank in the sights, and everywhere he looked, the face of his lover intruded.

Benno listened to his father sparring with Berenson. It amused him, but he kept his ears open just the same for bits of insight and pieces of information to file away in his own mind. Benno had always been self-possessed; his parents treated him like an adult. He had done poorly at school, refusing to adjust to the rules and language of the classroom, so his mother had taken him out for a year to be tutored at home. His teachers were terrified of his talmudic knowledge, his fellow students made fun of him and grew angry when he ignored them or joined in their laughter. He was open to every sort of person and every kind of experience; his curiosity was boundless. He ingested ideas the way he ate—with gusto and an immense appetite.

Elias thought they ought to go and see the Ambrogio Lorenzetti and Simone Martini frescoes inside the Palazzo Pubblico. B.B. made disagreeable noises but was overruled. He smiled at Emma, who gave him a kindly look in return. He understood that she would come to his aid if she felt he was threatened. It was clear to him that he must bring out her protective instincts.

Edu paid all their entrance fees with a matter-of-factness that brooked no opposition. Nevertheless, he was fully conscious of how others reacted to his generosity. He noted with satisfaction that Kurt was embarrassed and that B.B. gave it not a thought.

"You must come and study with me," B.B. said to Emma while they were looking at the paintings.

"Do you have regular classes?"

"No, my child, not regular classes. I detest unwashed students. I take a few select individuals under my wing and give them the benefit of my long years of study. They live at my villa and become part of my household. I should like to count you among the chosen."

Emma felt flattered, as the old man knew she would; it seemed to her now that she had been unfair to him. The satyr's face was no longer visible to her, she saw only the sage.

After a morning spent among great works of art they were all hungry. They ate at a simple trattoria on the Piazza del Campo where the food was delicious, and lingered for a long while over the meal.

"What shall we do this afternoon?" asked Emma finally.

"Perhaps we could separate," Elias said. "I have someone to see at the museum."

"I have a friend here whose house is always open to me. Would you like to go and look at his Sassettas?" B.B. spoke to Emma, but he meant to be heard by everyone.

"The fraudulent Sassettas," Elias murmured, but only Edu knew what he had said.

"Why don't you and Benno and I go back to the Duomo?" Bettina suggested to Edu. "Museum people bore me, whereas the marble 'graffiti' on the Duomo floor can be looked at for hours."

"Your word is my command," said Edu and called the waiter over. He paid the bill with several large lira notes. This time B.B. reached for his wallet half-heartedly, murmuring, "You must let me pay my own way," but he was satisfied to put it back as soon as Edu shook his head. "The treat is mine," he said.

The waiter, happy with the German gentleman's generosity, bowed several times, pulled their chairs back from the table, and helped the women into their jackets. B.B. noticed that Emma wore a single strand of pearls about her graceful neck. He felt a strong urge to draw her close to him and kiss her.

They walked slowly to the house of his friend, the count with the Sassettas. A man-servant in uniform, wearing a large striped apron, admitted them. He told them that the count was still resting but would soon be up. While they waited, B.B. and Emma spoke quietly in English, and the old man complimented her once again on the fluency of her speech.

"You ought to make use of your gift for languages," he said. "Have you ever thought of becoming a translator?"

"I haven't the patience," said Emma, "Nor the literary facility. I can only *speak*. I do not like to be silent for long, so I must learn languages in order to be able to talk wherever I am."

"Do you write letters?"

"Letters? Of course I write letters. That's not the same as literature, you can simply babble on as though you were talking."

"Will you write to me when you return to Frankfurt?"

"With pleasure."

The old art historian squeezed her hand. "*Some* of his paintings are not authentic," he said, "but oh, the Sassettas!"

The count came in presently. "Ah, Signore Berenson," he said in a high, nasal voice, "you have brought another lovely young creature to see my paintings, my little Sassettas."

He served them sherry in small gold-rimmed glasses, no larger than thimbles.

"The Sassettas are all that interest him," the count continued. "I ask him to look at the rest of the children, but he says 'No no no!' very emphatically." His imitation of the old man was very good, and Emma laughed.

B.B. drank to her health and to his host's good fortune, and then, as though he owned the place, he led the way to a distant study. He stopped in front of three small panels showing a saint going about his business in a bare but characteristic Tuscany landscape.

"Beautiful!" said Emma.

"Naïve and charming," said Berenson. "Not a great painter, but one of the most endearing. It is necessary to love the little masters, too, now and then." He turned to the count. "Are you still not interested in selling them?"

Emma had the fleeting impression that the question was always asked, in just this way, when the two men met.

"Only an American could put it so bluntly," the count said, with his whinny of a laugh. "Americans think that everything is for sale.

If they see something they like, immediately they want to have it —and if it can't be bought off the wall of the castle, they buy the entire castle and bring it home with them to Chicago stone by stone."

Emma felt certain that this little piece of the conversation—even the way in which the count pronounced "Chicago" so carefully, like a word it had taken a long time to learn—was familiar, rehearsed. B.B. shrugged his shoulders, rubbed his hands together, smiled raffishly. The subject of the Sassettas seemed closed. The room was growing darker, Emma saw the sky over the courtyard become a deeper blue. A clock chimed the hour; it was six o'clock.

"We must go to meet our friends," B.B. said. "This charming young person is the niece of Edu Wertheim," he confided to the count artlessly. "You have heard of him?"

"Ah, indeed!" The count's smile spread over his face like a blush. "Does he own a Sassetta?"

"I do not believe so," said Emma.

They got back to the Duomo a few minutes before six-thirty and agreed after a short debate on how to arrange themselves for the trip back to Florence. Edu and Bettina rode with Berenson and Emma; Benno and his father with Andreas and Kurt. Edu listened politely to B.B., who spoke highly of the count and did not mention the Sassettas. They let the old man off at a taxi stand. He kissed Emma's hands.

"Come to my villa next Thursday for tea," he whispered. "There will be others, but I want you to come alone. I will send my chauffeur." He nodded to Edu and Bettina.

"Charmed," he said, in Italian, and it sounded like a curse.

Several days later, walking across the Ponte Vecchio to see the Pontormos in the church of Santa Felicita, Emma found herself beside Edu, for the moment alone and not within earshot of the others. She mentioned the invitation she had received from Berenson for tea.

"He invited only you?" Edu asked.

"Yes," she said and felt, when she noticed how bare the word sounded, that she ought to qualify it. "He is having some other people, he said, but doesn't want to have too large a crowd."

"Watch out for him," he warned her, "I understand he's an old lecher." Edu was annoyed that he had not been invited. Berenson, despite his airs, was nothing but a rude American Jew, after all. "And tell me how good his pictures are," Edu said, "so that I'll know what I've missed."

"Those Sassettas at the count's were really lovely paintings," Emma answered. She thought she owed B.B. something, and Edu's irritation struck her as petty.

"They're fakes."

"What?"

"The count's Sassettas are copies. Elias told me. You know I trust him. He said it was uncertain when they were done. They may well be old, but they are not by the hand of Sassetta, and perhaps not even by the hand of a follower."

"Oh . . ." Emma tried to remember if there was anything about the pictures that might have made this obvious to her.

"Did the old crook tell you to try to sell me one of them?"

"No!" Emma said, a bit too vehemently. "He wouldn't do such a thing. I just heard them talking, that's all."

"No doubt they have the same conversation in front of every rich man's niece," said Edu.

EMMA HAD a wonderful time at the party. B.B. had sent his old Bentley for her. The young Italian at the wheel drove with great éclat. Many people had been invited to the house nestled in the sunny hills above the Arno, and Emma proved to be a huge social success. The villa could have accommodated all the others of her party, but B.B. had—as he said to Emma—"suffered enough at the hands of all those Frankfurt Jews. I understand even Goethe's mother complained about them." He winked at Emma, to let her know he was joking with her, and she forgave him. She understood perfectly his wish to put distance between a Jewish past and the cosmopolitan present.

He liked mixing his company, and there were guests of every nationality in the terraced garden and the flagstoned patio of the great villa. Emma's quickness with languages stood her in good stead. She chatted with several handsome aristocratic Italians and with some American students spending their summer in Florence, with titled English women, very rich Bostonians and with stuffy professors, all of whom seemed to have the same small spade-shaped beard as Bernard Berenson. B.B. would take her hand now and then and lead her to a corner, quizzing her on her impressions of the guests.

"My wife is jealous of you," he confided, "that's an excellent sign. It means you are a person she thinks capable of exciting my interest. Don't worry yourself," he said, seeing the look of consternation on Emma's face, "her jealousy is only a game she plays, she always ends up adoring my friends."

Emma had not been introduced to the art historian's wife. "I should like to meet her," she said.

"Mary is not a well person," he said with the mock concern of those who are healthy and old, looking forward to being older yet. "She makes one appearance and then returns to her bed. You'll see her another time. Let me introduce you to someone you really *must* get to know."

B.B. steered Emma toward a large woman in a flowing gown who had taken her place in a cushion-filled wicker chair where she clearly expected to spend the next several hours. She smoked a cigarette from an exquisitely carved holder and wore heavy jewelry about her neck and arms and upon her fingers. She made such a striking picture that Emma could not have said whether she was beautiful or ugly. She exuded neither charm nor kindliness, nor did she seem possessed of ill will. She was merely *there*, like a mountain. One could like her or not but one could not ignore her.

Mabel Hennessy Supino-Botti had at one time been married to an Italian of questionable origins. No one remembered him, but everyone had heard stories about the tempestuous romance. It did not, in any case, last very long. Mabel was left with her new drawn-out name and a villa, the Villa Botti, which was large and drafty but had a "divine" view. The source of her money was as mysterious as the origins of her husband. She was not an American heiress, but neither was she dependent on the largess of rich friends. Some income derived from the rooms and apartments she rented out at the villa. She was a shrewd manager but clearly did not live solely from the income of her *pensione*. For one thing, she liked to eat too well. The greatest pleasure of staying at her place was her table. On weekends the dining room was open to select visitors. Reservations had to be made weeks in advance, and she refused steadfastly to be included in any guidebook.

Mabel's Italian was atrocious, but she spoke loudly, forcefully and with feeling. Emma liked her immediately. There was something so open about Americans; it offered friendship without the convolutions of a protracted acquaintance. And Mabel herself had so powerful a personality that Emma, who liked strength in women but had forsworn it in men, felt carried away in her presence.

The two women conversed in English and in Italian, sharing information and opinions on a variety of subjects. They quickly discovered how much they had in common, from their views on the Italians (quick-witted and kindly but with inexplicable cruel streaks) to their assessment of the latest popular novelists. Both women were voracious readers.

Mabel had lit her fourth cigarette. "I smoke too much," she said, "and I eat too much. But life is short and temptation great. You must come to dinner at the Villa Botti. You will love it. Come next Monday."

"We're leaving Sunday."

"Come tomorrow, then. I must see you again before you go. We must have a *long* conversation. And you look as if you could use a square meal. There's a bus that goes to within a mile of my place. I'll send the man with the cart to look for you around one o'clock."

"I ought to check with my uncle. Can I call you in the morning?"

"My dear, you will have to learn independence. If you stay entangled with family until your dying day, you will wither and shrivel up. Families suck the lifeblood from single women. Believe me, I know."

"If I could become independent, I certainly would!"

"Nothing is impossible, if only you *will* it. I shall teach you, my sweet. Tomorrow at one!"

She turned away to speak to one of the students and left Emma no room for an answer.

When Emma mentioned the engagement to Edu, he said he had

thought they might make a final visit to Santa Maria del Carmine to see the Masaccios in the Brancacci chapel once more.

"We can go first thing in the morning," Emma said, but Edu claimed to have made other plans.

"You're getting very independent," he said, and his irony veiled the censure sufficiently for Emma not to feel it necessary to apologize.

The visit proved memorable in every way. The villa was situated on a small hill overlooking the valley of the Arno. A shaded terrace and bright, well-kept, unostentatious rooms gave the place the aura of being outside of time, suspended in delicious, sensuous pleasures without regard for everyday realities. The cook was as good as her reputation, and Emma found herself eating with more appetite than she normally did.

"Do you put some secret ingredient into the food?" she asked.

"It is only the magic of the place and the spell of the owner." Mabel, who was wearing one of her voluminous robes, stopped smoking only long enough to eat large portions of vitello tonnato, baked peppers and arugula salad. "Why don't you come and spend a month here next spring?" she asked. "It would please me to have you as one of my 'regulars.' "

Emma again felt the sense of freedom she had experienced the day before.

"And don't tell me that you have to ask permission, I won't hear of it. I'll make a reservation for you for March, and you'll come. That's all there is to it."

Her frank gray eyes appraised Emma shrewdly. She saw that she gave her courage, that Emma was someone who had had a terrible scare. Perhaps her parents had beaten her, perhaps she had been raped. This was an acute American insight; Mabel did not see Emma at a European distance, defined by class and nationality.

"You will get letters from me during the winter. I shan't let you forget me. I have the idea that you will love it here. You will fit in beautifully. And my prices are not exorbitant. Bernard Berenson will tell you. If you are one of those women who're attracted to his mewling, finicky conversation, you can go over there and listen to him whenever you want."

"He asked me if I would be one of his students."

"Watch out for the old lecher!"

"That's just what my uncle said."

"It's obvious you need to learn a thing or two. *I* shall be your teacher. B.B. knows he can't mess with me."

They parted late in the afternoon, with a kiss.

That evening, sitting with Andreas and Kurt in the bar of the hotel, sipping a Fernet-Branca, Emma mentioned the invitation she had received.

"Should I accept?" she asked. "I'd love to."

"By all means do," said Andreas.

"I wouldn't want to go against anyone's wishes," she said. "You know how Mama and Papa defer to Uncle Edu. He seems to think there's something shady about the people I've met here."

"That's only because *he* didn't introduce you." Andreas felt at peace with the world and able to make impersonal judgments. He had never been so happily in love before. "Edu likes to keep you on a string. I think you should begin to work on freeing yourself from him. Just because he's set up a trust fund for you is no reason for you to become his puppet. It was done because *Grosspapa* Wertheim asked that it be done . . ."

"He could have been less generous, no one would have said a word."

"That's not the sort of person he is, you know that. He has a rigid sense of right and wrong—and he likes to exercise the power doling out his money gives him."

"What's the name of your friend, the American lady?" asked Kurt. Conversations about Edu bored him.

"Mabel Hennessy Supino-Botti—why?"

"Haven't you heard about her?" Kurt asked.

"No."

Emma and Andreas both looked puzzled, but neither seemed to want to hear the gossip. Kurt saw them draw close to each other; they seemed to breathe as one. But having contributed so little to the general conversation on the trip, he could not suppress this tidbit. "She's a notorious lesbian," he said.

There was a moment of silence.

"And what is that supposed to mean to me?" Emma asked.

Kurt looked a little embarrassed. "Nothing, I presume. Far be it from *me* to make a moral judgment!" He was sorry he had spoken, but he was anxious to have Andreas to himself again. He was jealous of Emma. He wished that all the Wertheims would vanish. Never again would he agree to accompany Andreas on a family outing.

"Never mind him," Andreas told his sister. "Do exactly what you want to do. I doubt that this woman will corrupt you."

Emma felt a rush of affection for him and put her hand on his. He did not take it away but lifted it softly to his lips and kissed it.

PAUL LEOPOLD was sent to Berlin that summer to do a series of articles for the *Frankfurter Zeitung*. The day before he left he called Lene.

"How long have you known you were leaving?" she asked.

"A couple of days," he lied. "Newspapers never give you time to do anything more than pack your bags."

Lene knew he was lying. There was ice in her voice. "I wish you success," she said. "Send me a postcard if you have a minute."

"Come and visit me, why don't you?" Paul said on the spur of the moment. He did not like to make plans in advance.

"Where would I stay?"

"In the hotel with me, where else?"

"That will be hard to explain to my parents."

"Why must you explain everything to your parents?" Paul took the offense. He was more comfortable throwing out challenges than he was justifying himself. "I've never known anyone as bourgeois as you, my dear child," he said. The word "bourgeois" was the worst epithet in his vocabulary. With it he had reduced many women to tears.

"I do what I want to do, but I believe in preserving the façade of respectability. I don't want to shock my parents, nor do I want to enter into a discussion with them at this moment about my marriage. Can you understand that?"

"Nothing so hypocritical is worth the trouble it takes to understand it."

"Very well, then. Good-bye and have a good time in Berlin." Lene measured her words out as if with tongs.

"You won't come to see me? Berlin is a wonderful city. Much

more cosmopolitan than Frankfurt. You really should see it with me."

"I'll let you know."

"When?"

"When I'm ready."

"I love you, Lene—even if you are impossibly bourgeois."

"Must you qualify everything, including your love?"

Paul left for Berlin full of the glee such a change of place always provoked in him. He accumulated little problems and annoyances whenever he stayed somewhere too long, and he liked moving on, even briefly, when they began to complicate his life. He did not always see eye to eye with his colleagues, he had debts—it was good to leave Frankfurt. He hoped something would turn up soon so that he might never have to return.

But he sent postcards to Lene every other day, full of cryptic messages. Fräulein Gründlich could not decipher them, but she counted the postcards that came from Berlin and the ones that came from Weimar, and the latter did not measure up to the former.

"Are you going to get divorced?" she asked Lene one day, and Lene instantly replied that she didn't know.

"You can hardly call what you've got there a marriage," Fräulein Gründlich said, trying to sound as calm and as gentle as possible.

"I haven't talked to Tom about it," said Lene, "and he hasn't talked to me. So I try not to think about it."

It was to Fräulein Gründlich that she first confided her plan to visit Berlin.

"I shall go to see Ernst," she said.

"And the postcard sender?"

"Him too."

Ernst was surprised to hear from Lene. He rarely visited Frankfurt but sent brief letters to his mother and occasional cards to the rest of the family. Most of the notes Lene received were filled with advice about what she should read on the subject of Zionism and on the problem of German anti-Semitism.

"I'm coming to Berlin," she told him on the telephone one Sunday evening.

"How nice," he said. He sounded wary. "What's the occasion?"

"I just want to get away from Frankfurt for a bit."

"In the middle of summer? Why don't you go to the seashore or the mountains?"

"I'm meeting a friend in Berlin."

"That's something else, of course. Whatever happened to your husband? You *do* have a husband?"

"He's in Weimar."

"But you're coming to Berlin."

"I don't want to surprise him in Weimar."

"That's understandable. I hope he doesn't surprise *you* in Berlin."

"You'll alert me, if he does. I'm telling Mama that I'm coming to see you."

"I hope you know what you're doing. Who is your friend?"

"A journalist named Paul Leopold."

"I've read his articles. He's a smart man. Congratulations. Let me know when you get divorced."

"I haven't come to that bridge yet."

"He's married?"

"How did you know?"

"I didn't. It was a question. But let me guess the rest. He cannot get free of her because she's mad?"

"She has TB."

"Well, I was close. It sounds just perfect."

"You'll meet him—and like him, I think."

"I might as well tell you that I'm in love as well, and you'll meet *her*, but I'm not certain you'll like her."

"How can you say that? I think it's wonderful that you've found someone . . ."

"You didn't think I was . . . like Andreas?"

"Not at all. I thought you were too serious, too buried in your books and your politics."

"Miriam shares my politics, my books seem to have less and less revelance to my life. I think we'll soon go to Palestine. How is Mama? Papa?"

"Papa is morose, and more and more a stranger to the world. Mama retreats to her painting. She spends an hour a day with the baby, writes about it in her diary, and then closes the door and draws

flowers and dream landscapes. Papa dandles the baby on his knee before supper. It is the only time I see him smile. They both seem to have gone into permanent interior exile."

"They may have to go into real exile if things stay as they are. Tell them that."

"They'd sooner die."

"They won't like Miriam."

"They won't pay attention enough to say one way or the other. Why do you keep saying no one will like her?"

"She's from Poland. My beloved is *Ostjüdin.*"

"So is Paul!"

"Does he admit it?"

"Not very often."

"Miriam not only admits it but is proud of it. She has changed my life, Lene."

"Are you speaking Yiddish these days?"

"No, but I'm learning Hebrew."

"You're not becoming Orthodox?"

"Nothing like that. I just think it would be a mistake to arrive in Tel Aviv speaking only German."

"Can I come with you?"

"You'd have to work hard, Lene. It's not a vacationland. It requires commitment."

"What makes you think I'd mind hard work? Just because I never *had* to do it doesn't mean I couldn't."

"Yes, yes, I know. You took cooking lessons, you could go to work tomorrow as a cook. But—for three hundred people in a kibbutz?"

"I'll see you Friday, Ernst. I'm leaving on the morning train and will call you from the hotel."

"All right. Say hello to my brother Andreas and tell him to write. *Shalom!*"

"What was that?"

But Ernst had hung up.

EMMA RETURNED from Florence full of stories about Bernard Berenson and Mabel Hennessy Supino-Botti. Lene had not seen her so

animated in a long time. The two sisters talked until late in the night. Lene wanted to mention Paul, to let his name drop gently into the conversation and say, "I am going to meet him in Berlin," but there seemed to be no occasion for it, and she could not bring out the words—was she afraid that Emma would be against her?

Emma did not question Lene about her plans. She was content with the explanation that she had been given and happy at the prospect of being in charge of Clara. She adored the fat little girl and was surprisingly patient with her. She had the secret idea that she was capable of being a far better mother than Lene, for Lene's head seemed easily turned to other matters—she put men before children.

The train trip to Berlin was uneventful. Lene had brought a book, but she spent most of the time looking out the window, dreaming about the weekend before her. Paul had given her the name of his hotel and told her to take a taxi there. She did not think that he would surprise her by being at the station himself, but she looked for him anyway and felt a pang of disappointment when he was not there. She even made a brief foray into the restaurant on the chance that he might have stopped to have a glass of beer. She could not, she realized, imagine him on the platform of a railroad station, but she could at the polished table of a restaurant, his notebook and a glass of beer before him. But he wasn't there, either.

Lene finally gave up and hailed a cab. Her slight sensation of disappointment was forgotten as soon as she found herself in the midst of the busy, throbbing, noisy city. She had not been there for a number of years and had forgotten how different it was from Frankfurt, how much more like a world metropolis, full of different faces, pulsating with the racket of cars and trams and the cries of street hawkers speaking in dialects of every sort, sassy, musical, full of curses and laughter.

The tryst belonged to this city. Lene could not imagine meeting Paul in some country place, could not imagine making love to him among the birches of the forest or in an old-fashioned hotel by the seashore. Paul belonged in this great, pounding city, and she would lose herself with him here. It might be for only a short time—she recognized that it could not be sustained, but it would be intense and unforgettable. She tipped the taxi driver outrageously and wanted to tell him why. She didn't dare, but she thought perhaps he knew, he gave her such a knowing look.

She had brought only a very small suitcase. She wore her pearl necklace and a thin silk scarf about her head. The freckles on her face stood out, making her look young and strong like a country girl, even in the delicate matched outfit of a proper young lady from Frankfurt am Main. Paul was waiting for her at a table beneath the colorful awning of the street café. He was alone with his familiar paraphernalia—papers and notebook and cigarettes, glasses and bottles and coasters and ashtray.

They embraced, and Lene's beating heart felt as though it would burst from her ribs. "Let's go upstairs right away," she whispered into Paul's ear. "I've missed you so, I want to make love to you this very minute!"

"What a way to talk," he said to her mockingly. "Here she is, just arrived from the provinces, a young woman from a good home, wearing her pearls, with shoes that match her pocketbook, and what does she say to me?"

"Let's go to bed!"

"Not even 'Hello, how are you?' "

"Hello, Paul, how are you?"

"Fine, my love." He stroked her cheek, and his touch went right through her.

Paul sent the porter up to his room with Lene's bag. "Only one paragraph," he said to her. "Just to the end of the page, then I'll be yours forever. Here—I'll order you a sherry. Drink it like a good girl and say nothing until you see me close my book."

Lene sat down next to him and watched the afternoon crowds passing on the street. It was pleasant to sip her sherry and feel so close to Paul. He finally capped his pen, straightened his papers and leaned back to look at her. His eyes were bloodshot, his movements slow and deliberate, like those of a very old man. "It's good to see you," he said. "I thank you for coming."

Lene felt a moment of uncertainty that was close to panic. She was alone. Suppose something happened? No one would come to her aid. "You don't look well," she said.

"That's not something a person likes to hear," he said, "but, of course, you're right." His smile was theatrical. He appeared to be playacting. "I cannot stand this place," he said. Lene thought he meant that he missed Frankfurt.

"You haven't got to stay much longer, have you?" she asked. "You'll be back in Frankfurt before you know it."

"You don't understand me," he said and swallowed half a glass of Calvados. "It's not Berlin I dislike, it's Germany I detest. In Berlin I see it more clearly than in Frankfurt. That's one of the problems with your hometown—it allows you to put blinders on. This is the heart of Prussia, don't forget that. And what is done here will be felt in every corner of the country. This is where Karl Liebknecht and Rosa Luxemburg were murdered, my love, not far from where we're sitting. And Walther Rathenau too. There are assassins everywhere in this city, waiting for their victims. It is a frightening place—exhilarating and frightening. I can't escape the future in Berlin, much as I want to, and it depresses me. I escape into my novel, but my newspaper articles offer no such relief. I must act as a mirror, and what I show the world is ugly. Even the art. I thought it wouldn't affect me, I thought I could reflect on it and then be wiped clean again. But it leaves a residue, an imprint. And I can't free myself from it. I want to leave, Lene. I want to go abroad."

"Has something *happened* to you? I mean, I never heard you sound so distraught. Did something happen?"

"If you mean did I get beat up or arrested—no. It isn't that dramatic. But something happens every day. I observe. That's my job. I am alone and I observe, and the violence, the hatred, are there for me to see. I don't know where to turn. I cry out, but no one believes me. My reports are said to be brilliant, but they change nothing. They are read, they are discussed, and the assassins go on plotting Germany's future. There are the unspeakably rich and the unspeakably poor, and they will unite to conquer Europe and kill the Jews . . . Hatred is a bond stronger than all others. You don't believe me?"

"I don't understand you."

Paul took Lene's hand, held it, squeezed it until she cried in pain and leaned so close to her that she smelled his liquored breath as though it came from her own mouth.

"If I can't make you understand, how can I make anyone else

understand? The times are terrible!" he shouted. "Save yourself!"

Lene understood his terror, but there was nothing on this sunny afternoon with which to couple it. She still believed that the elections had been a sign that the danger was past. She thought that the left was stronger than the right. She went by the hope in her heart, like almost everyone else. "Weimar is a house of cards," he said, "ready to fall as soon as world events shake it a little."

"I think you are drinking a lot," said Lene.

"And you don't understand why?"

She saw the red of his eyes, the quiver in his mouth, his hands clenching hers and fire across the street, all at once. "Look!" she shouted, but it was only the sun reflected in the windows, glowing orange in the city's haze. But the fire remained, looking like fire, even after she knew it was not, and Paul's tone clung to her mind after the words had faded. She, too, was suddenly afraid again, and the city no longer looked dashing.

"Drink is the answer," he said and suddenly sounded drunk. "Calvados is the secret potion, the key to my inner peace. Drink it, and the mirror becomes smooth and clean again and I can work. Lene, I must block out my vision of the future! Only alcohol does the job. When I escape . . ."

"Where will you escape to?"

"I don't know. I can't think about it when I'm sober, and I won't think about it when I'm drunk. Paris, maybe."

"It's always Paris, isn't it? Where are we going tonight? Have you made any plans for my visit?"

"Lots of plans," he said. "We'll eat dinner and we'll go to my café and meet my friends, my fellow sufferers."

"I didn't come to Berlin to sit in cafés all night," said Lene. "Isn't there a play . . . or a concert?"

"Closed for the season. Only the poor are with us, shouting slogans in the streets. You'll see plenty of theater."

"Who's in the cafés?"

"My famous friends, my drinking companions, the only intelligent people around. Don't think you can save me, I'm a lost cause. Go see your brother if you want to blow a Salvation Army trumpet. Talk to him about *his* obsessions. Leave me alone."

He put his hands in front of his face, and it seemed to Lene that he was crying. But no sound escaped him. After a minute he drew a handkerchief from his pocket and blew his nose. "Let's go upstairs," he said and walked to the elevator in his short, bowlegged stride. He had trouble putting the key in the keyhole, and when he reached the bed he flung himself on it, face down, and was asleep in a second.

Lene sat at his side, watching the light of day fade from the sky. She did not call Ernst. She did not know what to say to him.

When Paul awoke, it was night. Lene was sitting beside the desk, reading her book by the light of a small lamp. It took him no time at all to pull himself together. A hot bath, a clean shirt, a new suit, and he was ready. He embraced Lene, he promised her his love, he brought a smile to her face. They were both hungry and walked through the summer night to eat at Kempinski's.

Paul ordered an expensive, exquisite meal. He knew the waiter; he was familiar with every detail of the menu. Lene saw the dandy in him, noticed his gold cufflinks and felt estranged from him. He was from a different world, swept by dark memories, haunted by uncertainty. He chose the best wine. They sat a long time over dinner, and Lene was won over again by the stories he told. She thought she loved him. Even if he was a stranger, she still desired him.

Paul told stories of his youth, stories of his service in the Austrian army. They were not true stories, but he made them seem so real that Lene believed them. Bits and pieces of Sholom Aleichem cropped up in his narrative, but Lene had never heard of Sholom Aleichem. Paul knew that he could win her back with stories. By the time he had finished the second bottle of wine, he had made himself an officer of the Imperial Austrian Army and was telling her tales borrowed from Kleist.

They left the restaurant quite late. "Let's walk," said Lene, "the fresh air will do us good."

"I never walk," said Paul grandly and did a small dance step for her. "We'll go by taxi."

The café was small and oppressively hot. The tables outside were apparently reserved for tourists, the regulars all sat inside. They gave a shout when Paul appeared, and several of the men leered at Lene. It was a tougher crowd than the one in Frankfurt. There were almost no women, and Paul was the only one who wore a tie. Someone apparently made a lewd remark about Lene, which she did not hear, but Paul's sudden fury made it plain. "I challenge you to a duel!" he screamed. "Never speak like that again or I'll kill you!" and he started to shake the man. But then, as quickly as it had come, the moment passed. Paul smiled benignly and ordered a round of cognac for all.

"I'll have coffee," said Lene. "You should too, after so much wine."

"I need to relax," Paul said. "If I drink coffee, I'll be a nervous wreck in no time flat." Lene's heart sank. She was drained of all desire, she wanted only to go home.

Paul grew loquacious. His conversation began to meander, but he always brought it back somehow. Lene sat beside him utterly still, unhappy, longing for sleep. She barely noticed what went on around her. Finally she excused herself. No one noticed. She found a toilet tucked away in the hall of the building where a couple stood pressed against the wall in close embrace. The toilet stank, but Lene used it, anyway. The couple in the hall were rocking back and forth when Lene passed them again. The woman's skirt was bunched about her stomach. Then Lene saw that the man's pants were down and his bare white buttocks were visible below his jacket. For a moment, the conjunction of sex and dissolution seemed a thrilling phenomenon to Lene. But only for a moment. Then her sense of collapsing order, of lawlessness, overpowered her. She walked into the street, but the street was threatening too. Lightning flickered in the sky. She did not know where she was.

She called Ernst from a public telephone. He had been asleep. "I was worried about you," he said. "You were supposed to call when you got to Berlin. Where are you?"

"In some dive," Lene said. "Oh, Ernst—it's awful here!" She sounded like a little girl. Then she thought of Clara and remembered who she was.

"Do you want me to come and fetch you?" he asked, but it was clear that he was barely awake and hoped she would decline his offer.

"It's enough simply to hear your voice," said Lene. "Can I come over tomorrow?"

"We planned to have you two here for supper."

"I'll see about Paul—but I'll definitely come."

"Are you sure you're all right?"

"Yes, yes."

"Where is it?"

"I have no idea. Don't worry, Ernst. Good night!"

When she got back to the table, Paul was holding forth on the disintegration of Germany. "I have my Austrian passport," he cried. "I can leave any time I want."

His friends were growing restive. The thickness of his tongue betrayed him. He repeated himself over and over.

"I'm going to Paris," he said. "Or to America. You know America? Lene—there you are—do you want to come to America with me?"

Lene shook her head.

"They'd never let you in," one of his friends said. "You'd be miserable there," said another. "No coffeehouses, no imperial splendor. Democracy."

"America is the land of the future," said Paul. "In fifty years the world will be divided up between the Soviet Union and the United States of America. Mark my words."

"We'll all be dead then."

"I'll be dead long before the rest of you," said Paul. "Dead of a rotted liver. But I'll look down from heaven—which looks like the Hapsburg Empire, I'm sure—and see the Russians and the Americans fighting each other. The Russians will sell the Revolution, and the Americans will sell jazz and capitalist baubles. And everyone will come running, wanting to buy them. It's easier to sell baubles than to sell ideology."

"What do the Brown Shirts sell?"

"Hatred and baubles made of Jewish blood."

"Let's go home, Paul," Lene begged.

"Have you read Kafka?" Paul asked her.

"No."

"You should read him. You should leave your nice bourgeois Jewish home for the boulevards of Paris, taking a volume of Kafka along. My respect for you would rise if you did that. But what does a nice girl from Frankfurt need to know about the jails of the mind and the prisons of the bureaucracy?" He turned to the others, "My girl's from Kafka!" he cried. "I mean—she's from Frankfurt . . ."

"We're going home," said Lene, rising, "right now. At least I am. If you want to stay, I'll go to my brother's."

Paul put his hat on his head. He seemed barely to know what he was doing. "Steady, steady," he muttered. His friends had turned away in order not to watch him. He rose ceremoniously and bowed. Now he was the stage-drunk. He kissed the ringed fingers of strange women and playfully bit on their diamonds. One cut his lip, and he tasted blood. He looked blankly at Lene. "What happened?" he asked.

She went into the street to call a cab, feeling strong and competent all at once. "I'm the gentleman! I'll get the cab!" Paul shouted. He staggered out behind Lene and stood on the sidewalk waving his arms, but there was no cab in sight. Lene walked to the nearest corner. Just as she spotted a taxi coming toward them, a band of brown-shirted young men sprinted past her. They pushed her roughly out of the way, and she saw that they had rocks in their hands. They were singing. She caught only a few words: ". . . *wir blitzen—unsere Messer—am Judenblut* . . ."—"we flash—our knives —on Jewish blood."

Lene had stepped into a puddle of water in the gutter; her pale-beige shoes were muddy. She got the cab to stop for her. In front of the café, Paul's tottering figure blocked the sidewalk. The brown-shirted youths pounced on him. They did it quickly, like lightning; they'd had their eyes on him, and they were well trained in street violence. Lene had no time to cry out. They knocked him down, kicked him, pummeled him and ran off again as quickly as they'd come. The sound of broken glass followed them as they let fly their rocks against the windows of stores and shops closed for the night but not sealed with iron doors.

Lene ran over to help Paul. He sat on the curb groaning, his suit filthy, one white bony knee showing through a slit in his pants. "I just died," he said.

Lene saw the taxi starting to drive past. "Stop!" she cried, but it rolled on. She grabbed the door handle and pulled open the door. "If you don't stop, I'll not let go of the door, and you can drag me through the streets," she shouted. "Will you do that?"

The cabbie braked. "I don't get mixed up in politics," he said. "I don't want to know about it. I have a living to make, and it's hard enough without getting mixed up with politics. If you're Jewish, that's your tough luck. I don't want trouble."

But he stayed. He did not help them, but neither did he drive off. He looked ahead, stiff as a rock, while Lene helped Paul into the back seat. A small crowd had gathered. They, too, made not a move. Faces gazed from the interior of the café, but no one came out.

All the way back to the hotel Paul sat silent, his head back against the cushion, breathing hard, plucking at the rip in his pants. Lene paid the driver, who barely acknowledged her and drove off as soon as the cab door was shut. Paul crept up the staircase. He did not want to be seen. Lene followed him. Once in his room, he sat on the edge of the bed, cold sober now, trembling.

"You see how right I was?" he said. "Always believe your Uncle Paul—he even makes of himself the first object lesson. The German is a beast, a beast who loves order, which makes him that much more dangerous. He will commit his beastly acts and do it neat and clean and according to the precepts he's learned at his father's knee. He hates freedom."

He reached his hand out to Lene. "Come hold my hand," he said, "I have much to tell you." He had regained his dignity; his voice was clear. "The German does not know what to do with freedom. It frightens him. In freedom resides responsibility. He wants to lose himself in bondage and avoid all blame for what goes wrong. He says, 'Look what happened when we gave freedom to the Jews. They took over the country.' Anyone who yearns so desperately for past glories must demand a return to past evils. The strength of the Nazis lies in combining the dreams of a pure and perfect past with an awareness of mass movements of the future, of seeing the people's lust for sacrifice as being eminently suitable for purposes of the state."

When he stopped talking, Lene was silent. He undressed himself with dignity, declining her help. With all his clothes off he looked like a delicate pale wraith, but he touched Lene, and they fell into each other's arms. As soon as they finished their love-making, Paul got up and went into the bathroom. Lene heard him vomiting. Then he ran water for his bath, washed himself thoroughly and emerged in white silk pajamas. There was a single bruise on his face.

Paul slept late the next morning, but Lene was up soon after dawn. She went downstairs, bought a newspaper and breakfasted by herself in the dining room of the hotel. She read the paper carefully, almost expecting to see an item in it about the assault on Paul Leopold, but of course there was none. There were no dispatches at all about violence in the streets. Paul had been right. "It happens too often to report," he had told her. "The newspapers only report the *news*. And crimes of passion, which are always in demand."

Lene went back upstairs. Paul was still asleep. She found it impossible to approach him. The smell of his breath and the distortion of sleep and his bruise repelled her. She did not want to stay in the room with him. Grabbing a piece of hotel stationery, she wrote a note and left it on top of Paul's clean shirts: "Back for lunch. Going to the museum." That seemed both clear and vague enough. She had no idea where she was going, she only knew she had to leave the room and the crumpled body of her lover.

It was a hot summer's day, cleansed by the thunderstorms of the previous night which seemed to have washed away the specters as well. Strolling along the Kurfürstendamm, Lene felt herself unfettered, adventurous. There were smiles on the faces in the crowd. When she met another's gaze, it was usually filled with admiration for her own radiance, with flirtatious shrewdness, with anything but anger or challenge. Berlin looked clean and prosperous. Lene did not go to the museum; she climbed on a sightseeing bus and toured the city. When she got back to the hotel, it was after two o'clock. She found Paul in the café sitting amid his papers. He had deep circles under his eyes and his face was badly discolored, but his shirt was clean, his suit immaculate, and he wore a red bow tie. Next to his coffee and the remains of his croissants stood his second glass of brandy.

"To take away my aches and pains," he said, lifting the glass to Lene. "How was the museum?"

"I didn't go."

"But your note *said* . . ."

"I changed my mind."

"Listen, Lene"—Paul sounded his gentlest, sweetest note—"I am sorry about last night. I know I drank too much. I must have been a bore. I know I spoiled your evening, and I want to give you my apologies. I will make it up to you. Trust me, forgive me."

"You're drinking already," said Lene. "Don't promise me you'll reform if you can't even be sober the morning after a drunk!" She thought she sounded like Emma, and this realization was painful. But she knew she must resist his blandishments. She knew she must put the whole of her strength behind her will to resist his call.

"It isn't morning and I didn't promise to reform," he said. "I would never do such a thing. I merely said I was sorry for last night, and that I would offer to return your money—since you were clearly not satisfied."

"We all have to learn our lesson."

"So it's been a 'lesson' to you? I served some purpose, after all."

"I didn't mean to make it sound so—cruel."

"But you *are* cruel. You have no idea what it's like to be *me*, to wake up every morning with the ghastly realization that you are still inside this leprous skin, that you are still alive, haven't changed, will always be the same. If I didn't see so clearly, it wouldn't be so bad. But I have the sharpest eyes in creation. I drink in order to blind myself. You can't understand it. No one can. I walk in relative safety only when I write. But I can't write *all* the time. I have to stare at the world too—and at my ghastly, crawling self—in order to find more things to tell my newspaper readers. My fantasies are turned into fiction—that is my hope for immortality—but no one wants to read my fiction. Everyone wants to read my facts. My journalism is considered 'superior' . . ." He looked straight at Lene with his sunken eyes. She suddenly noticed that he had long dark lashes. "Be glad you are who you are," he said, "and leave me . . . as soon as possible."

"I don't want to leave you," said Lene, but even as the words came out of her mouth she knew they were false. The wish to leave Paul had been formed in the darkness of the night before and had been growing steadily since then. Lene had recognized her deep aversion to the disorder through which he wandered, and once acknowledged, the aversion could lead only to flight.

"Ernst invited us over tonight, and I told him we would be there about six-thirty."

"I have a lot of work to do, Lene. Two deadlines to meet, and feeling as I do, I'll have a hard time working. I thought we were going to the theater later. It was what you wanted . . ."

"You were so vague about it, and I promised Ernst. He wants me to meet his fiancée."

"Go then without me, and I'll return the tickets."

"Maybe we can meet at the theater."

"Why don't you take *my* ticket, and you can go to the theater with Ernst. I don't mind. I've plenty to do." He was eager to end the discussion. "Do what you wish," he said brusquely, "I have work to do."

Lene ordered a light lunch of cold cuts. She drank a glass of red wine. While Paul wrote rapidly, she thought about Tom. She had never seen *him* work with such precision or passion. He always seemed to look for an excuse to put his work aside. He was easily discouraged, did only what was absolutely necessary and spent the best hours of the day dreaming. She could not stay with Paul, but neither could she return to Tom. She wanted a man who worked with passion but led an ordered life as well. A man who did something she could admire but had his feet planted on the ground. Once upon a time she had thought he needed to be handsome, then she had believed brilliance was enough.

The cigarette butts piled up beside Paul, the brandy glasses accumulated. The wine had made Lene sleepy. She excused herself and went upstairs to lie down. The maid had been in to clean up. No wonder Paul likes living in hotel rooms, thought Lene.

When she woke from her nap, she saw that it was after five o'clock. She washed her face, put on the clean dress she'd brought and ordered black coffee to be brought to her room.

Downstairs there was a note from Paul and two tickets for the theater. "Had to go out," the message read, "will I see you *late* tonight? Love, Paul."

Lene took a taxi to the address Ernst had given her. He lived quite a distance from the center of town, in a lower-middle-class Jewish quarter. Lene spent the ride preparing herself to meet him and his girl friend. Ernst had received a Doctor of Jurisprudence degree but had no intention of practicing law. He had a small teaching position at the university, but there was no hope of advancement, given his political views. He seemed to have forgotten his past and denied his class, obsessed as he was with Zionism, impatient, almost rude to all who did not think as he did. Nathan was helpless before him. He refused to understand how anyone—let alone one of his children— could believe in the necessity of a Jewish homeland.

"I could understand it if you were some poor ghetto dweller from the Russian pale, dealing in rags, speaking Yiddish. Then, if it were the only way to drop your filthy habits and escape the stifling orthodoxy of your surroundings and the vicious anti-Semitism of the peasants among whom you live, I could see it," he wrote, "but as a German Jew, you have the opportunity to live any kind of life you want to. You are free. You *have* a homeland."

Lene had defended Ernst against her father, who, having once articulated this lengthy diatribe, never tired of repeating it. Edu was more cautious in his assessment, but he thought it foolish of his nephew to throw away a law degree in order to feed chickens in the desert. Lene, riding through the Berlin summer evening, was not certain she believed her own spirited defense of Ernst. She sympathized with his stubborn resistance to Nathan and could understand his wish to return to the soil—was this idea not one the Germans were always pushing as well? Yet she could not quite imagine any of *them*, even Ernst, tilling the soil or sowing grain. Nor did she see him with a gun at some border settlement, defending it against the Arabs.

"Here we are," said the cab driver. He had stopped in front of a shabby apartment building, the kind that had been built throughout Germany in the 1880s, to provide rooms for the artisans and shopkeepers who were beginning to proliferate in the cities. Ernst's apartment was on the top floor. Lene was glad she was wearing her low-heeled shoes.

"Our location allows us to judge who our true friends are," said Ernst, standing on the landing, waiting to welcome his sister.

"It also prevents the elderly or infirm from ever seeing you," said Lene.

They hugged and kissed. Ernst held her tightly. She felt relief. Had anyone else ever crushed her to his chest like this? He smelled of toothpaste, clean laundry, scrubbed skin. *She* would not hesitate to go to Palestine with him.

Ernst said, "Come in and meet Miriam."

The apartment consisted of a living room and a small bedroom just large enough to hold a double bed. The ceilings were angled to the slope of the roof, and the windows looked directly into the sky. A toilet was down the hall. There was a stove in a corner of the living room, and it was here Miriam stood, wearing an apron, tasting the soup that was cooking on the stove.

The two women looked at each other for only the briefest of moments, then Miriam, having first wiped her hands on her apron, came forward to embrace Lene, who stiffened for a second. It was not her habit to be demonstrative, certainly not with a stranger. But she felt her resistance melt in Miriam's strong arms, so she kissed her back.

They had taken swift measurement of each other, and each saw how different the other was. Yet they felt a great sympathy. Had they been soldiers in battle together, they would have entrusted their lives to each other.

"I'm so glad to meet you at last," said Miriam. "Ernst talks about you more than he does about all the rest of the family put together."

"I must say that he's been very mysterious about *you*," said Lene, "I almost think he wanted to keep you safe from our family. There are snipers among us."

"Miriam needs no protection. She's well able to take care of herself," Ernst said. "Nevertheless, it's true the family is formidable. But I think that I was protecting myself."

"You're planning to marry?"

"Next spring, we hope, before we make *aliyah.* "

" 'Make *aliyah*'?"

"Settle in Palestine. We intend to emigrate."

"You're *really* going, then?"

"Absolutely," said Miriam, and Lene saw a look of proud love pass between her and Ernst. "I'll be finished with my studies then, I'll have my license, and I'll be able to be of real use there . . ."

"What do you do?"

"I'm a nursery-school teacher. I specialize in pre-school and pre-kindergarten children. Didn't Ernst tell me that you also studied child care?"

"Not really." Lene looked at her brother, embarrassed to have to admit her failure. "I began but never finished. As a matter of fact, I didn't get very far. Didn't Ernst mention that?"

"He only tells me the good parts."

"I couldn't handle the children," said Lene. "I was finally asked to leave. It's one of the things in my life I don't like to be reminded of."

"It's never too late to go back to something like that. Oftentimes one needs only a little more maturity to succeed where one's failed before." Miriam had a slight accent. She was smaller than Lene, with a head of short black curly hair. Her legs were sturdy, like her arms, and she had full breasts. She wore sandals and no make-up. She set the table for three while they talked.

"Well, yes," said Lene, "but I'm the sort who has to be forced to stick to a job. I'm afraid I'm one of the idle rich."

A brief, uncomfortable silence prevailed.

"How are you enjoying your stay in Berlin?" Miriam asked.

Lene suddenly remembered Paul. "Not very much," she said.

Miriam looked surprised. She had expected a positive reply. Most people loved Berlin. She herself did. She had been there for five years and knew that she would miss the city when they went to Palestine. She had no illusions—it would not be easy for them there. They were city Jews through and through.

"We had an unpleasant experience last night," Lene explained. Ernst had poured sherry into squat glasses, the kind one buys in hardware stores, while Miriam sliced a loaf of braided white bread. "Paul was beaten up by a gang of thugs."

"Nazis?" Ernst asked.

Lene's first impulse was to deny it, but she said yes with a deep sigh.

"It happens all the time," said Ernst.

"Let's eat," Miriam interjected. She served a rich vegetable soup and a plate of cheese. Small, delicate matzoh balls floated among the carrots and cabbage.

"It would have been interesting to meet Paul Leopold," said Ernst. "Was he badly hurt?"

"No—that wasn't what was terrible," said Lene. "It was the randomness of the attack. Those kids just ran wild and unchecked through the streets, breaking windows, knocking down people, smashing up cars. And no one did anything. No one helped Paul. They stared. They might have been at the theater looking at a performance."

"People feel helpless," said Miriam.

"The Nazis' violence answers some deep need in the Germans," said Ernst. "They'd like to do those things themselves. But they don't yet dare. They're waiting for permission—for someone to say, 'It's all right, you can go ahead, it's permitted to beat up Jews.' "

"You sound so dispassionate," said Lene.

"We've made up our minds how we're going to respond. We are going to Palestine. We happen to think it's the only answer for Jews, even if people laugh at us. I just hope we won't have to say 'I told you so,' but I'm afraid it will turn out exactly as we predict."

"You are the only people I know who seem calm in the face of things."

"It comes from having an ideology—a faith."

"Aunt Eva has an ideology and a faith."

"It isn't complete. It leaves out the most important element—her Jewishness."

"You *are* single-minded. You talk as though there were nothing else."

"There isn't," said Miriam.

"You're not *serious* about Paul Leopold?" Ernst asked. "He's a wonderful journalist, but he seems to be a wanderer."

"He's married, as you know."

"That wouldn't keep you from becoming serious."

"I'm not staying with him."

"Are you still married?" Miriam asked.

"Yes," said Lene, "I think so."

Miriam looked puzzled.

"My sister is notoriously unable to confront reality," said Ernst. He dipped great chunks of bread into his soup, and Miriam watched him eat with pride and joy. "I doubt that she has ever had a serious discussion about the state of her marriage—with Tom or anyone else."

"Tom doesn't like to talk about it either," said Lene. "We drifted into marriage, I suppose we'll drift out too."

"It's easier to drift in than to drift out," said Ernst, "and I tell you that not as a brother, but as a lawyer."

For dessert Miriam served honey cake and fresh peaches with brown sugar and thick cream. There was something stolid and maternal about her, and Ernst had responded to it by becoming more dogmatic, tougher. There was a coarseness. Lene did not want to see it.

"I have two tickets to a play," she said. It was already eight o'clock.

"Who are they for?" asked Ernst, his mouth full of cake.

"They were supposed to be for Paul and me. But he said I should take one of you."

"Ernst can go," said Miriam.

"Miriam can go," said Ernst.

"Why don't we all stay home?" said Lene. She felt suddenly comfortable there. They had a thousand and one things to talk about.

"The tickets shouldn't go to waste," Miriam said. "Maybe we can find someone in the building who'll take them."

"Leave it to Miriam to think of that," Ernst said. "She's got the peasant's instinct to save and make things over."

"I wasn't raised in as prodigal a household as you two were . . ."

"Let's see if the Zemlinskis downstairs want to go." Ernst took the tickets and disappeared into the hall. They heard his steps, running down the stairs.

"Will your parents be angry if we marry?" Miriam asked Lene. She stared at her with frank and intense eyes, and Lene could not equivocate.

"Probably yes," she answered, "though 'angry' isn't the right word. My parents rarely get angry. They'll be annoyed, they'll pout, my father may even give a long discourse citing chapter and verse of a learned treatise on the subject, proving that the marriage won't work. But he'll not shout or rant, and my mother will simply sigh. That doesn't mean they'll not, deep down, be resentful—but you'll be far away by then, so why worry?"

"I don't want to feel that I've come between Ernst and his family. I've moved out of the world of my own people so completely, I don't think I'll ever find my way back. But that's not good. It's inevitable in a society like the one I come from, but that's part of what I want to change. In *Eretz Israel* we'll not grow distant from our children, we'll all dwell in the modern world. An ancient land, but a modern world—*that's* the wonderful thing!"

Ernst returned panting from his run up the stairs. "They were delighted," he said. "They're poor students," he explained to Lene, "they never get to go anywhere, except when it's free, and most free things are either badly done or blatantly propagandistic: you think you're going to listen to a poetry reading and it turns out you've blundered into a meeting on moral rearmament."

They spent the next several hours deep in talk. Finally Ernst said, "I must see you home, Lene. We're taking a bunch of kids from our youth group on a trip to the country, and that means getting up at dawn, practically."

"I don't want to go back to the hotel," said Lene.

"Then stay here," Miriam said. "We have room on the couch. People are always sleeping over."

"What about Paul?" Ernst asked.

"I'll go there before he wakes up to pick up my things and leave him a note. He'll probably be so drunk he'll never miss me."

"I like your sister," Miriam said when they were in bed behind the closed door of their tiny room. The night was hot; they slept naked. Thunder rolled overhead.

"I wonder what will become of her," Ernst said, drawing his finger across Miriam's shoulder.

"What do you mean?" she asked.

"Girls from good Jewish families don't have it easy these days. They've learned none of the lessons of survival."

"I thought Lene was different from the others."

"Which others?"

"The others in your family. The ones you don't want me to meet."

"I told you you wouldn't like them."

"But I like Lene. You're just afraid *they* won't like *me.*"

"I don't want them intruding in my life, that's all."

"Do you think it will make you a different sort of person not having anything to do with them?"

"Yes."

"But that's not true. We all carry the baggage of our history and our family to our graves. I think you don't want me to meet them because you're ashamed of me. Deep deep down you're uncertain about me and only by keeping me in a compartment separate from your family can you avoid conflict."

"There isn't any conflict."

"What an absurd statement! Our cultures clash everywhere. We may both be Jewish, but we grew up worlds apart. You safe behind that garden wall among precious flowers, me in a courtyard filled with garbage."

"You exaggerate."

"I use metaphors, but they're accurate."

"When we go to Palestine, it'll all be solved. We'll start life fresh. We'll both be strangers in a new land."

"I hope you're not exaggerating the benefits. Going to Palestine shouldn't become an escape from reality."

"I'm aware of that."

Ernst's voice sounded testy, but Miriam persisted, "You'll have to face your family sooner or later. If you don't, you'll carry the conflict with you."

"It's getting late, Miriam."

"I'd like the chance to show them who I am. Lene seemed to like me. Maybe they would too."

"You're very sure of yourself."

"But you aren't—is that it?"

"If we don't get some sleep, we'll both be impossible in the morning," Ernst said, turning away from her to the very edge of the bed. Closing his eyes, he made a determined effort to stop his mind from thinking, to drown it in sleep.

"I just don't want you to do something you'll regret for the rest of your life," Miriam whispered.

"Good night," he said, his voice so firm that it was brusque. In a little while he heard her even breathing and knew she was asleep.

PAUL LEOPOLD had gone to look for Lene at the theater, seen she was not there and returned to the hotel to wait for her. He longed to have her beside him, and when she failed to turn up, he got very drunk, sitting up with a bottle of Calvados until the early hours of the morning. When he could no longer keep his eyes open, he dropped exhausted and fully clothed on the bed, which was how Lene found him when she came into the room the next morning at about nine o'clock. Seeing the empty bottle and the crumpled figure confirmed her worst premonitions, and she left quickly with her small leather suitcase to wait in the railroad station for the train home to Frankfurt. Her note to him said simply: "You were right —I'm leaving you."

Paul never returned to Frankfurt. A week after Lene left, he went to the railroad station and took a train to Prague, from where he continued for several years to send his lucid reports to the *Frankfurter Zeitung*.

EDU WERTHEIM spent four weeks in Baden-Baden every year from late August until the first day of autumn. Here, too, he might invite one or another of his relatives to keep him company for several days or a week. He was quite arbitrary about it; one could never *count* on being invited and never knew, from one year to the next, whether the invitation, if it came, would be for August or September, for a weekend or a week.

In the summer of 1928 Nathan, who had been ailing, canceled his

usual vacation in Grindelwald, Switzerland being considered too
mountainous and bad for the heart. Caroline felt cheated by this turn
of events and complained—in a veiled way, of course—to everyone.
She told Edu that it was a terrible shame that poor Nathan had to
stay in the hot city, and she wondered what she ought to do about
giving Anna her vacation. Fräulein Gründlich always left in August
to go home, and besides, she didn't know how to cook, it would be
an insult even to ask her. Lene had her own life to lead, it wouldn't
be fair to ask her to be the cook. It never occurred to Caroline that
she herself might fix a meal.

"I get your point," Edu finally said, and the current of words
stopped. He waited three days, however, before he extended his
invitation. "You'll be my guests for two weeks," he said. "Anything
longer than that you must pay for yourselves."

Lene returned from Berlin uncommunicative and sullen. She
stayed by herself a great deal and went walking in the Palmengarten,
pushing Clara in her carriage. The little girl was sitting up now and
looked about her with lively interest. She made funny sounds and
waved her arms around. She laughed a lot and played hide-and-seek
behind her blanket. For an hour every morning she visited with
Caroline, who was a late riser, staying in bed until after ten o'clock,
and then Lene would fetch her and take her out.

"How did you find Ernst?" Caroline asked her.

"Fine," said Lene. "He seems very happy with his friend and is
thinking of marrying her."

Caroline shook her head. "I wish *one* of my children would make
a sensible marriage," she said.

"Ernst will probably do better than the rest of us," said Lene.
"Miriam is really very nice."

"She's either the cause of his crazy idea to go to Palestine, or the
result of it. In either case, she's clearly not one of us."

"She doesn't have to be, if she makes Ernst happy."

"My dear child, happiness is a state of mind that does not last
when there's no common ground on which the lovers stand."

"They'll both be standing on the ground of their Palestinian
homeland before long," said Lene.

Fräulein Gründlich was the only one who knew that Lene had
gone to Berlin to see Paul Leopold. Lene told her exactly what

happened. It was a relief to her to talk about it, and Gründlich never passed judgment. All she said was, "One day you will find the right person."

"I never liked the atmosphere at Baden-Baden," Nathan confided to his brother Edu when they lunched together, as they did once a week to discuss family and business matters. "All those doddering antiques, those drooling ancients." He realized he was being ungrateful. "I forget I'm becoming old myself," he said. "Soon I'll be one of them."

"You needn't go," said Edu dryly. "I can always cancel your reservation."

"I'm sorry, Edu, forgive me. It's not that I don't value your invitation . . ."

"What is it then?"

"I am very glum about the future. Depressed about the country, about my children, about my health. Death has been knocking at my door. There are times when I think I might welcome it, but I know it's a coward's way out."

Talk of death always embarrassed Edu. He behaved as if death were a venereal disease, which one could escape if one lived properly and did not consort with whores. Nathan's insistence on talking about it he put down as self-indulgence. He was just like Hannchen in that respect, and Nathan couldn't stand it. The old lady still sat —fat and bright and chipper—in her apartment in Edu's house, fighting death merrily and triumphantly. She told Nathan that his complaints were all in his head and prescribed camomile tea and exercise. She stirred out of her apartment only to take her vacation. She drank too much coffee and ate too many dabs of butter, but her opinions were conveyed crackling across the telephone wires as they had always been. "I'm seventy-five," she said, "I've earned the right to give advice, even if it's wrong." Edu made certain that she went to Baden-Baden at such times as he was not there. In August she went with her maid to Travemünde.

"You'll come to visit us all for a weekend," Edu told Lene when he had done with Nathan. "Julia is coming too, if she can leave her current lover long enough. She needs the rest. I think she deliberately choses men who'll give her pain and trouble."

Lene had thought the same thing, many times.

"I ought to devote myself to Clara for the rest of the summer," Lene said. She rather enjoyed the peaceable life she'd been living since her return from Berlin. Edu had avoided that subject assiduously.

"It's a lovely idea, and I give you credit for being a good mother, but I know Emma is looking forward to having the baby to herself a little while. You needn't make the sacrifice."

Edu always caught them out in the little self-righteousnesses they allowed themselves, always knew when they cheated or pretended to be more humble or considerate than they were.

Emma had been put at the head of the volunteers at the *Frauenspital*, the women's hospital. It should, by rights, have been a paid job, but Emma was so loath to take on work for which she would receive money that she offered to donate her paycheck to charity. The director kept her on without renumeration, and Eva scolded her angrily: "Women have it hard enough without the likes of you working for nothing."

"I don't want to be beholden to anyone," said Emma. "This way I remain free to do as I wish. I can take time off when I want to, I do not owe them anything."

"No wonder they pay women badly when they have a whole army of them who'll work for free—you're no better than a scab."

"Oh, for heaven's sake, Aunt Eva, leave me alone," and Emma stalked out of the room.

Emma wrote weekly to both Bernard Berenson and Mabel Hennessy Supino-Botti. She had the gift of taking the experiences of a humdrum life and translating them into a series of amusing encounters.

"Imagine my surprise," she might write, "to discover the smell of garlic in the maternity ward. It turned out to emanate from a young woman who was rubbing it on her breasts to stimulate the flow of milk. Poor baby!" Both Mabel and B.B. were enchanted with their new friend and made elaborate plans for her visit in the spring.

THOSE WHO had been to Baden-Baden before the war claimed that those days of elegance had vanished forever. Families had arrived in rented railway carriages with a retinue of servants and enough baggage to require horse-drawn wagons to take them from the station to the hotel. The hotels were as splendid as palaces—indeed, royalty stopped there from time to time. In certain of the better hotels, one never saw Jews. Small armies of servants were always in attendance, the glitter of diamonds dazzled the eye.

Now the place seemed gray and dingy, the furniture worn, the help at the hotels mean-spirited, and there were Jews everywhere. The silver wasn't as heavy and the glasses weren't as thin, the flowers on the tables were not as fresh, and the tone of the waiters was impertinent. Even the doctors had changed. They were less optimistic. People complained all the time about these things, but they returned whenever they could afford it.

Edu, who was more sensitive than most of his contemporaries to the political currents swirling about him, found the conversations this year at Baden-Baden fraught with a new and dangerous substance. There was a bitter nationalist edge to the sentiments. Men were not only talking about the "good old days" but setting forth a multitude of ideas on how best to return to them. There were mutterings about the need to purge Germany of "foreign" elements, whispers about arms and armies and the need to establish another German Reich, which would extend the boundaries of the present rump of a state to its "natural" limits.

These and other opinions were most frequently voiced by businessmen and bankers who were Gentile. While they continued to be cordial, even deferential, to Edu Wertheim, he was repelled by their talk. He took aside several of his Jewish confreres to ask them their feelings on the subject. One or two agreed with him, the rest felt that he was unduly pessimistic, overly sensitive, or simply unrealistic. "One must make accommodation," they told him. It was easy to ignore his warnings, he was so clearly a man out of touch with his times.

Lady Samuel had chosen to while away two weeks at Baden-Baden while Edu was there. She stayed at the same hotel, the best in town. Lady Samuel came to the Continent every summer and spent a few weeks here, a few weeks there, dividing her time between pleasure and culture. She traveled by auto with her chauffeur and personal maid. The two servants sat together in the front seat of the car while she rode alone in the back, her small white spitz beside her. She would gaze out the window continuously and steadily, as though she expected the landscape to yield up some secret to her. She was, in fact, watching for points of interest, small churches in hidden villages, forgotten castles above meandering streams, simple country restaurants in a bucolic setting.

Lady Samuel had not informed Edu that she would be in Baden-Baden the first two weeks of September. She knew it was his habit to be there then, but this particular summer she had found herself in an especially unsettled frame of mind, had traveled about more aimlessly and distractedly than she usually did. Was it the political climate on the Continent or her impending "change of life"? She did not know. She hoped that Edu, whom she loved as much as it was in her cool English heart to love anyone, would reach out his hand to her, offer her companionship and affection at a moment in her life when she badly needed both.

They met, apparently by chance, in the Kurpark on their morning promenade. Lady Samuel had the spitz on a leash, Edu was walking alone, his cane in one hand, in the other Count Harry Kessler's newly published biography of Walther Rathenau. He planned to find a bench along one of the hillside paths and sit reading for a while in the fresh morning air. Since he did not expect her, he recognized her only at the last minute.

"Dorothea!" he cried, confused, pleased, startled and put out at the same time. He did not like surprises. She, on the other hand, adored them and felt extremely pleased that she had come upon him in this particular manner. She smiled her dazzling smile—it had been praised by prime ministers as well as painters, shop clerks as well as kings—and they kissed, not without passion.

"What are you doing here?" Edu asked. His mind instantly began to rearrange his entire schedule, and he could not quite rid himself of the touch of annoyance that had entered his heart when he recognized her.

"I couldn't bear it in the mountains," she said. "I felt fat and ugly and coarse like a peasant. I had to come here, to make myself over, to feel good again."

"Why didn't you let me know you were coming?"

"I wasn't certain, until the last minute, that I *would* come here," she lied. "I had considered Marienbad for a time."

"It would have been my pleasure to make plans to spend all my time here with you."

"I didn't want you to make plans. I wanted to surprise you. I wanted our meeting to be spontaneous . . ."

They wandered through the park arm in arm for more than an hour, chatting amiably, and Edu forgot his annoyance. The spitz trailed along behind them on his blue leash. He had a tiny Union Jack attached to his collar.

An hour before lunch they returned to the hotel and parted in the lobby. Edu returned to his room and Lady Samuel to hers. They had promised each other to meet for tea. Dorothea took off her hat and gloves and sat down on her bed. She was flushed and unsettled. After a few minutes, she got up and went to the desk where a number of books were stacked in disordered piles. They were all new, and a silver paper knife to cut their pages lay beside them. Dorothea picked up one volume after another, finally chose a slim one—a collection of short stories by D. H. Lawrence—and wrote something on its flyleaf. Using the stairs rather than the elevator, she climbed two floors to Edu's suite. The door was ajar and she entered without knocking.

"I brought you the stories you asked for," she said in an unnaturally ringing voice, just before she closed the door behind her and flung herself into Edu's arms.

That night, at dinner, Edu introduced her to Nathan and Caroline. "Dorothea is an old friend," he said. "I've invited her to have her meals with us while she is here."

Lady Samuel saw that Caroline's soft eyes were noncommittal, uncomprehending, while Nathan appraised her like a hospital patient being introduced to the head nurse.

"Edu has told me so much about you and your family," she said smoothly in her throaty English voice. "I am so happy finally to get to know you. Actually," she continued, smiling, "we met before. Years and years ago, just after my husband, Viscount Samuel, died. He was frequently in Frankfurt on business, as was my brother Dicky, who owned the firm of Simon and Seligmann. You might almost say that I'm an adopted citizen of Frankfurt am Main, I have spent so many enjoyable hours there."

"Ah yes," said Nathan, "I knew your brother. I did not know he was your brother, though."

"So *that* is the connection," said Caroline.

"The girls are coming tomorrow," Edu said, changing the subject. "Two of my nieces," he explained to Dorothea. "Helene, the youngest daughter of Nathan and Caroline here, and Julia, daughter of my brother Siegmund. Julia is the house intellectual."

"She writes," said Caroline.

"And quite well, too," said Nathan.

"You really think so?" Edu inquired. "To me it always seems as though she is being deliberately provocative. She flings down a gauntlet in every sentence to show you how modern and daring she is. Except for a rather clever way of using slang expressions to capture contemporary speech rhythms, she's not terribly original. Few women writers are."

"I have always liked her short fiction," said Caroline. "She may not be original, but she's got a sensitive eye."

"Just hope that she doesn't turn it on you and put you into one of her stories someday," said Edu.

"That's a perennial problem," said Lady Samuel. "I know a good many writers and always take care to stay on their good side."

"That's no guarantee they'll not use you," said Nathan. "Then they may write, 'She always endeavored to keep on our good side.'"

"And Helene?" Lady Samuel asked. "Did I not meet her once?"

"Where could that have been?" Caroline said.

"In Venice?"

"No," said Edu.

"In the Palmengarten. At a concert. Of course. And what does Helene do?"

"Her talents blossom in many ways," Edu said.

"She loves to eat," said Caroline. Nathan threw her a look of annoyance.

"Good for her!" said Dorothea. "I like people who like to eat. They're usually good-natured. It's the ones who do not appreciate good food who are dangerous to mankind. They become fanatics."

"Are you going to the concert at the Kursaal this evening?" Caroline asked Lady Samuel.

"If Edu invites me."

"Of *course* you'll be my guest," Edu said.

Caroline, looking up from her plate of steamed crevettes, saw that he looked at the Englishwoman with affection.

"What's the news from Frankfurt?" Nathan asked. "You read the paper, Edu, as I do not."

"The war veterans staged a large demonstration in support of the Republic," said Edu. "I hear it was a rousing success. I believe they had eighty thousand in the march, and many more watching and cheering them on. The paper says that a lot of demonstrators carried '48 flags."

"Perhaps there's some hope," said Nathan. "A coalition of the left seems the only chance."

"If there's a world-wide financial crisis, we can forget it," said Edu. "Then the Nazis will sweep right in."

"And the English?" Caroline asked Lady Samuel.

"We have no problems," Dorothea answered airily. "Not from the right, not from the left. The British have a sound tradition of freedom—unlike the Germans."

Silence settled over the table. As soon as she had finished her dessert, Lady Samuel excused herself. "I must dress for the concert," she said. "It's been such a pleasure meeting you."

Edu sat at the table for a while longer, smoking a cigar.

"Are you in love with her?" Caroline asked suddenly.

"That's none of your business."

"The question was not out of line," Nathan remarked. "I have never interfered in anyone's life. I keep my opinions to myself, but I do take an interest—even if it's only a distant one—in the affairs of members of my immediate family."

"You sound pompous," said Edu.

"I don't often have a chance to sound pompous, indulge me this once. Pomposity may well become the single indulgence of my old age."

"Let's not have an argument," said Caroline. "I'm sorry I asked an indiscreet question. In any case, I thought your lady exceedingly handsome."

"I thank you," said Edu and wondered why he was so absurdly pleased with the compliment.

After he left the table, Caroline turned to Nathan. "I *do* believe he loves the woman. If he marries her, you can be sure she'll carry him off."

"What do you mean?"

"She'll come between him and all of us."

"I don't believe he'll marry her." Nathan felt his heart beat with an uncertain, painful beat. "It's time for me to lie down," he said.

LENE AND JULIA arrived the following day, early in the afternoon. They decided to walk to the hotel. They wore large hats to shield their faces, and both were tanned, for they had gone swimming in the Main that summer as often as the weather permitted. Most of their friends were married, living conventional lives, and this cut them off from the two young women—one unmarried, the other married but alone—who found it possible to share experiences with each other that no one else would have understood. Lene liked to shape her days without much purpose, taking them as they came. Julia was a good companion. She had to work hard for her little bit of independence, the family pressure to make her conform was very great. She often doubted her gifts, and at those moments she would fall in love again, but even here her defiance of her family played a crucial role.

Julia felt threatened on every side by demands that she give up her career. Rudi, her present lover, did nothing but criticize her work and humiliate her in public. She was defenseless against him because, having never listened to her family when they warned her against men like him, she had not been able to build up the necessary defensive shield. Her rebelliousness made her choose precisely the wrong man every time. Rudi was only the last in a long line of faithless lovers. He could talk to her about literature—he was a playwright—and could analyze her prose down to the last comma, but he was totally amoral and thought only of his own career. He did not want her to be a writer, he wanted her to be his woman.

"*Your* talent isn't big enough," he'd say, or, "The world will thank you for taking care of me a whole lot quicker than it will thank you for your scribbling."

Julia had been confessing all this to Lene on the train, trying hard not to cry. Rudi was a bastard, but she loved him and missed him desperately. He was angry with her for leaving him for the weekend.

Lene had her own secret to confide, but her cousin was too distraught to allow her a moment to broach it. She had in her pocket a letter from Tom, a letter she had read just once when it came in that morning's mail. It had been written and mailed the day before in Weimar, and it said—in poetic and beautiful language, to be sure—that he had fallen in love with someone else. The news had stung Lene, if only because it was stark, unequivocal, written on a piece of blue stationery, and made it necessary for her to confront her own feelings and actions. It had suddenly made her love Tom fiercely, jealously. She had grown used to her single state, she could put Paul Leopold—now that he was gone—in proper context, but she found Tom's confession unbearable. The letter rustled in her pocket as she walked.

They arrived at the hotel only to be ignored by the porters, who were unused to guests who walked in off the street in the middle of the hot day. "Do they think we're prostitutes?" Julia whispered loudly. But as soon as Lene said that they were Eduard Wertheim's nieces, the entire staff sprang to attention, and a porter was found to escort them to their rooms.

They found a bouquet of late-summer flowers in the suite, and a note from Edu saying: "Welcome! Meet me on the terrace for tea at four o'clock." They washed up in the bathroom, which was all marble and tile with an immense tub and spigots of brass in the shape of swans' heads.

"What wonderful decadence," said Julia. "If it were not such a cliché, I'd write a story about Baden-Baden. This place is removed from time, and it tries to deny death. It promises you eternal life if only you will take care of yourself. How splendidly imperial all these buildings are—and it's all for the same purpose. Our idea of heaven is a Roman bath, a villa of marble, or an eighteenth-century palace, like Versailles . . ."

"I think Versailles was built in the seventeenth century."

"Don't be a stickler. I'm talking about illusions! I love the splendor and the make-believe. It's almost enough to make me forget Rudi. Do you know what he said?"

"No."

" 'Take me with you,' that's what he said. The nerve."

"I would have loved to see Uncle Edu's face."

"He needn't have known. I could have put Rudi up in a cheap hotel and met him on the sly . . ."

"It's not easy to get away with anything under Edu's nose. He smells out everything, like a bird dog."

"Did I ever tell you, Lene, that Rudi's mother was my mother's seamstress?"

"No. But I thought you were going to forget him, for the weekend."

"You're right, I am. But it's so odd and amusing. Mama always went there, to that awful dump of a house on the Kaiserhofstrasse. Once or twice I went with her. The kids who played in the courtyard were so filthy and foul-mouthed. Rudi was one of them! I bet he looked up my skirt when I walked up the stairs with Mama. He refuses to meet Pauline and Siegmund."

"Would they meet him?"

"Now that he's become a noted playwright, of course!"

Promptly at four they appeared on the terrace wearing fresh blouses and clean underwear. They felt like children. Would they feel like children, Lene wondered, when they were fifty, and Edu seventy?

Lady Samuel and her spitz sat nibbling on bits and pieces of Streuselkuchen, a crumb cake.

"Here come my stunning nieces," Edu said.

"Will you look who's with him," Lene whispered under her breath.

"His lady love!" said Julia. "The plot of my story thickens. I *must* write it now!"

They shook hands with Dorothea and kissed Edu on the cheek. He noticed their wise, knowing faces. "You've met?" he asked.

"Five years ago in Frankfurt," said Lene.

"You have an excellent memory," said Lady Samuel.

"When it comes to Uncle Edu, we are all very interested," said Julia. "Besides, Lene talks of little else."

Both Lene and Edu threw furious glances at Julia but she liked playing the *enfant terrible*.

"I'm delighted to receive such attention," said Dorothea. "Jealousy is always flattering."

"How are things in Frankfurt?" Edu asked. "Did you see the veterans' parade?"

"It was touching," Lene said, "and what a turnout! They carried banners of the 1848 revolution, and the Nazis stayed away."

"Hitler's sympathizers hold forth here," said Edu. "The air is poisonous with slander."

They talked about the latest family news, about books and theater and music. Edu asked after Clara and wanted to know how Julia's writing was coming along. "When you get the Nobel Prize, let me know," he said. Lady Samuel was almost entirely excluded from the conversation. She seemed to be listening with amused detachment, but her mind was elsewhere. She was not used to being ignored, and her German was not good enough to catch the nuances that lent interest to the conversation.

At five-thirty Nathan and Caroline joined the group. Lene, who had not seen her father for some days, thought he looked poorly. She tried to blame the sunny, sparkling surroundings, so different from the backdrop against which she usually saw him, but she worried, nonetheless.

Lady Samuel sighed audibly. It would be impolite to leave now, but she was coming down with a headache. The spitz was restless too. She had given him too much of the Streuselkuchen, and he broke wind constantly. Lene embraced her parents.

"Has anything interesting happened in Frankfurt since we've been gone?" Nathan asked.

Lady Samuel was afraid she might hear another description of the veterans' parade, but Lene obviously had other things on her mind. "I had a letter from Tom today," she said. What if her father was going to die? It was best to be honest. To get the unpleasant matter out of the way. She hadn't meant to blurt it out like this, it was simply, suddenly *there*. "He's in love with someone else." She had not meant to cry, but suddenly she could not stop the tears. They came rolling down her cheeks, and a sob escaped from deep within her.

Lady Samuel took the opportunity to rise and beg to be excused. The spitz yapped nervously.

"You'll want to be alone to talk," she said. "Edu—will I see you later?"

"Yes, of course." He rose from his chair to take her hands in his and kiss them.

Nathan made as if to rise but only moved forward somewhat stiffly. "Do you have the letter with you?" he asked Lene.

"It's in the pocket of my other skirt," Lene said. "What will I do?" The drama of it now belonged to them all. She no longer needed to cry.

"Ignore him," Julia said.

"Your advice has not been asked for," Edu said.

"My dearest daughter," Caroline said, "I'm truly sorry. But you should have known it was coming. It wasn't a sensible arrangement you two had."

"It's too late to talk about that now," said Nathan.

"You will give him a divorce," Edu said.

"But he didn't ask for a divorce, he simply confessed that he's in love. It may not be forever . . ."

"It's forever, as far as you're concerned," Julia said darkly.

"I will make all the arrangements," Edu said. "He won't get off easily. You must give me the letter, and I'll take it to my attorney. We'll draw up a plan of action."

"Do *you* still love him?" Julia asked.

"I do—I always will," said Lene. "That's how I am. But we've drifted apart and he's so far away—I can hardly remember him." The script was absurd. She wiped the tears from her face. Now that they all had a part, she felt that it would turn out all right. Uncle Edu patted her knee. "It's better this way," he said.

At dinner Lene and Julia shared a table with Nathan and Caroline; Lady Samuel dined with Edu. He told her as much as he knew of the story of Lene's marriage to Tom, even though she had not asked about it.

"It's awfully hot in here," Dorothea said when they had finished their meal. "Why don't we take a stroll outside? I'll fetch a sweater."

They wandered down the paths of the hotel garden. A full moon shone on them. Edu saw Dorothea's face in its light; it made her look younger and lovelier than ever.

"You are like a Shakespeare heroine," he said to her.

"As long as it isn't Lady Macbeth," she replied.

"I would like to marry you," he burst out, quite as abruptly as Lene had announced Tom's infidelity.

"What in heaven's name brought that on?" For years Dorothea had expected him to declare himself, but it had not occurred to her that moonlight would finally provide the necessary impetus. Just that day she had decided that he would never marry her, and been surprised that she felt relief.

"I've wanted to ask you for a long time," he said.

"But you never did."

"There were always obstacles . . ."

"And now there are not?"

"The times make choices necessary—who knows what the future will bring?"

"You wish to hold me as security for the future?"

"That's not a kind way to put it. Your appearance here, unannounced, seemed to me fortuitous. A sign of some sort. It may be the last time we can live like this—here."

"You are a pessimist. Where would you suggest we live?"

"In Frankfurt—but only until I've completed arrangements to leave."

"And then?"

"It depends. I would love to live in Italy, but the Fascists are in power, and things will come to a bad end there as well. Switzerland is the only safe place."

"Switzerland? I detest the Swiss! They are a nation of hotelkeepers, good for nothing else."

"They are a nation of bankers as well. That's what's going to keep them safe forever."

"You wouldn't want to live in England?"

"Much as I enjoy visiting there, no, I would not. I detest the climate. Besides, England will go down the drain too. Germany is doomed. Sooner or later it will turn to the Nazis, and then it will go to war to avenge Versailles, and conquer England and France. The moment has passed when the working class will listen to the Communists. The Nazis offer them much the same and the heads of Jews besides. *Their* myth doesn't hold out any hope for world brotherhood, it is narrow and Teutonic and more easily grasped, narrow ideologies always are . . ."

"Edu?"

"What is it?"

"No more political lectures! You asked me to marry you, did you not?"

"I hope you'll say yes."

"No, Edu. I will not say yes. I have loved you all these years. I've waited for you to ask this question for longer than I care to admit. I think we have many things in common; we would have made a splendid pair. But I think it's too late now. The time is past. I am glad I came here, it gave me a chance to watch you among your own, your family. I've seen you, hour upon hour—my God, it seems like week upon week—and I've made up my mind that I can't marry you. I can never take my place in your heart beside them. I'd be crushed by them. I might be able to live in the house with your mother—I assume you will take her with you when you remove to Switzerland—but your mother is, if you will excuse the expression, only the tip of the iceberg. You have brothers, sisters-in-law, nieces and nephews. They all make demands on you . . ."

"I would ask them to stop."

"You cannot ask them to stop, you encourage them to do it. You need them to do it. You expect to rule their lives—"

"Rule their lives?"

"Indeed you do. You'll see to Helene's divorce, won't you? I see how much you love those young women—I could never find happiness with you if I had to share your love with them."

"They're children—little girls! Charming and sweet, of course, and I *do* love them, but only as their uncle. Do you mean to say you are jealous?"

"Yes. Perhaps I am. But you delude yourself if you think they are 'children.' They are no such thing. They are young women who adore you, put on their best dresses for you, flirt with you, dab perfume behind their ears for you . . . even when they marry or have affairs or make babies. Little Clara will, no doubt, carry the tradition into the next generation. I cannot, I will not, challenge them for a place in your heart."

"You've thought about this a long time?"

"No. But I've thought about it *hard*. I've thought about nothing else in the last twenty-four hours."

"You don't need to mull over your decision? Perhaps in another place, away from here?"

"No, Edu. I know exactly what's right—for both of us, I think."

"I'm sorry."

"There's nothing to be sorry about. I think you'll recognize, once the moon sets and the bright daylight shines on me again, that it's better for us not to marry. I shall not stop seeing you. I am too fond of you for that. We can continue to meet, but our lives will go on circling in their own orbits."

They kissed, and it was not, at that moment, a kiss of passion but one of tenderness and mutual affection. It did not lack the element of desire, but that was muted for now.

"Do you want to know something?" Dorothea asked. "Those 'girls' of yours have been watching us, talking about us, for years. I always thought so."

"It never occurred to me at all."

"Of course not. Men are blind to such things. The details you observe and classify all have to do with palpable things—money in the bank, words on paper. But I collect other information. A glance here, a turn of phrase there, things that don't translate into facts. But when I put them all together, it helps me to make clever deductions."

They parted very late that night, and Dorothea took back her small volume of D. H. Lawrence. The next day she made plans to leave, and within twenty-four hours she was once more riding in her Rolls-Royce down the country lanes toward the Rhine, toward France. The chauffeur and the maid rode in the front seat and the spitz beside her in the back. She looked out the window, in search of beautiful vistas.

No one—neither Nathan nor Caroline nor Lene nor Julia—suspected that anything had occurred between Edu and his beloved.
They returned to Frankfurt, one after another, and took up their
lives again. Changes were made here and there, but they did not
seem earth-shaking or apt to have a lasting effect. Why, then, did
Lene feel such a longing for those late-summer days at Baden-
Baden? They were with her at all times, like pictures of the Garden
of Eden. It had been, Edu said, a summer like no other.

VI

1933

NATHAN WERTHEIM died in January of 1933. Coming at a moment of terrible political upheaval, his death touched the members of his family far more deeply than it would have in more normal times. Nathan missed, by a matter of days, the news that Hindenburg had named Adolf Hitler Chancellor of Germany.

"Thank God he was spared that," Siegmund said again and again during the period of mourning.

"What difference would it have made?" Caroline asked. "He knew it was coming." She wept at night, alone in her bed, but was composed and impassive in the company of others.

"For years everyone believed it was a bad dream and would go away," said Edu, who had moved his entire household, including Hannchen, to an estate just outside Zürich, overlooking the lake. Hannchen Wertheim had barely been aware of the move. She sat, weak and pasty-faced, in her old chair in the new room, like a doll slowly losing its sawdust. Day by day there seemed to be less of her. She was not always lucid, but her heart beat on and her skin, like the tough membrane of an egg, held her together. The doctors said she had had a stroke, perhaps several of them. Edu, on the other hand, desperately missed his beloved house, which he had sold, and his native city. The language of the Swiss grated on his ears. But he knew he was safe.

He returned to Frankfurt when his brother's death seemed imminent. Declining Caroline's offer of hospitality, he stayed at the Frankfurter Hof, from which he was able to see and hear several demonstrations by bands of well-organized Nazis. The swastika was now in evidence everywhere. It was bitter cold, and the ground was covered with frozen, dirty snow.

The house in the Guiollettstrasse was in a sorry state. During Nathan's final illness there had been no one to supervise repairs. The garden had gone untended, and it looked wild even in the dead of winter. Yellowed weeds choked the rosebushes, which no one had bothered to wrap in burlap. The garden wall was losing its stucco sheath and showed crumbling brick; the barbed wire strung along the top was so rusted it would not have kept anyone out. Edu felt a desperate sadness at the deterioration. He made every effort to ignore it, but the very air he breathed filled him with anxiety.

Lene and Clara, now a chubby five-year-old tomboy with a round, well-shaped head and her hair in a pageboy cut, still lived upstairs, and Fräulein Gründlich continued to look after them, to sort the linens and sew the sheets that needed it, to darn socks and make potholders out of the clean rags of the sheets that couldn't be saved. Anna still presided over the kitchen, and a *Putzfrau* came in once a week to do the heavy cleaning.

Death had so long been a dweller in this house that every room held the medicinal odor of its presence. Dr. Schlesinger had attended Nathan in his last hours as he had for years, with the gentleness of a friend as well as a physician. He closed Nathan's eyes and gazed for a time at the face, which looked far older than his sixty-three years. Then he went to see Caroline, to tell her that it was over. She had been waiting, sleepless, in the living room. Edu had just come in—it was early morning—and he let her go to Nathan alone, after embracing her for a minute. As he went to sit beside Emma on the couch, she took his hand in hers and held it.

"What will I do now?" Caroline asked when she returned. Her voice was as dry as firewood.

"You'll be all right," said Edu. "You're healthy, you have your children, and I'll look after your money. When you're done with the worst of your grief, I'll talk to you about leaving Frankfurt . . ."

"That's not what I mean," she said. "After all these years, I have unlearned the habit of social intercourse. No one understands me any longer, and I don't understand them. Who'll listen to my foolish stories? Who'll forgive me all my failings?"

Edu had no answer for that. He went to the telephone to call his brothers, leaving Emma to be kind to her mother. He called Jacob first.

"Will you tell Mama?" Jacob asked.

"Certainly not over the telephone," Edu said. "I'll take care of it when I go back to Zürich."

"Sometimes I envy the dead," said Jacob. "Oblivious to all that's going on around us now."

"I think you should leave Germany."

"I'm too old to start over again in some foreign place, Edu. I'll await the end right here in Frankfurt."

"It may come sooner than you think. When Hitler and his followers consolidate their power, there'll be no hope for us. He controls tens of thousands of followers and an apparatus so well oiled he'll be able to implement every directive, crush all opposition."

"I don't want to hear any more," said Jacob. "I have, myself, been prophesying doom for years. Now that it's at hand I feel only paralysis and a kind of relief."

The assistant rabbi at the synagogue knew them only slightly. He asked Edu when he had last been to temple. It was ostensibly a request for information, but it sounded like an accusation to Edu, who demanded to see the senior rabbi. Told that he was away for the week, Edu turned on his heel and walked out. Siegmund completed the arrangements. It was the first time in anyone's memory that Edu had not seen something through.

Lene stayed in bed the morning of the funeral, and when Fräulein Gründlich came to tell her it was time to dress, she said that she was not going. She sat in bed, the covers pulled up to her chin, and told them all, one by one, that she would not go.

Uncle Edu went to talk to her. "It's your duty to go," he said.

"Papa would have understood," she answered stubbornly.

"You're not doing it for him, but for the rest of us," said Edu.

Clara, seeing the black figures come to her mother's room, hearing the voices, sensing the grief and confusion, began to wail. She ran to Lene, burying her face in the bedclothes, which smelled of her mother and night and comforting oblivion. Lene let her climb into bed beside her and held her while the little girl put her face against her mother's neck, in the soft place between the ear and the collarbone, and wet her nightgown with tears.

"I'm staying with my child," said Lene.

The house was very quiet when they had all gone. Lene let Clara remain in bed with her and told her stories from Hans Christian Andersen as well as she remembered them.

Anna wore her good black dress to the funeral. The older Wertheim women were swathed in black veils, the men had broad mourning bands on their sleeves and black hats. Jacob insisted on walking behind the hearse from the West End Synagogue to the old Jewish cemetery on the Rat-Beil Strasse. The black automobiles followed slowly.

As the funeral cortege wound its way through the snow-covered streets of Frankfurt, children stared at the walking figure of Jacob; several threw snowballs after him. The skies were gray, and the only color to greet them along the way was the red-and-black flag of the Nazis, hanging from innumerable windows of slate-gray apartment houses. The white circles that held the crossed black wings of the swastikas were whiter than the snow. The mourners tried not to see them. There was no wind; the banners did not stir, but formed a mocking backdrop to the cortege.

The rabbi spoke eloquently, even Edu admitted that. He talked not so much about Nathan Wertheim, whom he had barely known, as about the death of a Jew of Frankfurt in the dangerous days of January 1933. He mentioned the Judengasse, which Nathan's family had come from full of hope, leaving their piety behind them, to sup at the German table, to partake of the German spirit, to believe in the fullness of their German citizenship. He wondered whether the country loved this man as much as this man loved his country. Here there was a slight movement in the small crowd, an unclasping of hands and a shuffling of feet. Several Gentile associates of Nathan's were there and a friend from his childhood, a distinguished judge.

The rabbi said that it would take more than a few men of good will to bring the country back from the ledge where it was poised, ready to leap into dictatorship. He warned that if the intolerance and the hatred preached by "the brown hordes" held sway in the land, there would be a return to the confinement of the Judengasse much worse than that which Nathan's ancestors had known. The sound of weeping accompanied his words, but the black-veiled faces of the women gave no hint of who it was that cried.

It was not possible, from the spot beside the open grave, to see the street beyond the wall. The cemetery was suspended in winter darkness, the snow along its paths still clean and white, its stone markers like anchors holding the dead for eternity. They were all, for the moment, embraced by the peace of death. This piece of Jewish earth, thought Edu, will be here when the swastikas are gone. But it was of no comfort to him.

The rabbi ended his talk by saying that Nathan Wertheim was spared the future that they all might have to face. He hoped that his family would draw strength from his memory. He looked around him and his face was kind as he prayed *"el moleh rachamim"* and said the *Kaddish.*

The coffin was lowered into the earth, and a cry—the only one —escaped Caroline's mouth just as the box struck bottom. It was a wild and piercing sound like the cry of a wild beast in that still, wintry cemetery. From a distance, far beyond the walls, one could hear martial music. The men took turns shoveling dirt on the coffin, the women held each other, and when the rabbi closed his book and began to shake the mourners' hands, they knew it was over and they must go back out into the street from the shielded park of the dead.

Edu thanked the rabbi and gave him his money. He did it unobtrusively, of course; he was used to paying the bill. They walked over the rough, unkempt ground of the old cemetery, through the snow, which left spots on the women's black stockings and on the cuffs of the men's trousers. To their left was the brick wall that sealed off the Orthodox section, a wild plot with crooked tablets stuck in the earth, pridefully separate, insisting on its superior piety. They heard the noise in the street more loudly now—it was a mixture of shouts and songs and the tramp of booted feet. The gatekeeper stood by the locked door, peeking out of a small hole.

"Don't go out there now," he said. "They're running wild and shouting for Jewish blood. They might attack you. I'll show you the way out through the Christian cemetery. Your cars will meet you there, and the mob won't notice you."

They could see the brown shirts through the iron pickets of the large gate that led into the street. The mob moved in ragged groups, running to join a greater march forming on the Eckenheimer Landstrasse to take them down to the Römer, to shout their triumph to all Frankfurt: their Führer had been elevated to the leadership of the nation. "*Sieg Heil!*" they screamed. One could hear them in the very depth of the cemetery. "*Sieg Heil!*" echoed through the wintry streets, bringing ecstatic joy to those who believed and dread fear to those who did not.

The mourners walked, single file and in pairs, along the walks of the Frankfurt burial ground on byways that had not been trod in weeks, even months, not since the last warm days of fall. The gatekeeper knew the cemetery in all its parts as well as he knew the city. He had been born in Frankfurt, and he lived in a small house next to the locked gate with a housekeeper, a good Christian woman, who was punctilious about cooking him his kosher food and turning on the lights for him on the Sabbath. He preferred the cemetery, he said, to the city of the living. It was his favorite jest, but today it seemed as if he were speaking the truth.

The family got back to the Guiollettstrasse safely. Anna fetched out the food that had been prepared, and Emma went upstairs to look for Lene. She found her in bed still, asleep, with Clara beside her, curled up in her arm so that her straight blond hair mingled with Lene's black locks. Emma kissed both mother and child and did not wake them.

They scarcely touched the food and spoke in voices so low they were almost whispers. Anna and Fräulein Gründlich sat together in the kitchen, united in their concern for the family they had served all these years. They sensed that bad times were coming for them, even as they understood that for Germany there would be rejoicing and jubilation. Anna, who voted Socialist, hated the Nazis, because she understood that they ruled by coercion. Fräulein Gründlich, who voted for the Centrists, feared them, because she understood that they left no room for any religion save that of the state. They both knew—they were good women who recognized goodness in others—that it was impossible to build a decent world on a foundation of hatred. When the *Putzfrau* came, they did not talk to her. She was one of those who coveted a place in the sun; she wanted to "clean up" the country. "I'm not a cleaning woman for nothing," she cackled as she scrubbed the floors on hands and knees and cursed the people who walked on them.

The house at least felt safe for now, thought Andreas, shutting the door behind him. The judge still hoped that the next elections would turn the tide; one of Edu's former associates believed that once the country was back on its feet, the measures the Chancellor had proposed would be withdrawn. Even some of the Jews had voiced the opinion that one must wait and see, that panic would solve nothing. But Andreas had been afraid. His body was chilled, either from the cold of January or the grip of fear. He stood near the radiator, rubbing warmth back into his hands. It seemed to him that perhaps it would be wise to move back into this, his father's house. The idea had taken hold as he stood next to the open grave. The dark earth reminded him of the garden at home. He looked at it now through the windows of the living room, saw its devastation and told himself that he would look after it.

"I think I'll come back and live at home," he said to Emma.

Edu poured cognac and talked to each one. He had not seen the family together like this in many a year. Only Ernst, who was in Palestine, was missing.

"Things are very bad," Eva Süsskind said to him. "The left is in disarray, many comrades are fleeing to Russia."

"Why are you telling *me* that?" Edu asked her. She looked careworn and old-maidish with her short hair now turned quite gray and a chin full of whiskers. She still wore her Russian scarf, even under her plain black wool dress, which smelled of mothballs and sweat. But Edu was struck all at once by what he perceived to be the innocence of her heart. He had been shaken to his very bones by the events of the day and could, just this once, understand this woman and her foolish convictions. "Are *you* going to Russia?" he asked.

"No . . ." She hesitated a minute. "Actually, I broke with the Party some time ago. Not with my beliefs," she hastened to add, "only with the organization. I disagreed with too many things, and they would brook no disagreement from the likes of me—not from anyone, I suppose. They're authoritarian, and I'll have no one dictate to me. It horrified me when they joined the Nazis in the transport workers' strike last November. The police chased and beat the Reds and let the Brown Shirts go free."

"I have, as you know, no sympathy for those who put themselves in a position to be chased by the police, whatever their color. You may have given up on the Communist Party, but that doesn't seem to have given you a better opinion of the forces of law and order."

"The 'forces of law and order,' as you call them, are becoming an arm of the fascist state, upholding no law and maintaining order only by terror."

"Still talking nonsense, Eva?" Jonah Süsskind, who had come from Wiesbaden for the funeral, looked lean and healthy. He was the only one who had eaten heartily of Anna's food. Nothing appeared to have disturbed him. "It's my opinion that the democratic state has been too permissive," he added.

"Where is your wife?" Eva asked him. Edu withdrew. He had never liked Jonah.

"She couldn't make it. Something came up at the last minute."

"Hitler, I suppose?"

"Please don't start with me, Eva," Jonah said testily. "I'm here to pay my last respects to my brother-in-law, not to argue with you."

The contempt in Eva's face could not escape him. "Poor Nathan," he said, to change the subject, "circulatory diseases are most unpleasant. I hope *I* don't go that way. Was he senile at the end?"

"Not a bit." Eva could tell from the sound of his voice how he talked to the rich spa patients. "That was a nasty sight today," she went on. She could not bear to let him go scot-free.

"What do you mean?"

"The rowdies outside the cemetery—the Nazis."

"Their complaints are legitimate."

"Their methods are not."

"Perhaps we need a strong man at the helm."

"That sounds like your wife's kind of talk. Have you given up thinking altogether?"

"You must admit that the country drifted in the days of the Republic. If I recall, you were trying to overthrow it yourself."

"The revolution *I* believe in is one that frees the oppressed. It is a revolution of ideals and ideas, it puts the worker in control of his destiny, and it does not have any end but democracy and equality."

"One could describe Hitler's revolution like that."

"One could, if one were his follower."

"Millions are."

"Including you?"

"Don't be absurd, Eva. You must, however, admit that it isn't good for the Jews to be seen in positions of power such as they held in the Republic . . ."

"What's become of you, Jonah? I do not understand you at all. You sound as though you were a ventriloquist's puppet. Is your wife—"

"Leave her out of this, Eva. My opinions are my own. I'm entitled to them. I see a different aspect of this country from the one you see. I don't live in a large industrial city. I share the view of the *real* Germans who consider cities cesspools, the root of anarchism, and degeneracy. We need a return to the values of preindustrial society."

"It is not possible to return—ever."

"I don't see Ernst here," Jonah said, changing the subject. "Why didn't he come?"

"Ernst went to Palestine. Didn't you know?"

"No one ever tells me anything." Jonah's voice was plaintive. "I'm ostracized by my entire family—and why? Because I followed the dictates of my heart and married an Aryan."

"It seems to me that it was *she* who would have nothing to do with *us.*" Eva was overcome with loathing for her brother.

"You've always misunderstood her and misinterpreted her actions. She's a sterling woman."

"I hope, for your sake, you're right." Seeing her nephew Benno approaching, she turned abruptly from Jonah and linked her arm in Benno's. "Come," she said, "we have to talk. Tell me how you are."

Benno still weighed too much, smoked too much and breathed heavily. He was still vague about practical matters and well aware that only his brilliance saved him from reprimands. Jonah, who had never brought his own children to visit his Frankfurt relatives, now thought of them with affection. He was well aware that Benno, too, was the product of a mixed marriage and considered him a bad advertisement for such an alliance.

"Still working on the Pergamon altar?" Eva asked.

"I had to give that up," said Benno. "A senior colleague claimed I was encroaching on his territory. I've begun a study of the influence of the antique on German artists of the late eighteenth century. A fascinating field of inquiry."

Benno was ready to launch into a detailed explanation, but Eva cut him off anxiously. "What do you make of the political situation?" she asked.

Benno looked puzzled.

"In relation to the Enlightenment or the French Revolution?" He saw Eva's startled eyes. "Oh, you mean here and now—the Nazis . . . Well, I don't know. I doubt they'll mess around in my field."

Jacob, looking wan from his cold and lonely trek, came up just then and prevented Eva from launching into an exhaustive lecture.

"Wasn't that awful today?" he asked. Jacob was bone-thin and walked with a pronounced stoop, though he was, as he said, "tough as parchment." He had become a creature of the night and left his shop almost entirely in the loyal hands of Alois.

"Benno here thinks his ivory tower will keep him safe." Eva was clearly exasperated.

"He'll learn. Wait until my apartment-house super storms the steps of the museum. You know, he stood in the courtyard the other day and shouted imprecations. He watches who hoists the swastika and who doesn't. He's king of the roost now. I have to take my garbage out myself. The elderly gentleman across the hall from me —a kind and decent person named Elfenbein—got into an argument with the super's wife, and she spat at him."

Jacob had developed a kind of courage in his solitude. Having rejected Edu's help, he lived frugally on his earnings and even managed to save something every month.

"May I come and see you one day soon?" Benno asked him. "I have found some fascinating documents relating to the Füssli circle in Rome, and I need to talk to someone who is familiar with the esthetic theories of his contemporaries."

"I'd love to share whatever knowledge I have with you," said Jacob. "The time is ripe for us to concern ourselves with matters of scholarship, not politics. Just take care you don't meet up with the super's wife."

"I am trying to compare the attitude toward classical sources of eighteenth-century Germans with that of earlier painters. Elsheimer, for instance—"

"For God's sake, Benno, come down to earth!" Eva exclaimed. "We're in the midst of a political disaster!"

"There is absolutely nothing I can do about it," Benno said. "I might as well think about the eighteenth century. *Someone* has to think about it. Dictators come and dictators go, but the light we can throw on our past burns at all times and gives future generations truths no ruler can ever challenge."

"The 'truth' you speak of is not absolute—politics shape it, destroy it, distort it."

Benno looked dismayed. "Things will calm down again," he said. "This government is not going to last."

"I hope you're right." Andreas was on his third glass of cognac. He was no longer afraid, no longer cold, his heart beat calmly. He could talk about what he had seen. "These demonstrations are frightening for what they tell us about the human condition. Barbarism of the sort we identify with earlier, more primitive times, taking place right here in Frankfurt in the twentieth century. In the land of Schiller and Goethe and Beethoven . . ."

"Even to the sound of their words and tunes, mind you," said Jacob.

"Hitler prefers Wagner, I hear," said Benno.

"We'll no doubt be treated to a *Götterdämmerung*," said Andreas. "Germans like immolation, the sense of being swept away by some great force, acting without will of their own."

"All this is abstract talk," said Eva, "discussion instead of action . . ."

"What can we do?" Jacob asked.

"Hush, here comes Aunt Caroline," said Benno.

Caroline had breathed a sigh of relief as soon as the front door had shut behind them all and she found herself among the familiar artifacts of home. Nothing, she thought, could befall her here. She would not leave again, ever.

"I expected the cleaning woman today," Caroline said. "She didn't come."

"The house looks fine," Eva told her.

"Where is my granddaughter," Caroline asked, "my little Clärchen?"

"Upstairs, asleep with Lene."

"Lene did not come to her father's funeral," Caroline said. "Does anyone know why?"

There was a guilty moment of silence as they all tried to think of some excuse to make for Lene.

"She simply couldn't face it," Jacob said finally.

"I don't blame her," Benno said. "Death is scary, especially when accompanied by the murderous shouts of the mob."

"Lene lets herself go limp in the face of trouble," said Andreas, "and waits for rescue."

"I must get myself a new *Putzfrau*," Caroline sighed. "It won't be easy. Not in such times."

Lene appeared just then, holding Clara by the hand. Both of them still had the flush of sleep on their cheeks. The little girl wore a smocked challis dress covered with tiny yellow flowers. Lene had on a lavender skirt and blouse with a low V-neck, and a sleeveless sweater. Among the black-dressed women she stood out like a creature from another world. It seemed to Eva that she held on to her daughter as if for protection. Clara was not at all shy and beamed at the company.

"Let me have her," Caroline said, and the little girl ran to her grandmother, who kneeled to hold her.

"Opapa's gone," Clara said. "Fräulein Gründlich told me so. She says he won't be back, but I'll see him in heaven."

Tears started in Caroline's eyes, but she fought them back. When she was composed again, she kissed the child on the cheek and said, "Opapa sent you his very special love before he left."

"I want to see him, but I don't think I'll go to heaven just yet," Clara told her grandmother. Wiggling to get out of her arms, she said, "I'll get my pencils and paper and draw a picture of Opapa in heaven and *pretend* I'm going there."

"Maybe you'll become an artist when you grow up," said Emma.

Pauline caught the little girl as she was trying to dodge out of the room and pinched her cheek. She did all things to excess. "I wish I had a grandchild like you," she said. "I wish I had a grandchild, period! My children are not to be depended upon in that regard."

"I told you I'd give you a grandchild," Julia said, "but you insisted I had to be married."

Clara managed to elude her great-aunt and ran upstairs to return with a sketch pad and a handful of colored pencils.

"You ought to have her portrait painted," Edu said to Lene. "I'll pay for it, on the condition that you get a good man to do it."

Clara could not pass the tray with cookies that stood on the coffee table without helping herself to a handful.

"Don't stuff yourself," said Lene.

"You don't want to look like Uncle Benno," Emma whispered to her niece.

"I like Uncle Benno," said the little girl, "and I can't look like him —he's a man and I'm a girl, and when I grow up I'll be a woman."

"A lady, I hope," said Emma.

"Do 'ladies' have to wear dresses, Aunt Emma?"

"Mostly they do."

"Well, then I don't want to be one. I want to be able to wear my blue sweat suit *all* the time."

"The dress you're wearing is much prettier, Clara."

"The dress scratches. My sweat suit is nice and soft."

Andreas had given her the suit, a small bright-blue—to bring out the color of her eyes—version of an athlete's training suit. It had pants with elastics at the waist and ankles, and a top with a collar that closed with a zipper. Clara loved the zipper.

"When you come with me to Italy in the spring, you may wear the sweat suit every day when you go out to play. But we wear dresses to dinner and when there's company on Sundays."

Lene had agreed to let her sister take Clara to Italy with her in May for her annual spring visit. Emma had become a regular visitor in the house of Mabel Hennessy Supino-Botti and had extended her visits each year, so that she went one month in the spring and two months in the autumn. These visits were something she had no intention of giving up, even for her good works at the hospital. They were the primary reason she would not take a paid job.

The friendship between the two women had ripened, even though Emma rejected the homosexual dimension, which was in any case of a subtle nature, not insisted upon but veiled in allusions. Emma was sympathetic to her friend's love life but repelled by the very idea of physical love between women. To be touched any-where by another, to feel the moist lips and hot breath of desire, to smell another's body—she shuddered at the thought. And yet she understood the difficulties, jealousies and ridicule that dogged Mabel's steps, and she heard her out in her grievances. She felt comfortable and sheltered among women. One day she told Mabel that she thought the story of the Garden of Eden was clearly one that could have been invented only by men, for it had the effect of keeping women in their place and establishing them for all time as untrustworthy. Mabel had laughed her big round American male laugh, a sound that always conjured up to Emma visions of Brecht's city of Mahagonny, and slapped her on the knee, telling her she had better keep her opinions on such things to herself if she didn't want her Uncle Edu to cut off her allowance. Emma did not like it when her friend mocked her family, but she only frowned and changed the subject quickly.

Emma longed deeply, even desperately, to keep Clara with her. She loved children and would have tried to adopt one had Edu not counseled against it. So all her maternal affections were lavished on her niece. It seemed to Emma that the child was neglected by her mother, who, when she wasn't in love, was pining to be. She had just met another "interesting" man, a Jew. Emma feared the worst. Manfred Solomon played the piano and had a musician's extravagant temperament. If Lene ran off with him—and Emma suspected she would—what would become of Clara? The pianist, egotist that he was, might well refuse to share Lene with her child. Emma believed the time had come to wean Clara from her mother and to take over most of her care herself.

These were, of course, fragmented ideas. Emma could only occasionally admit that she believed her sister was a bad mother.

Her present reveries were interrupted by Edu, whose mind was on Lene too. He had been deeply offended at her refusal to attend the funeral and was casting about for plausible explanations.

"I hear that your sister has a new admirer," he said to Emma. She nodded, hoping he would not ask her for an opinion. Her thoughts made her guilty; she felt she had been caught out in them.

"I hope nothing comes of it," Edu went on. "I met the young man in Zürich when he played there. He asked to be introduced to me and told me quite boldly that he was in love with my niece. I was appalled! He's got an extraordinary talent, no doubt about that, but he's an impossible person. He spoke as though he already *owned* Lene. I was convinced he'd inquire about her dowry next."

"Lene doesn't talk much about him," Emma said. This was true, for Lene trusted no one to understand the prompting of her heart and kept her love life secret. She and Emma talked at length about a thousand different things, but never this.

"He acted as though we were old friends. He tried to intimate that we were somehow equals, members of a common lodge . . ."

"Manfred was raised here in Frankfurt."

"He was at pains to remind me of that. But you know, he comes originally from Poland. If I remember the story correctly, his family was very poor and couldn't afford to keep him, so when they discovered his talent they simply *sold* him—to the highest bidder, as it were. That happened to be Alexander Buchsbaum—a *nouveau riche* if ever I met one—and that's how the boy came to Frankfurt. But how did your sister meet him?"

"I believe they met at Andreas'. His place has become the center for all the musicians of Frankfurt. He has musical evenings . . ."

"Does he still live with that . . . man?"

"Kurt? Yes. Kurt is really very nice."

"I have no doubt of that." He returned briskly to the subject of Lene. "Try to discourage your sister in this affair," he said. "She's only thirty years old. She has a beautiful child, and a family who loves her. With conditions in Germany as they are, it will be difficult for Jews like Manfred Solomon to continue to make a career, and he's not the sort who will be a loving husband when things don't go well in his professional life."

"You know Lene well enough to know that it's hard to tell her *anything.*"

"Indeed," Edu agreed. "That's why we both have to exert as much influence as we can."

"I always liked Tom," said Emma wistfully. "He was pleasant to have in the house . . ."

"He wasn't so pleasant to deal with when I had to arrange the divorce. He asked for all sorts of things."

"He wanted to be permitted to see Clara."

"Who told you that?"

"*He* did."

"He also wanted to be free of the responsibility of paying for the support of the child. He couldn't have it both ways."

"I know nothing about all that."

"It's best you don't. But you *do* know that your father could not, in his last years, be counted on to take charge of anything whatsoever. I had to handle all the details of his investments. I put Eisenstein on pension. I paid the rent of his office. Now I'll have to see that the secretary is taken care of and the last remaining clients informed of his demise. How anyone still went to him is a puzzle to me."

"He was wise in his profession in some odd way."

"Yes, I know all about that. But he failed utterly to keep the proper reins on his wife and children. He allowed your mother to wallow in her artistic dimness—she still refuses to be 'bothered' to deal with her life—and he gave his sons no direction. And, I'm sorry to say, he did not put his foot down when it came to his daughters' making . . . unsuitable matches."

Emma reddened. She still could not bear to hear reference made to her unhappy experience. Edu did not notice her discomfort.

"You are the most level-headed in some respects," he said, "that's why I tell you these things. I can talk to you, I know you no longer allow your head to be turned by men who whisper sweet nothings in your ear."

Emma could not look at her uncle just then. She felt a wound within her open. He loved her less than Lene; why had she not recognized this all these years? He was jealous because Lene had found herself a new lover. He didn't think at all the way she thought. Men were disgusting, like frogs, all of them! Just because one of them might, now and then, turn into a prince, women put up with them, and it wasn't worth it. She felt the wound ache.

Julia joined them at that moment, unaware that she was interrupting. "What a terrible day it's been," she said, "and me without sleep for nights on end."

Edu looked at her, and Emma saw that he found her beautiful, especially now that she looked haunted and somewhat wan. She had been writing a novel about her love affair with Rudi. It was said to be very good.

"Don't you think there's something symbolic about the disturbance today," she asked, "virtually on top of Uncle Nathan's grave? They will not let us bury our dead!"

"Nonsense," Edu said. "Your imagination is running away with you again. Things are bad enough, but you writers make them worse."

Someone had sent him a small avant-garde magazine which contained a story by Julia. He thought he recognized himself in it. Edu did not want to think about that now. He turned to find Elias, and Julia noticed the pointed effort he had made to be rude.

"He's read my story," she said to Emma, "and he'll never forgive me."

She had not thought—she never did—about the consequences.

She had hoped her success would impress him favorably. Now she was confused and uncertain, and it made her feel as if she stood before a deep pit and was in danger of falling.

"Did you write about him?" Emma asked. "That was foolish."

"Don't let's talk about it," Julia said. "Have you ever wished you were dead but been afraid to die?"

"I don't know what you mean . . ."

"You're all alike—here's Uncle Jacob, let me catch him before he goes."

She left Emma alone beside the window. Emma drew the curtains. The room grew smaller, its lamps brighter. Lene was now talking to Edu. Clara on the floor at her feet was playing with pick-up sticks. "You'll get dirty," Emma called out nervously.

Julia took Jacob by the arm. "I've insulted Edu," she said.

"Good for you," said Jacob, "it's time someone did. What did you say to him?"

"It was nothing I said—never mind, you wouldn't understand."

"Are you all right?"

"No, I'm not, but I will be, once I get away from the edge of the abyss. You know I dislike heights."

"Wouldn't you like to lie down? I'm sure you could find a bed upstairs. Caroline must have some valerian drops . . ."

"Rest is not the answer," said Julia morosely. "Will you get me some brandy?"

Emma saw that Clara's knees were dirty from kneeling on the carpet. "Get up, get up, child," she said and pulled her from the spot where she sat. The pick-up sticks were crunched under her feet. Clara began to cry.

"Leave her alone," Lene said.

"She's getting filthy," Emma said.

"The *Putzfrau* must be fired," Caroline sighed.

Clara wailed more loudly, hearing disharmony in the voices of the adults. "You broke my sticks!" she cried.

"I'll buy you some new ones," Emma told her. "Hush now and I'll go upstairs with you and we'll read a story."

"I don't want to go upstairs with you. I want to stay here with Mummy."

"You're being a bad girl," said Emma. She sat at the very edge of a chair and collected the broken pick-up sticks in her hand. Clara held on to her mother's skirt.

Julia drank the brandy Jacob brought her as if she were quenching a terrible thirst.

"How is your friend Rudi?" Jacob asked.

"He's no longer my friend. A good playwright but a terrible lover. Brecht liked his last play, but he can't get it performed. Everyone is afraid. They are running. Abandoning ship. My sister Jenny has had herself baptized."

Jacob looked for Jenny in the crowd of relatives. She sat in a corner by herself, staring into space. Her brother Willy was standing nearby, reading a book he had taken down from the bookshelf.

"Aren't we all very odd?" Julia asked.

"Willy is terribly thin," Jacob said. "Stand him beside Benno, and they'd look like cartoon characters out of *Max und Moritz.*"

"He's just been fired again," Julia said. "Papa keeps buying him into jobs. He lasts about the length of time it takes to run through Papa's money and then—out he goes. But he seems happy enough, drifting through life, dispensing pfennigs to poor children and playing the recorder."

"Does Jenny think it will help her?"

"What?"

"Being baptized."

The brandy had had the desired effect on Julia. The abyss was no longer directly in front of her. She thought it might be on the other side of the window.

"I believe she fell in love with the minister who converted her. Wouldn't it be fun to have a clergyman in the family?"

"No, it wouldn't."

"Just look at her, the silly goose. Not a brain in her head. She merely sits around looking pretty. I hate her."

"Don't waste your energy."

"Uncle Edu thinks she's adorable."

"My brother seems to be sticking in your craw today."

"He judges women on the most superficial levels."

"Most men do."

"But he considers himself such a superior person."

"Even superior people like a well-turned ankle or a juicy pair of buttocks . . ."

"*You're* not like that."

"And you see where it's gotten me. *I'm* not the uncle in the family who stirs his nieces' hearts—or makes them stamp their feet in anger, for that matter."

Night had fallen. A bitter cold wind had risen. Bonfires burned here and there, and shouts of *"Sieg Heil!"* still rang in the streets. But the freezing wind cleared them well before dawn and turned the water in the Justitia Fountain downtown into a block of ice.

The family stayed very late in the house on the Guiollettstrasse. None of them wanted to face the cold streets nor hear the echoing shouts of the Brown Shirts roaming the alleys. But the dawn brought no relief.

ERNST, who had changed his name to Uri once he reached Palestine, learned of his father's death in a telegram from Edu. He and Miriam were at midday dinner in their cabin.

"My father is dead," he told her.

"I'm sorry," she said. "May he rest in peace." She got up from her chair and put her arms around him.

"No, no," he muttered, pulling away, "I can't breathe."

"What's the matter?"

He bent over the telegram. "Only Uncle Edu could have sent it," he said. "Just listen to this: 'Sorry to have to inform you Nathan Wertheim passed away this morning. His death grieves us all. Edu.' "

"What should he have said?" Miriam asked. "What *can* one say in a telegram?"

He shrugged.

"I think you're trying to blame someone else for your mixed feelings," she said.

"You're quite perceptive."

"Isn't that why you married me?"

Leaving her to clean up, he went outside. It was a raw wintry day. Rain clouds hovered above the mountains to the east. He walked down to the edge of the Sea of Galilee. This was the quiet time of year on the kibbutz. Chores remained to be done, as always, but the spring planting was still some weeks away.

He had known that he would not see his father alive again when he went to make his farewells just before emigrating. It had saddened him, but he had put it out of his mind. Nothing of consequence had been said; they spoke like strangers. Even Lene seemed withdrawn. Emma hardly spoke to him at all, and Andreas, who seemed to want to speak, could do no more than reminisce. He had been glad to leave. When he went to see Edu, who had summoned him for tea, he was given a large check and much advice. "He sounded like Polonius," Ernst told Lene. "He's not that dense or foolish," she replied. "But equally pompous," he had answered.

He wandered along the water's edge. The fishing boats were all safely moored, the sky hung like a gray dome over the Golan Heights. The next hour might bring a thunderstorm and snow flurries in the mountains or brilliant sunshine. One never knew at this time of the year. What a strange land it was!

He managed, most of the time, to press the past into the distant chambers of his mind. He worked hard; he had begun to feel rough and callused, his hands were a laborer's hands, his arms and shoulders had grown as strong as a drayman's. Sometimes, when he saw himself in a mirror, he did not recognize himself. Had he really grown up in Frankfurt's West End and seen his face reflected in his mother's polished silver tea service?

He decided he must write a letter home that very day, but to whom? Miriam would tell him to begin, "Dear Family . . ." But it wasn't a family he remembered, it was a place, a quality, a mood. It was another country, and his relatives lived there like shadows. No, he thought, not like shadows, like mummies. That was how he saw them. He would have to write a separate letter to each one. Except Emma; he could think of nothing to say to her. She was the one who most deplored the choices he had made. She had been hateful to him, and he turned his thoughts elsewhere. He remembered the walks in the Palmengarten, Uncle Jacob's bookstore. He almost smelled the pines of the Christmas market on the Römer and the steaming sausages. He remembered the summer at Travemünde and that strange writer—what was his name?—who had, he believed, seduced Andreas. He had later become involved in some scandal and committed suicide. Had *he* been responsible for Andreas' sexual orientation? Where did they all go wrong?

He walked through the orange groves, past the stands of eucalyptus and the newly planted banana trees. Thunder rumbled from the Syrian mountains, but above the western shore of the lake there was already a band of clear blue sky. A tractor approached him, coming down the dirt road that led to the barbed-wire fence that bounded the kibbutz.

"Hey! Uri! Hey there!" the driver yelled over the sound of the chattering motor. "What are you doing here?" His Hebrew was scratchy with the whirring *r*'s of the "Yekkes"—the looked-down-upon German Jews. Ernst waved back to him. "I'm walking," he shouted.

"Be careful!" The man had a gun slung over his shoulder. He had been a printer in Leipzig.

Ernst nodded. It was true, one had to be careful. It wasn't wise to stray too far alone without protection. Reluctantly he turned back and found a spot near the fishing boats where he could sit unobserved, looking out toward Tiberias across the lake. He wrote the letters to his family on the pages of the small account book he always carried with him.

By the time he got back to the cabin, the sun was out. Miriam had gone back to the nursery where she worked. She had left him a piece of honeycake on the clean table and a glass of red wine. Ernst sighed. Why was he not content with her love? Why was this beautiful land still so strange to him? Why did he still miss the German winter, the silent forests of his native land?

Ernst copied out the letters one by one. When he was finished, he went out into the sunshine, down to where the field was being cleared for a new orchard. He hauled rocks until the sun began to set and cold mist rose from the lake. His mind was numb with exhaustion, and he no longer felt his sorrow so keenly.

ON FEBRUARY 27, fire destroyed the Reichstag building in Berlin. Police arrested a half-witted young Dutch national by the name of Van der Lubbe, who promptly confessed to the arson and implicated the Communists in the plot. This gave the Nazis the necessary excuse to order a sweeping crack-down on the Left. Not only the Communists but Socialists and trade unionists were arrested by the thousands, their papers shut down, their offices ransacked. All this was calculated to place the opposition at a disadvantage from which they would not be able to recover in time for the March elections. Without a press, their organizations in disarray, they nevertheless managed to keep the Nazis from capturing a majority of the seats in the Reichstag. But they could not, finally, prevent Hitler from marshaling enough votes to push through the Enabling Act, which made him dictator. The entire apparatus of government was now in his hands. Weimar was dead.

A few evenings later Eva Süsskind appeared at Jacob's door. She had not called to say she was coming, she simply appeared. Jacob was in the midst of eating his usual hard-boiled egg and rye bread with goose fat. A pot of black coffee and a bowl full of apples stood on the desk. Crumbs, eggshells and grease spots were everywhere.

Eva rang the bell impatiently, and Jacob looked out from behind the chain of his door to see who it was. The superintendent, Strüpler, had been harassing him these last several weeks. Relieved to find Eva, he let her in. "What brings you here?" he asked.

"I need your help."

"Of course, I realize that. Are you in trouble?"

"Not yet. I'm not very important. But many of my friends are. We have to be terribly careful. That's why I came now, when your super is likely to be at dinner. I'm going to ask you to do something that may bring you danger, so I want you to be honest with me— you may refuse me right now if you don't wish to become involved."

"I have very little to lose."

"Good, then I'll tell you. A good friend of mine, a woman named Lore—and I won't tell you her last name—is homeless. She can't return to her apartment; the Nazis have already raided it and are watching for her. They beat a neighbor almost senseless when she tried to keep them out at two A.M. Lore is at my place now, but we think that it's being watched. Will you put her up here?"

"Is she a Communist?"

"Does it matter to you?"

"No. Maybe. I guess not."

"Good. But she's *not* a Communist, just a very active opponent of the Nazis in every way. She's been in the trade-union movement since her days in the *Arbeiterjugend,* the young workers' league, which was where we met. If you think the Nazis are hunting down only Communists, you're mistaken. *All* opposition will be rooted out."

"How long will she need to be here?"

"No more than a week, we hope. Plans are being made to send her to the Saar, and from there perhaps on to Holland or Switzerland or France. We have to get papers for her. And we don't have experience in undercover activities or resistance. We didn't really believe it would ever come to this. In fact, the Communists will probably be the only ones with enough organization and ruthlessness to survive a long period of oppression. *They* have the Soviet Union behind them."

"And you have only your good hearts. Eva—please make certain that Strüpler doesn't see her. If he so much as suspects something's afoot, he'll bring his SA cronies in here in a minute. He's only waiting for an opportunity."

"I'll be careful. We have worked out a plan. I'll come here around this time without being seen. Then you must go out late at night to meet Lore, who'll be dressed like a streetwalker and act like one."

"Strüpler knows I don't come here with whores."

"We hope he won't see you. That's only just in case, and for the others. After a while I'll go out again, in Lore's clothes, so that they will think you are now alone. No one comes to your apartment?"

He shook his head. "Frau Koeppening quit working for me some time ago."

"Why?"

"She said she couldn't work for Jews."

"I'll leave some old clothes here, the kind a *Putzfrau* would wear, so that Lore can put them on and, if necessary, pretend that she's in the apartment merely to clean it up."

It had been years since Jacob had acted decisively, years since he had done anything that might be considered socially useful. The prospect of becoming, even briefly, part of a conspiracy filled him with excitement. Was it really possible to escape the morass of his

life, the lassitude he had sunk into since the death—so long ago!—
of Gerda?

"Would you like something to eat or drink?" he asked Eva.

"No, thank you," she said. She was touched by the eagerness with
which he had offered his help. She squeezed his hand, looking
harried, shabby. Jacob wanted to do her a kindness. He had never,
in all the years he had known her, been kind to her. Like everyone
else, he had assumed that she went her way surely and happily, that
she needed no affection, that her commitment to a cause was the
result of a clear choice from which she never wavered. He accompanied her to the door, but he could not bring himself to kiss her.

"I'll see you tomorrow at the same time," Eva said and went
hurrying down the stairs on her rubber-soled shoes.

Jacob sat at his desk far into the night, thinking about the responsibility he had taken on, the ragged bit of heroism he had been
offered.

Eva returned at the appointed time. The Strüplers were listening
to a broadcast of the Führer, promising them all the things they had
craved for so long in vain. Revenge for the stab in the back of
Versailles. An end to degeneracy, an end to the shame of Weimar,
the Jews' Republic. No more music that sounded like the rending
of cloth and the clatter of falling boxes. No more paintings in which
nothing was recognizable. No more books laced with too subtle
casuistry, with portraits etched in irony and derision. No more
affronts against the Fatherland . . . Herr Strüpler balled his fists.
Here was a man he could understand, a man who spoke his language.

Jacob was startled at Eva's appearance when she entered his apartment. For a moment he thought it was a stranger. Her clothes were
much too large for her, and she wore layers and layers of them. The
bright colors were odd, too, and the cloche hat. Eva never wore real
hats.

"These are Lore's clothes," she said. "I wore as many as I could."
She carried a large package wrapped in brown paper and tied with
string. "And this is her suitcase. It attracts less attention in the streets
this way." Stamps were pasted on it, and a fictional address.

"Does she always wear such cheerful flowered dresses?" Jacob asked. He had not wondered about the woman at all until this moment.

"I really never noticed," said Eva. "I don't see such things."

At midnight Jacob went downstairs. The night was black as pitch, the streetlights glistened dully. Three blocks away was a tavern; it stayed open late and was a known gathering place for whores. Jacob went in. Only a few people were left at their tables. He felt ill at ease. He did not belong here, and he was certain it showed. Two whores sat at a table near the door. Another woman, alone, sat at a rear table leaning on her elbows with a small bottle of chianti in front of her. That was the sign. Jacob went over to her. He saw that the clothes she wore were much too tight. She had a round, kindly face, excessively rouged and powered. She looked like a child playing at dressing up, not at all like a woman of the streets. He had been told to ask her, "Are you the lady from Rödelheim recommended to me by the greengrocer Lustig?" and he said the words exactly as he had been bidden. He felt quite ridiculous.

"Yes," the woman answered, "I'm the lady from Rödelheim. I talked to the greengrocer Lustig yesterday."

That was the agreed-upon answer, and Jacob sat down at the table and ordered a glass of apple wine. Eva had told him not to leave right away with Lore but to drink for a while and pretend to get tipsy. "Look natural," Eva had said.

Lore started the conversation. She chatted amiably about visits to the hairdresser, trips to the Taunus. She had a pronounced Frankfurt accent, and this endeared her to Jacob immediately. After about ten minutes she got up, stumbling a little, and said, "Pay the bill, if you please." Jacob obeyed, and she hung on his arm as they walked out the door. Only the whores looked after them.

Lore was silent all the way to Jacob's house. But she clung to him fiercely, and he realized all at once that she was frightened. Her chatter in the bar had been a nervous response. No one was stirring in the hallways of the house, the lights at the Strüplers' were out. Eva had nodded off in the armchair and woke with a start when Lore and Jacob came in. "Thank God you're safe," she said, tears welling in her eyes. Jacob made some tea, and they sat and talked softly for an hour or more.

Jacob had tried to clear out of the "spare" room as best he could so that Lore would have a place to sleep. The cartons of papers, which had stood on top of the bed, were all piled in the hall now. He had even made a little space in the wardrobe and freed a chair from its stacked books and magazines. He had found fresh sheets and left them on the silk-lined quilt, along with a towel and washcloth. Eva and Lore exchanged clothes behind the door, and when they came out again, Jacob for the first time saw Lore clearly.

"I'd better not meet a 'customer,' " Eva said, with her typically self-deprecating laugh. "He'd drop dead to see me walking the streets, looking as I do."

"So much the better, you'll stay safe," said Lore. She was a woman of about forty, and in her flowered dress her natural joyfulness shone from her even at this moment and in these circumstances. She had already made the bed and put some order in the room. "Be careful," she said to Eva, before hugging her tightly to her high bosom and giving her a farewell kiss.

The next morning when Jacob awoke, he had to remember, first of all, that he was not alone. Smelling coffee brewing, he could not recall the day or the month or the year, or even whether he was at home, until the awareness "I have a guest in the house" made the details click into place.

Lore had gotten up early and found everything necessary to prepare breakfast. She had even set a place for Jacob at the kitchen table and washed the dirty dishes in the sink. She did not open the curtains at the windows and walked carefully in felt slippers, and when she was done, she waited for Jacob, reading one of the books she had found in her room. The doorbell rang once. She did not answer it but held her breath until whoever it was had left again.

Jacob was annoyed for one brief, angry second when he saw that Lore had made herself at home in his kitchen. How dare she take over the disorder he had been fifteen years creating, and straighten it out in a single morning? But he looked at her friendly, open face, tasted the strong coffee and forgave her. She did not talk to him, and he saw that she respected his privacy and need for morning silence.

During the next fortnight Lore kept out of his way at all times except late at night, when they allowed themselves to talk quietly in the large room behind the thick drapes. Jacob found that she was a person who took hold of a problem and resolutely set out to solve it. Her thoughts did not run to abstractions; she saw everything in its most practical light. Even the reading she had done, and she had read Bebel and Lenin, Hegel and Marx, had left no residue of didacticism. She cared for people in a most natural way. She had been in Jacob's apartment no more than three days before it was subtly altered, and the odd thing was, he was happy to have it so.

The boycott of Jewish businesses on April 1 was proclaimed throughout the nation. Signs and placards everywhere called upon the populace to defend itself against the Jews of the world "who wish to annihilate Germany." Jacob had told Alois not to open the store that morning, so its metal gate remained shut. Rotten eggs and paint were splattered against it during the day, and uniformed hood-lums smeared the words "Death to the Jews" across the metal sur-face in the night. Alois washed it off the next day, although he was threatened with reprisal by a passer-by.

Frau Strüpler stood in the courtyard and shouted obscenities below the windows of her Jewish tenants, threatening them with eviction—something over which she had no control, though it pleased her to think that now, at last, she had a whole segment of the population targeted to be her victims. Jacob did not venture out except after dark; Alois brought him the necessities of life, and Lore busied herself about the apartment silently, on bare feet. Eva stopped by every few days but had nothing encouraging to tell them.

And then, toward the middle of April, Eva brought the necessary papers. Lore was free to go. At dusk they sat together in Lore's room, where one could see the sky and not be seen. The water of a brief April shower gurgled in the gutters.

"What will you do?" Jacob asked her.

"I will try to find my comrades and see what work they have for me."

"Where will you go?"

"The ticket they gave me is to a small town in the Saar, but after that, I don't know. And you?"

"What about me?"

"Will you stay here and listen to the Strüplers curse you?"

"What else is there to do?"

"Flee! Do you think they'll stop at a few shopwindows? Go now, while you still can, before they put your name on a list to stop you at the border. You haven't a family to worry about. You're not a poor man, you'll manage."

"I haven't been away from here for more than a brief vacation in fifteen years. I can't leave all my things!"

"You see me—I'm traveling with this one small suitcase. What do you have that you want to save that's worth more to you than your life?"

"It's a question of what my life is worth, stripped of all that it contains and that contains it."

Lore knew what the houses in the West End looked like, on the inside as well as the outside. Her mother had been a cook, her father a carpenter. She had sometimes, on Christmas or Pentecost, gone with her mother to the house where she worked. They had been nice to her there, but she was very much aware that they did not really see her as she was. She had the same problem in school. She had a scholarship because she was clever, but her classmates judged her by the clothes she wore, and her teachers told her to know her place. As a result, her view was obstructed too, she saw only the crystal chandeliers and tasted leftovers. Jacob was the first person she had met from that other world who did not seem frozen into a caricature. She saw the upper class refracted through his eyes and suddenly understood the traps it set for its children, even those like Jacob, who had left its precincts but not its assumptions. His past was there, folded away like his linen napkins moldering in a drawer.

"If anyone could make me leave my lair, it would be you," Jacob said.

The admission startled them both. The night before, Jacob had thought that it was odd how quickly he had adjusted to having a woman in the house. And then, lying in bed, listening to her breathing in the next room, he realized that she was not "a woman in the house," but Lore, warm and generous, who wore flowered dresses and was hiding from the Nazis. He was in danger while she was here, yet he wanted her to stay. He suspected he had fallen in love with her. Of course it was impossible for him to leave. How could he find his way through strange streets in a strange city? No one would understand him, and they would live in squalor, in rooming houses, quarreling about the rent money.

"I'm grateful to you for taking me in," she said. "I was afraid when Eva suggested I come here, I thought you'd be difficult, but now I am glad I came. I learned to know you."

"Did you think I would swallow you whole like the wolf in Little Red Riding Hood?"

"Not quite. But I did think I might have to— I wasn't afraid that you might denounce me, but I thought you might try to take advantage of me."

Jacob thought, as he seldom did, of his brother Gottfried. He remembered the bold way he had always looked at the girls in the shops. It had made him hate his brother.

"Lore!"

"Be careful," she said. "I think I know what you're going to say . . ."

"Lore, my friend, my good new-found friend, I can't let you go before I tell you how much I have come to like you. Indeed, I may say, I believe, truly—I love you."

Her eyes were merry. "I'm glad," she said, "glad that you love me, glad that it occurred to you to mention it. I've come to the same conclusion: I love you too."

"You sound so happy!"

"Isn't it a happy thing to be in love?"

"At this moment in our lives?"

"This moment is better than no moment at all. We aren't standing at the edge of a ditch, about to be executed, are we?"

Jacob had not been in the company of a woman for whom he felt tenderness for a long time. Though he had sought out whores now and then, the desire he felt at such moments was disconnected, blind; he wanted only to relieve an ache, as he might lance a boil. He never brought one home with him. The bad habits of his years of solitude weighed heavily on him. He was afraid that his body was a wreck, that his breath was stale, his fingernails dirty. He could not believe that Lore could see him any other way, he dared not think that love had altered her perceptions. And yet he found the courage to get up from his chair and kiss her. When she responded, he felt his own body grow tense and tender; he felt like a young man again.

They made love in the small room. They drew the curtains over the spring sky. They had the night before them; it seemed like all the time in the world. They used it well.

Eva came by in the late morning. "I thought you would have left by now. You must go as soon as possible," she urged Lore. "Many people are leaving—no one knows how long it will still be possible."

She had, Jacob noticed, seen nothing of the love that had blossomed between them. She was worried, distracted. The joy on Lore's face did not strike her as anything more than a sign of her friend's good nature.

"I'll go tomorrow," said Lore. "On the first train of the day. I'll get up before Herr Strüpler does and be gone by daybreak."

Jacob took Lore's hand. "Shall we tell her?" he asked.

"Tell me what?" Eva said.

"We love each other," Lore said.

It was only then that Eva saw them in the light of their affection. She kissed them both.

That night they made love again, and in the early hours of the morning they bid each other farewell. They had made a romantic pact. They would meet again in a month, in Strasbourg. They had chosen the exact spot—the south portal of the cathedral, under the clock by the figure of the synagogue at noon on May 13. "She's the blindfolded woman," said Jacob, "with the broken staff, holding the tablet of the law."

By then, they thought, some view of the near future might be vouchsafed them. Their love would have been tested by the thoughts they expended on it in solitude. At the cathedral—if they both reached it—they could decide what to do.

MANFRED SOLOMON had come into the world as Moshe. His parents pronounced it *Meish*. They were from Poland's Baltic provinces. There were eight children in the family, six of them boys, and they were desperately poor. The father was a shoemaker, the mother tried to keep bread on the table by sometimes helping out in the houses of the rich Jewish merchants. It was a life of incredible hardness. The winters were endless, the children always hungry. It was this hunger Manfred never forgot, for it had a spiritual dimension too; it was not merely a hunger for food. "We lacked everything," he once told Lene, "but especially *joy*. The hunger killed it all. The children were always crying, the grownups quarreled."

He did not like to talk about those early years, but once, leafing through a book of photographs taken in the Jewish villages of Eastern Europe, he reminisced. "I don't remember laughing or seeing sunny skies—there must have been some days without rain or snow —or having the kinds of pleasures even poor Jews can enjoy. No Purim games, no spinning tops at Hanukkah, no wedding feasts. I hardly remember hearing music, though music is what, if I forget everything else, I remember. Was there a band concert in the town square? Perhaps. I hear some martial airs. Jewish musicians playing in a stuffy hall? I hear the scraping of a violin. The cantor singing his prayers in the synagogue? I hear a heartrending wail. It seems to come from the back of the nose."

He had demonstrated his gift for music at an early age. There was no money for an instrument, no one to loan the boy a violin, but there was a piano in one of the merchant's houses where his mother worked. She would bring him with her, and he would sneak into the room where the piano stood and play on it. He was heard by the merchant, or his wife; there were exclamations of astonishment, amazement. Excited conferences were held, the child was kissed, washed, hugged and given piano lessons by the teacher who came once a week from Vilna to teach the rich little girls and boys. The lessons were not supposed to cost his family anything, but the ladies took it out of his mother in sweat and toil. They withheld a zloty here and a zloty there and expected the poor woman to be grateful. The only one who did not exact promises and ask for a "return on his investment" was the piano teacher, who recognized immediately what a great talent the boy possessed. He spent as much time as he decently could with the prodigy and was the first to recognize that there was only so much *he* could teach him. "He understood more and played better than I from the moment his fingers touched the keys!" the man cried. It was he who eventually found Moshe another teacher and arranged for his "escape."

Because of all this, his brothers and sisters as well as his fellow pupils resented him bitterly. He was made the butt of cruel childish tortures. Only his mother showed him kindness and love.

At the age of eleven he was sent to Vilna to continue his studies. He lived at the house of a Jewish family who normally took in boys who studied at the yeshivah. It was an unhappy arrangement on both sides. Moshe was not used to so strictly observant a home, and Reb Farbshtein did not appreciate his boarder's musical gifts.

It was almost a matter of providence that Alexander Buchsbaum happened to come through Vilna on a business trip and heard the young boy play. Buchsbaum had no sons, only a daughter. When the piano teacher introduced him to the gifted Moshe Solomon, Buchsbaum saw immediately how he could perform a *mitzvah*, a good deed, and acquire a son at the same time. He journeyed the hundred kilometers to meet Moshe's parents and was appalled by the grim countryside, the primitive conditions of travel and the abject poverty of his co-religionists.

When he offered to educate Moshe in Germany—he said "Germany" as though he were saying "paradise"—to send him to study with the finest teachers, to give him a home and good clothes and enough to eat and a pair of shoes for every occasion, they jumped at the chance. At least that was how Alexander Buchsbaum always told the story.

In fact—and Manfred Solomon remembered this detail all his life and never ceased to think of it when his stepfather told of his adoption—both parents were deeply grieved at the idea of losing their child. They knew that it would be forever. What chance had they against this smooth-talking *daitcher*, this rich and powerful man, should they want one day to assert their parental rights? And they wept bitterly. They knew that Moshe would not be allowed to write them, that he would never come to visit them, would not send for them, no matter how rich and famous he became. He'd be as lost to them as if he'd been swallowed up by the Czar's army and spit out in the Sea of Japan. Despite the story that he had "bought" the child—the story Edu heard from Alexander Buchsbaum's own lips—no money ever changed hands.

The scene that Manfred was to remember as though it had been tattooed on his heart took place as he was saying good-bye. Buchsbaum had gone out of the house to wait in his carriage ("My God, it stinks in there," he said), and his father sat down with him at the kitchen table while his mother, who never sat, leaned against the stove, tears coursing down her face. The other children had all been sent outside, but the bigger ones looked in at the window. *"Meish,"* his father said, in his *litvishe* Yiddish, which Buchsbaum drove out of Manfred's head soon enough, "I want this for you because I know you will go far in this life. But don't think I am happy to see you go. I know we will never see you again. It will be as though you are dead for us, and we must sit *shivah.* We love you, but we can't give you the education you need to make something of your great gift. So we are letting you go. But with great sadness."

His mother sobbed and clenched her hands before her. "I don't know what it will be like for you there, in Frankfurt—a city of which I know nothing except that it is the place where the great Rothschilds come from—but you will have enough to eat and clothes to wear and a piano all of your own to play. Buchsbaum will, no doubt, treat you well. He is not a cruel man. And he will probably say to you that Moshe is not a good name for a son of his, that it sounds funny on the tongues of the *goyim,* and he will say to you, 'Let's change it.' That is all right, even though it was the name of your grandfather of blessed memory. But keep the name all of us have, don't let him change that name too. It is the name, as you know, of a great and wise king of Israel. And also, should I be alive in twenty years or so and open the newspaper one day and read something about a great musician, I want to know if it is my son they are talking about."

When they drove away in the carriage Buchsbaum said, "Look back, my boy, they're all waving to you." But the boy would not turn his head. There was a storm of tears in his breast.

Alexander Buchsbaum had flung a handful of coins at the remaining children, making them scatter in the mud to hunt for their bounty. Moshe was renamed "Manfred" and carried his Teutonic name into all the concert halls of Europe. But he did not, true to his father's wish, alter his last name by one iota.

Lene had met Manfred, as Emma told Edu, at one of Andreas' Sunday-afternoon musicales. These monthly gatherings were largely for young musicians. It gave them a chance to play, to be heard by their peers, to try their hand at contemporary music. Andreas had got to know all the leading musicians of Germany since he became a regular music critic for the *Frankfurter Zeitung*. He was, in part because of his liaison with Kurt, whose work, although minor, was distinctly avant-garde, especially interested in gaining an audience for modern music. Paul Hindemith was a regular visitor to his apartment, as was Hans Wilhelm Steinberg, who had conducted the premiere of the Brecht-Weill *Mahagonny* at the Frankfurt Opera. Klemperer, Scherchen, Schnabel, Serkin, Morini, Gareis, Slezak, Schönberg, Dessau, Hubermann—they had all been there and written their names in the guest book on the hall table.

Lene attended the musicales faithfully. She found the atmosphere convivial and enjoyed the music. She had a privileged position as Andreas' sister and soon came to know all the musicians who were "regulars." Emma showed up now and then, but she claimed that the new music gave her a headache. Julia had once brought a very unpleasant man, who had been asked to leave by Kurt, and this put a virtual end to her visits. Benno came when he remembered, Jenny when she had nothing better to do, and Willy with his recorder and a score was often there, waiting to be asked to join in.

Lene got into the habit of preparing food for the guests, and the gatherings became almost as well known for her dishes as for the latest trio in the twelfth-tone mode. The polite, slightly fey quality that Andreas, Kurt and their homosexual friends contributed gave Lene a sense of both comfort and daring. Comfort because it was Andreas' world and did not cast her out, daring because she knew that she was among people whose activities put them beyond the pale of bourgeois respectability. They were subdued and casual, their habits did not caricature women's bitchiness. Andreas no more wanted to be pointed out in the street as a fag than he wanted to be recognized as a kike.

On a Sunday afternoon early the previous winter, Manfred Solomon had been asked to play some piano sonatas by Schönberg. Manfred was not well known in Frankfurt. Even though he had grown up there, the discipline to which his young life had been subjected had kept him apart from his West End contemporaries.

Lene could not recall meeting him at all, though she had heard him play and seen him at the opera and the museum concerts. She was predisposed not to like him for he had become a figure of local adulation, and she was certain that he had a swelled head under his mane of black hair and would prove to be arrogant. She had no idea that he knew who she was.

Manfred played superbly. He was thirty-two years old, just coming into his own, growing stronger, more assertive, surer, season by season. Hindemith, who was there, congratulated him warmly.

It was a gray Sunday, the kind on which changes in the light are almost imperceptible and night falls almost unnoticed, but the company was in a good mood. The music had been beautiful, Lene's food delectable, and the group congenial. Manfred was the center of everyone's attention. He was of medium build, with the large and powerful hands of a pianist. His big head was made to seem even bigger by the mane of black hair around it, "like Struwwelpeter," Lene said. He had a handsome face and a high forehead. He was well aware that he was vain but thought that by making fun of his vanity he could deny it.

He had been conscious of Lene from the moment he walked into the apartment and was waiting for her to introduce herself to him; most women did. But Lene hung back, talking to Kurt. Growing impatient, Manfred turned abruptly from the person to whom he was speaking and hailed Lene. "You there, *gnädige Frau*, where do I know you from? Where have I seen you before?"

"I'm Andreas' sister Lene. I don't know where you've seen me before. Perhaps walking the streets."

"Is that what you do for a living?"

"Only on weekends."

Manfred found it impossible to tell whether she meant her answer to be humorous or not. "Lene! You're the one who prepares the delicious food—the one we have to thank for our heartburn."

He smiled ingratiatingly to let her know this time that he had made a joke. But Lene was not one to appreciate barbed wisecracks. On the other hand, she could tell that Manfred made fun of her because he was embarrassed and shy. He was clearly unused to speaking to people in a normal way.

"You played beautifully," she said.

"I bet you say that to all the pianists," he replied.

Immediately he saw that the carelessly tossed off remark had angered her. She looked at him, and it was almost as though she had slapped him.

"If you think *that,*" she said, "there's no need for us to have a conversation. I'm not someone who flatters people indiscriminately."

She left him abruptly, pushing her way through the crowd around him, and went into the kitchen. He followed her.

"Forgive me," he said, "I ought not to be flip with you, I understand that. But the words fly into my mouth and out before I can stop them."

She frowned, but he saw that the frown was less a sign of displeasure than an attempt to maintain a serious mien.

"May I take you out this evening?" he asked. "We can go see a film. I find that very relaxing after a concert. Especially if it's an American film. When my schedule is heavy, I go to the cinema two, three afternoons a week. I manage to forget the music for a while."

"Is that good?"

"As long as you remember it later, when you sit down at the piano. Will you join me?"

"If you'll let me go home first to put my little girl to bed. I promised her I'd see her after Andreas' party. She sometimes comes with me to concerts or the museum; it's fun to hear a five-year-old comment on things. Of course she loves the zoo and the dinosaur bones at the Senckenberg Museum best. And she can't get enough of the martyred saints at the Städel . . ."

"I always go to the Städel to feast my eyes on the Rembrandts," said Manfred. It was his standard answer. He met too many strangers to be able to think up original responses. He realized as soon as he had made the remark that Lene would challenge it.

"Which one?"

"You know, the big one."

" 'The Night Watch'?"

"That's the one."

"But that's in Amsterdam."

Manfred Solomon had the grace to laugh. "You must take me on a personal tour, and I promise I won't make such a gaffe again."

A tense sort of attraction had sprung up between them. Lene wanted to cut him down to size and at the same time to warm herself at his fiery intensity. He could hold a thousand or more people spellbound, merely by running his hands up and down a piano keyboard! Manfred liked her stubborn insistence on keeping herself out of the immediate emanation of his charm.

"When shall I call for you?" he asked.

"Eight o'clock?"

"That will give us plenty of time."

He took down her address and went to talk to Kurt. "Tell me all about her," he said, and Kurt told him as much as he knew.

"I'm going to the cinema with Manfred Solomon," Lene said to Emma when she came home.

Emma was reading Clara a story. Her face took on a look of distaste. "That dreadful man!" she said.

"You object?"

"I've seen him at parties and always given him a wide berth. He's a complete egotist and a boor."

"Be careful what you say. I might marry him."

"You're not serious?"

"Not altogether. But I like him—just so he doesn't know that too soon—and I'm tired of being alone. This house is too full of women."

"What about Clara?"

"It wouldn't hurt her to have a father."

"She *has* a father."

"He never sees her."

"Is that *his* fault?"

Lene did not answer.

"I would be happy to look after Clara," Emma said.

"Thank you," Lene said, but she had not really been listening.

THE APRIL I boycott against the Jews was clearly just the beginning. The next step was to exclude Jews from the civil service. After that, other measures were enacted. At the same time the dictatorship increased its stranglehold on the state and eliminated free trade unions. On May 10, students at the University of Berlin burned hundreds upon thousands of books. It was an "action," the *Frankfurter Zeitung* reported, against the "un-German spirit." The writers on the list comprised a pantheon of the great and near-great of contemporary German literature, from Schnitzler and Freud to Remarque, Heinrich Mann and the brothers Zweig.

Emma was preparing for her trip to Florence with Clara. The little girl was full of excitement. She was dimly aware that the grownups always looked serious and preoccupied these days, and she was glad to be going on a journey. Edu had sent them repeated letters, urging them to emigrate. And now Andreas was in danger of losing his job.

Emma's bags had been ready since the night before. She liked to pack early. Most of Clara's clothes had been neatly folded by Fräulein Gründlich and put into two of Lene's suitcases. There was only the small valise—her very own—which had to be packed, and Clara was chosing what would go into it. She had put all her favorite things on the floor around her and was stuffing first one and then the other in the bag. The teddy bear clearly had to go, and so did her box of crayons and the blue-bound notebook in which she made her drawings. She sat next to Omama every morning and made her own pictures while Omama painted. But there were other, less important toys about which she had not made up her mind. Clara put the tin box of marbles next to the teddy bear. Was it right to pack teddy into so small a space? Maybe she ought to carry him in her arms. Then she'd have room for the marbles. And if she put the little wooden train at the very bottom and the picture book next to it, she'd have room for the rubber ball and could also squeeze in the miniature zoo animals, which liked to travel on the wooden train.

The smell of fresh grass and damp earth came through the open windows from the desolate garden. Andreas had stopped by to eat supper at his mother's house. He had not experienced so intense a fear since the day of his father's funeral. Frankfurt was plastered with signs and banners exhorting the populace to follow the dictates of the new state. All the terrible slogans that had formerly been scrawled secretly on walls by rowdies in the night now appeared officially in black Gothic type reminiscent of the imperial past. Every trace of the clear, straightforward letters of Weimar was gone. Roving troops—made up of cadres of SA and SS men, once only an underground force—were in control of the streets. It was the moment of revolution when the victors have not yet consolidated their power and must therefore display it ruthlessly. Only when every scrap of dissent had been crushed could the thugs be called off and the city return to a picture of normalcy. Then the savagery could be done behind closed doors, in cellars and jails.

Andreas wore a wool sweater, but he shivered in the spring air. He had put off his return to the Guiollettstrasse week by week ever since Nathan's funeral, looking for signs of hope every morning, putting his fear to sleep with a whiff of cocaine every night. He could not bring himself to leave Kurt, who was a *Mischling*, only half Jewish, and therefore still in a kind of limbo. He begged Andreas to stay with him, and Andreas, who loved him, had promised. There were large buds on the peonies, and the unpruned roses climbed in rich profusion over trellis and wall. Jacob had promised to come by after dark. He had gone to say good-bye to Siegmund and Pauline, who were departing for France that night, leaving Willy and Jenny to help the servants pack and store their belongings. They had bought tickets to Paris on the night express, telling everyone that it was a pleasure trip. They had not decided where they would finally go. Edu urged them to come to Zürich, but Siegmund thought he preferred London. The English had always appealed to him.

The business had with great care and the aid of a good attorney been "sold" to an Aryan partnership, but Edu still ran it from a small office in the heart of Zürich. He had also kept his directorship in the bank, which merged with a private Swiss banking firm. The worldwide depression had a deleterious effect on the wholesale cloth business, but Edu's shrewd and conservative leadership kept losses to a minimum. "People must be clothed, in any case," he said. His woolens continued to find their way into the coats and pants and jackets that were worn by people of the better sort in any number of countries.

Lene had spent the afternoon with Manfred Solomon at his apartment on the Beethovenstrasse. She had once asked him if he had moved there merely because of the name, and he had told her that when the choice was between the Mendelssohnstrasse and the Beethovenstrasse, he had faced a truly difficult decision, which he resolved in favor of Beethoven only because the living room was larger. Indeed, it was an immense room in which he kept nothing but a grand piano and a day bed. Lene would sit on the day bed for hours and listen to him practice. When he was done, he would sometimes make love to her.

In the wake of the Nazi boycott of Jewish businesses had come a prohibition against Jewish artists performing on the German stage and in German concert halls. The rapidity with which these decrees were enacted was both shocking and alarming. Hundreds of actors, musicians and others lost their jobs; museum, school and university staffs were decimated. Manfred's answer to the cancellation of his concerts was to go on practicing eight, ten, even twelve hours a day. He had decided to rework his interpretation of the entire opus of Beethoven piano sonatas.

"I'll go crazy if I don't keep working," he told Lene. His manager had left the country and was trying to arrange recitals and concerts for his Jewish artists elsewhere, but the market was being glutted by émigrés, and times were still hard.

Andreas had lost a great deal of weight and looked very much as Emma had looked as a young woman—dark and pale and haggard. He could not sit still, his movements were abrupt, and he turned around quickly whenever he heard a sound.

Caroline, on the other hand, was sunk in a torpor from which she only rarely emerged. Neither the sound of the spoken word nor the rattle of dishes nor the slamming of a door could bring her out of her reveries. She might lift her head and ask a question now and then, but it was not always clear from the questions where her mind had strayed.

"I'm not leaving," she said when Jacob came into the room. He had said nothing except "Good evening."

"How are Pauline and Siegmund?" Lene asked him.

"Nervous, like all of us."

"You can't make me leave," Caroline repeated.

"I'll stay with you," said Andreas. "We'll lock all the doors and never go out."

"What will happen to Anna and Fräulein Gründlich?" Jacob asked. "They'll soon be told they can't work for Jews."

"They'll never agree to it!" said Emma.

"They may have to."

"I can't stand it here anymore!" Lene cried. "I feel as if the whole country is an immense prison. I want to leave!"

"Where will you go?" Emma asked. "You can't just pack up and leave, like a gypsy."

"I can go to Palestine, like Ernst."

"Oh, please, Lene, be serious!"

"Ernst is picking oranges now, living in a shed and eating his meals from a single metal pot along with a lot of other tanned workers with dirty fingernails." Andreas' sharp voice was sharper yet with mockery. "I couldn't survive there!"

"Of course you could," Lene said sternly.

"I wouldn't want to," Andreas answered quietly. "Better to die with your face pressed against the cold window of your own cell, your home, than to live among strangers in a harsh land under endlessly burning skies."

"I don't understand you," said Emma. "Not that I'd want to live there myself, but you sound as if you're bent on cutting off your nose to spite your face."

"Clichés abound," said Caroline.

"Manfred says they're establishing Jewish cultural groups under whose auspices musicians will be able to play and actors will be able to act . . ."

"I told you we'd all be back in the ghetto," said Jacob. "Locked in every night and not allowed to show our faces in the public squares on national holidays. We'll wear a special hat and be deprived of real estate."

"I could live with that," said Andreas.

"*Your* kind will go to jail," Jacob said dryly.

"The garden must be maintained," Caroline said. "Where did the gardener go? I need to buy some alizarin crimson. Remind me, when the stores open again."

"What are we doing here?" Lene asked. "I thought there was some purpose to our being together."

"I think I'm also out of chrome yellow and Prussian blue," Caroline mused.

"Stop it, Mama!" Emma said furiously. "You know you aren't making sense. Pay attention to what's going on. Our future is at stake."

"Edu left us," said Caroline. "And don't forget the burnt sienna."

"I'm going to leave with Manfred," Lene said, "just as soon as it's possible."

EMMA AND CLARA took the train to Florence. It was longer and bigger than any of the trains Clara knew from the excursions she had taken into the Taunus, and there were men with white jackets who smiled at her and said, "Can I get you anything?" She had a compartment with Aunt Emma, just the two of them, and the seats were of soft plush. Clara sat with teddy next to her and looked out the window. Aunt Emma read a book and asked her now and then if she was hungry and whether she was happy to be on the train going to Florence with her. Clara thought that was a silly question. Of course she was happy! It was very exciting and she was sorry when it got dark and she couldn't see anything outside but lights dashing by and the reflection of her own face. But the dining car was also an adventure, because the men there served you while the train rocketed on at enormous speeds and everything shook and slithered around, so they had to have an edge around the table to keep things from sliding off, and the waiters were like acrobats, carrying trays full of food on the palm of one hand.

After dinner Aunt Emma told the porter to make the beds, and he turned the compartment into a bedroom just by turning the seats around and pulling down part of the ceiling. There were clean, smooth white sheets, and Clara slid between them in her nightgown, which she had to put on while sitting on the bed.

Aunt Emma seemed to enjoy it all as much as her niece did. She hugged the child every once in a while to Clara's surprise, but not always to her delight. Emma's kisses were awkward and hurried, her embrace clumsy. She had no practice. Love never translated itself into physical terms for her. "You're all corners," Clara said once when her aunt's arms pressed her too tightly.

When Clara awoke the next morning they were in Italy, where everything looked entirely different from Frankfurt. She pressed her face against the window, and Aunt Emma had to speak sharply to her to get her to dress. They had to hurry through breakfast, too; Aunt Emma didn't want them to miss their stop. Clara said she didn't like to hurry, and at that her aunt made funny clucking sounds and drummed on the table. Clara saw that she was angry. She wasn't allowed to finish her hot chocolate, which almost led to tears, and they practically ran back to the compartment, where they waited for a considerable amount of time, dressed in their hats and coats, until the train actually arrived in Florence.

Emma commandeered a porter for all their luggage, speaking in her rapid Italian, which fascinated Clara because it made her aunt seem to be another person entirely. Emma was nervous and agitated because the porter was slow and the cab that usually brought her to the Villa Botti was nowhere to be seen. Clara stood on the curb outside the railroad station, holding on to her teddy bear, while Emma harangued the Italians. Two great tears started up in Clara's eyes and rolled down her cheeks.

"What in the world is the matter with you?" Emma said to her. "There's nothing to cry about. Just stay close to me and you'll be fine. Don't act like a baby."

They finally got tucked away in the cab, and Emma, breathing more easily, kissed her niece and said, "Sorry, my poor baby, but these Italians, you don't know how they can provoke me. I love them dearly, still . . ."

"What a lovely lovely child!" Mabel Hennessy Supino-Botti said when she saw Clara, who curtsied nicely as she shook hands. She kissed the child on her round cheeks, and Clara found her bulky body softer than her aunt's.

Emma sent Clara to her room with the maid and walked arm in arm with Mabel out to the terrace. Clara could hear the sound of her voice trilling in high laughter, next to Mabel's growling lower voice. The house was dark and cool and full of heavy furniture and bright flowers and colorful bedspreads and walls that were whitewashed and hung with old pictures. Clara was glad to be away from her aunt for a while. She did not understand a word the maid said to her, but her gestures were expansive and she brought her a bowl full of fruit to eat and left her alone to unpack her things.

She set all the toys she had brought on the dresser and then sat by the window, trying to see exactly how this foreign place looked. The houses especially were not at all like the houses at home. They all had red roofs and were the color of sand. She would get to use that one crayon she never had a chance to use at home, because there nothing much had that sandy color. There was a cross around the maid's throat, a gold cross on a thin gold chain, and Clara wished she had one too. She remembered her bracelet and took it out of its little silk-lined case to wear. She would ask Aunt Emma if she could have a little cross just like the maid's.

Mabel came to fetch her after rest time. She wore many beads and pendants and silver jewelry, but Clara did not see her wearing a cross. Aunt Emma was waiting for them downstairs. Clara saw her sitting among a group of chattering women and again felt that odd and disconcerting change in her. She was speaking English, and the sound was quite unlike Italian; it was as if a different kind of music were being played. And her aunt, though she made a fuss over Clara, was intent on amusing her friends. Clara felt a pang of homesickness for her mother, for Fräulein Gründlich and Omama's sunny bedroom.

"Isn't it beautiful?" Aunt Emma cried, in German but in the exaggerated voice she seemed to find natural here. "We never have days like this at home," she said and gestured toward the deep-blue sky and the oleander heavy with pink and white and purple blooms. "This is the time of year I like best in Florence. How I wish I could live here." She did not usually talk like this to Clara. The little girl saw all the women looking at her, and her lips trembled a little, but she didn't want to cry. Fortunately, Mabel saw her and thought that she must be entertained in some way, so she begged Emma's leave and led the child down to the kitchen where the maid was polishing silver. She asked her to take Clara for a walk down to the barn to look at the cows and pigs and chickens. The estate had a tenant farmer and produced its own milk and butter and eggs as well as fresh garden vegetables. The lettuce was growing large, the tomato plants were in bloom and there were great yellow blossoms on the zucchini vines. Clara was allowed to touch the cows on their soft pink noses and to look at the piglets, nursing contentedly at their fat mother's teats. There was even a donkey and a large old dray horse, and the farmer put Clara on the back of the horse and let her ride around the farmyard. His grandchildren stood shyly in the doorway of their long low farmhouse and watched her curiously. They found they could talk to Concetta, the maid, about Clara and she wouldn't understand; she only smiled, like a deaf person. One of the boys called her a bad word, and Concetta slapped him, but Clara kept right on smiling.

EMMA ALWAYS felt at home the moment she saw Mabel's cheerful American face.

"You've put on weight again," Emma said.

But Mabel only laughed her raucous American laugh. "I have an interesting group of people here," she said. "It's a good time for me. The Depression keeps the riffraff away."

Emma was liked and respected by Mabel's guests and friends. Many of them assumed that the child was hers, and this flattered her. She began to think that Clara really belonged to her.

"How's B.B.?" Emma asked Mabel.

"The same as ever, nasty and clever and charming when he wants to be."

"I must go see him."

"He tells me he adores your letters."

"I try to entertain him."

Emma called B.B. that very evening. He cackled his delight at hearing from her and said she must come over the very next day.

"My little niece is with me," Emma said.

"You know I can't bear small children," B.B. said. "You'll have to leave her at Mabel's."

Florence sparkled in the May sunshine. Emma had ordered the taxi driver to go slowly so that she might enjoy the trip into the city and out again, up toward Fiesole. Bernard Berenson kissed her hand. His own seemed cold as the grave. He wore a white wool cardigan and a blanket about his shoulders. His small beard was very white, but his bright dark eyes shone.

"Your letters are a delight," he said to Emma. "You are that rare letter writer who makes the small details of daily life into the stuff of great adventures."

"It's getting harder and harder to find anything pleasant to write about from Germany. My Uncle Eduard left, and my father has died since last I saw you . . ."

"I am sorry to hear that. Was he old?"

"Only sixty-three."

B.B. clucked his tongue in sympathy. He took great satisfaction in hearing of the deaths of those younger than he.

"Does your Uncle Eduard suggest you follow him into exile?" he inquired.

"He thinks we should leave. But my mother and my brother— the one in Frankfurt—seem unwilling to take him seriously. My sister will probably go as soon as her lover leaves . . . I have been thinking, myself, of moving to Florence."

"What a grand idea. You know I've been after you to do that for years. You never *did* become my pupil, and now I am too old, I'm afraid. I can see only those ladies who'll cheer me up. I am too frail to lecture.

"What about the Fascists?"

"A rotten bunch. But I leave them alone and they don't bother me. Italians don't make good anti-Semites, and they're not easily turned into soldiers. Neither have they any taste for police work. It's what makes life among them such a joy."

"Of course," he continued, "some of my American friends tell me that the authorities have warned them about me. I know I'm watched. I've never made my anti-Fascist opinions a secret. The authorities tell the Americans I am senile. 'Don't bother with him anymore,' they say."

He chuckled. He was inordinately vain about his age. "I plan to keep my wits about me to the end," he said. "Tell me about your Uncle Wertheim's collection. I hear it's marvelous. If I were a little younger, I would go and see it—even if I am not invited. But it is no pleasure traveling these days. The world is falling into the hands of the rabble, and there's no room left for our kind."

Emma listed Edu's works of art in some detail. B.B. grew bored
quickly.

"Too many moderns," he said. "Is it catalogued?" Emma said she
thought not. "A shame, a shame. Tell him so for me. I'm certain he
has no Sassetta." There was a malicious twinkle in his mahogany
eyes. "He should have bought the count's. He was foolish to pass
it up."

"He was told it wasn't genuine."

"By that fat young man, no doubt! A typical German scholar!"

With a little flattery, Emma got the old man to smile again. He
forgot his petulance and patted her knee. He no longer had any
desire for her, but he found her pretty still. And it was marvelous,
being adored.

MUCH AS EMMA loved her niece, she left her in the servant's care most
of the time, and Clara began to find life pleasant and in some ways
like home. She made friends with the children and learned a few
words of Italian. Sometimes she missed her mother, but that happened rarely, largely in the morning right after she awoke, when the
sun left a long yellow rectangle on the cover of the bed.

At mealtimes she sat beside her Aunt Emma like a small Buddha
on a chair with a pillow and ate busily. She devoted herself to the
food with such love that Mabel never tired of watching her. When
they ate outside on nice days, the sun filtered down through the fig
tree and lit up her soft blond hair. At those moments Emma would
think, "She looks like her father. You wouldn't think she was Jewish." An only child, Clara never minded being alone.

After dinner she was sent to bed for her nap. She seldom slept,
but it was an hour she liked; she was all by herself, her room was
silent and—if she made no noise—she could play all she wanted. She
was free to do even the forbidden things she sometimes did, which
gave her pleasure.

Punctually at three one afternoon Emma fetched Clara from her
room. "We're going into town today," she said. "Hurry now."

They had a wonderful time. They visited the Uffizi Gallery,
where Clara saw a great scene of battle and a naked lady standing
on a sea shell, her hair blowing all about. When they had had their

fill of pictures, they went to the Piazza della Signoria outside and ate delicious chocolate and vanilla and lemon ice cream. A man came around selling postcards and little Florentine flags and silk hangings with gold tassels.

"Don't look at that junk," Emma said sternly. "If you want to buy a souvenir, we'll go to a real shop, and you can pick out something nice."

"Can I get a chain with a cross on it like Concetta's?" Clara asked.

"Good heavens, what an idea!" Emma said and laughed quite loudly. "That's something only maids wear, Italian maids especially. They get them blessed by the Pope. You wouldn't want *that.*"

"Why not?"

"You aren't Catholic," Emma said.

They took a bus back to the house, and while the grownups watched the sun setting behind the Tuscan hills, Clara drew pictures of things she remembered from the museum. She drew one of the lady in the shell (they had bought a postcard of her) and put a cross around her neck. The company laughed, but kindly, and praised her. "What a talented child you are!" they said.

They were all having their evening meal—Clara was proud that she was allowed to eat with the grownups—when Concetta came to tell Emma that there was a long-distance call for her. An icicle of panic stabbed her heart. But it was Lene at the other end, and she sounded happy.

"Where are you?" Emma asked. "Is everything all right?"

"Everything is fine. Wonderful. I'm in Zürich. I just visited Uncle Edu. He sends regards. It's good to be out of Germany. How's my Clärchen?"

"Having a wonderful time. We went to the Uffizi today, and she was very good and loved the pictures. Everyone adores her, especially the help. But why are you in Zürich?"

"Manfred is playing a concert here. They were able to get a small tour together for him. That's why I called. We'll be in Rome next week, and then he has a concert in Florence on Wednesday, and I'll be able to see you both then. Isn't that nice?"

Emma was not so certain.

"Haven't you seen any posters for the recital?" Lene asked.

"No, I haven't."

"I'll tell Manfred to get in touch with his Italian manager. We don't want him playing before an empty hall. Now let me say hello to Clara."

"How's Mama?"

"She was fine when I left. It will be great to see you, I have some gossip for you; stories that only you would appreciate. By the way, we're staying at the Excelsior. I'll leave you tickets."

Emma called to Clara. The little girl was not easily hurried. When Emma ran to fetch her, she was just wiping her mouth. "Hurry, hurry," she said, "your mama's on the phone." She pulled her away from the table with unseemly haste. "An impatient soul," said Mabel to an American woman from Philadelphia.

"Mummy, Mummy!" Clara babbled into the phone. "Where are you?"

Lene talked to her for a few minutes. Clara listened with her face wreathed in a smile so beatific that Emma was consumed with jealousy.

"Don't talk too long," she said, "it costs a lot of money."

"Mummy's coming here!" said Clara. "She's going to visit us next week, with Manfred."

"You must call him Mr. Solomon," Emma said. "Now say good-bye."

The little girl made the sounds of many kisses into the telephone. "I love you, too, Mummy," she said. "I miss you a lot. Can I come to the concert?"

"No, no, no," Emma hissed at her, "it'll be much too late for you."

"Mummy said I could!" Clara began to pout. She knew instinctively how to play her aunt off against her mother.

"Let me speak to her again," Emma said. "You're not serious?" she asked Lene. "Do you know how late concerts here begin? The child's not used to staying up so late—and it's a long way back to here."

"If worst comes to worst, she can stay with us at the hotel," said Lene. "Don't make such a fuss. You take things like this too seriously. Tell her to take a nap that afternoon, and let's you and I do something alone together. I *so* look forward to seeing you there.

Remember our trips with Edu? I think of them all the time. But enough now. *Ciao!*"

Clara had skipped back into the dining room. "My mummy's coming, hurrah, hurrah!" she crooned, and the company smiled at her pleasure.

Emma followed her, and there was a smile on her face as well, but it was strained. Her world had suddenly been invaded. She had thought that she was in a place that was hers alone, a place in which she was in charge. She had this feeling nowhere else, most certainly not in Frankfurt, where even at the hospital they knew her as Emma Wertheim, niece of Eduard Wertheim, director of Wertheim & Sons, the woman who had made that, you know, "unfortunate" marriage.

In Florence, at the Villa Botti, she was free of all this; she lived within a new skin. And she had brought Clara along hoping to make her forget Frankfurt, her mother, the whole of the little world she knew except for the part that had Emma at its center. Children had short memories, she thought. But the jubilant face, the cry "My mummy's coming!" belied her claim. Emma was distracted the rest of the evening and put Clara to bed with only a very brief story.

"Are you angry with me?" the little girl asked, and tears came into Emma's eyes. She hugged Clara fiercely and said, "Of course not, I love you."

Clara counted the days, and before long it was Wednesday. Lene called at one o'clock. Clara was eating her dinner on the terrace, listening for the telephone.

"Hello, my darling," Lene said.

"Mummy, Mummy, Mummy!"

Emma's face was full of pain. "You had best go and take your nap now," she said, "or else you won't be able to go to the concert."

"That's not what my mother said," Clara told her, "and my mother is my boss."

Emma took the receiver away from her niece with more force than she had intended. "Lene," she said, "are you telling the child she doesn't need a nap?"

"No, of course not," Lene said cheerfully. "She ought to nap, but we won't deprive her of the concert if she doesn't. Are you still coming in to meet me?"

"Do you want me to come?"

"Of course, I've made my plans around it. I'm free as a bird while Manfred takes *his* nap. We're having a bite to eat first, just something light. The concert starts at nine. Manfred is very strict about his schedule on concert days, otherwise I'd tell you to join us for dinner. But he doesn't like to be with strangers then."

"Am I a stranger?"

"Oh, you know what I mean," Lene said airily.

"Where shall we meet, you and I? If you're certain you want to see me, that is. It's a long way into town and back."

"We won't do anything tiring, just sit and chat. Is that fabulous café still there at the Piazza della Signoria? Remember when Uncle Edu would meet us there and say, 'Five o'clock sharp!' "

"I certainly do remember—and if it hadn't been for me, you and Julia would never have got there on time! Remember when you missed the train?"

"And you were at the station on time and we were still wandering through the town—was it Arezzo?"

"I think so. I went to get on the train to wait for you and save a compartment, so we could all sit together . . ."

". . . and before you knew it the train started to move, and we were still a couple of blocks away, looking in store windows . . ."

"I was *furious*—and worried too, I want you to remember *that*. I was certain you two would come to no good, alone there in Arezzo. But Edu laughed and laughed . . ."

Emma felt the old love for her sister flood through her. At that moment she thought there was no one who had ever been closer to her or with whom she got on better.

They met at the café and almost wept with gladness. The next several hours were filled with talk punctuated by laughter. Even the long shadow of Manfred Solomon, sleeping at the Hotel Excelsior with a black shade over his eyes and stoppers in his ears did not come between them.

Clara was afraid she would not fall asleep during her rest period.

She knew that if she didn't she would be tired at night and doze off at the concert, and then Aunt Emma would say, "I told you so." She closed her eyes tightly and tried not to think about sleeping, and when Concetta came in at five o'clock to wake her, she opened her eyes with the happy realization that she *had* slept. She felt warm under her covers and her eyes were stuck together a little. Why was waking up in the afternoon so unlike waking up in the morning? You carried sleep with you a lot longer in the afternoons.

Aunt Emma had just come home and was resting, so Clara ate her supper alone at a table in the breakfast room. Concetta helped her put on one of the pretty Florentine dresses Aunt Emma had bought her, and then Aunt Emma appeared, wearing a long dress.

The crowd at the concert hall was quite large—they had got the posters up in time—and Emma was visibly nervous as they waited for Lene in the vestibule. Lene was late, as always. Emma looked at her watch constantly and made the clucking noises in her throat that Clara hated. Her mother was never impatient like that, and Clara began to wish desperately that she would appear. She did not understand that Lene used sluggishness as a weapon against her sister's agitation.

Clara saw her mother immediately, coming down the flight of stairs. She tore herself loose from her aunt's grasp and raced to meet her. "Here I am, Mummy!" she cried and flung herself at Lene, who picked her up in her arms and squeezed her. "You weigh a ton!" she laughed.

It was good to feel that embrace. No matter how nice the others were, no matter how much she loved Aunt Emma, there was only one spot in the world where she felt completely protected and sheltered. The Italians smiled at mother and child. Emma said, "You're late," but she said it quietly. She noticed that Lene wore a silver necklace instead of her pearls. "Manfred gave it to me," Lene said when she saw her sister's glance. "Isn't it beautiful?" "I hope your pearls are safe," Emma answered.

They found their seats, and shortly thereafter the houselights dimmed and Manfred Solomon walked on stage. Applause broke out, and he bowed several times to each side of the house. He spent a long time adjusting the bench on which he sat to the proper height, then he waited until the audience was perfectly quiet before he began, with a loud crashing chord, to launch into his first piece.

Lene sat at the edge of her seat, her hands clenched in her lap. She relaxed only after Manfred was well into the first movement and had demonstrated complete mastery and control. Clara sat next to her with wide-open eyes. She had never been to a concert at night, and this was the first time she had ever heard Manfred play anywhere but at his house, on his own piano. Sometimes he took her on his lap and played nursery tunes for her and guided her fingers until she learned to play "All my Little Ducklings." She was going to try very hard to stay awake.

During the intermission the little girl went backstage with her mother while Emma stayed in the lobby to make small talk with some members of the American colony who raved about the pianist, but Emma would not admit that she knew him.

Clara sat on a high stool in the dressing room and watched while Manfred changed his shirt and Lene rubbed him dry with a towel. "How was it?" Manfred asked Lene.

"*Very* good," she said.

"The hall is *not* one of my favorites," he said. "Did the low notes come through where you sat?"

"There was a slight deadness."

"I know, I know," said Manfred, "but I played well?"

"Superbly."

He paid scant attention to Clara, but she was perfectly happy to sit on the stool alone with her mother and Manfred Solomon.

"Aren't you bored by so much music?" he asked her. Clara shook her head.

"I took a nap today," she told him, as if that explained it.

"You're a good girl," he said and went back to his toilette. He put eau de cologne all over his neck and face and looked in the mirror a very long time. His smile when he patted Clara on the head, just before going back to the wings, was better than the one he turned on his audience.

"*Cinque minuti,*" said the man who knocked on the door. "You must go now," Manfred told Lene. He no longer seemed to know them. "Break a leg," said Lene, and they returned to the hall. Clara held her hand tightly.

"Omama always tells *me* not to look in the mirror so long," Clara said.

"*You* don't have to perform on a stage in front of hundreds of people," Lene said. "Would you like Manfred to be your father?"

"I'll have to think about it," Clara said. "Is my own father dead?"

"No, but he's moved to a faraway place. Don't tell your Aunt Emma."

"About my father?"

"No. About Manfred Solomon. Promise?"

Clara nodded her head vigorously. Now she had a secret with her mother, and she could think about that whenever she got lonely. She wasn't often lonely, but Aunt Emma sometimes didn't understand her at all.

She nodded off several times during the second half of the concert, but the encores were loud, and she awoke and clapped very hard for Manfred Solomon.

"I'd better take her home," Emma said as the audience began to file out.

"Aren't you coming backstage?"

"There's always such a crowd."

Clara was holding on to her mother's dress. "Don't do that," Emma told her. The child remembered her secret and said, "It's none of your business." She was ashamed as soon as she had said it, for she saw that she had hurt her aunt.

"Don't be fresh," Emma hissed. For an awful instant she did not like Clara at all.

"That wasn't nice," Lene told Clara softly. "Manfred expects us backstage," she said to Emma. "Artists are very sensitive about that. They always know who's been there and who hasn't."

Manfred tried to kiss Emma's hand, but she withdrew it quickly. "No, no, no," she said, as if her gesture alone had not been enough. Lene sat on the narrow couch among Manfred's damp shirts and undershirts. He received in a pale-gray cashmere jacket, which had been a gift from Lene.

Clara slept soundly all the way home.

"Your sister doesn't like me," Manfred Solomon said to Lene over pasta and scampi in a restaurant near the concert hall.

"It has nothing to do with you," said Lene.

"That's no consolation. Besides, I think you're wrong."

"She doesn't like men, or Jews for that matter. And you're both."

"And a musician to boot."

"That's right."

"She liked your first husband."

"Not at the time that I married him. She only likes him in retrospect."

"Compared to me, you mean?"

"That's not what I said."

"It's what you implied."

"She's a person boxed in by fears."

"You're not like that at all. It's amazing how two sisters can be so different."

"I'm the youngest. I always managed to appear cute and cuddly. She was the gauche one. And then there was Otto Radowitz."

"You're lovely and strong and full of kindness. I never want to be without you again, Lene. You must stay with me always. We'll leave Germany together. I'm not afraid, as long as I know I can be with you."

He kissed her. Lene knew that everyone was looking, but she didn't care.

THE FOLLOWING Sunday, Emma and Clara set out on their usual morning walk. Because the day was cool and they walked more briskly, they strayed farther from the Villa Botti than usual. They followed a road that curved through olive groves. Coming around a bend where the road dipped unexpectedly, they found themselves at the gate of a walled garden. Beyond stood a stone house with green shutters. It was closed, vines grew up its sides, the garden had fallen into neglect. Several gnarled pines leaned over the wall, and when Emma turned to discover where the road led, she saw the valley of the Arno in the morning sun.

"Isn't it pretty here?" she asked Clara. The little girl felt a rush of love. They were alone together and had discovered a secret house.

"There's a sign on the door," said Clara. "Tell me what it says."

" 'For Sale or Rent,' " Emma read. At that moment she saw herself in this house with breath-taking certainty. "I must have it," she whispered and knew that her life had found a new center. "And you can stay with me—always."

A salamander raced across the stones into its hiding place.

"All by myself?"

"Maybe Fräulein Gründlich will come too."

"And Mummy and Manfred Solomon?"

"They'll be able to visit whenever Manfred plays a concert in Florence."

Clara grew very still. They had begun the walk home.

"What are you thinking about?" Emma asked.

"I want to be with Mummy and Manfred."

Emma shook her head and made her clucking sounds.

"I want Manfred Solomon to be my father."

"But you already have a father."

"He never comes to see me."

"That's not his fault. He loves you very much."

"Whose fault is it?"

"He and your mummy had a quarrel."

"And they never made up?"

"They never made up."

"Did Manfred Solomon make them quarrel?"

The question startled Emma. "Not really," she said. She knew one should not lie to children, but she wanted to benefit from the conversation. "Do you like Manfred Solomon?" she asked.

"Yes. Do you, Aunt Emma?"

"I like his piano playing very much."

"If he comes to live with us, I'll never have to leave Mummy again."

"Who told you that?"

"Mummy did."

"If he comes to live with your mother, he might very well be happy to have you stay with me."

"Why?"

Emma ignored the question. "Wouldn't it be fun?" she said gaily.

"Just the two of us, in that beautiful house. I'll fix it all up, and there'll be a room just for you. And maybe we can invite your papa to visit us. We'll have a party for him."

"I don't like parties," Clara suddenly sobbed, "I want to go home! I miss my room and Fräulein Gründlich and Omama . . ."

"You'll do what the grownups think is best for you," said Emma, "and please don't cry."

Clara saw that she had somehow made Emma angry with her tears. The day, which had started out so well, was spoiled.

When Emma mentioned the house, it turned out that Mabel knew it well. She knew everything there was to know about her neighbors for ten miles around. "So they finally decided to let go of it," she said. "It would be grand to have you for a neighbor, even if it meant losing a houseguest." She was tempted to kiss Emma but remembered her stiffness. "I know the owners. Shall I tell them you're interested? You'll save a broker's fee that way—unless you'd like to pay it to me." She laughed as if she had made a joke.

The next afternoon Mabel said, "I found out the price. It's very good. And if you haven't got the money, you can rent it with an option to buy. A depression isn't bad for *all* people," she chuckled.

Emma called Uncle Edu that night. He was full of advice. Emma had not caught his attention so strongly in years. He told her to have a trustworthy person go over the house with her and to report the findings back to him. "If we decide that it's a good investment, you may offer them 30 percent less than the asking price," he said.

It was all accomplished in a matter of weeks. Mabel brought around an architect she said was excellent and honest. He gave an estimate of repairs which sounded reasonable, but Edu told Emma to double that, because all Italians were thieves. Mabel agreed that this was so. Emma offered 30 percent less than the asking price and bought the house—with a loan from Edu—for 15 percent more than the owners had expected to get. Mabel put a few thousand lire into her pocket from both sides.

"Leave Frankfurt as soon as you can," Edu said, "and try to convince your mother and Andreas to go with you."

JACOB WOKE late on the morning before the day of his departure to meet Lore in Strasbourg. He had a slight headache. He made his breakfast exactly as he always did, and he thought of Lore, as he had been doing ever since she left. The realization that this was to be his next-to-last day in Frankfurt, in an apartment that had been home to him for almost twenty years, struck him with great sadness. He picked things up and put them down again, wondering idly whether he could make room in his suitcase for one thing or another. There were still a number of errands to be done before he could leave.

He had been very cautious, no one but Eva knew of his plans. When he crossed the border and was safe, he would telephone Andreas. His most valuable books and papers had been stored in the basement of the house on the Guiollettstrasse under the pretext that Herr Strüpler had promised to paint the apartment. Alois was now the official owner of the bookstore. The arrangement had been made through an old employee of Edu's who was trustworthy as well as honest. An amount of money sufficient to yield him a reasonable income was in a Swiss bank. The apartment looked as it always had. He planned to pack his suitcase just before he left.

He tried to focus his attention on what he must do that day. He had to check on the bookstore for a last time; he wanted to take his silver tea service to Caroline; Eva wanted to see him. She had also decided to leave the country. She knew a chemist who worked in Paris and she planned to go there, to see if he had a job for her. If not, she would wash beakers, clean lavatories. "You're not apprehensive?" Jacob had asked her. "I don't think about it," she said. "I've always managed. But I will miss Frankfurt."

Jacob's reveries were interrupted by a harsh voice and forceful pounding on his door. No one knocked on his door like that. There was a bell downstairs and another one upstairs with a brass plate that had his name on it. His neighbor had been taken away in handcuffs one evening, but the building had been still since that night. The force of the pounding increased, the voices grew louder. Jacob got up slowly from the table. When he reached for his gold cigarette case—he had seen it glimmer and decided to slip it into the pocket of his dressing gown, he did not really know why—he knocked over his half-filled cup of coffee. The brown liquid ran across the newspaper before it soaked into the ink-stained blotter.

There were four men outside Jacob's door. They were not in uniform, but each one had a swastika in his lapel.

"Are you Jacob Wertheim?" the youngest of the four asked.

"Yes, I am."

"Is there anyone here with you?"

"No," said Jacob, "I live alone."

"But you entertain?"

"Rarely, if ever." Jacob held the cigarette case in his hand, deep in the pocket. It was smooth and flat. The men crowded him but did not touch him. He smelled their breaths.

"Your superintendent says that women come up here all the time."

"He's lying," Jacob said. The men filled the doorway, and he stepped back involuntarily. He had not meant to give way. "I have some relatives who are of the female gender," he said, "maybe Strüpler meant them."

"*Herr* Strüpler," one of the large men said, "and don't be funny with us."

They pushed past him. Jacob was painfully aware that he was still dressed in his pajamas and had slippers on his feet. It made him feel exposed, almost as if he were naked. It was close to noon. He saw a square of sky through the window at the end of the hall and pushed all coherent thought out of his mind, concentrating on the pale-blue square instead. He felt that he would not be hurt if he did not think. He said any number of things to the men, whose backs were to him as they searched all the rooms of the apartment. "There's nothing here," he babbled. "You are free to look. I have nothing. I'm hiding no one. I'm an unpolitical man. Strüpler . . . Herr Strüpler knows that."

"Shut up," the young man said.

Jacob held on to the cigarette case with all his might. There was not even a copy of Karl Marx among his books. He had no weapons. There was no *reason* to arrest him. But, of course, they needed no reason. That was what people like him refused to understand. He began to sweat.

The men made a shambles of the apartment. They did not break anything, but they opened every drawer, threw the contents on the floor, pulled books down from the shelves, knocked over chairs, emptied closets. They pulled the sheets off his bed and the linens from the closet and the pillows off the couch. They found nothing, if in fact they were looking for something; their actions were reflexive, as if they did this routinely, to create chaos, to issue a warning. They were out of breath when they were done. Jacob heard them panting. They finally gathered around him again and cursed him, saying they would be back for him another time. Several times they said *"Saujud","* Jewish swine, and the words lodged in Jacob's mind. He knew they could still harm him, could turn at the last minute and shoot him or beat him senseless with blackjacks. But they backed away. It was just a warning.

"Herr Strüpler will keep his eye on you," the young man said. "If he says something is fishy with you, then you better believe he's right. You aren't as smart as you think. Your time will come."

They opened the door, and Jacob saw that across the hall in the next apartment the door was open. There were painters at work; everything had been cleared out. Herr Strüpler stood a few feet behind the door, craning his neck to see what had happened. Jacob still held the cigarette case in the pocket of his robe.

"Hello there, Herr Strüpler," he cried, "how are you you today?" The super moved out of sight.

Only after the door had slammed shut did Jacob feel the terror well up within him. Bits and pieces of the scenes just past kept flaming up in his mind, then the relief flooded back like a wave. He realized how much he had sweated; his slippers stuck to his feet and he smelled like an animal. He brewed some tea and decided not to leave the apartment until the next morning. Nothing mattered anymore but to get out of the country.

On May 12 he boarded the evening train to Strasbourg, carrying a single valise. He wore a winter coat, even though it was a warm and sunny day. No one saw him off. He had not wanted to leave Frankfurt, now he did not want to return. He had given no thought to what he would do should Lore not be there.

He arrived in Strasbourg shortly before nine o'clock. It was dark, and he had fifteen hours to wait. He wandered through the streets near the station, vaguely looking for a hotel and at the same time keeping his eyes open for Lore. He hoped he might run into her sooner than their appointed time, hoped that she might, like him, be wandering through the city looking for him. He was afraid to walk as far as the cathedral. Jacob was not normally superstitious, but his anxiety led him to look for signs and portents. He heard a clock strike ten, then eleven, and it occurred to him that he had better find a room for the night. The first hotel he entered had flies crawling over a stained table in the lobby. He walked out again.

There was another hotel across the street. Its lobby was filled with heavy furniture and smelled of cheap cigar smoke. But there were no flies, perhaps, he thought, because of the smoke. He asked for a room. The man at the desk appeared to be mute. He shoved a card at Jacob and gave him a pencil to fill it out with. Jacob made up a name and address but put down "Frankfurt am Main" for the city of his origin. The man did not ask to see his passport; he handed him a key and pointed to the elevator. Jacob did not immediately find the room, the numbers seemed to conform to no rational system. He began to think he had become trapped in a rabbit warren, the kind Franz Kafka might have designed. He was out of breath and his heart beat rapidly by the time he came upon the room, on the very top floor of the hotel.

The room was neither dirty nor particularly clean. The sheets were fresh but shabby. He undressed in the dark so that he would not be tempted to look around him and fell asleep within minutes. He had set his alarm clock for nine in the morning.

He slept soundly until the clock went off. As he groped his way out of deep, dreamless sleep, he thought, This is the day. His mouth was dry with excitement. Please God that she comes, he thought. Doubt had entered his mind for the first time since he and Lore parted.

He washed his face and brushed his teeth at the little sink in the corner of the room and relieved himself in it as well. He did not want to walk into the hall to look for a toilet. He packed his toiletries and his pajamas in the valise again. The room bore no more sign of his presence than the rumpled sheets on the bed.

Breakfast was served in a bare dark hallway at two long tables covered with oilcloth. The bread and croissants were surprisingly good, the butter fresh. Jacob ate so much of both that he was charged for an extra portion. He remembered that he had gone without dinner the night before. He paid his bill, looked at his watch and saw that it was ten o'clock. Two hours to wait. He decided to take his suitcase to the railroad station and leave it at the baggage check.

He took a trolley and by the time he was done and ready to head back toward the cathedral it was still not quite eleven o'clock, so he decided to walk. He reached the cathedral square at about eleven-thirty. The warmth of the May sunshine was a welcome sensation, and the sight of the cathedral itself gave him a feeling of such jubilation that he wanted to break into song. He stood for several minutes, letting the sun warm him, gazing at the ornate edifice rising like a transcendent mountain into the infinite blue sky. Suddenly he was struck by panic and hurried to the south portal. Lore, too, might be early; he hadn't a minute to spare. But only pigeons strutted on the steps under the garish clock.

Synagogue and Church Triumphant stood on either side of the portal, the latter with chalice in one hand, cross in the other, looking steadily at the pathetic figure across the way. How much more beautiful and delicate, thought Jacob, was the blindfolded Synagogue! Had the sculptor been more deeply touched by the symbol of the dejected maiden? Had the queenly Church, crowned and straight-backed, elicited less sympathy from the carver than her vanquished sister?

Jacob looked at his watch again; it was ten minutes to twelve. What if she didn't come? How long should he wait? Where would he go? He would stay in Strasbourg, return every day for a week, cling to hope. He would not return to Frankfurt.

The idea of suicide occurred to him; he realized it had been crawling through his mind for days, and he was simultaneously frightened and exhilarated by it. He felt a rumble in his bowels and realized that he must get to a toilet. He searched the periphery of the square. There was no public toilet, the restaurants looked closed, only a shop selling souvenirs was open. He entered the cathedral. Postcards were on sale here, too, but, of course, there was no lavatory. Whoever heard of a Gothic cathedral with a toilet? He managed to smile and sat down on one of the hard wooden pews, hoping the attack would go away. But his bowels continued their insistent grumbling. He went outside again; it was nearly twelve. There was no sign of Lore. Jacob saw that a Baroque building beyond the trees, near the canal, was a museum. Surely they must have a toilet.

Jacob paid the entrance fee and walked cautiously inside. In order to seem casual, he looked at a few objects in the hall before sidling up to a guard to ask him where the men's room was. The man told him to go up the stairs. The little, odd-shaped room was on the first landing. Emptying his bowels, he felt an extraordinary relief. The world made sense again. Just as he was leaving, he heard the clock strike twelve. He walked as quickly as he could without actually running, down the stairs and out the building. Once outside, he *did* run. People were suddenly everywhere, clustered on the steps, looking up at the clock. He didn't see her until he was almost there, and then she cried out his name, and they embraced and held each other so close that they heard their hearts beat as one.

They took the next train out. Lore had a single suitcase as well, but she had brought bread and cheese and a bottle of Alsatian wine, which they had in their compartment on the way to Amsterdam. The landscape of France and Holland rushed past them, but they did not see it. They saw only each other.

They were married soon after their arrival. Amsterdam was full of German refugees, and they found a circle of acquaintances, the seeds of new life. They took a flat in a building on one of the canals, near the Jewish quarter. When they were settled, Jacob called Alois and asked him to send him some books. It was then he found out that a week after he had left, Herr Strüpler had led the Gestapo into his apartment. They had carried all his books and papers into the courtyard and burned them. The conflagration had gotten out of control and almost set the building on fire. The fire engines had to be called. Jacob's apartment was given to a party official.

IN DECEMBER, just as the first snowstorm of the season swirled into northern Europe, Hannchen Wertheim suffered a severe hemorrhage. Zürich lay under its snowy blanket, and Edu could not get help in time. When the doctor arrived, Hannchen was dead.

Among her things Edu found an unopened letter from America. He looked at the date stamped on the envelope: January 22, 1930. The letter was in English and not very long. Edu read it quickly. It was from Blanche Worth, who introduced herself as "the daughter-in-law you never met" and went on, without flourishes or sentimentality, to explain that her husband, Gerald, had died some months before in a plunge from his office window. Most of his fortune had vanished in the Wall Street crash, and he was unable to recover from the blow. The loss of his money seemed to strike at the very heart of his being, Blanche wrote, and he sank deeper and deeper into despair. "It is only right that I should tell you these facts," she went on; "he was your son. I don't know, nor do I care to know, what came between you, but I feel an obligation to inform you of the facts of his death. The children and I mourn him. He was a good husband and father."

Edu carried the letter around with him for several days and then put it away in a corner of his desk. He could not bring himself to throw it out.

VII

1938

IN 1938 the new directors of the Städel—Elias had been fired five years before—shut down its galleries of contemporary art and dispersed the collection. It had been one of the finest in Germany and counted Edu Wertheim among its most generous donors. Seventy-five works of modern art, largely those of the Expressionists, were sent abroad to be auctioned off. Edu's blue Matisse was snapped up by an American collector. The same year saw the expropriation of Jewish businesses; it was no longer deemed sufficient to have an Aryan "front." Mass arrests began in May. In August, Jews had their passports amended to include either the name Israel or Sarah.

Caroline and Andreas Wertheim continued to live in the house on the Guiollettstrasse, their lives ruled by Caroline Wertheim's madness. Sometime during the previous winter she had chosen to retreat before the advancing specters; her sense of reality vanished. Andreas saw her condition as an accurate reflection of the world outside their crumbling garden wall. The house itself was a shambles. The windows were shuttered to the sidewalk. Children crossed the street to avoid walking past it and averted their eyes. They said the house was haunted, they claimed to hear screams coming from inside its unpainted walls, they said they had seen ghosts in the garden. The legend grew that a Jewish witch lived there among laughing devils who munched all night on the bones of Gentile children. If the witch caught your eye, you were turned into a zombie. You lost control of your mind and your limbs and had to walk into the clutches of her Jewish bogeymen, who tortured their victims by cutting them to pieces, draining out their blood and roasting them for dinner.

Only Anna still showed her face at the door. She shopped and cooked and cleaned; no one had been able to convince her to do otherwise. She was paid directly by Eduard Wertheim. Her cousin, whom she visited in the Kaiserhofstrasse, was her only friend. All the other people she had known turned their backs on her or had themselves been arrested or had gone away. Anna was single-minded in her belief that she must hold out, that these times would pass, that it was only by behaving as her conscience dictated that she could ever, in other, better times, be able to look herself in the face. She did not believe in heaven, but she believed that God was her judge.

Fräulein Gründlich accompanied Lene and Clara on their travels with Manfred Solomon and spent the school year with the child at Emma's house outside Florence, where Clara had been enrolled in a private girls' school. The governess had little time to miss her homeland, there was too much to see and to do, her life had become assimilated with the lives of her employers. She kept a picture of Frankfurt in her mind. It was clear and beautiful, a city full of sunlight and sparkle, and even its nights were suffused with the light of fireworks. The moors of her childhood had less reality; they were somber pictures, filled with dour peasants who folded their hands tightly before them. She did not wish to remember the gnarled, toothless faces, though they appeared now and then in her dreams.

Andreas had moved in with his mother in 1933. Kurt still lived in the apartment overlooking the Main. As an uncircumcised *Misch-*

ling, he managed to hold out in a nether world, barely tolerated, working as a waiter in a restaurant. He went on composing music that would, in any case, be banned. He hoped to survive until things had righted themselves again. He could not believe that there would not be a reckoning. He hoped for war. Because he feared being denounced for his homosexuality, he remained celibate. He even flirted with women, though he could never bring himself to take one to bed. There were many women who were amenable to this, but he lived in constant fear of denunciation.

Until March of 1938, Andreas had held a minor position with the Kulturbund Deutscher Juden, which bravely tried to employ Jewish musicians, Jewish actors, Jewish painters. He helped to organize concerts given before all-Jewish audiences at the West End Synagogue. More and more Jews, however, emigrated—the musicians to Palestine with Bronislaw Hubermann, the violinist, and Hans Wilhelm Steinberg, the conductor; the actors to Hollywood and New York. Many of the Communists had fled to Russia, only to fall victim to Stalin's purges. But then it grew harder to emigrate—what country in the world would take so many Jewish refugees?

The park benches in Frankfurt were forbidden to Jews, as were the public baths, the theaters and the schools. Jews became increasingly invisible to their fellow citizens, who discovered soon enough that it was better not to worry about shadows. "What you don't know won't hurt you" was the burghers' motto. It was easy enough to believe the world was bright and beautiful, every sign on the street announced it. The placards always showed the same smiling faces, the bands played happy airs. Could anyone be blamed for not looking behind the stage sets or listening at closed doors for screams of anguish?

Andreas had returned to practicing the piano many hours each day. If he did not, he thought he heard the sound of the hangman rapping at the gate. He played most often at dusk when Caroline was asleep, exhausted from a wakeful night and a day spent painting her black, dense paintings of bodies writhing in the torment of the Last Judgment. Andreas had grown heavy with the pale fat of one who neither moves nor tastes fresh air. He was flabby, bloated, and walked with a cane. He could not stand straight because of a mysterious pain in his back. He would not leave Germany, but he could not say why he stayed. Edu had urged him again and again, had promised to find asylum for Caroline, but Andreas merely sat staring into the overgrown garden, taking pills against his pain. He did not answer the letters; after a while he disconnected the phone. All his other relatives but one had fled. That one was Jonah Süsskind.

Jonah came to Frankfurt now and then and looked in on Caroline. He prescribed drugs for her and gave Andreas morphine. He never spoke about his wife and children, he said not a word against the regime, but he was gentle with his sister and his nephew. He was afraid his wife would leave him, and the fear had made him grovel before her. He saw the contempt in her eyes whenever he approached her with gifts and favors. She had become muscular and more beautiful than ever with the conviction of her racial superiority. She swam and sunbathed and worked out in the gymnasium; her strength was unbelievable. Most of Jonah's patients refused to come to him now. He sometimes begged the doctors—the ones he trusted —to send him cases. He had even performed abortions, but the regime was against this, and it would have gone badly with him, a Jew, if he had been caught doing away with the unborn child of an Aryan woman. "Why don't you leave?" Andreas asked him.

"I refuse to yield to them," Jonah said. "When this is over, I'll be here to pick up the pieces. Do you think those who leave, like rats running from a sinking ship, will ever be allowed to come back?"

"The ship hardly seems to be sinking. I'd say it was steaming full strength ahead and before long will conquer the world."

"Nonsense," Jonah said. "They may seek to regain some lost territories or to unite the German-speaking people, but nothing more."

"I find your capacity for self-delusion quite amazing," Andreas said.

"If the Jews had behaved differently . . ." Jonah began, but Andreas cut him off. "I don't want to hear," he said. "We're damned if we do and damned if we don't."

"I'm proud to have fought for my country in the Great War,"

Jonah said, "and they have honored my service. The Confederation of Jewish Front-line Soldiers has been spared reprisals."

"Will your membership in that organization save you from your wife?" Andreas asked.

"Shut up!" his uncle shouted. "She loves me! It's very hard for her."

Caroline saw her own demons. She was convinced that there was a conspiracy to deprive her of her house and all her possessions. She would not leave, she said, to go anywhere, because the place would be torched. She awoke at all hours of the night and checked the rooms for a sign of fire. She was convinced that the noises in the radiator were made by men planting bombs and incendiary devices. She knew that a plot existed to drive her mad. Under the leaves in the garden and in the bottles of wine on the racks in her basement grew slimy white slugs, fed on a special diet, who would grow into immense snails trained to crawl up her legs and into her womb, and up her arms into her armpits and from there into her hair and through her ears into her mind. She sometimes felt that her mind was already gnawed at, that little pieces had been nibbled away. One night she saw Hitler's face at the window and threw a bottle of perfume at it. The glass shattered and the cold air rushed in, carrying drops of rain, and Anna had to mend it the next day with a heavy piece of cardboard.

Andreas, knowing that his mother, mad as she was, was right, could only watch her with increasing melancholy. They *were* in danger, there was no doubt about that; they had been systematically deprived of every right, they had no recourse, neither judge nor jury would hear their pleas. They were no longer citizens, they did not exist—and yet they were counted, each and every one; the gallows were being made ready for them.

Caroline's mood changed daily, sometimes hourly. There were times she could not bear to be crossed, other times when to agree with her was to move her to frenzy. Once or twice she threatened to harm Andreas.

Jonah said it was schizophrenia and would not yield to treatment. "She should be hospitalized," he told Andreas.

"I can't put her away," Andreas said, "not in these times. They'll kill her, I know they will."

"She may try to kill herself, or you . . ."

"I'll take my chances on that, but I won't have it on my conscience that I imprisoned her. You know, when a modicum of sanity returns to her mind—and those moments come very rarely now—she'll suddenly look at me and say, 'Don't put me behind bars.' It is not a cry of desperation, it isn't meant to induce pity, it is almost an order. She sits straight up and her face loses its distorted look. Sometimes my heart melts and I feel like a child. I want to put my head on her lap and weep . . ."

"You must take me seriously, Andreas. It's not an idle threat. I have seen many like her. You cannot predict what they'll do."

"She spends her rage mostly in violent talk," Andreas said. "She talks and screams and uses foul language, but that night she smashed the window, thinking she saw Hitler, that was the only time she actually went on a rampage."

"It may happen tomorrow or not until next month."

"The day she smashed the window, you know, she had a *reason*. I heard terrible sounds coming from her room—it turned out the radio was on, she was listening to a propaganda broadcast. Goebbels was yelling, a thousand people screamed back. Have you ever heard the roar of thousands screaming?"

"Yes."

"I believe it triggered the violence in her. I took the radio away."

"You persist in thinking of it in rational terms. I tell you that won't work. You can't know what the mad will do unless you are mad, because they function outside of the discourse and the logic of reason. Their world is not your world, is not governed by its laws . . ."

Jonah was terribly tired that day. He could barely follow the thread of his own conversation. He envied Andreas, who had, it seemed to him, chosen the easier way—Caroline's madness had an element of the sublime to it, his own wife's hatred was mean, the way the actions of a criminal are mean. Yes, he thought, Hildegard is a criminal. But it didn't help to think that, it made his situation no easier. He loved her.

"People who are mad inhabit a different country," he went on as if by rote, "they follow their own sets of rules and have secret codes to decipher the mysteries that surround them . . ."

"It sounds like Germany under the Nazis to me," said Andreas. "Have you ever contemplated suicide?"

"It's a coward's way out," said Jonah.

"But have you thought about it?"

"I've got a family. A wife and four children."

"You haven't answered my question."

"I've thought about it."

"And . . ."

"That's it. I have given it some thought. But as long as I see even a glimmer of hope . . ."

"I can't see any hope at all, but I still— I can't contemplate suicide. I've tried, but the thought slithers out of my grasp. I sit and wait for something to happen. I can't make the motion to hold the razor against my wrist, or find the pills, or learn to pull the trigger on a gun."

Jonah looked at his watch. He wore an old-fashioned pocket watch, which had been his father's.

"Time to go home," he said. "I promised to bring Hildegard something from Frankfurt. The pickled tongue in the Fressgass' is like no other, she says."

He got up. His movements were those of an old man, and Andreas thought that he, too, saw the world with eyes of death.

"Let me know if there are any changes," Jonah said. "I'll leave you more sedatives. Is there anything you need?"

"I don't think so."

"I'm finding it hard to get drugs," Jonah said.

"I can tell you where the bars are"—Andreas smiled—"in which you can get *anything.*"

"No more," Jonah whispered. "The government is against sin."

Andreas locked the door behind his uncle and bolted it. He had had metal bars put up over all the windows, and iron grills against all the doors. Caroline, when she had seen the workmen fastening these contraptions in place, confronted Andreas in his room. "You've made me a prisoner!" she screamed.

"I'm doing it to keep people *out,*" he said patiently, "not to keep you in." And he showed her how the locks worked and how she could, any time she wanted to, open the doors. The windows, of course, were another matter. "A prison is a prison is a prison," she mumbled. "We're trapped, whatever you call it."

She wore her painter's smock, and Andreas smelled her body odor mingled with the linseed oil and paint.

"You really should bathe now and then, Mama," he said very gently, taking her hand in his. Caroline turned to look at herself in his oval mirror, as if it were possible to tell something about her cleanliness from that.

"I was beautiful once," she said and stroked her ashen cheeks with her bony, paint-stained hands. "Now I'm Jewish."

"You've always been both," said Andreas.

"You were a boy once," Caroline mused. "What are you now? You aren't a girl?"

"I'm a man."

"A real man? You haven't got a wife!"

"Uncle Jacob doesn't have a wife."

"But he had someone who let him put his thing in her." She looked at Andreas with a sharp, birdlike look. Her eyes flickered. "Or is that what you do to Kurt? Do you put your thing in him?" She giggled. "Is Kurt your wife?"

"That's enough, Mama. I don't want to talk about it with you—now."

"You always say 'enough' to me, and 'not now.' Especially when I have said something that is true. Crazy people are not supposed to tell the truth. You think I'm crazy?" Her voice rose. Andreas steeled himself. But she simply said, "I am crazy, you know: c-r-a-z-y. Like Emma. You know Emma is crazy too?"

"No, I didn't know that, Mama."

"She couldn't stand for that man, Otto, to put *his* thing in her. So she became a nun."

"What are you talking about?"

"She is a C-h-r-i-s-t-i-a-n."

"That's absurd."

"Mark my word, it's true. She didn't want to be Jewish, because she didn't want them to nail her to the cross. First she thought that

Otto would take the Jewish out of her, but she found out he wanted to put his Christian thing *in* her. And so she screamed and screamed, until he let her go. She said she would rather eat the body and the blood. You can't do that when you're Jewish."

"How do you know all this?"

"My voices tell me. They speak in the bare branches of the chestnut tree all winter long."

"And in the spring and summer?"

"They speak through the bees." She put her finger to her lips. "If you're quiet, you can hear them. But you have to be absolutely quiet."

LATER THAT month on a Saturday afternoon, Anna asked Andreas if she might go early that day. She had struck up a friendship with the shoemaker who lived across the landing from her cousin's flat on the Kaiserhofstrasse. He was a widower. A decent, honorable man who had applauded her decision to stay in the Wertheims' employ. He wanted her to go out with him while it was still light to Königstein to visit an old friend whose birthday it was. Andreas gave his assent gladly. "I'll leave supper for you and your mother," Anna said. She had steadfastly refused to have her meals in the dining room with them. Andreas had asked her again and again, but she was adamant. "I'm too old to learn new tricks," she said. "And don't think you're doing me any favors. I'm happy with *my* way. I don't particularly want to leave off eating by myself, down in my comfortable kitchen."

When Andreas came downstairs in the late afternoon, he found that Anna had set the table for two and left him a note telling him exactly where the cold cuts were and the potato salad, and what he must do to heat up the soup. He went to call his mother, but there was no answer. He knocked several times on her locked door, but she did not respond, although he heard her moving about. He went back downstairs, put a record on the phonograph and prepared to eat by himself. Caroline often refused to eat or came slipping into the kitchen at odd hours to stuff herself on nuts or carrots or cheese. She had once wolfed down a whole loaf of bread.

Andreas had bought a great many phonograph records and the best machine he could find on which to play them. He always listened to music when he ate alone. He thought it kept him from the awareness that he was like an animal, mindlessly stuffing food in his mouth, if he engaged in some cultivated pursuit. That evening he was eating his cold cuts to the sound of Artur Schnabel playing the Beethoven sonata "Les Adieux" when he heard Caroline come down the stairs. She entered the dining room, and he saw that she was wrapped in a bloody sheet.

"Contrary to what you may think," she said, "this is not a bloody sheet. It is a sheet painted with carmine red. Do you like it?"

"I'm eating supper, Mama. Come and join me." He had become used to his mother's bizarre behavior and her theatrical getups. He did not see that she was carrying a pair of shears in her hand like a dagger. Even when he noticed them, he did not believe they were of concern to him. He continued to eat. Schnabel had reached the rondo, Andreas' attention was on the music. Not until Caroline lunged at him did he think himself in danger. She had raised her hand, the shears a flashing blade between her fingers. He jumped out of her way. "What are you doing?" he cried.

"I'm on to you!" she said. "You are part of the plot against me. I found it out just now as I was preparing my shroud. The voices in the trees whispered to me. They told me that your head is full of propaganda. The Nazis put it in your food and spray into your room. Anna is their agent. She told you to put up the bars, and you followed her directions."

"Anna is as innocent of wrongdoing as anyone in this whole world," Andreas cried, "and I told you that the bars are to keep people *out*. I'll walk on the street with you this very minute, to show you that you're not locked in."

"They've called off the dogs for a day," Caroline said and came at Andreas again. Her strength was phenomenal. He struggled with her and twisted her hand until the scissors fell to the floor. He kicked them under the table. Caroline let out a long, piercing scream. It rose above the Beethoven sonata and echoed for many minutes. Then she wept.

She dropped the sheet and put her hands over her face. Her nails cut into the flesh of her cheeks. "I can't go back!" she cried. "I lost the way. Had I gotten where I was going and found the meadow,

I might be picking flowers now. Instead I'm here, attacked by voices that never stop. They tell me secrets, and they rub my ear and filter into the soft parts of my head. Oh, help me, Andreas! They told me to kill you, but it was them I was after."

"I mean you no harm," he said. "I love you. I am the only one of your children who is here with you. You must trust and believe me. No one else can help you. They're all gone. They've saved themselves. Let us save each other."

He went to the hall closet, fetched an old coat, wrapped it around her shoulders and led her to her room. She was still and had stopped weeping. Andreas made her take one of the pills and put her to bed. He drew the quilt over her and once again caught her bad odor. Nevertheless, he kissed her and sat beside her until he heard her even breathing. Then he went to his room, locked the door and read until he felt himself nodding off to sleep.

Several hours later he awoke, uncertain of his bearings, bathed in sweat. He went to open the window and saw the sliver of a new moon. For a second he felt happy. He had forgotten where he was; the sky looked like the sky over Travemünde. He thought he heard the ocean's roar. But it was the water in the bathroom overflowing its basin. Caroline had found a razor blade and cut her wrists. The wounds were not very deep, Andreas bandaged them himself, but they seeped continuously onto the white gauze. For the rest of the night he sat next to his mother and listened while she muttered her answers to the voices.

In the morning, he slipped out of the house and called Jonah from a public telephone. Jonah came as soon as he could and said there was only one place for her now.

"You must allow her to be put in an institution," he said. "It would be utterly frivolous to keep her here. No matter how bad things are, they're not so bad as to justify such irresponsibility."

It took him two days to find a sanatorium that would take Caroline. Most of them, finding that she was Jewish, said they were full. A private clinic in the Taunus finally agreed to have her. They cited an outrageous price for her keep.

"I'm only taking her because I've known you for so many years," the director told Jonah, who had been his classmate in medical school. Caroline Wertheim was admitted under an assumed name, even though the money for her board was transmitted from Switzerland on the account of Eduard Wertheim.

By the time the ambulance came to take her away, her posture had been frozen into one of medieval martyrdom. She saw only the blinding light of a brilliant sun and heard her voices dancing a dance of death on its beams. She had to listen very hard to hear the murmurs of farewell which her brother, her son and her cook, the only witnesses, whispered into her ear.

ON JULY 25 the government issued a decree forbidding Jewish physicians from practicing medicine as of September 30 of that year. Their licenses would all expire that day and would not be renewed.

"Well," Hildegard Süsskind said to her husband, "now what are you going to do?" She had sent the children to Hitler Youth camps to learn "strength through joy." They were registered as full-blooded Aryans. She planned to leave Jonah, but she worried that she could not take any of her belongings with her. She wished Hitler would confiscate every bit of Jewish property, then she could take what was rightfully hers and stop thinking about what he would do. She had heard talk among her friends that plans were afoot to resettle the Jews in ghettos, preferably in Poland, once this territory was returned to Germany.

Hildegard wanted desperately to serve the Fatherland. She wished she'd find it easier to bid Jonah farewell or to denounce him to the Gestapo. If the Jews were as evil as Hitler said they were, it was up to *him* to take the necessary steps to clear them out. It was too much to leave such a task to ordinary citizens!

Hildegard was a typical example of her caste and class. She had fallen in love with Jonah when he came home from the war a hero, which was not at all like her idea of a Jew—and not at all like the man who faced her now. She had not known then that he had betrayed his country, caused licentiousness to be let loose in its precincts, painted objectionable pictures and written dirty books. Whenever she looked at him now, she shuddered with moral revulsion.

Because he belonged to the Jewish War Veterans, Jonah had

hoped against hope that the storm would pass him by. When the decree of July 25 was handed down, he brought all his army papers, decorations and citations with him to the licensing board. They laughed at him.

The children had come home for the weekend, tanned and healthy, beaming with life, full of stories which they told to their mother without looking at Jonah. They knew he was no longer a doctor. Hitler had decreed it. It was a sign of their strength and devotion to their country to demonstrate their new-found hatred of their father. When Lieselotte, the youngest, said that she knew that it was the Jews who had engineered Germany's defeat in the war, Jonah, unable to stand it any longer, slapped her across the face. He had never done such a thing before. "We must rid Germany of her Jews!" the child screamed.

At that moment Jonah felt something break forever into a thousand pieces. It was not, he knew, his heart, but something more delicate; as a doctor he knew how strong the heart was. He thought he actually heard the sound of breaking crystal, and he felt a moment of dizziness, as if the shattering—whatever it was—had affected his sense of equilibrium. He went around the table to embrace his children and ask their forgiveness. They accepted his embrace, but their gaze was averted and their posture rigid. Not one softened to his touch. Hildegard watched it all with pursed mouth. The child Lieselotte was, in her eyes, blameless. Her anger at what Jonah had done cut her loose from him at last.

That evening she asked him what he intended to do. "We cannot live like this," she said. "Your every opportunity to practice in the community is gone. Perhaps you should move in among your own people—in Frankfurt, not here—and work with them."

"Is that your only response?"

"What other response could I possibly have?"

Jonah shrugged his shoulders.

"It is all for the best," she said. "A great good will come to our country from all this. Our Führer wills it." She no longer spoke proper German. Jonah had noticed it before. There was a kind of bureaucratic gibberish in which she liked to indulge; she made an effort to speak a language free of all foreign influences. She had thus been able to expunge all that might, in tone or language, remind her of old times, old love. She felt no pity. She felt no contempt, either. In her eyes Jonah was like a figure one sees on film being led blindfolded to his execution. The figure might be real, but who could tell? Next there would be the words THE END.

"Why don't you leave the country?" Hildegard asked.

"With two and a half marks in my pocket? That's all they allow you to take."

"You have connections. Caroline's in-laws are very rich. Ask them for help."

"It never occurred to me that I might have to go," Jonah said, "never in my entire life."

"You haven't told me what it is you're going to do."

"I didn't see this coming. I didn't believe it would happen. What is there to do?"

"I'll tell you what *I* will do, you can make your own mind up after that. I'm taking the children away. Home to Altona. We can start a new life there. No one will have to know about our past. The children can be raised as I want them raised. You will put the money we have in our name—I don't want the government to confiscate it from us. They'll take it from you soon enough."

"Where do you get your advice and information from?" Jonah had never seen her so resolute. He had always taken charge of things, allowed her to manage the household on an allowance. He had not thought she had any ideas in her head beyond the usual ones, and here she had become a tough business woman overnight.

"I talked with my father. I am following his directives. I should, long ago, have looked after my own interests. Heaven knows what shady Jewish deals you've engaged in."

Jonah understood what was being said to him, but something in his wife's conversation escaped him. He thought she might be committed to some grand hoax, that she was creating an elaborate scheme to save him.

"I haven't changed," he said. "I've been a decent husband and father these twenty years. And faithful too." He raised his voice a little. "Yes, I've been faithful and a good doctor. I made a home for us all . . ." He felt his voice break. He would not cry in front of her. He turned away and did not utter another word.

For a single moment Hildegard felt remorse. Then she choked down the feeling of pity, the feeling of guilt. She must be strong. She must lead her children out of the darkness and into the light. The Führer had called her to account. She conjured up his face, imagined millions shouting his name, heard the thunder of the voices rushing in her ears, *"Sieg Heil!"* they cried. She turned on her heel and walked out of the room.

The next morning she and the children were gone. Not one of them came to say good-bye. Jonah sat all night in his chair behind his desk until, toward dawn, he fell asleep, his head buried in his arms.

LENE WAS expecting a second child. She had married Manfred Solomon in 1935, when it seemed to them both that their relationship would weather the inner storms and be a bulwark against the outer ones. Manfred had shown himself to be greatly in need of a wife. He liked to lead an orderly, well-regulated life. In the turbulent years of his youth he had played the role of the virtuoso, affecting a mane of unruly hair and Byronic collars to frame his scowling mien. But just as his piano playing had cooled to a more cerebral style, his temperament had become more settled. Lene had been told by a woman to whom she had sent a piece of his handwriting for analysis that he was insecure. The woman had said a great many other things as well, and Lene had felt it necessary to hide the letter at the very bottom of her trunk. She wondered if it was his insecurity that made him insist so strongly upon his bourgeois habits. He was a great admirer of Thomas Mann, who seemed to him to embody all the virtues and none of the vices of a "great" artist.

They had been to visit Mann in his villa outside Zürich, and Manfred spoke of it whenever the opportunity presented itself. He had been deeply impressed by the writer, by the adulation his wife bestowed upon him, and by the sense he projected that he lived an idyllic and perfectly modulated life. Lene had been less impressed. Katja Mann's adoration seemed to her insipid. It was a trap she herself would take care not to fall into. She was, she hoped, too skeptical and straightforward a woman to worship any man, however great his genius. After one broken marriage and a failed affair, she would be cautious. She saw the dark side of Manfred, and feared it, saw the furies of his childhood, which he had tried to bury. She knew she would never be able to fill all his hungers, but they seemed to make him more desirable than any man she had ever known. And over all his dark desires hung the mantle of his immense talent. It was something Lene never talked about, but it was a large part of the attraction the pianist held for her. It was pleasant to bask in Manfred Solomon's fame, to hear herself pointed out as his wife. She was admired, and it cost her no effort. She had never liked to be envied for her wealth or her beauty—both seemed to her spurious attributes—but she was gladdened by the envy of people who thought she was infinitely lucky to be connected to a man of genius.

She worked very hard at being Manfred Solomon's wife. She had to take care of everything on their journeys, had to be his servant as well as his manager, had to prepare for his entrances and clean up after his final bow. She had to learn not to be critical at the wrong moment; he welcomed her opinions, but not in the heat of battle— *never* right after a concert. She was ready with his towel at intermission and a glass of wine at the concert's end. It was fun the first year. Later it became a chore, but it never entirely lost its glamour, and the music he made was a perpetual delight to her.

They had made Paris their base and rented a large furnished apartment, which came with a grand piano. They had not been back to Germany except to settle legal matters and to oversee the packing of their things into large "lifts" which were stored in a Parisian warehouse. On tour they lived in hotels. Lene saw Germany as a dreadful prison, and its citizens as obnoxious jailers. Frankfurt especially seemed to her steeped in evil—she could not forgive her exile. When she heard the sentimental songs she had loved so well as a child and had taught to Clara, songs about soldiers bidding farewell to their beloveds, songs about the small villages and their place in a wanderer's heart, she closed her ears, and tears of rage rose to her eyes. In the songbooks she had packed, whole sections were devoted to songs about the *Heimat,* the homeland, for which the travelers' souls pined in *Heimweh*. She detested them all except "Die Lorelei," whose author had been wiped from the German mind by a decree from Berlin. Instead of H. Heine, it now said "Author unknown."

Manfred Solomon, more sentimental than Lene and less certain about his own claim to being German, did not share her rage. He did not feel dispossessed by the turn of events, having been dispossessed many years before. Besides, he tried as best he could not to think about politics. He practiced the piano and studied his scores. When that was done, there was very little time left in the day for anything else. He never joined the heated discussions of his émigré colleagues, thinking their concerns were of little practical use and darkly suspecting some of them of being Communists.

By the summer of 1938 their stay in Paris had become a source of constant irritation. Both Manfred and Lene disliked the French and found the anxiety and malaise of the refugees oppressive. Since March, when Austria was annexed by Germany, a flood of Austrians had joined the stateless Germans in the French capital. Hysteria ran high, quarrels erupted, the heat of summer and the contempt of the citizenry did nothing to allay the prevailing bitterness and fear.

Manfred had applied for a visa to America for them all; he had been promised a position at a small Catholic girls' school outside New York. The pay was ridiculous, Manfred knew he was being taken advantage of, but at least it was a job, and one needed a job to enter the United States. Manfred was clearly not equipped to be a teacher, particularly a teacher of untalented young women, but a job was a job. The administration of the school was proud to be offering the job to a needy refugee.

Clara remained in Florence with Fräulein Gründlich. Emma had promised to bring the child to Paris to stay with Lene while they waited for the visa to America, but Emma had become evasive. She said she thought it wiser to keep her niece in "settled" circumstances in these unsettled times. She even suggested that Lene and Manfred find a place to live and make all their arrangements before sending for Clara. She told her sister in no uncertain terms that it was irresponsible of her to drag a small child through such wrenching experiences. She even hinted that Manfred was less than an ideal candidate for the role of stepfather.

All these discussions went on via telephone and the mails. The sisters wrote a minimum of two letters a week to each other and spoke on the phone every Sunday morning. School was out for the year, but Emma had arranged for a tutor to give Clara English lessons so that her arrival in an American school would be easier for her. The child was bored with the new language, which was unconnected with anything around her. Besides, the teacher frightened her, she was one of Emma's "cases," an Englishwoman in reduced circumstances who had to give up her position as a director of a travel agency because she suffered from crippling arthritis and could barely get around. Clara, whose imagination was vivid, saw Miss Johnson as a person of wicked disposition who liked to torture children in the small hours of the night. It did not matter that Fräulein Gründlich told her that the woman was poor and in need of assistance, that Emma stressed her intelligence and the importance of the lessons, Clara dreaded them, and the words she memorized every night in her room seemed to flee from her mind the next day when she sat beside Miss Johnson and watched her twisted fingers creep over the pages of the primer.

Lene called Emma on the first Sunday in August, determined to confront her, though she detested confrontation, with the demand that she bring Clara to Paris that very week. The connection was not very good.

"Are you coming on Friday?" she asked, after they had done with their usual pleasantries.

"Do you really want to have her with you now?" Emma said. Her voice quivered, but that might have been the shaky wires.

"Why in God's name shouldn't I want her?"

"It must be terribly hot there."

"No hotter than in Florence."

"We're in the country, it's very pleasant."

"But we may be called upon to leave at any minute. What if that happens and she's not here?"

"I can always bring her in the autumn—or perhaps next spring."

"Next spring we may all be trapped in war. They say it's coming, it can't help but come."

"Clara is safe here. Italy won't go to war."

"You don't know about that. You don't know about anything. You just don't like Manfred . . ."

"What if September comes and you haven't left and it's time for her to go to school?"

"She's only ten years old, a few weeks, even months, without school won't hurt her. We can always get her a tutor."

"All this moving around, all this confusion and uncertainty *could* damage her. You're being blind to reality."

"*I'm* blind to reality? I think it's *you* who won't face up to it. A child belongs with her mother."

"That all depends—a child needs love . . ."

"Are you saying I don't love my child?"

"Not as much as I do!"

There was static on the line, but Lene could hear the pleading cry in her sister's voice. "You're having another baby, Lene . . . all I have is Clara!"

The raw note of desperation frightened Lene. She didn't want to hear any more. "The connection is horrible," she said, "I can barely understand you. Listen," she shouted, "I'll write you! I'm sure we can work something out. Maybe you can come to America too. That's an idea," she said. "You come with us."

It was only after she had hung up that the gist of the conversation became clear to her. Emma wanted to keep Clara with her, for now, perhaps for always! Emma loved her, had always loved her, would not give her up. Lene sank back in the shabby chair and covered her eyes. The baby in her moved softly, gently.

The apartment was not only ugly but dark as well. The only advantage of the gloom was that it made it harder to see the hideous furniture. Manfred had seen the piano when they let the place, that was all that mattered to him. He was practicing now in the adjoining room. The telephone was back in its cradle and blessedly silent. Lene had been afraid that Emma might call back. Her sister's voice, full of anguish, kept ringing in her head. Manfred played on and on. Most of the time Lene enjoyed Manfred's practicing. The music always lifted her spirits, and in the privacy of their own rooms it was as if it were directed to her, as if he made love by bringing her the gift of his music. When she sat in the darkened concert hall among hundreds of other listeners, she always felt pleased with the thought that though the others might find Manfred's performance thrilling, they could never know how it felt to hear his heart beat as he lay atop her, covering her body with his kisses. When he practiced she did not take it as an actual act of love, but as a gift, a kind of prelude —the way a man brings flowers and a book of poems to the woman he loves.

But today in the damp heat, among the unfriendly furniture, the music sounded threatening, like the drumbeat of an army marching to war. Lene strode into the next room. Manfred did not stop playing, he did not even look up. He was totally absorbed; his concentration was so great he seemed to be in a trance. His head was thrown back, his eyes almost closed. Lene barely drew breath. She did not want to break in on him, even though a cold tongue of panic licked at her heart. She started toward a chair in the corner of the room where she often sat and listened to him, but she did not watch her steps and bumped into a low table. Something dropped to the floor with a loud sound. Manfred stopped playing, almost in the middle of a note, it seemed. He raised his hands and did not let them fall to the keys again. He looked about him aghast, like a man wakened from a deep and pleasant sleep, and then he stood up, rage darkening his face.

"What are you doing here?" he screamed, slamming down the lid over the keyboard. His voice was louder than the sound of the music had been, even louder than the sound of the cover crashing down. Lene had never seen him like this.

"What do you want?" he cried, his voice high like a woman's. "I've told you never to interrupt me when I'm practicing. Never, do you hear me? Never! Especially with noise, all at once, like a sneak, like a thief . . ." He could not quite bring out coherent sentences.

"Has something happened?" he asked, trying to get control of himself again. "Did war break out? Have they killed Hitler?"

"No, no, no," Lene said. "Forgive me, please do. It was nothing much. A conversation I had with Emma. I just spoke to her." He had frightened her and nearly driven every other concern out of her head.

"Couldn't that wait?" he asked, and his voice was almost normal again. "What's so important about a stupid conversation with your sister that makes you come barging in here while I'm practicing?"

"Emma wants to keep Clara," she said. "She wants to take her away from me. Oh, Manfred—what will I do?"

Manfred suddenly recognized his wife. He saw that it was Lene who stood before him. Lene in a light summer maternity dress, her dark hair combed back from her forehead, her eyes brimming with tears.

"I'm sorry," Manfred said. "I didn't know it was you. It was a shock to see you. I told you never to do that to me. Never."

"I know, I know." Unable to hold the tears back any longer, she flung herself against him. "I'm sorry," he whispered, holding her tightly to contain her sobbing. He looked down over her head at the piano, hoping he hadn't damaged anything when he banged down the lid. Street sounds climbed along the façade of the house and filtered into the room. The language was incomprehensible. Even the horns of the cars sounded French.

"Forgive me," he said. "I was so deep in my work. Please forgive me."

"I must go to Florence," Lene said in a voice still quivering with tears and muffled by his shoulder. "I'll fetch the child myself. I hope you won't mind."

"As long as the doctor agrees. You musn't endanger your health or the baby's life. Remember you're pregnant."

"That's hard to forget."

"I thought travel frightened you?"

"Only if it's to Germany. But Italy—even under the Fascists— is relatively benign. I might learn to fear the French, but never the Italians."

He kissed her face and tasted her salty tears. "May I finish my work now?" he asked.

His hand rested on the instrument. Lene wanted him to come with her out into the hot light of the street, out of the dismal apartment. She craved ice cream, something sweet and rich, and wanted to sit with him eating it at a small table. But he had already moved back into the embrace of his music. He was there—his one hand still rested on her neck—but he was *not* there. That was how it always was. A part of his strength was kept from her, unavailable, reserved for his work.

Lene went out alone and ate a dish of coffee ice cream with a rich bittersweet chocolate sauce. She sat under a leafy tree on a busy boulevard, trying to see it through the eyes of, say, Pissarro. She had loved this city in the days when she was a visitor; now it oppressed her. The great long blocks of buildings were too huge, looked too much alike. The people were hostile and abrupt. They made no effort to understand her schoolgirl French. She spent her time alone or among other refugees, even though she felt little sympathy for most of them and had made no friends.

The sound of Manfred's piano seemed to follow her. She had often wondered why there were no complaints from the neighbors. Perhaps the walls were thick, perhaps those around them were deaf, perhaps they worked during the daylight hours when he did all his playing. Lene listened for the language of home—it was the only reason she frequented the refugee cafés. She needed to hear German spoken now and then if only to feel some connection to the living world around her.

It was midafternoon and the place was largely empty. The news-paper readers were the most prominent early arrivals. They de-voured every line of print in several languages, hoping for a sign, for some news that might give them hope. Lene ordered a demitasse. She felt as she had back home in Frankfurt among the Bohemians. Most of those who passed her on their way to the rear of the place knew her and nodded a greeting. Few ever sat beside her. She was not counted among the intellectuals; she was a housewife, a preg-nant woman, wife of Manfred Solomon. She was not politically engaged like her Aunt Eva, who lived nearby and still bustled among the various left-wing groups, arguing and pounding the table. Lene held no strong opinions on any subject.

A French novel was in her lap. She carried it with her in her pocketbook all the time so that she would have something to read. It shielded and protected her, but it did not really help her French, as it was meant to do.

A shadow crossed her table, rested on the page of her novel, held fast. Lene was murmuring the words of an incomprehensible sen-tence, trying to make them come out right, first in French, then in translation. "Lene!" a familiar voice said, and she looked up into a face she knew but did not for an instant recognize.

Paul Leopold took her hand from the pages of the French novel and kissed it. Old, familiar gesture! He sat down beside her. A spasm shook him, and he began to cough into a gray rag of a handkerchief. He turned away from her, and Lene had a moment to compose her face and cover up the disbelief it mirrored. She looked at his body while his face was averted. The clothes were as fine as ever, clean and pressed and of the best quality. But they no longer fit the man. And when he stopped coughing and turned toward her, she saw the ravages of illness on his face: the eyelids so swollen that his eyes were nearly invisible; the mustache, once trim and neat, now like a tattered brush; the hair thin and sparse like the last long grasses of winter, stuck to a damp, pale forehead.

"Paul," Lene whispered.

He smiled, wheezing all the time. "Damn hay fever," he said, and his smile put the old face back together again for an instant. He summoned the waiter and ordered a drink.

"Make that two—doubles!" he called after him. "I'm not well at all," he said, but his tone was jaunty.

"Did you just arrive?"

"I've been traveling around. All over. After Austria fell—let's not talk about it. How are you?"

"Pregnant. Married."

"I didn't notice. You know my wife is dead."

"How would I know that?"

"She was getting better. We all thought she'd recover. She was up and walking around, she went into the town, the nurses thought she was trying to escape. They called me and I went there and found her looking amazingly well. We spent three days together, it was like old times, and then I left. Two weeks later they called me. She was dead. One night she'd hemorrhaged in her sleep and choked. She died suffocated by her own blood."

He had obviously told the story many times. He drank his first drink quickly but lingered for a moment or two over the second one. His hands shook less now. He called the waiter over. "I might as well take a bottle," he said.

"You're fat," he told Lene.

"I'm pregnant," she said. "You weren't listening."

"You found a father. That was what you wanted. Who is the lucky man?"

"Manfred Solomon."

"The pianist?"

"You know him?"

"I've heard of him. Music is not my strong point." He poured himself a full glass of Calvados. "I must catch up," he said. "It's already three o'clock and I'm still sober. That won't do at all. It gives me the shakes and makes a bad world look even more terrible."

"I seem to remember that you *always* thought things were hopeless."

"I have discovered that there are degrees of hopelessness. Both inside and outside of myself. There is the hopelessness of three in the night, and the hopelessness of three in the afternoon, let alone that of seven o'clock in the morning. By then nothing helps. There is the hopelessness of seeing Germany fall to the Nazis, and the hopelessness of Austria falling to Germany . . ."

"You're not looking well, Paul."

"That's hardly news, but thanks for telling me."

"You're drinking too much . . ."

"I knew I could count on you for moral uplift. I told you I am a very sick man." He drank greedily. "How can you bring a child into this world?" he asked.

"We're going to America."

"That's no answer, my dear. I don't believe in America. She is a state of mind, and going there destroys the mind. I have friends who have gone there and write me melancholy letters. I answer them by return mail, saying that they are lucky, Europe is doomed. They respond by hanging themselves by the bedsheet in their hotel rooms. Hollywood, New York—what dreadful places to exit from. If one must die, one should at least die in this city where the sun sparkles on the Seine and the trees shiver gaily above the heads of the pretty girls. That's the last view I'd want to have before I knocked over the chair."

"It sounds as though you'd given it some thought."

"I think about death all the time. But there's no need for me to kick over any chairs—nature will come to my rescue. My liver is almost gone. God needs to give me only a tiny shove. I just hope that He'll let me finish my novel."

"You're still writing novels?"

"And you're still dubious?" Paul looked at her gravely. "I know what I'm doing. I've discovered that it's no longer possible to report on current events. They're so terrible, they defy interpretation. I began this novel the day after the *boches* marched into Vienna. They were greeted by tens of thousands of my countrymen, all of them waving the swastika, beside themselves with happiness. *I* had to leave in the dark of night, on the last train, with only the clothes on my back. On that journey I saw that what I wanted to say could be said only in the name of fiction, that the truth of our situation can be told only in allegory."

"What's your novel about?"

"I don't want to talk about it."

Lene looked offended. "After so long an introduction you won't even tell me your subject?"

"My subject is the human condition," he said grandly. "The novel will be about a small corner of the world, a corner I know. It will be 'historical,' but more I won't say."

"I'm amazed at you. *You*, the person who always talked about everything, whose life was centered on the café where there was nothing *but* talk! But you still come to the café, I see."

"One reason I won't consider going to America is the absence of cafés in that country. You're right about me, talk has always been more natural to me than even sleep. Tell me, Lene, do you fear the loss of your mother tongue? Do you think you'll be able to live in America with a new language after—what is it, thirty-five years— spent with an old one?"

"I'm not a writer. I'm not even a talker. I'm a mother and a wife, and Manfred speaks through his music. He can play for the Hotten-tots . . ."

"Of course!" Paul Leopold cried mockingly, "Manfred Solomon, the pianist, speaks the universal language. He may be stupid, but everyone understands him."

"I believe you're jealous, Paul."

"I believe you're right, Lene."

He had, by now, consumed half the bottle of Calvados. The café was beginning to fill up inside.

"I must go and join my friends and compatriots," Paul said. "At this hour they expect me to sit with them and amuse them. You're welcome too."

"It's time for me to leave. Manfred will be done practicing and I have to prepare dinner."

Paul rose heavily. It was clear from the way he moved that he was very ill. His face had grown white, and he held on to the chair for a minute, then the ironic smile reappeared on his face. *"Küss' die Hand,"* he said and lifted Lene's hand to his lips in a perfectly executed gesture.

Lene walked down the street, but her steps were slow. She did not feel like returning to the dark apartment. She'd ask Manfred to take her out to dinner.

Before long, she realized she was lost. Anxious and tired, she hailed a taxi. She gave the driver an address and realized only when she heard him repeat it that the address was Eva's.

Eva was at home, writing letters. "Come in, come in, my child," she greeted Lene, truly happy to see her. Eva lived in a furnished room in a house owned by a trusted French friend. She had nothing in the way of possessions, her job was well beneath her capabilities, but her circle of acquaintances was immense and not a day went by that she did not see at least a dozen people. "Let me make you some coffee," she said.

"Don't bother," said Lene, and suddenly a long, low sob like a child's escaped her. Eva looked at her, startled, and immediately put her arms around her.

"There, there," she said, "tell me what's wrong. Everyone else does."

"It's been one of those days," Lene said a little sheepishly. "First I had a conversation with Emma, who wants to keep Clara, then Manfred screamed at me as I've never been screamed at before, then I met Paul Leopold at a café, looking like death. Then I got lost and ended up here. What shall I do, Aunt Eva?"

"About which of your troubles?"

"Clara. There's nothing much I can do to save Paul, and I'll have to learn to live with Manfred's temper."

"No woman should 'learn to live' with any man's rage."

"I thought I'd go to Florence and fetch her myself."

"But don't go in a fury. You might be wrong. Are you *certain* she wants to keep her?"

"She said she loved her better than I did."

"Poor thing."

"She was never your favorite."

"That doesn't mean I can't feel sorry for her. Such a sad life. She thinks the child will provide an anchor. Don't let her keep her—she might end up becoming a slave, like Emma."

"Emma a slave?"

"Yes, she has a slavish nature. She likes to be under the control of others. She has never thought anything through, she takes on the protective coloring of those around her." Eva sighed. "Shall I go with you?"

"No, thanks, Aunt Eva. I'm capable of going by myself. I'll take your advice, though."

"I'm sorry about Paul Leopold," Eva said. "He was a wonderful journalist. When he wrote for the *Frankfurter Zeitung* I never missed a single one of his pieces. What's the matter with him?"

"He's in exile." Lene did not realize until after she had said it how truly she had spoken.

"We're *all* in exile," Eva said.

"What's to become of us?" Lene asked.

"We can't afford to worry about it. We must simply stay ahead of the hangman, trying to save as many others as we can. You go and have your baby. There'll be so much death when the war comes that every sign of life will be a blessing."

"You think we'll have war?"

"I'm certain of it. But let's not talk about it now. I have something happy to tell you. I had a letter from Lore yesterday. She and Jacob are coming to Paris for a visit next weekend. I thought we'd all have dinner together. A little celebration. God knows when we'll be able to have another."

Lene was late getting home. Manfred was napping on the couch and did not chastise her. He was sorry for the scene he had made, and they ate a quiet dinner in a small bistro nearby.

Jacob and Lore arrived at noon the following Saturday. Eva had gone to a great deal of trouble to find a restaurant for their family reunion. She wanted the occasion to be memorable, for she was certain that they would never meet like this again. She bought an album with roses on the cover so that they could all write down a verse or a prophesy, and she told Julia to bring her camera and make certain she had plenty of film.

The restaurant where they met, in a back room all to themselves, was owned by a friend of Eva's landlord, a staunch and stubborn Parisian who had fought with the Loyalists in Spain. There were seven of them: Julia Wertheim, Benno Süsskind, Lene and Manfred Solomon, Eva, and the guests of honor.

They were served *saucissons* with a sharp mustard sauce, and a most delicate cold leek-and-potato soup with a mysterious hint of curry. The salad was fresh garden greens; the leg of lamb was fragrant with garlic and accompanied by *petits pois*, small roast potatoes and an excellent red wine. For dessert there was a meringue and *fraises du bois*.

Lore and Jacob captivated all the guests. Happiness crowned them like a halo. Lene had never seen her uncle so much in tune with his surroundings. He had lost the brusqueness of his lonely years, his laughter was clearer, his smile gentler. He seemed completely at ease for the first time in his life. Lore's openness and warmth charmed everyone. Lene particularly liked her.

"You look years younger!" Julia said to Jacob.

"It's all my wife's doing," he replied, "and you know, I never worked as hard as I do now. I keep the accounts at her refugee agency and I've learned Dutch and I know how to cook and I've started a new, smaller library. If the Nazis don't invade Holland, my life will have changed for the better permanently." He took Lore's hand. "And even if we have to flee again, these years will have been happy enough to last through whatever happens."

Julia always scrutinized the faces of her companions with unblinking eyes. She was well aware that she looked older than her years. She smoked too much and had spent too many unhappy nights. She was thin, but she worried constantly about her figure, dieting excessively whenever she gained a pound or two. Her hair was dyed red and frizzy, and there was mascara under her eyes. Her work had been banned in Germany, and this gave her a certain cachet, but she had not written a serious book for some time now and was trundling around Paris after yet another lover. "Don't bring him," Eva had told her. "I didn't intend to," Julia had said petulantly.

Benno had moved to Switzerland with his parents. Elias Süsskind had become curator of the drawing collection at the Basel Museum, and Benno was finishing an article, "Neoclassic Revival: What Are Its Perimeters ?," for which he was doing research in Paris. It was to be published in England. Eva was amazed that there were still people wandering the streets of Europe pursuing elusive scholarly subjects. Benno had remained fat and good-natured, and his suit was still wrinkled and baggy. He found the restaurant exceptionally good. "I shall have to remember it," he said. "Next time I'm in Paris, I'll make sure to come here."

"Do you think there'll be a next time?" Lene asked.

Benno looked puzzled. "I have a new project in mind," he said, "and it'll require a period of study in the Louvre. Ucello's 'Battle of San Romano'—"

"Oh, Benno," Julia cried, "that isn't what we're talking about. There might be war!"

"War will put an end to Hitler," Benno said, "though it may take a while."

"So you *do* know a little of what's going on," said Eva.

"We must talk about happy things," said Lene. "We aren't here to moan and groan but to celebrate Jacob and Lore's fifth anniversary!"

"There's little else to cheer about," said Lore. "None of us can close our eyes to the reports in the papers. And they don't tell the worst."

"Before it's over, Hitler will have staged a *Götterdämmerung* the likes of which has never been seen," said Jacob.

"What makes you say that?" Manfred had been aroused from his thoughts by the mention of *Götterdämmerung*.

"He'll surely turn on Russia eventually, and repeat Napoleon's mistake. The Wehrmacht will turn to ice. I can give you the whole scenario. First Czechoslovakia, then Poland, and finally Mother Russia."

"And the Allies will let him?" Lene asked.

"Until he attacks *them*. There's no taste for war here, the French think they're safe behind their Maginot Line. And England lost a whole generation in the 1914 war. They'll try to appease Hitler."

"That's a mistake," Eva said.

"I've been offered a job in a museum in America," Benno said. "Shall I take it?"

"Of course, you must," Lene said. "What a question to ask, Benno. There are people begging for jobs to allow them to emigrate."

"But it's such an unscholarly country . . ."

"Which museum?"

"It's in a place called Brooklyn on the eastern coast, near Boston, I think. Boston is a cultivated place, I hear."

"I'd love to go," Julia said. "You ought to say you have a wife and take me, Benno."

"I've already sent them all the information on myself . . ."

"I was only teasing." But Julia's laughter was contradicted by her drawn face. "I *would* love to go to America, though. It's a wild and woolly place. Everything here has fallen apart. My work's not going well—not going at all, in fact. I'm thirty-six and never been married. I have no children, no hope of ever having them. No one will marry me . . ."

"You are a writer," said Eva. "That is a noble profession, you have your freedom . . ."

"And it's never too late to marry," said Lore.

"My work is not very good. The critics never praise it. I took a wrong turn somewhere . . . if only I could change my life completely!"

"Critics are often wrong," Manfred said. He was bored with the company. He thought Lene's relatives were people of little consequence, except for Edu. He drummed on the table with his fingers, keeping them loose and limber for a particularly difficult passage in the cadenza of the Emperor Concerto. The group fell silent.

"There's an angel passing through the room," said Lore.

Jacob had finished pouring the last of the wine into the glasses. Eva said, "Let us propose a toast. We must drink to Jacob and Lore on their wedding anniversary and remember to write in their album. Take pictures, Julia, take us all together and separately, and be sure you don't shake the camera."

Everyone rose, except for Lore and Jacob, and raised a glass.

"May you always be happy," said Manfred, who thought he had a talent for the *bon mot.*

"May you live together in peace and harmony," said Julia, and her eyes sparkled with tears.

"May you see an end to this madness," said Eva, "and the dawn of a better world."

"May you return home to Frankfurt one day," said Lene, "along with the rest of us, and find it to be the city you carry in your hearts."

"I drink to all that," said Benno.

They drained their glasses, wrote in the album, had their pictures taken. The sunlight flickered a last time across the room. "Catch it!" Eva cried. "We must preserve it all."

EMMA CALLED Lene as always the following Sunday. Their conversation was pointedly centered on the party for Lore and Jacob. Emma wanted to know every detail and grew exasperated when Lene could not remember what everyone wore.

"Is it so important?" Lene asked.

"No, of course not," said Emma, "but it would be fun to know. It's part of the story you're supposed to be telling me. It adds a touch of the real . . ."

"I remember the *menu,*" Lene said, and they both laughed. The good feeling between them seemed to be restored. There was no mention of the issue that was on both their minds.

"By the way," said Lene just as they were about to ring off, "I'm coming down to Florence for a visit. I'll be on the express this Thursday."

"Why?" Emma asked.

Lene could not tell her the truth. "To see you," she said, "and Clara too. I need to get away from Paris for a bit."

"What about Manfred?"

"He's practicing for a concert—as always."

"Won't he mind your leaving?"

"He's expecting an old friend from Frankfurt."

"A man or a woman?"

"A woman, I think."

"Be careful, Lene."

"No one can take my place. I have no need to fear another woman."

"I'll see you then."

Lene hung up, relieved that she had not provoked a quarrel.

The journey was long, the train hot and crowded. Lene tried to empty her mind of its concerns, to swallow the nervous fluttering in her heart. Panic, she knew, lay just behind the flutter. She concentrated on the sounds of the clacking wheels, tried to read the novel she had brought with her, gazed out the window. Her fellow passengers had the look of the dispossessed. Were they refugees, or did she merely see them with the eye of one who was herself homeless? The crowds at every station appeared to her harried and volatile as if they might at any moment break into a riot. She was afraid of being crushed and losing her baby. She arrived in Florence in a terrible state of anxiety and was so happy to see Emma waiting for her at the end of the platform that she almost decided not to make a fuss about Clara. She fell into her sister's arms, and her heartbeats slowed their pace.

They were driven to the country by the chauffeur hired for such occasions. Emma owned an American car, a Ford, and had learned to drive it but still preferred being chauffeured into the heart of the city. She and Lene talked constantly and affectionately on the drive out to the villa, christened La Favorita by its owner, and Lene felt herself relax and grow happy again. As they pulled up in front of the house, something seemed to whisper to her, "Stay here!" Why not remain here in this beautiful place, mother to her children, sister to Emma, all of them cherished by Fräulein Gründlich who was even now beaming at them from the shade of the portico? Why not leave Manfred? The thought caught at her throat for a moment, she blushed in fright at her own audacity. How could she think such a thing? Was it because she knew she faced an unpleasant task here and was afraid of it, or was it really the sliver of a true wish, asserting itself for the first time?

Fräulein Gründlich, looking hale and tanned, could not keep the tears from her eyes when she saw Lene. They embraced.

"You look wonderful, wonderful," she said again and again, as if to reassure herself.

"It's good to see you," Lene said. "It feels as though I'm home."

Fräulein Gründlich sobbed loudly at those words. She did not like Italy. The people frightened her with their emotion-laden gestures and loud language, always just a shade away from a scream. She longed to be gone from there, settled safely in America, in a country she thought she would understand. Clara had been studying her English lessons with Fräulein Gründlich, and they had picked up some of the language together. Emma helped them out; they already knew quite a number of phrases.

Lene patted the governess on the shoulder. She felt too tired to cry. "Where's Clara?" she asked.

"Here I am, Mummy!" Clara had been in the garden picking flowers for her mother and had watched the scene at the door from behind an oleander bush. She knew that there was tension in the air, so she ran toward Lene as fast as she could and hugged her with all her strength. "You'll squeeze the baby out of me if you're not careful," Lene said, but the intensity of her daughter's affection was like a soothing balm. She had often wondered whether it wasn't possible, after all, for Emma to steal the child's love. At her worst moments she feared that Clara would say to her, "I want to stay with Aunt Emma." But the powerful embrace cleared all doubts from her mind. She felt sorry for Emma; she tried again to think of another solution. Perhaps Emma *could* be persuaded to come to America.

"Be careful not to hurt your mother," Emma said, and her voice was sharp. "Let's get out of the heat." She led the way into the living room, where the maid waited, smiling at the foreigners, her hands folded on her starched white apron.

"Take my sister's bag upstairs," Emma said to her, "and bring us something cold to drink." Theresa understood that there was pain in her mistress' heart and did not resent the gruff order. What this house needs is the presence of a man, she thought. If they had a man here, they'd be in better shape, all of them.

Emma had done a superb job in restoring the house. Each time Lene saw it, she admired her sister's taste anew. It was, she realized, not only taste but a flair for translating it into practical solutions. One felt at peace in the house the minute one entered it, no matter how fussy and spinsterish the owner herself was. Lene sometimes thought there must be a secret room where Emma stored terrible instruments of torture, which she used to vent her rage on some innocent creature from the lower depths.

Clara did not leave her mother's side for the next several hours. She sat beside her on the couch while the grownups talked. Her knees were skinned from her tree climbing and running and wrestling with the peasant children. This last was forbidden by Emma, but Fräulein Gründlich would not put a stop to it. She loved to see the child laughing and enjoying herself with others. Poor creature, she often thought, so alone in the world, growing up without a home to call her own, no sisters or brothers, no grandparents to spoil her—and a *Mischling* to boot.

The sun had begun to lose some of its strength and grow orange in the western sky when Clara finally interrupted the conversation. She had not been listening, but she had begun to hear an edge to the talk, and she knew it was time to take her mother away. "Come with me!" she said, tugging at Lene's hand. They strolled outside and Clara showed off the garden and the view from its lower end.

"Are you going to take me with you?" Clara asked.

"Of course I am," said Lene. "What do you think I'm doing here?"

"You've come for a visit."

"I've come to fetch you, so we can be ready to go to America just as soon as our papers are ready."

"Are there papers for me and Fräulein Gründlich?"

"We've applied for them."

"But how can you be sure they'll give them to you?"

"They will, Clärchen, don't worry."

"Will you go if our papers don't come?"

"Only if we know that yours are on the way. Then we might let Aunt Emma bring you over on the boat."

"You won't leave me behind?"

"Never!"

"I love Aunt Emma, but I want to be with you."

Lene put a kiss on the crown of her hair where it swirled in every direction, like water in a whirlpool.

"Aunt Emma can visit us. But I don't want her to stay with us all the time, I want to be just with you. I want to see the new baby when it comes. Aunt Emma isn't as nice to me when you're here."

"You just imagine that, Clärchen. Aunt Emma loves you dearly. But she's a nervous person."

"Fräulein Gründlich says she has lots on her mind, but you have lots on your mind too, and you're not nervous."

"I just hide it better," said Lene with a laugh.

"I heard Aunt Emma telling Fräulein Gründlich that Manfred wouldn't be nice to me."

"That's absurd," Lene said angrily. "She has no business saying that. It isn't true in the first place, and in the second, it's not right to talk in front of you about such things."

"They don't say it in front of me," Clara said, and her cheeks grew red with embarrassment. "I heard them through the door of Aunt Emma's sitting room. I wasn't going to listen, but I was walking by and I heard their voices and they were talking about *us.* Please don't tell her, Mummy! *Promise* me?"

"Don't get upset, Clärchen. I won't tell her, really I won't. Why are you so worried?"

"She'll think I'm sneaky, she'll be angry with me. She doesn't like me to tell you things like that."

"I'll pretend I never even heard what you said. I will strike it from my mind."

Clara looked so upset that Lene sat down on one of the small stone benches that lined the flagstone walk and took her on her lap, although she was ten years old and too big for that. And Clara put her head on Lene's shoulder and cried until all the sorrows on her heart had melted away.

"Is Aunt Emma ever unkind to you, baby?" Lene asked.

"She gets impatient sometimes, but Fräulein Gründlich says it's only her weak nerves and I shouldn't mind, she can't help it. So I try not to mind, even when she hollers at people."

"We'll be in America soon, all of us together and the new baby too. Be patient, all right?"

Clara nodded. Lene took the linen handkerchief from the pocket of her smock and wiped the little girl's face. The tears had left dirty streaks on her round cheeks.

"You know what, Mummy?"

"No. What?"

"Aunt Emma goes to church every week."

"She does?"

"You mustn't tell her I told you that, either. She took me several times."

"Which church?"

"The one all the Americans go to. When I asked Aunt Emma whether it was all right to go with her, she said I wasn't really Jewish. Is that true?"

"Your father isn't Jewish, but I am. We all are, Emma too, and Manfred and Omama and Uncle Andreas. Uncle Ernst, whom you don't even remember probably, is in Palestine."

"That's the land of the Bible. The minister talks about it all the time, Aunt Emma says. He spoke English and I didn't understand him, so she stopped taking me. But she tells me the stories she hears from him every Sunday."

"About God?"

"And Jesus Christ, too."

Lene sighed deeply. "It's time we left," she said.

The statement was ambiguous and Clara thought for a moment that they were leaving for Paris that very second. "I have to say good-bye," she said.

"There's time," Lene told her, and they walked hand in hand up the garden path.

"Aunt Emma said that going to church was restful," Clara said, chatty now, not telling secrets but discussing facts, reporting on the small events of her daily life. She felt completely happy again, having cried on her mother's shoulder, and confessed the thing that had weighed guiltily upon her. Lene wished she had as simple a way out of the task that faced her. "She said that one of the reasons she loved going was that she could just sit calmly and listen to the beautiful stories and sing the lovely songs. She likes the sermons too, they tell you to *be* good and to *do* good. But I was bored."

Lene was listening with only half an ear. She was, she discovered, profoundly shocked at Clara's revelations. She found it unsettling to imagine Emma sitting in church paying rapt attention to the platitudes of an Anglican cleric. And more unsettling yet to think that she discussed Manfred with everyone. If she discussed him with Gründlich, surely she discussed him with Bernard Berenson, who would spill the information out to all who came to pay their respects. Lene stopped for a minute at the top of the garden where the slopes of the hills and distant mountains were visible. Clara, beside her, reached almost to her shoulder; her face was sometimes startlingly like her father's, even though everyone always said that the child looked exactly like her. The blue eyes were Tom's, in their clarity and color, even if the way they were framed, the lids and the melancholy weight of the brows were hers.

"Where have you two been?" Emma asked when they entered the large living room, whose western end faced the garden. Lene felt that Emma had been watching them.

"We took a walk to the bottom of your beautiful garden," she said, "and sat for a while, talking to each other."

"B.B. called while you were out of the house. He would love to see you. He said, 'You know how I adore beautiful women.' It's amazing how spry he is, and he's over seventy." Emma was fussing with the flowers in a vase, picking out the dead ones, snapping off a bloom here, adding a sprig of greenery there. "And there's a telegram for you, which the postman just brought. From Paris. I suppose it's from Manfred. You've hardly left and he's already communicating with you."

"He misses me."

"He misses your care. Your ministrations and your good cuisine. You know all men are like that. And you play right into it, spoiling him madly. You'll regret it one day."

"I wish you wouldn't give me advice on marriage."

Lene wondered how she could ever have thought it would be possible to live with her sister. She took the telegram and sat down in a corner by the window to read it. Manfred had cabled that he loved her.

"It's time for Clara's bath," said Emma.

"At this hour?" Lene said.

"She bathes early here, so she's clean for dinner."

"She's not a baby anymore, Emma. I find her very grown-up. I trust you allow her to eat with the adults?"

"When there's no company."

Clara sat dangling her legs on a chair that was pulled as close as possible to her mother's. She felt protected now and knew that any attack she made on her aunt would be joined by her mother.

"Take your bath," Emma said sternly.

"I don't have to!" Clara answered sassily.

"Tell her," Emma said to her sister, her voice aquiver.

"Please do as Aunt Emma says." Lene rumpled her hair. "Go upstairs now. Fräulein Gründlich is no doubt waiting for you. When in Rome, you must do as the Romans do . . ."

"We're not in Rome, we're in Florence," said the child, and laughed at her own joke.

"Then do as the Florentines do," said her mother with a smile. "Florentines apparently bathe early."

Clara skipped across the room and up the stairs, casting an impudent look at her aunt.

Fräulein Gründlich was in her room sewing. Once upon a time it would have seemed demeaning to her to do those things that others were hired to do. She was neither cook nor laundress, chambermaid nor seamstress. She held to that belief for a long time. But when she saw Lene do the cooking and Emma help with the polishing of the silver, she realized that her own strict rules must bend as well. She lent a hand as best she could—you got better at things after a while, she noticed—and put her foot down only at doing the cooking. She felt that the *Herrschaft* had less to lose than she did. For them it was merely a matter of royalty playing at peasant games; for her it was a distinct comedown on the social ladder. Soon she'd be back among her grim ancestors, her hands rough, her mind dull. She still spent at least half an hour a day improving herself, with either Clara's English lessons or a good book.

"I'm to take my bath," Clara announced. It was always a relief to be with Fräulein Gründlich. She understood things better than the other adults, her life didn't take place outside the house. She focused on domestic details, she lived in the protected atmosphere of childhood with children and other servants. She did not get on with Theresa, but the antagonism between them remained muted, for neither spoke the other's language.

"Did you have a nice visit with your mama?" Fräulein Gründlich asked. She put her mending away carefully and tied on the apron she always wore to bathe the little girl. It had never occurred to either of them that it might be time for Clara to take her own bath —they both liked the occasion too much. The governess drew the water, kneeling on the bathmat before the great old-fashioned tub. She poured some salts into the steaming water, then sat back on her heels while Clara undressed. The child's arms and face were tanned, her knees dirty, her legs scratched. She had a well-formed body, which she dearly loved, even if it was still a little on the chubby side. She cavorted about, slyly looking into the mirror until her reflection disappeared in the mist. Fräulein Gründlich scrubbed her hard with a washcloth full of soap that smelled of lilacs. "Ouch!" said Clara when a little soap got into her eye.

"You know you must keep your eyes shut," the governess admonished her.

When the bath was over, Fräulein Gründlich held up the large white bath sheet in front of her as she waited for the child to climb out of the tub. She wrapped her in the thick terry cloth and rubbed her dry until Clara's skin tingled and she was pink all over.

At seven-thirty they both appeared in the dining room. Emma seemed nervous and criticized Theresa. Lene was morosely silent. Both Clara and the governess felt the tension in the air. Fräulein Gründlich, thinking it was unhealthy to ingest food under these circumstances, tried to chat with Clara about trivialities. But the child kept her eyes glued on her mother.

Dessert was a wonderfully delicate peach cake. It was one of the cook's specialties, made with fresh ripe peaches from the orchard below the olive grove.

"B.B. expects us for Sunday dinner," Emma said as Theresa served the espresso.

"Really?" Lene said, in a distracted manner.

"It's a great distinction to be invited to B.B.'s Sunday dinners," Emma said. "I have been there for only a few of them, but they are always gala events. It will be an experience for you."

"I won't be here Sunday," Lene said.

"What do you mean? I thought you were staying for a week at least. You said . . ."

"I find I can't stay the week. I must get home to Manfred. He's all alone, and besides, we might hear at any moment about our visas."

"You get a telegram from your husband and race home to him," Emma said. "I don't understand why you even came. What did the telegram say that was so important? Did it give a date for your ocean voyage?"

"The telegram has nothing to do with it," Lene said. "It was merely a reminder—which I sometimes need—to tell me where my place is."

"Woman's place is in the home," Emma said with all the sarcasm she could muster.

"Don't be angry with each other," Fräulein Gründlich said, even as she realized that the power she had once had over them was gone.

"My place is with my husband," Lene said. "And I don't want to hear any more about it."

But Emma, driven by her demons, fighting a battle she knew to be hopeless, could not give up. "Your husband is a parasite," she said, her voice low, as if only a scream could reach her niece, whose big eyes showed her fright. "He married you to make you into a slave. It's disgusting to watch . . ."

"Enough!" Lene said, and her voice, too, was quiet.

"Allow me to finish. He married you because he can exploit you and because you have money. I know this for a fact. His adoptive father left him nothing because he did not trust him. He gave it all away to charity. Edu told me, and you know that Edu, gossip that he is, always turns out to tell the truth. Manfred needs your money!"

"Emma . . ." Fräulein Gründlich warned.

"I forbid you to go on," said Lene. She felt a rage grow within her that threatened to erupt in a bellowing scream. But the sight of Clara, shrunk in her chair, her lower lip trembling, gave her the strength to swallow it. She balled her hands into fists to keep from slapping her sister. Years of rage swept through her. Emma had teased her like this once years ago, though she could not remember where and when it was; she remembered only the rage and the face set in a mask of arrogance and contempt. She did not see the fearful bravado Fräulein Gründlich saw.

"You leave me alone," Lene hissed, "do you hear? I won't allow you to slander my husband and defame my marriage. And I won't allow you to take away my child!"

"Stop it!" Fräulein Gründlich cried. "The child is listening."

"Go upstairs with her," Emma said.

"Don't," Lene countermanded, "she can hear us. I will live my life without advice from you. Who do you think you are, telling me these lies?" She was angry enough to put into words, for the first time, the thing that would wound her sister the most. She began to articulate Otto's name. She wanted to use him to avenge her own hurt. But she could not. At the last moment she knew that to use the ultimate weapon was a cruelty of which she was incapable. She cursed Emma with an angry word. But it was only a word.

"I will take the child upstairs myself," Emma said. "There's no excuse for your language."

"I'm certain she'll hear more of it in her life."

"No need to begin here and now. This is my house." Emma got up and took Clara by the arm. The girl pulled away, but Emma grabbed her wrist in a grip like an iron vise. "You're hurting me!" Clara cried, though it was not pain she felt, only the unyielding clutch of her aunt's cool hand.

"I'm not hurting you and I won't if you obey me," Emma said. "You are a nasty, ungrateful child."

"Mummy says I can stay," Clara said.

"I say you go upstairs." Emma began to tug at her niece to try to move her out of the chair, but the child went limp and sank to the floor, heavy as a sack of potatoes. Emma, her spare body tensed with furious strength, began dragging her toward the hall. "Leave me alone!" Clara screamed. "You're not my mother! You can't tell me what to do! I want to stay with my mother! I hate you!"

Emma slapped her very hard across the cheek. Clara's wail rose to a shriek. She relished the drama she was creating; for a moment she knew she was faking. The slap had stung her, but she had hurt her aunt more. Her scream drowned out her thoughts.

"Let go of her," Lene said, but Emma had already relaxed her hold. Clara scrambled to her feet and dove into her mother's lap. She wept into the bulging belly while Lene stroked her head. Emma had gone into the living room, where she sat in the dark. Fräulein Gründlich's face was distorted by helplessness. Lene led her daughter upstairs to her room and sat for a while without speaking. Clara undressed and slipped into her pajamas. The night smelled of summer, of mown hay and a multitude of flowers. Clara was very tired. "I love you, Mummy," she whispered. She felt washed clean through and through by her tears, and a note of triumph buzzed in her chest. She was too young to feel pity.

Lene sat next to the bed and watched Clara drift off into sleep. She missed Manfred. In the silence of the bedroom she thought of what she had done and felt remorse. It was true that Emma's life was empty beside her own. She had neither husband nor child, she was a creature haunted by unfulfilled dreams. Lene's anger vanished. Pity for her sister took its place. But that was only because she had won her point.

Downstairs Gründlich sat with Emma, who was dry-eyed. The old governess held Emma's hand in her own, and the words she uttered were like a bird's cooing. She had always known how to give comfort.

Two days later Lene, accompanied by Clara and Fräulein Gründlich, boarded the train for Paris. Clara was a little afraid that her aunt would make a scene, but she didn't. She did not even cry. She only said, "Remember me." As the train pulled slowly out of the station, Clara called out to her aunt, "Come to visit us in America!" Emma walked rapidly alongside the train until she could no longer keep pace. She waved and blew Clara a kiss. The child watched her until the train rounded a curve and she could no longer see her.

IN A SECRET corner of Manfred's heart he had hoped that his sister-in-law Emma would be successful in her efforts to keep Clara with her. Now he felt guilty, but he had had no experience with children and did not know what to say to his stepdaughter. He was convinced that she had the power to look into his heart and discover his secret. He was frightened, too, at the prospect of seeing his own child come into the world, and he kept his distance from Lene as though she carried a bomb under her skirts.

The month of August later seemed to all of them a blank, a hole in their lives between past and future. As a matter of fact, everyone went about the daily business of living quite normally. It was only that thought was suspended and every act overshadowed by the agonizing wait for the visa. Manfred practiced longer hours than usual, Fräulein Gründlich and Clara visited the Louvre again and again, Lene sat in the musty living room of their apartment and read French novels.

The visas arrived on August 29, a Monday. The call from the American consulate came punctually at nine-thirty in the morning. That night they held a small celebration, drinking champagne until they were giddy and the world spun about their heads. They had a little less than three weeks to wind up their affairs, having booked passage on the *Nieuw Amsterdam* leaving Boulogne on September 17.

Lene called Uncle Edu to tell him the good news. All efforts to reach Andreas were in vain.

"Come and see me before you leave," Edu said. "God knows when and if we'll ever see each other again. I'll pay for your trip. But leave the child and your husband in Paris."

Lene made no reply. The remark did not strike her as tyrannical and thoughtless until she repeated it to Manfred.

"What an awful man your uncle is," Manfred said. "I hope you're not going to take him up on his offer?"

"I did think of going to see him, yes."

"After what he said?"

"None of us can tell what the future holds. I owe him a great deal; we all do."

"*I* don't. I'm quite capable of getting along without him. You're my wife now and don't need him."

"Who do you think provides the money to pay Gründlich?"

"I'm glad you brought that up. I really think we don't need her . . ."

"*I* need her. Not only do I need her, I love her. What will become of her if we leave her? She's too old to find a job and the Nazis will make trouble for her because of her past with us. Whatever happens, I'm taking her to America."

"But we have, as you just said, no idea what it'll be like . . ."

"There's no use trying to figure *that* out until we get there. And Uncle Edu's support can only be a help. I'm going to Zürich tomorrow."

Edu's chauffeur met her at the railroad station to drive her to Edu's house in suburban Küsnacht. The weather was sultry. It was one of those windless days, rare in that part of the country, when the cool air from the glaciers does not reach into the valleys, and the water of the lakes is tepid and smooth as glass.

Edu welcomed her with a kiss. He had re-created his Frankfurt house as best he could. His books and paintings and gobelins were arranged in comparable order, the garden bloomed with flowers of the same sort, the family photographs on his desk stood in precisely the places they had always stood. He served her a glass of sherry from his crystal decanter. Lene was aware of a single great difference casting its pall over the whole, and that was the silence of country life. On the Bockenheimer Landstrasse one never lost the sense of being in the city. There was traffic beyond the gate, and the walls that surrounded the garden abutted on other gardens. On a winter evening the lights of Frankfurt twinkled through the bare trees; in summer one heard the sirens of police cars and ambulances and the bells of the trolley cars. But here in Küsnacht on the shores of Lake Zürich, the country stillness permeated everything. There was a meadow between the road and the front gate, and a woods to the north. The garden was bounded by a very high stone wall with pieces of broken glass set on its rim; here and there the lake waters glimmered through the stately beeches. Lene felt marooned on a desert island. She was uncertain whether this feeling was pleasant or frightening. Edu seemed determined to spend the rest of his life making time stand still. He supervised the maids and the cook and gardeners and went to his office in Zürich every day to look after his affairs.

"I'm happy to see you," he said to Lene. "You look well. Pregnancy seems to become you."

"I'm a peasant girl at heart," Lene said. Edu showed her a Cézanne landscape he had just bought. It was an unfinished work; Lene thought that every stroke on the canvas had cost the painter untold hours of pain. "I don't like it," she said, "it's too fierce."

"What do you mean?" Edu did not wish to hear critical comments about his purchases.

"I have the feeling that there's something in his struggle that's inhuman," Lene said. She saw an expression of pursed disdain forming around her uncle's mouth. "Forgive me, Edu, but I'm always on edge these days. It affects all my responses. I can't find comfort in the signs of struggle."

"Have you heard anything from Andreas?"

"Now and then there's a letter, disjointed and scraggly. I think Kurt, his lover, is staying with him. Why won't he come out?"

"I've done my best to try to bring him here, but he seems determined, as far as I can tell, to do *nothing* on his own behalf."

Edu did not look at Lene as he said this. It occurred to her that he was making excuses to salve his conscience. The thought was disloyal and she banished it as soon as she could.

"And Mama?" Lene asked.

"She's still safe in the sanatorium. God knows how long that will last. I hear the Nazis plan to begin a program of euthanasia—to rid the country of its parasitic elements . . ."

"She might be better off dead."

"That's not for me to say."

Lene again felt the chill of his presence.

"Fräulein Gründlich worries about Andreas all the time. 'My poor child,' she says. She writes to him every week."

"She's a good person, Lene. I'm glad you have her."

The conversation was brittle, as if they were speaking the lines of a play or were being overheard.

"She thinks that Andreas is staying only because he'll not leave Kurt," said Lene.

"If that's true—and it may well be—it wouldn't be the first time that such a thing has happened. I wish sometimes that I'd known such a powerful love!"

Lene looked away. A mass of large black clouds threatened in the west. The maid, in a black dress and white apron, a starched cap over her hair, curtsied and announced dinner.

They sat down together at a table that was too large for just the two of them. Lene could not shake the feeling that she was taking part in a play.

"I'm not yet at home here," Edu sighed as he broke his crisp roll in half. The wine was delicate, the soup had a trace of saffron.

"Dear Lene," he said, his tone sweeter than she had ever heard it. The maid served the salad and Edu held his tongue until she was out of the room. Tears had come into his eyes. Lene had never thought him capable of such a display of emotion.

"It's hard to be exiled," he said. "I've been gone many years already, but it seems to strike me with greater and greater force as things get worse over there. I see no end in sight. My own safety is an affront. I'm doing my best to help others to leave . . ."

Lene did not want to hear any of this. It was a litany that seemed to her merely the echo of words Edu had spoken to himself in his loneliness and his guilt.

"The Swiss—I shouldn't say this aloud—are not very helpful."

The maid brought the cold salmon and the fresh-made mayonnaise and the tiny potatoes and broiled tomatoes.

"The salmon is out of this world," Lene said. "Your food has lost none of its quality. You always manage to find good cooks."

"Don't you know I cook it all myself?" Edu said, and his ironic smile made him seem familiar again because he was clearly still in charge.

"If only it were possible to bring you *all* together here," he said, "I would even put up with husbands and children. But I see you don't want me waxing sentimental. I'm sorry, Lene, I've allowed myself to fall into the trap of the aged. And I'm not yet old enough to be allowed such a luxury."

The raspberries they had for dessert were from the garden, and the *crème frêche* from the farm down the road. Lene noticed that the maid's apron was wrinkled and stained.

"Give the laundress your uniform to wash," Edu said, and his Frankfurt accent was overlaid with singsong Swiss sounds, though he did not actually speak the dialect. The woman nodded. "An unpleasant country in many ways," Edu said in English. "I take a nap now. You should also, since you're pregnant. We'll meet for tea at four-thirty."

Lene's memory filled with pictures of her childhood, she saw herself ring the bell of the gate on the Bockenheimer Landstrasse, saw Emma glancing at her watch to see if they were on time.

"I'll make certain to be punctual," she said. Edu bowed to her. For a moment he looked exactly like his brother Nathan.

"It would be better if Mama were dead," she said.

"Her heart is very strong," said Edu.

Alone in her room, overlooking the lake, Lene heard the drops of the thunderstorm's rain slap against the window pane. The lake had turned black, but the storm was passing to the south; there was blue sky just beyond the meadow. Lene had wished for thunder and lightning, she wanted to hide from the violence of a storm. She ached to go to bed and pull the covers over her head, but there was no need for it now, and if ever she did it—just like that—she wouldn't be able to control it, she might not know when to stop.

She did not want to sit still waiting for the clock to move on, she was nervous and too full of food. The room she was in had been her grandmother's, it was replete with little mementos of Hannchen Wertheim. They made her think of Frankfurt, of home. If only she could go back just one more time! Lene slipped out of the room, down the stairs, like a thief. She felt that the Swiss maids were watching her, but she could not bear the little room at that moment. The telephone was in Edu's study on the first floor. Lene had no trouble finding it. She sat at the desk, knowing that it was not the right thing to do, knowing that Edu would be angry if he saw her at his desk. She asked for her Paris number in a whisper, trying not to look at the letters scattered about or the open pages of a ledger. She turned away and stared at the wall, waiting for the phone in the apartment to ring and then waiting for someone to answer it. Fräulein Gründlich's voice sounded far away and tentative. "Hello? Hello?" she said.

"It's me, Lene. Is everything all right?"

"We're fine," said the governess, still distant but less tentative now. She was afraid of the French on the phone. "Mr. Solomon is out," she said, speaking rapidly so as not to waste money. "He won't be back until this evening, he said. Clara isn't here either. She's playing with her friend Yvette, downstairs. I thought it was all right to let her go, the mother's home. How is your Uncle Eduard?"

"The same as ever, just a tiny bit older-looking, and a touch milder. But he makes me remember Frankfurt and that saddens me. I keep thinking that I'll go to the station tomorrow and, against all reason, buy a ticket to Frankfurt, change trains in Basel and go home. I want to see Andreas, I want to visit my mother. I even feel like going back to Tom. I don't want to go to America! I'm afraid of America!"

"Don't do anything foolish, child," Fräulein Gründlich said. "There's no use you getting into trouble there. It won't help to endanger yourself. Promise me to be sensible? You have a baby to think about, and Clara, too . . ."

"Emma would take her in a minute, if I were gone."

"She needs her own mother. What's the weather like there? It's very hot here, and no sign of rain."

"We had a thunderstorm nearby."

Lene heard the rustle of footsteps on the stairs. "I must go now," she said, "I'll be home late tomorrow night. Give Manfred my love, and Clara, too."

The maid entered the room. She was wearing a light-blue uniform now. She stood for a minute looking at Lene, undecided whether she should speak.

"I'm sorry to have disturbed you," she said finally. "I heard a sound in Herr Wertheim's study and did not know it was you."

"I'm finished," Lene said. "It was necessary to call home."

"There is a phone in the kitchen downstairs. Herr Wertheim is very particular."

"I know that," said Lene and went for a walk in the garden. The sun was out and she sat on a bench and looked very carefully at everything around her, but she saw it all through the scrim of her anxiety. The wind bent the tops of the trees, turning the leaves from silver to gray and back again.

There was company for tea and in the evening Uncle Edu took her to a concert in Zürich. "It would be nice to have you beside me all the time," he said on the drive back to Küsnacht. "You know, you've never had a proper escort."

Lene was back in Paris the following night, an envelope with 200 Swiss francs in her handbag, a gift from Edu.

THE DAY they left for Boulogne was crisp and clear. Lene remembered it later as windy too, for she kept recalling the tricolor waving merrily at all the stations along the way to the sea. There was just a trace of autumn in the air. Clara was excited at the prospect of seeing the ocean for the first time, imagining great roiling waves such as she had read about in books. She was doomed to disappointment. The busy harbor of Boulogne was so full of ships that the water was barely visible. Besides, there was England, just across the way, and no sign of high waves or an unlimited horizon. The *Nieuw Amsterdam*, however, was immense, which made up a little for dashed hopes. Clara had not imagined such a great ship; it was like a whole village, floating in the harbor so far out that it was necessary to take a small boat to reach it. There were no sailing ships anywhere. Clara had had a persistent vision of the *Niña*, *Pinta* and *Santa María*, which she had studied about with the crippled English teacher who had taught her "I am, you are, he, she and it is . . ."

The *Nieuw Amsterdam* exceeded Fräulein Gründlich's expectations too, and her first sight of it brought with it the recognition that they were really going to a faraway place, crossing a vast sea to a new continent. The excitement that grips travelers embarking on adventurous voyages was suddenly hers—Fräulein Gründlich felt the age-old thrill and hugged Clara to her as they stood on the deck in the bright sunshine, looking back toward the shore.

"It'll be so exciting," she said to the child. "Are you looking forward to it too?"

Clara put a kiss on the governess' cheek. The wind blew her hair into a tangled mass.

"Can I wear braids when we get to America?" Clara asked. "Or get my hair cut very short?"

"Wait and see how the other children wear theirs."

Clara and Fräulein Gründlich shared a stateroom not far from Lene and Manfred's. Their cabin had a real porthole and was just the way Clara had seen it in the movies, compact and neat, with everything bolted to the floor and a double-decker bunk. "Can I please sleep on top?" she asked, and Fräulein Gründlich was only too glad to agree.

"Do you think we'll have a stormy sea?" Clara said. "I want to see some real waves."

"Not me, thank you," Fräulein Gründlich told her, "I'll take the waves as I see them in pictures and hope for a smooth crossing."

Clara was too excited to go to sleep. She kept looking out of the porthole, trying in the dark to catch a glimpse of something. At Southampton she watched the cranes loading boxes and luggage onto the ship in huge nets and heard the mournful toot of the foghorns. The next morning when they were on the high seas at last, Clara discovered to her amazement that the huge ship seemed all at once much smaller when you stood at the railing in the midst of the immensity of sea and sky, watching other boats pass on the horizon, mere specks on the line that separated the blue sea from the blue sky. Clara found herself a deck chair and sat down to write in her diary, trying to capture the important things, like the wonderful game room filled with pinball machines and mechanical football games, and the swimming pool on D-deck, which spilled its waters sloppily over the edge whenever the ship pitched a little. Clara wondered what would happen if someone fell overboard and got left behind in the white wake. The things she saw and could not put into words she drew. The sky and the horizon, meeting all around her, appearing wherever she looked but changing aspect depending on the light and the time of day—this was what fascinated her most, but she could not put it into either pictures *or* words.

Clara and Fräulein Gründlich wandered about the ship as they would through a village. They found the nursery where maids in white uniforms watched over a multitude of babies, and governesses with veils like those of nursing sisters tried to make conversation with one another, though they spoke different languages. "It's like the Tower of Babel in there," Fräulein Gründlich said. She kept her distance from the nursemaids. She was older by far than most of them and felt a mixture of pride and discomfort in their presence.

For Clara, the voyage was like a vacation in a grand hotel. Games of every sort were constantly being organized; there was Ping-Pong and billiards and gambling contests, including races that involved turtles trying to find their way out of a maze. She hardly saw Lene and Manfred. Lene came to say good night every evening, even when she had to leave a party in one of the glittering salons, and when she floated toward her daughter to hug and kiss her, she was like a princess descending from her castle in the heart of night. The moon coming through the porthole glinted on her pearl-and-diamond necklace. Clara would lie there, waiting for her, and lose herself in her waking dreams—imagining herself as a character in some movie she'd seen or book she'd read. Often she would think of herself in the role of an orphan who stands outside society, or a poor scullery maid looking in on the splendid doings of the rich. Of course, the maid was better off than they, being alone and unfettered by all those trappings and regulations. Sometimes she imagined herself rescued from neglect by her dashing father, more often it was *she* who rescued him from the hospital ward to which he'd been sent, burned, blinded and forgotten. Because she got her ideas from the children's movies she saw, she had romantic ideas about being an orphan or poor. It never occurred to her that it was *she*, Clara, who always ate the delicacies.

On their fourth day out, the ocean's swells grew very large, and the ship pitched and rolled so much that everyone was seasick. The floor came up to meet you wherever you walked, and people began to stay locked in their cabins. Fräulein Gründlich had taken to her bunk. Clara was still perfectly well and therefore feeling superior. When the governess dozed off from exhaustion, the little girl went out to explore the ship's passageways, which had by now become familiar to her. She wanted to find the place in the bowels of the ship where stowaways might be hiding. But what she found instead was the ship's movie theater. It was nearly empty, but the screen flickered temptingly, and so she slipped inside. This, too, was forbidden; the movie was not for children.

Clara sat down in one of the back rows. Within minutes she was mesmerized. The movie clearly took place in America, for it showed a city with fire escapes exactly like those she had seen in pictures of New York. There were a lot of boys with smudges on their faces and a handsome young man and a pretty young girl who talked a lot at the end of a pier in the midst of this city, which was indeed New York. Clara did not understand much of what was said, but she followed the action avidly, and every gesture, every detail of the movie's set impressed itself on her mind.

It was calmer the next day, but the wind was still strong. Fräulein Gründlich heard the news first. "We've been through the edge of a great hurricane," she told Clara. "They say it did terrible damage in America. We're lucky we only caught such a little bit. Though it was too much for me." She still felt shaky and uncertain on her usually sturdy legs.

The *Nieuw Amsterdam* docked at the port of New York toward midnight. Clara, who had been asleep, woke up when the familiar sounds of the ship's motors and the familiar ship's pitch ceased. The stillness was broken only by the clanging sounds of shore. Cranes were at work again; stevedores shouted in a new tongue. But there was little to see out the porthole except oily water with garbage floating on top. She had so hoped for a glimpse of the Statue of Liberty, for sight of the skyscrapers, for the look of New York from the sea. It wasn't worth waking Fräulein Gründlich. Clara took out her diary and by the light above her bunk wrote in it: "Our trip has ended in New York. All I can see is the dirty water of the harbor, but tomorrow morning the sun will rise for us all on a brand new country." She went back to sleep contentedly.

ON OCTOBER 28 the National Socialist government issued a decree banishing all "stateless" Jews. On November 7 a third secretary in the German embassy in Paris, Ernst vom Rath, was shot by a seventeen-year-old Polish-Jewish student, Hershl Grynszpan, whose parents—Polish nationals who had lived in Hanover since 1914—had been expelled from Germany by the decree. This provided the excuse, if one was needed, for the pogrom that has gone down in history as *Kristallnacht,* the night of broken glass. Vom Rath did not actually die until November 9, the same night the Nazi leaders had planned a celebration to commemorate the fifteenth anniversary of the Beer Hall Putsch in Munich. The conjunction of the two events gave the signal to all who listened that they were free to begin in earnest the Terror against the Jews.

That night, fires flamed in almost every synagogue in Germany. The windows of Jewish shops were smashed. Ninety-one Jews were killed, over 7,000 Jewish businesses were looted and destroyed, and 26,000 male Jews were arrested and sent to the concentration camps of Dachau, Buchenwald and Sachsenhausen. The streets were covered with the shattered panes of a thousand windows.

Jonah Süsskind had heard the news of Vom Rath's death on the radio. He was home, thinking about his children, alternately cursing his wife and praying for her return. He drank more than he ate, took his daily constitutional and puttered about the garden. The fact that there was very little to do there at this time of the year did not prevent him from finding some pretext to go out and check the burlap wrappings on the rosebushes or make certain the mulch around the flower beds was the proper depth. He had firmly rejected the idea, proposed to him by a Jewish colleague, of applying for a visa to some distant country where he could find work as a male nurse preparatory to taking exams and returning to the practice of medicine. He could not abandon the idea that Hildegard would come back to save him or, barring that, would put in a good word for him with the authorities. He had some savings she had not been able to get her hands on, and he could manage to live, doing an occasional furtive favor for an old patient.

When he heard the report, he knew that something terrible would surely happen now. He had become obsessed by the idea that the most logical step would be the re-establishment of ghettos. He thought that it would not be at all difficult to move the Jews who were left in and around Frankfurt back into the Altstadt, into the area where the Judengasse had once been, where they could live in a closed community, responsible only to one another, out of sight of the general population. He imagined himself a physician in this community. He would treat his patients for nothing, asking only for a roof over his head and bread on his table. Andreas, to whom he had confided this fantasy, stared at him with a startled gaze and announced that he would never submit to being herded behind the walls of a ghetto.

Evening fell, and Wiesbaden appeared quiet. Jonah went from window to window looking for the troop of Hitler Youth which had on several previous occasions painted slogans on the wall of his garden and marched past his house singing songs of hate. Hours passed and nothing seemed to happen.

Jonah lived on a quiet residential street. He was dozing in his study when the first sounds reached him. Bands of vandals were roaming the streets armed with clubs, stones, cans of gasoline, rags and boxes of matches. First they shattered windows, then they set the fires. Jonah woke up to the sounds of the mob and the light of a great conflagration. Sparks flew in the cold night air, and a charred smell crept over the city. Jonah did not know it was the synagogue that was burning, but he could tell that the fire went unchecked.

It was after midnight before the sky turned black again and the stars emerged from behind the clouds of smoke. The telephone rang. Jonah answered it automatically. The voice at the other end was hoarse. "They've burned the synagogue," the man rasped, "and they're going through the city arresting Jews, destroying their businesses, smashing windows. Save yourself!"

"Who's this?" Jonah asked, but the line was already dead.

Jonah realized then that it would not be a question of receiving a polite letter asking him to report to the city hall to be assigned to the Frankfurt ghetto. When the knock came at his door, he was ready for it. He was not afraid to die, and he was a doctor who knew how best to let death come without pain.

The knocks grew louder; there were shouts, the sound of clubs smashing at the wood. Jonah filled the syringe, as he had done a thousand times. He turned off the light and locked his study door. He put the narrow rubber tube around his upper arm and pulled it tight, using his teeth to keep his right hand free. The vein darkened, grew thick, bulged. Jonah deftly put the needle in, pressed the syringe, released the tourniquet. A sweet twittering filled his mind; it sounded like songbirds early on a spring morning. He thought of the melody from the second movement of the "Pastorale." Was it an oboe he heard, or a flute? Perhaps it was both. A loud, rushing noise like a waterfall took over and drowned the music. The roar grew louder and louder, and he no longer heard anything else. This isn't so bad, he thought, but I would like to feel the fresh water on my tongue. Then he lost consciousness.

When the SA men found him he was already dead. This angered them so much that they tore apart everything in his office. They had found nothing of value in the house. A small painting, a view of Frankfurt by Johann Friedrich Morgenstern, was removed the next day by the neighbors. No one claimed the body, and it was carted off to the Jewish cemetery to be interred by the Burial Society. They put up a small marker, which rusted and did not survive the war.

ANDREAS DID NOT listen to the radio, he no longer listened to anything but his records. Kurt had moved into the house after a visit by the Gestapo. The apartment overlooking the Main now belonged to a party official. Anna, who looked after them even though it was dangerous for her to do so, brought them all the important news.

"I think this is the final straw," she said, after hearing about the shooting of Vom Rath. "There'll be no holding them back now. They're saying they were right about the Jews. You can't go anywhere without hearing the sound of their screaming. Over and over and over they say, 'The Jews are our misfortune.' No wonder people begin to believe it. A nightmare, that's what it is."

Her round face had grown wrinkled. She was beginning to show her age, but she refused to consider retirement.

"I don't want anything to happen to you," Andreas said. "I don't want to be your misfortune."

Anna waved his concern away. "I promised your Uncle Edu I would look after you."

"You did? I never knew that."

"He's doing all he can to see that you'll not be harmed. I wish you'd leave. Why do you have to stay?"

"You know why. I can't go without Kurt, and there's no one to help *him*."

Anna sighed. Never in her life had she thought she would one day come to understand and accept such a relationship. But they had won her heart. The two men were courtly with each other, determined to preserve their dignity. They read aloud and kept regular hours. They could not be served in any restaurant, and they could not shop in many stores or sit in the Anlagen. But they held on and thought only about the day at hand.

The sound of breaking glass did not reach Andreas behind his walls and above the music he played; he did not see the synagogues burning. The West End Synagogue nearby was unaccountably spared. He went to bed as always, behind shuttered windows and locked doors.

Anna brought further news the next day. "They say the Jews have to pay damages. I heard that on the street. They say the fire departments didn't raise a finger to put the fires out. And they say that a lot of Jews are being arrested. I saw a group of them on the street, being led away. I know they were Jews. I recognized Mr. Horowitz and Mr. Ettinger. It's something I'll never forget, that sight. People stood and watched. Some even cheered. There's no hope here anymore. Andreas"—she had never called him by his first name before—"you must leave!"

"What more can they do?"

"They can kill you."

"What would be the use of that?"

"Don't talk of 'use'—where there's hate there's no rhyme or reason." The old woman was both kindly and shrewd. "They'll take all they can get from you, and then they'll throw you away. They don't believe that Jews are human. They do what they want, and they see that no one objects. My nephew shouted out against the mob and he was beaten up. Save yourself!"

Andreas took her hand and kissed it. The gesture was at once gentle and gentlemanly. Anna blushed.

"Let's wait and see what happens," he said.

ACROSS THREE thousand miles of land and ocean, that very day, November 10, Lene gave birth to a baby boy at New York Hospital.

There were no complications, no problems of any sort. The child weighed ten pounds, had his father's black hair and a lusty cry. He was named Peter Nathan Solomon. A small quarrel had erupted over the naming. Manfred wanted to flatter a well-known conductor by using his name, and Lene refused. "The name's ugly," she said, "and I don't believe in bowing and scraping before anyone."

"You don't want to help my career," said Manfred, but he was proud of his red-faced child with the strong lungs.

A month later, just before Christmas, Paul Leopold died in a Paris hospital of complications following an operation on his gall bladder. Lene heard about his death from Eva, who wrote:

We all knew he was ill, but none of us realized how ill he really was. They say now that his liver was already destroyed. He could not have lived, even if the operation on his gall bladder had been successful. But I suspect that he died for many different reasons, the liver being but one. The doctor on the case is said to be a quack. They don't care about us here, they wouldn't let one of our own look after him. They said he was not licensed. Paul collapsed one night at the café and was taken by ambulance to the nearest hospital. They cut him up the next day, and he lived for nearly a week. He had many visitors, but the surgeon never came to see him and the nurses turned a deaf ear to those who asked that he be called in. They claimed that Paul was recovering splendidly. Later they claimed that he had been too sick to recover. They shrugged their shoulders, as the French will, and said, *"Mais oui—Monsieur est un ivrogne!"*—a drunk—as though that explained it all.

They were callous and cruel. He suffered a great deal. They did nothing. When he called out for help in his pain, they brought him water and aspirin. He cried out again and again that he wanted to go "home" but no one knew quite what he meant. He had no home. He died on the shortest day, the very nadir of the year. There was a brief funeral service, and the whole refugee colony turned out to mourn him. We all know that more awful deaths occur daily in the concentration camps of Germany, but he seemed to symbolize all our predicaments. We are exiles. They say he wanted to die, that he could not bear to be away from his beloved Austria, that he mourned her demise this year with all his heart. I don't know about that. I am not one to believe in such explanations; they seem too romantic to me. Besides, Paul was always an exile. It was the natural state of his life. He never had hope. Lenin returned to Russia in triumph, *his* exile was temporary. He knew this. Paul knew that there was no place for him to return to, ever. He had become too cynical to believe in a political solution.

And this is where I differ from him. I do believe that the wretched of the earth—and more and more become wretched each day Hitler remains in power—*will* rise up. There is work to be done. It will take a long time, but we must devote ourselves to it. Hitler's Reich will never last a thousand years. This I firmly believe.

LENE PUT the letter away and did not tell Manfred about it. She was alone in the apartment when Fräulein Gründlich brought it to her, and she read it several times. For weeks and weeks she could not put it out of her mind, and almost every night she dreamt of Paul Leopold. "You're not looking well," Manfred said, "perhaps you should stop nursing the baby."

VIII

1939–1945

THE FIRST YEARS in America were difficult ones for Manfred Solomon, and he often made them difficult for his family. His career, which had been on the ascendancy in Europe before the Nazis, suffered an eclipse now that he was in the land of, as he derisively put it, Golden Opportunity. Had it not been for his teaching job at the small Catholic college in New Rochelle and the monthly check Lene received from Edu, they would have had difficulty getting by. As it was, Lene managed to retain the illusion that her life had not been much altered. They had escaped, after all. That was the most important thing.

For a month after their arrival they lived in a hotel on West Eighty-first Street. From there Lene ventured forth, pregnant as she was, to find a suitable apartment. The one she took was in a building on East Eight-second Street at the corner of Madison Avenue. It was large enough for all of them, including Manfred's Bechstein piano. Fräulein Gründlich had her own room, and there was a tiny nursery for the baby, who arrived within a week of their move and was put to bed, when Lene brought him home from the hospital, in a new American crib.

The rest of their furniture arrived in huge crates, and Clara watched them being unpacked with astonished delight. Every one of her prized possessions, which she had not seen since the day she left Germany, turned up in one or another safe place. The big newly painted apartment took on a familiar aspect as the rugs were laid out and the furniture set in place, until it seemed that the only thing that had not been brought from Frankfurt was the view out the window. The small enamel bowl on the marble-top table where Lene always kept her keys was in its accustomed spot in the hall. Clara's bedroom had the Bauhaus-inspired wood-and-chrome furniture Lene had bought in 1932 when she decided, with Emma's help, to "redo" the child's room under the eaves of the Guiollettstrasse.

Clara ran to show her mother every new thing she found, and before the day was out she had arranged her room to suit herself exactly, down to the Coptic wall hanging her Uncle Ernst had sent her from Palestine. She felt safe and happy. Even the view down Madison Avenue pleased her; she liked watching life in the streets.

Lene had sent Manfred out so that he would not be bothered. He always grumbled about living in a "house full of women" but expected—and got—their love and devotion. When he returned, the movers were gone, and order had almost been restored. Lene, in a housedress stretched tight over her bulging stomach, with a rag wrapped around her head, sat in the bedroom smoking a cigarette and watching the sun set over the Metropolitan Museum. Manfred, passing the open door, saw her and said, "You look wonderfully sluttish." She stared at him without comprehension; he had disturbed a reverie so deep that it was almost a trance.

"But there's also a touch of the saint about you," Manfred went on. "The combination is irresistible."

Closing the door behind him, he walked over to where she sat and kissed the nape of her neck. When he was not working, his desire always flared more passionately. He put his hand into the front of her housedress and touched her breasts. "I've always adored maids," he whispered and quoted Wilhelm Busch, who had said more or less the same thing. He rubbed his index finger across her nipple. "I love you," he said.

"Not now," Lene said, "I've too much to do."

"I love you now, I love you always."

"Clara may come in at any moment. Let me be."

"You've grown cold to me since we came here."

"Please don't begin accusing me. Do you see how I look? The baby . . ."

"It's always something!" Manfred stormed out the door. He locked himself in his room and appeared only when called for supper. That night he went to the movies alone.

The birth of his son cheered Manfred unaccountably. He had expected to find only pride in having a child, but he went again and again into the nursery to gaze at the baby sleeping on its stomach, the black curls clinging softly to its reddish forehead. For a few months Manfred forgot that his career was at a standstill. The music he practiced was romantic and lyrical. He visited other musicians and played chamber music with them.

On March 15, 1939, German armies marched into Czechoslovakia.

Lene developed a fear of tunnels and other subterranean places. It began quite suddenly one day as she was riding on the Lexington Avenue subway. She was overcome by the certain knowledge that the train, hurtling uptown at a thunderous speed, was about to be crushed by the collapse of the street above them. And when the train slowed to a stop, Lene felt herself grow so faint that she begged a kindly-looking elderly man to give her his seat. Biting her lip to keep from crying out, her eyes closed, her fingers clutched about her handbag, she sat there, waiting for death. When they reached Eighty-sixth Street she rushed from the train in a frenzy, and only the fresh air and the sight of the sky calmed her. She started to go places on the bus rather than the subway. Once when she had to travel to New Jersey, the panic assailed her in the middle of the Lincoln Tunnel. To avoid a return, she went only as far as Hoboken on her way back and took a cab from there over the George Washington Bridge. It cost a small fortune, and Manfred chided her for her fear. "Just grit your teeth and don't give in to it," he said. "I have more to put up with than you do, and you don't see me giving in to despair. These are only foolish little fears."

"They are my despair," Lene said, but Manfred did not understand her.

He began to practice longer and longer hours. The neighbors sometimes knocked on the ceiling and the floor. The music grew less lyrical and more dissonant. He quarreled with some of his old acquaintances. They, too, were glum and critical of America.

Manfred went by train twice a week for half a day to New Rochelle. He walked to the school and back again, a distance of several miles, and soon became a familiar figure to the merchants along North Avenue. His pupils were afraid of his pedantic, authoritarian manner. He did not enjoy teaching, and the girls, without discipline or dedication, seemed to him blank as ciphers. "My baby son has more temperament," he would grumble to Lene. But the school often asked him to give recitals, and even though the audience was largely made up of fellow refugees, it grew larger over the months, and this he took to be an encouraging sign.

His Town Hall recital in Manhattan—which cost him money, since most of the tickets had been given away—was attended by the third-string critic of the New York *Times,* who said that Manfred's playing was "masterful" and "occasionally brilliant" but qualified this by insisting that it was "Teutonic." Since this was in the spring of 1940 when the Wehrmacht was on its lightning drive through France, the criticism was unlikely to gain him a following.

But Fräulein Gründlich and Clara adjusted splendidly to the new land. Manfred would say to Lene with malice in his voice, "You see, I told you, this country was *invented* for children and servants."

Fräulein Gründlich discovered the friendliness of Americans before she had been in America six months. On her days off, when she went to the movies or to have a solitary Sunday dinner at Schrafft's, people would always begin conversations with her. She was invariably told that she had a "friendly face" or "such a nice smile," and before long she found herself with a small circle of acquaintances. These women, mostly widows and spinsters, did not look down on her because she was a governess. Some of them had worked for the telephone company or been clerks in department stores; others had never worked at all and lived on their husband's pensions, watching their purchases carefully and "making do." Fräulein Gründlich learned to play canasta—she had always had a weakness for cards and knew dozens of variations of solitaire—and regularly met her new friends over the card table. Because she had no place of her own to which she could invite them, she always stopped at a bakery and bought a cake to bring with her; now and then she would also pick up a bottle of Kirsch, which they would sip from tiny glasses at the end of the evening.

Clara went to public school, where she learned to jitterbug and play baseball. Her parents were often exasperated by the casual way in which children in America were instructed. There was neither Latin nor Greek, no one cared about penmanship, and an extraordinary amount of time was given over to such things as drawing and painting, planting tulip bulbs in window boxes and learning how to bake butterscotch brownies.

One day she came home with an A plus on a story she had written entitled "My Journey to America." She flew into the apartment to tell her mother the good news. It was the first time she had ever been so highly praised for an English composition.

"What's this?" Lene asked, pointing to the top of the page where Clara had written her name. "It says 'Claire Badolet.' I believe your first name is Clara, and your last name von Brenda-Badolet. I admit it's a long name, but it's a very distinguished one. Why did you change it?"

Clara/Claire blushed. "I didn't think you'd mind," she said. "It's so hard . . . Americans just don't have names like that." She suddenly felt her heart drop, seeing how disconcerted her mother looked. "Do you want me to change it back? I will if you really want me to." Had she done something awful?

Lene had been shocked at the sight of the new name. It seemed to represent an act of presumption, or even rebellion. Like casting oneself adrift or running away from home. Could it be that Clara —Claire—entertained such ideas? That she was unhappy? Lene looked at her, trying to penetrate the familiar face to catch a glimpse of the unexpected. But all she saw was an inquisitive look and an expression of apprehension.

"Is it only that, Clärchen?" Lene asked. "Really? Are you telling me the truth? You're not unhappy?"

"I want to be like the others," Clara said. "I don't want them looking at me as if I were a freak. Janice called me a 'refugee' the other day. And I want to cut off my braids too. Can I, Mummy? Can I have short hair?"

"Cutting off your hair isn't as big a step as changing your name."

"Because your hair can grow back?"

"Because your name is one of your connections to the past . . . to your father."

"But he's far away. He'll never know."

"If it's wrong to do something, then it's wrong, even if nobody ever finds out."

"I know that." She blushed suddenly. Fräulein Gründlich said that you always got back what you gave.

"I'm not saying that your papa would mind, but I want you to know what you're doing, that's all. It's a big step," Lene explained.

"Oh, I understand," she said, wondering whether she really did. "I'm changing my ways," she went on slyly. "I'm becoming American. You changed your ways too. You married Manfred. You didn't want to spend your whole life with my papa."

"What grownups do is different," said Lene, "I'll tell you about that one day—when you're older."

"Sometimes I wish that Manfred were my real father." The girl did not look at her mother but out the window across the street.

"He loves you, Clara, like a real father. But your papa loves you too, don't forget that. You're a lucky girl, you've got two fathers!"

"Can I keep my new name? You won't make me change it back? Can I be Claire Badolet?"

"Claire Badolet . . ."

"Doesn't it sound nice?"

"I guess so. May I still call you Clara?"

"Oh, Mummy!" Claire was so happy to have got her way that she hugged her mother tightly and buried her head in her shoulder as though she were a small child. A sigh escaped her.

"Is anything the matter?" Lene asked.

"No, no! It's only that I love you so very much. Nobody understands me the way you do." Though she spoke English fluently now, at home she continued to talk German. It remained for her the language of intimacy, of childhood joys and sorrows.

Manfred entered the living room at that moment and stood still for a second, observing mother and daughter. He felt removed from their embrace. They were a formidable pair. Claire was not as pretty as her mother, but there was something utterly straightforward about her, and she was always happy. He loved them both. But he loved them better when they were apart.

"Am I interrupting something?" he asked.

"Not at all," said Lene. She patted her daughter on her behind, and the girl left the room to tell Fräulein Gründlich that she was henceforth to be addressed by her new name.

"I've got something I want to discuss with you," Manfred said. "It's a serious matter and I don't want anyone to disturb us."

"Let's go into your room then. Once we close the door, nobody will come in."

They sat facing each other, Manfred in his straight-backed chair, Lene in the more comfortable armchair. She felt a knot of dread in the place where her rib cage separated. "Serious discussions" with Manfred always implied that he was contemplating some venture of which she was certain to disapprove. He spent an inordinate amount of the time that hung so heavy on his hands working out schemes and projects to aid his career. Since he was not by nature equipped to be a schemer, most of his ideas were harebrained plots patched together from snippets of information gathered from friends and acquaintances.

"I've decided what it is I need to make a career in this country."

"What's that?" Lene asked suspiciously.

"A good manager."

"But you've got a manager."

"Goldschmidt, a refugee too, a man with European ideas and principles, without contacts, without American—how do they say it?—'know-how.' What I like about the language," he added, "is its directness."

"He's always been your friend."

"That's quite irrelevant. He doesn't help my career."

"So you plan to leave him?"

"Yes." Manfred drummed on the arm of his chair with the third finger of his left hand. He was always working to strengthen it. "They tell me that the best manager in the United States is a man named Samitzky. He is the big man in the field, and if *he* takes me on, my career is made."

"Are you going to talk to him?"

"I already called him."

"You didn't tell me."

"I wanted to see what he would say before I discussed it with you. I was afraid you'd insist I stay with Goldschmidt."

"I happen to like Goldschmidt, but I can perfectly well understand your point that you need an American manager."

"An American Jewish manager with East European roots. That's the best they tell me. These men are shrewd and intelligent and a little bit unscrupulous. They know business, and they love art."

"Does Samitzky fill the bill?"

"So they say."

"When you talked to him, what did *he* say?"

"I didn't actually talk to him, I talked to his secretary—an officious woman—who said that he was busy and that if I wanted to see him I should make an appointment. She also told me that he had a 'full stable'—those were her exact words, can you believe it? A stable, like horses. They treat musicians, artists, like animals here in the land of Golden Opportunity!"

"What do you plan to do now?"

"I plan to see him. But there's something I am going to ask you to do for me first."

"What's that?" The knot in the middle of her rib cage grew larger.

"I want you to ask your Uncle Edu for five thousand dollars."

"What in the world for?"

"As they say in America, 'Money talks.' "

"You plan to offer Samitzky money?"

"They say that in America you can buy anything and anyone. I'm going to try."

"But that's bribery!"

"They don't call it that here. It's a gift. And once I am successful, I'll earn it back a hundred times over, and then, if he wants to give it back, he can. So it will only have been an advance, as it were, on future earnings . . ."

"It seems wrong to me."

"You don't know what you're talking about, Lene. This is America. Don't bring your silly European scruples to it. Tell Edu that it's a loan. Tell him that it's essential for my career, that my career is essential to your happiness. If I don't work, I earn no money. It's not that I lack ability—he must understand that—but that conditions here are such that I have to adjust to them before I can make my way."

"What if he refuses?"

"He can't refuse. Not if you ask him in the right way. Of course, if *you* don't believe in me, if you've lost your faith in me, if you think this is a pipe dream, then you might just as well not bother to ask him. You can forget it and resign yourself to being married to a failure. You can send me out to become a streetcar conductor or a mailman."

Manfred was very agitated. He had worked the whole thing out so carefully in his mind that it had become unassailable in its clarity and logic. Lene's hesitation threatened to throw the plan into doubt.

"Will you do it or not? There are only two answers, yes or no. Which is it?"

"I have to think about it."

"I must know by next week."

"Why the hurry?"

"When you make up your mind that something must be done, it's best not to procrastinate about it."

Lene lay awake that night for a very long time. She could not get over her feeling that it was wrong to offer a man a bribe, no matter what you called it. And she worried that Edu would be outraged at the idea, angry with her, insulted that she should think that he would be party to such an action. But she was more worried that Manfred in his overpowering ambition, his blind commitment to a career, would stop at nothing to force her to acquiesce to his wishes.

And it was Manfred she had to live with; Uncle Edu was thousands of miles away.

So she wrote a letter, properly vague about the uses to which the money was to be put but clear about its ultimate purpose—to help Manfred make a career in America. Edu wrote back a letter full of disapproval and righteous indignation. He said that he was not to be counted on as the family treasury, that he did his duty as he saw fit and that he would not bail out in-laws or support his nieces in foolish extravagances or a dissolute life. He said it was a loan, and if it was paid back within five years, he would ask no interest on it.

Manfred made an appointment to see the impresario. He brought clippings of his European reviews.

"I can't read those languages," the man said gruffly. "Take the papers away. What have you done *here*?"

Manfred mentioned his job, his several recitals. He had not brought the New York *Times'* review of his Town Hall concert.

"I read somewhere that your playing is Teutonic," Samitzky said. He motioned to a baby grand that stood in the corner of his lavishly appointed office. "Play something for me."

Manfred sat down, and remembering the word "Teutonic," played a Liszt Etude and a Chopin Polonaise.

"Very good, very good," said Samitzky, waving the stump of his cigar, "but there are dozens of pianists who are very good. The country's crawling with very good pianists. Especially since Hitler. You have to be more than very good for me to take you on. Only the *best* are admitted into my firm." He gave a small brittle laugh at the witticism.

"I am among the best. All the German critics said so."

"The German critics are laying waste to Europe right now and persecuting the Jews. Don't talk to me about the German critics. *I* don't think you're good enough for me. You may be good enough for me in another few years—but not now. Go home and practice!"

"I have a check here," Manfred said, "a check for five thousand dollars."

"I'm glad you're not poor," said Samitzky. "It's not good to be poor. Believe me, I know."

"The check is for you." Manfred realized that he was not prepared for this moment. He had assumed that the encounter would take a different turn. He thought that Samitzky would say to him, "What do you offer me?"

Instead he said, "For me? What do you mean, for me?"

"A gift," Manfred said. In his confusion, he found that he could not remember the correct English words. "I want you to have this check," he said. "It is for you. So you will take me on, as you say."

Samitzky looked uncomprehending. Manfred took the check from his wallet and showed it to the impresario.

"I'll be damned," he said. "I don't believe it. This *shmuck* is trying to bribe me!"

"Bribe? What do you mean 'bribe'?" Manfred suddenly became frightened. Samitzky seemed apoplectic. Clearly he had done something wrong. "I was told you are a businessman, and as a businessman you would understand the value of money. I was told that in America I could buy myself a manager. I paid money to have a recital in Town Hall . . ."

"Get out of my office," Samitzky shouted. "I never want to see you again! Do you think you can come in here and buy me as though I were some kind of whore?"

He stood behind his enormous desk, livid with rage, pointing to the door. "And take your check with you," he cried, flinging it after the pianist. It fluttered in the air briefly and settled on the Oriental carpet. Manfred bent to pick it up, stuffed it in his pocket and bowed to the small fat man. "If I did something wrong, I am sorry," he said. "I didn't know."

Manfred walked for hours through the city streets. He did not want to return home, though he knew that he must eventually face Lene. It was a hot, muggy day. He did not watch where he was going and bumped into people. "Watch it, buddy," they said, and he mumbled "Sorry."

He wandered so far from his usual haunts that he finally found himself in Harlem. The faces all around him were black, and he felt stranger and more alien than ever. What a savage country this is, he thought.

He came home just before dinner.

"I worried about you," Lene said. "Did the interview take all this time?"

"I prefer not to talk about it."

"It went badly?"

"I don't want to discuss it!"

"I was afraid it was a mistake," Lene said, almost to herself.

"Say no more!" Manfred took an ashtray from the coffee table and threw it into a corner of the room. It shattered, leaving a dent in the wall. Claire, who was in her room doing her homework, turned up the volume of her radio so that its sounds—Red Barber was broadcasting an extra-inning Dodger game—would drown out the quarrel. Fräulein Gründlich picked up Peter and rocked him in her lap. Ethel, the cook, made loud noises with her pots and pans and started humming a Negro spiritual.

Lene went to pick up the pieces. She was crying and did not want Manfred to see her. What will I do? What will I do? she thought, fully aware that the anger in Manfred was like lightning, likely to scatter destruction. She was afraid for herself, for her children. She huddled in the corner, putting the smallest shards into the palm of her hand. If one looked directly out of this window, one could see the delicate May green of the trees that grew in the convent garden across Eighty-second Street. All the rest was stone and brick. It was a strange, hard country. But Manfred's mistake—and she should have seen it for what it was immediately—had been his own, not the country's. Lene was overcome by a burning, awful shame for Manfred, for what he had done. She should have prevented him; it was her fault as well. She was his accomplice. But she loved him!

It was two days before Manfred spoke to her again. Lene returned the money to Uncle Edu without comment.

THE SANATORIUM in which Caroline Wertheim had lived since 1938 was about an hour's drive from Frankfurt. On the first of every month Eduard Wertheim sent its director, *Sanitätsrat* Hodler, a check for her care.

In midsummer of 1940 Edu received a letter from Dr. Hodler requesting him to remit 2,045 reichsmarks "for services rendered Frau Caroline Wertheim, who has been sent to another institution, where, it is hoped, she will receive the care her condition warrants." Edu demanded an itemized bill; he did not like to pay out money unless he knew exactly what it was for. Dr. Hodler wrote back saying that Frau Wertheim had been provided with "extras" of an unspecified kind during her last months there, and that repairs had had to be made after her departure, since, as Herr Wertheim well knew, she often displayed behavior of a most violent nature. The day on which she had been transferred had, in fact, been one on which she was quite out of control. It was also hoped that Herr Wertheim would see fit to contribute some monies to the personnel's Christmas fund.

Edu instructed his lawyers to undertake an investigation of the transfer, but they were unable to find out anything much beyond the fact that on July 7 certain "hopeless" cases had been taken away quite abruptly on directions sent down from the Ministry of Health and Eugenics. The lawyers' letters to the ministry went unanswered for a long time. It was not until a year later that an official notice reached the attorneys telling them that Caroline Sarah Wertheim, née Süsskind, had died on July 10, 1940, of "congestive heart failure" at an unnamed institution somewhere in Germany. A request was made for an additional 300 RM to defray the expenses connected with her funeral.

The lawyer advised Edu not to pay either bill. He felt that there had been some negligence on the part of Dr. Hodler in allowing patients to be transferred to other, unnamed institutions. He ran a private facility, after all; it was not as if Frau Wertheim had been incarcerated in a public asylum. Edu thanked the man and went home to send his relatives notice of Caroline's death.

THERE HAD BEEN moments—rare though they were—when Caroline was completely lucid. At such times she would engage the nurses in sharp and pungent conversation. She swore like a truck driver, but what she said in between the curses was perfectly logical. The nurses sometimes had to laugh with her, she told such amusing stories. "My brother-in-law is rich as Croesus," she said more than once. "He pays us all to kow-tow to him. And we do it! We never grumble or complain, we are good children. He pays everybody, you know. I bet he even pays the devil." She cast a sly sideways glance at the nurse who was making the bed. "You know the devil, don't you?" she asked. "His name is Adolf Hitler. H-i-t-l-e-r, and he wants us all killed."

The nurse said, "There, there now, Frau Caroline, you musn't make things up. Our Führer is a wonderful man and thinks only of the good of our country. You believe in your fatherland, don't you?"

"Fatherland . . . motherland . . . children'sland, I believe in them all," Caroline said, "but I don't have one anymore. No father, no mother, no children. They were all taken away from me by my brother-in-law. Hitler ordered it. The trouble is that I can't figure out why. That's always the trouble," she said, her voice growing louder, "why, why, why?" She began to scream, as she so often did when her stories ended in the despair of a question she could not answer.

Sometimes she confided to the nurses that she had a son who "fucks men" and a daughter who "fucks Martin Luther," and that her youngest was a fair virgin who had a baby just like the Blessed Mother of God. Several of the nurses encouraged her to tell them about these things and teased her about her revelations. But Caroline always recognized the moment when the tide of her monologues turned against her, and then she would turn to the wall and grow still, holding herself stiff, her eyes fastened to a spot on the wallpaper which she said was a map of heaven. Sometimes her body twisted slowly, as though she were performing a dance, into attitudes representing frozen emotions of terrible fear or loathing. She would hold these for hours, her eyes blank as marble. She heard noises of mice scurrying through the walls and the rip of a butcher's saw through bone. And when she grew afraid, when she recognized—often in a single blinding flash—that there were neither answers nor reasons, that she was being pursued and punished for some monstrous crime she could never fathom, she would begin to wail and scream and flail about, battering the heavenly map on her wall until the orderly came with a strait jacket and bound her into it.

When the directive came down from Berlin that all the "incurables" were to be transferred to a public institution, Dr. Hodler was chagrined. He made a tidy sum caring for such patients; they were unlikely ever to be discharged, and one could fleece their relatives of thousands of extra marks every year. The Jewish inmates—especially those with relatives abroad—provided him with a tidy (often secret) income. He had sent all those whose families could no longer pay their bills to public institutions long ago.

At the same time Dr. Hodler, like most of his compatriots, was in a high ecstasy that summer. Belgium, Holland and finally France had fallen, the English had slunk back to their small island. It looked as if the Thousand-Year Reich was a reality, the Führer invincible. Given the euphoria victory brings and the sense of individual strength a united and triumphant nation imposes upon each of its citizens, Dr. Hodler was soon able to overcome his chagrin and convince himself that the directive from Berlin was not only necessary and correct but might ultimately be of some benefit to him. Besides, he knew quite well that there were those who would denounce him were he to be anything but punctilious in the discharge of his duties.

Dr. Hodler bid each of his patients good-bye personally and with great good manners and kindness. He had chosen about twenty among the hundred or so in his care, making certain that each one was clearly "incurable"—i.e., senile or Jewish or suffering from a physical ailment. He brought a small gift with him in some cases and talked soothingly to those who appeared to be frightened by the proposed change. He promised a special treat for dinner, said that he himself had inspected the new facilities and that they were fine. None of the patients who understood what he said believed him. Caroline cursed him, spit at him and called him a liar. He bowed calmly to her and told the nurses that she must be bound into her strait jacket for the journey.

"You're planning to kill me!" she screamed and fought with all her strength against the attendants. They finally had to give her a shot to calm her. Her belongings were stuffed into a brown paper bag and carefully labeled before being put on the rack of the bus which was to take the group to its destination. Nurses and orderlies, all of them with cheerful expressions on their faces, herded the patients onto the bus. There was a large red cross painted on its white sides, and the driver shook hands with everyone who boarded, saying "Hello" or "Welcome." Because Caroline's hands were bound to her torso, he merely patted her on the shoulder and directed her to the seat she had been assigned.

They drove through a countryside rife with summer in all its lush green warmth. Caroline looked out the window. She had grown calm; the strait jacket no longer bothered her; she felt like a swaddled child. A fat man sat next to her. He sweated profusely and made sounds like a growling dog, but he did not bother her either. The landscape was familiar. Caroline had known it all her life. There were castle ruins atop the gently rolling hills, and the forests stopped abruptly for well-tended fields. The tiny villages through which they rode were placid. Children played in the shade of great chestnut or linden trees, the village fountains splashed and swallows darted among the red-tiled roofs of whitewashed cottages.

Caroline allowed her mind to return to her childhood. The calm she felt was like a miracle. She was going on a summer outing. Her father was happy over the glee his children felt at the prospect of a picnic in the Taunus. They had walked some miles to a *Gasthof*, an inn on the edge of the forest beside a stream. The sun was high in the sky and there were red-and-white checkered tablecloths on all the tables. It was cool in the shade, but one could smell the sweet hay drying nearby. Papa Süsskind ordered beer for himself and *Himbeersaft*, a tall, chilled drink made with raspberry syrup, for the children, but he allowed them a taste of the cold lager, and they got mustaches of foam on their upper lips. They ate cold cuts on dark bread with fresh butter and then played in the meadow nearby while Papa dozed over his volume of Heine. The girls picked flowers while the boys built a waterwheel. When the shadows had lengthened across the whole of the *Gasthof* courtyard, they set off again for the train station and home. They were tired, and to keep themselves marching steadily they sang folk songs. Their voices were clear, they sang in harmony, and sometimes when they passed other wanderers returning from the country, they would be joined in a chorus or two. Eva's voice was the purest; Elias' still broke now and then, Jonah sang out of tune.

Caroline smiled to herself. She heard the familiar songs and hummed them. The day was clear and hot, but not a window on the bus was open. It was sweltering. The villages and fields gave way to a more rugged terrain, to greater forests, higher peaks. Caroline no longer knew where she was and clung to the memory of that long-ago day.

They arrived at a place that looked very much like an old but clean hospital. There were angels painted above the doors, holding wreaths and flowers. The patients were brought to a large white waiting room. Many of them shook and wept and cried, but Caroline was very still.

"Please take off my jacket!" she said to one of the attendants. They were all men in long white coats. Caroline wondered briefly why they wore boots, but then she saw that they were hosing down the floors of an adjoining room and remembered how it was at the abbatoir where she had once been with Jonah. The memory frightened her for a moment, and she asked again to be rid of her "jacket." "When you take your shower," one of the men said. He wore a garrison cap. "Take it off now," she pleaded, but he shook his head. "They must have had a reason to put it on you," he said. "You've been bad."

"I'll be good," she wheedled, "I've seen the light." But the man continued to shake his head.

Finally they were all brought to a great hall encircled by rows of windows. Here they were stripped of their clothes and everything was put in neat piles on benches against the wall. Caroline was finally freed of her strait jacket, and she flung her arms about with abandon. She was stiff and sore, but she tried to do a little dance; she thought of the meadow in the Taunus. All around her people were moaning and crying. Some screamed in terror, but she was untouched by it. She danced as best she could in the small space allotted to her and grew afraid only when they sent her into the little tiled room where the showers were. It was crowded, and the other naked bodies repelled her; they were slippery with sweat, and some of the old people had dirtied themselves. But then the gas came pouring out of the spigots, and she breathed deeply. She thought she felt the waters of the gurgling stream about her feet and saw the blue sky above her head. It was a deep deep ultramarine blue, perfect, like the blue of . . . like the blue . . .

She could not remember.

Outside the shower room the soldiers looked at their watches and the man from I.G. Farben checked the gleaming brass valves and looked dispassionately through the glass spy hole in the massive door.

IT WAS on a warm day in October of 1941—weather the Americans call "Indian Summer" and the Germans "Old Wives' Summer"— that Andreas was visited by two men from the Gestapo and told that he must prepare himself for resettlement. The men were dressed in nondescript civilian clothes and carried small black notebooks filled with page upon page of careful notations.

Andreas had gone to open the door himself. When the knock came, Anna was in the basement washing clothes. She hurried upstairs, but Andreas had already let the men into the house. He had been expecting them. There was no longer any question in his mind that Germany was to be purged of its Jews. Kurt was not yet on the lists stamped URGENT, but his time would come as well. Andreas had talked with him about this moment. They had contemplated suicide but found it unacceptable. "If they want us dead," Andreas said, "they must be willing to do the job. We should not do it for them."

In their confinement they had discovered the secret of cohabitation. They had learned, slowly and painfully, how to love each other fully, how to make the best of a situation that threatened them each day with separation and reprisal. They did not say "death," but they knew it; they swore to each other that they would not fear it. They had constructed a world so private that it was like the world of children, and no one intruded upon it.

They had agreed to separate, when the time came, and to try to survive. Often they talked about the need to see their predicament in terms that would help them live another day. They had seen the film *La Grande Illusion* together more than once, and chose to accept its message. There would be an end, even to this madness. There was courage and hope in the performance of small civilities.

"You can stay in this house as long as they let you," Andreas had said, "but I don't think that Anna will come back once I am gone."

"What will they do with the house, do you think?"

"Make it the headquarters of some ministry or give it to a high party official."

Anna had taken many things of value to her cousin's house at night, stealthily, so the police would not see it.

"After the war your family will be happy that I saved these things," she told Andreas. She had prepared a list and sent it to Edu. Andreas had signed his name to it.

"I don't want him to think I made off with anything," she said.

"He wouldn't think such a thing," said Andreas.

"I know people like him better than you do," Anna said. "I know their mean and suspicious side. But that's all right, too. They have a lot more to lose than our kind."

The house was now only sparsely furnished. Where the paintings had hung there were great pale rectangles on the walls.

Andreas packed a suitcase full of clothes. "You may bring fifty kilos," the men had said. "No more than that. You will have to carry it, take only what you need." He chose several clean shirts, two sweaters, a spare suit, two pair of pants, socks, some warm wool underwear and a sturdy pair of shoes. At the last minute he added a book or two. In case I'm in a cell where I can read, he thought. He understood that he was going off to a prison, to do hard labor. The suitcase felt heavy in his hand. He wished he were stronger.

Kurt stood in the doorway watching him. "Put it into two separate containers," he said, "one for each hand." He shuddered with the cold. "Better yet, take one of your father's carpetbags and something you can hang over your shoulder to keep your hands free."

They looked at each other and smiled.

"Does it matter, really?" Andreas asked. He felt a great flush of love rise out of his heart for his friend. "Take care of yourself," he said. "Go away. Hide. We'll meet after it's over."

"Where?"

"At Maxim's. In Paris. The way they did in the film."

"I'm afraid this will be different," said Kurt.

They kissed and held each other tightly. Andreas struggled to find a glimmer of hope. "It may not be so bad," he said. "If I work hard and keep my mouth shut, maybe I'll come out of it all right."

He repacked his things carefully and added an extra sweater and a small notebook, in case he wanted to write something down. He wore his sturdy shoes and his warm suit even though the day was almost summery. The leaves on the chestnut tree in the garden were gold in the sun. The sight of it was almost more than Andreas could bear.

The two men walked one more time through the overgrown garden. Anna watched them from the kitchen window. The last of the potatoes she had planted were ready to be dug. Soon there would be a killing frost.

Punctually, two hours after the first visit, there was another knock on the front door. This time it was a man in uniform who stood there, a gun slung over his shoulder. Andreas embraced Anna, who wept bitterly. Kurt had hidden himself in the empty apartment on the third floor which had once been Lene's. The man from the SS walked beside Andreas, leading him without a word in the direction of the Opernplatz. Andreas noticed that all along the Guiollett-strasse and from the side streets for as far as he could see, men and women were walking in the direction of the Opera accompanied by uniformed men with guns. Most of them were elderly, all of them were dressed in winter clothes and laden down with their belongings in shopping bags and valises, rucksacks and duffel bags. Silently they streamed toward the familiar square in front of the great Opernhaus, on whose portal the words *Dem Wahren Schönen Guten* —"To Truth, Beauty, Goodness"—stood incised for all to see under the brilliant autumnal sky.

Hundreds were gathered there. It was late morning, but the streets were nearly empty of pedestrians—the citizens of Frankfurt averted their eyes from the spectacle in their midst. The silence was eerie. The Jews spoke in low voices and whispers. Many of them were so self-contained that they looked neither to the left nor right. Husbands and wives stood close but did not glance into each other's eyes. Andreas nodded to a few acquaintances but could find no words to say to them. The SS men formed a ring around the group. Now and then they uttered a command or gave a mirthless bark of a laugh.

After several hours of waiting, a car drove up; several officers got out and the order was given to march. Walking along the Taunus Anlage and the Mainzer Landstrasse, they headed toward the railroad station. Andreas caught a last glimpse of his parents' house. Tears came into his eyes and spilled down his cheeks.

They were not taken to the *Hauptbahnhof*, the main station, but to the freight yards nearby. Tables had been set up on the long platforms next to the tracks where freight trains stood with doors open. It was all quite orderly. The Jews had to find their proper registration point; they were divided alphabetically.

Andreas was numb from the heat, and hunger gnawed at his stomach. By now he usually ate his midday meal. Why hadn't he thought to take something to eat?

"We're not going in those cars?" an elderly woman standing ahead of him at the table under the letter *W* asked the official who sat at his ledger smoking a cigarette.

"You can't bring that camera," he said in reply. "You aren't going on a vacation."

"It's valuable," she said. "I didn't want to leave it at home."

"You will leave it here," the man said. "We'll put your name on it." The woman gave up her camera wordlessly.

Andreas was next.

"You're not wearing your star," the official said.

"I haven't got one," Andreas said. "I didn't know anything about a star."

"Since the fifteenth of September all Jews have been required to wear yellow stars with the word *JUDE* inside. Where in hell have you been? Look around—you'll see everyone else here has obeyed the order. What makes you think you're different?"

Andreas shook his head.

"Speak up!"

"I didn't hear about the star."

"Get to the back of the line, and when I see you next, I expect you to have obeyed the order."

Andreas picked up his things and trudged to the end of the line. Someone plucked at his sleeve as he passed by.

"I've got an extra star," he said. He was a man about Andreas' age with a fleshy face.

"Thank you. I really didn't know about it," said Andreas, reaching for the cloth object the man held in his hand.

"It's not free. You must pay me."

"How much?"

"Five marks."

"You're mad! I won't pay five marks for a scrap of cloth . . .!"

"The safety pin to fasten it to your coat comes with it."

Andreas looked into the man's ugly face.

"Another three marks and I'll sell you a piece of bread. I bet you brought none with you. You thought we'd be sent first class on the Orient Express!"

Andreas took the money out of his pocket and made his purchases. The yellow star went directly over his heart. He ate the crust of bread hungrily.

It was late afternoon and a cool gray fog had crept up from the river before the trains were actually loaded. Each person had been relieved of his passport and had his name checked against the ones in the ledger. To the question "Where are we going?" no answer was given. Portable steps had been set up on the platform to make it easier to enter the freight cars. When everyone had boarded, the sliding doors were shut and bolted.

Two hours later the train started up with a jolt. The good burghers of Frankfurt were sitting down to dinner listening to their radios, reading the newspapers. The weather report said there would be a cold spell; a mass of arctic air was sweeping down from the pole. The train rattled eastward. It did not reach its destination for several days.

AFTER ANDREAS had been taken away, Anna tidied up the house. She did not speak to Kurt. At about four o'clock an officer came to the door. Anna noticed that he was a "Green" one, not with the Gestapo but with the regular police. "I have orders to seal these premises. Is there anyone still here beside you?" Anna shook her head. He sounded almost apologetic. "I must make certain the lights and the gas are shut off."

"Some job you've got," she said.

He sighed. "I have to do what I'm told to do. I have no choice."

"The dirty work is done before you get here," Anna said. "I guess it's easy for you. You only have to lock the doors."

He shifted uncomfortably from foot to foot and bit at his lip. Anna judged him to be about her age. He made a cursory search of the house, "for valuables" he said. Being a rather portly man, he did not climb up to the third floor.

"What are they doing to the Jews?" Anna asked.

"I don't know."

"You must know *something.*"

"Have you worked here long?" he asked.

"It's the only job I've ever had."

"They were good people?"

Anna could not answer; the tears that rose in her throat choked off all speech. She nodded.

"It's a shame," the man said. "They ought to make distinctions between the good Jews and the bad ones. But maybe they won't have it so bad, your people. They have money, don't they? With money you can buy yourself special treatment."

Anna wiped her eyes with the corner of her apron. The lump in her throat would not go down no matter how hard she swallowed.

"You have a place to live?" the man asked. "You know you can't stay here. I have to seal the place and take the keys to the police station."

"I'll get ready to go." Anna went upstairs in her deliberate, slow way. Her legs ached. The varicose veins bulged and throbbed whenever she stood in one place for a while.

Kurt had packed a few of his things in a rucksack. "What's going on?" he whispered. "Are they coming after me too?"

"They're closing up the house. You must leave," Anna said. Now that Andreas had gone she remembered that she hadn't much liked this man. "Go down the back stairs and out the basement door."

Kurt looked frightened. "Where will I go?"

"I can't help you," Anna told him.

When she heard the back door swing shut, Anna returned to the policeman, who was waiting patiently in the front hall.

"I'll be ready to go as soon as I check to see if the dishes are washed. You caught me in the middle of my chores."

"It doesn't matter anymore," the man said. "They won't be back. Did I hear a noise in the basement?" Anna saw that he wanted not to know anything.

"We have a loose door there," she said. "It always bangs. Even the slightest wind rattles it. They always meant to get it fixed."

She put on her coat. Dusk and the fog had extinguished the last warm rays of the sun. The half-dark street lamps of wartime cast small circles of light about their stanchions. The policeman put his seal on the front door of the house and affixed a paper to it. Anna could not read what it said. She turned away. Everything shivered in a blur of tears.

"Things were better when we were young," the policeman said. "I don't like these times. Nothing good will come of them." He touched the tips of his fingers to the visor of his shiny policeman's cap. It was the gesture with which he greeted a lost traveler asking for directions or a storekeeper when he made his daily rounds. "They're taking the Jews to the East, I hear," he said to Anna, "resettling them in the ghettos of Poland."

With those words he turned abruptly, his eyes fastened to the pages of his black notebook. The keys to a dozen houses jingled softly in his pockets.

As soon as Anna reached home she fetched a piece of lined writing paper, and in her careful, old-fashioned hand she wrote a letter to Eduard Wertheim telling him that Andreas had been taken from his house that day. "I believe," she wrote, "that they have sent him to Poland, to live in a district reserved for Jewish people. Perhaps you will be able to find him and help him."

BY THE TIME the train in which Andreas was confined reached Lodz, many of its passengers had died. The cold air the survivors breathed as they jumped from the wagons to the hard ground seemed for a moment to be fresh and pure, for the stench inside the sealed train had been putrid beyond description. It was only after he had stood about in the freight yard for several hours under a leaden sky in a landscape wholly without color or warmth that Andreas began to feel its bitter chill. He had managed to hold on to his bags, and the dying and dead had yielded up enough crusts of bread and rinds of cheese to give the living sustenance. Andreas was giddy with hunger and soon became numb with cold, but there was a certain satisfaction in being alive.

In due time the several hundreds of Jews from Frankfurt who had been on this particular train were marched into the ghetto of Lodz.

There they joined the streams of Jews from the villages and towns of Poland and from the German countryside. A new brick wall surrounded their quarter. Anyone who approached it from the Jewish side was summarily shot. Those who came near it from the other side were ordered to "Halt!" and given a chance to retreat before they were executed.

Andreas had wrapped his scarf—it was cashmere, like all the scarfs he had ever owned—around his neck and pulled his coat collar up to his ears to meet the brim of his hat. He wore two sweaters and two pairs of socks. His leather gloves were useless against the cold, so he kept his hands in his pockets. His suitcases hung about him like the wares of a junkman. He knew where he was, having seen the sign on one of the signal towers that overlooked the web of tracks that led in and out of the city. For one used to German towns and the landscape of the valley of the Rhine, for one who had been to Paris, Florence and Rome, this Polish industrial city would have seemed ugly in any case; under the circumstances it seemed to him as desolate as the frozen plains of hell. Andreas tried to pay attention to the road they took and the buildings and street signs along the way. He thought that if he knew where he was going, he might be able to find his way back. Absurd thoughts like that still edged their way into his mind. The trek to the Lodz ghetto took them through the town itself. Again, the people did not look at them. They scurried down a side street whenever possible and left the avenue clear for the silent, shuffling column. Sometimes Andreas saw a face at the window of one of the gray apartment buildings, looking out from behind a white curtain. It was easy to imagine those dreary apartments—and yet they were better than what Andreas had, and he knew he would give anything to crawl into one of them and lie down to sleep, on the floor if necessary.

A teen-aged girl pulled two small children out of their line of march and put her hands over their eyes.

"We are the damned," said the man who walked beside Andreas, "and we smell of death. A plague upon every decent citizen. Look how they scurry away."

The words startled Andreas. He could not remember speaking to anyone since he boarded the train. The faces had been invisible in the darkness, and to open one's mouth was to gag on the foul air. "When the Germans give the order to kill us, the Poles will do their bidding with pleasure," the man said. "Have you ever visited this lovely country before?"

Andreas shook his head.

"Not like Frankfurt, is it?"

"Not like any place I've ever been."

"And it's not yet winter."

"Do you know Lodz?"

"I've traveled through these parts. This was always a hideous town."

They walked on without further words and entered the gates that led through the brick wall into the ghetto. Great rolls of barbed wire flanked the entrance, and there were small wooden shacks for the sentries who patrolled the area with submachine guns. The streets on the Jewish side of the wall were crowded with men, women and children. These, in contrast to the few fleeing pedestrians outside the wall, stared at the newcomers. Their eyes were dull and hard, unfriendly.

"They look as though they hated us," Andreas said.

"Every person who comes here takes another bite of food out of their mouths. Do you blame them for hating us?"

"We're all in the same boat."

"Don't *you* hate *them*?"

Andreas was startled that this man, whoever he was, had so quickly penetrated his mind and picked out exactly the thought that he had meant to hide.

"Why should I?"

"Because you think they are not like you. They are in the same boat, but still you think they belong in steerage and you belong in first class."

"Is the lettering on that sign in Hebrew?" Andreas asked, pointing to the window of what had once been a butcher shop.

"The letters are Hebrew, but the language is Yiddish. Yiddish is the language spoken by most Jews in this part of the world. It comes originally from Middle High German. You might say it was a corruption."

Andreas looked at the man for the first time.

"Andreas Wertheim," he said.

"Werner Epstein. I take it you're related to *the* Wertheims? Eduard Wertheim?"

"He's my uncle."

"And still you're here, like the rest of us *proste yidn,* vulgar yids."

"I was locked away in my house. I hoped it wouldn't come to this . . ."

The streets were filled with beggars and dirty children whose faces were old and gaunt. Women sat on stoops holding listless babies wrapped in rags. Horse-drawn wagons wound their way among the crowds. It seemed to Andreas that he had left the twentieth century behind, had been abandoned by civilization.

AS SOON as Anna's letter reached him, Edu tried to trace his nephew, but the German authorities were evasive. They answered the letters they received from Edu's upright Swiss lawyers with bureaucratic exactitude, saying precisely nothing. The lawyers persisted. They had connections, lawyers in Germany who might be able to do something. Would it help to offer money? Money always helped, but the task here was staggering. How was it possible to find a single individual among the hundreds of thousands being transported across the face of Europe? Andreas' papers were somewhere, stamped EVACUATED. The trains started, stopped, switched tracks, made detours. Those who were dead when the trains reached Poland were hurriedly thrown into mass graves. It was well-nigh impossible to find someone in all of that confused movement. And even if one found this single person, how could one transport him back? It was the stated intent of the government that Germany should be *Judenrein,* rid of the Jews. The Swiss lawyers were embarrassed and shook their heads. There was a ghetto in Czechoslovakia; they understood that conditions were better there. Privileged Jews were sent there. Our client is willing to pay . . .

And how do you expect us to transport this person from Lodz to

Theresienstadt? Do you think we provide individual service? There is a war going on! Send me 500 marks now, and I will see what I can find out. And what would your client be willing to pay to have his nephew transferred to this model community?

After a while the word "Theresienstadt" began to sound to Edu like the name of a resort. The atlas said it was a garrison town named after the Empress Maria Theresia, established in 1789, about sixty-three kilometers from Prague. Five hundred marks did not seem an excessive amount to pay to send Andreas to such a place. But what if he was untraceable, what if he was already dead?

There were more letters.

The Germans were exasperated. It was just like a Jew to be so persistent and so cheap at the same time. Did Herr Wertheim know that his nephew was also a degenerate, a pederast? It was on his record, writ large.

"*That* they can determine," Edu said and sent the lawyers 500 marks.

ANDREAS and Werner joined the other Jews standing in groups on the street corners of the Lodz ghetto. Soon they looked exactly like everyone else, gray and dull. They grew used to the beggars and the sight of the dying lying in the middle of the street. They bartered away their possessions one by one. They slept on sacks of straw in a dank basement near a furnace that didn't work.

They talked. That was really all there was to do. They did not particularly like each other, but they spoke the same language, they understood each other. Werner was ardent in his love of the Jews. He taught Andreas until Andreas began for the first time in his life to have some glimmer of knowledge about Jewish history, Jewish practice, ritual, belief. Werner had stayed in Frankfurt as long as possible to help others escape. He had been trained as a lawyer, but his passion was Judaism. He kept a meticulous journal "to bear witness" to his experiences. "How will you ever get it out?" Andreas asked. "I'll find a way," Werner answered.

It grew colder, and life became harsher yet. The two men went to work outside the ghetto. It was hard work, but it meant an occasional extra ration, a bit of sausage or an apple, some potatoes or a cigarette. Andreas grew accustomed to the life, grew to know the streets, the shops, even some of the faces. The city under its blanket of sooty snow was no longer totally alien. He began to think about spring. He did not realize that he was growing weaker. He had a bad cough, but on some days it was almost gone; surely it would clear up in the warm weather. Andreas put his mind to work, focusing on the moment. Sleep at night, talk, a glass of hot tea. Life was bound to get better come spring.

One morning in April he could not get up for work. He had a fever and kept falling back on his mattress whenever he tried to rise. "Stay here," Werner Epstein said. "Someone else will take your place. We'll find a doctor when I get home."

There were puddles in the streets and a pale sun was shining. It was shortly before Passover. Werner had promised that they would attend a clandestine Seder; all religious observances had been forbidden the Jews. Andreas felt better in the afternoon. He thought it would be good to sit in the sun and left the room, surprised at the weight of his feet. He looked down; he was not even wearing shoes, only slippers. It took a long time to put one foot before the other. In the courtyard, a few children were playing with marbles. Andreas waved to them. He set out to find a park. He had decided there must be a square somewhere in the vicinity where trees grew.

He walked in circles, growing more and more confused. His limbs were like lead. Near the ghetto wall there was an empty lot which had once held a building, now torn down, its wooden beams, doors and floorboards used for fuel. A small fenced-in vegetable garden had been planted there. Some of the hardier plants were beginning to sprout. There were greens and horseradish for the Seder. Andreas leaned against the fence and looked at the garden for a long time. He tried to imagine it in full bloom, surrounded by a border of zinnias and marigolds.

Feeling suddenly very weak, he dropped to his knees. The soil was damp. He put his head down, his fingers locked in the chickenwire. Now he could smell the earth, the emerging blades of grass.

"What are you doing?" said a voice, a woman's voice, speaking Yiddish.

Andreas did not at first realize that she was addressing him. But when she repeated the words, he looked up. The woman was young, wrapped in the usual ragged gray garments pinned together. But there was a gaily colored kerchief around her head, and she was pregnant. Andreas saw her great round belly above him. He tried to speak but could only say something that sounded like "la la, tra la . . ." His head dropped forward, and he fell to his side. His cheek came to rest on a sharp rock. The woman knelt beside him and lifted his head from the ground. Andreas' eyes were already sightless.

"*Halt! Halt!*" she heard a German voice. A flatbed truck was driving slowly down the narrow street. On it a man with a camera mounted on a tripod was taking pictures. For a second the woman thought it was a gun. She screamed. The truck driver laughed. He put out his thumb and index finger as if he did indeed hold a gun in them. "Bang, bang," he said and laughed again.

"Andreas died today," Werner Epstein wrote in his diary that night.

"He was not in the house when I returned from work. The children in the yard said he had gone out in the early afternoon. I walked back and forth through the streets of the ghetto trying to find him, even staying out after the curfew, but to no avail. Early the next morning there was a knock on my door. A woman in her eighth month of pregnancy (imagine it, in these conditions of life!) stood there, asking if this was where Andreas Wertheim lived. She said he had died in front of the garden plot at the corner of the alley leading from the old yeshivah to the Wall. A German photographer had taken her picture, kneeling beside him. She said that she reported the corpse to the burial detail, which combs the streets of the ghetto for the dead. She did not know if they had come to fetch him. I went with her to the spot, but nothing was there. I must assume that he was buried with all the other "*Unbekannten,*" unknowns, in a mass grave on the periphery of the Jewish cemetery. They no longer use coffins, I am told, even for the rich.

I shall miss him. He was a good companion and decent. May his soul rest in peace. He has probably been spared more suffering. I hope that our conversations were of some comfort to him. If I can find a minyan meeting somewhere in secret, I shall say *Kaddish* for him.

The German Kommandant who received Edu's request to extradite Andreas to Theresienstadt tossed the letter in the wastebasket.

"Do they think we have nothing better to do than search that foul ghetto for some rich Jew-boy to send him on a vacation?" His subalterns laughed, as they always did when they thought he was trying to make a joke.

IN MAY OF 1940, when Holland fell, Jacob and Lore were trapped, like countless others. In the beginning, emboldened by the solidarity of the Dutch people and their will to resist, they lived on as before. Their landlord, a Dutch Socialist, was an honorable man and courageous. He soon became involved in the Dutch Resistance. It was possible to believe that in this network of friends and comrades one could survive, one could be useful, one could even carry the fight to the Germans.

Then, on January 10, 1941, the inevitable happened: the German authorities ordered all Jews to register. Jacob, having spent all the years of his life in a society where a good citizen followed orders, presented himself to the census taker, as did over 160,000 others. Lore had tried to dissuade him, but he said that he did not wish to bring trouble down upon them—the penalties for nonregistration were severe. There followed a brief period of quiet, as if the registrations had, in fact, been all that was demanded.

But the police, now in control, conducted a raid on the Jewish quarter late in February. Dockworkers, seeing Jews set upon and beaten, came to their aid. In the melee a policeman was killed. Four hundred Jews were arrested in reprisal and publicly beaten. Amsterdam's workers called a general strike for February 25 and 26, which spread to other Dutch cities. Martial law was imposed; many workers were arrested, eighteen leaders of the Resistance were shot. All the Jewish hostages were deported to Buchenwald and thence to Mauthausen, where they were tortured to death.

On April 29, 1942, the Jews of Holland were ordered to wear the yellow star. Once again, Lore counseled noncompliance, while Jacob, citing the punishment meted out by the Nazis for those who defied their laws, urged obedience. After many hours of heated discussion, it was decided that Jacob would wear the star. It was a fact, he said, that the Jews of Frankfurt had lived under a variety of restrictions much like those of the Nazis, back in "what we call the Renaissance."

"Did you know," he lectured, "that the Jews had to pay a toll to leave the Judengasse on Sundays and Christian holidays? The city finally annulled that decree in 1798, after exacting a payment of eighteen hundred gulden from the Jews. Goethe's mother didn't like it at all," Jacob said, "and complained bitterly when she saw Jews wandering pell-mell through the Anlagen one pleasant Sunday in 1806."

By that summer, when Jews were being rounded up for deportation daily, Jacob had given up leaving the house. A closet under the eaves in the attic had been fixed up for him in which he might hide for days on end should it become necessary. It had a single small window facing the sky and enough room for him to lie curled on a mattress or to sit in a chair. He had brought books and papers there and often spent some part of the day working in the cramped quarters, even when it was not necessary. He found it unbearable to go into the street wearing the badge and had hung his coat on a nail in the hall so that the yellow star was invisible. The only fresh air he got was when he sat before one of the windows that faced the canal, his face turned to the mist-covered sun. The odor of salt water, of fish and ships' oil reached him faintly. His hands were pale and had begun to shake a little.

Hitler had been fighting the Russians since June, and in December 1941 the United States was pulled into the war. Lore went out regularly to shop and get the news, which grew more ominous every month even as it appeared that the tide of war was slowly beginning to turn against Hitler. Deportations were accelerated, and Jews who did not report voluntarily were often picked up in their residences at dawn. The weather was beautiful in those summer weeks, and the children played with their dolls and wooden horses while the adults stood in endless lines, waiting to register with the authorities at the assembly point. Men and women wore their traveling clothes and dark straw hats; some pushed their fifty kilos of belongings in baby carriages. The ubiquitous photographers with their press cameras recorded the scenes, which were tranquil enough. The Jews, except for their stars, looked like ordinary civilians fleeing some natural disaster or the threat of bombs.

Lore decided that come what might, she would endeavor to keep

Jacob in hiding. She had heard reports about what happened to the people who walked so compliantly into the detention camps and climbed into the cattle cars. It was said that all the trains led directly to the East and to death. On her way to work she had often seen the lines of people trudging through Amsterdam just as the sun rose. She could not help but watch. Sometimes tears ran down her stricken face, and one or another of the Jews would smile self-consciously at her. Often at night she could not sleep and lay in Jacob's arms.

"I can't believe it," she would say, "I cannot imagine it. They say that people are killed, hundreds, thousands a day. It is so monstrous that I recoil from the very thought. It must take an army of helpers to *do* it. It isn't possible!

"It was possible to destroy the entire Jewish community of Frankfurt several times—once in 1241, and again in 1349, during the Black Death, not to mention the persecutions during the crusades, or the pogroms in Russia. If you can kill two hundred people in one ghetto, you can kill two hundred thousand in a thousand ghettos. The Germans with their vaunted efficiency have surely found a way to do it with the least amount of fuss."

"I'll hide you and protect you," Lore said.

BY 1943 the German armies were everywhere in retreat. In February the Sixth Army surrendered at Stalingrad; in May the last German forces surrendered in North Africa; in June the British and Americans landed in Sicily. None of these events, however, stopped the systematic slaughter of the Jews. In fact, they hastened it; time was running out for the Nazi death machine, and its operation was given top priority to accomplish the Final Solution. On September 29 the last 5,000 Jews were deported from Amsterdam.

Conditions worsened in that last winter before the Allied invasion. Lore had found work in the kitchen of a Dutch hospital. She lived with forged papers and had succeeded in reporting the "death" of Jacob to prevent continued searches for him. Her job gave her access to some extra food; the landlord had family in the country, so it was possible to sneak potatoes and turnips into the house. On special occasions a liter of milk appeared or a basket of eggs. Lore worked with the Resistance, but in such utter secrecy that Jacob knew nothing about it, and even the landlord, who was active in another cell, had no information on the details of her activities.

In mid-May of 1944 Jacob took his fateful, foolish step. It was quite impossible later to explain it. Some thought there had been an informer, someone waiting for him to show himself. Lore came to suspect the landlord, trading one life for another. Everything was possible in those days.

Jacob had had a slight case of the flu and spent several days in bed. He felt well that day, and when he saw the blue sky out of the attic window, he was seized with a kind of wanton courage. The house was empty, everyone was at work. Jacob prowled about the small apartment, unable to sit down, read, write or study. He looked at the calendar and saw that the next day was May 13—the anniversary of the day eleven years before when he met Lore in Strasbourg. It was a day just like the one he remembered, cloudless and bright. He must celebrate it when Lore came home. He would buy her a gift. Surely there was a place somewhere in Amsterdam where he could find a little trinket for her, some small pendant or necklace.

He searched for money but found none. Should he go to a pawn-shop and trade them his watch—what did he need a watch for?—for a gift for his wife? He became so preoccupied with his plans that he forgot completely that he was a hunted man, a Jew in a city cleared of Jews, a stranger to everyone.

Jacob put on his light raincoat—his winter coat minus its star had long since been given to a worker who was doing forced labor at a factory outside of Amsterdam—and left the house. He felt no fear. The street was peaceful; an old woman was sweeping the stoop next door. Jacob turned in the opposite direction. He thought he remembered what the city looked like and where the pawnshops were. But he grew confused only a short distance from the house; nothing was where it was supposed to be. Shops were closed or had changed owners, the pawnshop was not to be found, even its sign had vanished. Exasperated, Jacob continued to think of nothing but the need to find a gift—any gift—for Lore. He would even trade his watch for a bouquet of flowers. The sun was quite hot and dulled his senses. He realized that he should have worn a hat. After a while he also began to feel his legs aching. The cobblestones were hard underfoot, and the thin soles of his shoes let him feel every one.

He found a bench in a small square far from his house and sat down. He had not realized how tired he was. From the open window of a house just behind him came the sounds of someone practicing the violin. Each false note sent a shudder through him, but the melody, however distorted, was sad and lovely and sang him to sleep.

The shouting did not immediately wake him. It was part of his dream. He had been running to school in Frankfurt, for he was late, and the teacher always closed the door on the dot of eight. He had stumbled on the top step—

"*Get up!*" a voice said, but it was the pain of the nightstick across his shin that woke him. Jacob opened his eyes and looked directly at a policeman's black belt. There were two of them. They were Dutch. Then he remembered everything. He saw the swastikas in their lapels.

"Your papers," the first policeman demanded.

"I left them at home."

"You know better than that, don't you?"

"I forgot," Jacob stammered.

"You're not Dutch. Are you Jewish?"

"No, no," Jacob said, but he could not think of what else he might be.

"We'll take you to your house and you'll show us your papers."

"I don't have a permanent home." Jacob knew that he could not, under any circumstances, bring them to his apartment.

"Then you go to jail," one of them said.

Jacob was beaten, but he did not tell where he lived. In truth, he could not remember after a while, which was just as well. They had undressed him, seen that he was circumcised and been disgusted that he was just another Jew who had escaped the dragnet.

Lore came home that afternoon, buoyed by the beauty of the day and the news of Russian advances. She entered the apartment quietly; she had learned to move noiselessly wherever she went. "Jacob?" she said softly. There was no answer. She felt panic all at once. She thought he was dead, she imagined him hanging in the closet or lying in the tub or slumped in a chair, his heart stopped. She had brought some jonquils home for the anniversary.

"Jacob!" she called again, louder this time. She searched the rooms, went into his secret hiding place. Then she saw the empty coat rack and knew that he had gone out. He had left the safety of the house—for what? To take a walk in the spring sunshine, she thought, looking out the window.

She knocked on the landlord's door. "Have you seen Jacob?" she asked.

He shook his head.

"Did the police come around?"

"Not as long as I was here."

Lore looked at him. He saw the searching, angry gaze. "I had nothing to do with it," he said.

The old woman next door said she had seen a man in a raincoat leave the house that morning. He had not come back.

Lore went to the police station. The officers professed ignorance. No one had been brought in that day. Not into *their* station, at any rate. Why was *she* interested? Lore said it was an uncle of hers who was kept in the house because he was confused, getting senile, you know.

They said they understood. Their faces were blank. Lore went to several other precincts, and in one she found a policeman willing to tell her something.

"He's a Jew," the man said. "They found him on the street without papers, asleep on a bench as if it was the most natural thing. In such times as these!" He shook his head.

"His wife is not Jewish," Lore said.

"They have already sent him to Westerbork," the policeman said.

"He's sixty-six years old!" Lore cried. "What do they want with him?"

"The Germans take them at any age," the man said.

Lore saw that it was no use to make a scene there. She thanked the man politely, and once outside again she made certain that she was not followed. A moon, very nearly full, shone above the city. She heard the bombers coming over from England a long way off. By the time she saw them, hundreds of dark shapes against the sky, the noise was deafening. They were heading for Germany. Their sound was music to her ears.

Lore came into the empty apartment silently. She did not switch on the light but found her way in the dark. She undressed and washed herself and crawled into the empty bed. It was only then that she realized that she had had nothing to eat since late morning. In the dark still, she fetched a piece of bread and took a very small piece of hard cheese from the shelf where she kept the provisions. She sat in an armchair near the window and ate slowly, trying to make the meal last. She thought about Jacob, determined to try to find him. If she could not save him, she would die with him. For the past eleven years her entire life had been built upon his; she could not imagine going on without him. She was nearly fifty now. She knew she looked older, but Jacob did not care. He had never looked at her with anything but love, and in his love she appeared beautiful. No one else had ever felt such a need for her, no one else had ever found her beautiful.

Lore slept fitfully that night and kept dreaming of trains. She heard the bombers coming back from their missions and rose just as the pallor of dawn spread over the sky. That evening she went to see one of her comrades in the Resistance.

"I must go to Germany," she said.

"That's suicidal," he told her.

"I'm prepared to die," Lore said. "If you have anything for me to do there, tell me. I'm going in any case." She spoke dispassionately, reciting her reasons, saying that Jacob had been arrested and deported and that she planned to search for him, in all of Germany if necessary.

"Have you heard of a town called Oświęcim?" he asked her. "The Germans call it Auschwitz."

"I'm ready to go to Poland as well," Lore answered.

He saw her determination, he saw a glimpse of the beauty Jacob saw.

"I'm afraid that it's going to be too late for the Jews," Lore said. "They're all doomed. But I must find Jacob, I must." She did her best to control the weeping that threatened to break through her voice. "You'll get me the papers I need?"

Two weeks later Lore received word that she was to pick up an old suitcase in a shop not far from the railway station. It contained shortwave equipment concealed in its sides. She was to deliver it to a shoemaker in Mainz. Her papers were also inside.

Lore packed everything of value, including all of Jacob's books and papers, into a steamer trunk and left it in the basement of the house. She did not think she would ever see any of these things again, but she felt curiously detached from them. They were the shell, not the life. Jacob carried *that* with him; all else could just as well be consumed by flames or left to dust and rot.

She made her way to the border on a train full of soldiers and Nazi officials, pretending to be a German mother searching for her four sons lost in the war. Everyone she spoke to was full of sympathy. She wore a tiny swastika of rhinestones on her blouse.

The delivery of the suitcase to the shoemaker in Mainz went off as planned. She was free now, and she headed for Frankfurt. It was said that the transports from Westerbork went to Buchenwald, to replenish the supply of forced labor there, but it was not said what they did with the Jews. Buchenwald was located on the Ettersberg, a hill overlooking Weimar. Lore planned to go from Frankfurt to Erfurt and thence to Weimar; she went to Frankfurt first because it was home.

The city had been the object of heavy bombardment for some months, but it was in March of that year that the fires that destroyed the Altstadt raged out of control, leaving the city's heart a smoking ruin. Lore came into Frankfurt from the east and walked through a desert of stone. There were the familiar streets to go by but little else to remind her of the places she had known so well. She stopped at a bar where she had once sat with her comrades, drinking beer and talking late into the night. Several of the old men were still there, but they were guarded, like prisoners, when they saw her, and it was only in the street that one or another gave her a sign that showed he had clung to his old beliefs. She found out that some of the young people went to secret meetings at an abandoned camp in the Taunus, that this one still printed leaflets, that one scrawled slogans on the ruined walls at night. They told her who had died and who had been lost in the prisons of the state. Many had fled to the country, to relatives in the villages and on the farms nearby. "It can't go on much longer," they said, more in hope than true belief. "When are the Allies going to come?" Lore did not know. She remembered the sounds of the bombers flying over Amsterdam. They had been coming here.

"We hope we'll be alive when it's over," they said. "Maybe we can rebuilt it in our image this time." It was, Lore thought, a touching faith.

She spent the night in Rödelheim, at the apartment of a widowed friend; they had killed her husband in Dachau. Her seventeen-year-old son was soon to be called up. "They're throwing everyone against the Russians," she said, "old men and children too." One by one the surviving comrades came to the door, embraced her and stayed for half an hour or so to talk to her. They told her as best they knew where the trains ran to the camps and where there might be friends. The most important thing, they said, was to know whom to trust.

Early the next morning Lore went to the train station, only to find that it would not be possible to catch a train to Erfurt until the following day. "Because of the war," they said. But the trains to Auschwitz ran day and night. Lore stood on the square in front of the station, ticket in hand, feeling lost. The spring sun shone on piles of dusty rubble, a battalion of Russian POWs were repairing a watermain.

Lore did not dare return to her friends for fear of implicating them by her presence—which was sure to have been noted. She felt a loneliness at once frightening and exhilarating. She was without ties, she carried nothing with her but her love, her convictions. She thought of Jacob constantly. She hoped that he was only being made to work at some menial task, like the Russian prisoners here. Her mind could not reach out to anything more awful than that. It had been less than a week since he was arrested. He couldn't possibly be dead!

Walking toward the Baseler Platz and the Main, Lore found herself looking down on the Nizza Anlage, once a lovely garden spot. Across the river, the Städel was only half there. Both wings had been destroyed, but from the top of the central section the black barrels of anti-aircraft guns pointed at the sky. Lore wondered idly what had become of the pictures. She continued walking through the ruins of the city. The house in which Jacob had lived still stood, but it was only a shell, adorned with torn fragments of wallpaper, banked by rubble.

By late afternoon she had reached the Palmengarten. It was miraculously green. Eduard Wertheim's villa stood empty and roofless; a bomb had fallen into the very center of the garden and flung earth and rocks against the façade. The detonation had knocked out every window, but there was a homeless family camping in the ruin. The nearby Rothschild palace was no more. A passer-by told Lore that the old baron had died in his own bed at the age of ninety-one the year before, in the last room left to him by his captors.

To Lore, the Palmengarten had always seemed a place reserved for the privileged. She had looked through its fence as a child, watched the nannies with their children, lacked the few pennies it took to gain entrance. It was not until she was a young working woman that she went there occasionally with her lunch wrapped in a piece of brown paper and sat among the rosebushes.

Now she saw that there was a small restaurant still open on the side of the great Palm House, and entrance to the park was free. The rich were all gone. Frankfurt, bombed out and charred, was abandoned to the poor and the middle class. Lore sat at one of the small tables on the terrace and ordered a cup of ersatz chocolate and a dry biscuit.

All at once she noticed a man at the next table. A gentleman, she thought, and bit her tongue that such an expression should have crossed her mind and brought disdain with it. She still made these distinctions, and always to the detriment of those she judged to be of the "better" class. Once again she saw the picture of Jacob in her mind, with his gentle, patrician face. The man at the next table was well-dressed. He had come on a bicycle, which was leaning against the chair next to him, and his clean suede gloves lay neatly folded on the table. He was the first person she had seen in years who carried himself with assurance and appeared to have kept his sense of style. Lore looked with a touch of contempt at his worn but well-cut sports jacket, his shirt of striped cotton, his creased worsted slacks. He returned her gaze with a soft smile. His hair was growing a little thin, but he was handsome. His eyes were a bright blue. Lore decided that he looked familiar, and she tried to decide why this was so. Had she worked with him once years ago? Was he someone she'd known? Ought she to fear him?

He looked utterly harmless. Clearly he was not a person who plunged into politics; she could not have known him in *that* connection. And yet they shared something. She looked at him again and realized all at once that he was in some way connected to Jacob. She searched her mind to try to discover how. She went down the row of pictures he had kept on his desk and listed the names of all the relatives he had talked about these eleven years. Her mind's eye stopped at a photograph of a young woman in a ski suit standing next to a handsome blond man in a field of snow . . . of course! It could only be Lene's husband Tom. "I always liked Tom," Jacob had said. "I liked him better than that Manfred Solomon."

Just then the man got up from his table, came over to hers, and bowing slightly, said, "Thomas von Brenda-Badolet."

"I know who you are," said Lore. "I figured it out just this minute. My name is Lore Wertheim. I'm Jacob's wife."

Tom looked around, Lore noticed, with the instinctive, roving glance of one who knows the hunters are everywhere, and said, "May I sit down?" Lore nodded. He brought his cup with him. It contained weak tea. "I carry my own teabags," Tom said, "and I'll be glad to share one of them with you. All we need do is order hot water."

Lore shook her head. For a moment, neither one knew what to say, where to begin.

"Tell me about them all," Tom said, leaning across the table, his face close to hers so she could speak directly at him within the closed shell of the branches dipping down from above them. "Are they safe? Where are they? What's become of Lene? What are you doing here?"

Seeing a shadow cross her face, Tom knew that Lore was doomed, that Jacob was missing. "And the others?" he asked. "Do you have any news of Clara—my little girl?"

"I saw Lene in Paris six years ago. They were going to America.

She was on her way to Italy to fetch the child, who was staying, if I recall it right, with an aunt?"

"Yes. Emma. I'd heard she moved to Florence."

"They never said good-bye?"

Tom looked away from her. The question had been indiscreet, but Lore was not aware of it.

"It had been decided . . ." Tom began. "I was to stay away . . . Edu made all the arrangements." He stopped. "What are you doing here? Or shouldn't I ask?"

"I'm looking for Jacob," Lore said. "He was arrested last week. I understand they send the deportees to Buchenwald."

"Do you think you will find him?"

"No," said Lore. The answer was unpremeditated and shocked them both. Lore's voice became hoarse. "But I have to try to see him once more. I never said good-bye to him. He was gone when I came home from work. I had something to tell him."

Her eyes were bright with tears. The sun had been obliterated by the thickening haze; there was rain in the air.

"The weather's turning ugly," said Tom. "Come with me to my apartment."

"Will you be able to put me up for the night?" Lore asked. "My train to Erfurt won't leave till morning." She knew the question was a bold one, but she had to make plans.

"My wife is very ill," Tom said and saw Lore's face stiffen and grow wary. "I don't mean you can't stay," he added. "I just wanted to warn you."

"Is it catching?"

"She has cancer."

"I'm sorry. I didn't mean to be flippant. But I must get to where I am going, and I can't be delayed. I didn't know you had married again." She kept talking to cover her confusion.

"I married the woman I fell in love with when Lene and I were separated. It's not been a happy marriage. She thinks of herself as a poet, but she never had much talent. She's willful and difficult. No doubt I'm difficult in my own way, too, but she's become like a sack I carry with me, weighing me down. I go out every day even when there's no work to be done, just to escape her."

"Poor soul."

Tom did not know whether Lore meant him or his wife. The first raindrops began to fall.

"Come," Tom said, "I'll ride you to my house on the crossbar of my bicycle."

"Do you know how many years it's been since I've done that?" Lore asked. "I bet I'm too big and fat. I'll break the bike."

"No, you won't. It's a sturdy bike, and I'm a very good rider. It's the only athletic thing I can do well. I used to ride Lene like that sometimes."

After a wobbly start they both got the hang of it. Tom rode along the Grüneburg Park, his knees pointed out. The hardest thing was to stop when they came to an intersection and had to let a cart or a truck go by. They laughed heartily on their short ride and very nearly forgot that they were wandering on the precipice of hell.

The apartment building where Tom lived had escaped bomb damage, but it looked shabby and unkempt. The neighborhood was genteel; its buildings dated from the early part of the century, its streets were tree-lined and quiet. A housekeeper greeted them at the door. She was bent by arthritis and ancient.

"Who's that?" she asked irascibly, pointing a finger at Lore.

"She's a friend of the family," Tom said.

"I don't remember such a friend."

"She worked for my parents," Tom said to Lore *sotto voce*.

"What did you say about your parents?"

"Nothing, Grete, nothing."

Tom excused himself and went to the rear of the apartment. Lore saw him open the door to a room and heard the complaining whine of a rasping voice, interrupted by coughs.

"Please sit down in the living room," said Grete, "and give me your rucksack."

"I'll keep it with me, thank you," said Lore. She was always disconcerted by the presence of servants.

Tom returned shortly with a bottle of wine. "We must keep some of the amenities," he said as he opened it and smelled the cork. "A good year from before the war."

They drank out of crystal goblets.

"I rescued a few things from my parents' house," Tom said. Then he offered a toast: "To the end of the war and the defeat of the Fatherland."

They were served dinner by Grete in a room that clearly saw little use these days. The china was chipped and the silver service tarnished, but Lore did not notice. The soup was thin, full of rutabagas and turnips, and for a main course there was canned meat and scrambled eggs made from powder. But the wine was superb. Lore felt it smooth the way for her, and she grew used to the idea of being there. She told Tom about her youth. They talked on and on and never reached the present. Lore asked about Jacob, she wanted to understand him in a different context. And she ached to tell him of the evening. How pleased he would be, how much he would want to know—she had better notice everything!

Tom was telling her about the time Jacob had quarreled with the electric company over a bill and lived by candlelight for a month. Lore was laughing so hard that Tom did not for a minute notice that the spasms that shook her were not part of her mirth.

"You're crying," he said.

"I never cry," Lore sobbed.

Tom sat still. He knew it would be useless to try to persuade her to abandon her mission.

"I'll stop in a minute," she said.

Tom covered her hand with his. The gesture was delicate and tentative. It preserved the distance between them. It told her that he was unable to help. He was, she thought, like a religious; he believed in some other order of things. He had a kind of faith, but he never risked it.

"I must go and talk to my wife," he said when they had finished dinner. Lore sat in the living room while Grete cleared the table.

"Just let's hope there's no air raid," Tom said when he returned. "My wife won't walk the stairs. We have to carry her to the basement shelter. Down there she cries all the time. She's near death and in great pain, yet she doesn't want to die."

"You wish for her death, don't you?"

"Yes. I've begun to hate her," Tom said.

The planes didn't come that night. The rain fell softly, the clouds were thick and covered the blacked-out city and the countryside all the way to the French border. Lore and Tom talked until very late.

Grete had made up the bed in the guest room, and Lore slept between linen sheets. It was a deep sleep that destroyed all its dreams before she woke. Tom accompanied her to the station and waited with her until the train left. A group of portly men were seeing one of their number off. *"Heil Hitler!"* they cried as the train began to pull out of the station. Lore saw Tom stand back from these men as if they had pushed him out of their way. He waved to her with his gloved hand. This gesture, too, was barely visible, his motion a painful reminder that he lived in the worst of times and was defenseless.

The man from the Gestapo rang Thomas von Brenda-Badolet's doorbell at eleven-thirty in the morning. Grete let him in but made him wait in the hallway. She had no idea who he was, but she knew he did not belong in the living room.

"You had a visitor last night?" the man from the Gestapo asked Tom. They stood facing each other across the width of the Oriental rug. Tom gave a noncommittal shrug. It was almost a Jewish gesture.

"May I come in and sit down?" asked the man from the Gestapo.

"No," said Tom, "there's no need for that. We can talk here. My wife is deathly ill."

"About your visitor?"

"She was a friend of my sister's passing through Frankfurt. We met by accident in the Palmengarten."

"What is her name?"

Tom chose a name at random—the name of the girl who had sat next to him at his first formal dinner party. "But I know nothing about her," he said.

"And yet you put her up for the night? While your wife is ill— dying, as you tell me—down the hall here!"

"It's hard to find a room these days. The Frankfurter Hof is bombed out . . ."

"Where was she going? You took her to the station."

"To Leipzig."

"What for?"

"Listen," Tom said, "I will tell you the truth. She came here to sleep with me." The man from the Gestapo leered. Tom knew he was on the right track. "You know how it is," he said. "My wife has been sick for a long time."

"Dying."

"Yes."

"You people are disgusting," the man said with sudden vehemence, "degenerate—like the Jews. Do you know the name Wertheimer?" He had turned sly again.

"I don't believe so."

"You were married to a Jewish woman. What was her name?"

"Wertheim."

"That's what I said."

"Not exactly. In any case, that was many years ago. We were divorced in 1930."

"And you had a child. Where is she now?"

"In America, I hope, safe and sound."

"The rest of the family, where are they?"

"Out of range of your power to harm them, I hope."

"We sent one of them to Poland, to the ghetto in Litzmannstadt. So it says in my notice. He perished, I believe. The accommodations weren't good enough for him. He was used to a better class of hotel."

Tom stared at him. "If you're done, you may go," he said.

"Don't rush me. I have a job to do."

Tom opened the door. The man from the Gestapo backed out. He replaced his hat once he was on the landing. "Better watch yourself," he said.

The door closed in his face.

THE TRAINS ran poorly, and Lore did not arrive in Erfurt until the middle of the afternoon. The weather had not cleared despite the rain. It felt heavy. People complained of headaches and said that the Allies were using a new kind of gas. Lore set out for Weimar on foot, hoping to cover the twenty kilometers by nightfall. She had always been a good walker.

The gently rolling countryside of Thuringia stretched before her.

Farmers were at work in the fields, planting late potatoes. Whenever she came to a rise in the road, she could see for miles in all directions. It seemed a gentle enough landscape. A passing truck, filled with soldiers, stopped beside her, and the driver leaned out to ask her if she needed a lift. For a moment Lore was frightened, but seeing the dull, tired faces of the men, she realized that they posed no threat. She climbed into the back of the truck and sat on the floor, which was covered with straw. Wordlessly, one of the soldiers offered her a piece of bread and a swig from his canteen. She ate and drank. No one asked her where she was going.

The truck let Lore off two blocks from the center of Weimar. It was not yet dusk, and she had a chance to admire the splendid eighteenth-century façade of the town—the very one Goethe and Schiller knew. Lore was not well educated, but she understood that, like Chartres or St. Peter's in Rome, this little town represented the flowering of an age, summed up all that was great and good and lasting in man. Walking past the theater, past the house of Schiller and the house of Goethe, Lore felt like a pilgrim.

She went down into the town park, where she sat for a while on a bench, eating the dried fruit she had brought with her. When it was dark at last, she went to look for a hotel. She planned to spend the night and to set out early the next morning. Every extra hour she spent there would put her in danger of discovery and interrogation.

She found a small hotel, the sort that in peacetime caters to traveling salesmen and in times of war to black marketeers and other petty criminals. She felt unaccountably at home and slept soundly.

The next morning, just before sunrise, she awoke with a start as if a hand had been placed on her shoulder. But she was alone. She dressed quickly, washing her face with cold water in the small sink. She put her money but not her false passport into the small leather pouch she had tied around her waist. All of her belongings were safely packed into the rucksack, which she left in the wardrobe of the hotel room. She ate the last of the dried fruit and left. There was no one at the desk, and the streets were still empty.

She did not walk on the main road but kept to the woods and fields that alternated along its curving ascent out of the town. It seemed to her that she saw dark smoke rising from the far side of the mountain. The wind blew it away from her, but she saw it constantly as she went up one rise and then another. Except for that, the sky was clear. The crowing of a rooster, the distant clanging of cowbells were all the sounds she heard. She had walked about an hour when she entered the forest of beech trees that ringed the summit of the Ettersberg. There she rested briefly. She knew she was drawing closer to the camp, and a sense of foreboding hollowed out her soul, but she felt safer in the silent woods.

A single railroad track was the first sign she had that she was nearing the camp. She crossed it cautiously. The forest had opened up, giving way to a new territory, a thick second growth of oak and pine choking in vines, brambles and raspberry bushes. From here she could see the sky above the crest of the hill, and spreading across it, the cloud of black smoke. A sweet, sickening smell lingered in the air. Lore was ravenously hungry. All at once, she saw the wide cement road and heard the approaching sounds of trucks, the shouts of men, the barking of dogs. She dropped to her knees. She was most frightened of the dogs—their senses were keener than men's, they could find her, smell her, where their masters could not. She lay on the dank earth, pressing her face down among the small stones and dead leaves, and waited until the sounds of the convoy had passed.

When it was still once more, she got up and walked, bent almost double, in the direction from which the trucks had come, toward the place where the black smoke rose in blurred puffs into the gentle wind. After about ten minutes she reached the barbed-wire fence that enclosed the camp. She saw the watchtowers, the building with the smokestack, a large open square and rows upon rows of barracks. She saw men moving in groups through the "streets" of the camp; each group had its guard with a submachine gun. It was hard to make out what went on, but clearly these were work details. She saw the motions of men swinging axes, pulling equipment, breaking stones, hauling a large roller across the central square. She kept out of sight and watched until her eyes ached and her neck was stiff. The sun beat on her shoulders, the harsh stubble of grass between the weeds and the wild-cherry trees cut into the skin of her legs.

Toward noon she moved into the shade of a small thicket. She felt faint, and for a brief time she lay on the ground and dozed off. Above her the sky was hot with the merciless haze of the sun; her eyes burned. What was she to do? She would never be able to get into the camp, and even if she did, what then?

Lore spent two days and two nights in the underbrush outside the camp, darting for cover the way rabbits and other small game do whenever she saw or heard something she had not seen or heard before. She circled the camp again and again on hands and knees. She never crossed the road that led through the main gate but returned the way she had come, back to the other side. She had seen the words in cast-iron letters neatly set above the gate between its two great towers. *JEDEM DAS SEINE*—"To Each His Own," it said.

By the end of the second day Lore knew the layout of the camp exactly. She had seen the prisoners assemble on the square for roll call morning and evening, seen the dead carried to the building from which the smokestack belched its black cloud. She had seen men marched out to work in the morning and back at night, had seen truck transports come and go, heard cries of terror and pain and the rat-tat-tat of guns. It was all too far away to be clear or distinct, but the outlines were always visible. At night, bright lights shone from the watchtowers, so there were no shadows in which to hide.

The closest she came to another human being was on the second day when a group of prisoners in their striped shirts and pants passed a hundred feet from where she crouched on their way to the quarry. Jacob was not among them, and none wore a yellow star. It occurred to her then that the Jews were doubtless kept separate, and on her next round she watched to see if any barracks were set apart. She was beside herself with hunger; her mind no longer formed thoughts according to a coherent sequence. She was filthy and her clothes were torn, scratches covered her body, her neck was burned red, her hair was matted with twigs. She ate leaves and sipped water from a trickling stream she had found, but it tasted of rot.

Early on the morning of the third day she saw which were the

Jewish barracks. They were on the west side of the camp, enclosed by additional strands of barbed wire, apparently the inmates were kept segregated from the rest of the prisoners.

The last star was fading from the sky. The dewy air was cool. It will be another beautiful day, Lore thought. She no longer had any plan, she wanted only to survive long enough to see Jacob. Once or twice, during the first day, she had thought of giving up her quest, returning to Frankfurt and hiding out among her old friends. They had said it was possible. The closer the war came to Germany's borders, the harder it would be for the Nazis to maintain total control. But Lore could not bring herself to leave. Once she had established the pattern of her vigil, she was committed to it.

It had rained only once in the forty-eight hours since she had arrived at Buchenwald. A sudden violent squall had arisen out of a black cloud and let loose a rain of hailstones. Gusts of wind swept dust and debris across the camp. It was like some biblical tale in which God appears to the prophet. But when the storm ended, as quickly as it had begun, nothing had changed.

Dreams of food pressed on Lore's mind. She saw plates full of sausages, smelled hot coffee, lusted after fresh loaves of bread and strong pungent cheeses. All night long, these visions haunted her dreams. She nested in the underbrush and stuffed roots into her mouth. She had stopped her circling now that she knew where Jacob was most likely to be. She crept as close to the fence as she dared and tried to distinguish between the figures scurrying about in the pre-dawn emptiness.

Slowly it grew lighter. The searchlights dimmed, went out. Lore saw several hundred men standing stock-still, dead statues in even rows. She saw them divided into two groups, like the blessed and the damned, she thought, in paintings of the Last Judgment. She watched for Jacob's familiar figure. She knew she would recognize him by his movements, the way he held his head and lowered one shoulder; the way his shuffling walk betrayed a slight touch of arthritis. The Jews were not in prison stripes but apparently in the clothes in which they had come. From where Lore was, the stars on their chests were like handprints, pale as the spectral faces.

As the sun rose in a yellow burst of light, the guards gave the command to march, and the men, both groups of them, started off toward the main gate. Soon they were running in ragged step. Those who fell were pulled to their feet by their comrades and dragged along. The road led to the railroad track and siding that Lore had come upon the first day. A long line of cattle cars waited here, festooned with strands of barbed wire. Lore followed them at a short distance through woods of birch trees and young beeches. At a sign from the guards, the men began to climb into the cars.

The wagons filled slowly. Lore had found a place to hide behind a crumbling stone wall. She was almost mad with hunger. But at last she saw Jacob. She knew him first by the way his hair was brushed back—he always ran his hand through it—and by the shape of his glasses. He looked incredibly frail and delicate. Lore leapt up from her hiding place and began to run through the short stretch of woods that separated her from the train. "Jacob!" she screamed. "Jacob!" Her foot was caught by a root, and she fell but got up again, waving her arms. "Here I am, here I am," she called. Her eyes were blinded by tears, but she rubbed them away and saw more clearly than ever. He had turned toward her . . .

The shots rang out without echo. For a minute the birds stopped their singing, but only for a minute. The guards saw the woman fall. The Jews continued climbing into the cattle cars. Nobody went to see who she was. A guard would be sent out to pick her body up later.

Lore's rucksack lay unclaimed in a corner of the hotel manager's office until he decided to appropriate it months later; his own had worn out. He gave away the clothes he found in it and threw the passport in the stove. Jacob's train was sent to Auschwitz, where he was gassed and cremated. No one who saw him there knew him, no one in his transport survived. The date of his death was unknown. It was probably on one of the last days of July in 1944.

THE ALLIED invasion of Normandy in June was followed in less than three months by the liberation of Paris. Among the thousands who lined the streets and avenues of the French capital on that August day was Eva Süsskind. She had survived the occupation largely because her *chef* at the chemical lab had seen to it that she remain unmolested. She had not had an easy time of it, but she was alive. A frail woman, now sixty-four, she looked older than her years, but she had maintained her belief in the perfectibility of human institutions and the essential goodness of man. She considered the years of Nazi hegemony an aberration. She did not yet know, except by hearsay, about the death camps. She continued to have high hopes for the Soviet Union, even though she had no illusions about Josef Stalin. Although she had long ago repudiated the Party, she still maintained her friendship with those who remained loyal to it. She was a woman alone; comrades mattered.

Eva had moved to a small apartment facing a courtyard in a working-class section of Paris, an apartment Professor Fonsagrive, her *chef*, had found for her when the Germans began rounding up Jews in Paris during the spring and summer of 1941. He had gone to the authorities, demanding that he be allowed to keep Eva at her job, saying that she was essential to the work being done in his laboratory. The apartment she occupied was only a short distance from her place of work, so she did not have to show herself in the streets too much.

She had developed the habits of an eccentric old age; she saved scraps of paper and pieces of string and lived so frugally that it always seemed to her acquaintances that she was on the verge of starvation. She also became careless about her dress. She refused to buy anything new but rummaged in her trunk, which held everything she had brought with her, yellowing underwear and brittle silk shifts, her kerchiefs from Russia and serge suits and towels bought at Pfuller in Frankfurt in 1923.

Eva stood for many hours in the fierce August sun to watch the entry of the Free French liberators, to see them marching in endless streams down the Boul' Mich, their tanks garlanded with flowers, the fluttering tricolor everywhere. She wept as she had never wept before. A young Frenchwoman beside her tried to comfort her.

"Did you lose your husband?" she asked. "Did your son fall for France?"

"I have never married," Eva said. "I have no children. But my brother killed himself when the Nazis came. The others . . ." She let her voice trail off. In truth, at that moment, she remembered nothing, no one else.

"You are Jewish?" the woman asked. Eva looked at her with a startled expression. She supposed it was all right to admit it now, or was it? She nodded tentatively.

"And you lived?" the woman said. "That is a miracle. I saw them drive the Jews to the Vélodrome d'Hiver two years ago. It was terrible."

Eva dried her tears. "And what did you do?" she asked in her sharp French, tinged with the accents of Frankfurt.

"Do?" the woman asked. "What could I do? What could any of us do?" She moved discreetly away to let a father and his child have her place. The man had lost an arm.

Returning to her apartment in the early evening, Eva realized that for the first time in years she saw the city not as a prisoner, but like the *flâneuse* who strolls where her feet take her, awake to all impressions, sensitive to all subtleties. For six years she had walked the straight line between her flat and the lab, speaking to no one, nodding only to a few shopkeepers along the way. Now she smiled, and they smiled back. The concierge in her building had a kind word for her. Eva was pleased, but it occurred to her that a kind word during the years of the occupation might have been welcome indeed. She banished these thoughts quickly. She did not care to dwell on gloomy matters; she was alive. She had not been denounced. She poured herself a glass of brandy from the bottle she kept for those nights when she had trouble sleeping, and drank it down. "To liberty, equality, fraternity!" she said aloud and laughed heartily, something else she had not done for a very long time.

On the first Sunday in September, not long after ten o'clock in the morning, an American soldier knocked on the door of Eva's apartment. The other tenants had seen him enter the building, and their doors had all opened a crack to allow them to watch his progress up the stairs to Mademoiselle Süsskind's apartment. Eva was surprised to hear a knock and did not immediately respond to it. She thought it was a mistake. Perhaps the children were playing tricks again. When the sound became more insistent, she went to the door, unlatched its many locks and stood face to face with her nephew Benno. She studied him for a long time, making certain that it was he. Benno smiled broadly ("Just like an American," Eva later said of him) and embraced her. She was so slight and bony and so unused to affection that she held herself stiffly and would not let him kiss her. She cried a little bit, but she had spent her tears the week before in front of strangers, and now she wanted to be done with them.

"Benno!" she said. "You—an American. It's wonderful. I would not have expected it of you!"

They laughed, a little awkwardly. Benno had grown thinner, but his khaki uniform fit as badly as his linen suits had, and he was as ungainly as ever. He had brought cigarettes and chocolate. "Give the chocolate to the children," Eva said. "I'm not used to sweets." She took a package of Chesterfields and opened them. Her hands were still agile and strong.

"It's a pleasure to smoke again," she said. "It always annoyed my sister Caroline to have me spill ashes on her rug. Is she dead?"

Benno nodded. "Andreas too, we think. And nothing has been heard from Jacob and Lore."

"Are the stories they tell . . . true?"

"I'm here to find that out. I volunteered when America went to war, and they put me in the OSS, the undercover service. Once we get to Germany, we'll see. But I hear they've killed hundreds of thousands of Jews. Perhaps millions."

"Millions? How can that be? I can't imagine it."

"None of us can. Anyway, Papa is fine and Mama too. I hope to see them soon. They write me that they have still not mastered the Swiss dialect, that Edu is the same as ever and has brought Emma to Zürich, where she continues her good works."

"What an odd lost soul she is!"

"She'd be furious to hear you say that. I understand she tried to take over Edu's house and he asked her to move to an apartment in town."

"She always loved him rather too well."

"You knew that?"

"It was so obvious, Benno. You still have your Frankfurt accent," Eva said. "It sounds good to my ears."

They went out to sit in a nearby café.

"I can't believe I'm free," she said. "And you're still unmarried, Benno?"

"I haven't found, as they say in America, 'the right person' yet. So I sit and wait."

"Don't wait too long."

"You never married, Aunt Eva."

"That was different. In my day it was almost impossible to find a man who'd take a working wife. Women were meant to devote themselves to children, the kitchen and the church. I never *wanted* to stay unmarried. I've often thought about it, regretted it. But I don't believe in regrets, so let's talk about something else. How's Lene? And Clara? She must be grown up by now."

Benno had brought some photographs.

"Is she like her mother? She looks so much like her! And what does she do?"

"She's an American child. And the boy, Peter, too. It's odd to see them growing up in such a different culture. It makes it hard to understand them."

"Is Lene happy in her marriage?"

"I'm not certain. We meet now and then for lunch. She has few friends. I think Manfred doesn't allow her the time . . ."

"I always thought he'd be difficult. He tries to bluster his way through life, playing the grand artist, but he's dependent like a child. He wants to have every bit of Lene's attention. How is his career?"

"Coming along much too slowly. He came to America at the wrong moment."

"That makes it hard for Lene, too, I'm certain."

"He needs the affection of other women . . ."

"Ahhhh . . ." Eva let out a sigh at once understanding and full of pity.

"Lene allows Claire—she Americanized her name—to go with him when he plays concerts out of town. I don't know whether it's to keep him on the straight and narrow or to unload some of the burden of his demands on her." Benno paused and looked directly into Eva's eyes. They were a long way from home; it was a moment such as sailors in a strange port know. "I'm very fond of Claire," he said, and his voice was low. He drew circles on the table with the end of his spoon. "She allows me a glimpse into her heart sometimes. I think that she has a yearning to 'belong'—to be like the others around her. At the same time she wants to be 'someone,' to stand out. Like you, she wants to save the world"—he put his hand on Eva's—"like Ernst, she wants to go to Palestine, reclaim the land, become a pioneer. She's full of contradictions, *Mischling* that she is. She walks always in light and shade. I've told her that she's freer than others, she has a choice, she can be who she wants to be—free of every kind of orthodoxy."

"That's surely too hard for her to understand," said Eva. "She's still young, almost a child, and a twice displaced one at that. She 'lost' first her father and then her home."

"She never mentions Tom. I think she's got a very complicated relationship with Manfred. I've seen him look at her with something very close to desire, and she responds to that. You know she's old enough, at seventeen, to seduce a man—though she's what they call a 'tomboy' in America. She becomes her mother's surrogate when she travels with Manfred, his pride and joy: a daughter, yet not a daughter . . ."

"You see a lot of her?"

"She comes over to Brooklyn once a week, to take an art class at the Brooklyn Museum. We lunch together. I'd like to make an art historian out of her. She's a sensitive child—young woman—and *sees* extremely well. Once you show her a painting, she never forgets it, even though she's scatterbrained about a lot of other things."

"This Brooklyn, is it far from New York?"

"It's a part of New York. You must come and visit us when the war is over, Aunt Eva."

"If I live so long. Tell me, are there Indians in Brooklyn or gangsters with masks on their faces and machine guns on their hips?" Benno was very nearly taken in by her bemused question but caught her smile just in time.

"And have you any news of Julia?" she went on.

"I was coming to that—you won't believe it!"

"Where is she? Not in America?"

"No, no, no. She's right here, not more than a few hours away. I plan to see her, come with me!"

"I'd love to! All I know is that she fled Paris when the Germans came. The French police—those pigs!—rounded up the Jews with great relish, let me tell you. But then I never heard from her again. You say she's safe?"

"She's married to a French farmer. God knows how she did it, but it probably saved her life."

"Julia? Impossible!"

"I swear it!"

"The man is probably another disaster."

"She always had that talent."

"When will you go?"

"As soon as possible. That is, as soon as I can commandeer a car or a jeep. You may have to ride on a hard seat if you come with me."

"I rode on tractors in Russia; I can ride on a jeep, even so many years later. It would be wonderful to leave the city for a day, to see fields for a change, orchards and wild flowers by the road . . ."

Benno came for his aunt on another Sunday, two weeks later. The Allies were almost at the German border; Benno's unit would soon be called to follow them. He had brought some jam and canned meat and powdered eggs for Eva's breakfast. She put most of the food away "for another day." Black coffee and a piece of dry toast was all she had so early in the morning.

They drove through the peaceful landscape without much conversation. The roads were empty. In the villages through which they passed, the children gathered to wave at them. Here and there American flags flew beside the tricolor.

They ate the cans of K-rations Benno had commandered along with the jeep, by the side of the road in the shade of an ancient oak. It was midafternoon when they arrived at the village nearest the farm of Julia's husband. Eva asked about him and was greeted by a suspicious silence. Even after she explained her mission, only a single person stepped forward to show them the way. He was a garrulous old man who asked to ride with them and demanded some cigarettes in return for his help.

The barnyard was alive with chickens, geese and ducks; the customary manure pile was heaped high beside the barn door. The house looked like countless others in this region. It needed a coat of whitewash. Apple trees, twisted and black with age, leaned over the stone wall, their branches full of ripening fruit. The grass in the orchard across the road had just been cut and lay drying in the sun; its sweet fragrance mingled with the more pungent aroma of the manure.

Benno got out of the jeep to help Eva down. A large tethered dog began barking and straining at his chain as an old woman appeared at the door to stare at them for a moment. She was dressed in a dark cotton dress covered by an even darker apron. "Julie's family has come," she called into the invisible rooms behind her. She offered no greetings but stood there while chickens pecked about her feet, staring at the guests. Eva stared back at her. Clearly, this was Julia's mother-in-law.

Julia appeared beside her, wiping her hands on an apron of the same dark color as the old woman's. Her face bore the expression of one who has been too long on short rations; Eva recognized it at once. She wondered if Julia was ill. She was quite gaunt and her eyes were large. The very walls of the house seemed to reject her. Even in her peasant clothes she stood out from her surroundings, if only because her pose remained that of a young woman of good family.

"Come into my house," she said, speaking French. She embraced Eva and Benno stiffly and without tears. Benno felt the bony wing of her shoulder, fragile as a bird's. They entered the cool and shady kitchen.

"This is Maurice," Julia said, "my husband."

He sat at the table and did not rise. Eva saw his face and knew that he was like every other lover of Julia's—handsome and cruel. It was amazing to see how beautiful this primitive man was, and yet his jaws seemed locked in silence. Benno saw only the muscular body and felt his heart bend at the size of his fists, the cunning of his black eyes. He was glad that he was in the uniform of a lieutenant in the army of the United States of America. It gave him a new presence and hid the other self—the one that would have nothing to do with heroics. The smell of manure and warm milk, the smell of the cow barn, was there, even in the kitchen, along with the smell of damp burned wood from the stove. *"Mon mari,"* Julia repeated. Maurice nodded. A glass of wine and an almost empty bottle stood before him. He offered none to his guests.

Benno, studying him, saw how quickly his handsomeness dissolved in sullen blankness. His mother had a comparable stolidity, but her weight and age had so swelled her flesh that the features of her face were immobilized by fat as well as stupidity. She looked at her son with dark, darting eyes, ready at any moment to do his bidding. A great bellow of a cry from the adjoining room startled Eva. "It's Maurice's father," Julia said. "He's had a stroke and is confined to the downstairs bedroom." No one paid any attention to the noise.

Conversation was difficult. Eva commented on the weather, and Benno, in his schoolboy French, praised the landscape of the region. Julia stood leaning against the stove, her arms folded, her eyes on Maurice. The old woman, too, stared at her son. She complained about the *boches* and said there was nothing to eat. She talked of locusts, pests and plagues, of freezes and droughts and diseased cattle. It had been the fault of the Germans, who had invented a rocket that interfered with the weather and carried a warhead of deadly germs. She had clearly not made up this theory but repeated it by rote; it was something she had heard and did not understand.

After a while Maurice got up and went to look in on his father. He spoke to him in a low voice. When he returned to the kitchen, he had with him a full bottle of wine. He set it before the guests and told Julia to bring some glasses. They sat sipping the raw, bitter liquid.

"We're glad to see you're alive and well," Benno said to Julia, speaking German, out of habit. "*Parle français, s'il te plaît,*" Julia said. "Speak French, we have no secrets here."

"We can't stay too long," Benno said. "It's a long ride back to Paris. Why don't you show us around a little? I brought my camera and I'd like to take some pictures—to show the family."

"I am her family," said Maurice.

Julia looked at him with a timid smile. "We'll take a short walk," she said, "I won't be long. It'll be time soon to fetch the cows." Eva noticed that she was pleading with him but trying to make it appear —for her sake and Benno's—that she was simply stating a fact. Maurice shrugged. "*Je m'en fiche,*" he said and turned toward his mother. It was a sign of dismissal.

Benno got his camera from the car, and Julia led the way across the orchard, downhill toward a small river, which wound in great loops through the valley, its banks crowded with bulrushes. A meadow descended gently from the orchard to the stream, and a half-dozen black-and-white cows stood near a low wall at its farthest end. For a while no one spoke, though Julia held Eva by the hand as they walked along a narrow rocky path at the edge of the orchard.

"He was in the Resistance," Julia said, "and he saved my life. He saved many lives. That's all I can tell you. I was traveling south with some others. Intellectuals from the coffeehouses, timid men with blisters on their feet, who talked of suicide. We became separated at a crowded railway terminal in some hideous city, and I continued alone. I met Maurice in a tavern where he had gone for a drink on his way home with some game he'd shot. I could not take my eyes off him, and he took me home with him. He did not touch me for a long, long time. It was a peculiar kind of courtship—but it *was* a courtship—and he had to contend with his parents, who didn't like me. But he kept me safe. He married me. I owe my life to him."

"The war will be over before long," said Benno. "France has been liberated, we're about to enter Germany. You're free."

"Everyone in the village knew I was Jewish." Julia had plucked a piece of wheat growing wild among the thistles and was chewing it. Her face, Eva noticed, had already grown softer, less pained, since they had left the house. "No one ever reported me to the *flics*. They didn't care for me, a stranger, and yet they didn't turn me in. The Gestapo hunted down the émigrés systematically, but I was spared. They shot one of my friends at the border . . ."

"I came through alive too," Eva said, "without selling myself into bondage."

Julia bristled. "I'm not a slave," she said. "I loved Maurice. He was so different from all the other men . . ."

"Was he?" Eva asked.

"I could not stay away from him. It was painful to spend the day without him. We had a strong, a frenzied passion for each other. I adored him . . ."

Eva bit her tongue to say no more. Women had such a need to defend their love of men; they were furies when challenged. She had defended her ideology like that, she supposed, but that was something else. A matter of principle. For a moment her life seemed empty.

"You never had children?" Benno asked.

"One. It died. I'm not certain it wasn't for the best. I would not have been a good mother. I'm not a very good wife. But Maurice mourned it and blamed me and my narrow hips for its death."

"Come back with us," Benno said.

"I can't."

"Why not?"

"I owe my life to him."

"You've paid for that," said Eva.

"I can never pay for it."

"That's absurd," said Benno. "You can't be expected to waste the rest of your life in gratitude for an act that was no doubt courageous but also self-serving."

"Does he beat you?" Eva asked. Julia did not answer. "They're cruel," Eva said. "Do you no longer see that? They have the cruelty of those who believe that there's no more to life than the struggle to survive."

"Aren't they right?"

They had sat down near the river on some rocks warmed by the sun. The flowing water ran swiftly here and calmly there, over snagged branches and smooth stones. Dragonflies skimmed across its surface.

"It's not what we were taught," said Benno.

"The concentration camps showed us the value of all we were taught," Julia said. "The good and the kind are the first to die."

"That's not reason enough to renounce goodness and kindness. We don't stop our search for beauty because the world is, on the whole, ugly. We don't scrap the fruits of intelligence because stupidity is rampant."

"Do you still write?" Eva asked.

"I haven't had anything of value to say for a long time. I was never a good writer. I was essentially a dilettante. One of those people the 'times' throw up. I rode the crest of a feverish wave. I was like all the rest in the Weimar Republic, living beyond my means."

"And now, you think, you live within your means?" Benno had taken off his shoes and dipped his feet in the water.

"Roll up your pants or they'll get wet," said Eva.

"I'm needed. I'm wanted. Another person depends on me. You seem to think I'm suffering." Julia spoke more in sadness than in defiance. "I'm not. Truly I'm not. It may look that way to you, but you see only a little glimpse." Her voice rose. "You come here and you judge things you know nothing about. You haven't the right!"

"Come with us, just for a visit with me," Eva said. "You needn't make any plans. Tell them you need a vacation."

"You do, you know," said Benno. He had almost forgotten the war, sitting in the sunshine by the river.

Julia shook her head. "I couldn't," she said.

"Does he understand how different you are from him? From them?"

"He understands me very well. Do you think that one needs to be an intellectual or a scholar to understand people? I've learned so much I never knew . . ."

"Being torn out by our roots, as we were, from the soil in which we grew up, has made us all peculiar," Benno said.

"I don't think I'm peculiar," Eva told him.

"We have had to reinvent ourselves," Benno said.

"I am the same as I always was," Eva insisted.

The shadows were beginning to lengthen.

"Time to go and bring in the cows," Julia said.

"I think we should leave too," said Benno.

Julia broke off a small switch from a willow tree, stripped it of its leaves and began walking toward the cows in the meadow. Benno saw that it gave her pleasure to show them how well she did this. An upper-class Jewish girl from Frankfurt am Main, driving home the cows.

The bell on the lead cow clanged merrily as the animals, followed by Julia, Eva and Benno, wandered up the meadow single file past the apple orchard and into the farmyard. There Maurice drove them, one by one, into the barn to be milked.

"*Au revoir,*" Benno shouted to him, "we must get back to Paris."

Maurice came over to the jeep. Eva had already climbed into it. "I have something for you," he said. "Wait just a minute." He went into the kitchen and brought back a basket of apples. He set it carefully in the back of the jeep and shook hands with Benno, nodding his head at Eva.

"Julie's place is here," he said. It was a statement not to be questioned, but an aura of uncertainty clung to the words. Both the visitors heard it. Julia was in the barn. She had started the milking and did not come out to say good-bye.

It was past midnight when they reached Paris. Eva had fallen asleep, her head back against the hard seat of the vehicle. Benno was very tired. "Take the apples," he said when they reached Eva's house. The smell of the country clung to them.

"Come back to see me when you've won the war," Eva said and kissed him.

"We'll have to save Julia," he answered.

EMMA ALWAYS attended church on Christmas Eve as well as on the morning of Christmas Day. Edu had invited her for dinner, as he had done every year since she moved to Zürich. He did not know that she drove to his house in Küsnacht directly from the Church of the Redeemer, where she had listened to Pastor Tschudi's annual sermon on the Nativity and its Meaning for these Troubled Times. In order to be sure of her regular seat—Emma did not miss a Sunday or holiday during the entire year—she had arrived early and sat alone and at peace with herself, thinking about Christ, who seemed to her more and more each passing year like a beloved friend, gentle and considerate, to whom she might confide her doubts and fears and innermost thoughts. He sometimes appeared to her at night, before she went to sleep, a husband who made no demands, who asked only to tender His spiritual love, and who, stretched out upon the cross suffering the agonies of a cruel crucifixion, might be embraced and held, as Mary held Him in her lap, like a child grown large but somehow crippled in body. "This is my blood, drink it . . ." Emma sometimes thought that she could taste the salty blood on her tongue, far stronger than the sacramental wine.

Emma felt at home in the church. She had made friends with

several women of her own age with whom she met regularly to read and discuss Scripture. They were widows, mostly, though one of them was married to a pious city councilman who belonged to the old Zürich aristocracy. It was well known that Emma had been born into a Jewish family, but no one held it against her. She seemed to have purged herself of all the unpleasant Jewish traits. She still had her lovely dark hair—there were only a few gray strands in it—and her Mediterranean black eyes, but she thought of these now as biblical; she felt a kinship with Rachel and Rebecca which had never before been clear to her. She told her friends that it was only through Christianity that she had come to know the Bible. They were amazed. Were not the Jews the People of the Book?

Emma worked with her Christian friends to rescue the persecuted from the other side of the border. She was indefatigable. One needed only to tell her of another poor soul escaped from the Nazi dragnet to get her assistance. But she never, by gesture or word, gave any indication that she and the rescued were in any way alike. She greeted their attempts to make common cause with her, to establish an intimacy based on a shared past, with icy politeness. Edu knew of her activities, but he did not know that she went to church. He did not move in these circles, and it would never have occurred to him that anyone might even wish to do so. Piety offended him; he thought the clergy hypocritical and sanctimonious.

By the winter of 1944 it had become clear to almost everyone, including the Germans, that the war could not last much longer. December was harsh that year, and Emma often thought with longing of her home in Florence. It had been closed since December of 1941, when the United States entered the war and Edu had ordered his niece to leave her villa and come to stay with him. Bernard Berenson had counseled against it. "I want you near *me*, my dear," he said. "There's no danger to us among the Italians; even the *Fascisti* are inclined only to harass the Jews, not to deport them."

But Edu was insistent. "You haven't his connections," he said peremptorily. "Lock your house well and leave for Zürich just as soon as you can."

Emma left the house in the care of the maid and her relatives. She wrote B.B. long letters every week, which he answered with brief and cryptic notes, saying just enough to flatter her into continuing her chatty, somewhat malicious correspondence.

Edu put her in one of the small guest rooms on the third floor of his house. Emma was offended. She said nothing to Edu, but she made a sarcastic reference to her "banishment to the maid's domain" in a letter to B.B. When Emma had been at Edu's for a month, he suddenly told her that she must find an apartment in Zürich. "I will pay your rent," he said. "You can't stay here indefinitely; it's better that we're independent of each other. In Zürich you'll have your own life."

Emma had been crushed, but she allowed nothing of her disappointment to become visible; she exercised an iron control over her feelings and her words. She told Lene, to whom she also wrote every week, that the choice had been hers, but Lene suspected the truth, for Edu had written "she *cannot* stay here," though he claimed to be enjoying her company. Emma found a handsome apartment near the museum with a balcony that looked down on the lake. She furnished it tastefully, one item at a time, buying just enough silver, just enough crystal and china, for herself and three guests. She took up bridge. And she began going to church every week, becoming a fixture there in a matter of months. The pastor had asked her whether she had been baptized. He was puzzled by her Jewish appearance the first time she came up to take communion, but a short conversation with her convinced him that she would make a diligent member of his flock. He went to visit her. Before long Emma became a member of the Altar Guild.

Edu continued to invite her to lunch with him once a week, and he sometimes took her to concerts and to dinner at the Bauer-au-lac Hotel on days when his help was out. Emma loved to be seen with him. He was distinguished in appearance and at sixty of an age that is most attractive in men who have a great deal of money. He drove a dark-blue British Jaguar. Emma had motored north in her American Dodge, which was kept in running order by an Italian mechanic from the Ticino who loved all things American, especially cars.

Emma had just enough time at the conclusion of the Christmas morning service to drive out to Küsnacht through the wintry, snow-dusted landscape. Edu gave the staff Christmas Eve and the second day of Christmas off, but he expected the goose and all its trimmings on December 25. Elias and Bettina Süsskind usually came for the festive meal, but Edu rarely mixed in any "outsiders" or Gentile guests. The sky was overcast. As she drove along, Emma noticed that even Zürich had begun to look a little down at the heels; the war had depressed the tourist business throughout Switzerland, and the soldiers of the Swiss army, ever at the ready, were visible at street corners throughout the city. The young men in their scratchy green uniforms looked uncomfortable weighed down by backpacks and rifles. The mountains were shrouded in a wintry mist, the lake rippled under a cold wind. Emma's thoughts returned again and again to Frankfurt, although she had resolutely closed that chapter of her life when she left and put a seal on it when she converted. The place now seemed a huge Judengasse to her. She hoped that Elias would not become boring about it, the way, she now recalled, her grandfather Süsskind had been. Elias and Bettina usually drove out to Küsnacht with her, but they had somewhat mysteriously declined her invitation this time, saying only that they had made other arrangements. Emma wondered whether they were spending the entire holiday with Edu, who was often lonely at this time of the year.

There was no other car in the driveway when Emma arrived at the familiar villa. The garden had been bedded down for the winter, everything was pruned back, the snow lay undisturbed on the lawn, the gravel paths were marked only by Edu's solitary footsteps. The maid answered Emma's ring and took her hat and coat wordlessly. She hated having to work on Christmas Day. Emma preceded her into Edu's study, and Edu looked up at her from his place behind the large desk. A light was on against the wintry darkness, and it cast a warm glow over his prized possessions. There was a small Etruscan bronze and the bust made of him in London by Jacob Epstein. An Egyptian cat sat beside the Etruscan Hercules, and next to it was a brass candlestick from the thirteenth century. There was also the usual flotsam and jetsam of a businessman's desk, papers and letters in neat piles, a gold letter opener, several paperweights. And then there were the family photos. The one of Hannchen in a gold frame was the most prominent. It was a youthful picture of her in a Victorian dress, holding the baby Edu on her lap. A sepia portrait of his father looked up from a large white china paperweight. It was pure *kitsch*, and Edu valued it all the more for that. On the wall was a rococo clock, which kept perfect time, and a watercolor by Caspar David Friedrich flanked by a pencil drawing of an elegant Empire lady by Ingres and a small gouache by Paul Klee.

Edu took off his reading glasses and offered his cheek to be kissed. Emma's peck was, as always, awkward and inept. "I have your present here," she said and handed him a flat box wrapped in tasteful Christmas paper. "I hope you like it. If not, you can exchange it, I won't mind. But there aren't many to be had, on account of the war."

Emma had brought him a sleeveless cashmere sweater, made in England by Pringle. It had been difficult to find in the proper size and color (a dark blue exactly the shade of his car), and Emma was never certain whether he needed these things. He was so unlike other people and seemed to have gone into emigration with a life-time supply of shirts, ties, shoes and gray-flannel suits. Emma was glad to see that an expression of pleasure crossed his face when he saw the gift. "It was totally unnecessary," he said, "but thank you anyway." Still, he had looked happy. He was about to throw the wrapping paper into the wastebasket when she stopped him.

"If you don't need it, I'll take it back," she said. "It will do nicely for the cleaning woman's gift."

She did not seem to think her request odd. "Waste not, want not," she said, and she folded the gaily colored paper neatly, smoothing out every wrinkle.

Edu reached into the top drawer of his desk and took out an envelope. Her name was written on it. "Merry Christmas to you," he said. Emma quickly put the envelope into her pocketbook. She knew that the crisp new bills within were in 100 Swiss franc denominations. There were ten of them. It was the same every year. "A thousand thanks," she said. "One for each franc?" he quipped. Her face betrayed no pleasure. She hated the ritual gift but did not have the courage to refuse it.

The money she lived on—frugally, of course—came from the trust and had nearly doubled in value since its establishment; by now it had lost its original connection to Edu. "Live from the interest on the interest!" he had said to her, half in jest, but she did, and she was proud of it. The money he gave her (and the rest of his nephews and nieces) went directly into the savings account. She sent Claire a check for her birthday and for Christmas. Lene had said it was unfair not to treat her two children alike, so Peter also received some money. But not as much. He also did not receive nearly the number of letters his sister did. Emma thought that the decidedly Jewish mark of his father was on the child, and she felt that he would have to redeem himself. He was, of course, as yet too young to do so. Claire was a faithful correspondent and answered her aunt's letters with long and imaginative epistles of her own. Emma was relieved to think that the bond between them had been strengthened during these years. "When the war is over and I'm back in Florence," she wrote her niece, "you'll come to visit me and we'll look at all the wonderful art together and travel to Venice and Pisa, Siena and Rome. I so look forward to it. Perhaps we can ask your father to join us." She never allowed Claire to forget who her *real* father was.

Edu led the way into the drawing room where the decanters of sherry, port and brandy stood. He poured Emma a tiny drink of sherry. "Merry Christmas and a Happy New Year," he said, "and may we see the end of the war in 1945." They touched their glasses and Emma sipped the sherry; Edu drank his down in a single swallow.

"It's nice to be here," Emma said, "just the two of us. I thought about Frankfurt today, driving here. I couldn't get it out of my mind, I don't know why."

"One always thinks of childhood at Christmas time," Edu said. "I have more company coming, by the way."

"Elias and Bettina refused my offer of a ride."

"They're coming with a friend," Edu said. The intonation he gave to the word "friend" was ambiguous.

"Oh," said Emma. Edu seemed less formidable in his drawing room, among the paintings, than he did at his desk. He was relaxed, his legs casually crossed. On his feet were the soft leather loafers with tassels that he preferred to regular shoes. Emma thought he looked especially well today.

"A charming American woman who's been living in St. Moritz. She's also a collector, and Elias thought we should meet. I liked her so well I had the idea of inviting her to share Christmas dinner with us. I hope you don't mind?"

"Why should I mind?"

"I think, sometimes, that you take a proprietary interest in me and my life."

"How can you say such a thing?"

"Don't take offense, Emma. I meant none. However, I think it's better to be shown one's foibles than to wonder at the resentment they breed. *I* certainly prefer to be told when I am wrong."

Emma did not think this was true. She was tempted to test her belief by telling him so but was saved from a possible *faux pas* by the entrance of the Süsskinds, accompanied by a striking blond woman in her mid-forties.

"I'm so happy to see you," Edu said as he rose to greet them. "We must speak English now," he said to Emma.

"How wonderful of you to invite me," the American woman said. Her accent was the kind affected by New York women of the upper class who have been to finishing school and learned to Anglicize their speech. Emma could not know this, but she was put off right away by the number of large rings on the woman's hands and the slightly brash color of her hair.

"My name is Diane Leventhal," she said to Emma with a bright smile but without shaking hands. Emma nodded curtly and went to embrace Elias, who, because he had arthritis, walked with a cane and was wrapped in a long shawl and many sweaters. "It's always cold in this house," he complained.

"Edu is saving money," Bettina said. "He'd rather buy paintings than coal. Speaking of which"—she had helped herself to a glass of sherry—"I saw a superb Rembrandt drawing last week which ought to be in your collection."

Bettina acted as Edu's spy. She accompanied Elias everywhere and kept her eyes and ears open while he puttered around, examining objects of art, peering through his magnifying glass at gold-leafed halos and at the carved folds of Byzantine ivories. She engaged family retainers and titled mothers-in-law in casual talk and was often privy to information that did not enter the polite conversations around the dinner table.

"Speak to me about it later," Edu said to her in German. Bettina nodded but looked puzzled.

"Have I told you the story about the postmaster's Dalmatian bitch?" Emma interjected gaily, aware that a change of subject was in order. The two women gossiped over tea on alternate Tuesdays and laughed together like schoolgirls.

"Did I understand you to say that the Russians are advancing rapidly?" Elias asked Edu.

"We were speaking of dogs," Edu smiled.

"What a charming little Christmas tree you've got!" Diane Leventhal addressed Edu, pointing to the miniature spruce that stood in a corner of the drawing room, festooned with old-fashioned ornaments. The American had spread herself casually on the Empire settee and Emma saw that she possessed a pair of exquisite legs.

"This whole place is utterly beguiling," she went on, "how lucky you are to have found it. You must have good connections. We Americans are only just discovering this sweet little country. Imagine—a war raging all around and we sit here, snug as a bug in a rug."

Emma wondered whether the conversation was going to languish in platitudes and small compliments. Her Uncle Elias was busily studying a delicate drawing that hung next to the mantlepiece.

"Did we decide that this was a Pisanello, after all?" he asked. "I've been having my doubts again."

"I saw a wonderful Matisse for sale in Lucerne the other day," Diane said. "It was a most beautiful shade of blue."

"Can you describe it?" Edu asked.

Diane tried valiantly to articulate her impressions of the painting.

"Shall *I* tell you what it looks like?" Edu said and launched into a detailed description of the work in question.

"You know it then?" Diane was astounded.

"I gave it to the Städel—our museum in Frankfurt—many years ago."

"The Nazis considered it degenerate," said Elias. "It disappeared in 1938."

"And now someone else needs money." Bettina helped herself to another sherry. "How much are they asking for it?"

"Forty thousand francs."

"That's ten times what you paid for it," said Elias.

The maid appeared just then to announce dinner.

"Not before the servants!" Edu warned.

"I didn't know they understood English," said Bettina.

" 'A slip of the lip can sink a ship,' " said Diane.

"Have you heard from Lene lately?" Emma asked Edu.

"She sent her usual Metropolitan Museum Christmas card."

"I must confess that I worry about Claire a lot," said Emma. "They're letting her go to public school. She's certain to be exposed to bad influences—and all because Manfred is too cheap . . ."

"Diane is not interested in our family affairs," Edu interrupted his niece.

"I'd love to meet them," said Diane brightly. "I know all the best schools in New York. I do miss it, this time of year," she sighed. "All those lovely parties!"

The light consommé which preceded the goose was delicately flavored with chives, and there were small, airy liver dumplings floating in it. Everyone praised the cook.

"I should be praised for hiring her," Edu said.

"It's amazing that things function so well here," said Diane. "A house without a woman in it is usually mismanaged by the servants."

There was a momentary, uncomfortable silence. Then the goose appeared and Bettina told a joke in broad Frankfurt dialect involving a goose. Everyone laughed, except Diane, who did not understand German. Emma thought back to her childhood, remembered the dinners around Hannchen's table. She saw at that moment that the memory was vivid but had no sting to hurt her. She could let the past lie there without regret. She was a happier person now. She had found a purpose in life. It didn't matter that she was the ugly Jewish duckling, Jesus was her friend.

The goose was filled with a chestnut stuffing laced with apples. Red cabbage and mashed potatoes accompanied it, together with a sharp cucumber salad. The maid brought a rich brown gravy around in one of the silver gravy boats with scenes of a hunt chased on it that Emma had loved as a child. She had often studied it with Lene. It was one of those images as powerful in its way as a religious one, though its meaning was private. She saw herself standing in the shadows while Lene, fat and jolly, was kissed by the grownups. She had hugged her too, hard enough to hurt her, and, of course, her sister had screamed. She had told Lene frightening stories to try to make her cry, but Lene wasn't easily scared. Even "Bluebeard" didn't bother her.

"You aren't listening, Emma," Edu said.

"I'm sorry," she answered, "my mind was on the gravy boat."

"Diane asked you about Bernard Berenson," Edu said. "She's a great admirer of his."

"I understand you know him well," said Diane.

"We're old friends," said Emma. "I had a letter from him only yesterday. Now that Florence has been liberated, he is his happy self again. He says he enjoys visits from dozens of Italians who ask him to vouch for them. 'We were no Fascists!' they say. I look forward to going back. Maybe by spring it will be possible . . ."

She would miss Pastor Tschudi, of course, and the ladies of the Altar Guild. Emma noticed that the mention of B.B. had oiled Diane Leventhal's smile.

"I'll come and visit you next time I'm in Florence," she said to Emma, who had no wish ever to see her again.

"I'm not certain when I'll be there," she said, "or whether I'll be ready to accept guests . . ."

Bettina plunged into the ensuing silence with another Frankfurt witticism, this time a line of poetry by Stolze. Dessert was served —a concoction of lemon ices, tangy and fresh, with meringues and whipped cream—and Emma heard Edu's voice murmuring to her, "You are quite rude." It was clear to her that Diane, the huntress, had conquered her uncle. What an old fool he was!

They went back to the drawing room to have coffee and brandy.

Diane flashed her pert smile at Edu. Emma noticed that she was dressed in clothes of classic simplicity, expensively made, probably by hand. But she would be fat when she grew older; her appetite for good things was great.

"I think I had better start home," Emma said, rising from her chair.

Diane let out a small shriek. "I forgot to give you your present!" she said to Edu and rushed out of the room. She returned in a few minutes with a plain white box. There was a cashmere sweater in it, not blue as Emma's had been, but a pearly gray to match his suits.

"I've already got one of these," Edu said.

Diane laughed. "I'll return it then," she said. "Give it back."

"I can use two"—Edu held on to it—"one for Mondays, Wednesdays and Fridays, another for Tuesdays, Thursdays and Saturdays. I can use still another for Sundays!"

Emma laughed with the others, but she was not amused. She stood next to her chair, her coffee untouched. "Forgive me," she told Edu, "I feel a headache coming on." Why did she ask his forgiveness? It was he who should apologize.

"I'll walk you to the door," he said gallantly. Emma said good-bye to the Süsskinds. Elias had begun to nod off. "Be good," he murmured as if she were still a child.

"You were impossible to Diane," Edu chided his niece as she waited for the maid to fetch her old Persian lamb coat and matching hat.

"She's after your money," Emma said.

"She doesn't need it," said Edu. "She's very rich." He smiled at Emma. "Maybe I'm after *her* money," he said. "You'll eat with me on New Year's Day?" he asked as he held the door open for her, "at the Bauer-au-lac?"

When Edu came back to join his guests, he found them looking at his paintings.

"Your niece is a pathetic creature," Diane said.

"It's mostly her own fault," Edu replied.

Later, when they were home again, Bettina said to Elias, "It is not her own fault!"

"What?"

"He leads her on. He likes to surround himself with women as though they were varieties of roses in his garden."

"He's a lonely man. He should have married the Englishwoman."

"She would have made him give up his nieces," Bettina said. "Besides, the English are boring."

On her way home Emma made a detour past a small country church she knew. It was open, and she sat down on one of the wooden benches and looked for a long time at the crucifix on the plain altar. When she had regained her peace of mind, she read a small prayer and left some coins in the poor box. Outside it was almost dark and had begun to snow.

JULY 4, 1945, would, Lene reckoned, be their seventh Independence Day in America. The previous year, just before the holiday, their citizenship papers had come through, and they had all gone to the courthouse in Foley Square to be sworn in. This year the celebration was still muted. The war in Europe had been over for two months, but it dragged on in the Pacific.

The German-speaking émigrés in New York did not pay much attention to the war against the Japanese; the war in Europe had been all that mattered. Germany had surrendered unconditionally on May 7, but the relief everyone expected to feel did not materialize. Too many lives had been lost, too much had been destroyed forever. Another hot New York summer lay ahead. The refugees complained, but they were used to it by now. "It's not the heat, it's the humidity," they said. They made their accommodations, rented cottages at the beach, in the mountains. There had not been any suicides for a while. When Stefan Zweig killed himself—"down in the jungles of Brazil," as they always said, even though it was not quite true—a shock had run through them all. They held memorial meetings, gave readings, sighed and clucked their tongues. They accused the New World of being the agent of his demise. But they also looked into their own hearts and found that they did not wish to die quite yet. Stefan Zweig, said a wag, is a hard act to follow.

Manfred Solomon thought the joke was in bad taste and did not repeat it to Lene. He, too, had made his adjustments and accommodations. He played pop concerts here and there, enough to earn the money to rent a cottage at the seashore. It was an old ramshackle house far out on Long Island where no one they knew ever went, but Lene had fallen in love with its grape arbor and its privet hedges and the porch that extended around three of its sides. Besides, there was a piano in the living room on which Manfred could practice.

The real estate agent even knew of a piano tuner. Mail had to be picked up at the post office in the small general store. It was Manfred's duty to go there each day. He would wear his white beach hat and sun glasses, and carry his walking stick "against the dogs." He greeted the potato farmers with a formal bow. He barely understood their curious accent, nor they his, but this did nothing to lessen anyone's cordiality.

The only other Jewish family in the village—the real estate agent had been so surprised when Lene presented herself to him that he was unable to explain to her that they did not, on the whole, rent to Jews—belonged to the man who ran the dry-goods store. He recognized Manfred as "kin" immediately and treated him like an old friend. Manfred grumbled about it but often allowed Mr. Goldstein to engage him in long conversations.

Claire had just graduated from the High School of Music and Art and been admitted to Barnard College. In the fashion of a serious seventeen-year-old, she had made plans to read three "great books" that summer, beginning with James Joyce's *Ulysses*. She took it with her to the beach each morning but kept her eye out as well for a likely candidate with whom to have an affair of the heart. Her fantasies had prepared her for such an encounter, but the beach was generally deserted. Peter was seven and hung around Fräulein Gründlich, who built sand castles with him. Each one of them had a separate room in the ramshackle house, and Lene did the cooking. She found herself thinking of Frankfurt hardly at all these days. New York seemed to have swallowed up every other place she had known. She loved the way she could be alone there and not alone, she loved the great size, the newness that left no room for yesterday's burdens. And this house on its acre of green grass was only a few minutes from the sea and the endless white beach. Lene, too, sometimes thought about having an affair of the heart. But then she would hear Manfred practicing and remember that she loved him.

The day before the Fourth promised to be hot; thundershowers were predicted for the holiday itself. Great clouds hovered in the blue sky, and there was scarcely a breeze, even here by the sea. The privet was in bloom, and the bees hummed steadily along the thick hedges covered with cream-colored blossoms. The village was crowded with summer people and overalled farmers buying provisions for the holiday. Manfred went for the mail at one-thirty every day, right after lunch; sometimes Claire accompanied him. He napped from two to four before going down to the beach. He liked his schedule to be ironclad, precise. The farmers nodded to him, and the summer people ignored him, thinking he was a relative of Goldstein's, the dry-goods merchant.

Claire had some letters of her own to mail this day and walked beside her stepfather, feeling happy. She had a deep tan and knew it became her. She had lost weight, and her short blond hair was bleached by the sun. The bond between her and Manfred seemed tight and close, and it exhilarated her. She often thought that she understood him better than her mother did. When they strolled together like this—Manfred called the fifteen-minute walk to the post office the "small Jewish tour" as opposed to the "big Jewish tour," which was the thirty-minute walk down to the inlet bridge —he talked about music, seriously and expansively, as he might to a grownup. He never asked her any personal questions, and Claire did not confide in him. She wondered sometimes if her mother did, but his conversations about music and the stories he told her about his life and early career were full of intimations of something deeper, forbidden. He courted her with them.

Manfred knew that he must be careful with his stepdaughter. One day he would have to let her go, but for now he needed her earnest devotion and respect too much; he hungered after adulation. Claire did not perceive these undercurrents, she wanted only to please Manfred and soak up his love. She imagined that if only he were her real father he could not reject her and she would never have to stand outside his life and world. She was sometimes burdened by the weight of her absent father's inheritance; it made her different, a half-breed. The Gentile girls she knew dwelt in one world, the Jewish ones in another, she had never been quite at home with either. Her best friend was, like herself, a *Mischling*, the child of refugees.

"We go to Philadelphia next week, you and I?" Manfred asked. His English was grave and he always spoke it in public to show he was a good American.

"It'll be great fun," Claire said. "I *love* Paul Robeson."

"I'm playing the Gershwin concerto before the intermission and a medley of Sousa marches arranged for the piano, at the very end. In between he sings the *Ballad for Americans*—a dreadful piece. What do you call it—a 'hutch-putch'? But in these times we must be patriotic. And the Negro has a wonderful voice. If only he would use it right, he could sing *any*thing."

"They wouldn't *let* him," said Claire, her tone of voice full of outrage.

"What do you mean?"

"Don't you know what a racist country this is?" Claire knew she was treading on thin ice. Manfred Solomon never bothered his head about "politics."

"He sings on the same program with *me*!"

"In a summer concert at Robin Hood Dell. That doesn't count."

Manfred looked offended. "The Philadelphia Orchestra plays. It is a good place for me to be heard."

"I wasn't talking about you," Claire said. "It's terrific that they asked you. I just mean that Paul Robeson will never sing, say, at the Met."

"A Negro at the Metropolitan Opera! What role could he sing, except Otello?"

Claire knew it was wiser not to continue. "You were practicing Schumann this morning," she said. "I recognized it."

Manfred launched happily into a detailed account of the work in question, which he was scheduled to perform in November at the YMHA. They reached the post office in no time at all. The mail contained a dividend check, an insurance notice, a dentist's bill and a thick letter from Benno Süsskind.

Manfred carried the mail home and left it on the kitchen table for Lene, who with Fräulein Gründlich's help was cleaning up the lunch and breakfast dishes. As soon as Manfred and Claire appeared, the governess hung up the dishtowel and went quietly to her room. "I think I'll get my book and go to the beach," said Claire. Peter was resting upstairs. He had the radio on, but the volume was turned very low, so as not to disturb the afternoon peace. He was listening to a baseball game.

Lene took the letters out to the grape arbor, which adjoined the kitchen. There was a rough-hewn picnic table here and half a dozen unmatched chairs. It was utterly still and dappled in shade. Lene opened Benno's letter last. She read through it slowly and carefully, her mouth dry, her heart ticking away loudly. When she was finished and had put it down, she noticed that Manfred stood at the other end of the table, watching her.

"What does it say?" he asked. "You look upset."

"Here, read it," said Lene.

"I haven't got my reading glasses, read it to me."

"It's long, and it's full of bad news."

"Read it."

At that moment Claire appeared on her way to the beach, the well-worn Modern Library edition of *Ulysses* under her arm. She knew she had chanced on a private moment, and her first fearful thought was that it concerned her or meant that a quarrel was brewing.

"What do you want?" Manfred asked. "Your mother is about to read me an important letter."

"May I listen to it too?" Claire asked.

"It's not for young ears," Lene said. "Go on to the beach. I'll tell you about it another time."

"I'll join you later," Manfred said.

"There'll be fireworks tonight. I saw the announcement at the library," Claire told them. "At the Jew-less Club."

"What do you mean, 'Jew-less'?"

"I mean, it's restricted. It only lets Christians in. One of the kids I met told me."

"They aren't our kind of people, anyway," said Lene. "We can watch the fireworks from the public beach."

"I just thought I'd tell you."

"Thank you," said Manfred.

Claire got on her bicycle and pedaled down the broad street, across the bridge over the inlet to the beach. The roses that grew over the split-rail fences were in full bloom, and the odor of honeysuckle and sea air mingled with the privet.

The beach was searing hot that day and full of sandflies. There was no surf; the sea was calm and smooth as a lake, and it was dead low tide. Claire tried to read, but the sweat ran into her eyes, the flies bit at her legs. The water was full of seaweed and kelp, twining about her legs like an octopus. She decided to leave early.

The house looked deserted in the stillness of midafternoon. Everyone was asleep. The murmur from Peter's radio was no louder than the sound of the bees in the privet hedge. Claire took a glass of milk from the refrigerator and went out to the grape arbor to drink it. She saw Benno's letter lying open under a vase filled with daisies. The dampness had made the blue pages soft as cloth, wavy at the edges. She picked the letter up and read it:

April 12, 1945

Dear Lene,

I am writing you this letter from a room in a small hotel in Weimar where I am quartered, along with several other officers of the U.S. Army. It is late at night and I must write these lines down now, because the horrors so haunt me that I cannot sleep. Perhaps I can exorcise them by telling someone else about them. Someone far away who has seen nothing of this terrible devastation of human life, someone with whom I can share the awful truth, the horror, while it is still vivid and unretouched. They will, no doubt, send photographs around the world, and the world will be shocked. They will make a memorial here, when it is all cleaned up, and think this reminder will satisfy those who come after, that they will have done their duty by the dead. Those of us who have seen it firsthand will become expert in the telling, like actors performing a role, making the audience weep each night, even as a little bit of the outrage and anger and pain are lost with each repetition.

The American Army liberated the Buchenwald Concentration Camp yesterday, April 11, 1945. I was not with the soldiers in that first wave. We did not reach the place until this morning ("we" being a group of former Germans, including a doctor from Berlin and a lawyer from Mannheim) but I understand that there was an uprising, led by a group of Communists, which took place just before the Americans arrived.

When the first of our soldiers reached the camp, I'm told they got sick at the spectacle before them. It is unbearable, especially if one multiplies it a thousand times and adds to it the death camps in the East, which the

Russians liberated. I understand that the Germans tried to destroy the gas chambers in which millions (indeed I mean it, we understand that the numbers may reach *ten million!*) died, but there is nothing on earth that can destroy the memories of those who saw those deaths and lived.

Buchenwald KZ is situated near the top of the Ettersberg, commanding a beautiful view of the plain that stretches north toward Magdeburg from here. (Why am I writing this? It has nothing to do with what I am trying to tell you!) It is filled with barracks made of planks and tarpaper in which the prisoners were stacked in tiers of bunks, hundreds of them to a barrack, thousands of them to the camp. They wear striped prison garb, but they no longer resemble human beings; they are cadavers, skeletons covered with skin, scarecrows too weak to stand on their feet, too weak to cry or to move. Many, they say, are dying unattended, because we cannot find them among those already dead. They cannot whimper even to make us hear them. The only way we will be able to bury the dead is to dig a hole in the ground and push them all in with a bulldozer. The Jews, those who are left—we understand that many were sent to be exterminated in Auschwitz as late as last October, and in the few days before we arrived, 15,000 of them were herded northeast, through what is left of Germany, so that we would not find them—were in the most pitiful state. I do not know how many will live, and if they live, how many will ever again become normal human beings.

I hear their voices now, pitiful reedlike voices, that seem to come from deep within some other species of life. They sob without shedding tears, they no longer know how to smile. I am supposed to "interview" them and write down what they tell me, but there is no way the formulas they give you for writing down data can encompass what these people have to tell me. They were used, most of them, for slave labor (the useless ones, especially the Jews, were sent to be gassed elsewhere. I said "Gassed?" when I first heard the word, and they said, "Yes, gassed") in factories and underground installations nearby, and kept on such small rations (it was easier to replace those who died with new slaves than to feed the workers enough to sustain them) that hundreds died each day. They were shoveled into the crematorium and burned; their ashes were used for fertilizer, their bones for landfill. The mountain here is covered with this pale gray ash. It is like being on the slope of a volcano.

As I wrote earlier, many of the survivors will not, in fact, live, though we have teams of doctors here, working around the clock. They can no longer take in ordinary nourishment. I saw one man throw himself on some K-rations with such animal-like greed that one could barely stand to watch him, and then he threw it all up. The threat of disease, typhus especially, is great. I spent the entire day wandering through this place, trying to take in the unbelievable sight, the indescribable horror. And all of it within a few minutes of Weimar—my very favorite town, the cradle of German Enlightenment, the home of our native son, Goethe, who left Frankfurt because it was so narrow and mercantile, to come here!

Most of the men with whom I talk find it impossible to believe that we (the Americans) are really here, that they have been saved, that the SS guards won't return and take them out to beat them or hang them up by their arms from a high stake, or make them stand for hours and hours in sleet and hail and snow and the broiling sun of August for a roll call that never comes out correct. They have—and if I said this before, please forgive me, I must keep writing things down as they rush into my head —suffered so severely they will be forever crippled. The Nazis have succeeded in destroying half of the Jews in the world and a generation of Russians, plus those of their own who died in the war, and—what's worse —did what they did here.

The lawyer from Mannheim who goes around with me and questions the survivors sounds very cool and professional, he keeps careful notes and seems the perfect, rational prosecutor. He tells me they plan to try the Nazi hierarchy after the war, for high crimes against humanity. But when we came back to our rooms tonight, he suddenly broke down and cried. He cried so hard I had to call the doctor to give him a shot to calm him. He kept saying, "That could have been my parents, my brothers . . . me." And the awful thing is that one's pity turns so quickly into revulsion, for how can we identify with these skeletons before us, most of them reeking of death and decay, vomit and shit, groveling before us with their yapping grief, like dogs.

Forgive me, Lene, for going on like this! But I know that you will understand why I write it all down. One of the men (he had not been here very long and was still relatively strong) said to me, "Before they died, before they were deported, men would turn to me and say, 'Tell them about it when the war's over. Tell the world what they did to us!' " Before long, before another generation has grown up and died, they'll not remember, or remember only a little, or remember and distort it, each to his own use. And I think that even as I write this, there are yet others still being killed. Some woman is carrying her old mother, ill with dysentery, on her back through German villages toward Berlin, toward the still beating "heart" of the Reich. They will destroy all they can of these installations and the witnesses who suffered in them. And pretend before the world that it didn't really happen.

Nothing I have ever seen or read could have prepared me for this day. It is as though a world existed here that was based on the absolute opposite of everything True and Beautiful and Good (remember those words, from the portal of the Opernhaus?) which the mind of man has ever imagined. As if it had been decided to base a whole society purely on evil, purely on ugliness and deceit. As if a deliberate attempt had been made to turn civilization inside out. The hell of this place is a hell far worse than any on all those panels and frescoes and mosaics I studied. Giotto in Padua, Bosch even, or Grünewald could not imagine their damned going through tortures like those devised here.

It is not an easy matter to kill millions of human beings, it takes a lot of planning, a lot of work, a lot of manpower. And it wasn't done by social misfits or criminals, no! One of the guards we captured here (he had hidden from the Communists during the uprising, afraid for his life) told me that it was not hard at all killing defenseless people, men, women and children. He had seen "action" in Poland, he said, and it was "just a job," you did as you were told. But, he admitted, when he would sit over his beer later smoking a cigar, he was assailed by doubts. He wondered what his mother would say. He was a perfectly ordinary German, a mailman back in his hometown of Fürth. How was it ever possible to convince people like him (and there must have been many of them doing the job) that it was perfectly all right to kill people as though they were flies, roaches, lice? Did they never for a minute think that these hundreds upon thousands whom they led to gas chambers or shot dead at the edge of an open grave were human? That they had dreams and hopes and love in their hearts?

What a monstrous perversion—done not by some savage tribe but by neighbors of ours, by people you and I surely knew and greeted each day of our lives! We thought we lived with them in peace and harmony, lo these hundreds of years, and now we come to find out that any of them, the greengrocer or the streetcar conductor, could just as quickly have shoved us into a cattle car as to say *"Guten Tag, Herr Professor!"* And when the time comes to interrogate them, they will act nonchalant, they will say in their most obsequious way, *"Jawohl, Herr Leutnant . . . bestimmt, Herr Leutnant, wir haben's getan . . .* we spent every day of our army service except for Sundays, which we had off, killing Jews and flogging slave laborers. We were told to do it. Our orders came directly from Berlin, and orders are orders, as you must know, *Herr Leutnant.*"

It was infuriating to listen to that mailman as he bowed and scraped before us! "You know, they were Bolsheviks," he said. "As Americans you ought to understand that those are our enemies." And every time the wind blows a little, some of the ashes of the 50,000 people who died here blow through the neighboring forest of beech and birch and pine.

Which brings me to a personal matter I hardly dare to broach. You remember I wrote you from Paris, saying that Eva had told me that she believed that Jacob had been deported, and that she had heard from some old comrades that Lore had returned to Germany to look for him. Nothing further is known. I plan to search through the records here, to see if I can find any information. The SS tried to burn their files, but much, much material was saved. You know how thorough the Germans are—there are heaps upon heaps of lists, of things saved from the prisoners, taken from the dying. Piles of eyeglasses, suitcases, shoes, crutches, artificial limbs, baskets of wallets and keys and photographs. Many of the larger items are carefully tagged, and the passports are all stamped, correctly, with the date and the German eagle over the swastika. I will hold this letter for a few days, to see if anything can be found out for you about Uncle Jacob's fate.

It is almost three o'clock in the morning now, and my eyes are about to fall shut with sleep. I must close. I have talked myself out for now. I keep saying to myself, how can I return to America and take up my life as art historian, working among the prints and drawings at the Brooklyn Museum? It seems impossible at this moment, but I am certain that I will return, the memories will fade, and I will begin to think once more about attributions and iconography. Imagine me, your fat cousin Benno, acting the part of "liberator." But it is true. I come as an American (I crossed the line from certain death to certain life) and that is how I am seen, by the wretched survivors as well as the groveling conquistadors, that is how I see myself. It is very odd and unsettling in its way. There are moments when I simply do not know who I am.

P.S.   It is now April 15. I have gone through all the records, and they have yielded up their sad news. I found the name of Jacob Israel Wertheim of Frankfurt am Main, lately of Amsterdam, born on 18 March, 1878, arrived in Buchenwald on 20 May, 1944, evacuated (it does not say to where) on 3 June, 1944. There is no mention of Lore, but the prisoners tell me that it was not unusual for the guards to shoot "intruders" and "trespassers" and these would not, of course, have been identified. With so many dead here —all the inhabitants of a good-sized city—they will never know them all.

I shall end this letter now. No doubt I will write you again. Each day uncovers further horrors, and we must now face the fact that your brother Andreas and your mother, too, died cruelly at the hands of these monsters. I only hope that they did not linger long in that hell between life and death. I realize that's a foolish wish, for a single day in such a place yields more suffering than most of us know in a lifetime. A journey of several hundred kilometers in a sealed cattle car, without food and water, must have made any destination—even death—seem welcome.

They tell me that there was a certain point at which prisoners in the camps gave up on life, that it was always possible to see when someone had reached that point, and that those who got there were always chosen for the gas chamber. They were called "Muslims" by the others. And they tell me, too, that the people waiting to be gassed at Auschwitz-Birkenau stood patiently in line until their turn came. They did not want to know that what awaited them was not a hot shower but a cloud of cyanide gas.

How can those who profess belief in God, explain what was done here? Enough.

Give all your family my love, but most especially Claire.

Your cousin and friend,
Benno

P.S. I've made up my mind that I'm going to return to France and fetch Julia. I will bring her to America.

Claire put down the letter and carefully placed the vase of daisies over it. There was still not a sound from the house except the drone of the radio in Peter's room, broadcasting the Dodger game. Claire closed her eyes a minute, but then she saw the dead bodies piled high, waiting to be carted to the ovens. She opened them and gazed hard at the grape leaves and the green clusters of grapes, looked at the sky, deep-blue between the white puffs of clouds. Still she saw the bodies; sight did not restore the summer day to her mind. She got up blindly, afraid that she would meet her mother or Manfred, would have to speak to Fräulein Gründlich or discuss the baseball scores with her little brother.

It seemed to her that she had been deceived all her life. No one had ever told her the truth about anything. Leaving the silent house

behind her, Claire set out to walk along the dusty streets of the small
seaside village. She did not know where she was going, she knew
only that she had to be alone. The trees were the deep moist green
of early summer, and the well-tended lawns smelled of cut grass. She
was safe. They were all safe. Everywhere she looked, the flat sunny
landscape was radiant with beauty. In the distance the ocean lay like
a glistening ribbon against the pale blue of the sky. There was
neither war nor death here. It was hard to imagine even being
hungry. It was the time of year Claire loved best of all, a season of
heat and sun when everything seemed good and beautiful. She
always wished she could preserve it for winter, and so she wrote
about it in her notebooks, but that only made her long for it more
intensely in January. There was no way to hold on to summer. She
imagined Manfred and Lene, with little Peter between them, walking to their deaths. What would have become of her? She was only
half Jewish. Would she have been spared?

Claire was barefoot, and the dust of the road clung softly to the
soles of her feet. She walked across a small meadow, down to the
bulrushes that grew by the brackish waters of the inlet. She followed
the shore until she reached the canal that led to the sea. A few
sailboats were anchored here, small waves lapped against their sides.
There was no other sound. Claire sat down in a dinghy tied to the
pilings of an old dock. What if she had been plucked from the
transport that led to the death camps only to see them—Lene and
Manfred and little Peter—in that long line of other Jews, staring at
her with sad, accusing eyes?

What if she had stayed with Aunt Emma? She wouldn't be here
now, that was for sure, an American, sitting in a small boat, trailing
her hand in the water. She would be under her aunt's fierce scrutiny,
forced to hide forever that part of her that was Jewish. It seemed to
Claire that Emma had always wanted to capture her, to win her soul,
as if she knew, as her mother did not, that to be Jewish meant that
you were destined to be killed.

Claire tried to recall the pictures she had seen in the newspapers
of the dead and dying of war, the starved children, the hollow-eyed
mothers, the prisoners in their striped garb. But they were from
another country, worlds away, they had not concerned her. No one

had ever told her that there was a connection between them and her family.

Claire's thoughts went again and again to that unbearable other world she had just glimpsed. If she had been chosen to remain alive, would she have been brave and defied the guards and gone to her death? Would she have tried to fight them, hurled herself at a brutal soldier, beaten him with her hands, with a rock from the earth of Poland? She saw it all, like a movie. The images were intense and powerful but she knew them to be bogus, less plausible than a nightmare. She was here on a pond sparkling with sunlight. It was a summer afternoon, they were all safe, winter was months away, unimaginable, no more real than death. Those who had been martyred would spit at her in disgust for trying to approach even the idea of their suffering.

She was late for dinner.

"Your mother worried about you," Manfred said. "Where have you been?"

Claire imagined him trudging along a frozen road, rags wrapped around his feet, driven on by German soldiers. He stumbled, dropped by the wayside.

"Answer me, please," he said, his voice stern.

"I went for a walk down to the inlet," said Claire, "and completely lost track of the time."

"The Dodgers won," said Peter, eating a piece of bread thickly spread with butter. His black hair was shiny, his tanned face clean.

"Do you feel all right?" Lene asked and put her cool hand on Claire's forehead. "You seem a little hot."

"It's only the sun," Claire told her.

After dinner, while Manfred practiced the Gershwin concerto, Lene and Claire went for a walk. The night was still and black as velvet; a waning moon rose over the sea.

"You read Benno's letter," Lene said.

"How did you know?"

"Mothers know everything."

"I wish I hadn't read it. I can't stop thinking about those horrors, and yet I know that I'm untouched. What can I ever do to make up for it?"

"Nothing, Clärchen, nothing."

"How could everyone stand by and let those things happen? Didn't they know? Couldn't they do something?"

"I don't know any more than you do about it. There may be questions to which there are no answers, problems no one—let alone a child—can solve."

"I'm not a child!" Claire was outraged. "What did *we* do to deserve to live?"

"I suppose we were lucky. Some of us, like Uncle Edu, saw the handwriting on the wall . . ."

"Was it because we had money?"

"Your grandmother died; so did your Uncle Andreas."

"I'm sorry, Mummy"—Claire sighed deeply—"and I wish I could cry. I want to lie on my bed and weep and weep, but I can't. The dumbest things bring tears to my eyes—but this . . . Is it because I have no feelings? Am I cold and hard?"

"Of course you have feelings." Lene spoke softly. "Never let anyone tell you that you don't. Some people simply find it harder to express what they feel deep down inside. And no one can cross over into another's land of grief."

They walked for a few minutes in silence. Claire linked her arm in Lene's. She was as tall as her mother. The sound of laughing voices rang out across a lawn strung with paper lanterns. The radio in a passing car sent out a melody.

"What do you want of me?" Lene suddenly asked, her voice full of desperation.

Claire did not reply. Lene's question frightened her. It was the first time she had been asked to reassure her mother. She wanted her childhood back and to be grown up, both at the same time.

"I love you, Mummy," she said. Lene squeezed her arm. The moon slid behind a bank of silver-edged clouds. A thin white mist rose from the calm waters of the inlet. Claire understood that from now on it would be impossible to cry in her mother's lap and be comforted. She would have to find strength in herself, learn to be alone with sorrow. Her mother's past lay shattered behind her like shards of glass broken beyond repair.

"You and your generation will do better than we did," Lene said in a voice that was almost a whisper. "You'll see to it that nothing as terrible as this will ever happen again."

There was a rumble in the distance, the sound of drums and firecrackers.

"I hear thunder," said Lene. "Let's go home, where we'll be safe."